33 by
Arthur Conan Doyle

33 by
Arthur Conan Doyle

COMPILED AND WITH AN INTRODUCTION BY
JOHN MICHAEL GIBSON AND
RICHARD LANCELYN GREEN

**Classic Stories by the
Creator of Sherlock Holmes**

AVENEL BOOKS
NEW YORK

This 1986 edition is published by Avenel Books,
distributed by Crown Publishers, Inc., 225 Park
Avenue South, New York, New York 10003, by
arrangement with Doubleday and Company, Inc.

Grateful acknowledgment to Dame Jean Conan
Doyle for permission to reprint "The Death
Voyage" and "The End of Devil Hawker"
by the late Sir Arthur Conan Doyle, protected by
copyright in the United States.
Printed and Bound in the United States of America

Library of Congress Cataloging-in-Publication Data

Doyle, Arthur Conan Sir, 1859–1930.
33.

I. Gibson, John Michael. II. Green, Richard Lancelyn.
III. Title. IV. Title: Thirty-three.
PR4621.G5   1986   823'.8   86–26527
ISBN: 0-517-62543-1
h g f e d c b a

CONTENTS

INTRODUCTION

───────────◆───────────

Arthur Conan Doyle's first published story was written in 1879 when he was acting as a paid assistant to Dr. Reginald Ratcliffe Hoare at Clifton House in Birmingham. He was encouraged to submit the manuscript by Dr. Hoare's nephew, Dr. Rupert Hoare Hunter, who was also an assistant. Hunter had been impressed by Doyle's vivid letters and by the stories he had written during his spare time for Dr. Hoare's children. Doyle later modestly professed that he had had no idea he could write decent prose: "I sat down, however, and wrote a little adventure story which I called 'The Mystery of Sasassa Valley'. To my great joy and surprise it was accepted by 'Chambers' Journal,' and I received three guineas." It was the second story he had submitted, but, as the first to be accepted, marked the beginning of his literary career. He always retained a kindly feeling for the magazine with its "mustard-coloured back" and a pleasant recollection of the delightful sensations he had experienced when he gazed upon his first cheque for a literary production. *Chambers's Journal* was based in his home city of Edinburgh and already had to its credit the earliest publication of work by eminent, or soon-to-be eminent, authors – such as a poem by George Meredith in 1849 or the first piece by Thomas Hardy in 1865.

The first story had appeared anonymously and so did Doyle's next piece in *Chambers's* ten years later. This was "The Bravoes of Market Drayton" which described the case of Thomas Ellson, a Shropshire peasant, who in 1827 had been saved from hanging by the murder of a witness and who then informed on those who had been responsible (they included his parents) in order to win favour when he was again on trial. In 1890 the magazine accepted "The Surgeon of Gaster Fell", a story set in Yorkshire. His mother had moved there after his father had been confined to an asylum and the story reflects this family tragedy. It was written in May

1886 and had already been offered to *Blackwood's*, the other great Edinburgh magazine, who returned it in November 1888. The only other story by Doyle to have appeared in *Chambers's* was "The Recollections of Captain Wilkie" in 1895. In the same issue there is a short article by the editor on "Some Notable Beginners in Chambers's Journal", which gives a little information about the story. After drawing attention to Doyle's first contribution, it continues: "From this and his other contributions, 'The Bravos (*sic*) of Market Drayton', 'The Surgeon of Gaster Fell', and 'Captain Wilkie', the story of a reclaimed thief and Salvation Army Captain, it was evident that Dr. Doyle was a born story-teller . . . The story 'Captain Wilkie', which has just been printed, seems a kind of forecast of his Sherlock Holmes narratives, and contains a reference to the influence upon him by one of his Edinburgh teachers, Dr. Joseph Bell, who was continually impressing upon his pupils the vast importance of marking little distinctions, and the endless significance, when followed out, of so-called trifles in appearance, manner, and conduct. In all probability Dr. Bell never dreamt of the use one brilliant pupil would make of his lectures." The date is not mentioned, though there is a footnote at the end which reads: " 'Captain Wilkie' was written by Dr. Conan Doyle several years ago, and is interesting, both as a vigorous story in itself and as being in the vein which he afterwards developed in the well-known Sherlock Holmes stories." This would suggest that it was written between 1880 and 1886, but it may have been earlier. At the time of the publication of *Chambers's* anthology *Peril and Prowess*, which included "The Mystery of Sasassa Valley", the *Westminster Gazette* recalled that it was written while the author was a medical student at Edinburgh University; the note continues: "A tale of the same period seems to have been held over, and was only published in *Chambers's Journal* in 1895." Whether "Captain Wilkie" was, in fact, the first story which he sent to the magazine, which was rediscovered when the editor was preparing his article, or whether Doyle found it among his own papers is not known – though the former is the more likely.

A few months after "Captain Wilkie" had appeared in England, it was published in *McClure's Magazine* in America under the title "Recollections of Captain Wilkie. A Story of an Old Offender". The rights had been taken by a syndicate, though whether it was they or the editor of the American magazine who made a small but not insignificant change in the text, none can say. Where *Chambers's Journal* (the text used here) has: "I had the advantage of studying under a Professor at Edinburgh who was a master of the art . . .", *McClure's* has: "I had the advantage of studying under a master of the art . . ." A small point, were it not that the professor, Dr. Joseph Bell, is given credit for being the original of Sherlock Holmes.

Only "The Surgeon of Gaster Fell", which appears in *Danger! and Other Stories* (1918), was collected by the author. But that and his first story were pirated on many occasions in America, and also included in *Chambers's* own anthologies. "The Mystery of Sasassa Valley" was also among the first of his stories ever to appear in book form, as it was included in George Redway's three-volume anthology, *Dreamland and Ghostland*, which was published in October 1887. Doyle was the only author to be mentioned by name in the preface, which notes that his stories were "written from material picked up in various countries" and that they "introduce some curious examples of the power of superstition, and a singular mixture of truth and error, as in the Diamond Story of the Sassassa (*sic*) Valley".

Doyle was delighted to see his first story in print – even though the editor had removed all the "damns" – and when he returned to Edinburgh was able to impress his fellow out-patient clerk, D. Marinus, who worked with him under Dr. Joseph Bell at the Royal Infirmary. Doyle was by no means idle; soon after word had reached him that his story had been accepted, he wrote another two stories, "The Haunted Grange of Goresthorpe" and "The American's Tale". The first went to *Blackwood's Magazine*, but, unlike many of his subsequent stories which came back with rejection slips, he had no word of it. Some years later, when sending another story, he mentioned that he had been "unfortunate enough to lose the only other m.s. I ever remember sending you". But he never retrieved it. It seems that his covering letter had been mislaid and the manuscript set to one side where it remained and still remains. The unpublished story is subtitled "A True Ghost Story" and describes one dreadful night in the life of a medical student who is the owner of a haunted grange. He and a friend sit up through the night and after observing blood dripping from the ceiling, go to investigate, whereupon the ghost of a drowned sailor and of a woman with marks upon her neck flee past them. The story bears no relation to a later story "Selecting a Ghost. The Ghosts of Goresthorpe Grange", except for the similarity in the title. The latter is a humorous account of a rich grocer who wishes to procure a ghost.

"Selecting a Ghost" was one of eleven stories, the first being "The American's Tale", which appeared in *London Society*. It may have been Doyle's father who first suggested that he try the magazine, as he had done a number of illustrations for it. "The

American's Tale" was included in the 1880 Christmas number. Another was taken the following year, by which time Doyle was sailing around the West Coast of Africa. When he returned he again went to Dr. Hoare and while there spent much of his time writing. There was a descriptive account of his African adventures for the *British Journal of Photography*, and a number of stories: "Bones", "Our Derby Sweepstakes", and "The Actor's Duel". The first two he placed with *London Society*, which paid £5 for each, the third he sent to *Blackwood's*. "Bones" was to be his first story published in an anthology, being included in a large collection of stories called *Tales from Many Sources* in 1885, but as the collection was American he had no copyright and was probably unaware of its existence.

Although Doyle was pleased that his stories were being accepted, he had special reason to thank the editor of *London Society*, James Hogg, after his partnership with Dr. George Budd in Plymouth had broken down and when he was a struggling doctor in Southsea. Money was very short, the pound promised by Budd had been stopped, and he had a younger brother to support. When not brushing the floors of Bush Villa, his new house, or blacking his boots, he was peering through the venetian blinds at his "patients" who were reluctant to do more than read his plate. He was soon in some financial difficulty. "I explained to Mr. Hogg how I was situated, and wrote for him a new tale for his Christmas number, entitled 'My Friend the Murderer'. Hogg behaved very well and sent me £10, which I laid by for my first quarter's rent."

Over the next few years he sent more stories to the magazine, the last being "Elias B. Hopkins. The Parson of Jackman's Gulch" in 1885. He would probably have thought no more about *London Society* had not the editor claimed the full copyright of his stories and produced them in a volume. Doyle had himself tried to find a publisher for a collection of eighteen stories in November 1885. He proposed to call the volume *Light and Shade*. But it was only after the success of *Micah Clarke* in 1889 that Longmans agreed to take some and these were published as *The Captain of the Polestar and Other Tales* in 1890. Before this appeared, Walter Scott had published *Mysteries and Adventures* which was the volume compiled by Hogg. Doyle was furious but there was nothing he could do. He explained to the editor of a Birmingham newspaper: " 'Mysteries and Adventures' is a pirated edition of tales written years ago in London Society — some of them when I was little more than a boy. It is rough on me having these youthful effusions brought out in this catchpenny fashion, but I have no legal redress." The volume was popular and once Sherlock Holmes had made Doyle's name familiar with the reading public it sold by the thousand under the revised title of *The Gully of Bluemansdyke*.

James Hogg did not stop at the English edition. At the end of 1893 Doyle saw the same stories with three further ones from *London Society* and his first story in a volume called *My Friend the Murderer* published by Lovell and Coryell in New York. He immediately wrote a letter of protest to the New York *Critic*. But the publisher explained that "these stories were purchased from Mr. James Hogg, acting as agent for Dr. Doyle, during November, 1892, and that the sum of twenty-five pounds was paid for them". There was nothing he could do except disavow Hogg. Years later he wrote of this incident: "Have a care, young authors, have a care, or your own worst enemy will be your early self."

Doyle stated in his autobiography that his early stories were "scattered about amid the pages of 'London Society', 'All the Year Round', 'Temple Bar', 'The Boy's Own Paper', and other journals." Of all these named magazines, *All the Year Round* stood out. No contribution was known, nor could any be traced. Ever since it had been founded by Charles Dickens, it had had a policy of strict anonymity for all but the serial stories. Those who searched did so in vain. J. Finley Christ, for example, spent seven years attempting to track down a story, ascribed to Doyle in a German book, which had the title "A Medical Secret". He located a story with the same title in *All the Year Round* and felt its style "might have been that of Doyle". But neither he nor anybody else tracked down the two stories which were by Doyle: "That Veteran" and "Gentlemanly Joe".

"Gentlemanly Joe" has internal evidence to show that it is by Doyle as it is set in Birchespool, Doyle's fictional name for Portsmouth which is also used in *The Stark Munro Letters* (1895) and in two of the stories in this volume, "The Voice of Science" and "The Colonel's Choice". Both stories were mentioned in his letters. In the late summer of 1882, he referred to the first in a letter to a friend in Edinburgh. *All the Year Round* owed him four guineas, the fee for "That Veteran". He also pasted the proofs of the story into the scrapbook which he started after his marriage. In March of the following year he told the same friend of the success of his medical practice: "There is comparative stagnation in literature however. Though I have a scientific article in this month's 'Good Words' and a story called 'Gentlemanly Joe' appears in April in 'All the Year Round'." (The story actually appeared at the end of March.) The article mentioned in the letter, "Life and Death in the Blood", was one of a number of medical articles which he intended to write – though he found that fiction was in greater demand. The clearest proof of Doyle's authorship of the *All the Year Round* stories is a short piece in the Portsmouth *Crescent* on 28 September 1888. This gives a sketch of his life and lists many of his stories with the places where they had appeared: " 'Gentlemanly Joe' and 'That Veteran' appeared in 'All the Year Round'." It goes on to list his two contributions to *Temple Bar*, "The Captain of the Polestar" and "The Heiress of Glenmahowley".

"The Actor's Duel" had been rejected by *Blackwood's* at the end of March 1882. When he sent it, he had written (from "The Elms", Gravelly Hill, Birmingham): "I venture to submit to your notice the accompanying tale 'The Actor's duel' . . . However defective the working out may be I am conscious that the denouement is both original and powerful, worthy, I hope of the traditions of your magazine." Later in the year, after it had been returned to his Edinburgh address, it was read by his friend, Mrs. Drummond, who wrote to say how much she had enjoyed it. Doyle replied that he considered it was "the most powerful thing I have ever written but I can get no publisher to share my views. Is it not extraordinary. Every friend who has read it likes it, and yet they won't accept it. I have sent it to the 'Boy's Own Paper' in disgust but I am quite prepared to see it come back." And it did! But by then another magazine, which has not been previously associated with Doyle, had been tried with success. It was *Bow Bells*, published by John Dicks, which had accepted "The Winning Shot". It then took "The Actor's Duel" which was published as "The Tragedians".

"The Winning Shot" is the narrative of a girl whose lover, caught in the inexplicable power of a mysterious stranger, fires the winning shot in a contest, but the bullet strikes at his heart. The inspiration behind the setting was Doyle's visit to Tavistock after he had left Budd and was attempting to find a suitable place in which to set up on his own. It is the companion piece to an article published in the *British Journal of Photography* called "Dry Plates on a Wet Moor". It is also of interest for certain passages which are echoed in the later Sherlock Holmes stories. The stranger, Octavius Gaster, is first glimpsed as a silhouette on a tor in Dartmoor: "The moon was just topping the ridge behind, and the gaunt, angular outlines of the stranger stood out hard and clear against its silvery radiance." This may be compared with *The Hound of the Baskervilles* in which Watson in his second report to Sherlock Holmes describes the man on the tor: "The moon was low upon the right, and the jagged pinnacle of a granite tor stood up against the lower curve of its silver disc. There, outlined as black as an ebony statue on that shining background I saw the figure of a man upon the tor." Then there is Gaster's account of his companion, Karl Osgood, who died eating his own ears, which returns in a different form in "The Adventure of the Cardboard Box" where Holmes is confronted by two human ears. But the most interesting parallel concerns Trevor who was, in the early story, a close friend of Charley Underwood at Cambridge: "Trevor had a remarkably savage bull-dog, which, however fond of its master fiercely resented any liberties from the rest of us." In "The Adventure of the 'Gloria Scott' ", Holmes tells Watson about his friendship with Victor Trevor formed during the two years he was at college: "Trevor was the only man I knew, and that only through the accident of his bull-terrier freezing onto my ankle one morning as I went down to chapel."

In 1894 John Dicks brought out a small sixpenny booklet entitled *An Actor's Duel and The Winning Shot*. It has mystified many people ever since. The *English Catalogue*, which lists new books, gave its month of publication as July 1894, but no copies were sent to the copyright libraries and no reference was ever made to the stories by the author or by his biographers. J. Finley Christ, who ascribed the publication to John Hicks, knew only that they were "not old wine in new skins". It is not known whether Doyle ever saw the publication; if he did he could have denied the authorship of one of the stories. Although John Dicks did publish "The Winning Shot" and soon afterwards Doyle's "The Actor's Duel", when he came to reprint them on their own he made the inexcusable mistake of using the wrong story. The reason for this was that he had published "The Actor's Duel" as "The Tragedians" and so could not find it in the index. There was though another story, "A Palpable Hit", which has a very similar plot, and this was the one which was used – even though it bore the signature "C.R.B.", while Doyle's own was signed "A.C.D." The "two captivating and sensational stories, full of exciting situations and thrilling incidents, almost bordering on the marvellous" may well have been withdrawn; if not, they were allowed to fade quickly into obscurity to conceal the blushes of the publisher. Finley Christ was closer to the truth than he knew when he mentioned old wine in new skins.

At the end of 1882, or thereabouts, Doyle was writing a book called "The Narrative of John Smith", which was "of a personal-social-political complexion". It is known only from a description which he gave in an article on his juvenilia as it was lost in the post before it reached the publisher: "Had it appeared I should have probably awakened to find myself infamous, for it steered, as I remember it, perilously near to the libellous." His description given in 1893 suggests that it may well have been an earlier version of *The Stark Munro Letters* which is dated 1882–1884 though it actually covers Doyle's extraordinary experiences with Dr. Budd in Plymouth during 1882. He began the novel in 1894; if not political, it was certainly personal and could just be described as "social". There is however a reference in a letter written in December 1882 to a work which is otherwise completely unknown: "I have a fearful political pamphlet scourging everybody which Routledge is reading now. It will make a sensation if it comes out (Anonymous of course), but I fear they will not have pluck enough to publish it." It could be that this pamphlet (later given the grander title of a book) was *en route* to Routledge when he wrote the letter, so he imagined they would be reading it, while in fact it had gone astray in the Christmas post. An amusing, though probably baseless, reminiscence was given by the Portsmouth City Coroner, P.H. Childs, in 1942. He recalled that when Doyle was in Southsea he played for the Portsmouth Football Club, but so as not to offend his lady patients used the name "John Smith". This was not the case, for example, in March 1887 when Portsmouth F.A. played Woolston Works – the goalkeeper on that occasion was A. Conan Doyle.

During the autumn of 1883 Doyle was busy preparing a lecture on the Arctic Seas for the Portsmouth Literary and Scientific Society. He was also "going in for the Seven roomed house which is offered by Tit Bits for the best Xmas story". His story was dispatched to *Tit Bits* and he had high hopes of winning. The magazine had been founded by George Newnes in 1881 and its success enabled him to start the *Strand Magazine* ten years later. The prize was offered for the "best Christmas story in prose or verse, not necessarily original", and the winner was to be announced in the Christmas number. When that came out there was general consternation. Not only had the eminent public man who was to adjudicate failed to materialise, but the prize went to Private William Mellish who had sent in a story by Max Adeler. It was one of 30,000 contributions sent in by 22,000 competitors. To add to the swindle (for so it seemed) the story had nothing whatever to do with Christmas. The editor explained that "as the Christmas pieces sent to us have simply been made so by fixing the date of one of the incidents as Christmas Day or Christmas Eve, we do not see that we were entitled to attach much weight to this objection". Doyle immediately wrote to the editor offering to put up £25 if he would do the same, and to send the manuscript of his story and that of the winner to an impartial judge like James Payn, the editor of the *Cornhill Magazine*. *Tit Bits*, smarting, no doubt, from 22,000 similar letters, made no reply.

If Doyle was angry, it was because he felt more sure of his talents. In July 1883 he had been sent twenty-nine guineas by the *Cornhill Magazine* for " 'Habakuk Jephson's Statement' not yet published". This was a high point in his career, but he had been equally fortunate at the end of the previous year when *Temple Bar* took "The Captain of the Polestar". They sent him ten guineas and a copy of the magazine.

While he waited to learn if his story had won the *Tit Bits* Competition, he sent "An Exciting Christmas Eve" to the *Boy's Own Paper*. This may have been intended as his entry for the competition which had been put aside in favour of a better one, or it could possibly have been the same. Doyle would have seen copies of the *Boy's Own Paper* in Edinburgh as it was the favourite reading of the son of a family friend, Mrs. Drummond. He told her at the end of November 1883: "I have put a story in the Xmas Number of the Boy's Own Paper in deference to Tommy's susceptibilities." This was his first story to be accepted. Over the next few years he submitted further stories when all else had failed. Two of these and a poem from later Christmas numbers were afterwards collected: "Crabbe's Practice", "Cyprian Over-beck Wells", and "Corporal Dick's Promotion". The second appears to have been written for the magazine as the date of composition is given as "about twenty minutes to ten on the night of the fourth of June, eighteen hundred and eighty-six". The author wished to be accurate as he was laying his experiences "before the readers of the BOY'S OWN". It was included in the 1886 Christmas number.

Doyle's attitude towards the *Boy's Own Paper* was generally dismissive. Unlike his friend, Major-General A.W. Drayson, who was happy to contribute to boys' journals, he felt the standards were lower than elsewhere though he was grateful that the paper accepted the stories when others had returned them.

The other uncollected stories are "The Fate of the Evangeline", "Uncle Jeremy's Household", and "The Stone of Boxman's Drift". The first appeared in the 1885 Christmas number though it was written considerably earlier. When he sent it to *Blackwood's* at the end of 1884 he wrote: "I am trying my fortune once more with 'The Fate of the Evangeline'." The story is of particular interest for the use of a phrase which is associated with Sherlock Holmes. In the story the *Scotsman*, discussing the fate of the

Evangeline, comments in an editorial on the absurdity of many of the speculations: " 'It would be well,' the 'Scotsman' concluded, 'if those who express opinions upon such subjects would bear in mind those simple rules as to the analysis of evidence laid down by Auguste Dupin. 'Exclude the impossible,' he remarks in one of Poe's immortal stories, 'and what is left, however improbable, *must* be the truth.' In *The Sign of Four*, it is Holmes who remarks to Watson: 'How often have I said to you that when you have eliminated the impossible, whatever remains, *however improbable*, must be the truth?"

If that story has one quotation which should interest students of the detective story, the next, "Uncle Jeremy's Household", has been given a rather exaggerated association with Sherlock Holmes because one of the characters lives in Baker Street and another is called John H. Thurston, which is similar to John H. Watson. "Uncle Jeremy's Household" was sent to *Blackwood's* in the summer of 1885. The author told them: "The story is a little long but it is divided in the centre so as to be capable of being continued. I think that anyone who read the first half would wish to read the second." It was returned on 10 August. As Doyle was writing *A Study in Scarlet* in March and April 1886, it is possible that he did have the manuscript of the earlier story at his side and could have been influenced by it in his choice of names. It was published in the *Boy's Own Paper* in seven weekly parts during January and February 1887, and was later used with the other stories from the paper to launch *Every Boy's Magazine* which started in 1905. "Uncle Jeremy's Household" was also published as a book in France in July 1909, the only occasion when one of Doyle's stories appeared in translation without being published in book form in England. The translation was made by René Lécuyer and it was published by the Librairie Félix Juven as *Notre Dame de la Mort* (the volume also contained *Loin de la Vie*, a translation of *Beyond the City*). The last of Doyle's stories to appear in the *Boy's Own Paper* was "The Stone of Boxman's Drift" in the 1887 Christmas number. It was probably written earlier, in fact the setting and style are very similar to those of his first published story.

Among the completely unknown stories, the two from *Cassell's Saturday Journal* are of interest. They appeared in 1884 and 1885, and followed his first contribution, "John Barrington Cowles", a long story about the power of mesmerism. That had appeared in two parts and was signed "A.C.D."; "The Cabman's Story" and "The Lonely Hampshire Cottage" were shorter and were both anonymous. The evidence that they are by Doyle comes from

Cassell's files, which were examined by Simon Nowell-Smith who gave the names of the stories in a footnote to *The House of Cassell* (p. 131). "The Cabman's Story", which is set in London, is in some ways a precursor of the first Sherlock Holmes book. He subsequently wrote the title "A Study in Scarlet" in an early notebook, and beneath it he put: "The terrified woman rushing up to the cabman. The two going in search of a policeman . . ." When he came to write the book, the murderer was discovered disguised as a cabman. The early story is also one of the first by Doyle to be set in London, and the reminiscences, which include the use of the cab for the disposal of a corpse, for forging banknotes, and for carrying dynamite disguised as a piece of coal, belong to the sensational detective story. "The Lonely Hampshire Cottage", on the other hand, is a successful reworking of one of the oldest themes in literature – the return of the son, unrecognised by his parents who plot to kill him for his money. *Cassell's* also accepted another story for their monthly magazine, "Touch and Go: A Midshipman's Story", which Doyle based on a visit to the Isle of Arran which he had earlier described in an article for the *British Journal of Photography*.

Arran, or Uffa, an imaginary island close to it, was also the setting for "Our Midnight Visitor" which was published in *Temple Bar* in 1891. Both concern the dangers of the sea. In the former the midshipman is saved from disaster, in the latter the narrator's father is drowned when attempting to murder a diamond thief and gain a jewel. Uffa is mentioned again in one of the Sherlock Holmes stories, "The Adventure of the Five Orange Pips", where an unrecorded case is referred to which concerned "the singular adventures of the Grice Pattersons in the island of Uffa". The Sherlock Holmes story was written in May 1891, three months after "Our Midnight Visitor" appeared in *Temple Bar*. The other story in this collection from *Temple Bar*, "The Heiress of Glenmahowley", had appeared in January 1884, having been preceded a year earlier by "The Captain of the Polestar". The story is partly based on Doyle's memories of Ireland which he had visited in 1881 as Lismore was the home of his relatives. The interview in the Portsmouth *Crescent* provided the evidence that this otherwise anonymous story was by Doyle, but more evidence has recently been made available with the publication of the third volume of the *Wellesley Index to Victorian Periodicals* which used the Bentley archives to give all the contributors to the magazine. This also revealed that "The Siege of Sunda Gunge", which had long been attributed to Conan Doyle as it had appeared in the first American edition of *The Sign of Four*, was by H. Greenhough Smith.

By a curious twist of fate, Greenhough Smith was appointed as the first editor of the *Strand Magazine* which quickly became associated with the name of Conan Doyle. The first number appeared in January 1891, and during that month the editor received Doyle's first contribution, "The Voice of Science". The story is set in Birchespool and makes use of a phonograph to warn a girl of her lover's seedy past. It had been sent by A.P. Watt who had just taken over as Doyle's literary agent, and the price was £4 per thousand words (about £80 less than the author received for the last Sherlock Holmes stories). Although Doyle's name did not appear under the title of the story this was an oversight – the early numbers being compiled rather hurriedly: it was given on the contents page and later in the index. The main article in the issue for March 1891 contained a drawing by Queen Victoria and the monthly part was therefore also printed in a special hardbound Royal Edition with blue silk covers. As well as appearing in this form, Doyle's story was also included in a series of *Penny Tales from the Strand Library*, but was otherwise un-collected. However, the first volume of the *Strand Magazine* is not scarce as it was reprinted to match the growing circulation which followed from the success of the first Sherlock Holmes stories.

Much less common, in fact unknown even by name, are the stories from the *People* and *Lloyd's Weekly Newspaper*. These, "A Pastoral Horror", "A Sordid Affair", and "The Colonel's Choice", each published under Doyle's name, had been completely forgotten. "A Regimental Scandal" is also unfamiliar, though has been known by name from its appearance in America, where it was widely distributed by McClure's newspaper syndicate.

With the success of *Micah Clarke* and of the two Sherlock Holmes books, and with the knowledge that *The White Company* had been accepted by the *Cornhill Magazine*, Doyle's reputation was becoming firmly established. After he had left Southsea, his intention was to become an eye specialist and to this end he visited Vienna. But he spent much of the time when he was there writing *The Doings of Raffles Haw* for Alfred Harmsworth's penny paper, *Answers*. Commissions were coming more rapidly and, although he did briefly establish himself in Wimpole Street during the first half of 1891, by October he had moved to 12 Tennison Road, South Norwood, sold his eye instruments and embarked on a purely literary career which had been made possible by the exceptional popularity of Sherlock Holmes. The unknown stories were those which immediately preceded the sudden upsurge of fame.

When Doyle was at work on *The White Company* in 1889, he also agreed to do a short novel for *Lippincott's Magazine* which became *The Sign of Four*, and to revise his early novel "Girdlestone & Co." for publication by the *People*. As *The Firm of Girdlestone* it began serial publication in October 1889 and ran until April of the following year. Then in December 1890 the paper published "A Pastoral Horror" (one of the few occasions when Doyle allowed himself a play on words). This is of particular interest as it contains a description of Feldkirch in Austria, which, as the author states, is remarkable "for nothing save for the presence of a large well-conducted Jesuit school". This was where Doyle completed his schooling after leaving Stonyhurst in 1875. The story itself is somewhat reminiscent of Mary Shelley's *Frankenstein*, and the theme of the werewolf is unusual in Doyle's work. The construction is less than perfect as the dénouement comes as no surprise. It attempts to do in a sensational way what *The Silence of Dean Maitland* had succeeded in doing, that is to allow the truth to dawn on the reader long before it is recognised by the community within the story.

In November 1891, when the Sherlock Holmes stories had been running for five months in the *Strand Magazine*, the *People* published "A Sordid Affair". It describes the tribulations of a poor costumier who copies a dress in a West End store only to find that her drunken husband has pawned it and disappeared. She uses her entire savings to buy the original dress which is then dismissed as inferior by her client. The story ends with the woman crooning over her husband with blind, angelic, foolish love. As Doyle's father had suffered from alcoholism this was not a subject which he would have treated lightly, and the affection of his mother and the hardships which she endured probably lay behind the tale. But the story is also interesting for the closely observed domestic and feminine details. His knowledge in this field came as a surprise to many people when *A Duet* was published, but it went back a long way. There are a number of stories in this collection which have women as narrators and they are in no way inferior to the others. He had the example of a strong-willed mother and some determined sisters who like him had had to face difficulties in their early years and earn their own livelihoods.

"A Sordid Affair" was one of the earliest stories taken by S.S. McClure for his newspaper syndicate. He had already taken *The White Company*, *The Doings of Raffles Haw*, and a number of the Sherlock Holmes stories, and on this basis could claim to be the person who had introduced Doyle to his American readers. His magazine and publishing house, in both of which Doyle had shares, were to play an important part in making the author's name familiar. "A Sordid Affair", however, was one of the few stories which did not appeal to editors and McClure had great difficulty in finding anybody prepared to take it.

Although Doyle had no military background or training, he was surrounded by many friends at Southsea who had seen service in the army like Major-General A.W. Drayson, and this led to a series of regimental tales which were written just before the first Sherlock Holmes series. Among them was "The Colonel's Choice", a story of honour in an old soldier, which was taken by *Lloyd's Weekly Newspaper* – then one of the most popular papers of its day – which a few years later serialised his short novel *The Parasite*.

After "A Regimental Scandal" there are only nine stories which were not collected. Two of these were written in 1898 and seem to belong among the "Round the Fire" series, most of which appeared in the *Strand Magazine*. They are "The Confession" and "The Retirement of Signor Lambert". The first was written for the tenth anniversary number of the *Star*, and is unusual as it makes use of Doyle's Catholic schooling and background. He may have based it on his earliest memories of Sister Mary Gertrude, of St. Catherine's Convent, who had instructed him in his first communion, or, as it is set in Lisbon, on the experiences of his sister Annette. The second, which appeared in *Pearson's Magazine*, was probably excluded because it involved an illicit love affair as well as the macabre act of destroying a singer's vocal chords. For nearly ten years Doyle refused to allow the whole series of "Round the Fire" stories to be republished in book form. This was in deference to his 'ideal of art' which, at the turn of the century, led him to forgo the serial publication of *A Duet* and to suppress *The Firm of Girdlestone*, both at some financial loss.

"A True Story of the Tragedy of 'Flowery Land' " was published in America in 1899. It describes an actual incident and is thought by some to belong among the "Strange Studies from Life", a series based on true crimes. Doyle had intended to do twelve of these studies, but was very dissatisfied with the three he did – had they not gone to Sidney Paget to be illustrated, he would have withdrawn them. The three were published in the *Strand Magazine*, but he did no more. The "Flowery Land" story deals with a mutiny on board ship, a subject which Doyle knew how to handle with skill. The studies from life, on the other hand, were an attempt to explore the psychology of murder, but he found that he had no sympathy for the individuals concerned and little understanding of their confused mentalities. The text of the piece on the "Flowery Land" is taken from an American newspaper (as no English appearance has been traced) and this is slightly shorter than the original manuscript. The unwieldy title is also that used by the Americans, Doyle had called it simply "The Voyage of the 'Flowery Land' ".

With "An Impression of the Regency", one catches a glimpse of Doyle's art as a novelist. This was probably the sketch he wrote after he had completed his reading around the subject and before he began work on the novel, in this case *Rodney Stone*. He did the same with his next novel, *Uncle Bernac*, for which he wrote an impression of Napoleon, but being displeased with the finished product when it was serialised, he incorporated the one into the other thereby extending the book by four chapters (which he afterwards said were the one redeeming feature of the book).

The Regency period was one which particularly interested Doyle. His earliest story set at that time was *The Great Shadow*, then came the Brigadier Gerard stories, *Rodney Stone* and a number of short stories such as "The Croxley Master". His fondness for boxing – he was himself a pupil of Charlie Ball, the champion of Scotland – partly explains his interest, but he was also well versed in the social background. One of his posthumously published stories, "The End of Devil Hawker", is a Regency tale. Like "A Regimental Scandal" before it, the story concerns an incident of cheating at cards. It is based on fact, and the detailed observation, which in all his writings set him above the average writer, is employed to excellent effect. The late story is interesting for the mention of his own link with the period through his grandfather, John Doyle, the "father of polite caricature" who was known to his contemporaries as "H.B."

The stories Doyle rated among his best were a series he began in 1910 and collected the following year as *The Last Galley*. These followed from his interest in archaeology which came late in his life after his move to Crowborough on the Sussex downs. He began collecting flints and axe heads, and also acquired a large plaster cast of a prehistoric footprint. A direct result was *The Lost World*, the first draft of which was written on the cover of an archaeological journal, but this was preceded by the impressions and tales which ranged over the spectrum of ancient history from Greece to Byzantium with the Roman Empire and the birth of Christ as the central theme.

When John Murray was in the process of bringing out a new collected edition of Doyle's stories, the first five volumes being published during July 1922, Doyle wrote two further stories for the last volume, *Tales of Long Ago*. They were "A Point of Contact" and "The Centurion" and both were taken by the *Storyteller*. The magazine used the first in October but held the other back until December. Murray could not wait until then, so the volume published in November did not include "The Centurion". In America *Hearst's International* printed the story in October and it was included in the American edition, *The Last of the Legions and Other Tales of Long Ago*. "The Centurion" was reprinted in England in the *Argosy*, but was not added to the omnibus volume in 1929 which brought the six separate volumes together.

When Doyle was revising his history of the war and adding new material on the Italian campaigns for its republication in 1928 as *The British Campaigns in Europe*, he pondered a great deal on the immediate past and made some prophecies about the future. It was this mood which produced "The Death Voyage", a curiously bleak impression of what might have happened if the Kaiser had come out with his fleet to die fighting. It reflects Doyle's own feelings about the dismal end of Napoleon in tetchy captivity on St. Helena. There is a note of desperation in the worthless sacrifice and the reduction of heroism to slaughter and human waste.

By contrast "The Parish Magazine", one of three posthumously published stories which appeared in the *Strand Magazine* during the latter half of 1930, is a humorous story. As such it was chosen by P.G. Wodehouse for his anthology *A Century of Humour*. Wodehouse had been fond of Doyle's writings since he was a student at Dulwich College, and had particularly enjoyed the boxing stories and the adventures of Sherlock Holmes. He chose the story because it caught his attention at the right moment – he was contributing to the magazine at the same time. But Doyle, though rarely thought of as an observer of the human comedy, had given better examples of his wit and humour, as some of the other stories in this collection will show.

The last story by Doyle and the last to be published in the *Strand Magazine* was called, appropriately, "The Last Resource". It attempts to capture the rhythms of American speech just as the very early story, "The American's Tale" had done. Doyle's earliest work was strongly influenced by his reading of American writers such as Bret Harte, Mark Twain, and Oliver Wendell Holmes, and he continued to follow new American writers throughout his life, though it was Fulton Oursler, T.S. Stribling, and Thornton Wilder (to name a few) whose work he was enjoying at the end of his career. "The Last Resource" concerns the boot-legging gangster-ridden world of prohibition America. It is a fantasy which Hitler was to make fact in a more dreadful and terrifying way than even Doyle's imagination could have envisaged.

Doyle was at his most brilliant as a writer of short stories. His powers of observation, which make the Sherlock Holmes stories so satisfying, are reflected in these stories. His reputation has suffered in the past from his excessive popularity, from the "Eminent Victorian" school of criticism, and from the resilience of his historical novels which, for all their merits, are textbook history, an accumulation of well-presented facts rather than experience. He has been taken too much at his own estimation. No author is a good judge of his work, nor perhaps does any author realise the limits of his creative ability and the extent of his natural ability. Doyle invariably exaggerated the importance of the works on which he had spent a considerable amount of time and underrated the ones which had come most easily, as did the short stories which include those involving Sherlock Holmes.

To many people Sherlock Holmes is as familiar as London and as tangible as John Bull, but his creator has been forced into the shadows. When he is glimpsed through the eyes of biographers, he has had the rather chipped appearance of an old statue commemorating distant battles, dead controversies, and the faded remnants of a lost age of innocence and power. These stories, and the companion volume containing his articles from the *British Journal of Photography* will provide new, indeed largely unknown material which will do much to enhance the author's reputation and which have the added attraction of being well-written and entertaining pieces in their own right.

Richard Lancelyn Green
John Michael Gibson

THE MYSTERY OF SASASSA VALLEY

Do I know why Tom Donahue is called "Lucky Tom?" Yes; I do; and that is more than one in ten of those who call him so can say. I have knocked about a deal in my time, and seen some strange sights, but none stranger than the way in which Tom gained that sobriquet and his fortune with it. For I was with him at the time. – Tell it? Oh, certainly; but it is a longish story and a very strange one; so fill up your glass again, and light another cigar while I try to reel it off. Yes; a very strange one; beats some fairy stories I have heard; but it's true sir, every word of it. There are men alive at Cape Colony now who'll remember it and confirm what I say. Many a time has the tale been told round the fire in Boers' cabins from Orange State to Griqualand; yes, and out in the Bush and at the Diamond Fields too.

I'm roughish now sir; but I was entered at the Middle Temple once, and studied for the Bar. Tom – worse luck! – was one of my fellow-students; and a wildish time we had of it, until at last our finances ran short, and we were compelled to give up our so-called studies, and look about for some part of the world where two young fellows with strong arms and sound constitutions might make their mark. In those days the tide of emigration had scarcely begun to set in towards Africa, and so we thought our best chance would be down at Cape Colony. Well – to make a long story short – we set sail, and were deposited in Cape Town with less than five pounds in our pockets; and there we parted. We each tried our hands at many things, and had ups and downs; but when, at the end of three years, chance led each of us up-country and we met again, we were, I regret to say, in almost as bad a plight as when we started.

Well, this was not much of a commencement; and very disheartened we were, so disheartened that Tom spoke of going back to England and getting a clerkship. For you see we didn't

know that we had played out all our small cards, and that the
trumps were going to turn up. No; we thought our "hands" were
bad all through. It was a very lonely part of the country that we
were in, inhabited by a few scattered farmers, whose houses were
stockaded and fenced in to defend them against the Kaffirs. Tom
Donahue and I had a little hut right out in the Bush; but we were
known to possess nothing, and to be handy with our revolvers, so
we had little to fear. There we waited doing odd jobs, and hoping
that something would turn up. Well, after we had been there
about a month something did turn up upon a certain night,
something which was the making of both of us; and it's about that
night sir, that I'm going to tell you. I remember it well. The wind
was howling past our cabin, and the rain threatened to burst
in our rude window. We had a great wood-fire crackling and
sputtering on the hearth, by which I was sitting mending a whip,
while Tom was lying in his bunk groaning disconsolately at the
chance which had led him to such a place.

"Cheer up, Tom – cheer up," said I. "No man ever knows what
may be awaiting him."

"Ill-luck, ill-luck, Jack," he answered. "I always was an unlucky
dog. Here have I been three years in this abominable country;
and I see lads fresh from England jingling the money in their
pockets, while I am as poor as when I landed. Ah, Jack, if you
want to keep your head above water, old friend, you must try your
fortune away from me."

"Nonsense, Tom; you're down in your luck to-night. But hark!
Here's some one coming outside. Dick Wharton, by the tread;
he'll rouse you, if any man can."

Even as I spoke the door was flung open, and honest Dick
Wharton, with the water pouring from him, stepped in, his hearty
red face looking through the haze like a harvest-moon. He shook
himself, and after greeting us sat down by the fire to warm
himself.

"Whereaway, Dick, on such a night as this?" said I. "You'll find
the rheumatism a worse foe than the Kaffirs, unless you keep
more regular hours."

Dick was looking unusually serious, almost frightened, one
would say, if one did not know the man. "Had to go," he replied –
"had to go. One of Madison's cattle has been straying down
Sasassa Valley, and of course none of our blacks would go down
that Valley at night; and if we had waited till morning, the brute
would have been in Kaffirland."

"Why wouldn't they go down Sasassa Valley at night?" asked
Tom.

"Kaffirs, I suppose," said I.

"Ghosts," said Dick.

We both laughed.

"I suppose they didn't give such a matter-of-fact fellow as you a sight of their charms?" said Tom from the bunk.

"Yes," said Dick seriously – "yes; I saw what the niggers talk about; and I promise you, lads, I don't want ever to see it again."

Tom sat up in his bed. "Nonsense, Dick; you're joking, man! Come, tell us all about it. The legend first, and your own experience afterwards. – Pass him over the bottle, Jack."

"Well, as to the legend," began Dick " – it seems that the niggers have had it handed down to them that Sasassa Valley is haunted by a frightful fiend. Hunters and wanderers passing down the defile have seen its glowing eyes under the shadows of the cliff; and the story goes that whoever has chanced to encounter that baleful glare, has had his after-life blighted by the malignant power of this creature. Whether that be true or not," continued Dick ruefully, "I may have an opportunity of judging for myself."

"Go on, Dick – go on," cried Tom. "Let's hear about what you saw."

"Well, I was groping down the Valley, looking for that cow of Madison's, and I had, I suppose, got half-way down, where a black craggy cliff juts into the ravine on the right, when I halted to have a pull at my flask. I had my eye fixed at the time upon the projecting cliff I have mentioned, and noticed nothing unusual about it. I then put up my flask and took a step or two forward, when in a moment there burst apparently from the base of the rock, about eight feet from the ground and a hundred yards from me, a strange lurid glare, flickering and oscillating, gradually dying away and then reappearing again. – No, no; I've seen many a glow-worm and firefly – nothing of that sort. There it was burning away, and I suppose I gazed at it, trembling in every limb, for fully ten minutes. Then I took a step forwards, when instantly it vanished, vanished like a candle blown out. I stepped back again; but it was some time before I could find the exact spot and position from which it was visible. At last, there it was, the weird reddish light, flickering away as before. Then I screwed up my courage, and made for the rock; but the ground was so uneven that it was impossible to steer straight; and though I walked along the whole base of the cliff, I could see nothing. Then I made tracks for home; and I can tell you, boys, that until you remarked it, I never knew it was raining, the whole way along. – But hollo! what's the matter with Tom?"

What indeed? Tom was now sitting with his legs over the side of the bunk, and his whole face betraying excitement so intense as to be almost painful. "The fiend would have two eyes. How many lights did you see, Dick? Speak out!"

"Only one."

"Hurrah!" cried Tom – "that's better!" Whereupon he kicked the blankets into the middle of the room, and began pacing up and down with long feverish strides. Suddenly he stopped opposite Dick, and laid his hand upon his shoulder: "I say, Dick, could we get to Sasassa Valley before sunrise?"

"Scarcely," said Dick.

"Well, look here; we are old friends, Dick Wharton, you and I. Now, don't you tell any other man what you have told us, for a week. You'll promise that; won't you?"

I could see by the look on Dick's face as he acquiesced that he considered poor Tom to be mad; and indeed I was myself completely mystified by his conduct. I had, however, seen so many proofs of my friend's good sense and quickness of apprehension, that I thought it quite possible that Wharton's story had had a meaning in his eyes which I was too obtuse to take in.

All night Tom Donahue was greatly excited, and when Wharton left he begged him to remember his promise, and also elicited from him a description of the exact spot at which he had seen the apparition, as well as the hour at which it appeared. After his departure, which must have been about four in the morning, I turned into my bunk and watched Tom sitting by the fire splicing two sticks together, until I fell asleep. I suppose I must have slept about two hours; but when I awoke, Tom was still sitting working away in almost the same position. He had fixed the one stick across the top of the other so as to form a rough **T**, and was now busy in fitting a smaller stick into the angle between them, by manipulating which, the cross one could be either cocked up or depressed to any extent. He had cut notches too in the perpendicular stick, so that by the aid of the small prop, the cross one could be kept in any position for an indefinite time.

"Look here, Jack!" he cried, whenever he saw that I was awake, "Come, and give me your opinion. Suppose I put this cross-stick pointing straight at a thing, and arranged this small one so as to keep it so, and left it, I could find that thing again if I wanted it – don't you think I could, Jack – don't you think so?" he continued nervously, clutching me by the arm.

"Well," I answered, "it would depend on how far off the thing was, and how accurately it was pointed. If it were any distance, I'd cut sights on your cross-stick; then a string tied to the end of it, and held in a plumb-line forwards, would lead you pretty near what you wanted. But surely, Tom, you don't intend to localise the ghost in that way?"

"You'll see to-night, old friend — you'll see tonight. I'll carry this to the Sasassa Valley. You get the loan of Madison's crowbar, and come with me; but mind you tell no man where you are going, or what you want it for."

All day Tom was walking up and down the room, or working hard at the apparatus. His eyes were glistening, his cheek hectic, and he had all the symptoms of high fever. "Heaven grant that Dick's diagnosis be not correct!" I thought, as I returned with the crowbar; and yet, as evening drew near, I found myself imperceptibly sharing the excitement.

About six o'clock Tom sprang to his feet and seized his sticks. "I can stand it no longer, Jack," he cried; "up with your crowbar, and hey for Sasassa Valley! To-night's work, my lad, will either make us or mar us! Take your six-shooter, in case we meet the Kaffirs. I daren't take mine, Jack," he continued, putting his hands upon my shoulders — "I daren't take mine; for if my ill-luck sticks to me to-night, I don't know what I might not do with it."

Well, having filled our pockets with provisions, we set out, and as we took our wearisome way towards the Sasassa Valley, I frequently attempted to elicit from my companion some clue as to his intentions. But his only answer was: "Let us hurry on, Jack. Who knows how many have heard of Wharton's adventure by this time! Let us hurry on, or we may not be first in the field!"

Well sir, we struggled on through the hills for a matter of ten miles; till at last, after descending a crag, we saw opening out in front of us a ravine so sombre and dark that it might have been the gate of Hades itself; cliffs many hundred feet high shut in on every side the gloomy boulder-studded passage which led through the haunted defile into Kaffirland. The moon rising above the crags, threw into strong relief the rough irregular pinnacles of rock by which they were topped, while all below was dark as Erebus.

"The Sasassa Valley?" said I.

"Yes," said Tom.

I looked at him. He was calm now; the flush and feverishness had passed away; his actions were deliberate and slow. Yet there was a certain rigidity in his face and glitter in his eye which shewed that a crisis had come.

We entered the pass, stumbling along amid the great boulders. Suddenly I heard a short quick exclamation from Tom. "That's the crag!" he cried, pointing to a great mass looming before us in the darkness. "Now Jack, for any favour use your eyes! We're about a hundred yards from that cliff, I take it; so you move slowly towards one side, and I'll do the same towards the other. When you see anything, stop, and call out. Don't take more than twelve inches in a step, and keep your eye fixed on the cliff about eight feet from the ground. Are you ready?"

"Yes." I was even more excited than Tom by this time. What his intention or object was, I could not conjecture, beyond that he wanted to examine by daylight the part of the cliff from which the light came. Yet the influence of the romantic situation and of my companion's suppressed excitement was so great, that I could feel the blood coursing through my veins and count the pulses throbbing at my temples.

"Start!" cried Tom; and we moved off, he to the right, I to the left, each with our eyes fixed intently on the base of the crag. I had moved perhaps twenty feet, when in a moment it burst upon me. Through the growing darkness there shone a small ruddy glowing point, the light from which waned and increased, flickered and oscillated, each change producing a more weird effect than the last. The old Kaffir superstition came into my mind, and I felt a cold shudder pass over me. In my excitement, I stepped a pace backwards, when instantly the light went out, leaving utter darkness in its place; but when I advanced again, there was the ruddy glare glowing from the base of the cliff. "Tom, Tom!" I cried.

"Ay, ay!" I heard him exclaim, as he hurried over towards me.

"There it is – there, up against the cliff!"

Tom was at my elbow. "I see nothing," said he.

"Why, there, there, man, in front of you!" I stepped to the right as I spoke, when the light instantly vanished from my eyes.

But from Tom's ejaculations of delight it was clear that from my former position it was visible to him also. "Jack," he cried, as he turned and wrung my hand – "Jack, you and I can never complain of our luck again. Now heap up a few stones where we are standing. – That's right. Now we must fix my sign-post firmly in at the top. There! It would take a strong wind to blow that down; and we only need it to hold out till morning. O Jack, my boy, to think that only yesterday we were talking of becoming clerks, and you saying that no man knew what was awaiting him too! By Jove, Jack, it would make a good story!"

By this time we had firmly fixed the perpendicular stick in between two large stones; and Tom bent down and peered along the horizontal one. For fully a quarter of an hour he was alternately raising and depressing it, until at last, with a sigh of satisfaction, he fixed the prop into the angle, and stood up. "Look along, Jack," he said. "You have as straight an eye to take a sight as any man I know of."

I looked along. There, beyond the further sight was the ruddy scintillating speck, apparently at the end of the stick itself, so accurately had it been adjusted. "And now, my boy," said Tom, "let's have some supper, and a sleep. There's nothing more to be done to-night; but we'll need all our wits and strength to-morrow. Get some sticks, and kindle a fire here, and then we'll be able to keep an eye on our signal-post, and see that nothing happens to it during the night."

Well sir, we kindled a fire, and had supper with the Sasassa demon's eye rolling and glowing in front of us the whole night through. Not always in the same place though; for after supper, when I glanced along the sights to have another look at it, it was nowhere to be seen. The information did not, however, seem to disturb Tom in any way. He merely remarked: "It's the moon, not the thing, that has shifted;" and coiling himself up, went to sleep.

By early dawn we were both up, and gazing along our pointer at the cliff; but we could make out nothing save one dead monotonous slaty surface, rougher perhaps at the part we were examining than elsewhere, but otherwise presenting nothing remarkable.

"Now for your idea, Jack!" said Tom Donahue, unwinding a long thin cord from round his waist. "You fasten it, and guide me while I take the other end." So saying he walked off to the base of the cliff, holding one end of the cord, while I drew the other taut, and wound it round the middle of the horizontal stick, passing it through the sight at the end. By this means I could direct Tom to the right or left, until we had our string stretching from the point of attachment, through the sight, and on to the rock, which it struck about eight feet from the ground. Tom drew a chalk circle of about three feet diameter round the spot, and then called to me to come and join him. "We've managed this business together, Jack," he said, "and we'll find what we are to find, together." The circle he had drawn embraced a part of the rock smoother than the rest, save that about the centre there were a few rough protuberances or knobs. One of these Tom pointed to with a cry of delight. It was a roughish brownish mass about the size of a man's closed fist, and looking like a bit of dirty glass let into the wall of the cliff. "That's it!" he cried – "that's it!"

"That's what?"

"Why, man, *a diamond*, and such a one as there isn't a monarch in Europe but would envy Tom Donahue the possession of. Up with your crowbar, and we'll soon exorcise the demon of Sasassa Valley!"

I was so astounded that for a moment I stood speechless with surprise, gazing at the treasure which had so unexpectedly fallen into our hands.

"Here, hand me the crowbar," said Tom. "Now, by using this little round knob which projects from the cliff here, as a fulcrum, we may be able to lever it off. — Yes; there it goes. I never thought it could have come so easily. Now, Jack, the sooner we get back to our hut and then down to Cape Town, the better."

We wrapped up our treasure, and made our way across the hills, towards home. On the way, Tom told me how, while a law-student in the Middle Temple, he had come upon a dusty pamphlet in the library, by one Jans van Hounym, which told of an experience very similar to ours, which had befallen that worthy Duchman in the latter part of the seventeenth century, and which resulted in the discovery of a luminous diamond. This tale it was which had come into Tom's head as he listened to honest Dick Wharton's ghost-story; while the means which he had adopted to verify his supposition sprang from his own fertile Irish brain.

"We'll take it down to Cape Town," continued Tom, "and if we can't dispose of it with advantage there, it will be worth our while to ship for London with it. Let us go along to Madison's first, though; he knows something of these things, and can perhaps give us some idea of what we may consider a fair price for our treasure."

We turned off from the track accordingly, before reaching our hut, and kept along the narrow path leading to Madison's farm. He was at lunch when we entered; and in a minute we were seated at each side of him, enjoying South African hospitality.

"Well," he said, after the servants were gone, "what's in the wind now? I see you have something to say to me. What is it?"

Tom produced his packet, and solemnly untied the handkerchiefs which enveloped it. "There!" he said, putting his crystal on the table; "what would you say was a fair price for that?"

Madison took it up and examined it critically. "Well," he said, laying it down again, "in its crude state about twelve shillings per ton."

"Twelve shillings!" cried Tom, starting to his feet. "Don't you see what it is?"

"Rock-salt!"

"Rock fiddle; a diamond."

"Taste it!" said Madison.

Tom put it to his lips, dashed it down with a dreadful exclamation, and rushed out of the room.

I felt sad and disappointed enough myself; but presently remembering what Tom had said about the pistol, I, too, left the house, and made for the hut, leaving Madison open-mouthed with astonishment. When I got in, I found Tom lying in his bunk with his face to the wall, too dispirited apparently to answer my consolations. Anathematising Dick and Madison, the Sasassa demon, and everything else, I strolled out of the hut, and refreshed myself with a pipe after our wearisome adventure. I was about fifty yards away from the hut, when I heard issuing from it the sound which of all others I least expected to hear. Had it been a groan or an oath, I should have taken it as a matter of course; but the sound which caused me to stop and take the pipe out of my mouth was a hearty roar of laughter! Next moment, Tom himself emerged from the door, his whole face radiant with delight. "Game for another ten-mile walk, old fellow?"

"What! for another lump of rock-salt, at twelve shillings a ton?"

" 'No more of that, Hal, an you love me,' " grinned Tom. "Now look here, Jack. What blessed fools we are to be so floored by a trifle! Just sit on this stump for five minutes, and I'll make it as clear as daylight. You've seen many a lump of rock-salt stuck in a crag, and so have I, though we did make such a mull of this one. Now, Jack, did any of the pieces you have ever seen shine in the darkness brighter than any fire-fly?"

"Well, I can't say they ever did."

"I'd venture to prophesy that if we waited until night, which we won't do, we would see that light still glimmering among the rocks. Therefore, Jack, when we took away this worthless salt, we took the wrong crystal. It is no very strange thing in these hills that a piece of rock-salt should be lying within a foot of a diamond. It caught our eyes, and we were excited, and so we made fools of ourselves, and *left the real stone behind*. Depend upon it, Jack, the Sasassa gem is lying within this magic circle of chalk upon the face of yonder cliff. Come, old fellow, light your pipe and stow your revolver, and we'll be off before that fellow Madison has time to put two and two together."

I don't know that I was very sanguine this time. I had begun in fact to look upon the diamond as a most unmitigated nuisance. However, rather than throw a damper on Tom's expectations, I announced myself eager to start. What a walk it was! Tom was always a good mountaineer, but his excitement seemed to lend him wings that day, while I scrambled along after him as best I could. When we got within half a mile he broke into the "double," and never pulled up until he reached the round white circle upon the cliff. Poor old Tom! when I came up, his mood had changed, and he was standing with his hands in his pockets, gazing vacantly before him with a rueful countenance.

"Look!" he said – "look!" and he pointed at the cliff. Not a sign of anything in the least resembling a diamond there. The circle included nothing but flat slate-coloured stone, with one large hole, where we had extracted the rock-salt, and one or two smaller depressions. No sign of the gem. "I've been over every inch of it," said poor Tom. "It's not there. Some one has been here and noticed the chalk, and taken it. Come home, Jack; I feel sick and tired. Oh! had any man ever luck like mine!"

I turned to go, but took one last look at the cliff first. Tom was already ten paces off.

"Hollo!" I cried, "don't you see any change in that circle since yesterday?"

"What d'ye mean?" said Tom.

"Don't you miss a thing that was there before?"

"The rock-salt?" said Tom.

"No; but the little round knob that we used for a fulcrum. I suppose we must have wrenched it off in using the lever. Let's have a look at what it's made of."

Accordingly, at the foot of the cliff we searched about among the loose stones.

"Here you are, Jack! We've done it at last! We're made men!"

I turned round, and there was Tom radiant with delight, and with a little corner of black rock in his hand. At first sight it seemed to be merely a chip from the cliff; but near the base there was projecting from it an object which Tom was now exultingly pointing out. It looked at first something like a glass eye; but there was a depth and brilliancy about it such as glass never exhibited. There was no mistake this time; we had certainly got possession of a jewel of great value; and with light hearts we turned from the valley, bearing away with us the "fiend" which had so long reigned there.

There sir; I've spun my story out too long, and tired you perhaps. You see when I get talking of those rough old days, I kind of see the little cabin again, and the brook beside it, and the bush around, and seem to hear Tom's honest voice once more. There's little for me to say now. We prospered on the gem. Tom Donahue, as you know, has set up here, and is well known about town. I have done well, farming and ostrich-raising in Africa. We set old Dick Wharton up in business, and he is one of our nearest neighbours. If you should ever be coming up our way sir, you'll not forget to ask for Jack Turnbull – Jack Turnbull of Sasassa Farm.

THE AMERICAN'S TALE

"It air strange, it air," he was saying as I opened the door of the room where our social little semi-literary society met; "but I could tell you queerer things than that 'ere – almighty queer things. You can't learn everything out of books, sirs, nohow. You see it ain't the men as can string English together and as has had good eddications as finds themselves in the queer places I've been in. They're mostly rough men, sirs, as can scarce speak aright, far less tell with pen and ink the things they've seen; but if they could they'd make some of your European's har riz with astonishment. They would, sirs, you bet!"

His name was Jefferson Adams, I believe; I know his initials were J.A., for you may see them yet deeply whittled on the right-hand upper panel of our smoking-room door. He left us this legacy, and also some artistic patterns done in tobacco juice upon our Turkey carpet; but beyond these reminiscences our American storyteller has vanished from our ken. He gleamed across our ordinary quiet conviviality like some brilliant meteor, and then was lost in the outer darkness. That night, however, our Nevada friend was in full swing; and I quietly lit my pipe and dropped into the nearest chair, anxious not to interrupt his story.

"Mind you," he continued, "I hain't got no grudge against your men of science. I likes and respects a chap as can match every beast and plant, from a huckleberry to a grizzly with a jaw-breakin' name; but if you wants real interestin' facts, something a bit juicy, you go to your whalers and your frontiersmen, and your scouts and Hudson Bay men, chaps who mostly can scarce sign their names."

There was a pause here, as Mr. Jefferson Adams produced a long cheroot and lit it. We preserved a strict silence in the room, for we had already learned that on the slightest interruption our Yankee drew himself into his shell again. He glanced round with a self-satisfied smile as he remarked our expectant looks, and continued through a halo of smoke,

"Now which of you gentlemen has even been in Arizona? None, I'll warrant. And of all English or Americans as can put pen to paper, how many has been in Arizona? Precious few, I calc'late. I've been there, sirs, lived there for years; and when I think of what I've seen there, why, I can scarce get myself to believe it now.

"Ah, there's a country! I was one of Walker's filibusters, as they chose to call us; and after we'd busted up, and the chief was shot, some on us made tracks and located down there. A reg'lar English and American colony, we was, with our wives and children, and all complete. I reckon there's some of the old folk there yet, and that they hain't forgotten what I'm agoing to tell you. No, I warrant they hain't, never on this side of the grave, sirs.

"I was talking about the country, though; and I guess I could astonish you considerable if I spoke of nothing else. To think of such a land being built for a few 'Greasers' and half-breeds! It's a misusing of the gifts of Providence, that's what I calls it. Grass as hung over a chap's head as he rode through it, and trees so thick that you couldn't catch a glimpse of blue sky for leagues and leagues, and orchids like umbrellas! Maybe some on you has seen a plant as they calls the 'fly-catcher,' in some parts of the States?"

"Dianœa muscipula," murmured Dawson, our scientific man *par excellence*.

"Ah, 'Die near a municipal,' that's him! You'll see a fly stand on that 'ere plant, and then you'll see the two sides of a leaf snap up together and catch it between them, and grind it up and mash it to bits, for all the world like some great sea squid with its beak; and hours after, if you open the leaf, you'll see the body lying half-digested, and in bits. Well, I've seen those flytraps in Arizona with leaves eight and ten feet long, and thorns or teeth a foot or more; why, they could – But darn it, I'm going too fast!

"It's about the death of Joe Hawkins I was going to tell you; 'bout as queer a thing, I reckon, as ever you heard tell on. There wasn't nobody in Montana as didn't know of Joe Hawkins – 'Alabama' Joe, as he was called there. A reg'lar out and outer, he was, 'bout the darndest skunk as even man clapt eyes on. He was a good chap enough, mind ye, as long as you stroked him the right way; but rile him anyhow, and he were worse nor a wild-cat. I've seen him empty his six-shooter into a crowd as chanced to jostle him agoing into Simpson's bar when there was a dance on; and he bowied Tom Hooper 'cause he spilt his liquor over his weskit by mistake. No, he didn't stick at murder, Joe didn't; and he weren't a man to be trusted further nor you could see him.

"Now at the time I tell on, when Joe Hawkins was swaggerin' about the town and layin' down the law with his shootin'-irons, there was an Englishman there of the name of Scott – Tom Scott, if I rec'lects aright. This chap Scott was a thorough Britisher (beggin' the present company's pardon), and yet he didn't freeze much to the British set there, or they didn't freeze much to him. He was a quiet simple man, Scott was – rather too quiet for a rough set like that; sneakin' they called him, but he weren't that. He kept hisself mostly apart, an' didn't interfere with nobody so long as he were left alone. Some said as how he'd been kinder ill-treated at home – been a Chartist, or something of that sort, and had to up sticks and run; but he never spoke of it hisself, an' never complained. Bad luck or good, that chap kept a stiff lip on him.

"This chap Scott was a sort o' butt among the men about Montana, for he was so quiet an' simple-like. There was no party either to take up his grievances; for, as I've been saying, the Britishers hardly counted him one of them, and many a rough joke they played on him. He never cut up rough, but was polite to all hisself. I think the boys got to think he hadn't much grit in him till he showed 'em their mistake.

"It was in Simpson's bar as the row got up, an' that led to the queer thing I was going to tell you of. Alabama Joe and one or two other rowdies were dead on the Britishers in those days, and they spoke their opinions pretty free, though I warned them as there'd be an almighty muss. That partic'lar night Joe was nigh half drunk, an' he swaggered about the town with his six-shooter, lookin' out for a quarrel. Then he turned into the bar where he know'd he'd find some o' the English as ready for one as he was hisself. Sure enough, there was half a dozen lounging about, an' Tom Scott standin' alone before the stove. Joe sat down by the table, and put his revolver and bowie down in front of him. 'Them's my arguments, Jeff,' he says to me, 'if any white-livered Britisher dares give me the lie.' I tried to stop him, sirs; but he weren't a man as you could easily turn, an' he began to speak in a way as no chap could stand. Why, even a 'Greaser' would flare up if you said as much of Greaserland! There was a commotion at the bar, an' every man laid his hands on his wepins; but afore they could draw we heard a quiet voice from the stove: 'Say your prayers, Joe Hawkins; for, by Heaven, you're a dead man!' Joe turned round, and looked like grabbin' at his iron; but it weren't no manner of use. Tom Scott was standing up, covering him with his Derringer; a smile on his white face, but the very devil shining in his eye. 'It ain't that the old country has used me over-well,' he says, 'but no man shall speak agin it afore me, and live.' For a second or two I could see his finger tighten round the trigger, an' then he gave a laugh, an' threw the pistol on the floor. 'No,' he says, 'I can't shoot a half-drunk man. Take your dirty life, Joe, an' use it better nor you have done. You've been nearer the grave this night than you will be agin until your time comes. You'd best make tracks now, I guess. Nay, never look black at me, man; I'm not afeard at your shootin'-iron. A bully's nigh always a coward.' And he swung contemptuously round, and relit his half-smoked pipe from the stove; while Alabama slunk out o' the bar, with the laughs of the Britishers ringing in his ears. I saw his face as he passed me, and on it I saw murder, sirs – murder, as plain as ever I seed anything in my life.

"I stayed in the bar after the row, and watched Tom Scott as he shook hands with the men about. It seemed kinder queer to me to see him smilin' and cheerful-like; for I knew Joe's bloodthirsty mind, and that the Englishman had small chance of ever seeing the morning. He lived in an out-of-the-way sort of place, you see, clean off the trail, and had to pass through the Flytrap Gulch to get to it. This here gulch was a marshy gloomy place, lonely enough during the day even; for it were always a creepy sort o' thing to see the great eight- and ten-foot leaves snapping up if aught touched them; but at night there were never a soul near. Some parts of the marsh, too, were soft and deep, and a body thrown in would be gone by the morning. I could see Alabama Joe crouchin' under the leaves of the great Flytrap in the darkest part of the gulch, with a scowl on his face and a revolver in his hand; I could see it, sirs, as plain as with my two eyes.

" 'Bout midnight Simpson shuts up his bar, so out we had to go. Tom Scott started off for his three-mile walk at a slashing pace. I just dropped him a hint as he passed me, for I kinder liked the chap. 'Keep your Derringer loose in your belt, sir,' I says, 'for you might chance to need it.' He looked round at me with his quiet smile, and then I lost sight of him in the gloom. I never thought to see him again. He'd hardly gone afore Simpson comes up to me and says, 'There'll be a nice job in the Flytrap Gulch to-night, Jeff; the boys say that Hawkins started half an hour ago to wait for Scott and shoot him on sight. I calc'late the coroner 'll be wanted to-morrow.'

"What passed in the gulch that night? It were a question as were asked pretty free next morning. A half-breed was in Ferguson's store after daybreak, and he said as he'd chanced to be near the gulch 'bout one in the morning. It warn't easy to get at his story, he seemed so uncommon scared; but he told us, at last, as he'd heard the fearfulest screams in the stillness of the night. There weren't no shots, he said, but scream after scream, kinder muffled, like a man with a serapé over his head, an' in mortal pain. Abner Brandon and me, and a few more, was in the store at the time; so we mounted and rode out to Scott's house, passing through the gulch on the way. There weren't nothing partic'lar to be seen there – no blood nor marks of a fight, nor nothing; and when we gets up to Scott's house, out he comes to meet us as fresh as a lark. 'Hullo, Jeff!' says he, 'no need for the pistols after all. Come in an' have a cocktail, boys.' 'Did you see or hear nothing as you came home last night?' says I. 'No,' says he; 'all was quiet enough. An owl kinder moaning in the Flytrap Gulch – that was all. Come, jump off and have a glass.' 'Thank ye,' says Abner. So off we gets, and Tom Scott rode into the settlement with us when we went back.

"An allfired commotion was on in Main-street as we rode into it. The 'Merican party seemed to have gone clean crazed. Alabama Joe was gone, not a darned particle of him left. Since he went out to the gulch nary eye had seen him. As we got off our horses there was a considerable crowd in front of Simpson's, and some ugly looks at Tom Scott, I can tell you. There was a clickin' of pistols, and I saw as Scott had his hand in his bosom too. There weren't a single English face about. 'Stand aside, Jeff Adams,' says Zebb Humphrey, as great a scoundrel as ever lived, 'you hain't got no hand in this game. Say, boys, are we, free Americans, to be murdered by any darned Britisher?' It was the quickest thing as ever I seed. There was a rush an' a crack; Zebb was down, with Scott's ball in his thigh, and Scott hisself was on the ground with a dozen men holding him. It weren't no use struggling, so he lay quiet. They seemed a bit uncertain what to do with him at first, but then one of Alabama's special chums put them up to it. 'Joe's gone,' he said; 'nothing ain't surer nor that, an' there lies the man as killed him. Some on you knows as Joe went on business to the gulch last night; he never came back. That 'ere Britisher passed through after he'd gone; they'd had a row, screams is heard 'mong the great flytraps. I say agin he has played poor Joe some o' his sneakin' tricks, an' thrown him into the swamp. It ain't no wonder as the body is gone. But air we to stan'by and see English murderin' our own chums? I guess not. Let Judge Lynch try him, that's what I say.' 'Lynch him!' shouted a hundred angry voices – for all the rag-tag an' bobtail o' the settlement was round us by this time. 'Here, boys, fetch a rope, and swing him up. Up with him over Simpson's door!' 'See here though,' says another, coming forrards; 'let's hang him by the great flytrap in the gulch. Let Joe see as he's revenged, if so be as he's buried 'bout theer.' There was a shout for this, an' away they went, with Scott tied on his mustang in the middle, and a mounted guard, with cocked revolvers, round him; for we knew as there was a score or so Britishers about, as didn't seem to recognise Judge Lynch, and was dead on a free fight.

"I went out with them, my heart bleedin' for Scott, though he didn't seem a cent put out, he didn't. He were game to the backbone. Seems kinder queer, sirs, hangin' a man to a flytrap; but our'n were a reg'lar tree, and the leaves like a brace of boats with a hinge between 'em and thorns at the bottom.

"We passed down the gulch to the place where the great one grows, and there we seed it with the leaves, some open, some shut. But we seed something worse nor that. Standin' round the tree was some thirty men, Britishers all, an' armed to the teeth. They was waitin' for us evidently, an' had a businesslike look about 'em, as if they'd come for something and meant to have it. There was the raw material there for about as warm a scrimmidge as ever I seed. As we rode up, a great red-bearded Scotchman – Cameron were his name – stood out afore the rest, his revolver cocked in his hand. 'See here, boys,' he says, 'you've got no call to hurt a hair of that man's head. You hain't proved as Joe is dead yet; and if you had, you hain't proved as Scott killed him. Anyhow, it were in self-defence; for you all know as he was lying in wait for Scott, to shoot him on sight; so I say agin, you hain't got no call to hurt that man; and what's more, I've got thirty six-barrelled arguments against your doin' it.' 'It's an interestin' pint, and worth arguin' out,' said the man as was Alabama Joe's special chum. There was a clickin' of pistols, and a loosenin' of knives, and the two parties began to draw up to one another, an' it looked like a rise in the mortality of Montana. Scott was standing behind with a pistol at his ear if he stirred, lookin' quiet and composed as having no money on the table, when sudden he gives a start an' a shout as rang in our ears like a trumpet. 'Joe!' he cried, 'Joe! Look at him! In the flytrap!' We all turned an' looked where he was pointin'. Jerusalem! I think we won't get that picter out of our minds agin. One of the great leaves of the flytrap, that had been shut and touchin' the ground as it lay, was slowly rolling back upon its hinges. There, lying like a child in its cradle, was Alabama Joe in the hollow of the leaf. The great thorns had been slowly driven through his heart as it shut upon him. We could see as he'd tried to cut his way out, for there was slit in the thick fleshy leaf, an' his bowie was in his hand; but it had smothered him first. He'd lain down on it likely to keep the damp off while he were awaitin' for

Scott, and it had closed on him as you've seen your little hothouse ones do on a fly; an' there he were as we found him, torn and crushed into pulp by the great jagged teeth of the man-eatin' plant. There, sirs, I think you'll own as that's a curious story."

"And what became of Scott?" asked Jack Sinclair.

"Why, we carried him back on our shoulders, we did, to Simpson's bar, and he stood us liquors round. Made a speech too – a darned fine speech – from the counter. Somethin' about the British lion an' the 'Merican eagle walkin' arm in arm for ever an' a day. And now, sirs, that yarn was long, and my cheroot's out, so I reckon I'll make tracks afore it's later;" and with a "Good-night!" he left the room.

"A most extraordinary narrative!" said Dawson. "Who would have thought a Diancea had such power!"

"Deuced rum yarn!" said young Sinclair.

"Evidently a matter-of-fact truthful man," said the doctor.

"Or the most original liar that ever lived," said I.

I wonder which he was.

BONES
THE APRIL FOOL OF HARVEY'S SLUICE

———————————◆———————————

Abe Durton's cabin was not beautiful. People have been heard to assert that it was ugly, and, even after the fashion of Harvey's Sluice, have gone the length of prefixing their adjective with a forcible expletive which emphasised their criticism. Abe, however, was a stolid and easygoing man, on whose mind the remarks of an unappreciative public made but little impression. He had built the house himself, and it suited his partner and him, and what more did they want? Indeed he was rather touchy upon the subject. "Though I says it as raised it," he remarked, "it'll lay over any shanty in the valley. Holes? Well, of course there are holes. You wouldn't get fresh air without holes. There's nothing stuffy about *my* house. Rain? Well, if it does let the rain in, ain't it an advantage to know its rainin' without gettin' up to unbar the door. I wouldn't own a house that didn't leak some. As to its bein' off the perpendic'lar, I like a house with a bit of a tilt. Anyways it pleases my pard, Boss Morgan, and what's good enough for him is good enough for you, I suppose." At which approach to personalities his antagonist usually sheered off, and left the honours of the field to the indignant architect.

But whatever difference of opinion might exist as to the beauty of the establishment, there could be no question as to its utility. To the tired wayfarer, plodding along the Buckhurst-road in the direction of the Sluice, the warm glow upon the summit of the hill was a beacon of hope and of comfort. Those very holes at which the neighbours sneered helped to diffuse a cheery atmosphere of light around, which was doubly acceptable on such a night as the present.

There was only one man inside the hut, and that was the proprietor, Abe Durton himself, or "Bones," as he had been christened with the rude heraldry of the camp. He was sitting in front of the great wood fire, gazing moodily into its glowing depths, and occasionally giving a faggot a kick of remonstrance when it showed any indication of dying into a smoulder. His fair Saxon face, with its bold simple eyes and crisp yellow beard, stood out sharp and clear against the darkness as the flickering light played over it. It was a manly resolute countenance, and yet the physiognomist might have detected something in the lines of the mouth which showed a weakness somewhere, an indecision which contrasted strangely with his herculean shoulders and massive limbs. Abe's was one of those trusting simple natures which are as easy to lead as they are impossible to drive; and it was this happy pliability of disposition which made him at once the butt and the favourite of the dwellers in the Sluice. Badinage in that primitive settlement was of a somewhat ponderous character, yet no amount of chaff had ever brought a dark look on Bones's face, or an unkind thought into his honest heart. It was only when his aristocratic partner was, as he thought, being put upon, that an ominous tightness about his lower lip and an angry light in his blue eyes caused even the most irrepressible humorist in the colony to nip his favourite joke in the bud, in order to diverge into an earnest and all-absorbing dissertation upon the state of the weather.

"The Boss is late to-night," he muttered as he rose from his chair and stretched himself in a colossal yawn. "My stars, how it does rain and blow! Don't it, Blinky?" Blinky was a demure and meditative owl, whose comfort and welfare was a chronic subject of solicitude to its master, and who at present contemplated him gravely from one of the rafters. "Pity you can't speak, Blinky," continued Abe, glancing up at his feathered companion. "There's a powerful deal of sense in your face. Kinder melancholy too. Crossed in love, maybe, when you was young. Talkin' of love," he added, "I've not seen Susan to-day;" and lighting the candle which stood in a black bottle upon the table, he walked across the room and peered earnestly at one of the many pictures from stray illustrated papers, which had been cut out by the occupants and posted up upon the walls.

The particular picture which attracted him was one which represented a very tawdrily-dressed actress simpering over a bouquet at an imaginary audience. This sketch had, for some inscrutable reason, made a deep impression upon the susceptible heart of the miner. He had invested the young lady with a human interest by solemnly, and without the slightest warrant, christening her as Susan Banks, and had then installed her as his standard of female beauty.

"You see my Susan," he would say, when some wanderer from

Buckhurst, or even from Melbourne, would describe some fair Circe whom he had left behind him. "There ain't a girl like my Sue. If ever you go to the old country again, just you ask to see her. Susan Banks is her name, and I've got her picture up at the shanty."

Abe was still gazing at his charmer when the rough door was flung open, and a blinding cloud of sleet and rain came driving into the cabin, almost obscuring for the moment a young man who sprang in and proceeded to bar the entrance behind him, an operation which the force of the wind rendered no easy matter. He might have passed for the genius of the storm, with the water dripping from his long hair and running down his pale refined face.

"Well," he said, in a slightly peevish voice, "haven't you got any supper?"

"Waiting and ready," said his companion cheerily, pointing to a large pot which bubbled by the side of the fire. "You seem sort of damp."

"Damp be hanged! I'm soaked, man, thoroughly saturated. It's a night that I wouldn't have a dog out, at least not a dog that I had any respect for. Hand over that dry coat from the peg."

Jack Morgan, or Boss, as he was usually called, belonged to a type which was commoner in the mines during the flush times of the first great rush than would be supposed. He was a man of good blood, liberally educated, and a graduate of an English university. Boss should, in the natural course of things, have been an energetic curate, or struggling professional man, had not some latent traits cropped out in his character, inherited possibly from old Sir Henry Morgan, who had founded the family with Spanish pieces of eight gallantly won upon the high seas. It was this wild strain of blood no doubt which had caused him to drop from the bedroom-window of the ivy-clad English parsonage, and leave home and friends behind him, to try his luck with pick and shovel in the Australian fields. In spite of his effeminate face and dainty manners, the rough dwellers in Harvey's Sluice had gradually learned that the little man was possessed of a cool courage and unflinching resolution, which won respect in a community where pluck was looked upon as the highest of human attributes. No one ever knew how it was that Bones and he had become partners; yet partners they were, and the large simple nature of the stronger man looked with an almost superstitious reverence upon the clear decisive mind of his companion.

"That's better," said the Boss, as he dropped into the vacant chair before the fire and watched Abe laying out the two metal plates, with the horn-handled knives and abnormally pronged forks. "Take your mining boots off, Bones; there's no use filling the cabin with red clay. Come here and sit down."

His gigantic partner came meekly over and perched himself upon the top of a barrel.

"What's up?" he asked.

"Shares are up," said his companion. "That's what's up. Look here," and he extracted a crumpled paper from the pocket of the steaming coat. "Here's the *Buckhurst Sentinel*. Read this article — this one here about a paying lead in the Conemara mine. We hold pretty heavily in that concern, my boy. We might sell out to-day and clear something — but I think we'll hold on."

Abe Durton in the mean time was laboriously spelling out the article in question, following the lines with his great forefinger, and muttering under his tawny moustache.

"Two hundred dollars a foot," he said, looking up. "Why, pard, we hold a hundred feet each. It would give us twenty thousand dollars! We might go home on that."

"Nonsense!" said his companion; "we've come out here for something better than a beggarly couple of thousand pounds. The thing is bound to pay. Sinclair the assayer has been over there, and says there's a ledge of the richest quartz he ever set eyes on. It is just a case of getting the machinery to crush it. By the way, what was to-days' take like?"

Abe extracted a small wooden box from his pocket and handed it to his comrade. It contained what appeared to be about a teaspoonful of sand and one or two little metallic granules not larger than a pea. Boss Morgan laughed, and returned it to his companion.

"We sha'n't make our fortune at that rate, Bones," he remarked; and there was a pause in the conversation as the two men listened to the wind as it screamed and whistled past the little cabin.

"Any news from Buckhurst?" asked Abe, rising and proceeding to extract their supper from the pot.

"Nothing much," said his companion. "Cock-eyed Joe has been shot by Bill Reid in McFarlane's Store."

"Ah," said Abe, with listless interest.

"Bushrangers have been around and stuck up the Rochdale station. They say they are coming over here."

The miner whistled as he poured some whisky into a jug.

"Anything more?" he asked.

"Nothing of importance except that the blacks have been showing a bit down New Sterling way, and that the assayer has bought a piano and is going to have his daughter out from Melbourne to live in the new house opposite on the other side of the road. So you see we are going to have something to look at, my boy," he added as he sat down, and began attacking the food set before him. "They say she is a beauty, Bones."

"She won't be a patch on my Sue," returned the other decisively.

His partner smiled as he glanced round at the flaring print upon the wall. Suddenly he dropped his knife and seemed to listen. Amid the wild uproar of the wind and the rain there was a low rumbling sound which was evidently not dependent upon the elements.

"What's that?"

"Darned if I know."

The two men made for the door and peered out earnestly into the darkness. Far away along the Buckhurst road they could see a moving light, and the dull sound was louder than before.

"It's a buggy coming down," said Abe.

"Where is it going to?"

"Don't know. Across the ford, I s'pose."

"Why, man, the ford will be six feet deep to-night, and running like a mill-stream."

The light was nearer now, coming rapidly round the curve of the road. There was a wild sound of galloping with the rattle of the wheels.

"Horses have bolted, by thunder!"

"Bad job for the man inside."

There was a rough individuality about the inhabitants of Harvey's Sluice, in virtue of which every man bore his misfortunes upon his own shoulders, and had very little sympathy for those of his neighbours. The predominant feeling of the two men was one of pure curiosity as they watched the swinging swaying lanterns coming down the winding road.

"If he don't pull 'em up before they reach the ford he's a goner," remarked Abe Durton resignedly.

Suddenly there came a lull in the sullen splash of the rain. It was but for a moment, but in that moment there came down on the breeze a long cry which caused the two men to start and stare at each other, and then to rush frantically down the steep incline towards the road below.

"A woman, by Heaven!" gasped Abe, as he sprang across the gaping shaft of a mine in the recklessness of his haste.

Morgan was the lighter and more active man. He drew away rapidly from his stalwart companion. Within a minute he was standing panting and bare-headed in the middle of the soft muddy road, while his partner was still toiling down the side of the declivity.

The carriage was close on him now. He could see in the light of the lamps the raw-boned Australian horse as, terrified by the storm and by its own clatter, it came tearing down the declivity which led to the ford. The man who was driving seemed to see the pale set face in the pathway in front of him, for he yelled out some incoherent words of warning, and made a last desperate attempt to pull up. There was a shout, an oath, and a jarring crash, and Abe, hurrying down, saw a wild infuriated horse rearing madly in the air with the slim dark figure hanging on to its bridle. Boss, with the keen power of calculation which had made him the finest cricketer at Rugby in his day, had caught the rein immediately below the bit, and clung to it with silent concentration. Once he was down with a heavy thud in the roadway as the horse jerked its head violently forwards, but when, with a snort of exultation, the animal pressed on, it was only to find that the prostrate man beneath its forehoofs still maintained his unyielding grasp.

"Hold it, Bones," he said, as a tall figure hurled itself into the road and seized the other rein.

"All right, old man, I've got him;" and the horse, cowed by the sight of a fresh assailant, quieted down, and stood shivering with terror. "Get up, Boss, it's safe now."

But poor Boss lay groaning in the mud.

"I can't do it, Bones." There was a catch in the voice as of pain. "There's something wrong, old chap, but don't make a fuss. It's only a shake; give me a lift up."

Abe bent tenderly over his prostrate companion. He could see that he was very white, and breathing with difficulty.

"Cheer up, old Boss," he murmured. "Hullo! my stars!"

The last two exclamations were shot out of the honest miner's bosom as if they were impelled by some irresistible force, and he took a couple of steps backward in sheer amazement. There at the other side of the fallen man, and half shrouded in the darkness, stood what appeared to Abe's simple soul to be the most beautiful vision that ever had appeared upon earth. To eyes accustomed to rest upon nothing more captivating than the ruddy faces and rough beards of the miners in the Sluice, it seemed that that fair delicate countenance must belong to a wanderer from some better world. Abe gazed at it with a wondering reverence, oblivious for the moment even of his injured friend upon the ground.

"O papa," said the apparition, in great distress, "he is hurt, the gentleman is hurt," and with a quick feminine gesture of sympathy, she bent her lithe figure over Boss Morgan's prostrate figure.

"Why, it's Abe Durton and his partner," said the driver of the buggy, coming forward and disclosing the grizzled features of Mr. Joshua Sinclair, the assayer to the mines. "I don't know how to thank you, boys. The infernal brute got the bit between his teeth, and I should have had to have thrown Carrie out and chanced it in another minute. That's right," he continued as Morgan staggered to his feet. "Not much hurt, I hope."

"I can get up to the hut now," said the young man, steadying himself upon his partner's shoulder. "How are you going to get Miss Sinclair home?"

"Oh, we can walk," said the young lady, shaking off the effects of her fright with all the elasticity of youth.

"We can drive and take the road round the bank so as to avoid the ford," said her father. "The horse seems cowed enough now; you need not be afraid of it, Carrie. I hope we shall see you at the house, both of you. Neither of us can easily forget this night's work."

Miss Carrie said nothing, but she managed to shoot a little demure glance of gratitude from under her long lashes, to have won which honest Abe felt that he would have cheerfully undertaken to stop a runaway locomotive.

There was a cheery shout of "Good-night," a crack of the whip, and the buggy rattled away in the darkness.

"You told me the men were rough and nasty, pa," said Miss Carrie Sinclair, after a long silence, when the two dark shadows had died away in the distance, and the carriage was speeding along by the turbulent stream. "I don't think so. I think they were very nice." And Carrie was unusually quiet for the remainder of her journey, and seemed more reconciled to the hardship of leaving her dear friend Amelia in the far-off boarding school at Melbourne.

That did not prevent her from writing a full, true, and particular account of their little adventure to the same young lady upon that very night.

"They stopped the horse, darling, and one poor fellow was hurt. And O, Amy, if you had seen the other one in a red shirt, with a pistol at his waist! I couldn't help thinking of you, dear. He was just your idea. You remember, a yellow moustache and great blue eyes. And how he did stare at poor me! You never see such men in Burke-street, Amy;" and so on, for four pages of pretty feminine gossip.

In the mean time poor Boss, badly shaken, had been helped up the hill by his partner and regained the shelter of the shanty. Abe doctored him out of the rude pharmacopœia of the camp, and bandaged up his strained arm. Both were men of few words, and neither made any allusion to what had taken place. It was noticed, however, by Blinky that his master failed to pay his usual nightly orisons before the shrine of Susan Banks. Whether this sagacious fowl drew any deductions from this, and from the fact that Bones sat long and earnestly smoking by the smouldering fire, I know not. Suffice it that as the candle died away and the miner rose from his chair, his feathered friend flew down upon his shoulder, and was only prevented from giving vent to a sympathetic hoot by Abe's warning finger, and its own strong inherent sense of propriety.

A casual visitor dropping into the straggling township of Harvey's Sluice shortly after Miss Carrie Sinclair's arrival would have noticed a considerable alteration in the manners and customs of its inhabitants. Whether it was the refining influence of a woman's presence, or whether it sprang from an emulation excited by the brilliant appearance of Abe Durton, it is hard to say – probably from a blending of the two. Certain it is that that young man had suddenly developed an affection for cleanliness and a regard for the conventionalities of civilisation, which aroused the astonishment and ridicule of his companions. That Boss Morgan should pay attention to his personal appearance had long been set down as a curious and inexplicable phenomenon, depending upon early education; but that loose-limbed easy-going Bones should flaunt about in a clean shirt was regarded by every grimy denizen of the Sluice as a direct and premeditated insult. In self-defence, therefore, there was a general cleaning up after working hours, and such a run upon the grocery establishment, that soap went up to an unprecedented figure, and a fresh consignment had to be ordered from McFarlane's store in Buckhurst.

"Is this here a free minin' camp, or is it a darned Sunday-school?" had been the indignant query of Long McCoy, a prominent member of the reactionary party, who had failed to advance with the times, having been absent during the period of regeneration. But his remonstrance met with but little sympathy; and at the end of a couple of days a general turbidity of the creek announced his surrender, which was confirmed by his appearance in the Colonial Bar with a shining and bashful face, and hair which was redolent of bear's grease.

"I felt kinder lonesome," he remarked apologetically, "so I thought as I'd have a look what was under the clay," and he viewed himself approvingly in the cracked mirror which graced the select room of the establishment.

Our casual visitor would have noticed a remarkable change also in the conversation of the community. Somehow, when a certain dainty little bonnet with a sweet girlish figure beneath it was seen in the distance among the disused shafts and mounds of red earth which disfigured the sides of the valley, there was a warning murmur, and a general clearing off of the cloud of blasphemy, which was, I regret to state, an habitual characteristic of the working population of Harvey's Sluice. Such things only need a beginning; and it was noticeable that long after Miss Sinclair had vanished from sight there was a decided rise in the moral barometer of the gulches. Men found by experience that their stock of adjectives was less limited than they had been accustomed to suppose, and that the less forcible were sometimes even more adapted for conveying their meaning.

Abe had formerly been considered one of the most experienced valuators of an ore in the settlement. It had been commonly supposed that he was able to estimate the amount of gold in a fragment of quartz with remarkable exactness. This, however, was evidently a mistake, otherwise he would never have incurred the useless expense of having so many worthless specimens assayed as he now did. Mr. Joshua Sinclair found himself inundated with such a flood of fragments of mica, and lumps of rock containing decimal percentages of the precious metals, that he began to form a very low opinion of the young man's mining capabilities. It is even asserted that Abe shuffled up to the house one morning with a hopeful smile, and, after some fumbling, produced half a brick from the bosom of his jersey, with the stereotyped remark "that he thought he'd struck it at last, and so had dropped in to ask him to cipher out an estimate." As this anecdote rests, however, upon the unsupported evidence of Jim Struggles, the humorist of the camp, there may be some slight inaccuracy of detail.

It is certain that what with professional business in the morning and social visits at night, the tall figure of the miner was a familiar object in the little drawing room of Azalea Villa, as the new house of the assayer had been magniloquently named. He seldom ventured upon a remark in the presence of its female occupant; but would sit on the extreme edge of his chair in a state of speechless admiration while she rattled off some lively air upon the newly-imported piano. Many were the strange and unexpected places in which his feet turned up. Miss Carrie had gradually come to the conclusion that they were entirely independent of his body, and had ceased to speculate upon the manner in which she would trip over them on one side of the table while the blushing owner was apologising from the other. There was only one cloud on honest Bones's mental horizon, and that was the periodical appearance of Black Tom Ferguson, of Rochdale Ferry. This clever young scamp had managed to ingratiate himself with old Joshua, and was a constant visitor at the villa. There were evil rumours abroad about Black Tom. He was known to be a gambler, and shrewdly suspected to be worse. Harvey's Sluice was not censorious, and yet there was a general feeling that Ferguson was a man to be avoided. There was a reckless *élan* about his bearing, however, and a sparkle in his conversation, which had an indescribable charm, and even induced the Boss, who was particular in such matters, to cultivate his acquaintance while forming a correct estimate of his character. Miss Carrie seemed to hail his appearance as a relief, and chattered away for hours about books and music and the gaieties of Melbourne. It was on these occasions that poor simple Bones would sink into the very lowest depths of despondency, and either slink away, or sit glaring at his rival with an earnest malignancy which seemed to cause that gentleman no small amusement.

The miner made no secret to his partner of the admiration which he entertained for Miss Sinclair. If he was silent in her company, he was voluble enough when she was the subject of discourse. Loiterers upon the Buckhurst road might have heard a stentorian voice upon the hillside bellowing forth a vocabulary of female charms. He submitted his difficulties to the superior intelligence of the Boss.

"That loafer from Rochdale," he said, "he seems to reel it off kinder nat'ral, while for the life of me I can't say a word. Tell me, Boss, what would *you* say to a girl like that?"

"Why, talk about what would interest her," said his companion.

"Ah, that's where it lies."

"Talk about the customs of the place and the country," said the Boss, pulling meditatively at his pipe. "Tell her stories of what you have seen in the mines, and that sort of thing."

"Eh? You'd do that, would you?" responded his comrade more hopefully. "If that's the hang of it I am right. I'll go up now and tell her about Chicago Bill, an' how he put them two bullets in the man from the bend the night of the dance."

Boss Morgan laughed.

"That's hardly the thing," he said. "You'd frighten her if you told her that. Tell her something lighter, you know; something to amuse her, something funny."

"Funny?" said the anxious lover, with less confidence in his voice. "How you and me made Mat Houlahan drunk and put him in the pulpit of the Baptist church, and he wouldn't let the preacher in in the morning. How would that do, eh?"

"For Heaven's sake, don't say anything of the sort," said his Mentor, in great consternation. "She'd never speak to either of us again. No, what I mean is that you should tell about the habits of the mines, how men live and work and die there. If she is a sensible girl that ought to interest her."

"How they live at the mines? Pard, you are good to me. How they live? There's a thing I can talk of as glib as Black Tom or any man. I'll try it on her when I see her."

"By the way," said his partner listlessly, "just keep an eye on that man Ferguson. His hands aren't very clean, you know and he's not scrupulous when he is aiming for anything. You remember how Dick Williams, of English Town, was found dead in the bush. Of course it was rangers that did it. They do say, however, that Black Tom owed him a deal more money than he could ever have paid. There's been one or two queer things about him. Keep your eye on him, Abe. Watch what he does."

"I will," said his companion.

And he did. He watched him that very night. Watched him stride out of the house of the assayer with anger and baffled pride on every feature of his handsome swarthy face. Watched him clear the garden paling at a bound, pass in long rapid strides down the side of the valley, gesticulating wildly with his hands, and vanish into the bushland beyond. All this Abe Durton watched, and with a thoughtful look upon his face he relit his pipe and strolled slowly backward to the hut upon the hill.

March was drawing to a close in Harvey's Sluice, and the glare and heat of the antipodean summer had toned down into the rich mellow hues of autumn. It was never a lovely place to look upon. There was something hopelessly prosaic in the two bare rugged ridges, seamed and scarred by the hand of man, with iron arms of windlasses, and broken buckets projecting everywhere through the endless little hillocks of red earth. Down the middle ran the deeply rutted road from Buckhurst, winding along and crossing the sluggish tide of Harper's Creek by a crumbling wooden bridge. Beyond the bridge lay the cluster of little huts with the Colonial Bar and the Grocery towering in all the dignity of whitewash among the humble dwellings around. The assayer's verandah-lined house lay above the gulches on the side of the slope nearly opposite the dilapidated specimen of architecture of which our friend Abe was so unreasonably proud.

There was one other building which might have come under the category of what an inhabitant of the Sluice would have described as a "public edifice" with a comprehensive wave of his pipe which conjured up images of an endless vista of colonnades and minarets. This was the Baptist chapel, a modest little shingle-roofed erection on the bend of the river about a mile above the settlement. It was from this that the town looked at its best, when the harsh outlines and crude colours were somewhat softened by distance. On that particular morning the stream looked pretty as it meandered down the valley; pretty, too, was the long rising upland behind, with its luxuriant green covering; and prettiest of all was Miss Carrie Sinclair, as she laid down the basket of ferns which she was carrying, and stopped upon the summit of the rising ground.

Something seemed to be amiss with that young lady. There was a look of anxiety upon her face which contrasted strangely with her usual appearance of piquant insouciance. Some recent annoyance had left its traces upon her. Perhaps it was to walk it off that she had rambled down the valley; certain it is that she inhaled the fresh breezes of the woodlands as if their resinous fragrance bore with them some antidote for human sorrow.

She stood for some time gazing at the view before her. She could see her father's house, like a white dot upon the hillside, though strangely enough it was a blue reek of smoke upon the opposite slope which seemed to attract the greater part of her attention. She lingered there, watching it with a wistful look in her hazel eyes. Then the loneliness of her situation seemed to strike her, and she felt one of those spasmodic fits of unreasoning terror to which the bravest women are subject. Tales of natives and of bushrangers, their daring and their cruelty, flashed across her. She glanced at the great mysterious stretch of silent bushland beside her, and stooped to pick up her basket with the intention of hurrying along the road in the direction of the gulches. She started round, and hardly suppressed a scream as a long red-flannelled arm shot out from behind her and withdrew the basket from her very grasp.

The figure which met her eye would to some have seemed little calculated to allay her fears. The high boots, the rough shirt, and the broad girdle with its weapons of death were, however, too familiar to Miss Carrie to be objects of terror; and when above them all she saw a pair of tender blue eyes looking down upon

her, and a half-abashed smile lurking under a thick yellow
moustache, she knew that for the remainder of that walk ranger
and black would be equally powerless to harm her.

"O Mr. Durton," she said, "how you did startle me!"

"I'm sorry, miss," said Abe, in great trepidation at having
caused his idol one moment's uneasiness. "You see," he continued, with simple cunning, "the weather bein' fine and my
partner gone prospectin', I thought I'd walk up to Hagley's Hill
and round back by the bend, and there I sees you accidental-like
and promiscuous a-standin' on a hillock." This astounding false-
hood was reeled off by the miner with great fluency, and an
artificial sincerity which at once stamped it as a fabrication. Bones
had concocted and rehearsed it while tracking the little footsteps
in the clay, and looked upon it as the very depth of human guile.
Miss Carrie did not venture upon a remark, but there was a gleam
of amusement in her eyes which puzzled her lover.

Abe was in good spirits this morning. It may have been the
sunshine, or it may have been the rapid rise of shares in the
Conemara, which lightened his heart. I am inclined to think,
however, that it was referable to neither of these causes. Simple as
he was, the scene which he had witnessed the night before could
only lead to one conclusion. He pictured himself walking as wildly
down the valley under similar circumstances, and his heart was
touched with pity for his rival. He felt very certain that the
ill-omened face of Mr. Thomas Ferguson of Rochdale Ferry
would never more be seen within the walls of Azalea Villa. Then
why did she refuse him? He was handsome, he was fairly rich.
Could it – ? no, it couldn't; of course it couldn't; how could it! The
idea was ridiculous – so very ridiculous that it had fermented in
the young man's brain all night, and that he could do nothing but
ponder over it in the morning, and cherish it in his perturbed
bosom.

They passed down the red pathway together, and along by the
river's bank. Abe had relapsed into his normal condition of
taciturnity. He had made one gallant effort to hold forth upon
the subject of ferns, stimulated by the basket which he held in his
hand, but the theme was not a thrilling one, and after a spasmodic
flicker he had abandoned the attempt. While coming along he
had been full of racy anecdotes and humorous observations. He
had rehearsed innumerable remarks which were to be poured
into Miss Sinclair's appreciative ear. But now his brain seemed of
a sudden to have become a vacuum, and utterly devoid of any
idea save an insane and overpowering impulse to comment upon
the heat of the sun. No astronomer who ever reckoned a parallax

was so entirely absorbed in the condition of the celestial bodies as honest Bones while he trudged along by the slow-flowing Australian river.

Suddenly his conversation with his partner came back into his mind. What was it Boss had said upon the subject? "Tell her how they live at the mines." He revolved it in his brain. It seemed a curious thing to talk about; but Boss had said it, and Boss was always right. He would take the plunge; so with a premonitory hem he blurted out,

"They live mostly on bacon and beans in the valley."

He could not see what effect this communication had upon his companion. He was too tall to be able to peer under the little straw bonnet. She did not answer. He would try again.

"Mutton on Sundays," he said.

Even this failed to arouse any enthusiasm. In fact she seemed to be laughing. Boss was evidently wrong. The young man was in despair. The sight of a ruined hut beside the pathway conjured up a fresh idea. He grasped at it as a drowning man to a straw.

"Cockney Jack built that," he remarked. "Lived there till he died."

"What did he die of?" asked his companion.

"Three star brandy," said Abe decisively. "I used to come over of a night when he was bad and sit with him. Poor chap! he had a wife and two children in Putney. He'd rave, and call me Polly, by the hour. He was cleaned out, hadn't a red cent; but the boys collected rough gold enough to see him through. He's buried there in that shaft; that was his claim, so we just dropped him down it an' filled it up. Put down his pick too, an' a spade an' a bucket, so's he'd feel kinder perky and at home."

Miss Carrie seemed more interested now.

"Do they often die like that?" she asked.

"Well, brandy kills many; but there's more gets dropped – shot, you know."

"I don't mean that. Do many men die alone and miserable down there, with no one to care for them?" and she pointed to the cluster of houses beneath them. "Is there any one dying now? It is awful to think of."

"There's none as I knows on likely to throw up their hand."

"I wish you wouldn't use so much slang, Mr. Durton," said Carrie, looking up at him reprovingly out of her voilet eyes. It was strange what an air of proprietorship this young lady was gradually assuming towards her gigantic companion. "You know it isn't polite. You should get a dictionary and learn the proper words."

"Ah, that's it," said Bones apologetically. "It's gettin' your hand on the proper one. When you've not got a steam drill, you've got to put up with a pick."

"Yes, but it's easy if you really try. You could say that a man was 'dying,' or 'moribund,' if you like."

"That's it," said the miner enthusiastically. " 'Moribund!' That's a word. Why, you could lay over Boss Morgan in the matter of words. 'Moribund!' There's some sound about that."

Carrie laughed.

"It's not the sound you must think of, but whether it will express your meaning. Seriously, Mr. Durton, if any one should be ill in the camp you must let me know. I can nurse, and I might be of use. You will, won't you?"

Abe readily acquiesced, and relapsed into silence as he pondered over the possibility of inoculating himself with some long and tedious disease. There was a mad dog reported from Buckhurst. Perhaps something might be done with that.

"And now I must say good-morning," said Carrie, as they came to the spot where a crooked pathway branched off from the track and wound up to Azalea Villa. "Thank you ever so much for escorting me."

In vain Abe pleaded for the additional hundred yards, and adduced the overwhelming weight of the diminutive basket as a cogent reason. The young lady was inexorable. She had taken him too far out of his way already. She was ashamed of herself; she wouldn't hear of it.

So poor Bones departed in a mixture of many opposite feelings. He had interested her. She had spoken kindly to him. But then she had sent him away before there was any necessity; she couldn't care much about him if she would do that. I think he might have felt a little more cheerful, however, had he seen Miss Carrie Sinclair as she watched his retiring figure from the garden-gate with a loving look upon her saucy face, and a mischievous smile at his bent head and desponding appearance.

The Colonial Bar was the favourite haunt of the inhabitants of Harvey's Sluice in their hours of relaxation. There had been a fierce competition between it and the rival establishment termed the Grocery, which, in spite of its innocent appellation, aspired also to dispense spirituous refreshments. The importation of chairs into the latter had led to the appearance of a settee in the former. Spittoons appeared in the Grocery against a picture in the Bar, and, as the frequenters expressed it, the honours were even. When, however, the Grocery led a window-curtain, and its opponent returned a snuggery and a mirror, the game was declared to be in favour of the latter, and Harvey's Sluice showed its sense of the spirit of the proprietor by withdrawing their custom from his opponent.

Though every man was at liberty to swagger into the Bar itself, and bask in the shimmer of its many coloured bottles, there was a general feeling that the snuggery, or special apartment, should be reserved for the use of the more prominent citizens. It was in this room that committees met, that opulent companies were conceived and born, and that inquests were generally held. The latter, I regret to state, was, in 1861, a pretty frequent ceremony at the Sluice; and the findings of the coroner were sometimes characterised by a fine breezy originality. Witness when Bully Burke, a notorious desperado, was shot down by a quiet young medical man, and a sympathetic jury brought in that "the deceased had met his death in an ill-advised attempt to stop a pistol-ball while in motion," a verdict which was looked upon as a triumph of jurisprudence in the camp, as simultaneously exonerating the culprit, and adhering to the rigid and undeniable truth.

On this particular evening there was an assemblage of notabilities in the snuggery, though no such pathological ceremony had called them together. Many changes had occurred of late which merited discussion; and it was in this chamber, gorgeous in all the effete luxury of the mirror and settee, that Harvey's Sluice was wont to exchange ideas. The recent cleaning of the population was still causing some ferment in men's minds. Then there was Miss Sinclair and her movements to be commented on, and the paying lead in the Conemara, and the recent rumours of bushrangers. It was no wonder that the leading men in the township had come together in the Colonial Bar.

The rangers were the present subject of discussion. For some few days rumours of their presence had been flying about, and an uneasy feeling had pervaded the colony. Physical fear was a thing little known in Harvey's Sluice. The miners would have turned out to hunt down the desperadoes with as much zest as if they had been so many kangaroos. It was the presence of a large quantity of gold in the town which caused anxiety. It was felt that the fruits of their labour must be secured at any cost. Messages had been sent over to Buckhurst for as many troopers as could be spared, and in the mean time the main street of the Sluice was paraded at night by volunteer sentinels.

A fresh impetus had been given to the panic by the report brought in to-day by Jim Struggles. Jim was of an ambitious and aspiring turn of mind, and after gazing in silent disgust at his

last week's clean up, he had metaphorically shaken the clay of
Harvey's Sluice from his feet, and had started off into the woods
with the intention of prospecting round until he could hit upon
some likely piece of ground for himself. Jim's story was that he
was sitting upon a fallen trunk eating his midday damper and
rusty bacon, when his trained ear had caught the clink of horses'
hoofs. He had hardly time to take the precaution of rolling off the
tree and crouching down behind it, before a troop of men came
riding down through the bush, and passed within a stone-throw
of him.

"There was Bill Smeaton and Murphy Duff," said Struggles,
naming two notorious ruffians; "and there was three more that I
couldn't rightly see. And they took the trail to the right, and
looked like business all over, with their guns in their hands."

Jim was submitted to a searching cross-examination that evening; but nothing could shake his testimony or throw a further
light upon what he had seen. He told the story several times and at
long intervals; and though there might be a pleasing variety in the
minor incidents, the main facts were always identically the same.
The matter began to look serious.

There were a few, however, who were loudly sceptical as to the
existence of the rangers, and the most prominent of these was a
young man who was perched on a barrel in the centre of the
room, and was evidently one of the leading spirits in the community. We have already seen that dark curling hair, lack-lustre
eye, and thin cruel lip, in the person of Black Tom Ferguson, the
rejected suitor of Miss Sinclair. He was easily distinguishable
from the rest of the party by a tweed coat, and other symptoms of
effeminacy in his dress, which might have brought him into
disrepute had he not, like Abe Durton's partner, early established
the reputation of being a quietly desperate man. On the present
occasion he seemed somewhat under the influence of liquor, a
rare occurrence with him, and probably to be ascribed to his
recent disappointment. He was almost fierce in his denunciation
of Jim Struggles and his story.

"It's always the same," he said; "if a man meets a few travellers
in the bush, he's bound to come back raving about rangers. If
they'd seen Struggles there, they would have gone off with a long
yarn about a ranger crouching behind a tree. As to recognising
people riding fast among tree trunks – it is an impossibility."

Struggles, however, stoutly maintained his original assertion,
and all the sarcasms and arguments of his opponent were thrown
away upon his stolid complacency. It was noticed that Ferguson
seemed unaccountably put out about the whole matter. Some-

thing seemed to be on his mind, too; for occasionally he would spring off his perch and pace up and down the room with an abstracted and very forbidding look upon his swarthy face. It was a relief to every one when suddenly catching up his hat, and wishing the company a curt "Good-night," he walked off through the bar, and into the street beyond.

"Seems kinder put out," remarked Long McCoy.

"He can't be afeard of the rangers, surely," said Joe Shamus, another man of consequence, and principal shareholder of the El Dorado.

"No, he's not the man to be afraid," answered another. "There's something queer about him the last day or two. He's been long trips in the woods without any tools. They do say that the assayer's daughter has chucked him over."

"Quite right too. A darned sight too good for him," remarked several voices.

"It's odds but he has another try," said Shamus. "He's a hard man to beat when he's set his mind on a thing."

"Abe Durton's the horse to win," remarked Houlahan, a little bearded Irishman. "It's sivin to four I'd be willin' to lay on him."

"And you'd be afther losing your money, a-vich," said a young man with a laugh. "She'll want more brains than ever Bones had in his skull, you bet."

"Who's seen Bones to-day?" asked McCoy.

"I've seen him," said the young miner. "He came round all through the camp asking for a dictionary — wanted to write a letter likely."

"I saw him readin' it," said Shamus. "He came over to me an' told me he'd struck something good at the first show. Showed me a word about as long as your arm — 'abdicate,' or something."

"It's a rich man he is now, I suppose," said the Irishman.

"Well, he's about made his pile. He holds a hundred feet of the Conemara, and the shares go up every hour. If he'd sell out he'd be about fit to go home."

"Guess he wants to take somebody home with him," said another. "Old Joshua wouldn't object, seein' that the money is there."

I think it has been already recorded in this narrative that Jim Struggles, the wandering prospector, had gained the reputation of being the wit of the camp. It was not only in airy badinage, but in the conception and execution of more pretentious practical pleasantries that Jim had earned his reputation. His adventure in the morning had caused a certain stagnation in his usual flow of humour; but the company and his potations were gradually restoring him to a more cheerful state of mind. He had been brooding in silence over some idea since the departure of Ferguson, and he now proceeded to evolve it to his expectant companions.

"Say, boys," he began. "What day's this?"

"Friday, ain't it?"

"No, not that. What day of the month?"

"Darned if I know!"

"Well, I'll tell you now. It's the first o' April. I've got a calendar in the hut as says so."

"What if it is?" said several voices.

"Well, don't you see, it's All Fools' day. Couldn't we fix up some little joke on some one, eh? Couldn't we get a laugh out of it? Now there's old Bones, for instance; he'll never smell a rat. Couldn't we send him off somewhere and watch him go maybe? We'd have something to chaff him on for a month to come, eh?"

There was a general murmur of assent. A joke, however poor, was always welcome to the Sluice. The broader the point, the more thoroughly was it appreciated. There was no morbid delicacy of feeling in the gulches.

"Where shall we send him?" was the query.

Jim Struggles was buried in thought for a moment. Then an unhallowed inspiration seemed to come over him, and he laughed uproariously, rubbing his hands between his knees in the excess of his delight.

"Well, what is it?" asked the eager audience.

"See here, boys. There's Miss Sinclair. You was saying as Abe's gone on her. She don't fancy him much you think. Suppose we write him a note – send it him to-night, you know."

"Well, what then?" said McCoy.

"Well, pretend the note is from her, d'ye see? Put her name at the bottom. Let on as she wants him to come up an' meet her in the garden at twelve. He's bound to go. He'll think she wants to go off with him. It'll be the biggest thing played this year."

There was a roar of laughter. The idea conjured up of honest Bones mooning about in the garden, and of old Joshua coming out to remonstrate with a double-barrelled shot-gun, was irresistibly comic. The plan was approved of unanimously.

"Here's pencil and here's paper," said the humorist. "Who's goin' to write the letter?"

"Write it yourself, Jim," said Shamus.

"Well, what shall I say?"

"Say what you think right."

"I don't know how she'd put it," said Jim, scratching his head in great perplexity. "However, Bones will never know the differ. How will this do? 'Dear old man. Come to the garden at twelve to-night, else I'll never speak to you again,' eh?"

"No, that's not the style," said the young miner. "Mind, she's a lass of eddication. She'd put it kinder flowery and soft."

"Well, write it yourself," said Jim sulkily, handing him over the pencil.

"This is the sort of thing," said the miner, moistening the point of it in his mouth. " 'When the moon is in the sky —' "

"There it is. That's bully," from the company.

" 'And the stars a-shinin' bright, meet, O meet me, Adolphus, by the garden-gate at twelve.' "

"His name isn't Adolphus," objected a critic.

"That's how the poetry comes in," said the miner. "It's kinder fanciful, d'ye see. Sounds a darned sight better than Abe. Trust him for guessing who she means. I'll sign it Carrie. There!"

This epistle was gravely passed round the room from hand to hand, and reverentially gazed upon as being a remarkable production of the human brain. It was then folded up and committed to the care of a small boy, who was solemnly charged under dire threats to deliver it at the shanty, and to make off before any awkward questions were asked him. It was only after he had disappeared in the darkness that some slight compunction visited one or two of the company.

"Ain't it playing it rather low on the girl?" said Shamus.

"And rough on old Bones?" suggested another.

However, these objections were overruled by the majority, and disappeared entirely upon the appearance of a second jorum of whisky. The matter had almost been forgotten by the time that Abe had received his note, and was spelling it out with a palpitating heart under the light of his solitary candle.

That night has long been remembered in Harvey's Sluice. A fitful breeze was sweeping down from the distant mountains, moaning and sighing among the deserted claims. Dark clouds were hurrying across the moon, one moment throwing a shadow over the landscape, and the next allowing the silvery radiance to shine down, cold and clear, upon the little valley, and bathe in a weird mysterious light the great stretch of bushland on either side of it. A great loneliness seemed to rest on the face of Nature. Men remarked afterwards on the strange eerie atmosphere which hung over the little town.

It was in the darkness that Abe Durton sallied out from his little shanty. His partner, Boss Morgan, was still absent in the bush, so that beyond the ever-watchful Blinky there was no living being to observe his movements. A feeling of mild surprise filled his simple soul that his angel's delicate fingers could have formed those great straggling hieroglyphics; however, there was the name at the foot, and that was enough for him. She wanted him, no matter for what, and with a heart as pure and as heroic as any knight-errant, this rough miner went forth at the summons of his love.

He groped his way up the steep winding track which led to Azalea Villa. There was a little clump of small trees and shrubs about fifty yards from the entrance of the garden. Abe stopped for a moment when he had reached them in order to collect himself. It was hardly twelve yet, so that he had a few minutes to spare. He stood under their dark canopy peering at the white house vaguely outlined in front of him. A plain enough little dwelling-place to any prosaic mortal, but girt with reverence and awe in the eyes of the lover.

The miner paused under the shade of the trees, and then moved on to the garden-gate. There was no one there. He was evidently rather early. The moon was shining brightly now, and the country round was as clear as day. Abe looked past the little villa at the road which ran like a white winding streak over the brow of the hill. A watcher behind could have seen his square athletic figure standing out sharp and clear. Then he gave a start as if he had been shot, and staggered up against the little gate beside him.

He had seen something which caused even his sunburned face to become a shade paler as he thought of the girl so near him. Just at the bend of the road, not two hundred yards away, he saw a dark moving mass coming round the curve, and lost in the shadow of the hill. It was but for a moment; yet in that moment the quick perception of the practised woodman had realised the whole situation. It was a band of horsemen bound for the villa; and what horsemen would ride so by night save the terror of the woodlands – the dreaded rangers of the bush?

It is true that on ordinary occasions Abe was as sluggish in his intellect as he was heavy in his movements. In the hour of danger, however, he was as remarkable for cool deliberation as for prompt and decisive action. As he advanced up the garden he rapidly reckoned up the chances against him. There were half a dozen of the assailants at the most moderate computation, all desperate and fearless men. The question was whether he could keep them at bay for a short time and prevent their forcing a passage into the house. We have already mentioned that sentinels had been placed in the main street of the town. Abe reckoned that help would be at hand within ten minutes of the firing of the first shot.

Were he inside the house he could confidently reckon on holding his own for a longer period than that. Before he could rouse the sleepers and gain admission, however, the rangers would be upon him. He must content himself with doing his utmost. At any rate he would show Carrie that if he could not talk to her he could at least die for her. The thought gave him quite a glow of pleasure, as he crept under the shadow of the house. He cocked his revolver. Experience had taught him the advantage of the first shot.

The road along which the rangers were coming ended at a wooden gate opening into the upper part of the assayer's little garden. This gate had a high acacia hedge on either side of it, and opened into a short walk also lined by impassable thorny walls. Abe knew the place well. One resolute man might, he thought, hold the passage for a few minutes until the assailants broke through elsewhere and took him in the rear. At any rate, it was his best chance. He passed the front door, but forbore to give any alarm. Sinclair was an elderly man, and would be of little assistance in such a desperate struggle as was before him, and the appearance of lights in the house would warn the rangers of the resistance awaiting them. O for his partner the Boss, for Chicago Bill, for any one of twenty gallant men who would have come at his call and stood by him in such a quarrel! He turned into the narrow pathway. There was the well-remembered wooden gate; and there, perched upon the gate, languidly swinging his legs backwards and forwards, and peering down the road in front of him, was Mr. John Morgan, the very man for whom Abe had been longing from the bottom of his heart.

There was short time for explanations. A few hurried words announced that the Boss, returning from his little tour, had come across the rangers riding on their mission of darkness, and over-hearing their destination, had managed by hard running and knowledge of the country to arrive before them. "No time to alarm any one," he explained, still panting from his exertions; "must stop them ourselves – not come for swag – come for your girl. Only over our bodies, Bones," and with these few broken words the strangely assorted friends shook hands and looked lovingly into each other's eyes, while the tramp of the horses came down to them on the fragrant breeze of the woods.

There were six rangers in all. One who appeared to be leader rode in front, while the others followed in a body. They flung themselves off their horses when they were opposite the house, and after a few muttered words from their captain, tethered the animals to a small tree, and walked confidently towards the gate.

Boss Morgan and Abe were crouching down under the shadow of the hedge, at the extreme end of the narrow passage. They were invisible to the rangers, who evidently reckoned on meeting little resistance in this isolated house. As the first man came forwards and half turned to give some order to his comrades both the friends recognised the stern profile and heavy moustache of Black Tom Ferguson, the rejected suitor of Miss Carrie Sinclair. Honest Abe made a mental vow that he at least should never reach the door alive.

The ruffian stepped up to the gate and put his hand upon the latch. He started as a stentorian "Stand back!" came thundering out from among the bushes. In war, as in love, the miner was a man of few words.

"There's no road this way," explained another voice with an infinite sadness and gentleness about it which was characteristic of its owner when the devil was rampant in his soul. The ranger recognised it. He remembered the soft languid address which he had listened to in the billiard-room of the Buckhurst Arms, and which had wound up by the mild orator putting his back against the door, drawing a derringer, and asking to see the sharper who would dare to force a passage. "It's that infernal fool Durton," he said, "and his white-faced friend."

Both were well-known names in the country round. But the rangers were reckless and desperate men. They drew up to the gate in a body.

"Clear out of that!" said their leader in a grim whisper; "you can't save the girl. Go off with whole skins while you have the chance."

The partners laughed.

"Then curse you, come on!"

The gate was flung open and the party fired a struggling volley, and made a fierce rush towards the gravelled walk.

The revolvers cracked merrily in the silence of the night from the bushes at the other end. It was hard to aim with precision in the darkness. The second man sprang convulsively into the air, and fell upon his face with his arms extended, writhing horribly in the moonlight. The third was grazed in the leg and stopped. The others stopped out of sympathy. After all, the girl was not for them, and their heart was hardly in the work. Their captain rushed madly on, like a valiant blackguard as he was, but was met by a crashing blow from the butt of Abe Durton's pistol, delivered with a fierce energy which sent him reeling back among his comrades with the blood streaming from his shattered jaw, and his capacity for cursing cut short at the very moment when he needed to draw upon it most.

"Don't go yet," said the voice in the darkness.

However, they had no intention of going yet. A few minutes must elapse, they knew, before Harvey's Sluice could be upon them. There was still time to force the door if they could succeed in mastering the defenders. What Abe had feared came to pass. Black Ferguson knew the ground as well as he did. He ran rapidly along the hedge, and the five crashed through it where there was some appearance of a gap. The two friends glanced at each other. Their flank was turned. They stood up like men who knew their fate and did not fear to meet it.

There was a wild medley of dark figures in the moonlight, and a ringing cheer from well-known voices. The humorists of Harvey's Sluice had found something even more practical than the joke which they had come to witness. The partners saw the faces of friends beside them – Shamus, Struggles, McCoy. There was a desperate rally, a sweeping fiery rush, a cloud of smoke, with pistol-shots and fierce oaths ringing out of it, and when it lifted, a single dark shadow flying for dear life to the shelter of the broken hedge was the only ranger upon his feet within the little garden. But there was no sound of triumph among the victors; a strange hush had come over them, and a murmur as of grief – for there, lying across the threshold which he had fought so gallantly to defend, lay poor Abe, the loyal and simple hearted, breathing heavily with a bullet through his lungs.

He was carried inside with all the rough tenderness of the mines. There were men there, I think, who would have borne his hurt to have had the love of that white girlish figure, which bent over the blood-stained bed and whispered so softly and so tenderly in his ear. Her voice seemed to rouse him. He opened his dreamy blue eyes and looked about him. They rested on her face.

"Played out," he murmured; "pardon, Carrie, morib –" and with a faint smile he sank back upon the pillow.

However, Abe failed for once to be as good as his word. His hardy constitution asserted itself, and he shook off what might in a weaker man have proved a deadly wound. Whether it was the balmy air of the woodlands which came sweeping over a thousand miles of forest into the sick man's room, or whether it was the little nurse who tended him so gently, certain it is that within two months we heard that he had realised his shares in the Conemara, and gone from Harvey's Sluice and the little shanty upon the hill for ever.

I had the advantage a short time afterwards of seeing an extract from the letter of a young lady named Amelia, to whom we have made a casual allusion in the course of our narrative. We have already broken the privacy of one feminine epistle, so we shall have fewer scruples in glancing at another. "I was bridesmaid," she remarks, "and Carrie looked charming" (underlined) "in the veil and orange blossoms. Such a man, he is, twice as big as your Jack, and he was so funny, and blushed, and dropped the prayer-book. And when they asked the question you could have heard him roar 'I do!' at the other end of George street. His best man was a darling" (twice underlined). "So quiet and handsome and nice. Too gentle to take care of himself among those rough men, I am sure." I think it quite possible that in the fullness of time Miss Amelia managed to take upon herself the care of our old friend Mr. Jack Morgan, commonly known as the Boss.

A tree is still pointed out at the bend as Ferguson's gum-tree. There is no need to enter into unsavoury details. Justice is short and sharp in primitive colonies, and the dwellers in Harvey's Sluice were a serious and practical race.

It is still the custom for a select party to meet on a Saturday evening in the snuggery of the Colonial Bar. On such occasions, if there be a stranger or guest to be entertained, the same solemn ceremony is always observed. Glasses are charged in silence; there is a tapping of the same upon the table, and then, with a deprecating cough, Jim Struggles comes forward and tells the tale of the April joke, and of what came of it. There is generally conceded to be something very artistic in the way in which he breaks off suddenly at the close of his narrative by waving his bumper in the air with "An' here's to Mr. and Mrs. Bones. God bless 'em!" a sentiment in which the stranger, if he is a prudent man, will most cordially acquiesce.

OUR DERBY SWEEPSTAKES

———◆———

"Bob!" I shouted.

No answer.

"Bob!"

A rapid crescendo of snores ending in a prolonged gasp.

"Wake up, Bob!"

"What the deuce is the row?" said a very sleepy voice.

"It's nearly breakfast-time," I explained.

"Bother breakfast-time!" said the rebellious spirit in the bed.

"And here's a letter, Bob," said I.

"Why on earth couldn't you say so at once? Come on with it;" on which cordial invitation I marched into my brother's room, and perched myself upon the side of his bed.

"Here you are," said I. "Indian stamp – Brindisi postmark. Who is it from?"

"Mind your own business, Stumpy," said my brother, as he pushed back his curly tangled locks and, after rubbing his eyes, proceeded to break the seal. Now if there is one appellation for which above all others I have a profound contempt, it is this one of "Stumpy." Some miserable nurse, impressed by the relative proportions of my round grave face and little mottled legs, had dubbed me with the odious nickname in the days of my child-hood. I am not really a bit more stumpy than any other girl of seventeen. On the present occasion I rose in all the dignity of wrath, and was about to dump my brother on the head with the pillow by way of remonstrance, when a look of interest in his face stopped me.

"Who do you think is coming, Nelly?" he said. "An old friend of yours."

"What! from India? Not Jack Hawthorne?"

"Even so," said Bob. "Jack is coming back and going to stay with us. He says he will be here almost as soon as his letter. Now don't dance about like that. You'll knock down the guns, or do some damage. Keep quiet like a good girl, and sit down here again." Bob spoke with all the weight of the two-and-twenty summers which had passed over his towsy head, so I calmed down and settled into my former position.

"Won't it be jolly?" I cried. "But, Bob, the last time he was here he was a boy, and now he is a man. He won't be the same Jack at all."

"Well, for that matter," said Bob, "you were only a girl then – a nasty little girl with ringlets, while now –"

"What now?" I asked.

Bob seemed actually on the eve of paying me a compliment.

"Well, you haven't got the ringlets, and you are ever so much bigger, you see, and nastier."

Brothers are a blessing for one thing. There is no possibility of any young lady getting unreasonably conceited if she be endowed with them.

I think they were all glad at breakfast-time to hear of Jack Hawthorne's promised advent. By "all" I mean my mother and Elsie and Bob. Our cousin Solomon Barker looked anything but overjoyed when I made the announcement in breathless triumph. I never thought of it before, but perhaps that young man is getting fond of Elsie, and is afraid of a rival; otherwise I don't see why such a simple thing should have caused him to push away his egg, and declare that he had done famously, in an aggressive manner which at once threw doubt upon his proposition. Grace Maberly, Elsie's friend, seemed quietly contented, as is her wont.

As for me, I was in a riotous state of delight. Jack and I had been children together. He was like an elder brother to me until he became a cadet and left us. How often Bob and he had climbed old Brown's apple-trees, while I stood beneath and collected the spoil in my little white pinafore! There was hardly a scrape or adventure which I could remember in which Jack did not figure as a prominent character. But he was "Lieutenant" Hawthorne now, had been through the Afghan War, and was, as Bob said, "quite the warrior." What ever would he look like? Somehow the "warrior" had conjured up an idea of Jack in full armour with plumes on his head, thirsting for blood, and hewing at somebody with an enormous sword. After doing that sort of thing I was afraid he would never descend to romps and charades and the other stock amusements of Hatherley House.

Cousin Sol was certainly out of spirits during the next few days. He could be hardly persuaded to make a fourth at lawn-tennis, but showed an extraordinary love of solitude and strong tobacco. We used to come across him in the most unexpected places, in the shrubbery and down by the river, on which occasions, if there was any possibility of avoiding us, he would gaze rigidly into the distance, and utterly ignore feminine shouts and the waving of parasols. It was certainly very rude of him. I got hold of him one evening before dinner, and drawing myself up to my full height of five feet four and a half inches, I proceeded to give him a piece of my mind, a process which Bob characterises as the height of charity, since it consists in my giving away what I am most in need of myself.

Cousin Sol was lounging in a rocking-chair with the *Times* before him, gazing moodily over the top of it into the fire. I ranged up alongside and poured in my broadside.

"We seem to have given you some offence, Mr. Barker," I remarked, with lofty courtesy.

"What do you mean, Nell?" asked my cousin, looking up at me in surprise. He had a very curious way of looking at me, had cousin Sol.

"You appear to have dropped our acquaintance," I remarked; and then suddenly descending from my heroics, "You *are* stupid, Sol! What's been the matter with you?"

"Nothing, Nell, at least, nothing of any consequence. You know my medical examination is in two months, and I am reading for it."

"O," said I, in a bristle of indignation, "if that's it, there's no more to be said. Of course if you prefer bones to your female relations, it's all right. There are young men who would rather make themselves agreeable than mope in corners and learn how to prod people with knives." With which epitome of the noble science of surgery I proceeded to straighten some refractory antimacassars with unnecessary violence.

I could see Sol looking with an amused smile at the angry little blue-eyed figure in front of him. "Don't blow me up, Nell," he said, "I have been plucked once, you know. Besides," looking grave, "you'll have amusement enough when this — what is his name? – Lieutenant Hawthorne comes."

"Jack won't go and associate with mummies and skeletons, at any rate," I remarked.

"Do you always call him Jack?" asked the student.

"Of course I do. John sounds so stiff."

"O, it does, does it?" said my companion doubtfully.

I still had my theory about Elsie running in my head. I thought I might try and set the matter in a more cheerful light. Sol had got up, and was staring out of the open window. I went over to him and glanced up timidly into his usually good-humoured face, which was now looking very dark and discontented. He was a shy man as a rule, but I thought that with a little leading he might be brought to confess.

"You're a jealous old thing," I remarked.

The young man coloured and looked down at me.

"I know your secret," said I boldly.

"What secret?" said he, colouring even more.

"Never you mind. I know it. Let me tell you this," I added, getting bolder, "that Jack and Elsie never got on very well. There is far more chance of Jack's falling in love with me. We were always friends."

If I had stuck the knitting-needle which I held in my hand into cousin Sol he could not have given a greater jump. "Good heavens!" he said, and I could see his dark eyes staring at me through the twilight. "Do you really think that it is your sister that I care for?"

"Certainly," said I stoutly, with a feeling that I was nailing my colours to a mast.

Never did a single word produce such an effect. Cousin Sol wheeled round with a gasp of astonishment, and sprang right out of the window. He always had curious ways of expressing his feelings, but this one struck me as being so entirely original that I was utterly bereft of any idea save that of wonder. I stood staring out into the gathering darkness. Then there appeared looking in at me from the lawn a very much abashed and still rather astonished face. "It's you I care for, Nell," said the face, and at once vanished, while I heard the noise of somebody running at the top of his speed down the avenue. He certainly was a most extraordinary young man.

Things went on very much the same at Hatherley House in spite of cousin Sol's characteristic declaration of affection. He never sounded me as to my sentiments in regard to him, nor did he allude to the matter for several days. He evidently thought that he had done all which was needed in such cases. He used to discompose me dreadfully at times, however, by coming and planting himself opposite me, and staring at me with a stony rigidity which was absolutely appalling.

"Don't do that, Sol," I said to him one day; "you give me the creeps all over."

"Why do I give you the creeps, Nelly?" said he. "Don't you like me?"

"O yes. I like you well enough," said I. "I like Lord Nelson, for that matter; but I shouldn't like his monument to come and stare at me by the hour. It makes me feel quite all-overish."

"What on earth put Lord Nelson into your head?" said my cousin.

"I'm sure I don't know."

"Do you like me the same way you like Lord Nelson, Nell?"

"Yes," I said, "only more." With which small ray of encouragement poor Sol had to be content, as Elsie and Miss Maberley came rustling into the room and put an end to our *tête-à-tête*.

I certainly did like my cousin. I knew what a simple true nature lay beneath his quiet exterior. The idea of having Sol Barker for a lover, however – Sol, whose very name was synonymous with bashfulness – was too incredible. Why couldn't he fall in love with Grace or with Elsie? They might have known what to do with him; they were older than I, and could encourage him, or snub him, as they thought best. Gracie, however, was carrying on a mild flirtation with my brother Bob, and Elsie seemed utterly unconscious of the whole matter. I have one characteristic recollection of my cousin which I cannot help introducing here, though it has nothing to do with the thread of the narrative. It was on the occasion of his first visit to Hatherley House. The wife of the Rector called one day, and the responsibility of entertaining her rested with Sol and myself. We got on very well at first. Sol was unusually lively and talkative. Unfortunately a hospitable impulse came upon him; and in spite of many warning nods and winks, he asked the visitor if he might offer her a glass of wine. Now, as ill luck would have it, our supply had just been finished, and though we had written to London, a fresh consignment had not yet arrived. I listened breathlessly for the answer, trusting she would refuse; but to my horror she accepted with alacrity. "Never mind ringing, Nell," said Sol, "I'll act as butler;" and with a confident smile he marched into the little cupboard in which the decanters were usually kept. It was not until he was well in that he suddenly recollected having heard us mention in the morning that there was none in the house. His mental anguish was so great that he spent the remainder of Mrs. Salter's visit in the cupboard, utterly refusing to come out until after her departure. Had there been any possibility of the winepress having another egress, or leading anywhere, matters would not have been so bad; but I knew that old Mrs. Salter was as well up in the geography of the house as I was myself. She stayed for three-quarters of an hour waiting for Sol's reappearance, and then went away in high dudgeon. "My dear," she said, recounting the incident to her husband, and breaking into semi-scriptural language in the violence of her indignation, "the cupboard seemed to open and swallow him!"

"Jack is coming down by the two o'clock train," said Bob one morning, coming in to breakfast with a telegram in his hand.

I could see Sol looking at me reproachfully; but that did not prevent me from showing my delight at the intelligence.

"We'll have awful fun when he comes," said Bob. "We'll drag the fish-pond, and have no end of a lark. Won't it be jolly, Sol?"

Sol's opinion of its jollity was evidently too great to be expressed in words; for he gave an inarticulate grunt as answer.

I had a long cogitation on the subject of Jack in the garden that morning. After all, I was becoming a big girl, as Bob had forcibly reminded me. I must be circumspect in my conduct now. A real live man had actually looked upon me with the eyes of love. It was all very well when I was a child to have Jack following me about and kissing me; but I must keep him at a distance now. I remembered how he presented me with a dead fish once which he had taken out of the Hatherley Brook, and how I treasured it up among my most precious possessions, until an insidious odour in the house had caused the mother to send an abusive letter to Mr. Burton, who had pronounced our drainage to be all that could be desired. I must learn to be formal and distant. I pictured our meeting to myself, and went through a rehearsal of it. The holly-bush represented Jack, and I approached it solemnly, made it a stately curtsey, and held out my hand with, "So glad to see you, Lieutenant Hawthorne!" Elsie came out while I was doing it, but made no remark. I heard her ask Sol at luncheon, however, whether idiocy generally ran in families, or was simply confined to individuals; at which poor Sol blushed furiously, and became utterly incoherent in his attempts at an explanation.

Our farmyard opens upon the avenue about half-way between Hatherley House and the lodge. Sol and I and Mr. Nicholas Cronin, the son of a neighbouring squire, went down there after lunch. This imposing demonstration was for the purpose of quelling a mutiny which had broken out in the henhouse. The earliest tidings of the rising had been conveyed to the house by young Bayliss, son and heir of the henkeeper, and my presence had been urgently requested. Let me remark in parenthesis that fowls were my special department in domestic economy, and that no step was ever taken in their management without my advice and assistance. Old Bayliss hobbled out upon our arrival, and informed us of the full extent of the disturbance. It seems that the crested hen and the Bantam cock had developed such length of wing that they were enabled to fly over into the park; and that the example of these ringleaders had been so contagious, that even such steady old matrons as the bandy-legged Cochin China had developed roving propensities, and pushed their way into forbidden ground. A council of war was held in the yard, and it was unanimously decided that the wings of the recalcitrants must be clipped.

What a scamper we had! By "we" I mean Mr. Cronin and myself; while cousin·Sol hovered about in the background with the scissors, and cheered us on. The two culprits clearly knew that they were wanted; for they rushed under the hayricks and over the coops, until there seemed to be at least half a dozen crested hens and Bantam cocks dodging about in the yard. The other hens were mildly interested in the proceedings, and contented themselves with an occasional derisive cluck, with the exception of the favourite wife of the Bantam, who abused us roundly from the top of the coop. The ducks were the most aggravating portion of the community; for though they had nothing to do with the original disturbance, they took a warm interest in the fugitives, waddling behind them as fast as their little yellow legs would carry them, and getting in the way of the pursuers.

"We have it!" I gasped, as the crested hen was driven into a corner. "Catch it, Mr. Cronin! O, you've missed it! you've missed it! Get in the way, Sol. O dear, it's coming to me!"

"Well done, Miss Montague!" cried Mr. Cronin, as I seized the wretched fowl by the leg as it fluttered past me, and proceeded to tuck it under my arm to prevent any possibility of escape. "Let me carry it for you."

"No, no; I want you to catch the cock. There it goes! There – behind the hayrick. You go to one side, and I'll go to the other."

"It's going through the gate!" shouted Sol.

"Shoo!" cried I. "Shoo! O, it's gone!" and we both made a dart into the park in pursuit, tore round the corner into the avenue, and there I found myself face to face with a sunburned young man in a tweed suit, who was lounging along in the direction of the house.

There was no mistaking those laughing grey eyes, though I think if I had never looked at him some instinct would have told me that it was Jack. How could I be dignified with the crested hen tucked under my arm? I tried to pull myself up; but the miserable bird seemed to think that it had found a protector at last, for it began to cluck with redoubled vehemence. I had to give it up in despair, and burst into a laugh, while Jack did the same.

"How are you, Nell?" he said, holding out his hand; and then in an astonished voice, "Why, you're not a bit the same as when I saw you last!"

"Well, I hadn't a hen under my arm then," said I.

"Who would have thought that little Nell would have developed into a woman?" said Jack, still lost in amazement.

"You didn't expect me to develop into a man, did you?" said I in high indignation; and then, suddenly dropping all reserve, "We're awfully glad you've come, Jack. Never mind going up to the house. Come and help us to catch that Bantam cock."

"Right you are," said Jack in his old cheery way, still keeping his eyes firmly fixed upon my countenance. "Come on!" and away the three of us scampered across the park, with poor Sol aiding and abetting with the scissors and the prisoner in the rear. Jack was a very crumpled-looking visitor by the time he paid his respects to the mother that afternoon, and my dreams of dignity and reserve were scattered to the winds.

We had quite a party at Hatherley House that May. There were Bob, and Sol, and Jack Hawthorne, and Mr. Nicholas Cronin; then there were Miss Maberley, and Elsie, and mother, and myself. On an emergency we could always muster half a dozen visitors from the houses round, so as to have an audience when charades or private theatricals were attempted. Mr. Cronin, an easy-going athletic young Oxford man, proved to be a great acquisition, having wonderful powers of organisation and execution. Jack was not nearly as lively as he used to be, in fact we unanimously accused him of being in love; at which he looked as silly as young men usually do on such occasions, but did not attempt to deny the soft impeachment.

"What shall we do to-day?" said Bob one morning. "Can anybody make a suggestion?"

"Drag the pond," said Mr. Cronin.

"Haven't men enough," said Bob; "anything else?"

"We must get up a sweepstakes for the Derby," remarked Jack.

"O, there's plenty of time for that. It isn't run till the week after next. Anything else?"

"Lawn-tennis," said Sol dubiously.

"Bother lawn-tennis!"

"You might make a picnic to Hatherley Abbey," said I.

"Capital!" cried Mr. Cronin. "The very thing. What do you think, Bob?"

"First class," said my brother grasping eagerly at the idea.

Picnics are very dear to those who are in the first stage of the tender passion.

"Well, how are we to go, Nell?" asked Elsie.

"I won't go at all," said I; "I'd like to awfully, but I have to plant those ferns Sol got me. You had better walk. It is only three miles and young Bayliss can be sent over with the basket of provisions."

"You'll come, Jack?" said Bob.

Here was another impediment. The Lieutenant had twisted his ankle yesterday. He had not mentioned it to any one at the time; but it was beginning to pain him now.

"Couldn't do it, really," said Jack. "Three miles there and three back!"

"Come on. Don't be lazy," said Bob.

"My dear fellow," answered the Lieutenant, "I have had walking enough to last me the rest of my life. If you had seen how that energetic general of ours bustled me along from Cabul to Candahar, you'd sympathise with me."

"Leave the veteran alone," said Mr. Nicholas Cronin.

"Pity the war-worn soldier," remarked Bob.

"None of your chaff," said Jack. "I'll tell you what I'll do," he added, brightening up. "You let me have the trap, Bob, and I'll drive over with Nell as soon as she has finished planting her ferns. We can take the basket with us. You'll come, won't you, Nell?"

"All right," said I. And Bob having given his assent to the arrangement, and everybody being pleased, except Mr. Solomon Barker, who glared with mild malignancy at the soldier, the matter was finally settled, and the whole party proceeded to get ready, and finally departed down the avenue.

It was an extraordinary thing how that ankle improved after the last of the troop had passed round the curve of the hedge. By the time the ferns were planted and the gig got ready Jack was as active and lively as ever he was in his life.

"You seem to have got better very suddenly," I remarked, as we drove down the narrow winding country lane.

"Yes," said Jack. "The fact is, Nell, there never was anything the matter with me. I wanted to have a talk with you."

"You don't mean to say you would tell a lie in order to have a talk with me?" I remonstrated.

"Forty," said Jack stoutly.

I was too lost in contemplation of the depths of guile in Jack's nature to make any further remark. I wondered whether Elsie would be flattered or indignant were anyone to offer to tell so many lies in her behalf.

"We used to be good friends when we were children, Nell," remarked my companion.

"Yes," said I, looking down at the rug which was thrown over my knees. I was beginning to be quite an experienced young lady by this time, you see, and to understand certain inflections of the masculine voice, which are only to be acquired by practice.

"You don't seem to care for me now as much as you did then," said Jack.

I was still intensely absorbed in the leopard's skin in front of me.

"Do you know, Nelly," continued Jack, "that when I have been camping out in the frozen passes of the Himalayas, when I have seen the hostile array in front of me; in fact," suddenly dropping into bathos, "all the time I was in that beastly hole Afghanistan, I used to think of the little girl I had left in England."

"Indeed!" I murmured.

"Yes," said Jack, "I bore the memory of you in my heart, and then when I came back you were a little girl no longer. I found you a beautiful woman, Nelly, and I wondered whether you had forgotten the days that were gone."

Jack was becoming quite poetical in his enthusiasm. By this time he had left the old bay pony entirely to its own devices, and it was indulging in its chronic propensity of stopping and admiring the view.

"Look here, Nelly," said Jack, with a gasp like a man who is about to pull the string of his shower-bath, "one of the things you learn in campaigning is to secure a good thing whenever you see it. Never delay or hesitate, for you never know that some other fellow may not carry it off while you are making up your mind."

"It's coming now," I thought in despair, "and there's no window for Jack to escape by after he has made the plunge." I had gradually got to associate the ideas of love and jumping out of windows, ever since poor Sol's confession.

"Do you think, Nell," said Jack, "that you could ever care for me enough to share my lot for ever? could you ever be my wife, Nell?"

He didn't even jump out of the trap. He sat there beside me, looking at me with his eager gray eyes, while the pony strolled along, cropping the wild flowers on either side of the road. It was quite evident that he intended having an answer. Somehow as I looked down I seemed to see a pale shy face looking in at me from a dark background, and to hear Sol's voice as he declared his love. Poor fellow! he was first in the field at any rate.

"Could you, Nell?" asked Jack once more.

"I like you very much, Jack," said I, looking up at him nervously; "but" – how his face changed at that monosyllable! – "I don't think I like you enough for that. Besides, I'm so young, you know. I suppose I ought to be very much complimented and that sort of thing by your offer; but you mustn't think of me in that light any more."

"You refuse me, then?" said Jack, turning a little white.

"Why don't you go and ask Elsie?" cried I in despair. "Why should you all come to me?"

"I don't want Elsie," cried Jack, giving the pony a cut with his whip which rather astonished that easy-going quadruped. "What do you mean by 'all,' Nell?"

No answer.

"I see how it is," said Jack bitterly; "I've noticed how that cousin of yours has been hanging round you ever since I have been here. You are engaged to him."

"No, I'm not," said I.

"Thank God for that!" responded Jack devoutly. "There is some hope yet. Perhaps you will come to think better of it in time. Tell me, Nelly, are you fond of that fool of a medical student?"

"He isn't a fool," said I indignantly, "and I am quite as fond of him as I shall ever be of you."

"You might not care for him much and still be that," said Jack sulkily; and neither of us spoke again until a joint bellow from Bob and Mr. Cronin announced the presence of the rest of the company.

If the picnic was a success, it was entirely due to the exertions of the latter gentleman. Three lovers out of four was an undue proportion, and it took all his convivial powers to make up for the shortcomings of the rest. Bob seemed entirely absorbed in Miss Maberley's charms, poor Elsie was left out in the cold, while my two admirers spent their time in glaring alternately at me and at each other. Mr. Cronin, however, fought gallantly against the depression, making himself agreeable to all, and exploring ruins or drawing corks with equal vehemence and energy.

Cousin Sol was particularly disheartened and out of spirits. He thought, no doubt, that my solitary ride with Jack had been a prearranged thing between us. There was more sorrow than anger in his eyes, however, while Jack, I regret to say, was decidedly ill-tempered. It was this fact which made me choose out my cousin as my companion in the ramble through the woods which succeeded our lunch. Jack had been assuming a provoking air of proprietorship lately, which I was determined to quash once for all. I felt angry with him, too, for appearing to consider himself ill used at my refusal, and for trying to disparage poor Sol behind his back. I was far from loving either the one or the other, but somehow my girlish ideas of fair play revolted at either of them taking what I considered an unfair advantage. I felt that if Jack had not come I should, in the fulness of time, have ended by accepting my cousin; on the other hand, if it had not been for Sol, I might never have refused Jack. At present I was too fond of them both to favour either. "How in the world is it to end?" thought I. I must do something decisive one way or the other; or perhaps the best thing would be to wait and see what the future might bring forth.

Sol seemed mildly surprised at my having selected him as my companion, but accepted the offer with a grateful smile. His mind seemed to have been vastly relieved.

"So I haven't lost you yet, Nell," he murmured, as we branched off among the great tree-trunks and heard the voices of the party growing fainter in the distance.

"Nobody can lose me," said I, "for nobody has won me yet. For goodness' sake don't talk about it any more. Why can't you talk like your old self two years ago, and not be so dreadfully sentimental?"

"You'll know why some day, Nell," said the student reproachfully. "Wait until you are in love yourself, and you will understand it."

I gave a little incredulous sniff.

"Sit here, Nell," said cousin Sol, manœuvring me into a little bank of wild strawberries and mosses, and perching himself upon a stump of a tree beside me. "Now all I ask you to do is to answer one or two questions, and I'll never bother you any more."

I sat resignedly, with my hands in my lap.

"Are you engaged to Lieutenant Hawthorne?"

"No!" said I energetically.

"Are you fonder of him than of me?"

"No, I'm not."

Sol's thermometer of happiness up to a hundred in the shade at the least.

"Are you fonder of me than of him, Nelly?" in a very tender voice.

"No."

Thermometer down below zero again.

"Do you mean to say that we are exactly equal in your eyes?"

"Yes."

"But you must choose between us some time, you know," said cousin Sol with mild reproach in his voice.

"I do wish you wouldn't bother me so!" I cried, getting angry, as women usually do when they are in the wrong. "You don't care for me much or you wouldn't plague me. I believe the two of you will drive me mad between you."

Here there were symptoms of sobs on my part, and utter consternation and defeat among the Barker faction.

"Can't you see how it is, Sol?" said I, laughing through my tears at his woe-begone appearance. "Suppose you were brought up with two girls and had got to like them both very much, but had never preferred one to the other and never dreamed of marrying either, and then all of a sudden you are told you must choose one, and so make the other very unhappy, you wouldn't find it an easy thing to do, would you?"

"I suppose not," said the student.

"Then you can't blame me."

"I don't blame you, Nelly," he answered, attacking a great purple toadstool with his stick. "I think you are quite right to be sure of your own mind. It seems to me," he continued, speaking rather gaspily, but saying his mind like the true English gentleman that he was, "it seems to me that Hawthorne is an excellent fellow. He has seen more of the world than I have, and always does and says the right thing in the right place, which certainly isn't one of my characteristics. Then he is well born and has good prospects. I think I should be very grateful to you for your hesitation, Nell, and look upon it as a sign of your good-heartedness."

"We won't talk about it any more," said I, thinking in my heart what a very much finer fellow he was than the man he was praising. "Look here, my jacket is all stained with horrid fungi and things. We'd better go after the rest of the party, hadn't we? I wonder where they are by this time?"

It didn't take very long to find that out. At first we heard shouting and laughter coming echoing through the long glades, and then, as we made our way in that direction, we were astonished to meet the usually phlegmatic Elsie careering through the wood at the top of her speed, her hat off, and her hair streaming in the wind. My first idea was that some frightful catastrophe had occurred — brigands possibly, or a mad dog — and I saw my companion's big hand close round his stick; but on meeting the fugitive it proved to be nothing more tragic than a game of hide-and-seek which the indefatigable Mr. Cronin had organised. What fun we had, crouching and running and dodging among the Hatherley oaks! and how horrified the prim old abbot who planted them would have been, and the long series of black-coated brethren who have muttered their orisons beneath the welcome shade! Jack refused to play on the excuse of his weak ankle, and lay smoking under a tree in high dudgeon, glaring in a baleful and gloomy fashion at Mr. Solomon Barker; while the latter gentleman entered enthusiastically into the game, and distinguished himself by always getting caught, and never by any possibility catching anybody else.

Poor Jack! He was certainly unfortunate that day. Even an accepted lover would have been rather put out, I think, by an incident which occurred during our return home. It was agreed that all of us should walk, as the trap had been already sent off with the empty basket, so we started down Thorny Lane and through the fields. We were just getting over a stile to cross old Brown's ten-acre lot, when Mr. Cronin pulled up, and remarked that he thought we had better get into the road.

"Road?" said Jack. "Nonsense! We save a quarter of a mile by the field."

"Yes, but it's rather dangerous. We'd better go round."

"Where's the danger?" said our military man, contemptuously twisting his moustache.

"O, nothing," said Cronin. "That quadruped in the middle of the field is a bull, and not a very good-tempered one either. That's all. I don't think that the ladies should be allowed to go."

"We won't go," said the ladies in chorus.

"Then come round by the hedge and get into the road," suggested Sol.

"You may go as you like," said Jack rather testily; "but I am going across the field."

"Don't be a fool, Jack," said my brother.

"You fellows may think it right to turn tail at an old cow, but I don't. It hurts my self-respect, you see, so I shall join you at the other side of the farm." With which speech Jack buttoned up his coat in a truculent manner, waved his cane jauntily, and swaggered off into the ten-acre lot.

We clustered about the stile and watched the proceedings with anxiety. Jack tried to look as if he were entirely absorbed in the view and in the probable state of the weather, for he gazed about him and up into the clouds in an abstracted manner. His gaze generally began and ended, however, somewhere in the direction of the bull. That animal, after regarding the intruder with a prolonged stare, had retreated into the shadow of the hedge at one side, while Jack was walking up the long axis of the field.

"It's all right," said I. "It's got out of his way."

"I think it's leading him on," said Mr. Nicholas Cronin. "It's a vicious cunning brute."

Mr. Cronin had hardly spoken before the bull emerged from the hedge, and began pawing the ground, and tossing its wicked black head in the air. Jack was in the middle of the field by this time, and affected to take no notice of his companion, though he quickened his pace slightly. The bull's next manœuvre was to run rapidly round in two or three small circles; and then it suddenly stopped, bellowed, put down its head, elevated its tail, and made for Jack at the very top of its speed.

There was no use pretending to ignore its existence any longer. Jack faced round and gazed at it for a moment. He had only his little cane in his hand to oppose to the half ton of irate beef which was charging towards him. He did the only thing that was possible, namely to make for the hedge at the other side of the field.

At first Jack hardly condescended to run, but went off with a languid contemptuous trot, a sort of compromise between his dignity and his fear, which was so ludicrous that, frightened as we were, we burst into a chorus of laughter. By degrees, however, as he heard the galloping of hoofs sounding nearer and nearer, he quickened his pace, until ultimately he was in full flight for shelter, with his hat gone and his coat-tails fluttering in the breeze, while his pursuer was not ten yards behind him. If all Ayoub Khan's cavalry had been in his rear, our Afghan hero could not have done the distance in a shorter time. Quickly as he went, the bull went quicker still, and the two seemed to gain the hedge almost at the same moment. We saw Jack spring boldly into it, and the next moment he came flying out at the other side as if he had been discharged from a cannon, while the bull indulged in a series of triumphant bellows through the hole which he had made. It was a relief to us all to see Jack gather himself up and start off for home without a glance in our direction. He had retired to his room by the time we arrived, and did not appear until breakfast next morning, when he limped in with a very crestfallen expression. None of us was hard-hearted enough to allude to the subject, however, and by judicious treatment we restored him before lunch-time to his usual state of equanimity.

It was a couple of days after the picnic that our great Derby sweepstakes was to come off. This was an annual ceremony never omitted at Hatherley House, where, between visitors and neighbours, there were generally quite as many candidates for tickets as there were horses entered.

"The sweepstakes, ladies and gentlemen, comes off to-night," said Bob in his character of head of the house. "The subscription is ten shillings. Second gets quarter of the pool, and third has his money returned. No one is allowed to have more than one ticket, or to sell his ticket after drawing it. The drawing will be at seven thirty." All of which Bob delivered in a very pompous and official voice, though the effect was rather impaired by a sonorous "Amen!" from Mr. Nicholas Cronin.

I must now drop the personal style of narrative for a time. Hitherto my little story has consisted simply in a series of extracts from my own private journal; but now I have to tell of a scene which only came to my ears after many months.

Lieutenant Hawthorne, or Jack, as I cannot help calling him, had been very quiet since the day of the picnic, and given himself up to reverie. Now, as luck would have it, Mr. Solomon Barker sauntered into the smoking-room after luncheon on the day of the sweepstakes, and found the Lieutenant puffing moodily in solitary grandeur upon one of the settees. It would have seemed cowardly to retreat, so the student sat down in silence, and began turning over the pages of the *Graphic*. Both the rivals felt the situation to be an awkward one. They had been in the habit of studiously avoiding each other's society, and now they found themselves thrown together suddenly, with no third person to act as a buffer. The silence began to be oppressive. The Lieutenant yawned and coughed with over-acted nonchalance, while honest Sol felt very hot and uncomfortable, and continued to stare gloomily at the paper in his hand. The ticking of the clock, and the click of the billiard-balls across the passage, seemed to grow unendurably loud and monotonous. Sol glanced across once; but catching his companion's eye in an exactly similar action, the two young men seemed simultaneously to take a deep and all-absorbing interest in the pattern of the cornice.

"Why should I quarrel with him?" thought Sol to himself. "After all, I want nothing but fair play. Probably I shall be snubbed; but I may as well give him an opening."

Sol's cigar had gone out; the opportunity was too good to be neglected.

"Could you oblige me with a fusee, Lieutenant?" he asked.

The Lieutenant was sorry — extremely sorry — but he was not in possession of a fusee.

This was a bad beginning. Chilly politeness was even more repulsing than absolute rudeness. But Mr. Solomon Barker, like many other shy men, was audacity itself when the ice had once been broken. He would have no more bickerings or misunderstandings. Now was the time to come to some definite arrangement. He pulled his armchair across the room, and planted himself in front of the astonished soldier.

"You're in love with Miss Nelly Montague," he remarked.

Jack sprang off the settee with as much rapidity as if Farmer Brown's bull were coming in through the window.

"And if I am, sir," he said, twisting his tawny moustache, "what the devil is that to you?"

"Don't lose your temper," said Sol. "Sit down again, and talk the matter over like a reasonable Christian. I am in love with her too."

"What the deuce is the fellow driving at?" thought Jack, as he resumed his seat, still simmering after his recent explosion.

"So the long and the short of it is that we are both in love with her," continued Sol, emphasising his remarks with his bony forefinger.

"What then?" said the Lieutenant, showing some symptoms of a relapse. "I suppose that the best man will win, and that the young lady is quite able to choose for herself. You don't expect me to stand out of the race just because you happen to want the prize, do you?"

"That's just it," cried Sol. "One of us will have to stand out. You've hit the right idea there. You see, Nelly – Miss Montague, I mean – is, as far as I can see, rather fonder of you than of me, but still fond enough of me not to wish to grieve me by a positive refusal."

"Honesty compels me to state," said Jack, in a more conciliatory voice than he had made use of hitherto, "that Nelly – Miss Montague, I mean – is rather fonder of *you* than of me; but still, as you say, fond enough of me not to prefer my rival openly in my presence."

"I don't think you're right," said the student. "In fact I know you are not; for she told me as much with her own lips. However, what you say makes it easier for us to come to an understanding. It is quite evident that as long as we show ourselves to be equally fond of her, neither of us can have the slightest hope of winning her."

"There's some sense in that," said the Lieutenant reflectively; "but what do you propose?"

"I propose that one of us stand out, to use your own expression. There is no alternative."

"But who is to stand out?" asked Jack.

"Ah, that is the question."

"I can claim to have known her longest."

"I can claim to have loved her first."

Matters seemed to have come to a deadlock. Neither of the

young men was in the least inclined to abdicate in favour of his rival.

"Look here," said the student, "let us decide the matter by lot."

This seemed fair, and was agreed to by both. A new difficulty arose, however. Both of them felt sentimental objections towards risking their angel upon such a paltry chance as the turn of a coin or the length of a straw. It was at this crisis that an inspiration came upon Lieutenant Hawthorne.

"I'll tell you how we will decide it," he said. "You and I are both entered for our Derby sweepstakes. If your horse beats mine, I give up my chance; if mine beats yours, you leave Miss Montague for ever. Is that a bargain?"

"I have only one stipulation to make," said Sol. "It is ten days yet before the race will be run. During that time neither of us must attempt to take an unfair advantage of the other. We shall both agree not to press our suit until the matter is decided."

"Done!" said the soldier.

"Done!" said Solomon.

And they shook hands upon the agreement.

I had, as I have already observed, no knowledge of the conversation which had taken place between my suitors. I may mention incidentally that during the course of it I was in the library, listening to Tennyson, read aloud in the deep musical voice of Mr. Nicholas Cronin. I observed, however, in the evening that these two young men seemed remarkably excited about their horses, and that neither of them was in the least inclined to make himself agreeable to me, for which crime I am happy to say that they were both punished by drawing rank outsiders. Eurydice, I think, was the name of Sol's; while Jack's was Bicycle. Mr. Cronin drew an American horse named Iroquois, and all the others seemed fairly well pleased. I peeped into the smoking-room before going to bed, and was amused to see Jack consulting the sporting prophet of the *Field*, while Sol was deeply immersed in the *Gazette*. This sudden mania for the Turf seemed all the more strange, since I knew that if my cousin could distinguish a horse from a cow, it was as much as any of his friends would give him credit for.

The ten succeeding days were voted very slow by various members of the household. I cannot say that I found them so. Perhaps that was because I discovered something very unexpected and pleasing in the course of that period. It was a relief to be free of any fear of wounding the susceptibilities of either of my former lovers. I could say what I chose and do what I liked now;

for they had deserted me completely, and handed me over to the society of my brother Bob and Mr. Nicholas Cronin. The new excitement of horse-racing seemed to have driven their former passion completely out of their minds. Never was a house so deluged with special tips and every vile print which could by any possibility have a word bearing upon the training of the horses or their antecedents. The very grooms in the stable were tired of recounting how Bicycle was descended from Velocipede, or explaining to the anxious medical student how Eurydice was by Orpheus out of Hades. One of them discovered that her maternal grandmother had come in third for the Ebor Handicap; but the curious way in which he stuck the half crown which he received into his left eye, while he winked at the coachman with his right, throws some doubt upon the veracity of his statement. As he remarked in a beery whisper that evening, "The bloke'll never know the differ, and it's worth 'arf a dollar for him to think as it's true."

As the day drew nearer the excitement increased. Mr. Cronin and I used to glance across at each other and smile as Jack and Sol precipitated themselves upon the papers at breakfast, and devoured the list of the betting. But matters culminated upon the evening immediately preceding the race. The Lieutenant had run down to the station to secure the latest intelligence, and now he came rushing in, waving a crushed paper frantically over his head.

"Eurydice is scratched!" he yelled. "Your horse is done for, Barker!"

"What!" roared Sol.

"Done for – utterly broken down in training – won't run at all!"

"Let me see," groaned my cousin, seizing the paper; and then, dropping it, he rushed out of the room, and banged down the stairs, taking four at a time. We saw no more of him until late at night, when he slunk in, looking very dishevelled, and crept quietly off to his room. Poor fellow, I should have condoled with him had it not been for his recent disloyal conduct towards myself.

Jack seemed a changed man from that moment. He began at once to pay me marked attention, very much to the annoyance of myself and of someone else in the room. He played and sang and proposed round games, and, in fact, quite usurped the rôle usually played by Mr. Nicholas Cronin.

I remember that it struck me as remarkable that on the morning of the Derby-day the Lieutenant should have entirely lost his interest in the race. He was in the greatest spirits at breakfast, but did not even open the paper in front of him. It was Mr. Cronin who unfolded it at last and glanced over its columns.

"What's the news, Nick?" asked my brother Bob.

"Nothing much. O yes, here's something. Another railway accident. Collision apparently. Westinghouse brake gone wrong. Two killed, seven hurt, and – by Jove! listen to this: 'Among the victims was one of the competitors in the equine Olympiad of to-day. A sharp splinter had penetrated its side, and the valuable animal had to be sacrificed upon the shrine of humanity. The name of the horse is Bicycle.' Hullo, you've gone and spilt your coffee all over the cloth, Hawthorne! Ah, I forgot, Bicycle was your horse, wasn't it? Your chance is gone, I am afraid. I see that Iroquois, who started low, has come to be first favourite now."

Ominous words, reader, as no doubt your nice discernment has taught you during, at the least, the last three pages. Don't call me a flirt and a coquette until you have weighed the facts. Consider my pique at the sudden desertion of my admirers, think of my delight at the confession from a man whom I had tried to conceal from myself even that I loved, think of the opportunities which he enjoyed during the time that Jack and Sol were systematically avoiding me, in accordance with their ridiculous agreement. Weigh all this, and then which among you will throw the first stone at the blushing little prize of the Derby Sweep?

Here it is as it appeared at the end of three short months in the *Morning Post:* "August 12th. – At Hatherley Church, Nicholas Cronin, Esq., eldest son of Nicholas Cronin, Esq., of the Woodlands, Cropshire, to Miss Eleanor Montague, daughter of the late James Montague, Esq., J.P., of Hatherley House."

Jack set off with the declared intention of volunteering for a ballooning expedition to the North Pole. He came back, however, in three days, and said that he had changed his mind, but intended to walk in Stanley's footsteps across Equatorial Africa. Since then he has dropped one or two gloomy allusions to forlorn hopes and the unutterable joys of death; but on the whole he is coming round very nicely and has been heard to grumble of late on such occasions as the under-doing of the mutton and the over-doing of the beef, which may be fairly set down as a very healthy sympton.

Sol took it more quietly, but I fear the iron went deeper into his soul. However, he pulled himself together like a dear brave fellow as he is, and actually had the hardihood to propose the bridesmaids, on which occasion he became inextricably mixed up in the labyrinth of words. He washed his hands of the mutinous sentence, however, and resumed his seat in the middle of it, overwhelmed with blushes and applause. I hear that he has confided his woes and his disappointments to Grace Maberley's sister, and met with the sympathy which he expected. Bob and Gracie are to be married in a few months, so possibly there may be another wedding about that time.

THAT VETERAN

---◆---

"Served, sir? Yes, sir," said my tattered vis-à-vis, drawing himself up and touching his apology for a hat. "Crimea and Mutiny, sir."

"What arm?" I asked lazily.

"Royal Horse Artillery. Thank you, sir, I take it hot with sugar."

It was pleasant to meet anyone who could talk English among those barren Welsh mountains, and pleasanter still to find one who had anything to talk about. I had been toiling along for the last ten miles, vowing in my heart never to take a solitary walking-tour again, and above all never, under any circumstances, to cross the borders of the principality. My opinions of the original Celt, his manners, customs, and above all his language, were very much too forcible to be expressed in decent society. The ruling passion of my life seemed to have become a deep and all-absorbing hatred towards Jones, Davis, Morris, and every other branch of the great Cymric trunk. Now, however, sitting at my ease in the little inn at Langerod, with a tumbler of smoking punch at my elbow, and my pipe between my teeth, I was inclined to take a more rosy view of men and things. Perhaps it was this spirit of reconciliation which induced me to address the weather-beaten scarecrow in front of me, or perhaps it was that his resolute face and lean muscular figure attracted my curiosity.

"You don't seem much the better for it," I remarked.

"It's this, sir, it's this," he answered, touching his glass with the spoon. "I'd have had my seven shillings a day, as retired sergeant-major, if it wasn't for this. One after another I've forfeited them — my badges and my good service allowance and my pension, until they had nothing more to take from me, and turned me adrift into the world at forty-nine. I was wounded once in the trenches and once at Delhi, and this is what I got for it, just because I couldn't keep away from the drink. You don't happen to have a

fill of 'baccy about you? Thank you sir; you are the first gentleman I have met this many a day.

"Sebastopol? Why, Lord bless you, I knows it as well as I know
this here village. You've read about it, may be, but I could make it
clear to you in a brace of shakes. This here fender is the French
attack, you see, and this poker is the Russian lines. Here's
the Mamelon opposite the French, and the Redan opposite the
English. This spittoon stands for the harbour of Balaclava.
There's the quarries midway between the Russians and us, and
here's Cathcart's hill, and this is the twenty-four gun battery.
That's the one I served in towards the end of the war. You see it all
now, don't you sir?"

"More or less," I answered doubtfully.

"The enemy held those quarries at the commencement, and
very strong they made them with trenches and rifle-pits all round.
It was a terrible thorn in our side, for you couldn't show your nose
in our advanced works, but a bullet from the quarries would be
through it. So at last the general, he would stand it no longer, so
we dug a covering trench until we were within a hundred yards of
them, and then waited for a dark night. We got our chance at last,
and five hundred men were got together quietly under cover.
When the word was given they made for the quarries as hard as
they could run, jumped down, and began bayonetting every man
they met. There was never a shot fired on our side, sir, but it was
all done as quiet as may be. The Russians stood like men – they
never failed to do that – and there was a rare bit of give-an'-take
fighting before we cleared them out. Up to the end they never
turned, and our fellows had to pitchfork them out of the places
like so many trusses of hay. That was the Thirtieth that was
engaged that night. There was a young lieutenant in that corps, I
disremember his name, but he was a terrible one for a fight. He
wasn't more'n nineteen, but as tall as you, sir, and a deal stouter.
They say that he never drew his sword during the whole war, but
he used an ash stick, supple and strong, with a knob the size of a
cocoa-nut at the end of it. It was a nasty weapon in hands like his.
If a man came at him with a firelock, he could down him before
the bayonet was near him, for he was long in the arm and active as
well. I've heard from men in his company that he laid about him
like a demon in the quarries that night, and crippled twenty, if he
hit one."

It seemed to me that the veteran was beginning to warm to his
subject, partly, perhaps, from the effects of the brandy-and-
water, and partly from having found a sympathetic listener. One
or two leading questions were all that he would require. I refilled

my pipe, settled myself down in my chair, put my weary feet upon the fender, and prepared to listen.

"They were splendid soldiers, the Russians, and no man that ever fought against them would deny it. It was queer what a fancy they had for the English and we for them. Our fellows that were taken by them were uncommon well used, and when there was an armistice we could get on well together. All they wanted was dash. Where they were put they would stick, and they could shoot right well, but they didn't seem to have it in them to make a rush, and that was where we had them. They could drive the French before them, though, when we were not by. I've seen them come out for a sortie, and kill them like flies. They were terribly bad soldiers — the worst I ever saw — all except the Zouaves, who were a different race to the rest. They were all great thieves and rogues, too, and you were never safe if you were near them."

"You don't mean to say they would harm their own allies?" said I.

"They would that, sir, if there was anything to be got by it. Look at what happened to poor Bill Cameron, of our battery. He got a letter that his wife was ailing and as he wasn't very strong himself, they gave him leave to go back to England. He drew his twenty-eight pound pay, and was to sail in a transport next day; but, as luck would have it, he goes over to the French canteen that night, just to have a last wet, and he lets out there that he had the money about him. We found him next morning lying as dead as mutton between the lines, and so kicked and bruised that you could hardly tell he was a human being. There was many an Englishman murdered that winter, sir, and many a Frenchman who had a good British pea-jacket to keep out the cold.

"I'll tell you a story about that, if I am not wearying you. Thank you, sir; I thought I'd just make sure. Well, four of our fellows — Sam Kelcey and myself, and Jack Burns and Prout — were over in the French lines on a bit of a spree. When we were coming back, this chap Prout suddenly gets an idea. He was an Irishman, and uncommon clever.

" 'See here, boys,' says he; 'if you can raise sixpence among you, I'll put you in the way of making some money to-night, and a bit of fun into the bargain.'

"Well, we all agreed to this, and turned out our pockets, but we only had about fourpence altogether.

" 'Niver mind,' says Prout. 'Come on with me to the French canteen. All you've to do is to seem very drunk, and to keep saying "yes" to all I ask.'

"All this time, sir, we hadn't a ghost of an idea of what he was driving at, but we went stumbling and rolling into the canteen, among a crowd of loafing Frenchmen, and spent our coppers in a drain of liquor.

" 'Now,' says Prout, loud out, so as everyone could hear, 'are you ready to come back to camp?'

" 'Yes,' says we.

" 'Have you got your thirty pounds safe in your pocket, Sam?'

" 'Yes,' says Sam.

" 'And you, Bill,' he says to me, 'have you got your three months' pay all right?'

" 'Yes,' I answers.

" 'Well, come on, then, an don't tumble down more'n you can help;' and with that we staggers out of the canteen and away off into the darkness.

"By this time we had a pretty good suspicion of what he was after, but when we were well out of sight of everybody, he halted and explained to us.

" 'They're bound to follow us after what we've said, and it's queer if the four of us can't manage to best them. They keep their money in little bags round their necks, and all you've got to do is to cut the string.'

"Well, we stumbled on, still pretending to be very drunk, so as to have the advantage of a surprise, but never a soul did we see. At last we was within a stone's-throw of our lines when we heard a whispering of 'Anglais! Anglais!' which is their jargon for 'English,' sir; and there, sure enough, was about a dozen men coming down against us in the moonlight. We stumbled along, pretending to be too drunk even to see them. Pretty soon they stopped, and one of them, a big stout man, sidles up to Sam Kelcey and says, 'What time you call it?' while the rest of them began to draw round us. Sam says nothing, but gives a terrible lurch, on which the Frenchie, thinking it all right, sprang at his throat.

"That was our signal for action, and in we went. Sam Kelcey was the strongest man in the battery and a terrible bruiser, and he caught this leader of theirs a clip under the jaw that sent him twice head over heels before he brought up against the wall, with the blood pouring from his mouth. The others made a run at us, but all they could do was to kick and scream, while we kept knocking them down as quick as they could get to their feet. We had all their little bags, sir, and we left the lot of them stripped and senseless on the road. Five-and-thirty golden pieces in English money and French we counted out upon a knapsack when we got back to our quarters, besides boots and flannel shirts and other things that were handy. There was never another drunken man followed after that night's work, for you see they never could be sure that it wasn't a sham."

The veteran paused for a moment to have a pull at his glass and listen to my murmur of appreciation. I was afraid that I had exhausted his story-telling capacities; but he rippled on again between the puffs of his pipe.

"Sam Kelcey – him that I spoke about – was a fine man, but his brother Joe was a finer, though a bit of a scamp in his day, like many a fine man is. When I was stationed at Gibraltar after the war Joe Kelcey was working at the fortifications as a convict, having been sent out of England for some little game or other. He was known to be a bold and resolute man, and the overseers kept a sharp look-out on him for fear he'd try to break away. One day he was working on the banks of the river and he seed an empty hamper come floating down – one that had come with wine, as like as not, for the officers' mess. He gets hold of the hamper, and he knocks the bottom out, and stows it away among the rushes. Next morning we were having breakfast when in rushes one of the guard and cries, 'Come on, boys; the five-of-spades is up!' – the five-of-spades being a name they gave to the spotted signal they ran up when a convict had escaped. Out we all tumbled, and began searching like hounds for a hare, because there was always a reward of two pounds for the finder. There wasn't a drain or a hollow but was overhauled, and never a sign of Joe, till at last we gave him up in despair, and agreed that he must be at the bottom of the river.

"That afternoon I was on guard on the ramparts, and my eye chanced to light on the old hamper drifting about half a mile or so from the shore. I thought nothing of it at the time, but in a quarter of an hour I happened to catch sight of the same object again. I stared at it in astonishment.

" 'Why,' I said to the sentry on the wall, 'that hamper's going further away towards the Spanish shore. Blest if it isn't moving against wind and tide and every law of Nature.'

" 'Nonsense!' says he, 'there's always a queer eddy in the straits.'

"Well, this didn't satisfy me at all, so I goes up to Captain Morgan, of our battery, who was smoking his cigar, and I saluted and told him about the hamper. Off he goes, and is back in a minute with a spy-glass, and takes a peep through it.

" 'Bless my soul!' he cries, 'why the hamper's got arms sticking out of it! Ah, to be sure, it's that rascal who escaped this morning. Just run up a signal to the man-of-war.'

"We hoisted it, and in a few minutes two boats were in pursuit of the convict. Now if we had left well enough alone, Joe would have been caught sure enough, for he never knew he was found out, and was taking things leisurely, being an uncommon fine swimmer. But Captain Morgan says:

" 'Just wheel round this thirty-two pounder, and we'll drop a shot beside him to show him that we see him, and bring him to a halt.'

"We slewed the gun round, sir, and the captain looked along the sights and touched her off. A more wonderful shot you never saw, and the whole crowd that was on the ramparts gave a regular shout. It hit the top of the hamper and sent the whole thing flying in the air, so that we made sure that the man was killed. When the foam from the splash had cleared away, he was still there though, and striking out might and main for the Spanish coast. It was a close race between him and the boats, and the coxswain actually grabbed at him with a boat-hook as he clambered up on land, but there he was, and we could see him dancing about and chaffing the men-o'-war's men. There was a cheer, sir, when we saw him safe, for a plucky chap like that deserves to be free, whatever he's been and done. You look tired. You've had a long walk maybe. Perhaps you'd best have some rest."

This remark, disinterested as it sounds, was given point to by the plaintive manner in which my companion gazed at the two empty glasses, as if it were evident that the proceedings of the evening had come to a close.

"It's not often," he murmured, "that a poor old soldier like me finds a gentleman as sociable-like and free as your honour."

I need hardly say that after that I had no alternative but to ring the bell and order up a second edition of the brandy-and-water.

"You were talking about the Russians," he continued, "and I told you they were fine soldiers. Some of their riflemen were as good shots as ever pulled a trigger. Excuse me, that glass is yours, sir, and the other is mine. Our sharpshooters used to arrange four sand-bags, one on each side, one in front, and one crossways on the top, so as to cover them all round. Then, you see, they shot through the little slit between the bag in front and the one on the top; maybe not more than two inches across. You'll hardly believe me, but I've seen at the distance of five hundred yards the bullets humming through the narrow slits as thick as bees. I've known as many as six men knocked over in half an hour in one of these sand-traps, as we used to call them; every one of them hit in the eye too, for that was the only part that showed.

"There is a story that that reminds me of which might interest you. There was one Russian fellow that had a sand-pit all of his own, right in front of our trenches. I never saw anybody so persevering as that man was. Early in the morning he'd be popping away, and there he'd stay until nightfall, taking his food with him into the pit. He seemed to take a real pleasure in it, and as he was a very fine shot, and never let us get much of a chance at him, he was not a popular character in the advanced trenches. Many a good fellow he sent to glory. It got such a nuisance that we dropped shells at him now and again, but he minded them no more than if they had been so many oranges.

"One day I was down in the trenches when Colonel Mancor, of the Forty-eighth, a splendid shot and a great man of sport, came along. A party with a sergeant were at work, and just as the colonel came up, one of them dropped with a ball through his head.

" 'Deuced good shot! Who fired that?' says the colonel, putting up his eye-glass.

" 'Never saw a neater shot,' says the colonel. 'He only showed for a moment, and wouldn't have shown then, only that the edge of the trench is a bit worn away. Does he often shoot like that?'

" 'Terribly dangerous man,' replies the sergeant; 'kills more than all the guns in the Redan.'

" 'Now, major,' says the colonel, turning to another officer as was with him, 'what's the odds against my picking him off?'

" 'In how long?'

" 'Within ten minutes.'

" 'Two to one, in ponies, I'll give you,' says the major.

" 'Say three, and it's a bargain.'

" 'Three to one in ponies,' answered the major, and the bet was made.

"He was a great man for measuring his powder, was the colonel, and always emptied out a cartridge and then filled it up again according to his taste. He took about half his time getting the sergeant's gun loaded to please him. At last he got it right, and the glass screwed well into his eye.

" 'Now, my lads,' says he, 'just push poor Smith here up over the trench. He's dead enough, and another wound will make little difference to him.'

"The men began to hoist the body up, and the colonel stood, maybe twenty yards off, peering over the edge with eyes like a lynx. As soon as the top of Smith's shako appeared, we saw the barrel of the gun come slowly out of the sand-pit, and when his poor dead face looks over the edge, whizz comes a bullet right through his forehead. The Russian he peeps out of the pit to see the effect of his shot, and he never looks at anything again until he sees the everlasting river. The colonel fired with a sort of a chuckle, and the rifleman sprang up in the air, and ran a matter of ten or twelve paces towards us, and then down on his face as dead as a door-nail. 'Double or quits on the man in the pit to the right,' says the colonel, loading up his gun again, but I think the major had dropped money enough for one day over his shooting, for he wouldn't hear of another try. By the way, it was handed over to Smith's widow, for he was a free-handed gentleman, was the colonel, not unlike yourself, sir.

"That running of dead men is a queer thing. Perhaps your eddication may help you to understand it, but it beats me. I've seen it, though, many a time. I remember the doctor of our regiment saying it was commoner among men hit through the heart. What do you think about it, sir?"

"Your doctor was quite right," I answered. "In serveral murder cases people who have been stabbed or shot through the heart have gone surprising distances afterwards. I never heard of such a case occurring in a battle, but I don't see why it shouldn't."

"It happened once," resumed my companion, "when Codrington's division were going up the Alma, and were close on the great redoubt. To their surprise a single Russian came running down the hill against them, with his firelock in his hand. One or two fired at him and seemed to miss him, for on he came till he got right up to the line, when a sergeant, as had seen a deal of service, gives a laugh, and throws his gun down in front of him. Down goes the Russian and lies there stone dead. He'd been shot through the heart at the top of the hill, and was dead before ever he began that charge. At least, that's what the sergeant said, and we all believed him.

"There was another queer incident of the same sort which happened later on in the war. Perhaps you may have heard of it, for it got into print at the time. One night a body, fearfully mangled and crushed, came crashing in among the tents of the light division. Nobody could make head or tail of it, until some deserters let it out long afterwards. It seems that they had one old-fashioned sort of gun with a big bore in a Russian battery. Now the night was cold, and the poor devil of a sentry thought he'd stow himself away where he'd never be seen, so he creeps inside the big gun, and goes to sleep there. In the middle of the night there was a sudden alarm of an attack, and an artilleryman runs up to the gun and touches it off, and the sentry was flying through the air at twenty miles a minute. It didn't much matter," added the veteran philosophically, "for he was bound to be shot any way, for sleeping at his post, so it saved a deal of useless delay."

"To a man who has seen so much of the world," I remarked, "this humdrum life in a Welsh village must be very slow."

"It is that, sir. It is that, sir. You've hit it there. Lord bless you, sir, if I had a gentleman like yourself to talk to every night I'd be a different man. I'll tell you one reason now for my coming to this place," here he leaned forward impressively. "I've got a wife in London, sir, but I came here to break myself of the drink. And I'm doing it, slow but sure. Why, three weeks ago I could never sleep unless I had my five glasses under my belt, and now I can manage it on three."

"Waiter, another glass of brandy-and-water," said I.

"Thank you, sir; thank you. As you said just now I have had a stirring life, and this quiet business is too much for me. Did I ever tell you how I got my stripes? Why, it was by hanging three men — three men with these very hands."

"How was that?" I asked sleepily.

"It was like this, sir. We were in Corfu — three batteries of us, in '50. Well, one of our officers — a lieutenant he was — went off into the mountains to shoot one day, and he never came back. His dog trotted into the messroom, however, and began to howl for all the world like a human being. A party was made up, and followed the dog, who led them right up among the hills to a place where there was a ditch. There, with a lot of ferns and such-like heaped over him, the poor young fellow was lying with his throat cut from ear to ear. He was a great favourite in the regiment, and more particularly with the officer in command, and he swore that he'd have revenge. There was a deal of discontent among the Greeks on the island at the time, and this had been encouraged by the priests — 'pappas' they call them. Well, when we got back to town, the captain calls all these pappas before him, and there were three of them who could give no sort of account of themselves, but turned pale and stammered, and were terribly put out. A court-martial was held, and the three of them were condemned to be hanged. Now came the difficulty, however, for it was well known that if anyone laid hands on a priest his life wasn't worth an hour's purchase. They are very strict about that are the Greeks, and uncommon handy with their knives. The captain called for a volunteer, and out I stepped, for I thought it was my duty, sir, seeing that I had been the dead man's servant. Well, the troops formed square round the scaffold, and I hung them as high as Haman. When the job was over, the captain says, 'Now, my lad, I'll save your life,' and with that he forms the troops up into close order, puts me in the middle, and marches me down to the quay. There was a steamer there just casting off her warps for England,

and I was shoved aboard, the crowd surging all round, and trying to get at me. You never heard such a howl as when they saw the ship steam out of the bay, and knew that I was gone. I have been a lonely man all my life, sir, and I may say that was the only time I have been honestly regretted when I left. We searched the ship when we got to sea, and blessed if there weren't three Greek stowaways aboard, each with his knife in his belt. We hove them over the side, and since I have never heard from them since, I fear they may possibly have been drowned;" and the artilleryman grinned in high delight. "They made me a corporal for that job, sir."

"By the way, what is your name?" I asked, getting more and more drowsy, partly from the heat of the fire, and partly from a curious feeling which was stealing over me, and the like of which I had never experienced before.

"Sergeant Turnbull, sir; Turnbull of B Battery, Royal Horse Artillery. Major Campbell, who was over us in the Crimea, or Captain Onslow, or any of the old corps, would be glad to hear that you have seen me. You'll not forget the name, will you, sir?"

I was too sleepy to answer.

"I could tell you a yarn about a Zouave that would amuse you. He was mortal drunk, and mistook the Russian lines for ours. They was having their supper in the Mamelon when he passes the sentry as cool as may be – prisoner – jumps – colonel – free –"

When I came to myself I found that I was lying in front of the smouldering fire, and that the candle was burning low. I was alone in the room. I staggered to my feet with a laugh, but my brain seemed to spin round, and I came down into my former position. Something was evidently amiss. I put my hand into my pocket to find out the time. It was empty. I gave a gasp of astonishment. My purse was gone too. I had been thoroughly rifled.

"Who's in there?" cried a voice, and a small dapper man, rather past the prime of life, came into the room with a candle. "Bless my soul, sir, my wife told me a traveller had come, but I thought you were in bed long ago. I'm the landlord, but I've been away all day at Llanmorris fair."

"I've been robbed," said I.

"Robbed!" cried the landlord, nearly dropping the candle in his consternation.

"Watch, money – everything gone," I said despondently. "What time is it?"

"Nearly one," said he. "Are you sure there is no mistake?"

"No, there's no mistake. I fell asleep about eleven, so he's got two hours' start."

"There was a train left about an hour and a half ago. He's clear away, whoever he is," observed the landlord. "You seem weak, sir. Ah!" he added, sniffing at my glass; "laudanum, I see. You've been drugged, sir."

"The villain!" I cried. "I know his name and history, that's one blessing."

"What was it?" asked the landlord eagerly.

"I'll make every police-station in the kingdom ring with it till I teach him. It is Sergeant Turnbull, formerly of B Battery."

"Why, bless my soul!" cried my companion. "Why, I am Sergeant Turnbull of B Battery, with medals for the Crimea and Mutiny, sir."

"Then who the deuce is he?"

A light seemed to break upon the landlord.

"Was he a tall man with a scar on his forehead?" he asked.

"That's him!" I cried.

"Then he's the greatest villain unhung. Sergeant, indeed! He never wore a uniform except a convict's in his life. That's Joe Kelcey."

"And do you mean to say he never was in the Crimea?"

"Not he, sir. He's never been out of England, except once to Gibraltar where he escaped very cleverly."

"He told me – he told me," I groaned; "and the officer with the stick, and the sporting colonel, and the running corpses, and the Greek priests – were they all lies?"

"All true as gospel, sir, but they happened to me, and not to him. He's heard me tell the stories many a time in the bar, so he reeled them off to you, so as to get a chance of hocussing the liquor. He's been reformed, and living here quiet enough, but being left alone with you, and seeing your watch, has been too much for him. Come up to bed, sir, and I'll send round and let the police know all about it."

And so, reader, I present you with a string of military anecdotes. I don't know how you will value them. They cost me a good watch and chain, and fourteen pounds, seven shillings and fourpence, and I thought them dear at the price.

GENTLEMANLY JOE

That was the name by which he was known in the banking-house of Ducat, Gulden, and Ducat, or at least in that branch of it which did a thriving business in the great commercial city of Birchespool. It did not require more than five minutes' acquaintance, however, to inform the uninitiated that the apparently complimentary epithet was bestowed rather from a keen sense of humour on the part of his five fellow-clerks, than on account of any exceptional claims to blue blood in the case of Mr. Joseph Smith himself. Even the casual customer, whose knowledge of Joe was limited to watching his self-satisfied smirk and enormous watch-guard, at the other side of the shining mahogany desk, or admiring the emphasis with which he utilised his moistened thumb in overcoming the gregarious leaves of his ledger, must have been struck by the misappropriate epithet. To us, however, who had, so to say, sat at his feet and marvelled at the war of independence which he was carrying on against the Queen's English – a guerilla warfare consisting in attacks upon aspirates, and the cutting off of straggling g's – to us our fanciful sobriquet was a joke of the first water. If anything could have enhanced our enjoyment of it, it was the innocent gravity with which our companion accepted the doubtful title, and, after one feeble remonstrance, adopted it for ever as his own prerogative and right.

The circumstances of the remonstrance deserve to be recorded. Before the arrival of Mr. Joseph Smith from the paternal training-stables – his father was a successful sporting tout who had developed into a trainer – our office had been a particularly aristocratic one. Welstead, our senior clerk, was a fine handsome young fellow of twenty-six, who came of a good Scotch strain, and was occasionally understood to make dark allusions concerning the extinct Earldom of Stirling. Dullan and Moreby were Oxford men, well-connected and well-read; Little Sparkins was the son of a High Church clergyman; and I had some of the best blood of Wales in my veins. No wonder, then, that our dignity was hurt by the appearance of a loudly-dressed scorbutic-looking youth, with horse-shoe pin, and a necktie suggestive of spectrum analysis, upon the very stool lately vacated by my old college friend Vernon Hawkins – most gentlemanly and quiet of mankind.

For a few days we contented ourselves with observing the habits and customs of the creature. There was an audacity about his vulgarity, and a happy unconsciousness of all offence, which fairly disarmed criticism. It was not until he began to address us as "old pals," and went the length of playing a small practical joke upon Little Sparkins, that a spirit of resistance began to stir within our bosoms, and that Welstead, as usual, was pushed forward as our mouthpiece.

"You see, Smith," he remarked in his most languid tones, "you have been in our office for a comparatively short period, and yet you have taught us many things which were new to us. There is a natural buoyancy about your character which points you out as one calculated to shine in the most select circles. Before your arrival we had never learned to designate ladies as 'fillies,' nor had we heard of the 'real gents' whom you mention as having frequented your father's establishment. These things interest and please us. Allow us to show some small sense of the honour your society confers upon us, by christening you as 'Gentlemanly Joe,' excusing the liberty we take with your name in consideration of the alliteration."

A great part of this speech must have been lost upon Mr. Joseph, but never did elaborate sarcasm fall so utterly flat. Instead of being offended, as we had fondly hoped would be the case, he burst into an uproarious fit of laughter, and slapped his gaitered leg with the ebony ruler as a token of delight. "Haw! haw!" he roared, writhing about on the top of the high stool. "Whatever'll father say! Oh, law, to think of it! 'Gentlemanly Joe' – eh? You're right, though; you're right, and not ashamed to own up neither. I said when I was comin' up, 'Father,' says I, 'I'll teach them a trick or two,' and I have, hain't I? Of course we're all gents here, for clerks is mostly reckoned such, but it do make a difference when a man has been brought in contac' with the real thing. You can call me Gentlemanly Joe, an' pleasure, but not as meaning to imply that there is any in this room not such, though, maybe, not one of you has seen a belted hurl give your father one in the short ribs and holler out, 'You're a deep old scoundrel, Smith, and one as knows how many beans make five!' "

Welstead's face at the idea of his gouty and dyspeptic governor receiving such an attention at the hands of nobility was so ludicrous that we all burst into a roar of laughter, which ended our first and last attempt to take a serious rise out of our bucolic companion. It is true that his life was spent under a continual shower of small jokes and chaff, and that his new name superseded his old one, but there was a massive simplicity about the man, and a marvellous power of converting the most unpromising remarks into compliments which rendered him a very disconcerting individual to attack. Allusions to his hat, necktie, or any other peculiarity of raiment were met by his eternal horse-laugh, and an earnest recommendation that we should allow him to send down to the country and procure facsimiles for all and each of us. "You hain't got nothin' spicy in Birchespool," he would remark. "Lord, I know a place at 'ome where you can get your collars spotted over with fox's 'eads instead of bein' plain white, which is a poor colour at best." I think he imagined that it was nothing but want of money which induced us to refuse to purchase these and other luxuries, and he was wont to throw out allusions as to "it's not costing us nothink," while he jingled the loose coins in his trouser-pockets.

Town life did not improve Joseph. On the contrary he deteriorated. During the first six months that he honoured the office with his presence, he not only lost none of the traits which he had brought with him from his father's stables, but he grafted upon them everything which is objectionable in the city snob. The premonitory symptoms were a suspicious waxiness of the half-dozen hairs which adorned his upper-lip, and the appearance of a large diamond-ring with a greenish and vitreous hue. His next venture was an eye-glass; and he finally launched forth into a light ulster, decorated with a large black check, which gave him the appearance of being inside a cage, with his head projecting at one end and his feet at the other. "It's a proper thing for a gent to wear," he remarked. "When you see a get-up like this you knows at a glance who's a cad and who ain't" — a sentiment which we all very cordially endorsed.

In spite of these peculiarities we learned not only to tolerate the Gentleman, but even to like him. Indeed, we hardly knew how strong this feeling was until he betook himself into the country on a fortnight's leave, carrying with him ulster, eye-glass, ring, and everything else which was calculated to impress the rustics and stamp him as the natural associate of the "belted hurl." He left quite a vacancy behind him. There was a dead level of equality about the five of us which deprived life of all its piquancy. Even Welstead, who had disliked him from the first, was fain to confess that he was good fun, and that he wished him back. After all, if his laugh was obtrusive it was hearty, and his quaint, vulgar face had sincerity and good-nature stamped upon every line of it. It was with unaffected pleasure that we heard a loud view-halloa in the street one morning just after the opening of the doors, and saw our friend swaggering in, more ugly, more dressy, and, if possible, more vulgar than before.

Newsome, our bank manager, was an excellent fellow, and on the best terms with all of us. As we were all single men, with a very limited circle of friends in Birchespool, he kindly gave us the run of his house, and it was seldom that a week passed without our enjoying a musical evening there, winding up with one of the choice little suppers for which Mrs. Newsome was celebrated. On these occasions, since distinctions would be invidious, Gentlemanly Joe used to be present in all his glory, with a very large white-frilled shirt-front, and another vitreous fragment sparkling gloomily in the middle of it. This, with a watch-chain which reminded one of the chain cable of a schooner, was his sole attempt at ornamentation, for, as he used to say, "It ain't good form to show you're richer than your neighbours, even if you are. Too much like a Sheeny, don't you know?"

Joe was an endless source of amusement to Cissy Newsome, a mischievous, dark-eyed little brunette of eighteen, the sole child of the manager. We had all fallen in love with Cissy at one time or another, but had had to give it up on finding her heart was no longer her own to bestow. Charles Welstead had known her from childhood, and the affection of early youth had ripened into love on both sides. Never was there a more fondly attached couple, nor one to whom the path seemed to lie so smoothly, for old Welstead had been Newsome's personal friend, and Charles's prospects were of the brightest.

On these pleasant evenings which I have mentioned, it was great fun to see Joe darting into the drawing-room and endeavouring to secure a seat in the neighbourhood of the young lady, with a profound disregard for any claims her parents might have upon his courtesy. If he attained the coveted position he would lean back in his chair with what he imagined to be an air of easy gentility, and regale her with many anecdotes of horses and dogs, with occasional reminiscences of the "big nobs" who had had professional relations with his father. On such occasions Miss Cissy would imitate him to his face in the most amusing way, looking all the time as demure as a little mouse, while Welstead leaned up against the piano, not quite sure whether to laugh or be angry. Even he usually broke down, however, when the two came to discuss "hetiquette," and Joe, in his character of gentleman, laid down his views as to when a "feller should raise 'is 'at," and when not. The argument was generally closed by a burst of laughter from all of us, in which Joseph would join, though protesting loudly that he was unable to see the joke.

It is a proverbially dangerous thing to play with edged tools. I have never been sure whether Smith knew how matters stood between Welstead and the young lady. I am inclined to think that at first he did not. Perhaps, if someone had informed him of it then, he might have mastered his feelings, and much misery have been averted. It was clear to us young fellows who had gone through the same experience how things were tending, but we held our tongues rather than spoil what we considered a capital joke. Cissy may have seen it too, and given him a little mischievous encouragement — at least, young ladies have the credit of not being blind in such cases. Certainly Smith pursued his hopeless suit with a vigour which astonished us. During business hours he lived in a sort of day-dream, musing upon his perch like some cogitative fowl, and getting into endless trouble over his accounts, while every evening found him interfering with Welstead's tête-à-tête at the high corner house in Eldon Street.

At last the crash came. There was no need to ask what had happened, when little Joe slunk quietly into the office one morning with dishevelled hair, melancholy face, and eyes bleared with the wakefulness of a restless night. We never learnt the particulars of his dismissal. Suffice it that he was informed once and for ever that a gap which there was no crossing lay between Miss Cissy Newsome and himself. He bore up bravely, and tried to hug his sorrow to his heart, and hide it from the vulgar gaze of mankind, but he became an altered man. What had been but a passing fancy with us, had taken root in his very soul and grown there, so that he, who had hardly known when it was planted, was now unable to wrench it out. The ordeal he had gone through chastened him to a great extent from his vulgarity by toning down his natural spirits, and though he occasionally ventured upon a "Haw! haw!" it was painfully artificial, and a good deal more suggestive of a dirge than of merriment. The worst feature of his case was that every week increased the gloom which hung over him. We began to suspect that our estimate of his character had been a superficial one, and that there were depths in the little man's soul of whose existence we had been ignorant.

Four months had passed away. None of us changed much during that time, with the exception of the Gentleman. We saw little of him except in office hours. Where he spent the rest of the day was a mystery. Once I met him late at night in the docks, stumbling along among ring-bolts and chains, careless of the fact that a trip or slip might send him into eternity. Another time I saw a cloaked figure lurking in the shadow beside the house in Eldon Street, which fled round the corner on my approach. His naturally unhealthy complexion had become so cadaverous, that the sandy eyebrows and moustache stood out quite dark against it. His clothes hung loosely on his figure. The eye-glass was discarded. Even the once gorgeous ring seemed to have assumed a sombre and melancholy lustre, as if in sympathy with the feelings of its owner. His manner had lost all its old audacity, and become timid and retiring. I doubt if any of his rustic acquaintances would have recognised their gaudy Joseph in the shambling unkempt figure which haunted the counting-house of Ducat, Gulden, and Ducat.

The termination of Welstead's engagement began to draw near. It had been arranged that after his marriage he was to be promoted to the management of another branch in a distant part of the country. This approaching break-up in our little circle drew us all closer together, and made us the more sorry that the general harmony should be destroyed by the unhappiness of one of our number. If we could have cheered him we would, but there was something in his look, for all his snobbishness, which forbade even sympathy on a subject so sacred. He endeavoured to put on a careless manner when he joined us all in wishing Welstead good luck at midday on the Saturday preceding the Monday on which the wedding was to take place. We expected then that we should not see our fellow-clerk again until he appeared in the character of bridegroom. How little did we guess the catastrophe which was impending.

I remember that Saturday evening well. It was in January, and a clear wintry sky, with a suspicion of an aurora in its northern quarter, spread over the great city. There was a slight frost in the air, and the ground clinked cheerily under foot. One of my fellow-clerks – Dullan – and I had kept by little Smith all day, for there was a wild look about his eyes which made us think it might be unsafe to leave him to his own devices. We dined at a restaurant, and afterwards dropped into a theatre, where Joe's ghastly face in the stalls had a very depressing effect upon the pantomime. We were walking slowly homewards after supper, it being then between twelve and one, when we saw a great crimson glow upon the heavens, such as aurora never threw, and a fire-engine dashed past us with a whistle and a clang, the big-boned shaggy horses whirling it along at such a rate that we only caught a glimpse of a flash of lights and a cluster of bearded, helmeted heads suspended, as it were, in the darkness.

I have always had a weakness for fires. There is something grand and ennobling in the irresistible sweep of a great volume of flame. I could moralise over a conflagration as Chateaubriand did over Niagara. Dullan is of the same bent of mind, and the Gentleman was ready to turn anywhere from his own thoughts. We all began running in the direction of the blaze.

At first we ran languidly, jogging along with many other people who were hurrying towards the same goal. Then, as we came into a quarter of the town which we knew well, we almost involuntarily quickened our pace, until, tearing round a familiar corner at racing speed, we pulled up, and gazed silently into each other's pale faces. There, not a hundred yards from us, stood the high house of Eldon Street – the house under whose hospitable roof we had spent so many happy hours – with the red flames licking round the whole lower storey, and spurting out of every chink and crevice, while a dense pall of smoke obscured the upper windows and the roof.

We dashed through the crowds together, and fought our way to the clear space on which the firemen were connecting their hose. As we reached them, a half-naked man, bare-footed and dishevelled, was pleading with the superintendent, clutching frantically at his arm, and pointing up into the dark clouds above him, already rent with jagged streaks of ascending flame.

"Too short!" he screamed in a voice which we were horrified to recognise as that of Mr. Newsome. "It can't be – it mustn't be! There are more escapes than one. Oh, man, man, she is burning – choking – suffocating! Do something! Save her! My child – my beautiful child – the only one I have!"

In the agony of his fear, he fell at the fireman's feet and implored his assistance.

I was paralysed by the horror of the thing. The situation was apparent at a glance. There, seen dimly through the smoke, was Cissy Newsome's window, while beneath it, separated by a broad expanse of wall, was the head of the fire-escape. It was too short by a good twelve feet. The whole lower storey was one seething mass of fire, so that there seemed no possibility of approach from that direction. A horrible feeling of impotence came over me. There was no sign of movement at the young lady's window, though crawling trails of flame had climbed up to it and festooned it round with their red garlands. I remember hoping in my heart that she had been suffocated in her sleep, and had never awoke to the dreadful reality.

I have said that we were paralysed for the moment. The spell was rapidly broken. "This way, lads!" cried a resolute voice, and Charley Welstead broke in among us with a fireman's hatchet in his hand. We pushed after him as he rushed round to the rear of the house, where there was a door usually used by the servants. It was locked, but a couple of blows shattered it to pieces. We hurried up the stone kitchen stairs, with the plaster falling in strips all round us, and the flags so hot that they burned into the soles of our boots. At the head of the stairs there was a second door, thicker and stronger than the first, but nearly charred through by the fire.

"Give me room!" gasped Welstead, swinging round his axe.

"Don't do it, sir," cried a stalwart fireman, seizing him by the wrist; "there's flames on the other side of that door."

"Let me go!" roared Charley.

"We're dead men if you break it!"

"Let me go!"

"Drop it, sir; drop it!"

There was a momentary struggle, and the axe clattered down upon the stone steps. It had hardly time to fall before some one caught it up. I could not see who for the dense blue reek of smoke. A man dashed past the fireman, there was the crashing of a parting lock, and a great lick of flame, like a hound unleashed, shot out and enveloped us. I felt its hot sear as it coiled round my face, and I remember nothing more until I found myself leaning against the door-post, breathing in the fresh sweet air of night, while Welstead, terribly burned, struggled furiously with the fireman who held him back to prevent him from reascending the staircase, which was now a solid sheet of fire.

"Hold back, sir!" I heard the honest fellow growl. "Ain't one life thrown away enough? That little cove – him with the gaiters – the same what broke the door – he's gone. I seed him jump right slap into the middle of it. He won't never come back no more!"

Together we led Welstead round to the front once more, all three staggering like drunken men. The flames were higher than before, but the upper storey and the roof still rose above them like a black island in a sea of fire. There was Miss Cissy's window dark and unopened, though the woodwork around it was in a glow. There was no sign of the flutter of a female dress. Poor Welstead leaned against me, sobbing like a child. A ghastly longing came into my heart that I might see flames in that room, that I might know it to be all over, and her pain and trouble at an end. Then I heard the crash of glass falling outwards, and I bent my head to avoid seeing the very thing that I had wished for; and then there broke upon my ear a shout from ten thousand voices, so wildly exultant and madly jubilant that I never hope to hear the like again.

Welstead and I looked up. Balanced upon the narrow ledge outside the window I had been watching, there was standing a man, framed as it were in fire. His clothes were hanging around him as a few tattered charred rags, and his very hair was in a blaze. The draught caused by knocking out the window had encouraged the flames, so that a lurid curtain hung behind him, while the ground was fully seventy feet below. Yet there, on the thin slip of stone, with Eternity on each side of him, stood Joe Smith, the uncouth and ungrammatical, tying two sheets together, while women sobbed below and men shouted, and every hand was raised to bless him. He staggered and disappeared so suddenly that we feared he had fallen, but he was back again in an instant, not alone this time, for the girl he had come to save was slung over his shoulder. The brave fellow seemed to have doubts of the strength of his impromptu rope, for he rested his own weight upon the nearly red-hot water-pipe during those twelve perilous feet, supporting Miss Newsome by the arm which clutched the sheet. Slowly, very slowly they descended, but at last his feet touched the topmost rung of the escape. Was it a dream that I heard a voice high above me say, "Hall right, missy," before a burst of cheering rang out which drowned every other sound.

Miss Cissy, more frightened than hurt, was delivered over into her half-distracted father's care, while I helped to lift Gentlemanly Joe from the escape. He lay panting upon the ground, burned and scorched, his sporting coat tattered and charred, while, strangely enough, the prismatic necktie and horse-shoe pin had escaped the general destruction, so as to present an absurd oasis amid the desert around. He lay without speaking or moving until Cissy Newsome was led past him on her way to a cab. Then he made a feeble gesture with his hand, which indicated that he wished to speak with her, and she stooped over him. No other ear but mine caught that whisper.

"Don't fret, miss," he said, " 'cause it was the wrong hoss came in. He's a good fellar – a deal better than me – and did as much, but hadn't the luck."

A vulgar little speech, but Cissy's eyes got very moist as she listened, and I'm not sure that mine didn't too.

The office was sadly reduced after that. With Welstead and the Gentleman on the sick-list, there were only four of us at the desk, and the reaction from the excitement had left us anything but lively. I can remember only one remark ventured upon during that first day. The dreary scratching of pens had lasted unbroken for over an hour, when Little Sparkins looked up from his ledger.

"I suppose you would call him a gentleman after all," he said.

"A very much better one than you will ever be," growled Dullan, and we relapsed into the scratching of pens.

I was present at the wedding of Charley Welstead and Cissy Newsome, when, after a long delay, it was finally celebrated. By the original arrangement I was to have figured as best man, but my post of honour was handed over to a certain very ugly young man whose appearance suggested the idea that he had spent the last few weeks in a mustard-poultice. Unromantic as it may seem, this youth not only went through his duties with all the nonchalance in the world, but danced at the subsequent festivities with the greatest vigour and grace. It is commonly rumoured that this activity of his, combined with sundry interesting anecdotes concerning horses and dogs, have so prevailed upon the heart of a susceptible young lady, that there is every probability of our having a repetition of the marriage ceremony. Should it be so, I trust that I may at last revert to my original position as best man.

THE WINNING SHOT

———————◆———————

"Caution. – The public are hereby cautioned against a man calling himself Octavius Gaster. He is to be recognised by his great height, his flaxen hair, and deep scar upon his left cheek, extending from the eye to the angle of the mouth. His predilection for bright colours – green neckties, and the like – may help to identify him. A slightly foreign accent is to be detected in his speech. This man is beyond the reach of the law, but is more dangerous than a mad dog. Shun him as you would shun the pestilence that walketh at noonday. Any communications as to his whereabouts will be thankfully acknowledged by A.C.U., Lincoln's Inn, London."

This is a copy of an advertisement which may have been noticed by many readers in the columns of the London morning papers during the early part of the present year. It has, I believe, excited considerable curiosity in certain quarters, and many guesses have been hazarded as to the identity of Octavius Gaster and the nature of the charge brought against him. When I state that the "caution" has been inserted by my elder brother, Arthur Cooper Underwood, barrister-at-law, upon my representations, it will be acknowledged that I am the most fitting person to enter upon an authentic explanation.

Hitherto the horror and vagueness of my suspicion, combined with my grief at the loss of my poor darling on the very eve of our wedding, have prevented me from revealing the events of last August to anyone save my brother.

Now, however, looking back, I can fit in many little facts almost unnoticed at the time, which form a chain of evidence that, though worthless in a court of law, may yet have some effect upon the mind of the public.

I shall therefore relate, without exaggeration or prejudice, all that occurred from the day upon which this man, Octavius

Gaster, entered Toynby Hall up to the great rifle competition. I know that many people will always ridicule the supernatural, or what our poor intellects choose to regard as supernatural, and that the fact of my being a woman will be thought to weaken my evidence. I can only plead that I have never been weak-minded or impressionable, and that other people formed the same opinions of Octavius Gaster that I did.

Now to the story.

It was at Colonel Pillar's place at Roborough, in the pleasant county of Devon, that we spent our autumn holidays. For some months I had been engaged to his eldest son Charley, and it was hoped that the marriage might take place before the termination of the Long Vacation.

Charley was considered "safe" for his degree, and in any case was rich enough to be practically independent, while I was by no means penniless.

The old Colonel was delighted at the prospect of the match, and so was my mother; so that look what way we would, there seemed to be no cloud above our horizon.

It was no wonder, then, that that August was a happy one. Even the most miserable of mankind would have laid his woes aside under the genial influence of the merry household at Toynby Hall.

There was Lieutenant Daseby, "Jack," as he was invariably called, fresh home from Japan in Her Majesty's ship *Shark*, who was on the same interesting footing with Fanny Pillar, Charley's sister, as Charley was with me, so that we were able to lend each other a certain moral support.

Then there was Harry, Charley's younger brother, and Trevor, his bosom friend at Cambridge.

Finally there was my mother, dearest of old ladies, beaming at us through her gold-rimmed spectacles, anxiously smoothing every little difficulty in the way of the two young couples, and never weary of detailing to them *her* own doubts and fears and perplexities when that gay young blood, Mr. Nicholas Underwood, came a-wooing into the provinces, and forswore Crockford's and Tattersall's for the sake of the country parson's daughter.

I must not, however, forget the gallant old warrior who was our host; with his time-honoured jokes, and his gout, and his harmless affectation of ferocity.

"I don't know what's come over the governor lately," Charley used to say. "He has never cursed the Liberal Administration since you've been here, Lottie; and my belief is that unless he has a good blow-off, that Irish question will get into his system and finish him."

Perhaps in the privacy of his own apartment the veteran used to make up for his self-abnegation during the day.

He seemed to have taken a special fancy to me, which he showed in a hundred little attentions.

"You're a good lass," he remarked one evening, in a very port-winey whisper. "Charley's a lucky dog, egad! and has more discrimination than I thought. Mark my words, Miss Underwood, you'll find that young gentleman isn't such a fool as he looks!"

With which equivocal compliment the Colonel solemnly covered his face with his handkerchief, and went off into the land of dreams.

How well I remember the day that was the commencement of all our miseries!

Dinner was over, and we were in the drawing-room, with the windows open to admit the balmy southern breeze.

My mother was sitting in the corner, engaged on a piece of fancy-work, and occasionally purring forth some truism which the dear old soul believed to be an entirely original remark, and founded exclusively upon her own individual experiences.

Fanny and the young lieutenant were billing and cooing upon the sofa, while Charley paced restlessly about the room.

I was sitting by the window, gazing out dreamily at the great wilderness of Dartmoor, which stretched away to the horizon, ruddy and glowing in the light of the sinking sun, save where some rugged tor stood out in bold relief against the scarlet background.

"I say," remarked Charley, coming over to join me at the window, "it seems a positive shame to waste an evening like this."

"Confound the evening!" said Jack Daseby.

"You're always victimising yourself to the weather. Fan and I ar'n't going to move off this sofa – are we, Fan?"

That young lady announced her intention of remaining by nestling among the cushions, and glancing defiantly at her brother.

"Spooning is a demoralising thing – isn't it, Lottie?" said Charley, appealing laughingly to me.

"Shockingly so," I answered.

"Why, I can remember Daseby here when he was as active a young fellow as any in Devon; and just look at him now! Fanny, Fanny, you've got a lot to answer for!"

"Never mind him, my dear," said my mother, from the corner. "Still, my experience has always shown me that moderation is an excellent thing for young people. Poor dear Nicholas used to think so too. He would never go to bed of a night until he had jumped the length of the hearthrug. I often told him it was dangerous; but he *would* do it, until one night he fell on the fender and snapped the muscle of his leg, which made him limp till the day of his death, for Doctor Pearson mistook it for a fracture of the bone, and put him in splints, which had the effect of stiffening his knee. They did say that the doctor was almost out of his mind at the time from anxiety, brought on by his younger daughter swallowing a halfpenny, and that that was what caused him to make the mistake."

My mother had a curious way of drifting along in her conversation, and occasionally rushing off at a tangent, which made it rather difficult to remember her original proposition. On this occasion Charley had, however, stowed it away in his mind as likely to admit of immediate application.

"An excellent thing, as you say, Mrs. Underwood," he remarked; "and we have not been out to-day. Look here, Lottie, we have an hour of daylight yet. Suppose we go down and have a try for a trout, if your mamma does not object."

"Put something round your throat, dear," said my mother, feeling that she had been outmanœuvred.

"All right, dear," I answered; "I'll just run up and put on my hat."

"And we'll have a walk back in the gloaming," said Charley, as I made for the door.

When I came down, I found my lover waiting impatiently with his fishing basket in the hall.

We crossed the lawn together, and passed the open drawing-room windows, where three mischievous faces were looking at us.

"Spooning is a terribly demoralising thing," remarked Jack, reflectively staring up at the clouds.

"Shocking," said Fan; and all three laughed until they woke the sleeping Colonel, and we could hear them endeavouring to explain the joke to that ill-used veteran, who apparently obstinately refused to appreciate it.

We passed down the winding lane together, and through the little wooden gate, which opens on to the Tavistock road.

Charley paused for a moment after we had emerged and seemed irresolute which way to turn.

Had we but known it, our fate depended upon that trivial question.

"Shall we go down to the river, dear," he said, "or shall we try one of the brooks upon the moor?"

"Whichever you like?" I answered.

"Well, I vote that we cross the moor. We'll have a longer walk back that way," he added, looking down lovingly at the little white-shawled figure beside him.

The brook in question runs through a most desolate part of the country. By the path it is several miles from Toynby Hall; but we were both young and active, and struck out across the moor, regardless of rocks and furze-bushes.

Not a living creature did we meet upon our solitary walk, save a few scraggy Devonshire sheep, who looked at us wistfully, and followed us for some distance, as if curious as to what could possibly have induced us to trespass upon their domains.

It was almost dark before we reached the little stream, which comes gurgling down through a precipitous glen, and meanders away to help to form the Plymouth "leat."

Above us towered two great columns of rock, between which the water trickled to form a deep, still pool at the bottom. This pool had always been a favourite spot of Charley's, and was a pretty cheerful place by day; but now, with the rising moon reflected upon its glassy waters, and throwing dark shadows from the overhanging rocks, it seemed anything rather than the haunt of a pleasure-seeker.

"I don't think, darling, that I'll fish, after all," said Charley, as we sat down together on a mossy bank. "It's a dismal sort of place, isn't it?"

"Very," said I, shuddering.

"We'll just have a rest, and then we will walk back by the pathway. You're shivering. You're not cold, are you?"

"No," said I, trying to keep up my courage; "I'm not cold, but I'm rather frightened, though it's very silly of me."

"By jove!" said my lover, "I can't wonder at it, for I feel a bit depressed myself. The noise that water makes is like the gurgling in the throat of a dying man."

"Don't, Charley; you frighten me!"

"Come, dear, we mustn't get the blues," he said, with a laugh, trying to reassure me. "Let's run away from this charnel-house place, and – Look! – see! – good gracious! what is that?"

Charley had staggered back, and was gazing upwards with a pallid face.

I followed the direction of his eyes, and could scarcely suppress a scream.

I have already mentioned that the pool by which we were

standing lay at the foot of a rough mound of rocks. On the top of this mound, about sixty feet above our heads, a tall dark figure was standing, peering down, apparently, into the rugged hollow in which we were.

The moon was just topping the ridge behind, and the gaunt, angular outlines of the stranger stood out hard and clear against its silvery radiance.

There was something ghastly in the sudden and silent appearance of this solitary wanderer, especially when coupled with the weird nature of the scene.

I clung to my lover in speechless terror, and glared up at the dark figure above us.

"Hullo, you sir!" cried Charley, passing from fear into anger, as Englishmen generally do. "Who are you, and what the devil are you doing?"

"Oh! I thought it, I thought it!" said the man who was overlooking us, and disappeared from the top of the hill.

We heard him scrambling about among the loose stones, and in another moment he emerged upon the banks of the brook and stood facing us.

Weird as his appearance had been when we first caught sight of him, the impression was intensified rather than removed by a closer acquaintance.

The moon shining full upon him revealed a long, thin face of ghastly pallor, the effect being increased by its contrast with the flaring green necktie which he wore.

A scar upon his cheek had healed badly and caused a nasty pucker at the side of his mouth, which gave his whole countenance a most distorted expression, more particularly when he smiled.

The knapsack on his back and stout staff in his hand announced him to be a tourist, while the easy grace with which he raised his hat on perceiving the presence of a lady showed that he could lay claim to the *savoir faire* of a man of the world.

There was something in his angular proportions and the bloodless face which, taken in conjunction with the black cloak which fluttered from his shoulders, irresistibly reminded me of a bloodsucking species of bat which Jack Daseby had brought from Japan upon his previous voyage, and which was the bugbear of the servants' hall at Toynby.

"Excuse my intrusion," he said, with a slightly foreign lisp, which imparted a peculiar beauty to his voice. "I should have had to sleep on the moor had I not had the good fortune to fall in with you."

"Confound it, man!" said Charley; "why couldn't you shout out, or give some warning? You quite frightened Miss Underwood when you suddenly appeared up there."

The stranger once more raised his hat as he apologised to me for having given me such a start.

"I am a gentleman from Sweden," he continued, in that peculiar intonation of his, "and am viewing this beautiful land of yours. Allow me to introduce myself as Doctor Octavius Gaster. Perhaps you could tell me where I may sleep, and how I can get from this place, which is truly of great size?"

"You're very lucky in falling in with us," said Charley. "It is no easy matter to find your way upon the moor."

"That can I well believe," remarked our new acquaintance.

"Strangers have been found dead on it before now," continued Charley. "They lose themselves, and then wander in a circle until they fall from fatigue."

"Ha, ha!" laughed the Swede; "it is not I, who have drifted in an open boat from Cape Blanco to Canary, that will starve upon an English moor. But how may I turn to seek an inn?"

"Look here!" said Charley, whose interest was excited by the stranger's allusion, and who was at all times the most open-hearted of men. "There's not an inn for many a mile round; and I daresay you have had a long day's walk already. Come home with us, and my father, the Colonel, will be delighted to see you and find you a spare bed."

"For this great kindness how can I thank you?" returned the traveller. "Truly, when I return to Sweden, I shall have strange stories to tell of the English and the hospitality!"

"Nonsense!" said Charley. "Come, we will start at once, for Miss Underwood is cold. Wrap the shawl well round your neck, Lottie, and we will be home in no time."

We stumbled along in silence, keeping as far as we could to the rugged pathway, sometimes losing it as a cloud drifted over the face of the moon, and then regaining it further on with the return of the light.

The stranger seemed buried in thought, but once or twice I had the impression that he was looking hard at me through the darkness as we strode along together.

"So," said Charley at last, breaking the silence, "you drifted about in an open boat, did you?"

"Ah, yes," answered the stranger; "many strange sights have I seen, and many perils undergone, but none worse than that. It is, however, too sad a subject for a lady's ears. She has been frightened once to-night."

"Oh, you needn't be afraid of frightening me now," said I, as I leaned on Charley's arm.

"Indeed there is but little to tell, and yet is it sorrowful.

"A friend of mine, Karl Osgood of Upsala, and myself started on a trading venture. Few white men had been among the wandering Moors at Cape Blanco, but nevertheless we went, and for some months lived well, selling this and that, and gathering much ivory and gold.

" 'Tis a strange country, where is neither wood nor stone, so that the huts are made from the weeds of the sea.

"At last, just as what we thought was a sufficiency, the Moors conspired to kill us, and came down against us in the night.

"Short was our warning, but we fled to the beach, launched a canoe and put out to sea, leaving everything behind.

"The Moors chased us, but lost us in the darkness; and when day dawned the land was out of sight.

"There was no country where we could hope for food nearer than Canary, and for that we made.

"I reached it alive, though very weak and mad; but poor Karl died the day before we sighted the islands.

"I gave him warning!

"I cannot blame myself in the matter.

"I said, 'Karl, the strength that you might gain by eating them would be more than made up for by the blood that you would lose!'

"He laughed at my words, caught the knife from my belt, cut them off and eat them; and he died."

"Eat what?" asked Charley.

"His ears!" said the stranger.

We both looked round at him in horror.

There was no suspicion of a smile or joke upon his ghastly face.

"He was what you call headstrong," he continued, "but he should have known better than to do a thing like that. Had he but used his will he would have lived as I did."

"And you think a man's will can prevent him from feeling hungry?" said Charley.

"What can it not do?" returned Octavius Gaster, and relapsed into a silence which was not broken until our arrival in Toynby Hall.

Considerable alarm had been caused by our nonappearance, and Jack Daseby was just setting off with Charley's friend Trevor in search of us. They were delighted, therefore, when we marched in upon them, and considerably astonished at the appearance of our companion.

"Where the deuce did you pick up that second-hand corpse?" asked Jack, drawing Charley aside into the smoking-room.

"Shut up, man; he'll hear you," growled Charley. "He's a Swedish doctor on a tour, and a deuced good fellow. He went in an open boat from What's-it's-name to another place. I've offered him a bed for the night."

"Well, all I can say is," remarked Jack, "that his face will never be his fortune."

"Ha, ha! Very good! very good!" laughed the subject of the remark, walking calmly into the room, to the complete discomfiture of the sailor. "No, it will never, as you say, in this country be my fortune," – and he grinned until the hideous gash across the angle of his mouth made him look more like the reflection in a broken mirror than anything else.

"Come upstairs and have a wash; I can lend you a pair of slippers," said Charley; and hurried the visitor out of the room to put an end to a somewhat embarrassing situation.

Colonel Pillar was the soul of hospitality, and welcomed Doctor Gaster as effusively as if he had been an old friend of the family.

"Egad, sir," he said, "the place is your own; and as long as you care to stop you are very welcome. We're pretty quiet down here, and a visitor is an acquisition."

My mother was a little more distant. "A very well informed young man, Lottie," she remarked to me; "but I wish he would wink his eyes more. I don't like to see people who never wink their eyes. Still, my dear, my life has taught me one great lesson, and that is that a man's looks are of very little importance compared with his actions."

With which brand new and eminently original remark, my mother kissed me and left me to my meditations.

Whatever Doctor Octavius Gaster might be physically, he was certainly a social success.

By next day he had so completely installed himself as a member of the household that the Colonel would not hear of his departure.

He astonished everybody by the extent and variety of his knowledge. He could tell the veteran considerably more about the Crimea than he knew himself; he gave the sailor information about the coast of Japan; and even tackled my athletic lover upon the subject of rowing, discoursing about levers of the first order, and fixed points and fulcra, until the unhappy Cantab was fain to drop the subject.

Yet all this was done so modestly and even deferentially, that no one could possibly feel offended at being beaten upon their own ground. There was a quiet power about everything he said and did which was very striking.

I remember one example of this, which impressed us all at the time.

Trevor had a remarkably savage bulldog, which, however fond of its master, fiercely resented any liberties from the rest of us. This animal was, it may be imagined, rather unpopular, but as it was the pride of the student's heart it was agreed not to banish it entirely, but to lock it up in the stable and give it a wide berth.

From the first, it seemed to have taken a decided aversion to our visitor, and showed every fang in its head whenever he approached it.

On the second day of his visit we were passing the stable in a body, when the growls of the creature inside arrested Doctor Gaster's attention.

"Ha!" he said. "There is that dog of yours, Mr. Trevor, is it not?"

"Yes; that's Towzer," assented Trevor.

"He is a bulldog, I think? What they call the national animal of England on the Continent?"

"Pure-bred," said the student, proudly.

"They are ugly animals — very ugly! Would you come into the stable and unchain him, that I may see him to advantage. It is a pity to keep an animal so powerful and full of life in captivity."

"He's rather a nipper," said Trevor, with a mischievous expression in his eye; "but I suppose you are not afraid of a dog?"

"Afraid? — no. Why should I be afraid?"

The mischievous look on Trevor's face increased as he opened the stable door. I heard Charley mutter something to him about its being past a joke, but the other's answer was drowned by the hollow growling from inside.

The rest of us retreated to a respectable distance, while Octavius Gaster stood in the open doorway with a look of mild curiosity upon his pallid face.

"And those," he said, "that I see so bright and red in the darkness — are those his eyes?"

"Those are they," said the student, as he stooped down and unbuckled the strap.

"Come here!" said Octavius Gaster.

The growling of the dog suddenly subsided into a long whimper, and instead of making the furious rush that we expected, he rustled among the straw as if trying to huddle into a corner.

"What the deuce is the matter with him?" exclaimed his perplexed owner.

"Come here!" repeated Gaster, in sharp metallic accents, with an indescribable air of command in them. "Come here!"

To our astonishment, the dog trotted out and stood at his side, but looking as unlike the usually pugnacious Towzer as is possible to conceive. His ears were drooping, his tail limp, and he altogether presented the very picture of canine humiliation.

"A very fine dog, but singularly quiet," remarked the Swede, as he stroked him down.

"Now, sir, go back!"

The brute turned and slunk back into its corner. We heard the rattling of its chain as it was being fastened, and next moment Trevor came out of the stable-door with blood dripping from his finger.

"Confound the beast!" he said. "I don't know what can have come over him. I've had him three years, and he never bit me before."

I fancy – I cannot say it for certain – but I fancy that there was a spasmodic twitching of the cicatrix upon our visitor's face, which betokened an inclination to laugh.

Looking back, I think that it was from that moment that I began to have a strange indefinable fear and dislike of the man.

Week followed week, and the day fixed for my marriage began to draw near.

Octavius Gaster was still a guest at Toynby Hall, and, indeed, had so ingratiated himself with the proprietor that any hint at departure was laughed to scorn by that worthy soldier.

"Here you've come, sir, and here you'll stay; you shall, by Jove!"

Whereat Octavius would smile and shrug his shoulders and mutter something about the attractions of Devon, which would put the Colonel in a good humour for the whole day afterwards.

My darling and I were too much engrossed with each other to pay very much attention to the traveller's occupations. We used to come upon him sometimes in our rambles through the woods, sitting reading in the most lonely situations.

He always placed the book in his pocket when he saw us approaching. I remember on one occasion, however, that we stumbled upon him so suddenly that the volume was still lying open before him.

"Ah, Gaster," said Charley, "studying, as usual! What an old bookworm you are! What's the book? Ah, a foreign language; Swedish, I suppose?"

"No, it is not Swedish," said Gaster; "it is Arabic."

"You don't mean to say you know Arabic?"

"Oh, very well – very well indeed!"

"And what's it about?" I asked, turning over the leaves of the musty old volume.

"Nothing that would interest one so young and fair as yourself, Miss Underwood," he answered, looking at me in a way which had become habitual to him of late. "It treats of the days when mind was stronger than what you call matter; when great spirits lived that were able to exist without these coarse bodies of ours, and could mould all things to their so-powerful wills."

"Oh, I see; a kind of ghost story," said Charley. "Well, adieu; we won't keep you from your studies."

We left him sitting in the little glen still absorbed in his mystical treatise. It must have been imagination which induced me, on turning suddenly round half an hour later, to think that I saw his familiar figure glide rapidly behind a tree.

I mentioned it to Charley at the time, but he laughed my idea to scorn.

I alluded just now to a peculiar manner which this man Gaster had of looking at me. His eyes seemed to lose their usual steely expression when he did so, and soften into something which might be almost called caressing. They seemed to influence me strangely, for I could always tell, without looking at him, when his gaze was fixed upon me.

Sometimes I fancied that this idea was simply due to a disordered nervous sytem or morbid imagination; but my mother dispelled that delusion from my mind.

"Do you know," she said, coming into my bedroom one night, and carefully shutting the door behind her, "if the idea was not so utterly preposterous, Lottie, I should say that that Doctor was madly in love with you?"

"Nonsense, 'ma!" said I, nearly dropping my candle in my consternation at the thought.

"I really think so, Lottie," continued my mother. "He's got a way of looking which is very like that of your poor dear father, Nicholas, before we were married. Something of this sort, you know."

And the old lady cast an utterly heart-broken glance at the bed-post.

"Now, go to bed," said I, "and don't have such funny ideas. Why, poor Doctor Gaster knows that I am engaged as well as you do."

"Time will show," said the old lady, as she left the room; and I went to bed with the words still ringing in my ears.

Certainly, it is a strange thing that on that very night a thrill which I had come to know well ran through me, and awakened me from my slumbers.

I stole softly to the window, and peered out through the bars of the Venetian blinds, and there was the gaunt, vampire-like figure of our Swedish visitor standing upon the gravel-walk, and apparently gazing up at my window.

It may have been that he detected the movement of the blind, for, lighting a cigarette, he began pacing up and down the avenue.

I noticed that at breakfast next morning he went out of his way to explain the fact that he had been restless during the night, and had steadied his nerves by a short stroll and a smoke.

After all, when I came to consider it calmly, the aversion which I had against the man and my distrust of him were founded on very scanty grounds. A man might have a strange face, and be fond of curious literature, and even look approvingly at an engaged young lady, without being a very dangerous member of society.

I say this to show that even up to that point I was perfectly unbiased and free from prejudice in my opinion of Octavius Gaster.

"I say!" remarked Lieutenant Daseby, one morning; "what do you think of having a picnic to-day?"

"Capital!" ejaculated everybody.

"You see, they are talking of commissioning the old *Shark* soon, and Trevor here will have to go back to the mill. We may as well compress as much fun as we can into the time."

"What is it that you call nicpic?" asked Doctor Gaster.

"It's another of our English institutions for you to study," said Charley. "It's our version of a *fête champêtre*."

"Ah, I see! That will be very jolly!" acquiesced the Swede.

"There are half a dozen places we might go to," continued the Lieutenant. "There's the Lover's Leap, or Black Tor, or Beer Ferris Abbey."

"That's the best," said Charley. "Nothing like ruins for a picnic."

"Well the Abbey be it. How far is it?"

"Six miles," said Trevor.

"Seven by the road," remarked the Colonel, with military exactness. "Mrs. Underwood and I shall stay at home, and the rest of you can fit into the waggonette. You'll all have to chaperon each other."

I need hardly say that this motion was carried also without a division.

"Well," said Charley, "I'll order the trap to be round in half an hour, so you'd better all make the best of your time. We'll want salmon, and salad, and hard-boiled eggs, and liquor, and any number of things. I'll look after the liquor department. What will you do, Lottie?"

"I'll take charge of the china," I said.

"I'll bring the fish," said Daseby.

"And I the vegetables," added Fan.

"What will you do, Gaster?" asked Charley.

"Truly," said the Swede, in his strange, musical accents, "but little is left for me to do. I can, however, wait upon the ladies, and I can make what you call a salad."

"You'll be more popular in the latter capacity than in the former," said I, laughingly.

"Ah, you say so," he said, turning sharp round upon me, and flushing up to his flaxen hair. "Yes. Ha! ha! Very good!"

And with a discordant laugh, he strode out of the room.

"I say, Lottie," remonstrated my lover, "you've hurt the fellow's feelings."

"I'm sure I didn't mean to," I answered. "If you like I'll go after him and tell him so."

"Oh, leave him alone," said Daseby. "A man with a mug like that has no right to be so touchy. He'll come round right enough."

It was true that I had not had the slightest intention of offending Gaster, still I felt pained at having annoyed him.

After I had stowed away the knives and plates into the hamper, I found that the others were still busy at their various departments. The moment seemed a favourable one for apologising for my thoughtless remark, so without saying anything to anyone, I slipped away and ran down the corridor in the direction of our visitor's room.

I suppose I must have tripped along very lightly, or it may have been the rich thick matting of Toynby Hall – certain it is that Mr. Gaster seemed unconscious of my approach.

His door was open, and as I came up to it and caught sight of him inside, there was something so strange in his appearance that I paused, literally petrified for the moment with astonishment.

He had in his hand a small slip from a newspaper which he was reading, and which seemed to afford him considerable amusement. There was something horrible too in this mirth of his, for though he writhed his body about as if with laughter, no sound was emitted from his lips.

His face, which was half-turned towards me, wore an expression upon it which I had never seen on it before; I can only describe it as one of savage exultation.

Just as I was recovering myself sufficiently to step forward and knock at the door, he suddenly, with a last convulsive spasm of merriment, dashed down the piece of paper upon the table and hurried out by the other door of his room, which led through the billiard-room to the hall.

I heard his steps dying away in the distance, and peeped once more into his room.

What could be the joke that had moved this stern man to mirth? Surely some masterpiece of humour.

Was there ever a woman whose principles were strong enough to overcome her curiosity?

Looking cautiously round to make sure that the passage was empty, I slipped into the room and examined the paper which he had been reading.

It was a cutting from an English journal, and had evidently been long carried about and frequently perused, for it was almost illegible in places. There was, however, as far as I could see, very little to provoke laughter in its contents. It ran, as well as I can remember, in this way:-

"Sudden Death in the Docks. – The master of the bark-rigged steamer Olga, from Tromsberg, was found lying dead in his cabin on Wednesday afternoon. Deceased was, it seems, of a violent disposition, and had had frequent altercations with the surgeon of the vessel. On this particular day he had been more than usually offensive, declaring that the surgeon was a necromancer and worshipper of the devil. The latter retired on deck to avoid further persecution. Shortly afterwards the steward had occasion to enter the cabin, and found the captain lying across the table quite dead. Death is attributed to heart disease, accelerated by excessive passion. An inquest will be held to-day."

And this was the paragraph which this strange man had regarded as the height of humour!

I hurried downstairs, astonishment, not un-mixed with repugnance, predominating in my mind. So just was I, however, that the dark inference which has so often occurred to me since never for one moment crossed my mind. I looked upon him as a curious and rather repulsive enigma – nothing more.

When I met him at the picnic, all remembrance of my unfortunate speech seemed to have vanished from his mind. He made

himself as agreeable as usual, and his salad was pronounced a
chef-d'œuvre, while his quaint little Swedish songs and his tales of
all climes and countries alternately thrilled and amused us. It was
after luncheon, however, that the conversation turned upon a
subject which seemed to have special charms for his daring mind.

I forget who it was that broached the question of the supernatural. I think it was Trevor, by some story of a hoax which
he had perpetrated at Cambridge. The story seemed to have a
strange effect upon Octavius Gaster, who tossed his long arms
about in impassioned invective as he ridiculed those who dared to
doubt about the existence of the unseen.

"Tell me," he said, standing up in his excitement, "which
among you has ever known what you call an instinct to fail. The
wild bird has an instinct which tells it of the solitary rock upon
the so boundless sea on which it may lay its egg, and is it disappointed? The swallow turns to the south when the winter is
coming, and has its instinct ever led it astray? And shall this
instinct which tells us of the unknown spirits around us, and
which pervades every untaught child and every race so savage, be
wrong? I say, never!"

"Go it, Gaster!" cried Charley.

"Take your wind and have another spell," said the sailor.

"No, never," repeated the Swede, disregarding our amusement. "We can see that matter exists apart from mind; then why
should not mind exist apart from matter?"

"Give it up," said Daseby.

"Have we not proofs of it?" continued Gaster, his gray eyes
gleaming with excitement. "Who that has read Steinberg's book
upon spirits, or that by the eminent American, Madame Crowe,
can doubt it? Did not Gustav von Spee meet his brother Leopold
in the streets of Strasbourg, the same brother having been
drowned three months before in the Pacific? Did not Home, the
spiritualist, in open daylight, float above the housetops of Paris?
Who has not heard the voices of the dead around him? I myself—"

"Well, what of yourself?" asked half a dozen of us, in a breath.

"Bah! it matters nothing," he said, passing his hand over his
forehead, and evidently controlling himself with difficulty.
"Truly, our talk is too sad for such an occasion." And, in spite of
all our efforts, we were unable to extract from Gaster any relation
of his own experiences of the supernatural.

It was a merry day. Our approaching dissolution seemed to
cause each one to contribute his utmost to the general amusement. It was settled that after the coming rifle match Jack was to
return to his ship and Trevor to his university. As to Charley and

myself, we were to settle down into a staid respectable couple.

The match was one of our principal topics of conversation. Shooting had always been a hobby of Charley's, and he was the captain of the Roborough company of Devon volunteers, which boasted some of the crack shots of the county. The match was to be against a picked team of regulars from Plymouth, and as they were no despicable opponents, the issue was considered doubtful. Charley had evidently set his heart on winning, and descanted long and loudly on the chances.

"The range is only a mile from Toynby Hall," he said, "and we'll all drive over, and you shall see the fun. You'll bring me luck, Lottie," he whispered, "I know you will."

Oh, my poor lost darling, to think of the luck that I brought you!

There was one dark cloud to mar the brightness of that happy day.

I could not hide from myself any longer the fact that my mother's suspicions were correct, and that Octavius Gaster loved me.

Throughout the whole of the excursion his attentions had been most assiduous, and his eyes hardly ever wandered away from me. There was a manner, too, in all that he said which spoke louder than words.

I was on thorns lest Charley should perceive it, for I knew his fiery temper; but the thought of such treachery never entered the honest heart of my lover.

He did once look up with mild surprise when the Swede insisted on relieving me of a fern which I was carrying; but the expression faded away into a smile at what he regarded as Gaster's effusive good-nature. My own feeling in the matter was pity for the unfortunate foreigner, and sorrow that I should have been the means of rendering him unhappy.

I thought of the torture it must be for a wild, fierce spirit like his to have a passion gnawing at his heart which honour and pride would alike prevent him from ever expressing in words. Alas! I had not counted upon the utter recklessness and want of principle of the man; but it was not long before I was undeceived.

There was a little arbour at the bottom of the garden, overgrown with honeysuckle and ivy, which had long been a favourite haunt of Charley and myself. It was doubly dear to us from the fact that it was here, on the occasion of my former visit, that words of love had first passed between us.

After dinner on the day following the picnic I sauntered down to this little summer-house, as was my custom. Here I used to wait until Charley, having finished his cigar with the other gentlemen, would come down and join me.

On that particular evening he seemed to be longer away than usual. I waited impatiently for his coming, going to the door every now and then to see if there were any signs if his approach.

I had just sat down again after one of those fruitless excursions, when I heard the tread of a male foot upon the gravel, and a figure emerged from among the bushes.

I sprang up with a glad smile, which changed to an expression of bewilderment, and even fear, when I saw the gaunt, pallid face of Octavius Gaster peering in at me.

There was certainly something about his actions which would have inspired distrust in the mind of anyone in my position. Instead of greeting me, he looked up and down the garden, as if to make sure that we were entirely alone. He then stealthily entered the arbour, and seated himself upon a chair, in such a position that he was between me and the doorway.

"Do not be afraid," he said, as he noticed my scared expression. "There is nothing to fear. I do but come that I may have talk with you.".

"Have you seen Mr. Pillar?" I asked, trying hard to seem at my ease.

"Ha! Have I seen your Charley?" he answered, with a sneer upon the last words. "Are you then so anxious that he come? Can no one speak to thee but Charley, little one?"

"Mr. Gaster," I said, "you are forgetting yourself."

"It is Charley, Charley, ever Charley!" continued the Swede, disregarding my interruption. "Yes, I have seen Charley. I have told him that you wait upon the bank of the river, and he has gone thither upon the wings of love."

"Why have you told him this lie?" I asked, still trying not to lose my self-control.

"That I might see you; that I might speak to you. Do you, then, love him so? Cannot the thought of glory, and riches, and power, above all that the mind can conceive, win you from this first maiden fancy of yours? Fly with me, Charlotte, and all this, and more, shall be yours! Come!"

And he stretched his long arms out in passionate entreaty.

Even at that moment the thought flashed through my mind of how like they were to the tentacles of some poisonous insect.

"You insult me, sir!" I cried, rising to my feet. "You shall pay heavily for this treatment of an unprotected girl!"

"Ah, you say it," he cried, "but you mean it not. In your heart so tender there is pity left for the most miserable of men. Nay, you shall not pass me – you shall hear me first!"

"Let me go, sir!"

Nay; you shall not go until you tell me if nothing that I can do may win your love."

"How dare you speak so?" I almost screamed, losing all my fear in my indignation. "You, who are the guest of my future husband! Let me tell you, once and for all, that I had no feeling towards you before save one of repugnance and contempt, which you have now converted into positive hatred!"

"And is it so?" he gasped, tottering backwards towards the doorway, and putting his hand up to his throat as if he found a difficulty in uttering the words. "And has my love won hatred in return? Ha!" he continued, advancing his face within a foot of mine as I cowered away from his glassy eyes. "I know it now. It is this – it is this!" and he struck the horrible cicatrix on his face with his clenched hand. "Maids love not such faces as this! I am not smooth, and brown, and curly like this Charley – this brainless school-boy; this human brute who cares but for his sport and his –"

"Let me pass!" I cried, rushing at the door.

"No; you shall not go – you shall not!" he hissed, pushing me backwards.

I struggled furiously to escape from his grasp. His long arms seemed to clasp me like bars of steel. I felt my strength going, and was making one last despairing effort to shake myself loose, when some irresistible power from behind tore my persecutor away from me and hurled him backwards on to the gravel walk.

Looking up, I saw Charley's towering figure and square shoulders in the doorway.

"My poor darling!" he said, catching me in his arms. "Sit here – here in the angle. There is no danger now. I shall be with you in a minute."

"Don't Charley, don't!" I murmured, as he turned to leave me.

But he was deaf to my entreaties, and strode out of the arbour.

I could not see either him or his opponent from the position in which he had placed me, but I heard every word that was spoken.

"You villain!" said a voice that I could hardly recognise as my lover's. "So this is why you put me on a wrong scent?"

"That is why," answered the foreigner, in a tone of easy indifference.

"And this is how you repay our hospitality, you infernal scoundrel!"

"Yes; we amuse ourselves in your so beautiful summer-house."

"We! You are still on my ground and my guest, and I would

wish to keep my hands from you; but, by heavens —"

Charley was speaking very low and in gasps now.

"Why do you swear? What is it, then?" asked the languid voice of Octavius Gaster.

"If you dare to couple Miss Underwood's name with this business, and insinuate that —"

"Insinuate? I insinuate nothing. What I say I say plain for all the world to hear. I say that this so chaste maiden did herself ask —"

I heard the sound of a heavy blow, and a great rattling of the gravel.

I was too weak to rise from where I lay, and could only clasp my hands together and utter a faint scream.

"You cur!" said Charley. "Say as much again, and I'll stop your mouth for all eternity!"

There was a silence, and then I heard Gaster speaking in a husky, strange voice.

"You have struck me!" he said; "you have drawn my blood!"

"Yes; I'll strike you again if you show your cursed face within these grounds. Don't look at me so! You don't suppose your hankey-pankey tricks can frighten me?"

An indefinable dread came over me as my lover spoke. I staggered to my feet and looked out at them, leaning against the door-way for support.

Charley was standing erect and defiant, with his young head in the air, like one who glories in the cause for which he battles.

Octavius Gaster was opposite him, surveying him with pinched lips and a baleful look in his cruel eyes. The blood was running freely from a deep gash on his lip, and spotting the front of his green necktie and white waistcoat. He perceived me the instant I emerged from the arbour.

"Ha, ha!" he cried, with a demoniacal burst of laughter. "She comes! The bride! She comes! Room for the bride! Oh, happy pair, happy pair!"

And with another fiendish burst of merriment he turned and disappeared over the crumbling wall of the garden with such rapidity that he was gone before we had realised what it was that he was about to do.

"Oh, Charley," I said, as my lover came back to my side, "you've hurt him!"

"Hurt him! I should hope I have! Come, darling, you are frightened and tired. He did not injure you, did he?"

"No; but I feel rather faint and sick."

"Come, we'll walk slowly to the house together. The rascal! It

was cunningly and deliberately planned, too. He told me he had
seen you down by the river, and I was going down when I met
young Stokes, the keeper's son, coming back from fishing, and he
told me that there was nobody there. Somehow, when Stokes said
that, a thousand little things flashed into my mind at once, and I
became in a moment so convinced of Gaster's villainy that I ran as
hard as I could to the arbour."

"Charley," I said, clinging to my lover's arm, "I fear he will
injure you in some way. Did you see the look in his eyes before he
leaped the wall?"

"Pshaw!" said Charley. "All these foreigners have a way of
scowling and glaring when they are angry, but it never comes to
much."

"Still, I am afraid of him," said I, mournfully, as we went up the
steps together, "and I wish you had not struck him."

"So do I," Charley answered; "for he was our guest, you know,
in spite of his rascality. However, it's done now and it can't be
helped, as the cook says in 'Pickwick,' and really it was more than
flesh and blood could stand."

I must run rapidly over the events of the next few days. For me,
at least, it was a period of absolute happiness. With Gaster's
departure a cloud seemed to be lifted off my soul, and a depression which had weighed upon the whole household completely disappeared.

Once more I was the light-hearted girl that I had been before
the foreigner's arrival. Even the Colonel forgot to mourn over his
absence, owing to the all-absorbing interest in the coming competition in which his son was engaged.

It was our main subject of conversation and bets were freely
offered by the gentlemen on the success of the Roborough team,
though no one was unprincipled enough to seem to support their
antagonists by taking them.

Jack Daseby ran down to Plymouth, and "made a book on the
event" with some officers of the Marines, which he did in such an
extraordinary way that we reckoned that in case of Roborough
winning, he would lose seventeen shillings; while, should the
other contingency occur, he would be involved in hopeless
liabilities.

Charley and I had tacitly agreed not to mention the name of
Gaster, nor to allude in any way to what had passed.

On the morning after our scene in the garden, Charley had
sent a servant up to the Swede's room with instructions to pack up
any things he might find there, and leave them at the nearest inn.

It was found, however, that all Gaster's effects had been already removed, though how and when was a perfect mystery to the servants.

I know of few more attractive spots than the shooting-range at Roborough. The glen in which it is situated is about half a mile long and perfectly level, so that the targets were able to range from two to seven hundred yards, the further ones simply showing as square white dots against the green of the rising hills behind.

The glen itself is part of the great moor and its sides, sloping gradually up, lose themselves in the vast rugged expanse. Its symmetrical character suggested to the imaginative mind that some giant of old had made an excavation in the moor with a titanic cheese-scoop, but that a single trial had convinced him of the utter worthlessness of the soil.

He might even be imagined to have dropped the despised sample at the mouth of the cutting which he had made, for there was a considerable elevation there, from which the riflemen were to fire, and thither we bent our steps on that eventful afternoon.

Our opponents had arrived there before us, bringing with them a considerable number of naval and military officers, while a long line of nondescript vehicles showed that many of the good citizens of Plymouth had seized the opportunity of giving their wives and families an outing on the moor.

An enclosure for ladies and distinguished guests had been erected on the top of the hill, which, with the marquee and refreshment tents, made the scene a lively one.

The country people had turned out in force, and were excitedly staking their half-crowns upon their local champions, which were as enthusiastically taken up by the admirers of the regulars.

Through all this scene of bustle and confusion we were safely conveyed by Charley, aided by Jack and Trevor, who finally deposited us in a sort of rudimentary grandstand, from which we could look round at our ease on all that was going on.

We were soon, however, so absorbed in the glorious view, that we became utterly unconscious of the betting and pushing and chaff of the crowd in front of us.

Away to the south we could see the blue smoke of Plymouth curling up into the calm summer air, while beyond that was the great sea, stretching away to the horizon, dark and vast, save where some petulant wave dashed it with a streak of foam, as if rebelling against the great peacefulness of nature.

From the Eddystone to the Start the long rugged line of the Devonshire coast lay like a map before us.

I was still lost in admiration when Charley's voice broke half-reproachfully on my ear.

"Why, Lottie," he said, "you don't seem to take a bit of interest in it!"

"Oh, yes I do, dear," I answered. "But the scenery is so pretty, and the sea is always a weakness of mine. Come and sit here, and tell me all about the match and how we are to know whether you are winning or losing."

"I've just been explaining it," answered Charley. "But I'll go over it again."

"Do, like a darling," said I; and settled myself down to mark, learn, and inwardly digest.

"Well," said Charley, "there are ten men on each side. We shoot alternately; first, one of our fellows, then one of them, and so on — you understand?"

"Yes, I understand that."

"First we fire at the two hundred yards range — those are the targets nearest of all. We fire five shots each at those. Then we fire five shots at the ones at five hundred yards — those middle ones; and then we finish up by firing at the seven hundred yards range — you see the target far over there on the side of the hill. Whoever makes the most points wins. Do you grasp it now?"

"Oh, yes; that's very simple," I said.

"Do you know what a bull's eye is?" asked my lover.

"Some sort of sweetmeat, isn't it?" I hazarded.

Charley seemed amazed at the extent of my ignorance. "That's the bull's-eye," he said; "that dark spot in the centre of the target. If you hit that, it counts five. There is another ring, which you can't see, drawn round that, and if you get inside of it, it is called a 'centre,' and counts four. Outside that, again, is called an 'outer,' and only gives you three. You can tell where the shot has hit, for the marker puts out a coloured disc, and covers the place."

"Oh, I understand it all now," said I, enthusiastically. "I'll tell you what I'll do Charley; I'll mark the score on a bit of paper every shot that is fired, and then I'll always know how Roborough is getting on!"

"You can't do better," he laughed as he strode off to get his men together, for a warning bell signified that the contest was about to begin.

There was a great waving of flags and shouting before the ground could be got clear, and then I saw a little cluster of red-coats lying upon the greensward, while a similar group, in grey, took up their position to the left of them.

"Pang!" went a rifle-shot, and the blue smoke came curling up from the grass.

Fanny shrieked, while I gave a cry of delight, for I saw the white disc go up, which proclaimed a "bull," and the shot had been fired by one of the Roborough men. My elation was, however, promptly checked by the answering shot which put down five to the credit of the regulars. The next was also a "bull," which was speedily cancelled by another. At the end of the competition at the short range each side had scored forty-nine out of a possible fifty, and the question of supremacy was as undecided as ever.

"It's getting exciting," said Charley, lounging over the stand. "We begin shooting at the five hundred yards in a few minutes."

"Oh, Charley," cried Fanny in high excitement, "don't you go and miss, whatever you do!"

"I won't if I can help it," responded Charley, cheerfully.

"You made a 'bull' every time just now," I said.

"Yes, but it's not so easy when you've got your sights up. However, we'll do our best, and we can't do more. They've got some terribly good long-range men among them. Come over here, Lottie, for a moment."

"What is it, Charley?" I asked, as he led me away from the others. I could see by the look in his face that something was troubling him.

"It's that fellow," growled my lover. "What the deuce does he want to come here for? I hoped we had seen the last of him!"

"What fellow?" I gasped, with a vague apprehension at my heart.

"Why, that infernal Swedish fellow, Gaster!"

I followed the direction of Charley's glance, and there, sure enough, standing on a little knoll close to the place where the riflemen were lying, was the tall, angular figure of the foreigner.

He seemed utterly unconscious of the sensation which his singular appearance and hideous countenance excited among the burly farmers around him; but was craning his long neck about, this way and that, as if in search of somebody.

As we watched him, his eye suddenly rested upon us, and it seemed to me that, even at that distance, I could see a spasm of hatred and triumph pass over his livid features.

A strange foreboding came over me, and I seized my lover's hand in both my own.

"Oh, Charley," I cried, "don't – don't go back to the shooting! Say you are ill – make some excuse, and come away!"

"Nonsense, lass!" said he, laughing heartily at my terror. "Why, what in the world are you afraid of?"

"Of him!" I answered.

"Don't be so silly, dear. One would think he was a demi-god to hear the way in which you talk of him. But there! that's the bell, and I must be off."

"Well, promise, at least, that you will not go near him?" I cried, following Charley.

"All right – all right!" said he.

And I had to be content with that small concession.

The contest at the five hundred yards range was a close and exciting one. Roborough led by a couple of points for some time, until a series of "bulls" by one of the crack marksmen of their opponents turned the tables upon them.

At the end of it was found that the volunteers were three points to the bad – a result which was hailed by cheers from the Plymouth contingent and by long faces and black looks among the dwellers on the moor.

During the whole of this competition Octavius Gaster had remained perfectly still and motionless upon the top of the knoll on which he had originally taken up his position.

It seemed to me that he knew little of what was going on, for his face was turned away from the marksmen, and he appeared to be gazing into the distance.

Once I caught sight of his profile, and thought that his lips were moving rapidly as if in prayer, or it may have been the shimmer of the hot air of the almost Indian summer which deceived me. It was, however, my impression at the time.

And now came the competition at the longest range of all, which was to decide the match.

The Roborough men settled down steadily to their task of making up the lost ground; while the regulars seemed determined not to throw away a chance by over-confidence.

As shot after shot was fired, the excitement of the spectators became so great that they crowded round the marksmen, cheering enthusiastically at every "bull."

We ourselves were so far affected by the general contagion that we left our harbour of refuge, and submitted meekly to the pushing and rough ways of the mob, in order to obtain a nearer view of the champions and their doings.

The military stood at seventeen when the volunteers were at sixteen, and great was the despondency of the rustics.

Things looked brighter, however, when the two sides tied at twenty-four, and brighter still when the steady shooting of the local team raised their score to thirty-two against thirty of their opponents.

There were still, however, the three points which had been lost at the last range to be made up for.

Slowly the score rose, and desperate were the efforts of both parties to pull off the victory.

Finally, a thrill ran through the crowd when it was known that the last red-coat had fired, while one volunteer was still left, and that the soldiers were leading by four points.

Even *our* unsportsman-like minds were worked into a state of all-absorbing excitement by the nature of the crisis which now presented itself.

If the last representative of our little town could but hit the bull's-eye the match was won.

The silver cup, the glory, the money of our adherents, all depended upon that single shot.

The reader will imagine that my interest was by no means lessened when, by dint of craning my neck and standing on tiptoe, I caught sight of my Charley coolly shoving a cartridge into his rifle, and realised that it was upon his skill that the honour of Roborough depended.

It was this, I think, which lent me strength to push my way so vigorously through the crowd that I found myself almost in the first row and commanding an excellent view of the proceedings.

There were two gigantic farmers on each side of me, and while we were waiting for the decisive shot to be fired, I could not help listening to the conversation, which they carried on in broad Devon, over my head.

"Mun's a rare ugly 'un," said one.

"He is that," cordially assented the other.

"See to mun's een?"

"Eh, Jock; see to mun's moo', rayther! – Blessed if he bean't foamin' like Farmer Watson's dog – t' bull pup whot died mad o' the hydropathics."

I turned round to see the favoured object of these flattering comments, and my eyes fell upon Doctor Octavius Gaster, whose presence I had entirely forgotten in my excitement.

His face was turned towards me; but he evidently did not see me, for his eyes were bent with unswerving persistence upon a point midway apparently between the distant targets and himself.

I have never seen anything to compare with the extraordinary concentration of that stare, which had the effect of making his eyeballs appear gorged and prominent, while the pupils were contracted to the finest possible point.

Perspiration was running freely down his long, cadaverous face, and, as the farmer had remarked, there were some traces of foam at the corners of his mouth. The jaw was locked, as if with some fierce effort of the will which demanded all the energy of his soul.

To my dying day that hideous countenance shall never fade from my remembrance nor cease to haunt me in my dreams. I shuddered, and turned away my head in the vain hope that perhaps the honest farmer might be right, and mental disease be the cause of all the vagaries of this extraordinary man.

A great stillness fell upon the whole crowd as Charley, having loaded his rifle, snapped up the breech cheerily, and proceeded to lie down in his appointed place.

"That's right, Mr. Charles, sir — that's right!" I heard old McIntosh, the volunteer sergeant, whisper as I passed. "A cool head and a steady hand, that's what does the trick, sir!"

My lover smiled round at the gray-headed soldier as he lay down upon the grass, and then proceeded to look along the sight of his rifle amid a silence in which the faint rustling of the breeze among the blades of grass was distinctly audible.

For more than a minute he hung upon his aim. His finger seemed to press the trigger, and every eye was fixed upon the distant target, when suddenly, instead of firing, the rifleman staggered up to his knees, leaving his weapon upon the ground.

To the surprise of everyone, his face was deadly pale, and perspiration was standing on his brow.

"I say, McIntosh," he said, in a strange, gasping voice, "is there anybody standing between the target and me?"

"Between, sir? No, not a soul, sir," answered the astonished sergeant.

"There, man, there!" cried Charley, with fierce energy, seizing him by the arm, and pointing in the direction of the target, "Don't you see him there, standing right in the line of fire?"

"There's no one there!" shouted half a dozen voices.

"No one there? Well, it must have been my imagination," said Charley, passing his hand slowly over his forehead. "Yet I could have sworn — Here, give me the rifle!"

He lay down again, and having settled himself into position, raised his weapon slowly to his eye. He had hardly looked along the barrel before he sprang up again with a loud cry.

"There!" he cried; "I tell you I see it! A man dressed in volunteer uniform, and very like myself — the image of myself. Is this a conspiracy?" he continued, turning fiercely on the crowd. "Do you tell me none of you see a man resembling myself walking from that target, and not two hundred yards from me as I speak?"

I should have flown to Charley's side had I not known how he hated feminine interference, and anything approaching to a scene. I could only listen silently to his strange wild words.

"I protest against this!" said an officer coming forward. "This gentleman must really either take his shot, or we shall remove our men off the field and claim the victory."

"But I'll shoot *him*!" gasped poor Charley.

"Humbug!" "Rubbish!" "Shoot him, then!" growled half a score of masculine voices.

"The fact is," lisped one of the military men in front of me to another, "the young fellow's nerves ar'n't quite equal to the occasion, and he feels it, and is trying to back out."

The imbecile young lieutenant little knew at this point how a feminine hand was longing to stretch forth and deal him a sounding box on the ears.

"It's Martell's three-star brandy, that's what it is," whispered the other. "The 'devils,' don't you know. I've had 'em myself, and know a case when I see it."

This remark was too recondite for my understanding, or the speaker would have run the same risk as his predecessor.

"Well, are you going to shoot or not?" cried several voices.

"Yes, I'll shoot," groaned Charley – "I'll shoot *him* through! It's murder – sheer *murder*!"

I shall never forget the haggard look which he cast round at the crowd. "I'm aiming *through* him, McIntosh," he murmured, as he lay down on the grass and raised the gun for the third time to his shoulder.

There was one moment of suspense, a spurt of flame, the crack of a rifle, and a cheer which echoed across the moor, and might have been heard in the distant village.

"Well done, lad – well done!" shouted a hundred honest Devonshire voices, as the little white disc came out from behind the marker's shield and obliterated the dark "bull" for the moment, proclaiming that the match was won.

"Well done, lad! It's Maister Pillar, of Toynby Hall. Here, let's gie mun a lift, carry mun home, for the honour o' Roborough. Come on, lads! There mun is on the grass. Wake up, Sergeant McIntosh. What be the matter with thee? Eh? What?"

A deadly stillness came over the crowd, and then a low incredulous murmur, changing to one of pity, with whispers of "leave her alone, poor lass – leave her to hersel'!" – and then there was silence again, save for the moaning of a woman, and her short, quick cries of despair.

For, reader, my Charley, my beautiful, brave Charley, was lying cold and dead upon the ground, with the rifle still clenched in his stiffening fingers.

I heard kind words of sympathy. I heard Lieutenant Daseby's voice, broken with grief, begging me to control my sorrow, and felt his hand, as he gently raised me from my poor boy's body. This I can remember, and nothing more, until my recovery from my illness, when I found myself in the sick-room at Toynby Hall, and learned that three restless, delirious weeks had passed since that terrible day.

Stay! – do I remember nothing else?

Sometimes I think I do. Sometimes I think I can recall a lucid interval in the midst of my wanderings. I seem to have a dim recollection of seeing my good nurse go out of the room – of seeing a gaunt, bloodless face peering in through the half-open window, and of hearing a voice which said, "I have dealt with thy so beautiful lover, and I have yet to deal with thee." The words come back to me with a familiar ring, as if they had sounded in my ears before, and yet it may have been but a dream.

"And this is all!" you say. "It is for this that a hysterical woman hunts down a harmless *savant* in the advertisement columns of the newspapers! On this shallow evidence she hints at crimes of the most monstrous description!"

Well, I cannot expect that these things should strike you as they struck me. I can but say that if I were upon a bridge with Octavius Gaster standing at one end, and the most merciless tiger that ever prowled in an Indian jungle at the other, I should fly to the wild beast for protection.

For me, my life is broken and blasted. I care not how soon it may end, but if my words shall keep this man out of one honest household, I have not written in vain.

Within a fortnight after writing this narrative, my poor daughter disappeared. All search has failed to find her. A porter at the railway station has deposed to having seen a young lady resembling her description get into a first-class carriage with a tall, thin gentleman. It is, however, too ridiculous to suppose that she can have eloped after her recent grief, and without my having had any suspicions. The detectives are, however, working out the clue. – EMILY UNDERWOOD

AN EXCITING CHRISTMAS EVE;

OR, MY LECTURE ON DYNAMITE

---◆---

I

It has often seemed to me to be a very strange and curious thing that danger and trouble should follow those who are most anxious to lead a quiet and uneventful life. I myself have been such a one, and I find on looking back that it was in those very periods of my existence which might have been most confidently reckoned on as peaceful that some unexpected adventure has befallen me, like the thunder-bolt from an unclouded sky which shook the nerves of old Horace. Possibly my experience differs from that of other men, and I may have been especially unfortunate. If so, there is the more reason why I should mourn over my exceptional lot, and record it for the benefit of those more happily circumstanced.

Just compare my life with that of Leopold Walderich, and you will see what I complain of. We both come from Mulhausen, in Baden, and that is why I single him out as an example, though many others would do as well. He was a man who professed to be fond of adventure. Now listen to what occurred. We went to Heidelberg University together. I was quiet, studious, and unassuming; he was impetuous, reckless, and idle. For three years he revelled in every sort of riot, while I frequented the laboratories, and rarely deserted my books save for a hurried walk into the country when a pain in my head and ringing in my ears warned me that I was trifling with my constitution.

Yet during that period his life was comparatively uneventful, while my whole existence was a series of hairbreadth perils and escapes. I damaged my eyesight and nearly choked myself by the evolution of a poisonous gas. I swallowed a trichina in my ham, and was prostrated for weeks. I was hurled out of a second-floor window by an English lunatic because I ventured to quote the solemn and serious passage in Schoppheim's "Weltgeschichte" which proves Waterloo to have been a purely Prussian victory, and throws grave doubts on the presence of any British force nearer than Brussels! Twice I was nearly drowned, and once I should have been precipitated from the parapet of the schloss but for the assistance of this same Englishman. These are a few of the incidents which occurred to me while endeavouring to read in seclusion for my degree.

Even in smaller matters this luck of mine held good. I can well remember, for example, that on one occasion the wilder spirits of the Badischer Corps ventured upon an unusually hare-brained escapade. There was a farmer about a couple of miles from the town whose name was Nicholas Bodeck. This man had made himself obnoxious to the students, and they determined to play a prank upon him in return. An enormous number of little caps were accordingly made with the colours of the corps upon them, and the conspirators invaded his premises in the middle of the night and gummed them upon the heads of all the fowls.

They certainly had a very comical effect, as I had an opportunity of judging, for I happened to pass that way in the morning. I suppose that Walderich and his friends carried out their little joke for excitement, knowing the farmer to be a resolute man. *They* got no excitement from it, however; it was I who got that. Activity was never my strong point, but certainly I ran those two miles that morning with incredible speed – and so did the five men with pitch-forks who ran behind me!

These things may seem trivial, but, as you say in England, a straw shows which way the wind blows, and these were only indications of what was to come.

I took my degree in medicine, and found myself Herr Doctor Otto von Spee. I then graduated in science, receiving much applause for my thesis, "On the Explosive Compounds of the Tri-methyl Series." I was quoted as an authority in works of science, and my professors prophesied that a great career lay before me. My studies, however, were suddenly put an end to by the outbreak of the great war with France.

Walderich volunteered into one of the crack regiments, fought in nearly every engagement, covered himself with glory, and came back unhurt to be decorated with the cross for valour. I was stationed in an ambulance which never even crossed the frontier, yet I succeeded in breaking my arm by tumbling over a stretcher, and in contracting erysipelas from one of the few wounds which came under my care. I got no medal or cross, and went back quietly to Berlin after it was all over, and there I settled as *privat docent* of chemistry and physics.

You will naturally ask what all this has to do with my Christmas story. You shall see in time that it is necessary I should tell you this, in order that you may appreciate that crowning event in my long list of misfortunes. You must remember also that I am a German and therefore somewhat long-winded perhaps, as my nation has the reputation of being. I have often admired the dashing, rattling manner of English story-tellers, but I fear if I were to attempt to imitate this it would be as if one of our own ponderous old Mulhausen storks were to adopt the pretty graceful airs of your Christmas robins. You shall hear in time all that I have to say about my Christmas Eve.

II

After I had settled in Berlin I endeavoured to combine the private practice of medicine with my labours as a *privat docent*, which corresponds to what you call a "coach" in England. For some years I pursued this plan, but I found that my practice, being largely among the lower classes, favoured my unfortunate propensity for getting into trouble, and I determined to abandon it.

I took a secluded house, therefore, in a quiet quarter of the city, and there I gave myself up to scientific research, pursuing principally the same train of investigation which had originally attracted me – namely, the chemistry of explosive compounds.

My expenses were small, and all the money which I could spare was laid out on scientific instruments and mechanical contrivances of different sorts. Soon I had a snug little laboratory which, if not as pretentious as that at Heidelberg, was quite as well fitted to supply my wants. It is true that the neighbours grumbled, and that Gretchen, my housekeeper, had to be quieted with a five-mark piece, after having been blown up three several times, and blown down once while engaged in fixing an electric wire upon the summit of an outhouse. These little matters, however, were easily settled, and I found my life rapidly assuming a peaceful complexion, of which I had long despaired.

I was happy – and what is more I was becoming famous. My "Remarks on Cacodyl" in the "Monthly Archives of Science" created no small sensation, and Herr Raubenthal of Bonn characterised them as, "meisterlich," though dissenting from many of my deductions. I was enabled, however, in a later contribution to the same journal to recount certain experiments which were sufficient to convince that eminent *savant* that my view of the matter was the correct one.

After this victory I was universally recognised as an authority in my own special branch, and as one of the foremost living workers at explosives. The Government appointed me to the torpedo commission at Kiel, and many other honours were bestowed upon me. One of the consequences of this sudden accession of celebrity was that I found myself in great request as a lecturer, both at scientific gatherings and at those meetings for the education of the people which have become so common in the metropolis. By these means my name got into the daily papers as one learned in such matters, and to this it is that I ascribe the events which I am about to narrate.

It was a raw windy Christmas Eve. The sleet pattered against the window panes, and the blast howled among the skeleton branches of the gaunt poplar-trees in my garden. There were few people in the street, and those few had their coats buttoned up, and their chins upon their breasts, and hurried rapidly homewards, staggering along against the force of the storm. Even the big policeman outside had ceased to clank up and down, and was crouching in a doorway for protection.

Many a lonely man might have felt uncomfortable upon such a night, but I was too interested in my work to have time for any sympathy with the state of the weather. A submarine mine was engaging my attention, and in a leaden tank in front of me I had sunk a small pellet of my new explosive. The problem was how far its destructive capacities would be modified by the action of the water. The matter was too important to allow me to feel despondent. Besides, one of Gretchen's lovers was in the kitchen, and his gruff expressions of satisfaction, whether with her charms or my beer, or both, were sufficiently audible to banish any suspicion of loneliness.

I was raising my battery on to the table, and was connecting the wires carefully so as to explode the charge, when I heard a short, quick step outside the window, and immediately afterwards a loud knock at the outer door.

Now I very seldom had a call from any of my limited number of acquaintances, and certainly never upon such a night as this. I was astonished for a moment; then concluding that it was a visitor of Gretchen's, I continued to work at my apparatus.

To my very great surprise, after Gretchen had opened the door there was some muttering in the hall, and then a quiet tap at the entrance of my sanctum, followed by the appearance of a tall lady whom I could vow that I had never seen in my life before.

Her face was covered by a thick dark veil, and her dress was of the same sombre colour, so that I concluded her to be a widow.

She walked in with a decisive energetic step, and after glancing round, seated herself quietly upon the sofa between the voltaic pile and my stand of reagents – all this without saying a word, or apparently taking the slightest notice of my presence.

"Good evening, madam," I remarked, when I had somehow recovered my composure.

"Would you do me a favour, doctor?" she replied, brusquely, in a harsh voice, which harmonised with her gaunt angular figure.

"Surely, madam," I answered, in my most elegant manner. I remember a girl at Heidelberg used to say that I had a very fascinating way sometimes. Of course it was only a joke, but still something must have put it into her head or she would never have said it. "What can I do for you?" I asked.

"You can send away that servant of yours, who is listening at the door."

At this moment, before I could move hand or foot, there were a succession of tremendous bumps, followed by a terrible crash and a prolonged scream. It was evident that my unhappy domestic had fallen downstairs in her attempt to avoid detection. I was about to rise, but the stranger arrested me.

"Never mind now," she said. "We can proceed to business."

I bowed my head to show that I was all attention.

"The fact is, doctor," she continued, "that I wish you to come back with me and give me your opinion upon a case."

"My dear madam," I answered, "I have long retired from the practice of my profession. If you go down the street, however, you will see the surgery of Doctor Benger, who is a most competent man, and who will be happy to accompany you."

"No, no," cried my companion, in great distress. "You or no one! You or no one! My poor dear husband cried out as I left him that Otto von Spee was the only man who could bring him back from the tomb. They will all be broken-hearted if I return without you. Besides, the professors at the hospital said that you were the only one in Europe who would be capable of dealing with it."

Now, devoted as I was to scientific research, I had always had a conviction in my mind that I had the makings in me of a first-class practical physician. It was inexpressibly consoling to hear that the heads of the profession had endorsed this opinion by referring a curious case to my judgment. The more I thought of it, however, the more extraordinary did it seem. "Are you sure?" I asked.

"Oh yes, quite sure."

"But I am a specialist – a student of explosives. I have had very little experience in practice. What is the matter with your husband?"

"He has a tumour."

"A tumour? I know nothing of tumours."

"Oh come, dear Doctor von Spee; come and look at it!" implored the female, producing a handkerchief from her pocket and beginning to sob convulsively.

It was too much. I had lived a secluded life, and had never before seen a female in distress.

"Madam," I said, "I shall be happy to accompany you."

I regretted that promise the moment it was uttered. There was a wild howl of wind in the chimney which reminded me of the inclemency of the night. However, my word was pledged, and there was no possibility of escape. I left the room with as cheerful an aspect as possible, while Gretchen wrapped a shawl round my neck and muffled me up to the best of her ability.

What could there be about this tumour, I wondered, which had induced the learned surgeons to refer it to my judgment — I who was rather an artillerist than a physician? Could it be that the growth was of such stony hardness that no knife could remove it, and that explosives were necessary for extraction? The idea was so comical that I could scarce refrain from laughing.

"Now, madam," I said re-entering the study, "I am at your disposal." As I spoke I knocked against the electric machine, causing a slight transmission of the current along the wires, so that the submarine mine exploded with a crash, blowing a little column of water into the air. Accustomed as I was to such accidents, I confess that I was considerably startled by the suddenness of the occurrence. My companion, however, sat perfectly impassive upon the sofa, and then rose without the slightest sign of surprise or emotion, and walked out of the room.

"She has the nerves of a grenadier," I mentally ejaculated, as I followed her into the street.

"Is it far?" I asked, as we started off through the storm.

"Not very far," she answered; "and I took the liberty of bringing a cab for you, for fear Herr Doctor might catch cold. Ah, here it comes."

As she spoke, a closed carriage dashed along the road, and pulled up beside us.

III

"Have you got Otto von Spee?" asked a sallow-faced man, letting down the window and protruding his head.

"Yes, here he is."

"Then shove him in."

For the moment I was inclined to regard the expression as a playful figure of speech, but my companion soon dispelled the delusion by seizing me by the collar and hurling me, with what seemed superhuman strength, into the vehicle. I fell upon the floor, and was dragged on to a seat by the man, while the other sprang in, slammed the door, and the horses dashed off at a furious gallop.

I lay back in a state of bewilderment, hardly able to realise what had occurred. It was pitch dark inside the carriage, but I could hear my two companions conversing in low whispers. Once I attempted to expostulate and demand an explanation of their conduct, but a threatening growl, and a rough hand placed over my mouth, warned me to be silent. I was neither a wealthy man nor particularly well connected, nor was I a politician. What, then, could be the object of these people in kidnapping me in such an elaborate fashion? The more I pondered over it, the more mysterious did it seem.

Once we halted for a moment, and a third man got into the carriage, who also inquired anxiously whether Otto von Spee had been secured, and expressed his satisfaction on being answered in the affirmative. After this stoppage we rattled along even more quickly than before, the vehicle rocking from side to side with the velocity, and the clatter of the horses' hoofs sounding above the howling of the gale. It seemed to me that we must have passed through every street in Berlin before, with a sudden jar, the coachman pulled up, and my captors intimated that I was to descend.

I had hardly time to look about me and realise the fact that I was in a narrow street in some low quarter of the city. A door opened in front of us, and the two men led me through it, while the herculean female followed us, effectually cutting off any hopes of escape.

We were in a long passage or corridor, feebly illuminated by a couple of flickering lamps, whose yellow glare seemed to intensify the darkness around them. After walking about twenty metres or more we came to a massive door, blocking our passage. One of my guardians struck it a blow with a stick which he carried in his hand, when it reverberated with a metallic clang, and swung open, closing with a snap behind us.

At this point I ventured to stop and expostulate with my companions once again. My only answer, however, was a shove from the individual behind me, which shot me through a half-opened door into a comfortable little chamber beyond. My captors followed in a more leisurely manner, and after turning the lock, they proceeded to seat themselves, motioning to me that I should do the same.

The room in which I found myself was small, but elegantly furnished. A fire was sparkling in the grate, and the bright colours of the handsome suite of furniture and variegated carpet helped to give it a cheering aspect. The pictures on the walls, however, went far towards neutralising this effect. They were very numerous, but every one of them treated of some un-pleasant or murderous passage of history. Many of them were so distant that I was unable to decipher the inscriptions. To a scholar like myself, however, the majority were able to tell their own story. There was the lunatic Schtaps in the garden, making his attempt upon the life of the First Napoleon. Above it was a sketch of Orsini with his cowardly bomb, waiting silently among the loungers at the opera. A statuette of Ravaillac was placed upon a pedestal in the corner, while a large oil-painting of the strangling of the unhappy Emperor Paul in his bedchamber occupied the whole of one wall of the apartment.

These things did not tend to raise my spirits, and the appear-ance of my three companions was still less calculated to do so. I had several times doubted the sex of the individual who had seduced me from my comfortable home, but the veil had now been removed and revealed a dark moustache and sunburnt countenance, with a pair of searching, sinister eyes, which seemed to look into my very soul. Of the others, one was gaunt and cadaverous, the other insignificant-looking, with a straggling beard and unhealthy complexion.

"We are very sorry, Doctor von Spee, to be reduced to this necessity," said the last-mentioned individual, "but unhappily we had no other method of securing the pleasure of your society."

I bowed – a little sulkily, I am afraid.

"I must apologise for any little liberties I have taken, above all for having deprived you of the satisfaction of beholding my husband's remarkable tumour," said my original acquaintance.

I thought of the manner in which he had bundled me about like an empty portmanteau, and my bow was even more sulky than before.

"I trust, gentlemen," I remarked, "that since your practical joke has been so admirably carried out, you will now permit me to return to the studies which you have interrupted."

"Not so fast, Herr Doctor – not so fast," said the tall man, rising to his feet. "We have a little duty which you shall perform before you leave us. It is nothing more nor less than to give a few inquirers into the truth a lesson upon your own special subject. Might I beg you to step in this direction?"

He walked over to a side door, painted of the same colour as the paper on the wall, and held it persuasively open. Resistance was useless, as the other confederates had also risen, and were standing on either side of me. I yielded to circumstances, and walked out as directed.

We passed down a second passage, rather shorter than the first, and much more brilliantly illuminated. At the end of it a heavy velvet curtain was hung, which covered a green baize folding-door. This was swung open, and I found myself, to my astonishment, in a large room in which a considerable number of people were assembled. They were arranged in long rows, and sat so as to face a raised platform at one end of the apartment, on which was a single chair, with a small round table, littered with a number of objects.

My companions ushered me in, and our entrance was greeted with considerable applause. It was clear that we had been awaited, for there was a general movement of expectation throughout the assembly. Glancing round, I could see that the majority of the company were dressed as artisans or labourers. There were some, however, who were respectably and even fashionably attired, and a few whose blue coats and gilt shoulder-bands proclaimed them to be officers in the army. Their nationalities seemed almost as varied as their occupations. I could distinguish the dolicho-cephalic head of the Teuton, the round, curl-covered cranium of the Celt, and the prognathous jaw and savage features of the Slav. I could almost have imagined myself looking into one of the cabinets of casts in my friend Landerstein's anthropological musuem.

However, I had not much time for wonder or reflection. One of my guardians led me across the room, and I found myself standing at the table, which I have already mentioned as being situated upon a raised dais. My appearance in this situation was the signal for a fresh outburst of applause, which, with clapping of hands and drumming of sticks upon the floor, lasted for some considerable time.

When it had subsided, the gaunt man who had come with me in the carriage walked up to the dais and addressed a few words to the audience. "Gentlemen," he said, "you will perceive that the committee have succeeded in keeping their promise and of bringing the celebrated – ("beruhmte" was the word he used) – Doctor Otto von Spee to address you." Here there was renewed applause.

"Doctor," he continued, turning to me, "I think a few words of public explanation will not be amiss in this matter. You are well known as an authority upon explosives. Now all these gentlemen and myself have an interest in this subject, and would gladly listen to your views upon it. We are particularly anxious that you should give us clear and precise directions as to the method of preparing dynamite, guncotton, and other such substances, as we sometimes have a little difficulty in obtaining such things for our experiments. You shall also tell us about the effect of temperature, water, and other agents upon these substances, the best method of storing them, and the way of using them to the greatest advantage. For our part, we shall listen attentively and treat you well, always provided that you make no attempt to summon aid or to escape. Should you be so ill-advised as to do either" – here he slapped his pocket – "you shall become as intimately acquainted with projectiles as you now are with explosives." I cannot say that this struck me as a good joke, but it seemed to meet considerable favour among the audience.

"I wish to add a few words to the remarks of our learned president," said a small man, rising up from among the first line of the company. "I have placed upon the table such materials as I could lay my hands upon in order that the learned doctor may be able to illustrate his discourse by any experiments which he may think appropriate. I may warn him, in conclusion, to speak somewhat slowly and distinctly, as some of his hearers are but imperfectly acquainted with the German language."

Here was my old luck again with a vengeance! At a time when Walderich and every gay dog in Berlin were snoring peacefully in their beds, I – I, Doctor Otto von Spee, the modest man of science, was lecturing to a murderous secret organisation – for my audience could be nothing else – and teaching them to forge the weapons with which they were to attack society and everything which should be treasured and revered. And on such a night as this too! Should I, then, put it in their power to convert a house into an arsenal, to destroy the stability of the Fatherland, and even perhaps attempt the life of my beloved kaiser? Never! I swore it – never!

Most small men who wear spectacles are obstinate. I am a small man with spectacles, and I was no exception to the rule. I clenched my teeth, and felt that *ruat cœlum*, never a word should pass my lips that might be of any help to them. I should not refuse to lecture, but I was determined to avoid those very points upon which they desired to be instructed.

I was not allowed much time for meditation. An ominous murmur among the audience, and a shuffling of feet upon the floor, betokened their impatience. I must say, however, that many of them seemed actuated with rather kindly feelings towards me, more particularly one stoutish individual of a well-marked Celtic type, who, not content with smiling all over his florid countenance, waved his arms occasionally in motions intended to indicate sympathy and inspire confidence.

I stepped up to the table, which was covered all over with such objects as were thought to have a bearing upon my subject. Some of them were rather curious – a lump of salt, an iron teapot, part of the broken axle of a wheel, and a large pair of kitchen bellows. Others were more appropriate. There was a piece of guncotton which could not have weighed less than a couple of pounds, coarse cotton, starch, various acids, a Bunsen burner, tubes of fulminate of mercury, some dynamite powder, and a large pitcher of water. There was also a carafe and tumbler for my own use, should I feel so disposed.

"Meine herren," I began, with perhaps a slight quaver in my voice, "we have met here tonight for the purpose of studying dynamite and other explosives." It flowed naturally from my lips, as it was the stereotyped formula with which my discourses at the Educationische Institut were usually commenced. My audience seemed, however, to be much amused, and the florid Celt was convulsed with admiration and merriment. Even the forbidding-looking man who had been referred to as the president condescended to smile his approval and remark that I adapted myself readily to my circumstances.

"These substances," I continued, "are powerful agents either for good or for evil. For good when used for the quarrying of rocks, the removal of impediments to navigation, or the destruction of houses during a conflagration. For evil –"

"I think you had better pass on to something more practical," said the president, grimly.

"On dipping starch into certain liquids," I resumed, "it is found to assume an explosive property. The attention of a learned countryman of ours, the chemist Schönbein, was directed to the fact, and he found that by treating cotton in a similar manner the effect was enormously increased. Schönbein was a man respected among his contemporaries, devoted to his country, and loyal –"

"Pass on!" said the president.

"After being treated in this fashion," I continued, "the cotton is found to gain eighty per cent. in weight. This substance is more susceptible to an increase of temperature than gunpowder, igniting at 300° Fahrenheit, while the latter requires a heat of 560° for its explosion. Guncotton can also be exploded by a blow, which is not the case with a mixture of carbon, sulphur, and saltpetre."

Here there were some angry murmurs among the company, and the president interrrupted me for the third time.

"These gentlemen complain," he said, "that you have left no definite impression upon their minds as to how the substance is manufactured. Perhaps you will kindly dwell more fully upon the point."

"I have no further remarks to make," I said.

There was another threatening murmur, and the president took something out of the pocket of his coat, and toyed with it negligently. "I think you had better reconsider your decision," he remarked.

Most little men with spectacles are timid. Again I was no exception to the rule. I am ashamed to say that the peril of my Fatherland and even of my kaiser suddenly vanished from my recollection. I only realised that I, Otto von Spee, was standing upon the brink of eternity. After all, I argued, they could find out for themselves in any book upon chemistry. Why should my valuable life be sacrificed for such a trifle? I resumed my lecture with somewhat undignified haste.

"Guncotton is manufactured by steeping cotton waste in nitric acid. The explosion is caused by the oxygen of the acid combining with the carbon of the wool. It should be well cleaned with water after manufacture, otherwise the superfluous nitric acid acts directly upon the wool, charring it and gradually reducing it to a gummy mass. During this process heat is often evolved sufficient to explode the cotton, so that it is a dangerous matter to neglect the cleaning. After this a little sulphuric acid may be used to get rid of the moisture, when the substance is ready for use."

There was considerable applause at this point of my discourse, several of the audience taking notes of my remarks.

While I had been speaking I had been making a careful survey of the room in the hope of seeing some possibility of escape. The daïs upon which I stood extended as far as the side wall, in which there was a window. The window was half open, and, could I reach it, there appeared to be a deserted looking garden outside, which might communicate with the street. No one could intercept me before I reached the window, but then there was the deadly weapon with which my cadaverous acquaintance was still trifling. He was sitting on the other side, and the table would partially protect me should I venture upon a dash. Could I screw up my courage to make an attempt? Not yet, at any rate.

"General von Link," I continued, "the Austrian artillerist, is one of our leading authorities upon guncotton. He experimented upon it in field-pieces, but –"

"Never mind that," said the president.

"After being manufactured, guncotton may be compressed under water. When compressed it is perfectly safe, and cannot be discharged. This sample which we have upon the table is not compressed. No amount of heat will have any effect upon the wet cotton. In an experiment tried in England a storehouse containing guncotton was burned down without there being any explosion. If, however, a charge of fulminated mercury, or a small piece of dry cotton, be fired in connection with a damp disc, it will be sufficient to discharge it. I shall now proceed to demonstrate this to you by an experiment."

An idea had come into my mind. Upon the table there was lying a mixture of sugar and chlorate of potash, used with sulphuric acid as a fuse for mining purposes. A bottle of the acid was also ready to my hand. I knew the white dense cloud of smoke which is raised by the imperfect combustion of these bodies. Could I make it serve as a screen between the weapon of the president and myself?

For a moment the plan seemed wild and unfeasible; still, it offered some chance of escape, and the more I thought it over the more reconciled I became to it. Of course, even after getting through the window there was the possibility that the garden might prove to be a *cul-de-sac*, and that my pursuers might overtake me. But then, on the other hand, I had no guarantee that I might not be murdered at the conclusion of my lecture. From what I knew of the habits of such men I considered it to be extremely probable. It was better to risk – but no, I would not think of what I was risking.

"I am now going to show you the effect of fulminate of mercury upon a small piece of damp cotton," I said, shaking out the sugar and chlorate of potash upon the edge of the table and pushing the large piece of cotton to the other end to be out of danger from the effects of the explosion.

"You will observe that the fact of the substance having been soaked with water does not in any way hinder its action." Here I poured the sulphuric acid over the mixture, dropped the bottle, and fled for the window amid a perfect cloud of smoke.

Most little men with spectacles are not remarkable for activity. Ha! there at last I proved myself to be an exception. I seemed hardly to put my foot to the ground between leaving the table and shooting out through the window as the equestrians fly through hoops in the circus. I was well outside before the sharp crack which I was expecting sounded in the chamber behind me, and then –

Ah! what then? How can I ever hope to describe it? There was a low, deep rumble, which seemed to shake the ground, swelling and swelling in sound until it culminated in a roar which split the very heavens. Flames danced before my eyes, burning wood and stones and *débris* came clattering down around me, and as I stared about me in bewilderment I received a crushing blow upon the head, and fell.

How long I may have remained unconscious it is difficult to say. Some time, at any rate, for when I came to myself I was stretched upon the bed in my own little chamber at home, while the devoted Gretchen bathed my temples with vinegar and water. In the doorway were standing a couple of stalwart *polizei diener*, who bobbed their helmeted heads and grinned their satisfaction on seeing that I was returning to consciousness.

It was some while before I could recall anything of what had passed. Then gradually came the recollection of my mysterious visitor, of the wild drive through the storm, of the impromptu lecture on dynamite, and lastly of some strange and unaccountable accident. Strange it still remains, but I think that when we reflect that the table was between the bullet and me, and that on that table were two pounds of guncotton liable to ignition at a blow, we have not very far to go for an explanation. I have fired a pistol at a distance into a small piece of the same substance since that occasion with very much the same result.

And where was the house? you will ask, and what was the fate of its inmates? Ah! there my lips are sealed. The police of the Fatherland are active and cunning, and they have commanded me to say nothing – not even to my dearest friend – upon either point. No doubt they have their reasons for it, and I must obey. Perhaps they wish other conspirators to imagine that more has been found out than is actually the case. I may say, however, that it is not conducive to long life or perfect health to be present on such an occasion. That, at least, no one can object to.

I am nearly well again now, thanks to Gretchen and Dr. Benger, who lives down the road. I can hobble about, and my neighbours are already beginning to complain of the noxious vapours which I evolve. I fear I have not quite the same enthusiasm, however, upon the subject of explosives as I entertained before my midnight lecture on dynamite. The subject seems to have lost many of its charms. It may be that in the course of time I may return to my first love once again; at present, however, I remain a quiet *privat docent* of the more elementary branches of chemistry. It is that very quietness which weighs upon my mind. I fear that I am on the verge of some other unexpected adventure. There is one thing, however, upon which I am unalterably determined. Should every relative that I have in the world, with the Imperial family and half the population of Berlin, be clamouring at my door for medical advice, I shall never again protrude my head after nightfall. I am content to work away in my own little groove, and have laid aside for ever the pretensions to be looked upon as a practical physician which I entertained before that eventful Christmas Eve.

———————◆———————

SELECTING A GHOST

THE GHOSTS OF GORESTHORPE GRANGE

———◆———

I am sure that Nature never intended me to be a self-made man. There are times when I can hardly bring myself to realise that twenty years of my life were spent behind the counter of a grocer's shop in the East End of London, and that it was through such an avenue that I reached a wealthy independence and the possession of Goresthorpe Grange. My habits are conservative, and my tastes refined and aristocratic. I have a soul which spurns the vulgar herd. Our family, the D'Odds, date back to a pre-historic era, as is to be inferred from the fact that their advent into British history is not commented on by any trustworthy historian. Some instinct tells me that the blood of a Crusader runs in my veins. Even now, after the lapse of so many years, such exclam-ations as "By'r Lady!" rise naturally to my lips, and I feel that, should circumstances require it, I am capable of rising in my stirrups and dealing an infidel a blow – say with a mace – which would considerably astonish him.

Goresthorpe Grange is a feudal mansion – or so it was termed in the advertisement which originally brought it under my notice. Its right to this adjective had a most remarkable effect upon its price, and the advantages gained may possibly be more senti-mental than real. Still, it is soothing to me to know that I have slits in my staircase through which I can discharge arrows; and there is a sense of power in the fact of possessing a complicated apparatus by means of which I am enabled to pour molten lead upon the head of the casual visitor. These things chime in with my peculiar humour, and I do not grudge to pay for them. I am proud of my battlements and of the circular uncovered sewer which girds me round. I am proud of my portcullis and donjon and keep. There is but one thing wanting to round off the mediævalism of my abode, and to render it symmetrically and completely antique. Goresthorpe Grange is not provided with a ghost.

Any man with old-fashioned tastes and ideas as to how such establishments should be conducted, would have been disappointed at the omission. In my case it was particularly unfortunate. From my childhood I had been an earnest student of the supernatural, and a firm believer in it. I have revelled in ghostly literature until there is hardly a tale bearing upon the subject which I have not perused. I learned the German language for the sole purpose of mastering a book upon demonology. When an infant I had secreted myself in dark rooms in the hope of seeing some of those bogies with which my nurse used to threaten me; and the same feeling is as strong in me now as then. It was a proud moment when I felt that a ghost was one of the luxuries which money might command.

It is true that there was no mention of an apparition in the advertisement. On reviewing the mildewed walls, however, and the shadowy corridors, I had taken it for granted that there was such a thing on the premises. As the presence of a kennel presupposes that of a dog, so I imagined that it was impossible that such desirable quarters should be untenanted by one or more restless shades. Good heavens, what can the noble family from whom I purchased it have been doing during these hundreds of years! Was there no member of it spirited enough to make away with his sweetheart, or take some other steps calculated to establish a hereditary spectre? Even now I can hardly write with patience upon the subject.

For a long time I hoped against hope. Never did rat squeak behind the wainscot, or rain drip upon the attic floor, without a wild thrill shooting through me as I thought that at last I had come upon traces of some unquiet soul. I felt no touch of fear upon these occasions. If it occurred in the night-time, I would send Mrs. D'Odd – who is a strong-minded woman – to investigate the matter, while I covered up my head with the bedclothes and indulged in an ecstacy of expectation. Alas, the result was always the same! The suspicious sound would be traced to some cause so absurdly natural and commonplace that the most fervid imagination could not clothe it with any of the glamour of romance.

I might have reconciled myself to this state of things, had it not been for Jorrocks of Havistock Farm. Jorrocks is a coarse, burly, matter-of-fact fellow, whom I only happened to know through the accidental circumstance of his fields adjoining my demesne. Yet this man, though utterly devoid of all appreciation of archæological unities, is in possession of a well-authenticated and undeniable spectre. Its existence only dates back, I believe, to the reign of the Second George, when a young lady cut her throat upon hearing of the death of her lover at the battle of Dettingen. Still, even that gives the house an air of respectability, especially when coupled with blood stains upon the floor. Jorrocks is densely unconscious of his good fortune; and his language when he reverts to the apparition is painful to listen to. He little dreams how I covet every one of those moans and nocturnal wails which he describes with unnecessary objurgation. Things are indeed coming to a pretty pass when democratic spectres are allowed to desert the landed proprietors and annul every social distinction by taking refuge in the houses of the great unrecognised.

I have a large amount of perseverance. Nothing else could have raised me into my righful sphere, considering the uncongenial atmosphere in which I spent the earlier part of my life. I felt now that a ghost must be secured, but how to set about securing one was more than either Mrs. D'Odd or myself was able to determine. My reading taught me that such phenomena are usually the outcome of crime. What crime was to be done, then, and who was to do it? A wild idea entered my mind that Watkins, the house-steward, might be prevailed upon – for a consideration – to immolate himself or someone else in the interests of the establishment. I put the matter to him in a half-jesting manner; but it did not seem to strike him in a favourable light. The other servants sympathised with him in his opinion – at least, I cannot account in any other way for their having left the house in a body the same afternoon.

"My dear," Mrs. D'Odd remarked to me one day after dinner, as I sat moodily sipping a cup of sack – I love the good old names – "my dear, that odious ghost of Jorrocks' has been gibbering again."

"Let it gibber!" I answered, recklessly.

Mrs. D'Odd struck a few chords on her virginal and looked thoughtfully into the fire.

"I'll tell you what it is, Argentine," she said at last, using the pet name which we usually substituted for Silas, "we must have a ghost sent down from London."

"How can you be so idiotic, Matilda?" I remarked, severely. "Who could get us such a thing?"

"My cousin, Jack Brocket, could," she answered, confidently.

Now, this cousin of Matilda's was rather a sore subject between us. He was a rakish, clever young fellow, who had tried his hand at many things, but wanted perseverance to succeed at any. He was, at that time, in chambers in London, professing to be a general agent, and really living, to a great extent, upon his wits. Matilda managed so that most of our business should pass through his hands, which certainly saved me a great deal of trouble; but I found that Jack's commission was generally considerably larger than all the other items of the bill put together. It was this fact which made me feel inclined to rebel against any further negotiations with the young gentleman.

"O yes, he could," insisted Mrs. D., seeing the look of disapprobation upon my face. "You remember how well he managed that business about the crest?"

"It was only a resuscitation of the old family coat-of-arms, my dear," I protested.

Matilda smiled in an irritating manner. "There was a resuscitation of the family portraits, too, dear," she remarked. "You must allow that Jack selected them very judiciously."

I thought of the long line of faces which adorned the walls of my banqueting-hall, from the burly Norman robber, through every gradation of casque, plume, and ruff, to the sombre Chesterfieldian individual who appears to have staggered against a pillar in his agony at the return of a maiden MS. which he grips convulsively in his right hand. I was fain to confess that in that instance he had done his work well, and that it was only fair to give him an order – with the usual commission – for a family spectre should such a thing be attainable.

It is one of my maxims to act promptly when once my mind is made up. Noon of the next day found me ascending the spiral stone staircase which leads to Mr. Brocket's chambers, and admiring the succession of arrows and fingers upon the whitewashed wall, all indicating the direction of that gentleman's sanctum. As it happened, artificial aids of the sort were entirely unnecessary, as an animated flap-dance overhead could proceed from no other quarter, though it was replaced by a deathly silence as I groped my way up the stair. The door was opened by a youth evidently astounded at the appearance of a client, and I was ushered into the presence of my young friend, who was writing furiously in a large ledger – upside down, as I afterwards discovered.

After the first greetings, I plunged into business at once.

"Look here, Jack," I said, "I want you to get me a spirit, if you can."

"Spirits you mean!" shouted my wife's cousin, plunging his hand into the waste-paper basket and producing a bottle with the celerity of a conjuring trick. "Let's have a drink!"

I held up my hand as a mute appeal against such a proceeding so early in the day; but on lowering it again I found that I had almost involuntarily closed my fingers round the tumbler which my adviser had pressed upon me. I drank the contents hastily off, lest anyone should come in upon us and set me down as a toper. After all there was something very amusing about the young fellow's eccentricities.

"Not spirits," I explained, smilingly; "an apparition – a ghost. If such a thing is to be had, I should be very willing to negotiate."

"A ghost for Goresthorpe Grange?" inquired Mr. Brocket, with as much coolness as if I had asked for a drawing-room suite.

"Quite so," I answered.

"Easiest thing in the world," said my companion, filling up my glass again in spite of my remonstrance. "Let us see!" Here he took down a large red note-book, with all the letters of the alphabet in a fringe down the edge. "A ghost you said, didn't you? That's G. G – gems – gimlets – gas-pipes – gauntlets – guns – galleys. Ah, here we are. Ghosts. Volume nine, section six, page forty-one. Excuse me!" And Jack ran up a ladder and began rummaging among the pile of ledgers on a high shelf. I felt half inclined to empty my glass into the spittoon when his back was turned; but on second thoughts I disposed of it in a legitimate way.

"Here it is!" cried my London agent, jumping off the ladder with a crash, and depositing an enormous volume of manuscript upon the table. "I have all these things tabulated, so that I may lay my hands upon them in a moment. It's all right – it's quite weak" (here he filled our glasses again). "What were we looking up, again?"

"Ghosts," I suggested.

"Of course; page 41. Here we are. 'J.H. Fowler & Son, Dunkel Street, suppliers of mediums to the nobility and gentry; charms sold – love philtres – mummies – horoscopes cast.' Nothing in your line there, I suppose."

I shook my head despondently.

" 'Frederick Tabb,' " continued my wife's cousin, " 'sole channel of communication between the living and the dead. Proprietor of the spirits of Byron, Kirke White, Grimaldi, Tom Cribb, and Inigo Jones.' That's about the figure!"

"Nothing romantic enough there," I objected. "Good heavens! Fancy a ghost with a black eye and a handkerchief tied round its waist, or turning summersaults, and saying, 'How are you to-morrow?' " The very idea made me so warm that I emptied my glass and filled it again.

"Here is another," said my companion, " 'Christopher McCarthy; bi-weekly séances – attended by all the eminent spirits of ancient and modern times. Nativities – charms – abracadabras, messages from the dead.' He might be able to help us. However, I shall have a hunt round myself to-morrow, and see some of these fellows. I know their haunts, and it's odd if I can't pick up something cheap. So there's an end of business," he concluded, hurling the ledger into the corner, "and now we'll have something to drink."

We had several things to drink – so many that my inventive faculties were dulled next morning, and I had some little difficulty in explaining to Mrs. D'Odd why it was that I hung my boots and spectacles upon a peg along with my other garments before retiring to rest. The new hopes excited by the confident manner in which my agent had undertaken the commission, caused me to rise superior to alcoholic reaction, and I paced about the rambling corridors and old-fashioned rooms, picturing to myself the appearance of my expected acquisition, and deciding what part of the building would harmonise best with its presence. After much consideration, I pitched upon the banqueting-hall as being, on the whole, most suitable for its reception. It was a long low room, hung round with valuable tapestry and interesting relics of the old family to whom it had belonged. Coats of mail and implements of war glimmered fitfully as the light of the fire played over them, and the wind crept under the door, moving the hangings to and fro with a ghastly rustling. At one end there was the raised dais, on which in ancient times the host and his guests used to spread their table, while a descent of a couple of steps led to the lower part of the hall, where the vassals and retainers held wassail. The floor was uncovered by any sort of carpet, but a layer of rushes had been scattered over it by my direction. In the whole room there was nothing to remind one of the nineteenth century; except, indeed, my own solid silver plate, stamped with the re-suscitated family arms, which was laid out upon an oak table in the centre. This, I determined, should be the haunted room, supposing my wife's cousin to succeed in his negotiation with the spirit-mongers. There was nothing for it now but to wait patiently until I heard some news of the result of his inquiries.

A letter came in the course of a few days, which, if it was short, was at least encouraging. It was scribbled in pencil on the back of a playbill, and sealed apparently with a tobacco-stopper. "Am on the track," it said. "Nothing of the sort to be had from any professional spiritualist, but picked up a fellow in a pub yesterday who says he can manage it for you. Will send him down unless you wire to the contrary. Abrahams is his name, and he has done one or two of these jobs before." The letter wound up with some incoherent allusions to a cheque, and was signed by my affectionate cousin, John Brocket.

I need hardly say that I did not wire, but awaited the arrival of Mr. Abrahams with all impatience. In spite of my belief in the supernatural, I could scarcely credit the fact that any mortal could have such a command over the spirit-world as to deal in them and barter them against mere earthly gold. Still, I had Jack's word for it that such a trade existed; and here was a gentleman with a Judaical name ready to demonstrate it by proof positive. How vulgar and commonplace Jorrocks' eighteenth-century ghost would appear should I succeed in securing a real mediæval apparition! I almost thought that one had been sent down in advance, for, as I walked round the moat that night before retiring to rest, I came upon a dark figure engaged in surveying the machinery of my portcullis and drawbridge. His start of surprise, however, and the manner in which he hurried off into the darkness, speedily convinced me of his earthly origin, and I put him down as some admirer of one of my female retainers mourning over the muddy Hellespont which divided him from his love. Whoever he may have been, he disappeared and did not return, though I loitered about for some time in the hope of catching a glimpse of him and exercising my feudal rights upon his person.

Jack Brocket was as good as his word. The shades of another evening were beginning to darken round Goresthorpe Grange, when a peal at the outer bell, and the sound of a fly pulling up, announced the arrival of Mr. Abrahams. I hurried down to meet him, half expecting to see a choice assortment of ghosts crowding in at his rear. Instead, however, of being the sallow-faced, melancholy-eyed man that I had pictured to myself, the ghost-dealer was a sturdy little podgy fellow, with a pair of wonderfully keen sparkling eyes and a mouth which was constantly stretched in a good-humoured, if somewhat artificial, grin. His sole stock-in-trade seemed to consist of a small leather bag jealously locked and strapped, which emitted a metallic chink upon being placed on the stone flags in the hall.

"And 'ow are you, sir?" he asked, wringing my hand with the utmost effusion. "And the missus, 'ow is she? And all the others — 'ow's all their 'ealth?"

I intimated that we were all as well as could reasonably be expected, but Mr. Abrahams happened to catch a glimpse of Mrs. D'Odd in the distance, and at once plunged at her with another string of inquiries as to her health, delivered so volubly and with such an intense earnestness, that I half expected to see him terminate his cross-examination by feeling her pulse and demanding a sight of her tongue. All this time his little eyes rolled round and round, shifting perpetually from the floor to the ceiling, and from the ceiling to the walls, taking in apparently every article of furniture in a single comprehensive glance.

Having satisfied himself that neither of us was in a pathological condition, Mr. Abrahams suffered me to lead him upstairs, where a repast had been laid out for him to which he did ample justice. The mysterious little bag he carried along with him, and deposited it under his chair during the meal. It was not until the table had been cleared and we were left together that he broached the matter on which he had come down.

"I hunderstand," he remarked, puffing at a trichinopoly, "that you want my 'elp in fitting up this 'ere 'ouse with a happarition."

I acknowledged the correctness of his surmise, while mentally wondering at those restless eyes of his, which still danced about the room as if he were making an inventory of the contents.

"And you won't find a better man for the job, though I says it as shouldn't," continued my companion. "Wot did I say to the young gent wot spoke to me in the bar of the Lame Dog? 'Can you do it?' says he. 'Try me,' says I, 'me and my bag. Just try me.' I couldn't say fairer than that."

My respect for Jack Brocket's business capacities began to go up very considerably. He certainly seemed to have managed the matter wonderfully well. "You don't mean to say that you carry ghosts about in bags?" I remarked, with diffidence.

Mr. Abrahams smiled a smile of superior knowledge. "You wait," he said; "give me the right place and the right hour, with a little of the essence of Lucoptolycus" – here he produced a small bottle from his waistcoat pocket – "and you won't find no ghost that I ain't up to. You'll see them yourself, and pick your own, and I can't say fairer than that."

As all Mr. Abrahams' protestations of fairness were accompanied by a cunning leer and a wink from one or other of his wicked little eyes, the impression of candour was somewhat weakened.

"When are you going to do it?" I asked, reverentially.

"Ten minutes to one in the morning," said Mr. Abrahams, with decision. "Some says midnight, but I says ten to one, when there ain't such a crowd, and you can pick your own ghost. And now," he continued, rising to his feet, "suppose you trot me round the premises, and let me see where you wants it; for there's some places as attracts 'em, and some as they won't hear of – not if there was no other place in the world."

Mr. Abrahams inspected our corridors and chambers with a most critical and observant eye, fingering the old tapestry with the air of a connoisseur, and remarking in an undertone that it would "match uncommon nice." It was not until he reached the banqueting-hall, however, which I had myself picked out, that his admiration reached the pitch of enthusiasm. " 'Ere's the place!" he shouted, dancing, bag in hand, round the table on which my plate was lying, and looking not unlike some quaint little goblin himself. " 'Ere's the place; we won't get nothin' to beat this! A fine room – noble, solid, none of your electro-plate trash! That's the way as things ought to be done, sir. Plenty of room for 'em to glide here. Send up some brandy and the box of weeds; I'll sit here by the fire and do the preliminaries, which is more trouble than you'd think; for them ghosts carries on hawful at times, before they finds out who they've got to deal with. If you was in the room they'd tear you to pieces as like as not. You leave me alone to tackle them, and at half-past twelve come in, and I lay they'll be quiet enough by then."

Mr. Abrahams' request struck me as a reasonable one, so I left him with his feet upon the mantelpiece, and his chair in front of the fire, fortifying himself with stimulants against his refractory visitors. From the room beneath, in which I sat with Mrs. D'Odd, I could hear that, after sitting for some time, he rose up and paced about the hall with quick impatient steps. We then heard him try the lock of the door, and afterward drag some heavy article of furniture in the direction of the window, on which, apparently, he mounted, for I heard the creaking of the rusty hinges as the diamond-paned casement folded backward, and I knew it to be situated several feet above the little man's reach. Mrs. D'Odd says that she could distinguish his voice speaking in low and rapid whispers after this, but that may have been her imagination. I confess that I began to feel more impressed than I had deemed it possible to be. There was something awesome in the thought of the solitary mortal standing by the open window and summoning in from the gloom outside the spirits of the nether world. It was with a trepidation which I could hardly disguise from Matilda that I observed that the clock was pointing to half-past twelve, and that the time had come for me to share the vigil of my visitor.

He was sitting in his old position when I entered, and there were no signs of the mysterious movements which I had overheard, though his chubby face was flushed as with recent exertion.

"Are you succeeding all right?" I asked as I came in, putting on

as careless an air as possible, but glancing involuntarily round the
room to see if we were alone.

"Only your help is needed to complete the matter," said Mr.
Abrahams, in a solemn voice. "You shall sit by me and partake of
the essence of Lucoptolycus, which removes the scales from our
earthly eyes. Whatever you may chance to see, speak not and
make no movement, lest you break the spell." His manner was
subdued, and his usual cockney vulgarity had entirely disappeared. I took the chair which he indicated, and awaited the
result.

My companion cleared the rushes from the floor in our neighbourhood, and, going down upon his hands and knees, described
a half-circle with chalk, which enclosed the fireplace and ourselves. Round the edge of this half-circle he drew several hieroglyphics, not unlike the signs of the zodiac. He then stood up and
uttered a long invocation, delivered so rapidly that it sounded
like a single gigantic word in some uncouth guttural language.
Having finished this prayer, if prayer it was, he pulled out the
small bottle which he had produced before, and poured a couple
of teaspoonfuls of clear transparent fluid into a phial, which he
handed to me with an intimation that I should drink it.

The liquid had a faintly sweet odour, not unlike the aroma of
certain sorts of apples. I hesitated a moment before applying it to
my lips, but an impatient gesture from my companion overcame
my scruples, and I tossed it off. The taste was not unpleasant;
and, as it gave rise to no immediate effects, I leaned back in my
chair and composed myself for what was to come. Mr. Abrahams
seated himself beside me, and I felt that he was watching my face
from time to time, while repeating some more of the invocations
in which he had indulged before.

A sense of delicious warmth and languor began gradually to
steal over me, partly, perhaps, from the heat of the fire, and
partly from some unexplained cause. An uncontrollable impulse
to sleep weighed down my eyelids, while at the same time my
brain worked actively, and a hundred beautiful and pleasing
ideas flitted through it. So utterly lethargic did I feel that, though
I was aware that my companion put his hand over the region of
my heart, as if to feel how it were beating, I did not attempt to
prevent him, nor did I even ask him for the reason of his action.
Everything in the room appeared to be reeling slowly round in a
drowsy dance, of which I was the centre. The great elk's head at
the far end wagged solemnly backward and forward, while the
massive salvers on the tables performed cotillons with the claret-
cooler and the epergne. My head fell upon my breast from sheer

heaviness, and I should have become unconscious had I not been recalled to myself by the opening of the door at the other end of the hall.

This door led on to the raised dais, which, as I have mentioned, the heads of the house used to reserve for their own use. As it swung slowly back upon its hinges, I sat up in my chair, clutching at the arms, and staring with a horrified glare at the dark passage outside. Something was coming down it – something unformed and intangible, but still a *something*. Dim and shadowy, I saw it flit across the threshold, while a blast of ice-cold air swept down the room, which seemed to blow through me, chilling my very heart. I was aware of the mysterious presence, and then I heard it speak in a voice like the sighing of an east wind among pine-trees on the banks of a desolate sea.

It said: "I am the invisible nonentity. I have affinities and am subtle. I am electric, magnetic, and spiritualistic. I am the great ethereal sigh-heaver. I kill dogs. Mortal, wilt thou choose me?"

I was about to speak, but the words seemed to be choked in my throat; and, before I could get them out, the shadow flitted across the hall and vanished in the darkness at the other side. while a long-drawn melancholy sigh quivered through the apartment.

I turned my eyes toward the door once more, and beheld, to my astonishment, a very small old woman, who hobbled along the corridor and into the hall. She passed backward and forward several times, and then, crouching down at the very edge of the circle upon the floor, she disclosed a face the horrible malignity of which shall never be banished from my recollection. Every foul passion appeared to have left its mark upon that hideous countenance.

"Ha! ha!" she screamed, holding out her wizened hands like the talons of an unclean bird. "You see what I am. I am the fiendish old woman. I wear snuff-coloured silks. My curse descends on people. Sir Walter was partial to me. Shall I be thine, mortal?"

I endeavoured to shake my head in horror; on which she aimed a blow at me with her crutch, and vanished with an eldritch scream.

By this time my eyes turned naturally toward the open door, and I was hardly surprised to see a man walk in of tall and noble stature. His face was deadly pale, but was surmounted by a fringe of dark hair which fell in ringlets down his back. A short pointed beard covered his chin. He was dressed in loose-fitting clothes, made apparently of yellow satin, and a large white ruff surrounded his neck. He paced across the room with slow and majestic strides. Then turning, he addressed me in a sweet, exquisitely modulated voice.

"I am the cavalier," he remarked. "I pierce and am pierced. Here is my rapier. I clink steel. This is a blood stain over my heart. I can emit hollow groans. I am patronised by many old Conservative families. I am the original manor-house apparition. I work alone, or in company with shrieking damsels."

He bent his head courteously, as though awaiting my reply, but the same choking sensation prevented me from speaking; and, with a deep bow, he disappeared.

He had hardly gone before a feeling of intense horror stole over me, and I was aware of the presence of a ghastly creature in the room, of dim outlines and uncertain proportions. One moment it seemed to pervade the entire apartment, while at another it would become invisible, but always leaving behind it a distinct consciousness of its presence. Its voice, when it spoke, was quavering and gusty. It said: "I am the leaver of footsteps and the spiller of gouts of blood. I tramp upon corridors. Charles Dickens has alluded to me. I make strange and disagreeable noises. I snatch letters and place invisible hands on people's wrists. I am cheerful. I burst into peals of hideous laughter. Shall I do one now?" I raised my hand in a deprecating way, but too late to prevent one discordant outbreak which echoed through the room. Before I could lower it the apparition was gone.

I turned my head toward the door in time to see a man come hastily and stealthily into the chamber. He was a sunburnt powerfully built fellow, with ear-rings in his ears and a Barcelona handkerchief tied loosely round his neck. His head was bent upon his chest, and his whole aspect was that of one afflicted by intolerable remorse. He paced rapidly backward and forward like a caged tiger, and I observed that a drawn knife glittered in one of his hands, while he grasped what appeared to be a piece of parchment in the other. His voice, when he spoke, was deep and sonorous. He said, "I am a murderer. I am a ruffian. I crouch when I walk. I step noiselessly. I know something of the Spanish Main. I can do the lost treasure business. I have charts. Am able-bodied and a good walker. Capable of haunting a large park." He looked toward me beseechingly, but before I could make a sign I was paralysed by the horrible sight which appeared at the door.

It was a very tall man, if, indeed, it might be called a man, for the gaunt bones were protruding through the corroding flesh, and the features were of a leaden hue. A winding-sheet was wrapped round the figure, and formed a hood over the head, from under the shadow of which two fiendish eyes, deep set in their grisly sockets, blazed and sparkled like red-hot coals. The lower jaw had fallen upon the breast, disclosing a withered, shrivelled tongue and two lines of black and jagged fangs. I shuddered and drew back as this fearful apparition advanced to the edge of the circle.

"I am the American blood-curdler," it said, in a voice which seemed to come in a hollow murmur from the earth beneath it. "None other is genuine. I am the embodiment of Edgar Allan Poe. I am circumstantial and horrible. I am a low-caste spirit-subduing spectre. Observe my blood and my bones. I am grisly and nauseous. No depending on artificial aid. Work with grave-clothes, a coffin-lid, and a galvanic battery. Turn hair white in a night." The creature stretched out its fleshless arms to me as if in entreaty, but I shook my head; and it vanished, leaving a low, sickening, repulsive odour behind it. I sank back in my chair, so overcome by terror and disgust that I would have very willingly resigned myself to dispensing with a ghost altogether, could I have been sure that this was the last of the hideous procession.

A faint sound of trailing garments warned me that it was not so. I looked up, and beheld a white figure emerging from the corridor into the light. As it stepped across the threshold I saw that it was that of a young and beautiful woman dressed in the fashion of a bygone day. Her hands were clasped in front of her, and her pale proud face bore traces of passion and of suffering. She crossed the hall with a gentle sound, like the rustling of autumn leaves, and then, turning her lovely and unutterably sad eyes upon me, she said. "I am the plaintive and sentimental, the beautiful and ill-used. I have been forsaken and betrayed. I shriek in the night-time and glide down passages. My antecedents are highly respectable and generally aristocratic. My tastes are æsthetic. Old oak furniture like this would do, with a few more coats of mail and plenty of tapestry. Will you not take me?"

Her voice died away in a beautiful cadence as she concluded, and she held out her hands as if in supplication. I am always sensitive to female influences. Besides, what would Jorrocks's ghost be to this? Could anything be in better taste? Would I not be exposing myself to the chance of injuring my nervous system by interviews with such creatures as my last visitor, unless I decided at once? She gave me a seraphic smile, as if she knew what was passing in my mind. That smile settled the matter. "She will do!" I cried; "I choose this one;" and as, in my enthusiasm, I took a step toward her I passed over the magic circle which had girdled me round.

"Argentine, we have been robbed!"

I had an indistinct consciousness of these words being spoken, or rather screamed, in my ear a great number of times without my being able to grasp their meaning. A violent throbbing in my head seemed to adapt itself to their rhythm, and I closed my eyes to the lullaby of "Robbed, robbed, robbed." A vigorous shake caused me to open them again, however, and the sight of Mrs. D'Odd in the scantiest of costumes and most furious of tempers was sufficiently impressive to recall all my scattered thoughts, and make me realise that I was lying on my back on the floor, with my head among the ashes which had fallen from last night's fire, and a small glass phial in my hand.

I staggered to my feet, but felt so weak and giddy that I was compelled to fall back into a chair. As my brain became clearer, stimulated by the exclamations of Matilda, I began gradually to recollect the events of the night. There was the door through which my supernatural visitors had filed. There was the circle of chalk with the hieroglyphics round the edge. There was the cigar-box and brandy-bottle which had been honoured by the attentions of Mr. Abrahams. But the seer himself – where was he? and what was this open window with a rope running out of it? And where, O where, was the pride of Goresthorpe Grange, the glorious plate which was to have been the delectation of generations of D'Odds? And why was Mrs. D. standing in the grey light of dawn, wringing her hands and repeating her monotonous refrain? It was only very gradually that my misty brain took these things in, and grasped the connection between them.

Reader, I have never seen Mr. Abrahams since; I have never seen the plate stamped with the resuscitated family crest; hardest of all, I have never caught a glimpse of the melancholy spectre with the trailing garments, nor do I expect that I ever shall. In fact my night's experiences have cured me of my mania for the supernatural, and quite reconciled me to inhabiting the humdrum nineteenth-century edifice on the outskirts of London which Mrs. D. has long had in her mind's eye.

As to the explanation of all that occurred – that is a matter which is open to several surmises. That Mr. Abrahams, the ghost-hunter, was identical with Jemmy Wilson, *alias* the Nottingham crackster, is considered more than probable at Scotland Yard, and certainly the description of that remarkable burglar tallied very well with the appearance of my visitor. The small bag which I have described was picked up in a neighbouring field next day, and found to contain a choice assortment of jemmies and centre-bits. Footmarks deeply imprinted in the mud on either side of the

moat showed that an accomplice from below had received the
sack of precious metals which had been let down through the
open window. No doubt the pair of scoundrels, while looking
round for a job, had overheard Jack Brocket's indiscreet inquiries, and promptly availed themselves of the tempting opening.

And now as to my less substantial visitors, and the curious
grotesque vision which I had enjoyed – am I to lay it down to any
real power over occult matters possessed by my Nottingham
friend? For a long time I was doubtful upon the point, and
eventually endeavoured to solve it by consulting a well-known
analyst and medical man, sending him the few drops of the
so-called essence of Lucoptolycus which remained in my phial. I
append the letter which I received from him, only too happy to
have the opportunity of winding up my little narrative by the
weighty words of a man of learning:

"ARUNDEL STREET
"Dear Sir: Your very singular case has interested me extremely.
The bottle which you sent contained a strong solution of chloral,
and the quantity which you describe yourself as having swallowed
must have amounted to at least eighty grains of the pure hydrate.
This would of course have reduced you to a partial state of
insensibility, gradually going on to complete coma. In this semi-
unconscious state of chloralism it is not unusual for circumstantial
and *bizarre* visions to present themselves – more especially to
individuals unaccustomed to the use of the drug. You tell me in
your note that your mind was saturated with ghostly literature,
and that you had long taken a morbid interest in classifying and
recalling the various forms in which apparitions have been said to
appear. You must also remember that you were expecting to see
something of that very nature, and that your nervous system was
worked up to an unnatural state of tension. Under the circumstances, I think that, far from the sequel being an astonishing one,
it would have been very surprising indeed to any one versed in
narcotics had you not experienced some such effects. – I remain,
dear sir, sincerely yours,

"T. E. STUBE, M.D.

"Argentine D'Odd, Esq.
"The Elms, Brixton."

THE HEIRESS OF GLENMAHOWLEY

———————◆———————

"Bob," said I, "this won't do; something must be done."

"It must," echoed Bob, as he puffed away from his pipe in a mouldy little sitting room in the Shamrock Arms, at Glenmahowley.

Glenmahowley attained any importance which it possessed by being the centre of an enormous area of peat cuttings and bog land which stretched away with exasperating monotony to the horizon, unbroken by the slightest irregularity. In one place only, along the Mountsimon Road, there was a single belt of thick woods, whose luxuriance only served to aggravate the hopeless waste around them. The village itself consisted of a long straggling line of thatched cottages, each with an open door, through which entered bare-legged children, gaunt pigs, cocks and hens, ragged-looking, short-piped men and slatternly women. Bob Elliott seemed rather to admire the aborigines. No doubt it tickled his vanity to hear admiring exclamations as we went down the street; such as "Look at him now; look at the illigant fut on him!" or, "Oh, then, an' isn't he a beautiful gintleman entoirely!" But I don't care for these things. Besides, though far more handsome than Bob, my beauty is of an intellectual type, and is lost upon these savages. My nose is pronounced, my complexion pallid, and my head denotes considerable brain power. "There's no harm in the crayter!" was the least offensive of the opinions which these idiots expressed of me.

We had been located in this barbarous place about a week. Bob and I were second cousins, and a distant mutual relation whom neither of us had seen had bequeathed us each a small property in the West. The clearing-up of business attendant on this, and the necessity of consulting with the old lady's pragmatical country attorney, had kept us for a week in the Shamrock Arms, and promised to keep us for at least another one in that unenviable retreat, if we could survive the tedium of our existence so long.

"What can we do?" groaned Bob again.

"Where's Pendleton? Let's get Pendleton up and take a rise out of him," I suggested with a flickering attempt at vivacity. Pendleton was our fellow-lodger at the inn – a quiet young fellow of artistic proclivities, with a weakness for solitary rambles and seclusion. All our attempts to pump him had failed as yet to elicit any explanation of the objects and aims which had led him to Glenmahowley, unless it were that its bleak morasses harmonised with his misanthropic turn of mind.

"It's no use," said my companion. "He's as dismal as a tombstone and as shy as a girl. I never saw such a fellow. I wanted him to come with me this morning when you were writing your letter and to aid and abet me in a little mild chaff with the two girls at the draper's – you need help against these Irish girls, you know – but he flushed up quite red and wouldn't hear of such a thing."

"No, he is hardly cut out for a lady-killer," I remarked, adjusting my necktie before the flyblown mirror, and practising a certain expression which I have found extremely effective with the weaker sex – a sort of Lara-like piratical cock of the eye which gives the impression of hidden griefs and a soul which spurns the commonplaces of existence. "Perhaps he will come in though, and play dummy whist."

"No, he never touches cards."

"Milksop!" I ejaculated. "We'll send for the landlord, Bob, and ask him if there is nothing we can see or do."

This was recognised to be the most rational proceeding under the circumstances, and a messenger was despatched in hot haste to summon Dennis O'Keefe, our worthy host. Let me remark, while he is shuffling upstairs in his slipshod carpet slippers, that I am the mortal known as John Vereker, barrister-at-law, popularly supposed to be a rising man, though the exact distance that I have risen during the four years that I have been in practice is not calculated to turn my brain. Several nice little actions have however during that time been taken against me, in county courts and otherwise, so that I have put the machinery of the law into motion, though my personal profit in the matter must be acknowledged to have been somewhat remote.

O'Keefe was a fine specimen of the aboriginal Celt – freckle-faced and rough-haired, with shrewd grey eyes and a deep rich, Milesian voice. "Good-morrow to ye, gintlemen," he began as he entered, his large flat feet and uncouth gait giving him a sort of plantigrade appearance. "What would your honours be afther to-day?"

"The very thing we wanted to ask you, O'Keefe," said Bob. "What in the world *are* we to do? Can't you suggest anything?"

"There's the church," remarked O'Keefe, scratching his red hair in perplexity. " 'Tis a foine building. There was a gintleman came here the year before last just for to look at it. Maybe your honours—"

"Hang the church!" roared Bob, with as much vehemence as a Radical advocate for Disestablishment; "we were there five times last week – in fact every day except Sunday. Try again, old Pict and Scot."

Our host, who was serenely indifferent to the many unintelligible epithets applied to him by Bob's exuberant fancy, pondered once more over the problem. "There's the hole in the bog," he suggested with diffidence. "The same where the boys threw Mr. Lyons of Glenmorris – bad scran to him! – afther they shot him. May be you'd loike to see where they found him wid his head in the mud, an' his feet stickin' up. Ah, it was a glad soight, sorrs, for the pisantry that had worked and slaved – the craturs – and then for him to step in wid a dirty foive and twinty per cint. reduction in the rint, and serve notices on them as wouldn't pay. Sure you could take your food – or a gossoon could carry it – and picnic by the hole."

"The prospect is alluring," I remarked, "but there seems to me to be too much chance of the inoffensive tillers of the soil taking a fancy to plant a couple more Saxons upside down in the bog-hole. I negative that suggestion."

"What are those trees to the eastward?" asked Bob. "Surely there is something to be seen down there."

"It's proivate. It's the Clairmont family's ground, an' you'd be shot as loike as not if you so much as put your nose over the wall."

"Pleasant land this, Jack!" remarked my companion ruefully. "I almost wish old O'Quibble would unearth a codicil leaving the place to somebody else."

"Ah sure you can't judge of the counthry now while its quoiet," said our host. "Wait till the throubles come round agin – next year maybe, or the year afther. It's a loively land when the bhoys is out – sorra a taste of scenery would you think about; and bein' landlords yourselves by that toime, you'd see the cream of the divarsion."

"How about these Clairmonts?" I asked at a venture. "Do they live upon their own land?"

"Begorra – you've got it there!" cried O'Keefe. "They do nothing *but* live on their own land. They've niver stirred off it for more'n fifteen years."

"Never stirred off it!"

"Sorra a fut beyond the park gates and the great brick wall. No man's oi has ever rested upon Miss Clairmont's face bar ould Dennis the lodgekeeper – the blackmouthed spalpeen – more be token they say she's grown into the purtiest girl in the county, forbye having foive and twinty thousand in her own right."

"What!" we both roared.

"Foive and twinty thousand pound," repeated O'Keefe solemnly; "and when her ould cat of a mother dies she'll come in for the whole family estate."

"What is she?" "Where is she?" "Who is she?" "What the devil is the matter with her?" shouted Bob and I, forming a sort of strophe and antistrophe to the landlord's chorus.

O'Keefe's account of the past history of the Clairmont family was a remarkable one, and when curtailed of his many Hibernian digressions and meanderings, amounted to this. A certain Major Clairmont had come into the county some sixteen years before, bearing with him a large sum in hard cash, a showy-looking wife of rather foreign appearance, and a pretty little daughter about two years old. Having expended a portion of the first item upon the purchase of a considerable estate near Glenmahowley, he had taken up his residence there, and awaited some recognition from the county families. This came soon enough in the case of the Major, who, as an old Guardsman, possessed a recognised social position, which was secured by his own many admirable qualities. It was different with Madame. The men might drink the old claret of the soldier, or take a day's shooting in his pheasant preserves, but their wives made no sign. Strange rumours were in circulation as to the antecedents of Mrs. C. Some said that she had been upon the stage before her marriage, some that her career had been more equivocal still. There were individuals who ventured to doubt that she possessed even now the little blue slip of paper which civilisation demands. It was this rumour which some busybody brought to the ears of the Major, coupling with it the name of a neighbouring landed proprietor. The Major was a bull-necked, choleric man. He chose out his heaviest hunting crop, and galloped furiously down the avenue to interview the traducer of his wife's character. The lodgekeeper was surprised to see the veteran horseman reel in his saddle as he shot through the gates, and then fall backwards with a dull thud on to the dusty road. The local practitioner pronounced it to be apoplexy, while the family physician favoured heart disease – but whatever the cause, the Major's spirit had drifted far away from Glenmahowley. It was then that that fiery foreign strain which showed itself on his wife's face asserted itself in her character. She would live on the estates still because he had been fond of them, but her life should be spent in mourning her loss, and in educating her daughter in her own way. Above all, never should she again exchange word or look with any living being belonging to the county which had insulted her, and indirectly caused her husband's death. The great gates were walled up, and only small slits left through which provisions and other necessaries, ordered by Dennis the lodgekeeper, were handed. A formidable row of spikes was planted on the brick wall which had always surrounded the estate. In this extraordinary seclusion, cut off from the whole world, Mrs. Clairmont and her daughter had now passed fifteen years of their lives unseen by human eyes, save those of the few English domestics who remained with them, and perhaps of an occasional daring urchin who might penetrate into the wood, which surrounded the great house. It was these irregular scouts no doubt who had brought word of the exceeding beauty of the young lady, though no adult male had ever yet had the privilege of being able to form an opinion upon it. She was at present close upon her eighteenth birthday.

Thus far O'Keefe; while Bob and I sat, with elbows upon the table and chins upon our hands, drinking in every word. Neither of us broke the silence for some little time after he had concluded. Bob Elliott puffed furiously at his pipe, while I looked dreamily out of the window at the thatched roofs of the cottages and the long monotonous stretch of bog land in the distance.

"She is beautiful?" asked Bob at last.

"She is that!"

"And rich?" I queried.

"Divil a doubt of it."

We relapsed into another silence, in the midst of which our worthy landlord, evidently thinking us the worst of company, stole out of the room, walking for some unknown reason upon the tips of his toes as if he were afraid of waking us.

Left to ourselves we became even more meditative than before. Bob strolled restlessly up and down in front of the door; I whistled and continued to stare out of the window. We were both lost in our own thoughts.

"Fancy a girl who has never even seen a male fellow-creature!" ejaculated Bob at last.

"Who is unfettered by the conventionalities of civilisation!" said I.

"How artless she must be, and how simple!" rendered my companion, twisting his moustache.

"What a depth of pent-up affection there must be in that heart!" I exclaimed, with my corsair-like look of slumbrous passion.

"How charmingly childlike and romantic!" said Bob, smoothing his hair in the glass.

"How easy for a dashing young fellow to win!" I returned, smiling at my own reflection over Bob's shoulder.

It is a curious fact, that for the remainder of the day, though nothing in the shape of a distraction turned up, neither of us complained of the *ennui* of a residence in Glenmahowley. We both seemed suddenly reconciled to a contemplative existence, and even became tolerant of Pendleton, whose contentment under existing circumstances had struck us hitherto as nothing less than an insult. He came in about supper-time with his sketch-book and his mud-bespattered boots, apparently as happy as if he were among the most artistic scenery in the world. If it were not for his shyness and reserve he would be rather a pleasant fellow — that is, in gentlemen's society, for his diffidence would ruin him among women. He is tall, slim, and fair-haired, rather a good-looking young man — decidedly more so than Bob.

I did not sleep very well that night, neither did my companion. He showed his tousled head round the corner of my door somewhere about two o'clock in the morning.

"Hullo, Jack," he said, "are you asleep?"

"No."

"What was the figure again?"

"Twenty-five," I growled.

"I thought it was twenty. Thanks! Good-night!"

"Good-night!" and the head disappeared like the apparition in "Macbeth." It was evident that our thoughts were running in very much the same groove. As for me, my plans were matured, and I could afford to smile at Bob's cogitations. While he hankered aimlessly for the prize I should swoop down and carry it off. The Verekers were always noted for their iron determination. I chuckled to myself while I dropped to sleep as I thought of the march which I should steal upon him on the morrow.

The day broke without a cloud on the sky. Both Elliott and Pendleton were somewhat silent at breakfast, and as I was engaged in planning the details of the enterprise to which I had determined to commit myself, I did not attempt to enter into conversation with them. After the meal Pendleton remarked that he would take a short stroll in search of effects, and Bob almost immediately afterwards sallied out for a mouthful of fresh air. This was a most unexpected piece of luck. I had ransacked my brain for some excuse which would enable me to get rid of my companion, and here he had solved the problem of his own accord. Giving him half an hour's grace to take him well out of the way, I slipped out through the back-door of the Shamrock Arms and made my way rapidly down the Morristown Road in the direction of the Clairmont estate.

My sole doubt and anxiety was as to how I was to succeed in obtaining an interview with the young lady. Should fortune befriend me in that matter the rest appeared simple enough. I pictured to myself her mental condition, the sense of desolation which must oppress her young soul. Cooped up away from the world, her heart must yearn for some manly bosom upon which to rest her head, some strong arm to break her fetters. Besides, I was a man with exceptional personal advantages. Without being conceited, I have a just appreciation of my own merits. To eyes accustomed to nothing but an occasional glance of Dennis the lodgekeeper I should appear an Adonis. By-the-way, how about Dennis? Might he not resent my intrusion? Pooh! he was an old man. I remember the landlord saying so. What would I not risk for the girl whom I was prepared to adore! Perhaps he would have a gun though! These Irishmen are hotheaded and blood-thirsty. I grew thoughtful and slackened my pace.

By this time I had come to the place where a high brick wall, with a conical coping bristling with spikes and pieces of broken bottles, ran along by the side of the road. This I recognised from O'Keefe's description as being the boundary line of the Clairmont estate. At the other side of the wall there was, as far as I could see, a thick forest. Should I do it, or should I not? I thought of the five and twenty thousand pounds. Besides, what would a gatekeeper be doing with a gun! What a sell for Bob Elliott – and for Pendleton, the shy Pendleton! Would they not curse their want of energy when they saw the prize which had slipped through their fingers? How the fellows would talk in London, too, even if I failed! It would make my name as a Don Juan. I could imagine Clinker or Waterhouse or some of the old set coming into the Temple wine bar and beginning. "I say, you chaps, have you heard of Vereker's latest? Very devil among women, is Vereker. He was in Ireland a few weeks ago" – and so on, and so on. "By Jove!" I cried, as I approached the wall in a paroxysm of recklessness, "I'll do it if I have to skin my knee!"

I did skin my knee, in fact I skinned them both. I also removed portions of integument from my scalp, shoulder, elbow, hand and ankle, besides splitting my coat and losing my hat. I was recompensed for all this, however, as I sat astride upon the top of the wall and looked down into the forbidden land beyond. I could have laughed at the thought of the march I was stealing on my two companions. I would have done so had it not been for a spike which was running into the calf of my leg.

The drop on the other side did not look very deep. I held on to the largest projection I could see, and lowered myself until my feet were not more than a yard or so from the ground. Then I let go, but only to find that I hung suspended by a hook which had passed through my waist-band. This impediment however gave way, and I fell with a crash for about nine feet into a sort of trench, which had been dug apparently all round the inner side of the wall, and was so artistically covered with grass and sticks that it was impossible to detect it from the top. All this I discovered after I crawled out of it, for during the few minutes that I lay at the bottom every idea was shaken out of my head beyond a general impression that I had been struck by lightning.

The trees grew so thickly together that it was impossible to see for any distance into the wood, and the brushwood was so dense that it was no easy matter to move in any direction. After emerging from the ditch I hesitated for a moment as to my next step, and then was about to keep to what appeared to be some sort of path on the left when my eye was attracted by a small placard attached to the trunk of a tree. I made my way towards it eagerly, pushing aside the intervening briars and brambles. It might contain some directions which would enable me to find my way, or — romantic thought! — it might be that the lonely Beatrice I was in search of had inscribed her pinings and longings where they might meet the eye of an adventurous stranger. As I stood before the inscription and read it, I felt a kind of cold flush, if the expression be permissible, pass along my spine and up to the roots of my hair, while my knees, or what was left of them, knocked together like castanets. Scrawled upon the paper in a rough bold hand were the three words, "Bloodhounds — Spring-guns — Mantraps" — unpleasant words at any time, but most particularly so amid the gloom of a forest with a ten-foot wall in one's rear. The announcement was a concise one, and yet I felt as I re-perused it that it contained more food for reflection than any volume which I had ever read. Was I to abandon my enterprise now that the first difficulty had been successfully overcome? Possibly the notice was a mere empty threat. Surely no one would allow such things to remain in their shrubberies. The combination of ideas was so dreadful. Suppose that I was caught in a mantraps whatever that might be, and was then attacked by a bloodhound. The mere supposition made me shudder. But then if these frightful dogs were really roaming about over the forest, how was it that none of them were shot by the spring-guns or caught in the traps? This consideration revived my drooping spirits, and I pushed on through the thick underwood.

As I advanced it opened up somewhat, so that I made better progress. A few half-overgrown paths meandered here and there, but I avoided these and kept under the concealment of the trees. Never shall I forget that dreadful walk! Every time a twig snapped I sprang into the air under the impression that I was shot. No hero of romance ever underwent such an ordeal for his lady, and indeed no lady was ever worth it. Five and twenty thousand pounds however are enough to steel the heart of the most timorous, but even they would hardly recompense me for the frights which were in store for me.

I had got to one of the deepest and one of the most secluded parts of the wood, when I stopped suddenly and crouched down, trembling in every limb. Was it the sound of footsteps which had been wafted towards me on the breeze? I listened intently, and then with a long sigh of relief was about to rise, convinced that I had been mistaken, when the same sound came to my ears, but much louder than before. There could be no question that it was approaching me. I lay down upon my face among the prickly brambles, hoping to escape observation. The footsteps continued to come nearer and nearer. They were those of a man – but put down stealthily and softly as if he were also shunning observation. Could it be that some ruffian had observed me and was hunting me down as one stalks a deer? He was coming nearer and nearer. I could hear the rustle of the leaves as he brushed past them. It seemed to me that I could even distinguish the sound of his breathing. Nearer he came and nearer still – he was close to me, and the next moment the brambles in front of me parted and a man stepped out almost upon the top of me, and staggered back with a shout as I sprang to my feet. The voice seemed familiar – so did the figure. Could it be! Yes; there was no mistaking the identity of Mr. Robert Elliott of Lincoln's Inn.

Sed quantum mutatus ab illo! The stylish coat was torn and covered with mud. The aristocratic face was stained with dust and perspiration, and interlaced with scratches where the brambles had left their mark. His hat had been knocked in and was a hopeless wreck. His watchguard and the studs in his shirt seemed to stand out as oases of respectability in a great desert of desolation.

"Bob!" I ejaculated.

It was a few moments before any sign of recognition came over his face. Then gradually the ghost of a smile appeared in his astonished eyes, which deepened and deepened until he burst into an uproarious fit of laughter.

"Vereker, by Jove!" he yelled. "What ever have you been doing to yourself?"

I looked down at my own costume and was forced to acknowledge that there was very little to choose between us. What with the wall and the ditch and the underwood and the briars, there was hardly an article of clothing which was fit to be worn again. The two of us looked more like a couple of scarecrows on tramp and in search of employment, than two prominent members of the junior bar. "What are you doing here, Elliott?" I asked.

"Exploring," he answered evasively; "what are you?"

"Explor – No, hang it, why can't we be frank to one another, Bob? You know very well you came after that girl."

My companion looked sheepish. "Well, I suppose you did the same?" he said.

"Of course I did. What fools we were to try and bamboozle each other! If we had stuck together we might never have got into such a plight."

"I'm very sure I should never have tumbled into that infernal ditch if I had seen you go in," said Bob ruefully.

"Oh, you've been in the ditch too, have you?" I remarked, with the first approach to satisfaction which I had felt since I left O'Keefe's hospitable roof.

"Yes," groaned Bob. "I think I have been through the whole performance. Did you see any notices on the trees?"

"I did."

"Has old Dennis been round to you yet?"

"No; have you seen him!"

"Yes; he passed within ten yards of me a short time ago. At least I suppose it was him – a big gaunt fellow with a great stick."

"Heaven save us!" I ejaculated.

"However he has passed now, and the question is what are we to do?"

"Persevere," I responded manfully. "It would be more dangerous to go back than to go on since that truculent gatekeeper is behind us."

"Right you are!" said Elliott, with a melancholy attempt at cheerfulness. "You lead on, and I'll follow."

"No, you go first," I answered, not I am bound to say from any innate courtesy or feeling of politeness, but with an idea that dangers from the abominations mentioned on the placard would be lessened thereby.

We threaded our way through the forest in Indian file, and after advancing for about half a mile were evidently close to the edge of it. The trees were smaller and the unplanted spaces larger. Suddenly Bob pulled up and pointed in front of him.

"There's the house," he said.

There it was sure enough, a stern looking edifice of grey stone with a large number of small glimmering windows. There was a lawn in front of it, very tastefully laid out, which somewhat relieved the gloomy and prison-like appearance of the building. No one was to be seen either outside or at the windows. We held a council of war as to what our next step should be.

"We can't walk right up to the house under some excuse or other, can we?" said Bob.

"It would be too dangerous," I remarked. "There is no saying what they might do to us. They seem to be very savage people."

"Besides, it would be the very last way to have any chance of saying a few words to the young lady," added my companion.

"The whole thing makes a deuced romantic situation," I observed.

"I wonder what Pendleton would think of us if he saw us?"

"Poor shy Pendleton! I think he would put us both down as madmen."

"It's a pity he's so retiring," said Bob. "But I say, Jack, what do you intend to say to the young lady when you see her?"

"Why, I propose to tell her of my love straight off, and ask her to fly with me. It must be all done to-day. I'm not coming in here again on any consideration. Besides, I think it will not be difficult to carry a romantic girl of that sort by a kind of *coup de main*."

"But that's exactly my plan," said Bob plaintively.

"The deuce it is?" I ejaculated. "By George! There she is!"

The last exclamation was drawn from me by the appearance, upon the steps of the house, of an elegantly-dressed young lady. Her features were invisible, owing to the distance, but her erect carriage and the long, graceful curves of her figure showed that report had not exaggerated her charms. She turned as she came out to address an elder woman, her mother probably, who followed her. The latter seemed, as far as we could make out, to be weeping, for she raised her handkerchief to her eyes several times, while the girl passed her arm round her neck as if to console her. In this she appeared to succeed, for the elder went back into the house, and the younger sprang down the three steps at a single bound and hurried away with long elastic steps down the path which led into the shrubbery.

"We must follow her!" I cried.

"Take your time," said Bob. "We must come to some agreement before we start. It would be too ridiculous for the two of us to plunge at her together and begin pouring out two confessions of love."

"It might startle her," I remarked, "especially as she has never seen either of us before."

"Who is to have the preference then?"

"I am the elder," I observed.

"But then I left the inn first," objected Elliott.

"Well, suppose we toss for it."

"I suppose we must," said Bob gloomily, producing a penny and spinning it up in the air. "Heads, so it is. Just my luck. Of course, if after your proposal the young lady thinks fit to refuse you, I am at liberty to do whatever I choose. Is that agreed?"

"Certainly," I answered, and we both pushed on rapidly through the shrubbery, gaining confidence as we saw some prospect of attaining our object.

"There she is!" whispered Bob, as we saw the flutter of a pink dress among the trees in front of us."

"There's a man talking to her!"

"Impossible!"

"There is."

If there was he must have disappeared very rapidly on hearing our approach, for when we got near enough to her to see her whole figure she was alone. She turned with a start of surprise, and seemed inclined for a moment to run away from us, but then recovering herself she came towards us. As she advanced I saw that she was one of the most lovely girls that I had ever seen in my life – not at all the doll-like sort of beauty that I had imagined from what I knew of her training, but a splendid, well-developed young woman with a firmly set lower jaw and delicately moulded chin which would have been almost masculine in their force had they not been relieved by a pair of pensive blue eyes and a sweetly sensitive mouth. Somehow, as I found her steady gaze directed at me, all the well-turned speeches which I had rehearsed in my mind seemed to fade entirely from my memory and leave nothing but an utter blank behind. The amorous gallop with which we bore down upon her subsided into a ridiculous trot, and when eventually I pulled up a few yards in front of her I could no more have uttered a word of explanation than I could have recovered my lost hat or concealed the gaps in my clothing.

"I fancy you must have mistaken your way," she said in a low sweet voice without the slightest appearance of being affected by this apparition of young men.

I felt Bob nudge me from behind and whisper something about "going ahead" and "making the running," but my only inclination under the gaze of those calm, tranquil eyes was to make the running in the opposite direction at the top of my speed.

"The house is over there," she observed, pointing through the trees. "I suppose that you are the bailiffs."

"Bailiffs!" I gasped.

"Excuse me if I do not give you your proper title," she continued with a melancholy smile. "It is the first time that we have ever been brought in contact with the officers of the law, and hardly know how to address them. We have expected you for two days."

Bob and I could only stare at her in silent bewilderment.

"There is one thing I should like to ask you," she went on, drawing nearer to us with her hands clasped and a beautiful pleading expression upon her face. "Though my mother and I are almost beggars now, remember that she is a lady, delicately reared and sensitive. Above all, remember that she has no one to protect her or to take her part. Be gentle with her therefore, and do your duty without wounding her feelings more than you can help."

"Bob," I whispered, drawing my companion aside, though he still continued to stare idiotically over his shoulder at the young lady. "Do you realise it? They expect the bailiffs. There's no money in the concern. What are we to do?"

"She's an angel!" was all Bob could evolve.

"So she is, but she's got no money."

"Then you give her up?"

"I do," said I with a sentimental twinge at my heart. Sentimentalism has always been my weak point.

"You won't propose?" asked Bob excitedly.

"No, marriage is an expensive luxury. Besides —"

"Besides what?"

"I am convinced she would not have me."

"Then, by Jove, I'll do it!" said Bob, facing round with a look of determination upon his dirty face.

Miss Clairmont had been standing looking considerably surprised and a little frightened during our hurried conclave. She drew back a few feet as Bob took a step towards her with his two arms thrown out in eloquent entreaty like an animated semaphore.

"Young lady," he began, "I am not a bailiff. I belong to another and a higher branch of the legal profession. I am a Londoner and a gentleman."

Bob paused for a moment to allow this statement to sink into his listener's mind. Miss Clairmont looked more amazed than impressed, though it was evident from her shrinking figure that she was considerably startled.

"In a foreign land," cried Bob, warming to his work – "A land beyond the seas – I allude to England – I heard of your charms and of your solitary existence, and I swore – that is to say, we both did, only I lost the toss, – to save you and bring you out into the great world which you are so fitted to adorn. We crossed the deep – which made us both exceedingly unwell, – and flew to your rescue. We have scaled this inhospitable wall of yours; if you doubt my statement you will find a large portion of the sleeve of my coat upon one of the spikes which adorn it. We also ran the gauntlet of the many unpleasant things which your amiable parent seems to have littered about for the benefit of the casual stranger. Dear girl," continued Bob advancing with an imbecile grin upon his countenance, which he imagined no doubt to be a seductive smile, "fly with me! Be mine! Share with me the wild free life of a barrister! Say that you return the love which consumes my heart – oh, say it!" Here Bob put his hand over a hole in his waistcoat and struck a dramatic attitude.

During this extraordinary address the young lady had been gradually edging away from us, and at its conclusion she burst into a merry peal of laughter.

"Edward!" she cried – "Ned! Do come out! It's really too ridiculous, but I don't know what to say to them."

At this summons a man emerged from behind a tree where he had concealed himself, and flew to her side. Imagine our petrifying and all-absorbing astonishment when we recognised in him Pendleton, our retiring companion of the inn.

"Don't be frightened, darling," he said passing his arm round her slender waist, to Bob's intense and audible disgust. "I can understand, gentlemen," he went on, "the romantic motives which have led you here, but you will see how futile they are when I tell you that this lady is my wife."

"Your what?" roared Bob and I in chorus.

"My wedded wife. You are the first that have heard our secret, though Mrs. Clairmont must learn it to-day. It does not matter to you how we met or how we married – suffice it that it is so. To-day the ruin which I had long foreseen has come upon the household; Mrs. Pendleton thinks it may have softened the hard heart of her mother, and we are going up now to see her together, to confess what we have done, and to offer her a home for the rest of her life at my place in Devon. You will see, gentlemen," he continued,

"that a delicate matter of the sort must be done without interruption and at once; you will therefore excuse us from showing
you off the grounds. I may say, however, that if you will keep to
that path on the left you will soon find yourselves at the boundary
– and now, gentlemen, my wife and myself must wish you a very
good-morning," with which he offered the young lady his arm
and the two strolled off together in the direction of the house.

How long Bob and I stood there gazing after them and at each
other, neither of us could ever determine. Then we plodded
sullenly down the path pointed out, without exchanging a word,
and after sundry gymnastic exercises found ourselves in the road
once more.

Bob was inclined to be sentimental all day, and perhaps I was
hardly myself either. When night fell however, and a steaming
jug of hot water was brought up, flanked with a lemon on one side
and the sugar on the other, while the whisky bottle towered in the
rear, we began to get over our troubles; and I doubt if O'Keefe,
when he joined us, could have given a guess at the stirring events
which had occurred since he told us the story of the Clairmont
family the night before. Certainly by next morning there were no
traces left of our short matrimonial campaign.

Another week found us in our chambers in town, settling down
comfortably into the old routine. I do not know where our next
holiday will be spent, but I can confidently predict that it will *not*
be at Glenmahowley. I have heard nothing since of the Pendle-
tons beyond the fact that he is the owner of a large estate on the
borders of Dartmoor. Bob talks of visiting those parts in the
spring, but I think for his own peace of mind he had better steer
clear of those blue eyes and sweet features which are our only
pleasant recollection of the land of bogs.

THE CABMAN'S STORY

THE MYSTERIES OF A LONDON "GROWLER"

———◆———

We had to take a "growler," for the day looked rather threatening, and we agreed that it would be a very bad way of beginning our holiday by getting wet, especially when Fanny was only just coming round from the whooping cough. Holidays were rather scarce with us, and when we took one we generally arranged some little treat, and went in for enjoying ourselves. On this occasion we were starting off from Hammersmith to the Alexandra Palace in all the dignity of a four-wheeler. What with the wife and her sister, and Tommy and Fanny and Jack, the inside was pretty well filled up, so I had to look out for myself. I didn't adopt the plan of John Gilpin under similar circumstances, but I took my waterproof, and climbed up beside the driver.

This driver was a knowing-looking old veteran, with a weather-beaten face and white side whiskers. It has always seemed to me that a London cabman is about the shrewdest of the human race, but this specimen struck me as looking like the shrewdest of the cabmen. I tried to draw him out a bit as we jogged along, for I am always fond of a chat; but he was a bit rusty until I oiled his tongue with a glass of gin when we got as far as the "Green Anchor." Then he rattled away quickly enough, and some of what he said is worth trying to put down in black and white.

"Wouldn't a hansom pay me better?" he said, in answer to a question of mine. "Why, of course it would. But look at the position! A four-wheeler's a respectable conveyance, and the driver of it's a respectable man, but you can't say that of a rattling, splashing 'ansom. Any boy would do for that job. Now, to my mind money hain't to be compared to position, whatever a man's trade may be."

"Certainly not!" I answered.

"Besides, I've saved my little penny, and I'm got too old to change my ways. I've begun on a growler, and I'll end on one. If you'll believe me, sir, I've been on the streets for seven-and-forty year."

"That's a long time," I said.

"Well, it's long for our trade," he replied. "You see, there ain't no other in the world that takes the steam out of a man so quick – what with wet and cold and late hours, and maybe no hours at all. There's few that lasts at it as long as I have."

"You must have seen a deal of the world during that time," I remarked. "There are few men who can have greater oppor-tunities of seeing life."

"The world!" he grunted, flicking up the horse with his whip. "I've seen enough of it to be well-nigh sick of it. As to life, if you'd said death, you'd ha' been nearer the mark."

"Death!" I ejaculated.

"Yes, death," he said. "Why, bless your soul, sir, if I was to write down all I've seen since I've been in the trade, there's not a man in London would believe me, unless maybe some o' the other cabbies. I tell ye, I took a dead man for a fare once, and drove about with him nigh half the night. Oh, you needn't look shocked, sir, for this wasn't the cab – no, nor the last one I had neither."

"How did it happen?" I asked, feeling glad, in spite of his assurance, that Matilda had not heard of the episode.

"Well, it's an old story now," said the driver, putting a small piece of very black tobacco into the corner of his mouth. "I daresay it's twenty odd years since it happened, but it's not the kind o' thing as slips out of a man's memory. It was very late one night, and I was working my hardest to pick up something good, for I'd made a poor day's work of it. The theatres had all come out, and though I kept up and down the Strand till nigh one o'clock, I got nothing but one eighteenpenny job. I was thinking of giving it up and going home, when it struck me that I might as well make a bit of a circuit, and see if I couldn't drop across something. Pretty soon I gave a gentleman a lift as far as the Oxford Road, and then I drove through St. John's Wood on my way home. By that time it would be about half-past one, and the streets were quite quiet and deserted, for the night was cloudy, and it was beginning to rain. I was putting on the pace as well as my tired beast would go, for we both wanted to get back to our suppers, when I heard a woman's voice hail me out of a side street. I turned back, and there in about the darkest part of the road was standing two ladies – real ladies, mind you, for it would take a deal of darkness before I would mistake one for the other. One was elderly and stoutish; the other was young, and had a veil over her face. Between them there was a man in evening dress, whom they were supporting on each side, while his back was propped up against a lamp-post. He seemed beyond taking care of himself altogether, for his head was sunk down on his chest, and he'd have fallen if they hadn't held him.

" 'Cabman,' said the stout lady, with a very shaky voice, 'I wish you would help us in this painful business.' Those were her very hidentical words.

" 'Cert'nly, mum,' I says for I saw my way to a good thing. 'What can I do for the young lady and yourself?' I mentioned the other one in order to console her like, for she was sobbing behind her veil something pitiful.

" 'The fact is, cabman,' she answers, 'this gentleman is my daughter's husband. They have only just been married, and we are visiting at a friend's house near here. My son-in-law has just returned in a state of complete intoxication, and my daughter and I have brought him out in the hope of seeing a cab in which we could send him home, for we have most particular reasons for not wishing our friends to see him in this state, and as yet they are ignorant of it. If you would drive him to his house and leave him there, you would do us both a very great kindness, and we can easily account to our hosts for his absence.'

"I thought this rather a rum start, but I agreed, and no sooner had I said the word than the old one she pulls open the door, and she and the other, without waiting for me to bear a hand, bundled him in between them.

" 'Where to?' I asked.

" 'Forty-seven, Orange Grove, Clapham,' she said. 'Hoffman is the name. You'll easily waken the servants.'

" 'And how about the fare?' I suggested, for I thought maybe there might be a difficulty in collecting it at the end of the journey.

" 'Here it is,' said the young one, slipping what I felt to be a sovereign into my hand, and at the same time giving it a sort of grateful squeeze, which made me feel as if I'd drive anywhere to get her out of trouble.

"Well, off I went, leaving them standing by the side of the road. The horse was well-nigh beat, but at last I found my way to 47, Orange Grove. It was a biggish house, and all quiet, as you may suppose, at that hour. I rang the bell, and at last down came a servant – a man, he was.

" 'I've got the master here,' I said.

" 'Got who?' he asked.

" 'Why, Mr. Hoffman – your master. He's in the cab, not quite himself. This is number forty-seven, ain't it?'

" 'Yes, it's forty-seven, right enough; but my master's Captain Ritchie, and he's away in India, so you've got the wrong house.'

" 'That was the number they gave me,' I said. 'But maybe he's come to himself by this time, and can give us some information. He was dead drunk an hour ago.'

"Down we went to the cab, the two of us, and opened the door. He had slipped off the seat and was lying all in a heap on the floor.

" 'Now, then, sir,' I shouted. 'Wake up and give us your address.'

"He didn't answer.

"I gave another shake. 'Pull yourself together,' I roared. 'Give us your name, and tell us where you live.'

"He didn't answer again. I couldn't even hear the sound of his breathing. Then a kind of queer feeling came over me, and I put down my hand and felt his face. It was as cold as lead. 'The cove's dead, mate,' I said.

"The servant struck a match, and we had a look at my passenger. He was a young, good-looking fellow, but his face wore an expression of pain, and his jaw hung down. He was evidently not only dead, but had been dead some time.

" 'What shall we do?' said the flunkey. He was as white as death himself, and his hair bristled with fear.

" 'I'll drive to the nearest police station,' I answered; and so I did, leaving him shivering on the pavement. There I gave up my fare, and that was the last I ever saw of him."

"Did you never hear any more of it?" I asked.

"Hear! I thought I should never hear the end of it, what with examinations and inquests and one thing and another. The doctors proved that he must have been dead at the time he was shoved into the cab. Just before the inquest four little blue spots came out on one side of his neck, and one on the other, and they said only a woman's hand could have fitted over them, so they brought in a verdict of wilful murder; but, bless you, they had managed it so neatly that there was not a clue to the women, nor to the man either, for everything by which he might have been identified had been removed from his pockets. The police were fairly puzzled by that case. I've always thought what a bit o' luck it was that I got my fare, for I wouldn't have had much chance of it if it hadn't been paid in advance."

My friend the driver began to get very husky about the throat at this stage of the proceedings, and slackened his speed very noticeably as we approached a large public-house, so that I felt constrained to offer him another gin, which he graciously accepted. The ladies had some wine, too, and I followed the example of my companion on the box, so that we all started refreshed.

"The police and me's been mixed up a good deal," continued the veteran, resuming his reminiscences. "They took the best customer I ever had away from me. I'd have made my fortin if they'd only let him carry on his little game a while longer."

Here, with the coquetry of one who knows that his words are of interest, the driver began to look around him with an air of abstraction, and to comment upon the weather.

"Well, what about your customer and the police?" I asked.

"It's not much to tell," he said, coming back to his subject. "One morning I was driving across Vauxhall Bridge when I was hailed by a little crooked old man with a pair of spectacles on, who was standing at the Middlesex end, with a big leather bag in his hand. 'Drive where you like,' he said; 'only don't drive fast, for I'm getting old, and it shakes me to pieces.' He jumped in, and shut himself up, closing the windows, and I trotted about with him for nearly three hours, before he let me know that he had had enough. When I stopped, out he hopped with his big bag in his hand.

" 'I say, cabbie!' he said, after he had paid his fare.

" 'Yes, sir,' said I, touching my hat.

" 'You seem a decent sort of fellow, and you don't go in the break-neck way of some of your kind. I don't mind giving you the same job every day. The doctors recommend gentle exercise of the sort, and you may as well drive me as another. Just pick me up at the same place to-morrow.'

"Well, to make a long story short, I used to find the little man in his place every morning, always with his black bag, and for nigh on to four months never a day passed without his having his three hours' drive, and paying his fare like a man at the end of it. I shifted into new quarters on the strength of it, and was able to buy a new set o' harness. I don't say as I altogether swallowed the story of the doctors having recommended him on a hot day to go about in a growler with both windows up. However, it's a bad thing in this world to be too knowing, so though I own I felt a bit curious at times, I never put myself out o' the way to find out what the little game was. One day, I was driving up to my usual place of dropping him – for by this time we had got into the way of going a regular beat every morning – when I saw a policeman waiting, with a perky sort of look about him, as if he had some job on hand. When the cab stopped, out jumped the little man with his bag right into the arms of the 'bobby.'

" 'I arrest you, John Malone,' says the policeman.

" 'On what charge?' he answers as cool as a turnip.

" 'On the charge of forging Bank of England notes,' says the 'bobby'.

" 'Oh, then the game is up!' he cries, and with that he pulls off his spectacles, and his wig and whiskers, and there he was, as smart a young fellow as you'd wish to see.

" 'Good-bye, cabby,' he cried, as they led him off, and that was the last I saw of him, marching along between two of them, and another behind with the bag."

"And why did he take a cab?" I asked, much interested.

"Well, you see, he had all his plant for making the notes in that bag. If he were to lock himself up in his lodging several hours a day it would soon set people wondering, to say nothing of the chance of eyes at the window or key-hole. Again, you see, if he took a house all on his own hook, without servant nor anyone, it would look queer. So he made up his mind as the best way of working it was to carry it on in a closed cab, and I don't know that he wasn't right. He was known to the police however, and that was how they spotted him. Drat that van! It was as near as a touch to my off-wheel.

"Bless you, if I was to tell you all the thieves and burglars, and even murderers, as have been in my growler one time or another, you'd think I'd given the whole Newgate Calendar a lift, though to be sure this young chap as I spoke of was the only one as ever reg'lar set up in business there. There was one though as I reckon to be worse than all the others put together, if he was what I think him to be. It's often laid heavy on my mind that I didn't have that chap collared before it was too late, for I might have saved some mischief. It was about ten years ago – I never was a good hand for dates – that I picked up a stout-built sailor-sort of fellow, with a reddish moustache, who wanted to be taken down to the docks. After this chap as I told you of had taken such liberties with the premises I'd had a little bit of a glass slit let in in front here – the same that your little boy's flattening his nose against at this moment – so as I could prevent any such games in the future, and have an idea, whenever I wished, of what was going on inside. Well, something or another about this sailor fellow made me suspicious of him, and I took a look at what he was after. He was sitting on the seat, sir, with a big lump o' coal in his lap, and was a looking at it most attentive. Now this seemed to me rather a rum start, so I kept on watching of him, for as you'll see, my window's not a very large one, and it's easier to see through it than to be seen. Well, he pulls a spring or something, and out jumps one o' the sides of this bit of coal, and then I saw it was really a hollow box, painted, you see, and made rough so as to look like the other. I couldn't make head or tail of it anyhow, and indeed I'd pretty near forgot all about it when there came news of the explosion at Bremerhaven, and people began to talk about coal torpedoes. Then I knew as in all probability I'd carried the man who managed the business, and I gave word to the police, but they never could make anything of it. You know what a coal torpedo is, don't you? Well, you see, a cove insures his ship for more than its value, and then off he goes and makes a box like a bit o'coal, and fills it chock full with dynamite, or some other cowardly stuff of the sort. He drops this box among the other coals on the quay when the vessel is filling her bunkers, and then in course of time the box is shovelled on to the furnaces, when of course the whole ship is blown sky high. They say there's many a good ship gone to the bottom like that."

"You've certainly had some queer experiences," I said.

"Why, bless you!" remarked the driver, "I've hardly got fairly started yet, and here we are at the 'Alexandry.' I could tell you many another story as strange as these – and true, mind ye, true as Gospel. If ever your missus looks in need of a breath of fresh air you send round for me – Copper Street, number ninety-four – and I'll give her a turn into the country, and if you'll come up beside me on the box, I'll tell you a good deal that may surprise you. But there's your little lad a hollering to you like mad, and the wife wants to get out, and the other one's a tapping at the window with a parasol. Take care how you get down, sir! That's right! Don't forget number ninety-four! Good-day missus! Good-day, sir!" And the growler rumbled heavily away until I lost sight both of it and of its communicative driver among the crowd of holiday-makers who thronged the road which led to the Palace.

THE TRAGEDIANS

───◆───

I

Night had fallen on the busy world of Paris, and its gay population had poured out on to the Boulevards; soldier and civilian, artistocrat and workman, struggled for a footing upon the pavement, while in the roadway the Communistic donkey of the costermonger jostled up against the Conservative thoroughbreds of the Countess de Sang-pur. Here and there a *café*, with its numerous little tables, each with its progeny of chairs, cast a yellow glare in front of it, through which the great multitude seemed to ebb and flow.

Let us leave the noise and bustle of the Boulevard des Italiens behind us, and turn to the right, along the Rue D'Egypte. At the bottom of this there lies a labyrinth of dingy little quiet streets, and the dingiest and quietest of them all is the Rue Bertrand.

In England, we should call it shabby-genteel. The houses are two-storied semi-detached villas. There is a mournful and broken-down look about them, as if they had seen better days, and were still endeavouring to screen their venerable tiles and crumbling mortar behind a coquettish railing and jaunty Venetian blinds.

The street is always quiet, but it is even quieter than usual to-night; indeed, it would be entirely deserted but for a single figure which paces backwards and forwards over the ill-laid pavement. The man – for a man it is – must be waiting or watching for someone, as the Rue Bertrand is the last place which the romantic dreamer would select for his solitary reverie. He is here with a purpose, no doubt, and what that purpose may be is no business either of ours or of the gendarme who comes clanking noisily round the corner.

There is a house just opposite the spot where the watcher has stationed himself, which exhibits not only signs of vitality, but even some appearance of mirth. The contrast, perhaps, has caused him to stop and gaze at it. It is neater and more modern-looking than its companions. The garden is well laid out, and between the bars of the green *persiennes* the warm light glows out into the street. It has a cheery, English look about it, which marks it out among the fossils which surround it.

If the outside gives this impression, it is confirmed by the appearance of the snug room within. A large fire is crackling and sparkling merrily, as if in playful defiance of the stolid lamp upon the table. There are two people seated in front of the blaze, both of the gentler sex, and it would take no very profound student of humanity to pronounce at a glance that they were mother and daughter.

In both there is the same sweet expression and the same graceful figure, though the delicate outlines of the younger woman are exaggerated in her plump little mother, and the hair which comes from under the matronly cap is streaked with traces of grey.

Mrs. Latour has had an anxious time since her husband, the Colonel, died, but has battled through it all with the uncomplaining patience of her race. Her second son, Jack, at a university in England, has been a grief to her, for Jack is sowing his wild oats, and vague reports of the process are wafted across the Channel, and startle the quiet household in the Rue Bertrand. There is Henry, too, with his great talent for tragedy, and no engagement for more than six months. It is no wonder that the bustling, kind-hearted little woman is sad at times, and that her cheery laugh is heard less frequently than of old. The sum which the Colonel had left behind him is not a large one; were it not for the supervision exercised by Rose it would hardly have met their necessary expenses.

This young lady would certainly never be expected to have the household virtues, if it be a fact that ornament and utility are seldom united in her sex. It is true that she was no regal beauty; her features had not even the merit of regularity; yet the graceful girl, with her laughing eyes and winning smiles, would be a dangerous rival to the stateliest of her sex. Unconsciousness of beauty is the strongest adjunct which beauty can have, and Rose Latour possessed it in an eminent degree. You could see it in every natural movement of her lithe form, and in the steady gaze of her hazel eyes. No wonder that even in the venerable Rue Bertrand, which should have been above such follies, there was a parting of window blinds when the dainty little figure went tripping down it, and that the *blasé* Parisian lounger, glancing at her face, sauntered on with the conviction that there was something higher in womanhood than he had met with in his varied experiences of the "Mubille" and the *Cafés Chantants*.

"Remember this, Rose," the old lady was saying, emphasising every second or third word with an energetic little nod of the head, which gave her a strong resemblance to a plump and benevolent sparrow, "you are a Morton, and nothing but a Morton. You haven't one drop of French blood in you, my dear!"

"But papa was a Frenchman, wasn't he?" objected Rose.

"Yes, my dear; but you are a pure Morton. Your father was a dear good man, though he was a Frenchman, and only stood five feet four; but my children are all Scotch. My father was six feet two, and so would my brother have been only that the nurse used to read as she rolled him in the perambulator, and rested her book upon his head, so that he was compressed until he looked almost square, poor boy, but he had the makings of a fine man. You see, both Henry and Jack are tall men, so it is ridiculous to call them anything but Morton, and you are their sister. No, no, Rose; you haven't one drop of your father's blood in you!"

With which physiological deduction the good old lady dropped twenty stitches of her knitting and her ball of worsted, which rolled under the sideboard, with the strange instinct which all things dropped possess, and was only dislodged by Rose after ten minutes' poking in the dark with fire-irons.

This little interruption seemed to change the current of Mrs. Latour's ideas.

"Henry is later than usual to-night," she remarked.

"Yes; he was going to the Theatre National to apply for an engagement, you know. I do hope he won't be disappointed."

"I'm sure I can't conceive why they should ever refuse such a handsome young fellow," said the fond mother. "I think, even if he could not act at all, they would fill the house with people who wanted to look at him."

"I wish I were a man, mamma," said Rose, pursing her lips to express her idea of masculine inflexibility.

"Why, what would you do, child?"

"What wouldn't I do? I'd write books, and lecture, and fight, and all sorts of things."

At which summary of manly accomplishments Mrs. Latour laughed, and Rose's firmness melted away into a bright smile at her mother's mirth.

"Papa was a soldier," she said.

"Ah, my dear, there is no such thing as fighting now-a-days. Why, I remember, when I was a girl in London, how twenty and thirty thousand people used to be killed in a day. That was when young Sir Arthur Wellesley went out to the Peninsula. There was Mrs. McWhirter, next door to us – her son was wounded, poor fellow! It was a harrowing story. He was creeping through a hole in a wall, when a nasty man came up, and ran something into him."

"How very sad!" said Rose, trying to suppress a smile.

"Yes; and I heard young McWhirter say, with his own lips, that he had never seen the man before in his life, and he added that he never wished to see him again. It was at Baggage-horse."

"Badajos, 'ma."

"I said so, dear. The occurrence dispirited young McWhirter very much, and, indeed, threw a gloom over the whole family for the time. But England has changed very much since then in every way. Why, the very language seems to me to be altering in a marvellous manner. I doubt if I could make myself understood if I went back. There is Jack, at Edinburgh – he uses refinements of speech which you and I, Rose, have no idea of. We can't keep up to the day when we are living in a foreign country."

"Jack does use some queer words," said Rose.

"I had a letter from him to-night," continued the little old woman, diving first into her pocket, and then into her reticule. "Dear me! Oh, yes, here it is! I really can't understand one word of it, my dear, except that the poor lad seems to have met with some sort of an accident or misfortune."

"Acident, 'ma?"

"Well, something unpleasant, at any rate. He does not enter into any particulars. Just listen, Rose, for it is very short. Perhaps you will be able to make out what it means; but I confess it has puzzled me completely. Where are my spectacles? It begins, 'Dearest mother,' – that is intelligible enough, and very gratifying, too, as far as it goes – 'I have dropped a pony over the Cambridge-shire.' What do you suppose your brother meant by that, dear?"

"I'm sure I don't know, mamma," said the young lady, after pondering over the mysterious sentence.

"You know he could not really have dropped a pony over anything. It would have been too heavy for him, though he is a strong lad. His poor dear father always used to say that he would be sure to have a very fine muscle; but that would be *too* much. It must be his way of saying that a pony dropped him over something, and no doubt he means that the accident occurred in Cambridgeshire."

"Very likely, mamma."

"Well, now, listen to this. 'It was a case of scratching, so I was done for without a chance.' Think of that, Rose! Something has been scratching the poor, dear boy, or else he has been scratching something; I'm sure I don't know which. I shouldn't think the pony can have scratched him, for they have hoofs, you know."

"I don't think it could have been the pony," laughed Rose.

"It is all very mysterious. The next sentence is a little plainer. He says, 'If you have any of the ready, send it.' I know what he means by that, but it is the only intelligible thing in the letter. He wishes to pay his doctor's fees, no doubt, poor boy! He adds in a postcript that he may run over very soon, so he cannot be much the worse."

"Well, that's consoling," said Rose. "I hope he will come soon, and explain what it is all about."

"We'd better lay the table for supper," said the old lady. "Henry must come soon."

"Never mind ringing for Marie," said the daughter. "I am what Jack would call 'no end of a dab' at laying a table."

The mother laughed as she watched her darling flitting about the room, and coming to endless grief over the disposition of her knives and forks.

"You have given the carver four knives," she said, "while his right-hand neighbour has nothing but the steel to eat with. Listen, Rose; isn't that your brother's step?"

"There are two people."

"One of them is he, I fancy."

"So it is!" cried Rose, as the key was turned in the latch, and a masculine voice was heard in the hall. "How did you get on, Harry? Did you get it?"

And she took a spring into the passage, and threw her arms round her brother.

"Wait a bit, Rosey! Let me get my coat off before you begin to throttle me! It's all right this time, and I have got an engagement at the 'National.' "

"Didn't I tell you, Rose?" said the mother.

"Come in, do, and let us know all about it!" pleaded Rose. "We are dying to know!"

"I mustn't forget my politeness, though," said Henry. "Let me introduce Mr. Barker, an Englishman, and a friend of Jack's."

A tall, dark young man, with a serious face, who was standing in the background, stepped forward, and made his bow.

(I may remark, in parenthesis, before proceeding further, that I myself was that Mr. Barker, and that what follows in this startling narrative is therefore written from my own personal observation.)

We went into the snug little drawing-room, and drew up to the cheery fire.

Rose sat upon her brother's knee, while Mrs. Latour dropped her knitting, and put her hand into that of her son.

I leaned back in the shadow, at the other side of the hearth; while the gleam of the light played upon the golden tresses of the girl and the dark, stern profile of her brother.

"Well," said Henry, "to begin at the beginning, I went to a *café* after I set out, and it was there that I had the good fortune to come across Mr. Barker, whose name I know very well from Jack."

"We all seem to know you very well," said the mother.

I smiled and bowed.

It was pleasant to be in this miniature England in the heart of France.

"We went together to the National," continued Henry, "firmly believing I hadn't the ghost of a chance, for Lablas, the great tragedian, has much influence there, and he always does his best to harm and thwart me, though I never gave him cause of offence that I know of."

"Nasty thing!" said Rose.

"My dear, you really musn't!"

"Well, you know he is, 'ma. But go on, do!"

"I didn't see Lablas there, but I managed to get hold of the manager, old Monsieur Lambertin. He jumped at the proposal. He had the goodness to say that he had seen me act at Rouen once, and had been much struck."

"I should think so!" said the old lady.

"He then said that they were just looking out for a man to play an important *rôle* – that of *Laertes*, in a new translation of Shakespeare's 'Hamlet.' It is to come out on Monday night, so that I have only two days to learn it in. It seems that another man, Monnier by name, was to have played it, but he has broken his leg in a carriage accident. You have no idea how cordial old Lambertin was!"

"Dear old man!" said Rose.

"But come, you must be hungry, Barker, and the supper is on the table. Pull up your chairs, and just have some water boiling afterwards, Rose."

And so, with jest and laughter, we sat down to our little supper, and the evening passed away like a happy dream.

Looking back through the long vista of years, I seem to be able to recall the scene; the laughing, blushing girl, as she burned her fingers and spilt the water in her attempts at making punch; the purring little bright-eyed mother; the manly young fellow, with his honest laugh!

Who could have guessed the tragedy which was hanging over them? Who, except that dark figure that was then still standing in the Rue Bertrand, and whose shadow stretched across to darken the doorstep of number twenty-two?

II

It was the same night, or rather the following morning, for the cathedral clock had already struck three. The streets of Paris were deserted, save for an occasional gendarme or a solitary reveller hurrying home from some scene of pleasure.

Even in the Rue d'Anjou (the most dissipated of fashionable streets) there were but few houses which showed a light.

It is to one of these, however, that our story leads us.

In a large room, luxuriously fitted up, half a dozen men in evening dress were lounging and smoking. The great chandelier reflected its lustre cheerily in the mirrors around, and cast a warm glow on the red velvet of the furniture.

The carpet was so thick that hardly a footfall was heard, as one of the men rose from his seat and walked over to lean against the great marble mantelpiece.

Any *habitué* of the French theatres would have known at a glance who this man was. One could not easily forget the sinewy, upright form, and the dark, cynical smile of Lablas, the foremost tragedian of the Theatre National. A follower of Spurzheim would have prophesied great things, of good or of evil, from that broad, low forehead and massive jaw; and another glance at the cold grey eye and the sensual lip would have warned the physiognomist that off the boards of the National this was a man to be shunned, a selfish friend and a vindictive foe.

Our theatrical *habitué* would have found some other, and possibly some more agreeable, old acquaintances here.

Over there by the little glittering cabinet was Grossière, from the Variétés, cleverest and most unscrupulous of actors, whose duels and intrigues were only less notorious than those of his host, Lablas. Beside him was a *blasé* young officer of cavalry, and near him Turville, another well-known actor and "lion." Reposing on the couch, puffing at a meerschaum pipe, was Cachet, from the Gaieté; while one or two less known actors completed the group.

Lablas looked wearily at the table, all heaped with cards, dice, and odd pieces of coin.

"Well, gentlemen," he said, "you must please yourselves. Shall we have another turn or not?"

"We have plenty of time yet," said one of the actors; "but I fear there is such a run of luck against the unfortunate Lieutenant, that he will hardly dare to try again. Positively it is cruel to ask him."

The young officer looked up, with a flush upon his beardless face. He was a very young bird to endeavour to hold his own among these seasoned old vampires. It was evident from the way in which they glanced round at him when Grossière made the remark, that he had been elected as the butt of the company.

"What if I *have* bad luck?" he said. "It's all fair play and the fortune of war. I'll try again."

And he drank down a tumbler of champagne to try and drown the vision of a little woman down at Montpellier, in the sunny south, who was scraping and saving in order to keep her handsome boy like a gentleman in Paris.

"That's right! Pluckily said!" went up the chorus of voices from around the table.

"Don't drink your wine like that, though," said Cachet. "You'll make yourself unsteady."

"I'm afraid our military friend is unsteady already," remarked Lablas.

"Not at all, monsieur," said the young Lieutenant. "My hand is as steady as your own."

"There is no hand in Paris as steady as my own, young man," returned Lablas. "Lallacourt, of your own regiment, could tell you as much. You were with me, Cachet, when I shot away his trigger finger at Vincennes. I stopped his pistol shooting for ever and a day. Do you perceive a little dark spot which is fixed in the centre of the white sheet at the other side of the room? It is the head of a fusee, a mark which I generally use for the purpose of practice, as there can be no doubt as to whether you have struck it or not. You will excuse the smell of gunpowder, messieurs?" he continued, taking a small and highly-finished pistol from a rack upon the wall.

He seemed hardly to glance along the sights; but as he pulled the trigger, there was a crack and spurt of flame from the other side of the room, and the fusee, struck by the bullet, was scattered in burning splinters upon the floor.

"I hardly think you will venture to state that your hand is as steady as mine for the future," he added, glancing towards the young officer, as he replaced the dainty weapon in its stand upon the wall.

"It was a good shot, sir," returned the other.

"Hang the shooting!" said Grossière, rattling up the dice. "If you want your revenge, Lieutenant, now is your time!"

And once again money began to change hands, while a hush in the talk showed how all interest was concentrated upon the table. Lablas did not play, but he hovered round the green baize like some evil spirit, with his hard smile upon his lips, and his cold eye bent upon the man who was at once his guest and his dupe.

Poor lad! No wonder he lost when all were combining to play against him. He pushed his chair back at last in despair.

"It is useless!" he said. "The luck is against me! But, gentlemen," he added, beseechingly, "if I can raise a little money tomorrow, even though it be only a little, you will not refuse to play the same stakes – you will give me a chance?"

"We will play just exactly as long as your little lasts!" said Turville, with a brutal laugh.

The young officer was flushed and excited. He sat apart from the others, and seemed to hear the talk which ensued as in a dream. He had an uneasy feeling that all had not been fair, and yet, do what he would, he could not give one proof to the contrary.

"Pass over the wine," said Grossière. "Where were you till one o'clock, Lablas?"

Lablas showed his white teeth in a smile.

"The old story, I suppose?" said Turville.

"Bah! It is becoming too old a story," resumed Grossière. "A story without change or variety is apt to become monotonous. One intrigue is as like another as a pair of small swords, and success is always the end of them."

"They are too easily won," assented Cachet.

"I promise you this will not be too easily won," said Lablas. "Though she is a quarry worth flying for, as she is as beautiful as an angel, she is strictly preserved too; and there is a six-foot brother acting as gamekeeper, so there is a prospect of some little excitement."

"Have you made any advance yet?" asked Cachet.

"No; I have taken a few preliminary observations, however," returned the *roué*. "I fear it must be done by force, and it will need both courage and tact."

"Who is the girl, Lablas?" said Turville.

"That I won't answer."

"Come, do tell us her name."

"Curiosity sometimes verges on impertinence," said Lablas, looking from under his eyebrows at his brother actor. "Take care that you do not cross the border, for I never tolerate a liberty."

Turville was a brave man enough, but he sank his eyes before the fiery glance of the practised duellist.

There was a moment's silence, and then Lablas stretched out his hand and said, "Come, Turville, forgive and forget. I didn't mean to speak hastily, but you know my cursed temper. There, I can say no more. After all, there is no reason why I should not give you the name. I may need your assistance; and, in any case, you are men of honour, and would not thwart me in my plans. I don't suppose any of you know her. Her name is Rose Latour, and she lives in the Rue Bertrand.

"What? The sister of Henry Latour?" cried Grossière.

"Yes, the same. Do you know him?"

"Know him? Why he plays *Laertes* to your *Hamlet* on Monday night."

"The deuce he does!"

"Yes, old Lambertin closed with him last night. This will be a pretty complication! As good a fellow as ever breathed."

"I don't see that that affects the question of my carrying off his sister."

"I know the girl, too – as chaste as she is beautiful. You'll never succeed there, Lablas. She is an angel upon earth, and her brother is not the man to be trifled with."

"My dear fellow," said Lablas, "don't you see that every word you say is strengthening my resolution? As you said just now, intrigues become monotonous. There is some variety about an abduction."

"You will fail," said Grossière.

"On the contrary, I shall succeed."

"I would stake my head that you will fail."

"If you are willing to stake ten thousand francs, it will be more to the purpose. Shall it be a bet, and I claim twenty-four hours only in which to carry the little Puritan off."

"Done!" responded the comedian.

"You are my witnesses, messieurs," said Lablas, turning to the company, and entering the figures in an ivory writing-tablet.

There was a hush as he wrote, and then a youthful voice broke the silence.

"I will be no partner to this!" it said.

It was the young officer.

He had risen from his chair, and was standing opposite Lablas.

There was a murmur of surprise among the actors as their butt and plaything rose up and dared the arch-spirit of them all. They would have saved him if they could. Cachet grasped him by the sleeve, and half pulled him down.

"Sit down!" he whispered, – "sit down! He is the deadliest shot in France!"

"I will not sit down!" said the soldier. "I protest against this! If the young lady's helplessness and virtue are powerless to screen her, surely the fact that her brother is your fellow-actor should suffice to save her from your insulting wager."

Lablas never raised his eyes from the book in which he was writing.

"How long," he said, in the cold, measured voice which those who had heard it knew to be more dangerous than the bully's shout, — "how long have you turned moralist, Monsieur Malpas?"

"I have not turned moralist. I simply remain a gentleman, a title which I regret to say that you have forfeited."

"Indeed! You become personal."

"I don't pretend to be immaculate; far from it. But, so help me Heaven! nothing in the whole world would induce me to be an accomplice in such a cold-blooded, villainous seduction!"

There was a brave ring in the lad's voice as he spoke, and all the fire of the chivalrous South sparkled in his eyes.

"I only regret," he continued, "that your confiding your plans to our honour before revealing them will prevent my helping to frustrate them."

"Dear, innocent youth!" sneered Lablas. "I think I see the cause of your conversion to morality. You have some intentions in that quarter yourself, *mon cher*. Is it not so?"

"You lie, and you know that you lie!" said the soldier.

"Here, hold him — hold his arms, Cachet! Pull him back! Don't let them brawl like roughs!"

"Let me go, I say!" yelled Lablas. "He called me a liar! I'll have his life!"

"To-morrow, my dear fellow — to-morrow," said Grossière. "We will see that you have every satisfaction."

"There is my card," said the Lieutenant, as he threw it down upon the table. "You shall find me ready whenever it is convenient to you. Capitaine Haut shares my rooms; he will act as my friend. Adieu, gentlemen! — *au revoir*, monsieur!"

And the young fellow turned on his heel, and swaggered gallantly out of the room, leaving his money behind him.

In spite of his faults, the old lady in Montpellier would not have been ashamed of her son if she could have seen him then.

"You will call upon his friend to-morrow, Cachet," said Lablas, grimly. "In the meantime, to business. Can I rely upon your help in the matter of the girl — and yours, Turville?"

"We will do all we can."

"Well, I had a good look at the house to-night. It is a simple two-storey one, and she sleeps alone in one of the upper rooms.

So much I gathered, partly from observation, and partly from the servant. They go to bed early, and there is only the brother and the old lady in the house. They have no shutters to the bedrooms – only blinds."

"What will be your mode of action?"

"It is easy enough. You know the street is a very quiet one. We'll take my closed carriage; one of us can drive. Then, as you know, I have a ladder in three pieces for such little affairs. It can be brought with us. We leave the carriage; put up our ladder, open her window, gag her in her sleep, carry her down, and it is done. If she is awake and screams, surely the three of us can knock her brother on the head. They will have no clue as to who we are, or where we have gone. It will be a splendid triumph."

"So it will;" and the three men laughed heartily.

"The little prude! She will be tractable enough soon, I warrant. Well, I must be steady to-morrow, so I had better turn in for a few hours. I shall want you in the Rue Bertrand about two o'clock on Monday morning. They go to bed at eleven. Good night." And, throwing his half-finished cigar into the fire, the profligate actor sauntered out of the room, leaving his associates to discuss the diabolical deed in which they were called upon to assist.

III

It is strange how naturally Englishmen adapt themselves to the customs of the country in which they happen to be placed – more especially when those customs happen to accord with their own inclinations.

At home I am a rigid Churchman enough; but on that Parisian Sunday, the still small voice of conscience was even stiller and smaller than usual, as I sauntered round to the Rue Bertrand to see if my new friend, Henry Latour, would have pity on my loneliness, and venture out for a stroll.

Possibly the fair Rose had more to do with my visit than her brother; but, if so, I was disappointed, as that young lady had just tripped off to church, and I was compelled to put up with the male element of the household.

"You couldn't possibly have done better than come," said Henry, as he stretched his tall frame in a stupendous yawn. "I have been sitting in this confounded chair, making sure of my part, ever since breakfast, and I think I am right at last. I have been doing the *quarte tierce* business too with the poker, in preparation for the last scene. You know I used to be an excellent fencer, and it always brings down the house."

"I suppose your *Hamlet* can fence?" I remarked.

"He is notorious for it," Henry answered, as a dark shade passed over his handsome face. "But come, Barker; it's my last free day for some time to come, so we must make the most of it."

We certainly did make the most of it, and the young actor proved himself to be an admirable cicerone, doing the honours of picture galleries and museums with an amusing air of proprietorship. He was in excellent spirits about his engagement at the National, to which he often referred as being a splendid opening.

"There's only one drawback," he remarked, "and that is having to play second fiddle to that unmitigated scoundrel, Lablas. He is a profligate fellow, Barker. This very morning they say that he fought a duel in the Bois de Boulogne; shot a young officer of cavalry through the lungs. I shall have a quarrel with him, I fear; for, as *Hamlet* says, 'There is something sensitive in me,' and the man's manner jars upon me more than I can tell."

It was dark by this time, and we were both somewhat fatigued and hungry after our long peregrination.

"There's a *café* here," said Henry, "on the right-hand side, close to the railway station, where we can have a quiet little meal. That's it where the lights are. Shall we try it?"

"All right," I said. And we turned to enter.

Just at this moment, a tall young fellow, with a carpet-bag in his hand, who was coming out, ran against us.

"Pardon, messieurs," he said, turning half round and bowing, and was about to pass on, when Henry sprang forward, and caught him by the arm.

"Jack, my boy, where in the world did you come from?"

"Henry, and Barker, by all that is astonishing!" said the voice of my old college friend, Jack Latour, as he seized us alternately by the hand. "Why, what an extraordinary thing!"

"Extraordinary, indeed," cried his brother. "Why, we thought you were in Edinburgh, hundreds of miles away!"

"So I ought to be; but it struck me yesterday that a change of air would do me good. The insolent familiarity of the British tradesman was beginning to prey upon my mind. My tailor was exhibiting an increased hankering after his filthy lucre, so I thought I would deprive him for a few weeks of the refining influence of my society."

"The old game, Jack," said I.

"Yes, the old game; and I conclude you fellows are up to the old game, since I find you mooning about the first 'pub' I pass – I beg pardon, *café*. *Café* sounds better than 'pub'."

"How do you account for your own presence here?" laughed Henry.

"My dear fellow, you don't seriously suppose that I came in search of bibulous refreshment? No; it was a harmless eccentricity which led me within these walls. What do you fellows intend to do with yourselves? There is no use my knocking up Rose and the mother to-night, so I shall stay with you."

"We have nothing particular to do," I said.

"Then come up to the 'Anglais' with me. Two Edinburgh men are up there – Grant and Buckley. Will you come?"

"I am willing," said I.

"And I," said Henry.

So the bargain was concluded, and we all three repaired to the hotel, where we were introduced to Jack's friends, a couple of reckless, light-hearted medical students of his own kidney.

There is no reason why I should dwell upon the convivial evening which ensued. I have only alluded to these things as influencing the dark events which were impending.

It was close upon one o'clock before Henry Latour glanced at his watch, and announced that it was high time to break up.

"I must run over my part again to-morrow," he said. "You come along with me, Jack, and we can sleep together without disturbing anyone. I have a key."

"I'll walk round with you," said I; "I want to finish my pipe."

I am afraid that the sight of a certain window was becoming dearer to me than all the tobacco Virginia ever grew.

The brothers were delighted that I should come, so we bade our fellow countrymen adieu, and set off together.

We were a hilarious party as long as we kept to the well-lit Boulevards, but when we got into the quiet streets which branch off from them, a curious feeling of depression stole over us, which affected even the irrepressible Jack.

We strode on together, each buried in his own thoughts.

Everything was very still – so still that we all looked up in surprise when a closed carriage rattled past us, going in our own direction.

"That fellow is driving at a deuce of a rate," remarked Jack.

"Without lights either," I said.

"I wonder where he can be bound for? This is not much of a carriage neighbourhood, especially at such an hour."

"Well, anyway, he isn't going to visit us," laughed Henry; "so it's no business of ours."

And so saying, he quickened his pace, and we all three rounded the corner, and passed into the Rue Bertrand.

We were hardly round, before Jack stopped in amazement.

"Why, Harry!" he said; "what on earth is this? They just exactly *are* visiting us!"

There was no doubt about it. The moon had just come from behind a cloud, and was pouring a flood of cold light upon the dingy little street. And there, away down opposite number twenty-two, was a dark blur, which could be nothing but the carriage. It had pulled up.

"What is it?" said Henry.

"There are a couple of men on the pavement!"

"One of them has a lantern!"

"What a lark!" cried Jack. "It's my Edinburgh tailor, for a dollar!"

"They can't be burglars!" I whispered. "Let us watch them for a bit."

"By Heaven, there's ladder against a window — against Rose's window!" hissed a voice which we could hardly recognise as Henry's it was so altered.

The light fell upon his face, and I could see that it was dark with wrath, and that his jaw was fixed and hard, while his features worked spasmodically.

"The villains!" he said. "Come after me, but quietly!"

Swiftly and silently he started down the street.

Jack's rage was as great as his brother's, but he was of a less fiery disposition. He ground his teeth, and followed Henry with giant strides.

Had I been alone, I should have shouted my indignation, and hurried forward to the rescue. Henry Latour's was the leading mind among us, however, and it is on such occasions that mind asserts itself. There was something terrible in his very stillness.

We followed him implicitly down the road.

Rain had fallen during the evening, and the ground was very soft.

We made little noise as we approached the carriage. We might have made more without fear of detection, for the horses had been left to themselves, and the men we had seen were in the front garden, too much occupied with their own movements and those of their leader to be easily disturbed. The Rue de Bertrand was a *cul de sac*, and the possibility of being disturbed at their work was so slight as to be disregarded.

Henry slipped behind the carriage, and we followed him.

We were effectually concealed, and commanded a view of all that was going on in front of us.

Two of the men were standing at the foot of a ladder which was reared against one of the upper windows.

They were watching the movements of a third who appeared at that moment at the open casement bearing something on his arms.

My blood seemed to run in a fiery torrent through my veins as I saw the man place his foot upon the upper step and begin to descend. I glanced at Henry, but he held up his hand as if to ask for one more moment's forbearance. I could see that he knew as well as I did what the poor little white burden was which the man was clasping to his breast. I had lost sight of Jack, but a smothered curse from between the wheels showed me where he was crouching.

The leader came slowly and gingerly down the ladder. He must have been a powerful fellow, for the additional weight did not seem to inconvenience him. We could see that his face was covered with a mask. His friends below kept encouraging him in whispers.

He reached the bottom without an accident.

"Hurry her into the carriage!" he said.

Henry rose silently to his feet, with every muscle braced.

The time for action had arrived.

And at this very moment the prisoner's gag must have slipped, for a sweet, piteous voice rang out on the still night, – "Harry! Brother! Help!"

Never, surely, was an appeal so promptly answered. The spring was so swift, so sudden, that I never saw him leave my side. I heard a snarl like a wild beast's and a dull thud, and my friend with the man in the mask were rolling on the ground together.

It all happened in less time than I take to tell it. Jack and I ran forward to assist Rose into the house; but we were confronted by the two confederates.

I would have passed my antagonist in order to help the lady, but he flew at me with a savage oath, hitting wildly with both hands.

A Frenchman can never realise the fact that a segment is shorter than an arc; but I gave my opponent a practical illustration of the fact by stopping him with a facer before he could bring his hands round, and then toppling him over with what is known to the initiated as a Cribb's hit behind the ear.

He sat down upon a rose-bush with a very sickly smile, and manifested a strong disinclination to rise up; so I turned my attention to Jack.

I was just in time to see his adversary make a desperate attempt to practice the barbarous French *savate* upon him; but the student was a man of expedients, and springing aside, he seized the uplifted foot, and gave it a wrench, which brought the discomfited owner howling to the ground with a dislocated leg.

We led poor trembling Rose into the house, and after handing her over to her frightened mother, hurried back into the garden.

Neither of our acquaintances were in a condition to come up to time; but the struggle between their leader and Henry Latour was going on with unabated vigour.

It was useless to attempt to help our friend. They were so entwined, and revolving so rapidly upon the gravel walk, that it was impossible to distinguish the one from the other.

They were fighting in silence, and each was breathing hard.

But the clean living of the younger man began to tell. He had the better stamina of the two.

I saw the glint of the moonlight upon his sleeve-links as he freed his arm, and then I heard the sound of a heavy blow. It seemed to stun his antagonist for a moment; but before it could be repeated he had shaken himself free, and both men staggered to their feet.

The mask had been torn off, and exposed the pale face of the Frenchman, with a thin stream of blood coursing down it from a wound on the forehead.

"You infernal scoundrel! I know you now!" yelled Henry, and would have sprung at him again had we not restrained him.

"*Ma foi!* you'll know me better before you die!" hissed the man, with a sinister smile.

"You accursed villain! do you think I fear your threats? I'll fight you now if you wish; I have weapons! Run in for the pistols, Jack!"

"Quietly, old man – quietly," said I; "don't do anything rash."

"Rash!" raved Henry. "Why, man, it was my sister! Give me a pistol!"

"It is for me to name the time and place," said Lablas; for he it was. "It is I who have been struck."

"When, then?"

"You shall hear from me in the morning. Suffice it that you shall be chastised before all Paris. I shall make a public warning of you, my young friend."

And with the same hard smile upon his face, he mounted upon the box, and seized the reins.

"If this gentleman whose joint I have had the pleasure of damaging considers himself aggrieved," said Jack, "he shall always find me ready to make any amends in my power."

"The same applies to my friend on the right," said I. "I refer to the gentleman with the curious swelling under his ear."

Our friends only answered our kind attentions by a volley of curses.

The patron of the *savate* was hoisted into the carriage, and the other followed him; while Lablas, still white with passion, drove furiously off, amid laughter from Jack and myself and curses from Henry, whose fiery blood was too thoroughly roused to allow him to view the matter in its ridiculous aspect.

"Nothing like evaporating lotions for bruises," was the practical piece of advice which our medical student shouted after them as the carriage rumbled away like a dark nightmare, and the sound of its wheels died gradually in the distance.

At this moment a gendarme, true to the traditions of his order, hurried on to the scene of action; but after jotting down the number of the house in a portentous note-book, he gave up the attempt of extracting any information from us, and departed with many shrugs.

My heart was heavy as I trudged back to my hotel that night. There is always a reaction after such excitement, and I was uneasy at the thought of what the morrow might bring forth.

The allusion which Henry had made in the early part of the evening to the duelling proclivities of Lablas, and in particular to the sinister result of his encounter with the young French officer, had not been forgotten by me.

I knew the wild blood which ran in my friend's veins, and that it would be hopeless to attempt to dissuade him from a meeting. I was powerless, and must let events take their own course.

IV

When I came down to breakfast in the morning I found the two brothers waiting for me. Henry looked bright and almost exultant as he greeted me, but Jack was unusually serious.

"It's all right, old fellow," said the young actor.

"Yes; look here, Barker," explained Jack, evidently in considerable perturbation. "It's a most extraordinary business. The queerest challenge I ever heard of, though I confess that my experience of these things is very limited. I suppose we cannot get out of it?"

"Not for the world!" cried his brother.

"See here," said Jack; "this is the note I got. Read it for yourself."

It was addressed to the student, and ran thus:—

"Sir,–

"On the understanding that you act as second to Mr. Henry Latour, allow me to state that in the exercise of his right M. Lablas selects rapiers as his weapon. He begs you to accompany your principal to the theatre to-night, where you will be admitted to the stage as a supernumerary. You can thus satisfy yourself that the final scene is fought according to the strict rules of the duello. The rapiers will be substituted for stage foils without difficulty. I shall be present on behalf of M. Lablas. I have the honour to remain very sincerely yours,

"PIERRE GROSSIERE."

"What do you think of that?" said Jack.

"Why, I think that it is a preposterous idea, and that you should refuse."

"It wouldn't do," said Henry. "They would try and construe it into cowardice. Besides, what does it matter where I meet the fellow so long as I *do* meet him? I tell you, Barker," he continued, laying his hand upon my arm, "that when I do, I intend to kill him!"

There was something resolute in the ring of my friend's voice. I felt that, in spite of his advantages, Lablas would meet with a dangerous opponent.

"If you should fall, Henry," said Jack, "I will take your place, and either lick the blackguard or never leave the stage. It would make a sensation to have *Hamlet* run through by a super-numerary, wouldn't it?"

And he gave the ghost of a smile.

"Well, write an acceptance at once, Jack," said Henry. "My only fear is that my sister's name should get mixed up in the matter."

"No fear of that," said I. "It would not be their interest to talk about the ridiculous *fiasco* they have made."

"You will come to the National to-night, Barker?" asked Henry. "You can get a place in the front row of the stalls."

"I will," said I; "and if you should both fail to avenge your sister, Lablas will have to reckon with me before the curtain falls."

"You are a good fellow, Barker," said Henry. "Well," he added, after a pause, "my private quarrel mustn't interfere with my duty to the public, so I'll go back and read my part over. Good-bye, old man! We shall see you to-night."

And the brothers left me alone to my coffee.

How they got through the day I do not know. I should think even imperturbable Jack found the hours hung rather heavily upon his hands.

As for myself, I was in a fever of suspense. I could only pace up and down the crowded streets, and wait for the evening to come.

The doors did not open until seven o'clock, but the half-hour found me waiting at the entrance to the National.

A knot of enthusiasts, eager to secure places, were already clustering round it. I spent the time in perusing a poster, which was suspended to one of the pillars.

"Lablas" was written across it in great capitals, while in smaller print below there were a few other names, that of Henry Latour being one of them.

It seemed as if the door would never open. There is an end to all things, however, and the hour struck at last. We filed into the theatre one after another, in the orderly French fashion.

I was fortunate enough to secure what I wanted – namely, a centre seat in the front row.

Nothing but the orchestra intervened between me and the footlights. I would have given anything to have seen Jack now – to have had anyone with whom I could exchange a word on the topic which was nearest my heart; but my immediate neighbours were a stolid English manager, who had come over in the hope of picking up something worth imparting, and an enthusiastic young lady with her elderly mamma.

I had learned, even in our short acquaintance, to regard Henry as a dear friend; but I think it was the idea of his sister which gave me such a sinking at the heart, when I thought of the deadly science and diabolical vindictiveness of Lablas.

During the overture I was far too preoccupied to pay much attention to my neighbour the manager, who was pouring into my ears his views of the French stage.

"We can't approach them on 'touch-and-go' comedy," he said; "it's their strong point; but when it comes to Shakespeare, they are lost, sir – utterly lost. If you had seen the *Hamlets* I have seen – Macready, sir, and the older Kean –"

But here his reminiscences were providentially cut short by the rise of the curtain.

The first few scenes were tame enough. The translation lacked the rugged strength and force of our own glorious language. Old theatre goers became restless in their seats, and whispered that there was something amiss with their favourite actor.

His eye seemed to rest upon me with a dark and threatening scowl. The black, tight-fitting dress showed off his splendid figure to advantage, and was admirably adapted, as I could not help thinking, for the second and more tragic part which he was about to play.

My spirits revived when Henry entered. He looked cool and at his ease, though I could see a dangerous light in his eye when he glanced towards his brother actor.

The spirit and fire of his elocution semed to captivate his hearers. From pit to gallery there was not one who did not sympathise with the gallant young Danish nobleman, and he was applauded to the echo.

Hamlet was forgotten in *Laertes*. I shall never forget the torrent of indignation which rang out in the words–

"A sister driven into desperate terms.
Whose worth, if praises may go back again,
Stood challenger on mount of all the age
For her perfections. But my revenge will come."

"By Jove, sir!" said the manager, *sotto voce*; "those last words were nature itself."

Henry was called before the curtain at the end of the fourth act; but it was in the scene at *Ophelia*'s grave that he surpassed himself. His howl of "The devil take thy soul!" as he sprang at *Hamlet*'s throat, fairly brought down the house, and caused me involuntarily to spring to my feet; but he seemed to recollect himself in time, and shook himself clear of his rival.

Hamlet's invective, too was the strongest point in his character. The vast audience seemed to hang on every word which passed between them.

"You'll get an English actor to make more stage points," said the manager; "but there's a confounded naturalness about all this which is wonderful!"

His dramatic instinct had told him that, in spite of his forty years' experience, there was something here which he had never met before.

And now there was a great hush in the house as the curtain rose upon the final scene. It was magnificently put upon the stage. The rude, barbaric pomp of the Danish Court was pictured to the life. The king and queen were seated in the background, under a canopy of purple velvet, lined with ermine. The walls of the royal banquet-hall were gorgeous with strange trophies, supposed to have been brought from afar by Viking hands.

There was a clear space in the centre, and at either side a swarm of men-at-arms, courtiers, and all the hangers-on of the royal household.

Laertes was leaning carelessly against a pillar, while *Hamlet* stood with a smile of confidence upon his face, conversing with a courtier.

Beside *Laertes* I could see Jack Latour, got up in a suit of armour which was ridiculously out of proportion to his brawny limbs. There was a look upon his face, however, that would have forbidden a laugh at his expense.

To me the excitement was agonising, and all over the house a strange interest began to manifest itself in the proceedings.

Not a sound could be heard over the great theatre as *Osric* came tripping forward with the bundle of foils.

I surmised that the rapiers were lying among them, for *Hamlet* took some little time to satisfy himself, though *Laertes* seemed to choose his weapon without a moment's hesitation.

"Gad!" said the manager; "look at the man's eyes! I tell you it's unique!"

The salute was given, and the courtier with whom Lablas had been speaking drew up to his principal, while Jack took up his position behind his brother.

His honest face was pale with anxiety, and I could see that instead of the double-edged Danish sword, he had a delicate rapier slung to his side. I knew what was meant by that.

I turned away my eyes as the two men approached each other; but I glanced round again involuntarily as I heard a quick stamp, and the sharp ring of steel.

The silence was so profound that you might have heard the breathing of the combatants at the extreme end of the pit.

I caught a glimpse of the dark, savage face of Lablas, and the tall, lithe figure of his antagonist, and I turned my eyes away again from sheer nervousness.

Then there came a momentary cessation in the clash of the swords, and I heard the manager say, "The deception is admirable. You'd swear there was blood running down the leg of *Laertes*. Capital! capital! The business is perfect!"

I shuddered, and looked up again as they sprang at each other for the second time, and my eyes were riveted upon the stage for the remainder of the conflict.

The combatants were very evenly matched; first one, and then the other, seemed to gain a temporary advantage. The profound science of Lablas was neutralised by the fire and fury of his antagonist's attack.

I could see from Henry's face that he had determined to bring matters to a crisis. To kill or be killed had become his one idea.

He rushed at his opponent so furiously that he drove him back among the crowd of courtiers. I saw Lablas give a deadly lunge under the guard, which Henry took through his left arm; and then I saw my friend spring in, and there was a groan and a spurt of blood as *Hamlet, Prince of Denmark*, tottered forwards to the footlights and fell heavily upon his face.

The effect upon the audience was electrical. There was a hush for a moment, and then, from pit to boxes, and from boxes to gallery, there went up a cheer so spontaneous and so universal, that it was like the mighty voice of one man. The whole house sprang to its feet with round after round of applause.

It was the finest illusion of the year – it was the best *coup de theatre*, and most realistic stage duel that had ever been fought. But the English manager shuddered as he caught me convulsively by the wrist, and said, in an awe-struck whisper, "*I saw it come out at his back!*"

Yes, it was the finest illusion of the year; and still the audience applauded and applauded.

Surely he will rise and bow his acknowledgments? One more cheer may do it. But no; he lies there stiff and stark, with a scowl upon his white face, and his life-blood trickling down the boards.

And now there is a hot, heavy smell in the orchestra, which was surely never caused by a stage illusion. Why is that young man gesticulating so? A little crimson pool has trickled upon his music book, and he sees that it is still dripping down, liquid and warm.

And a hush comes over the pit, while the boxes are still applauding; and then the boxes grow quiet, and strange whispers go about. Then the audience above become silent, too, and a great stillness falls upon the theatre, and the heavy brown curtain is rolled down.

"Well, my boy," said Jack, when I met him, "it was all very terrible, but it ended right."

"Won't there be an inquiry into the matter?"

"No, not a bit. The initiated know that it was all fair play, and the rest are under the impression that a button slipped, or a foil snapped. Henry's name as an actor is made for ever – that's some consolation."

"How is he?" I asked.

"Oh, well enough to see company. You must come along and dine with us. He has a slight wound in the leg, and is run through the biceps; but there is no damage done. Rose and the mother are terribly cut up, but, of course, they think it was all an accident. They shall never know the truth."

And now, before I conclude, let me sketch another scene. It is that solemn and orthodox ritual with which fiction usually, and fact occasionally, as in the present instance, terminates. A man and a woman are kneeling at the foot of an altar, while a clergyman is pronouncing the words that refute the commonly-received doctrine that one and one are two. You will have no difficulty in recognising the pretty little girlish bride; she is altered but little since we saw her six months ago. The bridegroom is – No, most astute and sagacious reader, it is *not* myself; it is a young French officer of cavalry, with a boyish smile, and the scar of a bullet upon his left breast.

THE LONELY HAMPSHIRE COTTAGE

———◆———

John Ranter, ex-landlord of the "Battle of Dettingen" public-house in Southampton, was not a man whom one would desire as a friend, and still less would one relish him as a foe. Tall and strong in his person, dark and saturnine in his disposition, the two-and-fifty years which had passed over John's head had done little to soften his character or to modify his passions. Perhaps the ill-fortune which had attended him through life had something to do with his asperity, yet this same ill-fortune had been usually caused by his own violent and headstrong temper. He had quarrelled with his parents when a lad, and left them. After working his way up in the world, to some extent, he had fallen in love with a pretty face, and mated himself to a timid, characterless woman, who was a drag rather than a help to him. The fruit of this union had been a single son; but John Ranter beat the lad savagely for some trivial offence, and he had fled away to sea as a cabin-boy, and was reported to have been drowned in the great wreck of the *Queen of the West*. From that time the publican went rapidly down-hill. He offended his customers by his morose and sullen temper, and they ceased to frequent the "Battle of Dettingen," until, at last, he was compelled to dispose of the business. With the scanty proceeds he purchased a small house upon the Portsmouth and Southampton road, about three miles from the latter town, and settled down with his wife to a gloomy and misanthropic existence.

Strange tales were told of that lonely cottage, with its bare brick walls and great, overhanging thatch, from under which the diamond-paned windows seemed to scowl at the passers-by. Waggoners at roadside inns talked of the dark-faced, grizzly-haired man, who lounged all day in the little garden which adjoined the road, and of the pale, patient face, which peered out at them sometimes through the half-opened door. There were darker things, too, of which they had to speak, of angry voices, of the dull thud of blows, and the cries of a woman in distress. However tired the horses might be, they were whipped up into a trot, when, after nightfall, they came near the wooden gate which led up to that ill-omened dwelling.

It was one lovely autumn evening that John Ranter leaned his elbows upon that identical gate, and puffed meditatively at his black clay pipe. He was pondering within himself as to what his future should be. Should he continue to exist in the way in which he was doing, or should he embark what little capital he had in some attempt to better his fortunes? His present life, if unambitious, was at least secure. It was possible that he might lose all in a new venture. Yet, on the other hand, John felt that he still had all the energy of youth, and was as able as ever to turn his hand to anything. If his son, he reflected, who had left him fifteen years before had been alive, he might have been of assistance to him now. A vague longing for the comforts which he had enjoyed in more fortunate days filled and unsettled his mind. He was still brooding over the matter when, looking up, he saw, against the setting sun, a man dressed in a long grey overcoat, who was striding down the road from the direction of Southampton.

It was no uncommon thing for pedestrians of every type to pass the door of John Ranter, and yet this particular one attracted his attention to an unusual degree. He was a tall, athletic young fellow, with a yellow moustache, and a face which was tanned by exposure to the sun and weather. His hat was a peculiar slouched one, of soft felt, and it may have been this, or it may have been the grey coat, which caused the ex-publican to look closely at him. Over his shoulder the stranger had a broad leather strap, and to this was attached a large black bag, something like those which are worn by bookmakers upon a race-course. Indeed, John Ranter's first impression was that the traveller belonged to the betting fraternity.

When the young fellow came near the gate, he slowed down his pace, and looked irresolutely about him. Then he halted, and addressed John, speaking in a peculiar metallic voice.

"I say, mate," he said; "I guess I'd have to walk all night if I wanted to make Portsmouth in the morning?"

"I guess you would," the other answered, surlily, mimicking the stranger's tone and pronunciation. "You've hardly got started yet."

"Well now, that beats everything," the traveller said, impatiently. "I'd ha' put up at an inn in Southampton if I dared. To think o' my spending my first night in the old country like that!"

"And why dar'n't you put up at an inn?" John Ranter asked.

The stranger winked one of his shrewd eyes at John.

"There ain't such a very long way between an innkeeper and a thief," he said; "anyway, there's not in Californey, and I guess human natur' is human natur' all the world over. When I've got what's worth keepin' I give the inns a wide berth."

"Oh, you've got what's worth keeping, have you?" said the old misanthrope to himself, and he relaxed the grimness of his features as far as he could, and glanced out of the corner of his eyes at the black leather bag.

"Ye see, it's this way," the young man said, confidentially; "I've been out at the diggings, first in Nevada and then in Californey, and I've struck it, and struck it pretty rich too, you bet. When I allowed that I'd made my pile, I pushed for home in the *Marie Rose* from 'Frisco to Southampton. She got in at three to-day, but those sharks at the customs kept us till five 'fore we could get ashore. When I landed I let out for Portsmouth, where I used to know some folk; but you see I didn't quite reckon up how far it was before I started. Besides, this bag ain't quite the thing a man would lug about with him if he was walkin' for a wager."

"Are your friends expecting you in Portsmouth?" John Ranter asked.

The young man laid down his bag, and laughed so heartily that he had to lean against the gate for support.

"That's where the joke comes in," he cried; "they don't know that I've left the States."

"Oh, that's the joke, is it?"

"Yes; that's the joke. You see, they are all sitting at breakfast, maybe, or at dinner, as the case might be, and I pushes my way in, and I up with this here bag and opens it, and then ker-whop down comes the whole lot on the table;" and the young man laughed heartily once more over the idea.

"The whole lot of what?" asked John.

"Why, of shiners, of course – dollars, you understand."

"And d'ye mean to say you carry your whole fortune about with you in gold?" Ranter asked in amazement.

"My whole fortune! No, boss, I reckon not. The bulk of it is in notes and shares, and they're all packed away right enough. This is just eight hundred dollars that I put to one side for this same little game that I spoke of. But I suppose it's no use trying to get there to-night, and I'll have to trust to an inn after all."

"Don't you do that," the elder man said, earnestly. "They are a rough lot in the inns about here, and there's many a poor sailor found his pockets as empty in the morning as they were the day he sailed out of port. You find some honest man and ask him for a night's lodging; that's the best thing you can do."

"Well, pard, I guess I've lost my bearings in this neighbourhood," the gold-digger said. "If you can put me on the track of any such berth as you speak of, I'd be beholden to you."

"Why, for that matter," John Ranter said, "we have a spare bed of our own, and should be very glad if you would pass the night in it. We are simple folk, my wife and I; but as far as a fire and a warm supper go, you're very welcome to both the one and the other."

"Well, you can't say fairer than that," the traveller responded, and he walked up the little gravel walk with his companion, while the shadow of night spread slowly over the landscape, and the owl hooted mournfully in the neighbouring wood.

Mrs. Ranter, who had been a comely lass thirty years before, was now a white-haired, melancholy woman, with a wan face and a timid manner. She welcomed the stranger in a nervous, constrained fashion, and proceeded to cook some rashers of bacon, which she cut from a great side which hung from the rafters of the rude kitchen. The young man deposited his bag under a chair, and then, sitting down above it, he drew out his pipe and lit it. Ranter filled his again at the same time, eyeing his companion furtively all the while from under his heavy eye-brows.

"You'd best take your coat off," he said, in an off-hand way.

"No; I'll keep it on, if you don't mind," the other returned. "I never take this coat off."

"Please yourself," said John, puffing at his pipe; "I thought maybe you'd find it hot with this fire burning; but then, Californey is a hot place, I'm told, and maybe you find England chilly?"

The other did not answer, and the two men sat silently watching the rashers, which grizzled and sputtered upon the pan.

"What sort o' ship did you come in?" the host asked, at last.

"The *Marie Rose*," said the other. "She's a three-masted schooner, and came over with hides and other goods. She's not much to look at, but she's no slouch of a sea boat. We'd a gale off Cape Horn that would have tried any ship that ever sailed. Three days under a single double-reefed topsail, and that was rather more than she could carry. Am I in your way, missus?"

"No, no," said Mrs. Ranter, hurriedly. The stranger had been looking at her very hard while he spoke.

"I guess the skipper and the mates will wonder what has become of me," he continued. "I was in such a hurry that I came off without a word to one of them. However, my traps are on board, so they'll know I've not deserted them for good."

"Did you speak to anyone after you left the ship?" Ranter asked, carelessly.

"No."

"Why didn't you take a trap if you wanted to get to Portsmouth?"

"Mate, you've never come ashore from a long sea voyage, else you'd not ask me that question. Why, man, it's the greatest pleasure you can have to stretch your legs, and keep on stretching them. I'd have padded on right enough if the light had held."

"You'll be a deal better in a comfortable bed," said Ranter; "and now the supper's ready, so let us fall to. Here's beer in the jug, and there's whisky in that bottle, so it's your own fault if you don't help yourself."

The three gathered round the table and made an excellent meal. Under the influence of their young guest's genial face and cheery conversation, the mistress of the house lost her haggard appearance, and even made one or two timid attempts to join in the talk. The country postman, coming home from his final round, stopped in astonishment when he saw the blazing light in the cottage window, and heard the merry sound of laughter which pealed out on the still night air.

If any close observer had been watching the little party as they sat round the table, he might have remarked that John Ranter showed a very lively curiosity in regard to the long grey coat in which his visitor was clad. Not only did he eye that garment narrowly from time to time, but he twice found pretexts to pass close to the other's chair, and each time he did so he drew his hand, as though accidentally, along the side of the overcoat. Neither the young man nor the hostess appeared, however, to take the slightest notice of this strange conduct upon the part of the ex-publican.

After supper the two men drew their chairs up to the fire once more, while the old woman removed the dishes. The traveller's conversation turned principally upon the wonders of California and of the great republic in which he had spent the best part of his life. He spoke of the fortunes which were made at the mines, too, and of the golden store which may be picked up by whoever is lucky enough to find it, until Ranter's eyes sparkled again as he listened.

"How much might it take to get out there?" he said.

"Oh! a hundred pounds or so would start you comfortably," answered the man with the grey coat.

"That doesn't seem much."

"Why anyone should stay in England while there is money to be picked up there is more than I can understand," the miner remarked. "And now, mate, you'll excuse me, but I'm a man that likes to go to roost early and be up at cock-crow. If the missus here would show me my room I'd be obliged."

"Won't you have another whisky? No? Ah! well, good-night. Lizzie, you will show Mr. — Mr. —"

"Mr. Goodall," said the other.

"You will show Mr. Goodall up to his room. I hope you'll sleep well."

"I always sleep sound," said the man with the grey coat; and, with a nod, he tramped heavily, bag in hand, up the wooden staircase, while the old woman toiled along with the light in front of him.

When he had gone, John Ranter put both his hands into his trousers pockets, stretched out his legs, and stared gloomily into the fire, with a wrinkled brow and projecting lips. A great many thoughts were passing through his mind — so many that he did not hear his wife re-enter the kitchen, nor did he answer her when she spoke to him. It was half-past ten when the visitor retired, and at twelve John Ranter was still bending over the smouldering heap of ashes with the same look of thought upon his face. It was only when his wife asked him whether he was not going to bed that he appeared to come to himself.

"No, Lizzie," he said, in a more conciliatory tone than was usual with him. "We'll both stay up a short time to-night."

"All right, John," the poor woman said, with a glad smile. It was many a year since he had ever asked her for her company.

"Is he upstairs all right?"

"Who? Oh, Mr. Goodall? Yes; I showed him into the spare room."

"D'ye think he's asleep?"

"I suppose so, John. He's been there nigh an hour and a half."

"Is there a key in the door?"

"No, dear; but what queer questions you do ask."

John Ranter was silent for a time.

"Lizzie," he said at last, taking up the poker, and playing with it nervously, "in the whole world there is no one who knows that that man came here to-night. If he never left us again no one would know what had become of him, or care to make any search after him."

His wife said nothing, but she turned white to her very lips.

"He has eight hundred dollars in that bag, Lizzie, which makes over a hundred and fifty pound of our money. But he has more than that. He's got lumps of gold sewn into the lining of that grey coat of his. That's why he didn't care about taking it off. I saw the knobs, and I managed to feel 'em too. That money, my girl, would be enough to take the two of us out to that same country where he picked all this up –"

"For Heaven's sake, John," cried his wife, flinging herself at his feet, and clasping his knees with her arms, "for my sake – for the sake of our boy, who might be about this young man's age – think no more of this! We are old, John, and, rich or poor, we must in a few short years go to our long home. Don't go with the stain of blood upon you. Oh, spare him! We have been bad, but never so bad as this!"

But John Ranter continued to gaze over his wife's head into the fire, and the set sternness of his features never relaxed for one moment. It seemed to her, as she looked up into his eyes, that a strange new expression had come into them such as she had never seen before – the baleful, lurid glare of the beast of prey.

"This is a chance," he said, "such as would never come to us again. How many would be glad to have it! Besides, Lizzie, it is my life or this man's. You remember what Dr. Cousins said of me when we were at Portsea. I was liable to apoplexy, he said, and disappointment, or hardships or grief, might bring it on. This wretched life has enough of all three. Now if we had the money, we could start afresh, and all would be well. I tell you, wife, I shall do it!" and he clenched his large brown hand round the poker.

"You must not, John – and you shall not."

"I shall, and I will. Leave go of my knees."

He was about to push her from him when he perceived that she had fainted. Picking her up he carried her to the side of the room and laid her down there. Then he went back, and taking up the poker he balanced it in his hand. It seemed to strike him as being too light, for he went into the scullery, and after groping about in the dark he came back with a small axe. He was swinging this backwards and forwards when his eye fell upon the knife which his wife had used before supper in cutting the rashers of bacon. He ran his finger along the edge of it. It was as keen as a razor. "It's handier and surer!" he muttered; and going to the cupboard he drank off a large glass of raw whisky, after which he kicked off his boots and began silently to ascend the old-fashioned stair.

There were twelve steps which led up from the kitchen to a landing, and from the landing eight more to the bedroom of their guest. John Ranter was nearly half an hour in ascending those first twelve. The woodwork was rotten, and the construction weak, so that they creaked under the weight of the heavy man. He would first put his right foot lightly upon the board, and gradually increase the pressure upon it until his whole weight was there. Then he would carefully move up his left foot, and stand listening breathlessly for any sound from above. Nothing broke the silence, however, except the dull ticking of the clock in the kitchen behind him and the melancholy hooting of an owl among the shrubbery. In the dull, uncertain light there was something terrible in this vague, dark figure creeping slowly up the little staircase – moving, pausing, crouching, but always coming nearer the top.

When he reached the landing he could see the door of the young miner's room. John Ranter stood aghast. The door was on the jar, and through the narrow opening there shone a thin golden stream. The light was still burning. Did it mean that the traveller was awake? John listened intently, but there was no sound of any movement in the room. For a long time he strained his ears, but all was perfectly still.

"If he were awake," John said to himself, "he would have turned in his bed, or made some rustling during this time."

Then he began stealthily to ascend the eight remaining steps until he was immediately outside the bedroom door. Still all was silent within. No doubt it was one of his foreign customs to leave the light burning during the night. He had mentioned in conversation that he was a sound sleeper. Ranter began to fear that unless he got it over soon his wife might recover and raise an alarm. Clutching his knife in his right hand, he quietly pushed the door a little more open with his left and inserted his head. Something cold pressed against his temple as he did so. It was the muzzle of a revolver.

"Come in, John Ranter," said the quiet voice of his guest; "but first drop your weapon, or I shall be compelled to fire. You are at my mercy."

Indeed, the ex-publican's head was caught in such a way that it was difficult for him either to withdraw or to force his way in. He gave a deep groan of rage and disappointment, and his knife clattered down upon the floor.

"I meant no harm," he said, sulkily, as he entered the room.

"I have been expecting you for a couple of hours," the man with the grey coat said, holding his pistol still cocked in his right hand, so that he might use it if necessary. He was dressed exactly as he had been when he went upstairs, and the ill-fated bag was resting upon the unruffled bed. "I knew that you were coming."

"How – how?" John stammered.

"Because I know you; because I saw murder in your eye when

you stood before me at the gate; because I saw you feel my coat here for the nuggets. That is why I waited up for you."

"You have no proof against me," said John Ranter, sullenly.

"I do not want any. I could shoot you where you stand, and the law would justify me. Look at that bag upon the bed there. I told you there was money in it. What d'ye think I brought that money to England for? It was to give it to you – yes, to you. And that grey coat on me is worth five hundred pounds; that was for you also. Ah! you begin to understand now. You begin to see the mistake you have made."

John Ranter had staggered against the wall, and his face was all drawn down on one side.

"Jack!" he gasped. "Jack!"

"Yes; Jack Ranter – your son. That's who I am." The young man turned back his sleeve, and bared a blue device upon his forearm. "Don't you remember Hairy Pete put that 'J.R.' on when I was a lad? Now you know me. I made my fortune, and I came back, earnestly hoping that you would help me to spend it. I called at the 'Battle of Dettingen,' and they told me where to find you. Then, when I saw you at the gate, I thought I'd test my mother and you, and see if you were the same as ever. I came to make you happy, and you have tried to murder me. I shall not punish you; but I shall go, and you shall never see either me or my money any more."

While the young man had been saying these words, a series of twitchings and horrible contortions had passed over the face of his father, and at the last words he took a step forward, raising his hands above his head, and fell, with a hoarse cry, upon the ground. His eyes became glazed, his breathing stertorous, and foam stood upon his purple lips. It did not take much medical knowledge to see that he was dying. His son stooped over him and loosened his collar and shirt.

"One last question," he said, in quick, earnest tones. "Did my mother aid in this attempt?"

John Ranter appeared to understand the import of it, for he shook his head; and so, with this single act of justice, his dark spirit fled from this world of crime. The doctor's warning had come true, and emotion had hastened a long-impending apoplexy. His son lifted him reverentially on to the bed, and did such last offices as could be done.

"Perhaps it is the best thing that could have happened," he said, sadly, as he turned from the room, and went down to seek his mother, and to comfort her in her sore affliction.

*   *   *

Young John Ranter returned to America, and by his energy and talents soon became one of the richest men in his State. He has definitely settled there now, and will return no more to the old country. In his palatial residence there dwells a white-haired, anxious-faced old woman, whose every wish is consulted, and to whom the inmates show every reverence. This is old Mrs. Ranter; and her son has hopes that with time, and among new associations, she may come to forget that terrible night when the man with the grey coat paid a visit to the lonely Hampshire cottage.

THE FATE OF THE EVANGELINE

I

My wife and I often laugh when we happen to glance at some of the modern realistic sensational stories, for, however strange and exciting they may be we invariably come to the conclusion that they are tame compared to our own experiences when life was young with us.

More than once, indeed, she has asked me to write the circumstances down, but when I considered how few people there are in England who might remember the *Evangeline* or care to know the real history of her disappearance, it has seemed to me to be hardly worth while to revive the subject. Even here in Australia, however, we do occasionally see some reference to her in the papers or magazines, so that it is evident that there are those who have not quite forgotten the strange story: and so at this merry Christmastide I am tempted to set the matter straight.

At the time her fate excited a most intense and lively interest all over the British Islands, as was shown by the notices in the newspapers and by numerous letters which appeared upon the subject. As an example of this, as well as to give the facts in a succinct form, I shall preface this narrative by a few clippings chosen from many which we collected after the event, which are so numerous that my wife has filled a small scrapbook with them. This first one is from the "Inverness Gazette" of September 24th, 1873.

"PAINFUL OCCURRENCE IN THE HEBRIDES. — A sad accident, which it is feared has been attended with loss of life, has occurred at Ardvoe, which is a small uninhabited island lying about forty miles north-west of Harris and about half that distance south of the Flannons. It appears that a yacht named the Evangeline, belonging to Mr. Scholefield, jun., the son of the well-known banker of the firm Scholefield, Davies, and Co., had put in there, and that the passengers, with the two seamen who formed the crew, had pitched two tents upon the beach, in which they camped out for two or three days. This they did no doubt out of admiration for the rugged beauty of the spot, and perhaps from a sense of the novelty of their situation upon this lonely island. Besides Mr. Scholefield there were on the *Evangeline* a young lady named Miss Lucy Forrester, who is understood to be his fiancée, and her father, Colonel Forrester, of Teddington, near London. As the weather was very warm, the two gentlemen remained upon shore during the night, sleeping in one tent, while the seamen occupied the other. The young lady, however, was in the habit of rowing back to the yacht in the dinghy and sleeping in her own cabin, coming back by the same means in the morning. One day, the third of their residence upon the island, Colonel Forrester, looking out of the tent at dawn, was astonished and horrified to see that the moorings of the boat had given way, and that she was drifting rapidly out to sea. He promptly gave the alarm, and Mr. Scholefield, with one of the sailors, attempted to swim out to her, but they found that the yacht, owing to the fresh breeze and the fact that one of the sails had been so clumsily furled as to offer a considerable surface to the wind, was making such headway that it was impossible to overtake her. When last seen she was drifting along in a west-sou'-westerly direction with the unfortunate young lady on board. To make matters worse, it was three days before the party on the island were able to communicate with a passing fishing-boat and inform them of the sad occurrence. Both before and since, the weather has been so tempestuous that there is little hope of the safety of the missing yacht. We hear, however, that a reward of a thousand pounds has been offered by the firm of Scholefield to the boat which finds her and of five thousand to the one which brings Miss Forrester back in safety. Apart from any recompense, however, we are sure that the chivalry of our brave fishermen will lead them to do everything in their power to succour this young lady, who is said to possess personal charms of the highest order. Our only grain of consolation is that the Evangeline was well provided both with provisions and with water."

This appeared upon September 24th, four days after the disappearance of the yacht. Upon the 25th the following telegram was sent from the north of Ireland:

"Portrush. — John Mullins, of this town, fisherman, reports that upon the morning of the 21st he sighted a yacht which answered to the description of the missing Evangeline. His own boat was at that time about fifty miles to the north of Malin Head, and was hove-to, the weather being very thick and dirty. The yacht passed within two hundred yards of his starboard quarter, but the fog was so great that he could not swear to her appearance. She was running in a westerly direction under a reefed mainsail and jib. *There was a man at the tiller*. He distinctly saw a woman on board, and thinks that she called out to him, but could not be sure owing to the howling of the wind."

I have many other extracts here expressive of the doubts and fears which existed as to the fate of the Evangeline, but I shall not quote one more than is necessary. Here is the Central News telegram which quashed the last lingering hopes of the most sanguine. It went the round of the papers upon the 3rd of October.

"Galway, October 2nd, 7.25 p.m. – The fishing boat Glenmullet has just come in, towing behind her a mass of wreckage, which leaves no doubt as to the fate of the unfortunate Evangeline and of the young lady who was on board of her. The fragments brought in consist of the bowsprit, figurehead, and part of the bows, with the name engraved upon it. From its appearance it is conjectured that the yacht was blown on to one of the dangerous reefs upon the north-west coast, and that after being broken up there this and possibly other fragments had drifted out to sea. Attached to it is a fragment of the fatal rope, the snapping of which was the original cause of the disaster. It is a stout cable of manilla hemp, and the fracture is a clean one – so clean as to suggest friction against a very sharp rock or the cut of a knife. Several boats have gone up and down the coast this evening in the hope of finding some more *débris* or of ascertaining with certainty the fate of the young lady."

From that day to this, however, nothing fresh has been learned of the fate of the *Evangeline* or of Miss Lucy Forrester, who was on board of her. These three extracts represent all that has ever been learned about either of them, and in these even there are several statements which the press at the time showed to be incredible. For example, how could the fisherman John Mullins say that he saw a man on board when Ardvoe is an uninhabited island, and therefore no one could possibly have got on board except Miss Forrester? It was clear that he was either mistaken in the boat or else that he imagined the man. Again, it was pointed out in a leader in the "Scotsman" that the conjecture that the rope was either cut by a rock or by a knife was manifestly absurd, since there are no rocks around Ardvoe, but a uniform sandy bottom, and it would be preposterous to suppose that Miss Forrester, who was a lady as remarkable for her firmness of mind as for her beauty, would deliberately sever the rope which attached her to her father, her lover, and to life itself. "It would be well," the "Scotsman" concluded, "if those who express opinions upon such subjects would bear in mind those simple rules as to the analysis of evidence laid down by Auguste Dupin. 'Exclude the impossible,' he remarks in one of Poe's immortal stories, 'and what is left, however improbable, *must* be the truth.' Now, since it is impossible that a rock divided the rope, and impossible that the young lady divided it, and doubly impossible that anybody else divided it, it follows that it parted of its own accord, either owing to some flaw in its texture or from some previous injury that it may have sustained. Thus this sad occurrence, about which conjecture is so rife, sinks at once into the category of common accidents, which, however deplorable, can neither be foreseen nor prevented."

There was one other theory which I shall just allude to before I commence my own personal narrative. That is the suggestion that either of the two sailors had had a spite against Mr. Scholefield or Colonel Forrester and had severed the rope out of revenge. That, however, is quite out of the question, for they were both men of good character and old servants of the Scholefields. My wife tells me that it is mere laziness which makes me sit with the scrapbook before me copying out all these old newspaper articles and conjectures. It is certainly the easiest way to tell my story, but I must now put them severely aside and tell you in my own words as concisely as I can what the real facts were.

*　　*　　*

My name is John Vincent Gibbs, and I am the son of Nathaniel Gibbs, formerly a captain in one of the West Indian regiments. My father was a very handsome man, and he succeeded in winning the heart of a Miss Leblanche, who was heiress to a good sugar plantation in Demerara. By this marriage my father became fairly rich, and, having left the army, he settled down to the life of a planter. I was born within a year of the marriage, but my mother never rose again from her bed, and my father was so broken-hearted at his loss that he pined away and followed her to the grave within a few months.

I have thus never known either of my two parents, and the loss of their control, combined perhaps with my tropical birthplace, made me, I fear, somewhat headstrong and impetuous.

Immediately that I became old enough to be my own master I sold the estate and invested the money in Government stock in such a way as to insure me an income of fifteen hundred a year for life. I then came to Europe, and for a long time led a strange Bohemian life, flitting from one University to another, and studying spasmodically those subjects which interested me. I went to Heidelberg for a year in order to read chemistry and metaphysics, and when I returned to London I plunged for the first time into society. I was then twenty-four years of age, dark-haired, dark-eyed, swarthy, with a smattering of all knowledge and a mastery of none.

It was during this season in London that I first saw Lucy Forrester. How can I describe her so as to give even the faintest conception of her beauty? To my eyes no woman ever had been or could be so fair. Her face, her voice, her figure, every movement and action, were part of one rare and harmonious whole. Suffice it that I loved her the very evening that I saw her, and that I went on day after day increasing and nourishing this love until it possessed my whole being.

At first my suit prospered well. I made the acquaintance of her father, an elderly soldier, and became a frequent visitor at the house. I soon saw that the keynote of Miss Forrester's character was her intense devotion to her father, and accordingly I strove to win her regard by showing extreme deference and attention to him. I succeeded in interesting her in many topics, too, and we became very friendly. At last I ventured to speak to her of love, and told her of the passion which consumed me. I suppose I spoke wildly and fiercely, for she was frightened and shrank from me.

I renewed the subject another day, however, with better success. She confessed to me then that she loved me, but added firmly that she was her father's only child, and that it was her duty to devote her life to comforting his declining years. Her personal feelings, she said, should never prevent her from performing that duty. It mattered not. The confession that I was dear to her filled me with ecstasy. For the rest I was content to wait.

During this time the colonel had favoured my suit. I have no doubt that some gossip had exaggerated my wealth and given him false ideas of my importance. One day in conversation I told him what my resources were. I saw his face change as he listened to me, and from that moment his demeanour altered.

It chanced that about the same time young Scholefield, the son of the rich banker, came back from Oxford, and having met Lucy, became very marked in his attentions to her. Colonel Forrester at once encouraged his addresses in every possible way, and I received a curt note from him informing me that I should do well to discontinue my visits.

I still had hopes that Lucy would not be influenced by her father's mercenary schemes. For days I frequented her usual haunts, seeking an opportunity of speaking to her. At last I met her alone one morning in St. James's Park. She looked me straight in the face, and there was an expression of great tenderness and sadness in her eyes, but she would have passed me without speaking. All the blood seemed to rush into my head, and I caught her by the wrist to detain her.

"You have given me up, then?" I cried. "There is no longer any hope for me."

"Hush, Jack!" she said, for I had raised my voice excitedly. "I warned you how it would be. It is my father's wish and I must obey him, whatever it costs. Let me go now. You must not hold me any more."

"And there is no hope?"

"You will soon forget me," she said. "You must not think of me again."

"Ah, you are as bad as he," I cried, excitedly. "I read it in your eyes. It is the money – the wretched money." I was sorry for the words the moment after I had said them, but she had passed gravely on, and I was alone.

I sat down upon one of the benches in the park, and rested my head upon my hands. I felt numbed and stupefied. The world and everything in it had changed for me during the last ten minutes. People passed me as I sat – people who laughed and joked and gossiped. It seemed to me that I watched them almost as a dead man might watch the living. I had no sympathy with their little aims, their little pleasures and their little pains. "I'll get away from the whole drove of them," I said, as I rose from my seat. "The women are false and the men are fools, and everything is mean and sordid." My first love had unhappily converted me to cynicism, rash and foolish as I was, as it has many such a man before.

For many months I travelled, endeavouring by fresh scenes and new experiences to drive away the memory of that fair false face. At Venice I heard that she was engaged to be married to young Scholefield. "He's got a lot of money," this tourist said – it was at the table d'hôte at the Hotel de l'Europe. "It's a splendid match for her." For *her!*

When I came back to England I flitted restlessly about from one place to another, avoiding the haunts of my old associates, and leading a lonely and gloomy life. It was about this time that the idea first occurred to me of separating my person from mankind as widely as my thoughts and feelings were distinct from theirs. My temperament was, I think, naturally a somewhat morbid one, and my disappointment had made me a complete misanthrope. To me, without parents, friends, or relations, Lucy had been everything, and now that she was gone the very sight of a human face was hateful to me. Loneliness in a wilderness, I reflected, was less irksome than loneliness in a city. In some wild spot I might be face to face with nature and pursue the studies into which I had plunged once more, without interruption or disturbance.

As this resolution began to grow upon me I thought of this island of Ardvoe, which, curiously enough, had been first mentioned to me by Scholefield on one of the few occasions when we had been together in the house of the Forresters. I had heard him speak of its lonely and desolate position, and of its beauty, for his father had estates in Skye, from which he was wont to make yachting trips in summer, and in one of these he had visited the island. It frequently happened, he said, that no one set foot upon it during the whole year, for there was no grass for sheep, and nothing to attract fishermen. This, I thought, would be the very place for me.

Full of my new idea, I travelled to Skye, and from thence to Uist. There I hired a fishing-boat from a man named McDiarmid, and sailed with him and his son to the island. It was just such a place as I had imagined – rugged and desolate, with high, dark crags rising up from a girdle of sand. It had been once, McDiarmid said, a famous emporium for the goods of smugglers, which used to be stored there, and then conveyed over to the Scotch coast as occasion served. He showed me several of the caves of these gentry, and one in particular, which I immediately determined should be my own future dwelling. It was approached by a labyrinth of rocky paths, which effectually secured it against any intruder, while it was roomy inside, and lit up by an aperture in the rock above, which might be covered over in wet weather.

The fisherman told me that his father had pointed the spot out to him, but that it was not commonly known to the rare visitors who came to the island. There was abundance of fresh water, and fish were to be caught in any quantity.

I was so well satisfied with my survey that I returned to Scotland with the full intention of realising my wild misanthropical scheme.

In Glasgow I purchased most of the more important things that I wanted to take with me. These included a sleeping bag, such as is used in the Arctic seas; several mathematical and astronomical instruments; a very varied and extensive assortment of books, including nearly every modern work upon chemistry and physics; a double-barrelled fowling-piece, fishing-tackle, lamps, candles, and oil. Subsequently at Oban and Stornoway I purchased two bags of potatoes, a sack of flour, and a quantity of tinned meats, together with a small stove. All these things I conveyed over in McDiarmid's boat, having already bound both himself and his son to secrecy upon the matter – a promise which, as far as I know, neither of them ever broke. I also had a table and chair conveyed across, with a plentiful supply of pens, ink, and paper.

All these things were stowed away in the cave, and I then requested McDiarmid to call upon the first of each month, or as soon after as the weather permitted, in case I needed anything. This he promised to do, and having been well paid for his services, he departed, leaving me upon the island.

It was a strange sensation to me when I saw the brown sail of his boat sinking below the horizon, until at last it disappeared, and left one broad, unbroken sheet of water before me. That boat was the last tie which bound me to the human race. When it had vanished, and I returned into my cave with the knowledge that no sight or sound could jar upon me now, I felt the first approach to satisfaction which I had had through all those weary months. A fire was sparkling in the stove, for fuel was plentiful on the island, and the long stove-pipe had been so arranged that it projected through the aperture above, and so carried the smoke away. I boiled some potatoes and made a hearty meal, after which I wrote and read until nightfall, when I crept into my bag and slept soundly.

It might weary my readers should I speak of my existence upon this island, though the petty details of my housekeeping seem to interest my dear wife more than anything else, and ten years have not quite exhausted her questions upon the subject. I cannot say that I was happy, but I was less unhappy than I could have believed it possible. At times, it is true, I was plunged into the deepest melancholy, and would remain so for days, without energy enough to light my fire or to cook my food. On these occasions I would wander aimlessly among the hills and along the shore until I was worn out with fatigue. After these attacks, however, I would become, if not placid, at least torpid for a time. Occasionally I could even smile at my strange life as an anchorite, and speculate as to whether the lord of the manor, since I presumed the island belonged to some one, would become aware of my existence, and if so, whether he would evict me ignominiously, or claim a rent for my little cavern.

II

Three months had passed, as I knew by the regular visits of the worthy fisherman, when the event occurred which altered the course of my whole life, and led in the end to the writing of this narrative.

I had been out all day surveying my little kingdom, and having returned about four o'clock, had settled down to Ricardo's "Principles of Political Economy," of which work I was writing a critical analysis. I had been writing about three hours, and the waning light (it was in September) was warning me that the time had come to stop, when suddenly, to my intense astonishment, I heard a human voice. Crusoe, when he saw the footstep, could hardly have been more surprised. My first idea was that some unforeseen circumstance had induced McDiarmid to come across before his time, and that he was hailing me; but a moment's reflection showed me that the voice which I had heard was very different from the rough Gaelic accents of the fisherman. As I sat pen in hand, wondering and listening, a peal of laughter rose up from the beach. An unreasoning indignation at this intrusion on my privacy then took possession of me, and I rushed out of my cave and peered over the rocks to see who the invaders might be.

Down beneath me in the bay a trim little yacht of five-and-twenty tons or thereabouts was riding at anchor. On the beach two yachtsmen – a young man and an old – were endeavouring with the aid of a sailor to raise a canvas tent, and were busily engaged knocking pegs into the crumbling sand and fastening ropes to them. Between the shore and the yacht there was a small boat rowed by one man, and in the sheets there sat a lady. When the boat reached the shore one of the yachtsmen, the younger of the two, ran down and handed its passenger out. The instant she stood erect I recognised her. Even after the lapse of ten years I feel again the rush and whirlwind of emotion which came over me when I saw once more in this strange place the woman whom I loved better than all the world besides.

At first it seemed so extraordinary, so utterly inexplicable, that I could only surmise that she and her father and lover (for I had now recognised the two men also) had heard of my presence here and had come with the intention of insulting me. This was the

mad notion which came into my disordered brain. The unconcerned air of the party showed, however, that this could not be.
On second thoughts I convinced myself that it was no very
wonderful coincidence after all. No doubt Scholefield was taking
up the young lady and her father to pay a visit to his rich friends in
Skye. If so, what more natural than that in passing they should
visit this island concerning which I remembered that Lucy had
expressed interest and curiosity when Scholefield spoke of it
originally? It seemed to me now to be such a natural sequence of
events that my only wonder was that the possibility of it had not
occurred to me earlier.

The tent was soon up, and they had supper inside it, after
raising another smaller tent for the two seamen. It was evident
that the whole party intended to camp out for a time.

I crept down towards the beach after it was dark, and came as
near to them as I dared. After a time Scholefield sang a sea song;
and then, after some persuasion, she sang too – a melancholy
ballad, one which had been a favourite of mine in the old days in
London. What would she have thought, I wondered, could she
have seen me, unshaven and dishevelled, crouching like a wild
beast among the rocks! My heart was full, and I could bear it no
longer. I went back to my lonely cave with all my old wounds
ripped open afresh.

About ten o'clock I saw her in the moonlight go down to the
beach alone, and row to the yacht, where she fastened the dinghy
astern. She was always proud, I remembered, of being at home
upon the water. I knew then for certain that she was not married
yet, and a gush of senseless joy and hope rose up in my bosom.

I saw her row back in the morning, and the party breakfasted
together in the tent. Afterwards they spent the day in exploring
the island and in gathering the rare shells which are to be found
upon the beach. They never came my way – indeed the rocks
among which my cave lay were well-nigh inaccessible to any one
who did not know the steep and intricate pathway. I watched the
lady wandering along the sands, and once she passed immediately beneath my citadel. Her face was pale, I thought, and she
seemed graver than when I saw her last, but otherwise there was
no change. Her blue yachting costume with white lace and gilt
buttons suited her to perfection. Strange how small details may
stick in the memory!

It was on the evening of the second day of their visit that I
found that the stock of fresh water which I usually kept in my cave
had run short, which necessitated my going to the stream for
more. It was about a hundred yards off, and not far from the tent,

but it seemed to me that since darkness had set in I should be running no risk of discovery; so taking my bucket in my hand I set off. I had filled it and was about to return when I heard the footsteps and voices of two men close to me, and had hardly time to crouch down behind a furze bush when they stopped almost within arm's length of me.

"Help you!" I heard one of them say, whom I at once identified as old Forrester. "My dear fellow, you must help yourself. You must be patient and you must be resolute. When I broached the matter to her she said that she had obeyed me in not speaking to the other, but when I asked for more than that I exceeded the claims which a father has upon a daughter. Those were her very words."

"I can't make it out," the other said peevishly; "you always hold out hopes, but they never come to anything. She is kind to me and friendly, but no more. The fellows at the club think that I am engaged to her. Everybody thinks so."

"So you will be, my boy, so you will be," Forrester answered. "Give her time."

"It's that black chap Gibbs who runs in her head," said Schole-field. "The fellow is dead, I believe, or gone mad, as I always said he would. Anyway he has disappeared from the world, but that seems to make no difference to her."

"Pshaw!" the other answered. "Out of sight is out of mind, sooner or later. You will have exceptional opportunities at Skye, so make the most of them. For my part I promise to put on all the pressure I can. At present we must go down to the tent or she'll think we are lost," with which they moved off, and their steps died away in the distance.

I stood up after they were gone like one in a dream, and slowly carried back my bucket. Then I sat down upon my chair and leaned my head upon my hands, while my mind was torn by conflicting emotions. She was true to me then. She had never been engaged to my rival. Yet there was the old prohibition of her parent, which had no doubt the same sacred weight with her as ever. I was really no nearer her than before. But how about this conspiracy which I had overheard – this plot between a mer-cenary father and a mean-spirited suitor. Should I, ought I, to allow her to be bullied by the one or cajoled by the other into forsaking me? Never! I would appeal to her. I would give her one more chance at least of judging between her father and myself. Surely, I thought, I who love her so tenderly have more claim upon her than this man who would sell her to the highest bidder.

Then in a moment it came into my head how I could take her

away from them, so that no one should stand between us, and I might plead my cause without interruption. It was such a plan as could only have occurred perhaps to a man of my impetuous nature. I knew that if once she left the island I might never have the chance again. There was but one way to do it, and I was determined that it should be done.

All night long I paced about my cave pondering over the details of my scheme. I would have put it into execution at once, but the sky was covered with clouds and the night was exceptionally dark. Never did time pass more slowly. At last the first cold grey light began to show upon the horizon and to spread slowly along it. I thrust a clasp knife into my pocket and as much money as I had in the cave. Then I crept down to the beach, some distance from the sleeping party, and swam out to the yacht. The ladder by which Lucy had got on board the night before was still hanging down, and by it I climbed on board. Moving softly so as not to awake her, I shook out enough of one of the sails to catch the breeze, and then stooping over the bows I cut the thick rope by which we were moored. For a minute or so the yacht drifted aimlessly, and then getting some way on her she answered the helm, and stood out slowly towards the Atlantic.

Do not misunderstand me. I had no intention of forcing the lady's inclinations in any way, or compelling her to break her promise to her father. I was not base enough for that. My sole and only object was to have an opportunity of appealing to her, and pleading my cause for the last time. If I had not known, on the authority of her suitor, that she still loved me, I would have cut my right hand off as soon as cut that cable. As it was, if I could persuade her to be my wife we could run down to Ireland or back to Oban, and be married by special licence before the prisoners at Ardvoe could get away. If, on the other hand, she refused to have anything to do with me, I would loyally take the *Evangeline* back to her moorings and face the consequences, whatever they might be. Some have blamed me for putting the lady in such a compromising situation. Before they judge they must put themselves in my position, with but one chance of making life happy, and that chance depending upon prompt action. My savage life, too, may have somewhat blunted my regard for the conventionalities of civilisation.

As the boat slowly headed out to sea I heard a great outcry upon the beach, and saw Forrester and Scholefield, with the two sailors, running frantically about. I kept myself carefully out of sight. Presently Scholefield and one of the sailors dashed into the water, but after swimming a little way they gave it up as hopeless, for the breeze was very fresh, and even with our little rag of canvas we could not have been going less than five knots. All this time Miss Forrester had not been disturbed, nor was there anything to let her know that the yacht was under way, for the tossing was no greater than when she was at anchor.

III

The moorings had been at the south end of the island, and as the wind was cast, we headed straight out to the Atlantic. I did not put up any more sail yet, for it would be seen by those we had left, and I wished at present to leave them under the impression that the yacht had drifted away by accident, so that if they found any means of communicating with the mainland they might start upon a wrong scent. After three hours, however, the island being by that time upon the extreme horizon, I hoisted the mainsail and jib.

I was busily engaged in tugging at the halliards, when Miss Forrester, fully dressed, stepped out of her cabin and came upon deck. I shall never forget the expression of utter astonishment which came over her beautiful features when she realised that she was out at sea and with a strange companion. She gazed at me with, at first, terror as well as surprise. No doubt, with my long dark hair and beard, and tattered clothing, I was not a very reassuring object.

The instant I opened my lips to address her, however, she recognised me, and seemed to comprehend the situation.

"Mr. Gibbs," she cried. "Jack, what have you done? You have carried me away from Ardvoe. Oh, take me back again! What will my poor father do?"

"He's all right," I said. "He is hardly so very thoughtful about you, and may not mind doing without you now for a little."

She was silent for a while, and leaned against the companion rail, endeavouring to collect herself.

"I can hardly realise it," she said, at last. "How could you have come here, and why are we at sea? What is your object, Jack? What are you about to do?"

"My only object is this," I said, tremblingly, coming up closer to her. "I wished to be able to have a chance of talking to you alone without interruption. The whole happiness of my life depends upon it. That is why I have carried you off like this. All I ask you to do is to answer one or two questions, and I will promise to do your bidding. Will you do so?"

"Yes," she said, "I will."

She kept her eyes cast down and seemed to avoid my gaze.

"Do you love this man Scholefield?" I asked.

"No," she answered, with decision.

"Will you ever marry him?"

"No," she answered again.

"Now, Lucy," I said, "speak the truth fearlessly, let me entreat you, for the happiness of both of us depends upon it. Do you still love me?"

She never spoke, but she raised her head and I read her answer in her eyes. My heart overflowed with joy.

"Then, my darling," I cried, taking her hand, "if you love me and I love you, who is to come between us? Who dare part us?"

She was silent, but did not attempt to escape from my arm.

"Not your father," I said. "He has no power or right over you. You know well that if one who was richer than Scholefield appeared to-morrow he would bid you smile upon him without a thought as to your own feelings. You can in such circumstances owe him no allegiance as to giving yourself for mere mercenary reasons to those you in heart abhor."

"You are right, Jack. I do not," she answered, speaking very gently, but very firmly. "I am sorry that I left you as I did in St. James's Park. Many a time since I have bitterly regretted it. Still at all costs I should have been true to my father if he had been true to me. But he has not been so. Though he knows my dislike to Mr. Scholefield he has continually thrown us together as on this yachting excursion, which was hateful to me from the first. Jack," she continued, turning to me, "you have been true to me through everything. If you still love me I am yours from this moment – yours entirely and for ever. I will place myself in their power no more."

Then in that happy moment I was repaid for all the long months of weariness and pain. We sat for hours talking of our thoughts and feelings since our last sad parting, while the boat drifted aimlessly among the tossing waves, and the sails flapped against the spars above our heads. Then I told her how I had swum off and cut the cable of the *Evangeline*.

"But, Jack," she said, "you are a pirate; you will be prosecuted for carrying off the boat."

"They may do what they like now," I said, defiantly; "I have gained you, in carrying off the boat."

"But what will you do now?" she asked.

"I will make for the north of Ireland," I said; "then I shall put you under the protection of some good woman until we can get a special licence and be able to defy your father. I shall send the

Evangeline back to Ardvoe or to Skye. We are going to have some wind, I fear. You will not be afraid, dear?"

"Not while I am with you," she answered, calmly.

The prospect was certainly not a reassuring one. The whole eastern horizon was lined by great dark clouds, piled high upon each other, with that lurid tinge about them which betokens violent wind. Already the first warning blasts came whistling down upon us, heeling our little craft over till her gunwale lay level with the water. It was impossible to beat back to the Scotch coast, and our best chance of safety lay in running before the gale. I took in the topsail and flying-jib, and reefed down the mainsail; then I lashed everything moveable in case of our shipping a sea. I wished Lucy to go below to her cabin, but she would not leave me, and remained by my side.

As the day wore on the occasional blasts increased into a gale, and the gale into a tempest. The night set in dark and dreary, and still we sped into the Atlantic. The *Evangeline* rose to the seas like a cork, and we took little or no water aboard. Once or twice the moon peeped out for a few moments between the great drifting cloud-banks. Those brief intervals of light showed us the great wilderness of black, tossing waters which stretched to the horizon. I managed to bring some food and water from the cabin while Lucy held the tiller, and we shared it together. No persuasions of mine could induce her to leave my side for a moment.

With the break of day the wind appeared to gain more force than ever, and the great waves were so lofty that many of them rose high above our masthead. We staggered along under our reefed sail, now rising upon a billow, from which we looked down on two great valleys before and behind us, then sinking down into the trough of the sea until it seemed as if we could never climb the green wall beyond. By dead reckoning I calculated that we had been blown clear of the north coast of Ireland. It would have been madness to run towards an unknown and dangerous shore in such weather, but I steered a course now two more points to the south, so as not to get blown too far from the west coast in case that we had passed Malin Head. During the morning Lucy thought that she saw the loom of a fishing-boat, but neither of us were certain, for the weather had become very thick. This must have been the boat of the man Mullins, who seems to have had a better view of us than we had of him.

All day (our second at sea) we continued to steer in a south-westerly direction. The fog had increased and become so thick that from the stern we could hardly see the end of the bowsprit. The little vessel had proved herself a splendid sea boat, and we had both become so reconciled to our position, and so confident in her powers, that neither of us thought any longer of the danger of our position, especially as the wind and sea were both abating. We were just congratulating each other upon this cheering fact, when an unexpected and terrible catastrophe overtook us.

It must have been about seven in the evening, and I had gone down to rummage in the lockers and find something to eat, when I heard Lucy give a startled cry above me. I sprang upon deck instantly. She was standing up by the tiller peering out into the mist.

"Jack," she cried. "I hear voices, There is some one close to us."

"Voices!" I said; "impossible. If we were near land we should hear the breakers."

"Hist!" she cried, holding up her hand. "Listen!"

We were standing together straining our ears to catch every sound, when suddenly and swiftly there emerged from the fog upon our starboard bow a long line of Roman numerals with the figure of a gigantic woman hovering above them. There was no time for thought or preparation. A dark loom towered above us, taking the wind from our sails, and then a great vessel sprang upon us out of the mist as a wild beast might upon its prey. Instinctively, as I saw the monster surging down upon us, I flung one of the life-belts, which was hanging round the tiller, over Lucy's head, and seizing her by the waist, I sprang with her into the sea.

What happened after that it is hard to tell. In such moments all idea of time is lost. It might have been minutes or it might have been hours during which I swam by Lucy's side, encouraging her in every possible way to place full confidence in her belt and to float without struggling. She obeyed me to the letter, like a brave girl as she was. Every time I rose to the top of a wave I looked around for some sign of our destroyer, but in vain. We joined our voices in a cry for aid, but no answer came back except the howling of the wind. I was a strong swimmer, but hampered with my clothes my strength began gradually to fail me. I was still by Lucy's side, and she noticed that I became feebler.

"Trust to the belt, my darling, whatever happens," I said.

She turned her tender face towards me.

"If you leave me I shall slip it off," she answered.

Again I came to the top of a great roller, and looked round. There was nothing to be seen. But hark! what was that? A dull clanking noise came on my ears, which was distinct from the splash of the sea. It was the sound of oars in rowlocks. We gave a last feeble cry for aid. It was answered by a friendly shout, and the next that either of us remember was when we came to our senses once more and found ourselves in warm and comfortable berths with kind anxious faces around us. We had both fainted while being lifted into the boat.

The vessel was a large Norwegian sailing barque, the *Freyja*, of five hundred tons, which had started five days before from Bergen, and was bound for Adelaide in Australia. Nothing could exceed the kindness of Captain Thorbjorn and his crew to the two unfortunates whom they had picked out of the Atlantic Ocean. The watch on deck had seen us, but too late to prevent a collision. They had at once dropped a boat, which was about to return to the ship in despair, when that last cry reached their ears.

Captain Thorbjorn's wife was on board, and she at once took my dear companion under her care. We had a pleasant and rapid voyage to Adelaide, where we were duly married in the presence of Madame Thorbjorn and of all the officers of the *Freyja*.

After our marriage I went up country, and having taken a large farm there, I remained a happy and prosperous man. A sum of money was duly paid over to the firm of Scholefield, coming they knew not whence, which represented the value of the *Evangeline*.

One of the first English mails which followed us to Australia announced the death of Colonel Forrester, who fractured his skull by falling down the marble steps of a Glasgow hotel. Lucy was terribly grieved, but new associations and daily duties gradually overcame her sorrow.

Since then neither of us have anything to bind us to the old country, nor do we propose to return to it. We read the English periodicals, however, and have amused ourselves from time to time in noticing the stray allusions to the yacht *Evangeline*, and the sad fate of the young lady on board her. This short narrative of the real facts may therefore prove interesting to some few who have not forgotten what is now an old story, and some perhaps to whom the circumstances are new may care to hear a strange chapter in real life.

TOUCH AND GO: A MIDSHIPMAN'S STORY

What is there in all nature which is more beautiful or more inspiriting than the sight of the great ocean, when a merry breeze sweeps over it, and the sun glints down upon the long green ridges with their crests of snow? Sad indeed must be the heart which does not respond to the cheery splashing of the billows and their roar upon the shingle. There are times, however, when the great heaving giant is in another and a darker mood. Those who, like myself, have been tossed upon the dark waters through a long night, while the great waves spat their foam over them in their fury, and the fierce winds howled above them, will ever after look upon the sea with other eyes. However peaceful it may be, they will see the lurking fiend beneath its smiling surface. It is a great wild beast of uncertain temper and incalculable strength.

Once, and once only, during the long years which I have spent at sea, have I found myself at the mercy of this monster. There were circumstances, too, upon that occasion, which threatened a more terrible catastrophe than the loss of my own single life. I have set myself to write down, as concisely and as accurately as I can, the facts in connection with that adventure and its very remarkable consequences.

In 1868 I was a lad of fourteen, and had just completed my first voyage in the *Paraguay*, one of the finest vessels of the finest of the Pacific lines, in which I was a midshipman. On reaching Liverpool, our ship had been laid up for a month or so, and I had obtained leave of absence to visit my relations, who were living on the banks of the Clyde. I hurried north with all the eagerness of a boy who has been abroad for the first time, and met with a loving reception from my parents and from my only sister. I have never known any pleasure in life which could compare with that which these reunions bring to a lad whose disposition is affectionate.

The little village at which my family were living was called

Rudmore, and was situated in one of the most beautiful spots in the whole of the Clyde. Indeed, it was the natural advantages of its situation which had induced my father to purchase a villa there. Our grounds ran down to the water's edge, and included a small wooden jetty which projected into the river. Beside this jetty was anchored a small yacht, which had belonged to the former proprietor, and which had been included in the rest of the property when purchased by my father. She was a smart little clipper of about three-ton burden, and directly my eyes fell upon her I determined that I would test her sea-going qualities.

My sister had a younger friend of hers, Maud Sumter, staying with her at this time, and the three of us made frequent excursions about the country, and occasionally put out into the Firth in order to fish. On all these nautical expeditions we were accompanied by an old fisherman named Jock Reid, in whom my father had confidence. At first we were rather glad to have the old man's company, and were amused by his garrulous chat and strange reminiscences. After a time, however, we began to resent the idea of having a guardian placed over us, and the grievance weighed with double stress upon me, for, midshipman-like, I had fallen a victim to the blue-eyes and golden hair of my sister's pretty playmate, and I conceived that without our boatman I might have many an opportunity of showing my gallantry and my affection. Besides, it seemed a monstrous thing that a real sailor, albeit only fourteen years of age, who had actually been round Cape Horn, should not be trusted with the command of a boat in a quiet Scottish firth. We put our three youthful heads together over the matter. and the result was a unanimous determination to mutiny against our ancient commander.

It was not difficult to carry our resolution into practice. One bright winter's day, when the sun was shining cheerily, but a stiffish breeze was ruffling the surface of the water, we announced our intention of going for a sail, and Jock Reid was as usual summoned from his cottage to escort us. I remember that the old man looked very doubtfully at the glass in my father's hall, and then at the eastern sky, in which the clouds were piling up into a gigantic cumulus.

"Ye maunna gang far the day," he said, shaking his grizzled head. "It's like to blow hard afore evening."

"No, no, Jock," we cried in chorus; "we don't want to go far."

The old sailor came down with us to the boat, still grumbling his presentiments about the coming weather. I stalked along with all the dignity of chief conspirator, while my sister and Maud followed expectantly, full of timidity and admiration for my audacity. When we reached the boat I helped the boatman to set the mainsail and the jib, and he was about to cast her off from her moorings when I played the card which I had been reserving.

"Jock," I said, slipping a shilling into his hand; "I'm afraid you'll feel it cold when we get out. You had better get yourself a drop of something before we start."

"Indeed I will, maister," said Jock emphatically. "I'm no as young as I was, and the coffee keeps the cold out."

"You run up to the house," I said; "we can wait until you come back."

Poor old Jock, suspecting no treachery, made off in the direction of the village, and was soon out of sight. The instant he had disappeared six busy little hands were at work undoing the moorings, and in less than a minute we were clear of the land, and were shooting gallantly out into the centre of the Firth of Clyde. Under her press of canvas, the little boat heeled over until her lee-gunwale was level with the water, and as we plunged into the waves the spray came showering over the bows and splashing on our deck. Far away on the beach we could see old Jock, who had been warned by the villagers of our flight, running eagerly up and down, and waving his arms in his excitement. How we laughed at the old man's impotent anger, and what fun we made of the salt foam which wet our faces and sprinkled on our lips! We sang, we romped, we played, and when we tired of this the two girls sat in the sheets, while I held the tiller and told many stories of my nautical experiences, and of the incidents of my one and only voyage.

At first we were somewhat undecided as to what course we should steer, or where we should make for; but after consultation it was unanimously decided that we should run out to the mouth of the Firth. Old Jock had always avoided the open sea, and had beaten about in the river, so it seemed to us, now that we had deposed our veteran commander, that it was a favourable opportunity for showing what we could do without him. The wind, too, was blowing from the eastward, and therefore was favourable to the attempt. We pulled the mainsail as square as possible, and keeping the tiller steady, ran rapidly before the wind in the direction of the sea.

Behind us the great cumulus of clouds had lengthened and broadened, but the sun was still shining brightly, making the crests of the waves sparkle again, like long ridges of fire. The banks of the Firth, which are four or five miles apart, are well wooded, and many a lovely villa and stately castle peeped out from among the trees as we swept past. Far behind us we saw the long line of smoke which told where Greenock and Glasgow lay, with their toiling thousands of inhabitants. In front rose a great stately mountain-peak, that of Goatfell, in Arran, with the clouds wreathed coquettishly round the summit. Away to the north, too, in the purple distance lay ranges of mountains stretching along the whole horizon, and throwing strange shadows as the bright rays of the sun fell upon their rugged sides.

We were not lonely as we made our way down the great artery which carries the commerce of the west of Scotland to the sea. Boats of all sizes and shapes passed and re-passed us. Eager little steamers went panting by with their loads of Glasgow citizens, going to or returning from the great city. Yachts and launches, and fishing-boats, came and went in every direction. One of the latter crossed our bows, and one of her crew, a rough-bearded fellow, shouted hoarsely at us; but the wind prevented us from hearing what he said. As we neared the sea a great Atlantic steamer went slowly past us, with her big yellow funnel vomiting forth clouds of smoke, and her whistle blowing to warn the smaller craft to keep out of her way. Her passengers lined the side to watch us as we shot past them, very proud of our little boat and of ourselves.

We had brought some sandwiches away with us, and a bottle of milk, so that there was no reason why we should shorten our cruise. We stood on accordingly until we were abreast of Ardrossan, which is at the mouth of the river and exactly opposite to the island of Arran, which lies in the open sea. The strait across is about eight miles in width, and my two companions were both clamorous that we should cross.

"It looks very stormy," I said, glancing at the pile of clouds behind us; "I think we had better put back."

"Oh, do let us go on to Arran!" little Maud cried enthusiastically.

"Do, Archie," echoed my sister; "surely, you are not afraid?"

To tell the truth, I *was* afraid, for I read the signs of the weather better than they did. The reproachful look in Maud's blue eyes at what she took to be my faint-heartedness overcame all my prudence.

"If you wish to go, we'll go," I said; and we sailed out from the mouth of the river into the strait.

Hitherto we had been screened from the wind to some extent by the hills behind us, but as we emerged from our shelter it came upon us in fiercer and more prolonged blasts. The mast bent like a whip under the pressure upon the sail, and would, I believe, have snapped short off, had it not been that I had knowledge enough of sailing to be able to take in a couple of reefs in the great sail. Even then the boat lay over in an alarming manner, so that we had to hold on to the weather bulwarks to prevent our slipping off. The waves, too, were much larger than they had been in the Firth, and we shipped so much water that I had to bail it out several times with my hat. The girls clapped their hands and cried out with delight as the water came over us, but I was grave because I knew the danger; and seeing me grave, they became grave too. Ahead of us the great mountain-peak towered up into the clouds, with green woods clustering about its base; and we could see the houses along the beach, and the long shining strip of yellow sand. Behind us the dark clouds became darker, lined at the base with the peculiar lurid tint which is nature's danger signal. It was evident that the breeze would soon become a gale, and a violent one. We should not lose a moment in getting back to the river, and I already bitterly repented that I had ever left its sheltering banks.

We put the boat round with all the speed we could, but it was no light task for three children. When at last we began to tack for the Scotch coast, we realised how difficult a matter it was for us to return. As long as we went with the wind, we went also with the waves; and it was only a stray one which broke over us. The moment, however, that we turned our broadside towards the sea we were deluged with water, which poured in faster than we could bail it out. A jagged flash of lightning clove the dark eastern sky, followed by a deafening peal of thunder. It was clear that the gale was about to burst; and it was evident to me that if it caught us in our present position we should infallibly be swamped. With much difficulty we squared our sail once more, and ran before the wind. It had veered a couple of points to the north, so that our course promised to take us to the south of the island. We shipped less water now than before, but on the other hand, every minute drove us out into the wild Irish Sea, further and further from home.

It was blowing so hard by this time, and the waters made such a clashing, that it was hard to hear each other's words. Little Maudie nestled at my side, and took my hand in hers. My sister clung to the rail at the other side of me.

"Don't you think," she said, "that we could sail right into one of the harbours in Arran? I know there is a harbour at Brodick, which is just opposite us."

"We had better keep away from it altogether," I said. "We should be sure to be wrecked if we got near the coast; and it is just as bad to be wrecked there as in the open sea."

"Where are we going?" she cried.

"Anywhere the wind takes us," I answered; "it is our only chance. Don't cry, Maudie; we'll get back all right when the storm is over." I tried to comfort them, for they were both in tears; and, indeed, I could hardly keep my sobs down myself, for I was a very little fellow to be placed in such a position.

As the storm came down on us it became so dark that we could hardly see the island in front of us, and the dark line of the Bute coast. We flew through the water at a tremendous pace, skimming over the great seething waves, while the wind howled and screamed through our rigging as though the whole air was full of pursuing fiends intent upon our destruction. The two girls cowered, shivering with terror, at the bottom of the boat, while I endeavoured to comfort them as well as I could, and to keep our craft before the wind. As the evening drew in and we increased our distance from the shore, the gale grew in power. The great dark waves towered high above our mast-head, so that when we lay in the trough of the sea, we saw nothing but the sombre liquid walls in front and behind us. Then we would sweep up the black slope, till from the summit we could see a dreary prospect of raging waters around us, and then we would sink down, down into the valley upon the other side. It was only the extreme lightness and buoyancy of our little craft which saved her from instant destruction. A dozen times a gigantic billow would curl over our heads, as though it were about to break over us, but each time the gallant boat rose triumphantly over it, shaking herself after each collision with the waters as a seabird might trim her feathers.

Never shall I forget the horrors of that night! As the darkness settled down upon us, we saw the loom of a great rock some little distance from us, and we knew that we were passing Ailsa Craig. In one sense it was a relief to us to know that it was behind us, because there was now no land which we need fear, but only the great expanse of the Irish Sea. In the short intervals when the haze lifted, we could see the twinkling lights from the Scottish lighthouses glimmering through the darkness behind us. The waves had been terrible in the daytime, but they were worse now. It was better to see them towering over us than to hear them hissing and seething far above our heads, and to be able to make out nothing except the occasional gleam of a line of foam. Once, and once only, the moon disentangled itself from the thick hurrying clouds which obscured its face. Then we caught a glimpse of a great wilderness of foaming, tossing waters, but the dark scud drifted over the sky, and the silvery light faded away until all was gloom once more.

What a long weary night it was! Cold and hungry, and shivering with terror, the three of us clung together, peering out into the darkness and praying as none of us had ever prayed before. During all the long hours we still tore through the waters to the south and west, for the wind was now blowing from the north-east. As the day dawned, grey and cheerless, we saw the rugged coast of Ireland lining the whole western horizon. And now it was, in the first dim light of dawn, that our great misfortune occurred to us. Whether it was the result of the long-continued strain, or whether some gust of particular violence had caught the sail, we have never known, but suddenly there was a sharp cracking, rending noise, and next moment our mast was trailing over the side, with the rigging and the sails flapping on the surface of the water. At the same instant, our momentum being checked, a great sea broke over the boat and nearly swamped us. Fortunately the blow was so great, that it drove our boat round so that her head came to the seas once more. I bailed frantically with my cap, for she was half full of water, and I knew a little more would sink her, but as fast as I threw the water out, more came surging in. It was at this moment, when all seemed lost to us, that I heard my sister give a joyful cry, and looking up, saw a large steam launch ploughing its way towards us through the storm. Then the tears which I had restrained so long came to my relief, and I broke down completely in the reaction which came upon us, when we knew that we were saved.

It was no easy matter for our preservers to rescue us, for close contact between the two little craft was dangerous to both. A rope was thrown to us, however, and willing hands at the other end drew us one after the other to a place of safety. Maudie had fainted, and my sister and I were so weakened by cold and fatigue, that we were carried helpless to the cabin of the launch, where we were given some hot soup, after which we fell asleep, in spite of the rolling and tossing of the little vessel.

How long we slept I have no idea, but when we woke it appeared to be considerably past mid-day. My sister and Maudie were in the bunk opposite, and I could see that they were still sleeping. A tall, dark-bearded man was stooping over a chart which was pinned down to the table, measuring out distances with a pair of compasses. When I moved he glanced up and saw that I was awake.

"Well, mate," he said cheerily, "how are you now?"

"All right," I said; "thanks to you."

"It was touch and go," he remarked. "She foundered within five minutes of your coming aboard. Have you any idea where you are now?"

"No," I said.

"You're just off the Isle of Man. We're going to land you there on the west coast, where no one is likely to see us. We've had to go out of our course to do it, and I should have preferred to have taken you on to France, but the master thinks you should be sent home as soon as possible."

"Why don't you want to be seen?" I asked, leaning on my elbow.

"Never mind," he said; "we don't – and that's enough. Besides, you and these girls must keep quiet about us when you land. You must say that a fishing-boat saved you."

"All right," I said. I was much surprised at the earnestness with which the man made the request. What sort of vessel was this that we had got aboard of? A smuggler, perhaps, certainly something illegal, or else why this anxiety not to be seen? Yet they had been kind and good to us, so whatever they might be, it was not for us to expose them. As I lay speculating upon the point I heard a sudden bustle upon deck, and a head looked down the hatchway.

"There's a vessel ahead of us that looks like a gun-boat," it said.

The captain – for such I presumed the dark-haired man to be – dropped his compasses, and rushed upon deck. A moment later he came down, evidently much excited.

"Come on," he said; "we must get rid of you at once." He woke the girls up, and the three of us were hurried to the side and into a boat, which was manned by a couple of sailors. The hilly coast of the island was not more than a hundred or two yards away. As I passed into the boat, a middle-aged man, in dark clothes and a grey overcoat, laid his hand upon my shoulder.

"Remember," he said – "silence! You might do much harm!"

"Not a word," I answered.

He waved an adieu to us as our oarsmen bent to their oars, and in a few minutes we found our feet once more upon dry land. The boat pulled rapidly back, and then we saw the launch shoot away southward, evidently to avoid a large ship which was steaming down in the distance. When we looked again she was a mere dot on the waters, and from that day to this we have never seen or heard anything of our deliverers.

I fortunately had money enough in my pocket to send a telegram to my father, and then we put up at a hotel at Douglas, until he came himself to fetch us away. Fear and suspense had whitened his hair; but he was repaid for all when he saw us once more, and clasped us in his arms. He even forgot, in his delight, to scold us for the piece of treachery which had originated our misfortunes; and not the least hearty greeting which we received upon our return to the banks of the Clyde was from old Jock himself, who had quite forgiven us our desertion.

And who were our deliverers? That is a somewhat difficult question to answer, and yet I have an idea of their identity. Within a few days of our return, all England was ringing with the fact that Stephens, the famous Fenian head-centre, had made good his escape to the Continent. It may be that I am weaving a romance out of very commonplace material; but it has often seemed to me that if that gun-boat had overtaken that launch, it is quite possible that the said Mr. Stephens might never have put in an appearance upon the friendly shores of France. Be his politics what they may, if our deliverer really was Mr. Stephens, he was a good friend to us in our need, and we often look back with gratitude to our short acquaintance with the passenger in the grey coat.

UNCLE JEREMY'S HOUSEHOLD

———◆———

I

My life has been a somewhat chequered one, and it has fallen to my lot during the course of it to have had several unusual experiences. There is one episode, however, which is so surpassingly strange that whenever I look back to it it reduces the others to insignificance. It looks up out of the mists of the past, gloomy and fantastic, overshadowing the eventless years which preceded and which followed it.

It is not a story which I have often told. A few, but only a few, who know me well have heard the facts from my lips. I have been asked from time to time by these to narrate them to some assemblage of friends, but I have invariably refused, for I have no desire to gain a reputation as an amateur Munchausen. I have yielded to their wishes, however, so far as to draw up this written statement of the facts in connection with my visit to Dunkelthwaite.

Here is John Thurston's first letter to me. It is dated April 1862. I take it from my desk and copy it as it stands:

"My dear Lawrence, – if you knew my utter loneliness and complete *ennui* I am sure you would have pity upon me and come up to share my solitude. You have often made vague promises of visiting Dunkelthwaite and having a look at the Yorkshire Fells. What time could suit you better than the present? Of course I understand that you are hard at work, but as you are not actually taking out classes you can read just as well here as in Baker Street. Pack up your books, like a good fellow, and come along! We have a snug little room, with writing-desk and armchair, which will just do for your study. Let me know when we may expect you.

"When I say that I am lonely I do not mean that there is any lack of people in the house. On the contrary, we form rather a large household. First and foremost, of course, comes my poor Uncle Jeremy, garrulous and imbecile, shuffling about in his list slippers, and composing, as is his wont, innumerable bad verses. I think I told you when last we met of that trait in his character. It has attained such a pitch that he has an amanuensis, whose sole duty it is to copy down and preserve these effusions. This fellow, whose name is Copperthorne, has become as necessary to the old man as his foolscap or as the 'Universal Rhyming Dictionary.' I can't say I care for him myself, but then I have always shared Caesar's prejudice against lean men – though, by the way, little Julius was rather inclined that way himself if we may believe the medals. Then we have the two children of my Uncle Samuel, who were adopted by Jeremy – there were three of them, but one has gone the way of all flesh – and their governess, a stylish-looking brunette with Indian blood in her veins. Besides all these, there are three maidservants and the old groom, so you see we have quite a little world of our own in this out-of-the-way corner. For all that, my dear Hugh, I long for a familiar face and for a congenial companion. I am deep in chemistry myself, so I won't interrupt your studies. Write by return to your isolated friend,

"JOHN H. THURSTON."

At the time that I received this letter I was in lodgings in London, and was working hard for the final examination which should make me a qualified medical man. Thurston and I had been close friends at Cambridge before I took to the study of medicine, and I had a great desire to see him again. On the other hand, I was rather afraid that, in spite of his assurances, my studies might suffer by the change. I pictured to myself the childish old man, the lean secretary, the stylish governess, the two children, probably spoiled and noisy, and I came to the conclusion that when we were all cooped together in one country house there would be very little room for quiet reading. At the end of two days' cogitation I had almost made up my mind to refuse the invitation, when I received another letter from Yorkshire even more pressing than the first.

"We expect to hear from you by every post," my friend said, "and there is never a knock that I do not think it is a telegram announcing your train. Your room is all ready, and I think you will find it comfortable. Uncle Jeremy bids me say how very happy he will be to see you. He would have written, but he is absorbed in a great epic poem of five thousand lines or so, and he spends his day trotting about the rooms, while Copperthorne stalks behind him like the monster in Frankenstein, with note-book and pencil, jotting down the words of wisdom as they drop from his lips. By the way, I think I mentioned the brunettish governess to you. I might throw her out as a bait to you if you retain your taste for ethnological studies. She is the child of an Indian chieftain, whose wife was an Englishwoman. He was killed in the mutiny, fighting against us, and, his estates being seized by Government, his daughter, then fifteen, was left almost destitute. Some charitable German merchant in Calcutta adopted her, it seems, and brought her over to Europe with him together with his own daughter. The latter died, and then Miss Warrender – as we call her, after her mother – answered uncle's advertisement; and here she is. Now, my dear boy, stand not upon the order of your coming, but come at once."

There were other things in this second letter which prevent me from quoting it in full.

There was no resisting the importunity of my old friend, so, with many inward grumbles, I hastily packed up my books, and, having telegraphed overnight, started for Yorkshire the first thing in the morning. I well remember that it was a miserable day, and that the journey seemed to be an interminable one as I sat huddled up in a corner of the draughty carriage, revolving in my mind many problems of surgery and of medicine. I had been warned that the little wayside station of Ingleton, some fifteen miles from Carnforth, was the nearest to my destination, and there I alighted just as John Thurston came dashing down the country road in a high dog-cart. He waved his whip enthusiastic- ally at the sight of me, and pulling up his horse with a jerk, sprang out and on to the platform.

"My dear Hugh," he cried, "I'm so delighted to see you! It's so kind of you to come!" He wrung my hand until my arm ached.

"I'm afraid you'll find me very bad company now that I am here," I answered; "I am up to my eyes in work."

"Of course, of course," he said, in his good-humoured way. "I reckoned on this. We'll have time for a crack at the rabbits for all that. It's a longish drive, and you must be bitterly cold, so let's start for home at once."

We rattled off along the dusty road.

"I think you'll like your room," my friend remarked. "You'll soon find yourself at home. You know it is not often that I visit Dunkelthwaite myself, and I am only just beginning to settle down and get my laboratory into working order. I have been here a fortnight. It's an open secret that I occupy a prominent position in old Uncle Jeremy's will, so my father thought it only right that I should come up and do the polite. Under the circumstances I can hardly do less than put myself out a little now and again."

"Certainly not," I said.

"And besides, he's a very good old fellow. You'll be amused at our ménage. A princess for governess – it sounds well, doesn't it? I think our imperturbable secretary is somewhat gone in that direction. Turn up your coat-collar, for the wind is very sharp."

The road ran over a succession of low bleak hills, which were devoid of all vegetation save a few scattered gorse-bushes and a thin covering of stiff wiry grass, which gave nourishment to a scattered flock of lean, hungry-looking sheep. Alternately we dipped down into a hollow or rose to the summit of an eminence from which we could see the road winding as a thin white track over successive hills beyond. Every here and there the monotony of the landscape was broken by jagged scarps, where the grey granite peeped grimly out, as though nature had been sorely wounded until her gaunt bones protruded through their covering. In the distance lay a range of mountains, with one great peak shooting up from amongst them coquettishly draped in a wreath of clouds which reflected the ruddy light of the setting sun.

"That's Ingleborough," my companion said, indicating the mountain with his whip, "and these are the Yorkshire Fells. You won't find a wilder, bleaker place in all England. They breed a good race of men. The raw militia who beat the Scotch chivalry at the Battle of the Standard came from this part of the country. Just jump down, old fellow and open the gate."

We had pulled up at a place where a long moss-grown wall ran parallel to the road. It was broken by a dilapidated iron gate, flanked by two pillars, on the summit of which were stone devices which appeared to represent some heraldic animal, though wind and rain had reduced them to shapeless blocks. A ruined cottage, which may have served at some time as a lodge, stood on one side. I pushed the gate open and we drove up a long, winding avenue, grass-grown and uneven, but lined by magnificent oaks, which shot their branches so thickly over us that the evening twilight deepened suddenly into darkness.

"I'm afraid our avenue won't impress you much," Thurston said, with a laugh. "It's one of the old man's whims to let nature have her way in everything. Here we are at last at Dunkelthwaite."

As he spoke we swung round a curve in the avenue marked by a patriarchal oak which towered high above the others, and came upon a great square whitewashed house with a lawn in front of it. The lower part of the building was all in shadow, but up at the top a row of blood-shot windows glimmered out at the setting sun. At

the sound of the wheels an old man in livery ran out and seized
the horse's head when we pulled up.

"You can put her up, Elijah," my friend said, as we jumped
down. "Hugh, let me introduce you to my Uncle Jeremy."

"How d'ye do? How d'ye do?" cried a wheezy cracked voice, and
looking up I saw a little red-faced man who was standing waiting
for us in the porch. He wore a cotton cloth tied round his head
after the fashion of Pope and other eighteenth-century celeb-
rities, and was further distinguished by a pair of enormous
slippers. These contrasted so strangely with his thin spindle
shanks that he appeared to be wearing snowshoes, a resemblance
which was heightened by the fact that when he walked he was
compelled to slide his feet along the ground in order to retain his
grip of these unwieldly appendages.

"You must be tired, sir. Yes, and cold, sir," he said, in a strange
jerky way, as he shook me by the hand. "We must be hospitable to
you, we must indeed. Hospitality is one of the old-world virtues
which we still retain. Let me see, what are those lines? 'Ready and
strong the Yorkshire arm, but oh, the Yorkshire heart is warm?'
Neat and terse, sir. That comes from one of my poems. What
poem is it, Copperthorne?"

" 'The Harrying of Borrodaile'," said a voice behind him, and a
tall long-visaged man stepped forward into the circle of light
which was thrown by the lamp above the porch. John introduced
us, and I remember that his hand as I shook it was cold and
unpleasantly clammy.

This ceremony over, my friend led the way to my room, passing
through many passages and corridors connected by old-fashioned and irregular staircases. I noticed as I passed the thickness
of the walls and the strange slants and angles of the ceilings,
suggestive of mysterious spaces above. The chamber set apart for
me proved, as John had said, to be a cheery little sanctum with a
crackling fire and a well-stocked bookcase. I began to think as I
pulled on my slippers that I might have done worse after all than
accept this Yorkshire invitation.

II

When we descended to the dining-room the rest of the household
had already assembled for dinner. Old Jeremy, still wearing his
quaint headgear, sat at the head of the table. Next to him, on his
right, sat a very dark young lady with black hair and eyes, who was
introduced to me as Miss Warrender. Beside her were two pretty
children, a boy and a girl, who were evidently her charges. I sat

opposite her, with Copperthorne on my left, while John faced his uncle. I can almost fancy now that I can see the yellow glare of the great oil lamp throwing Rembrandt-like lights and shades upon the ring of faces, some of which were soon to have so strange an interest for me.

It was a pleasant meal, apart from the excellence of the viands and the fact that the long journey had sharpened my appetite. Uncle Jeremy overflowed with anecdote and quotation, delighted to have found a new listener. Neither Miss Warrender nor Copperthorne spoke much, but all that the latter said bespoke the thoughtful and educated man. As to John, he had so much to say of college reminiscences and subsequent events that I fear his dinner was a scanty one.

When the dessert was put on the table Miss Warrender took the children away, and Uncle Jeremy withdrew into the library, where we could hear the dull murmur of his voice as he dictated to his amanuensis. My old friend and I sat for some time before the fire discussing the many things which had happened to both of us since our last meeting.

"And what do you think of our household?" he asked at last, with a smile.

I answered that I was very much interested with what I had seen of it. "Your uncle," I said, "is quite a character. I like him very much."

"Yes; he has a warm heart behind all his peculiarities. Your coming seems to have cheered him up, for he's never been quite himself since little Ethel's death. She was the youngest of Uncle Sam's children, and came here with the others, but she had a fit or something in the shrubbery a couple of months ago. They found her lying dead there in the evening. It was a great blow to the old man."

"It must have been to Miss Warrender too?" I remarked.

"Yes; she was very much cut up. She had only been here a week or two at the time. She had driven over to Kirby Lonsdale that day to buy something."

"I was very much interested," I said, "in all that you told me about her. You were not chaffing, I suppose?"

"No, no; it's true as gospel. Her father was Achmet Genghis Khan, a semi-independent chieftain somewhere in the Central Provinces. He was a bit of a heathen fanatic in spite of his Christian wife, and he became chummy with the Nana, and mixed himself up in the Cawnpore business, so Government came down heavily on him."

"She must have been quite a woman before she left her tribe," I said. "What view of religion does she take? Does she side with her father or mother?"

"We never press that question," my friend answered. "Between ourselves, I don't think she's very orthodox. Her mother must have been a good woman, and besides teaching her English, she is a good French scholar, and plays remarkably well. Why, there she goes!"

As he spoke the sound of a piano was heard from the next room, and we both paused to listen. At first the player struck a few isolated notes, as though uncertain how to proceed. Then came a series of clanging chords and jarring discords, until out of the chaos there suddenly swelled a strange barbaric march, with blare of trumpet and crash of cymbal. Louder and louder it pealed forth in a gust of wild melody, and then died away once more into the jerky chords which had preceded it. Then we heard the sound of the shutting of the piano, and the music was at an end.

"She does that every night," my friend remarked; "I suppose it is some Indian reminiscence. Picturesque, don't you think so? Now don't stay here longer than you wish. Your room is ready whenever you would like to study."

I took my companion at his word and left him with his uncle and Copperthorne, who had returned into the room, while I went upstairs and read Medical Jurisprudence for a couple of hours. I imagined that I should see no more of the inhabitants of Dunkelthwaite that night, but I was mistaken, for about ten o'clock Uncle Jeremy thrust his little red face into the room.

"All comfortable?" he asked.

"Excellent, thanks," I answered.

"That's right. Keep at it. Sure to succeed," he said, in his spasmodic way. "Good night!"

"Good night!" I answered.

"Good night!" said another voice from the passage; and looking out I saw the tall figure of the secretary gliding along at the old man's heels like a long dark shadow.

I went back to my desk and worked for another hour, after which I retired to bed, where I pondered for some time before I dropped to sleep over the curious household of which I had become a member.

III

I was up betimes in the morning and out on the lawn, where I found Miss Warrender, who was picking primroses and making them into a little bunch for the breakfast-table. I approached her before she saw me, and I could not help admiring the beautiful litheness of her figure as she stooped over the flowers. There was a feline grace about her every movement such as I never remember to have seen in any woman. I recalled Thurston's words as to the impression which she had made upon the secretary, and ceased to wonder at it. As she heard my step, she stood up and turned her dark handsome face towards me.

"Good morning, Miss Warrender," I said. "You are an early riser, like myself."

"Yes," she answered. "I have always been accustomed to rise at daybreak."

"What a strange, wild view!" I remarked, looking out over the wide stretch of fells. "I am a stranger to this part of the country, like yourself. How do you like it?"

"I don't like it," she said, frankly. "I detest it. It is cold and bleak and wretched. Look at these" – holding up her bunch of primroses – "they call these things flowers. They have not even a smell."

"You have been used to a more genial climate and a tropical vegetation?"

"Oh, then, Mr. Thurston has been telling you about me," she said, with a smile. "Yes, I have been used to something better than this."

We were standing together when a shadow fell between us, and looking round I found that Copperthorne was standing close behind us. He held out his thin white hand to me with a constrained smile.

"You seem to be able to find your way about already," he remarked, glancing backwards and forwards from my face to that of Miss Warrender. "Let me hold your flowers for you, miss."

"No, thank you," the other said, coldly. "I have picked enough and am going inside."

She swept past him and across the lawn to the house. Copperthorne looked after her with a frowning brow.

"You are a student of medicine, Mr. Lawrence?" he said, turning towards me and stamping one of his feet up and down in a jerky, nervous fashion, as he spoke.

"Yes, I am."

"Oh, we have heard of you students of medicine," he cried in a raised voice, with a little crackling laugh. "You are dreadful fellows, are you not? We have heard of you. There is no standing against you."

"A medical student, sir," I answered, "is usually a gentleman."

"Quite so," he said, in a changed voice. "Of course I was only joking." Nevertheless I could not help noticing that at breakfast he kept his eyes persistently fixed upon me while Miss Warrender was speaking, and if I chanced to make a remark he would flash a glance round at her as though to read in our faces what our thoughts were of each other. It was clear that he took a more than common interest in the beautiful governess, and it seemed to me to be equally evident that his feelings were by no means reciprocated.

We had an illustration that morning of the simple nature of these primitive Yorkshire folk. It appears that the housemaid and the cook, who sleep together, were alarmed during the night by something which their superstitious minds contorted into an apparition. I was sitting after breakfast with Uncle Jeremy, who, with the help of continual promptings from his secretary, was reciting some Border poetry, when there was a tap at the door and the housemaid appeared. Close at her heels came the cook, buxom but timorous, the two mutually encouraging and abetting each other. They told their story in a strophe and antistrophe, like a Greek chorus, Jane talking until her breath failed, when the narrative was taken up by the cook, who, in turn, was supplanted by the other. Much of what they said was almost unintelligible to me owing to their extraordinary dialect, but I could make out the main thread of their story. It appears that in the early morning the cook had been awakened by something touching her face, and starting up had seen a shadowy figure standing by her bed, which figure had at once glided noiselessly from the room. The housemaid was awakened by the cook's cry, and averred stoutly that she had seen the apparition. No amount of cross-examination or reasoning could shake them, and they wound up by both giving notice, which was a practical way of showing that they were honestly scared. They seemed considerably indignant at our want of belief, and ended by bouncing out of the room, leaving Uncle Jeremy angry, Copperthorne contemptuous, and myself very much amused.

I spent nearly the whole of the second day of my visit in my room, and got over a considerable amount of work. In the evening John and I went down to the rabbit-warren with our guns. I told John as we came back of the absurd scene with the servants in the morning, but it did not seem to strike him in the same ridiculous light that it had me.

"The fact is," he said, "in very old houses like ours, where you have the timber rotten and warped, you get curious effects sometimes which predispose the mind to superstition. I have heard one or two things at night during this visit which might have frightened a nervous man, and still more an uneducated servant. Of course all this about apparitions is mere nonsense, but when once the imagination is excited there's no checking it."

"What have you heard, then?" I asked with interest.

"Oh, nothing of any importance," he answered. "Here are the youngsters and Miss Warrender. We mustn't talk about these things before her, or else we shall have her giving warning too, and that would be a loss to the establishment."

She was sitting on a little stile which stood on the outskirts of the wood which surrounds Dunkelthwaite, and the two children were leaning up against her, one on either side, with their hands clasped round her arms, and their chubby faces turned up to hers. It was a pretty picture and we both paused to look at it. She had heard our approach, however, and springing lightly down she came towards us, with the two little ones toddling behind her.

"You must aid me with the weight of your authority," she said to John. "These little rebels are fond of the night air and won't be persuaded to come indoors."

"Don't want to come," said the boy, with decision. "Want to hear the rest of the story."

"Yes – the 'tory," lisped the younger one.

"You shall hear the rest of the story to-morrow if you are good. Here is Mr. Lawrence, who is a doctor – he will tell you how bad it is for little boys and girls to be out when the dew falls."

"So you have been hearing a story?" John said as we moved on together.

"Yes – such a good story!" the little chap said with enthusiasm. "Uncle Jeremy tells us stories, but they are in po'try and they are not nearly so nice as Miss Warrender's stories. This one was about elephants –"

"And tigers – and gold –" said the other.

"Yes, and wars and fighting, and the king of the Cheroots –"

"Rajpoots, my dear," said the governess.

"And the scattered tribes that know each other by signs, and the man that was killed in the wood. She knows splendid stories. Why don't you make her tell you some, Cousin John?"

"Really, Miss Warrender, you have excited our curiosity," my companion said. "You must tell us of these wonders."

"They would seem stupid enough to you," she answered, with a laugh. "They are merely a few reminiscences of my early life."

As we strolled along the pathway which led through the wood we met Copperthorne coming from the opposite direction.

"I was looking for you all," he said, with an ungainly attempt at geniality. "I wanted to tell you that it was dinner-time."

"Our watches told us that," said John, rather ungraciously as I thought.

"And you have been all rabbiting together?" the secretary continued, as he stalked along beside us.

"Not all," I answered. "We met Miss Warrender and the children on our way back."

"Oh, Miss Warrender came to meet you as you came back!" said he. This quick contortion of my words, together with the sneering way in which he spoke, vexed me so much that I should have made a sharp rejoinder had it not been for the lady's presence.

I happened to turn my eyes towards the governess at the moment, and I saw her glance at the speaker with an angry sparkle in her eyes which showed that she shared my indignation. I was surprised, however, that same night when about ten o'clock I chanced to look out of the window of my study, to see the two of them walking up and down in the moonlight engaged in deep conversation. I don't know how it was, but the sight disturbed me so much that after several fruitless attempts to continue my studies I threw my books aside and gave up work for the night. About eleven I glanced out again, but they were gone, and shortly afterwards I heard the shuffling step of Uncle Jeremy, and the firm heavy footfall of the secretary, as they ascended the staircase which led to their bedrooms upon the upper floor.

IV

John Thurston was never a very observant man, and I believe that before I had been three days under his uncle's roof I knew more of what was going on there than he did. My friend was ardently devoted to chemistry, and spent his days happily among his test-tubes and solutions, perfectly contented so long as he had a congenial companion at hand to whom he could communicate his results. For myself, I have always had a weakness for the study and analysis of human character, and I found much that was interesting in the microcosm in which I lived. Indeed, I became so absorbed in my observations that I fear my studies suffered to a considerable extent.

In the first place, I discovered beyond all doubt that the real master of Dunkelthwaite was not Uncle Jeremy, but Uncle Jeremy's amanuensis. My medical instinct told me that the absorbing love of poetry, which had been nothing more than a harmless eccentricity in the old man's younger days, had now become a complete monomania, which filled his mind to the exclusion of every other subject. Copperthorne, by humouring his employer upon this one point until he had made himself indispensable to him, had succeeded in gaining complete power over him in everything else. He managed his money matters and the affairs of the house unquestioned and uncontrolled. He had sense enough, however, to exert his authority so lightly that it galled no one's neck, and therefore excited no opposition. My friend, busy with his distillations and analyses, was never allowed to realise that he was really a nonentity in the establishment.

I have already expressed my conviction that though Copperthorne had some tender feeling for the governess, she by no means favoured his addresses. After a few days I came to think, however, that there existed besides this unrequited affection some other link which bound the pair together. I had seen him more than once assume an air towards her which can only be described as one of authority. Two or three times also I had observed them pacing the lawn and conversing earnestly in the early hours of the night. I could not guess what mutual understanding existed between them, and the mystery piqued my curiosity.

It is proverbially easy to fall in love in a country house, but my nature has never been a sentimental one, and my judgment was not warped by any such feeling towards Miss Warrender. On the contrary, I set myself to study her as an entomologist might a specimen, critically, but without bias. With this object I used to arrange my studies in such a way as to be free at the times when she took the children out for exercise, so that we had many walks together, and I gained a deeper insight into her character than I should otherwise have done.

She was fairly well read, and had a superficial acquaintance with several languages, as well as a great natural taste for music. Underneath this veneer of culture, however, there was a great dash of the savage in her nature. In the course of her conversation she would every now and again drop some remark which would almost startle me by its primitive reasoning, and by its disregard for the conventionalities of civilisation. I could hardly wonder at this, however, when I reflected that she had been a woman before she left the wild tribe which her father ruled.

I remember one instance which sruck me as particularly characteristic, in which her wild original habits suddenly asserted themselves. We were walking along the country road, talking of Germany, in which she had spent some months, when she suddenly stopped short and laid her finger upon her lips. "Lend me your stick!" she said, in a whisper. I handed it to her, and at once, to my astonishment, she darted lightly and noiselessly through a gap in the hedge, and bending her body, crept swiftly along under the shelter of a little knoll. I was still looking after her in amazement, when a rabbit rose suddenly in front of her and scuttled away. She hurled the stick after it and struck it, but the creature made good its escape, though trailing one leg behind it.

She came back to me exultant and panting. "I saw it move among the grass," she said. "I hit it."

"Yes, you hit it. You broke its leg," I said, somewhat coldly.

"You hurt it," the little boy cried, ruefully.

"Poor little beast!" she exclaimed, with a sudden change in her whole manner. "I am sorry I harmed it." She seemed completely cast down by the incident, and spoke little during the remainder of our walk. For my own part I could not blame her much. It was evidently an outbreak of the old predatory instinct of the savage, though with a somewhat incongruous effect in the case of a fashionably dressed young lady on an English high road.

John Thurston made me peep into her private sitting-room one day when she was out. She had a thousand little Indian knickknacks there which showed that she had come well-laden from her native land. Her Oriental love for bright colours had exhibited itself in an amusing fashion. She had gone down to the market town and bought numerous sheets of pink and blue paper, and these she had pinned in patches over the sombre covering which had lined the walls before. She had some tinsel too, which she had put up in the most conspicuous places. The whole effect was ludicrously tawdry and glaring, and yet there seemed to me to be a touch of pathos in this attempt to reproduce the brilliance of the tropics in the cold English dwelling-house.

During the first few days of my visit the curious relationship which existed between Miss Warrender and the secretary had simply excited my curiosity, but as the weeks passed and I became more interested in the beautiful Anglo-Indian a deeper and more personal feeling took possession of me. I puzzled my brains as to what tie could exist between them. Why was it that while she showed every symptom of being averse to his company during the day she should walk about with him alone after nightfall? Could it be that the distaste which she showed for him before others was a blind to conceal her real feelings? Such a supposition seemed to involve a depth of dissimulation in her nature which appeared to be incompatible with her frank eyes and clear-cut proud features. And yet, what other hypothesis could account for the power which he most certainly exercised over her?

This power showed itself in many ways, but was exerted so quietly and silently that none but a close observer could have known that it existed. I have seen him glance at her with a look so commanding, and, as it seemed to me, so menacing, that next moment I could hardly believe that his white impassive face could be capable of so intense an expression. When he looked at her in this manner she would wince and quiver as though she had been in physical pain. "Decidedly," I thought, "it is fear and not love which produces such effects."

I was so interested in the question that I spoke to my friend John about it. He was in his little laboratory at the time, and was deeply immersed in a series of manipulations and distillations, which ended in the production of an evil-smelling gas, which set us both coughing and choking. I took advantage of our enforced retreat into the fresh air to question him upon one or two points on which I wanted information.

"How long did you say that Miss Warrender had been with your uncle?" I asked.

John looked at me slyly, and shook his acid-stained finger.

"You seem to be wonderfully interested about the daughter of the late lamented Achmet Genghis," he said.

"Who could help it?" I answered, frankly. "I think she is one of the most romantic characters I ever met."

"Take care of the studies, my boy," John said, paternally. "This sort of thing doesn't do before examinations."

"Don't be ridiculous!" I remonstrated. "Any one would think that I was in love with Miss Warrender to hear the way in which you talk. I look on her as an interesting psychological problem, nothing more."

"Quite so — an interesting psychological problem, nothing more."

John seemed to have some of the vapours of the gas still hanging about his system, for his manner was decidedly irritating.

"To revert to my original question," I said. "How long has she been here?"

"About ten weeks."

"And Copperthorne?"

"Over two years."

"Do you imagine that they could have known each other before?"

"Impossible!" said John, with decision. "She came from Germany. I saw the letter from the old merchant, in which he traced her previous life. Copperthorne has always been in Yorkshire except for two years at Cambridge. He had to leave the university under a cloud."

"What sort of a cloud?"

"Don't know," John answered. "They kept it very quiet. I fancy
Uncle Jeremy knows. He's very fond of taking rapscallions up
and giving them what he calls another start. Some of them will
give him a start some of these fine days."

"And so Copperthorne and Miss Warrender were absolute
strangers until the last few weeks?"

"Quite so; and now I think we can go back and analyse the
sediment."

"Never mind the sediment," I cried, detaining him. "There's
more I want to talk to you about. If these two have only known
each other for this short time, how has he managed to gain his
power over her?"

John stared at me open-eyed.

"His power?" he said.

"Yes, the power which he exercises over her."

"My dear Hugh," my friend said, gravely, "I'm not in the habit
of thus quoting Scripture, but there is one text which occurs
irresistibly to my mind, and that is, that 'Much learning hath
made thee mad.' You've been reading too hard."

"Do you mean to say," I cried, "that you have never observed
that there is some secret understanding between your uncle's
governess and his amanuensis?"

"Try bromide of potassium," said John. "It's very soothing in
twenty-grain doses."

"Try a pair of spectacles," I retorted, "you most certainly need
them;" with which parting shot I turned on my heel and went off
in high dudgeon. I had not gone twenty yards down the gravel
walk of the garden before I saw the very couple of whom we had
just been speaking. They were some little way off, she leaning
against the sundial, he standing in front of her and speaking
earnestly, with occasional jerky gesticulations. With his tall, gaunt
figure towering above her, and the spasmodic motions of his long
arms, he might have been some great bat fluttering over a victim.
I remember that that was the simile which rose in my mind at the
time, heightened perhaps by the suggestion of shrinking and of
fear which seemed to me to lie in every curve of her beautiful
figure.

The little picture was such an illustration of the text upon which
I had been preaching, that I had half a mind to go back to the
laboratory and bring the incredulous John out to witness it.
Before I had time to come to a conclusion, however, Copperthorne caught a glimpse of me, and turning away, he strolled
slowly in the opposite direction into the shrubbery, his com-

panion walking by his side and cutting at the flowers as she passed with her sunshade.

I went up to my room after this small episode with the intention of pushing on with my studies, but do what I would my mind wandered away from my books in order to speculate upon this mystery.

I had learned from John that Copperthorne's antecedents were not of the best, and yet he had obviously gained enormous power over his almost imbecile employer. I could understand this fact by observing the infinite pains with which he devoted himself to the old man's hobby, and the consummate tact with which he humoured and encouraged his strange poetic whims. But how could I account for the to me equally obvious power which he wielded over the governess? She had no whims to be humoured. Mutual love might account for the tie between them, but my instinct as a man of the world and as an observer of human nature told me most conclusively that no such love existed. If not love, it must be fear – a supposition which was favoured by all that I had seen.

What, then, had occurred during these two months to cause this high-spirited, dark-eyed princess to fear the white-faced Englishman with the soft voice and the gentle manner? That was the problem which I set myself to solve with an energy and earnestness which eclipsed my ardour for study, and rendered me superior to the terrors of my approaching examination.

I ventured to approach the subject that same afternoon to Miss Warrender, whom I found alone in the library, the two little children having gone to spend the day in the nursery of a neighbouring squire.

"You must be rather lonely when there are no visitors," I remarked. "It does not seem to be a very lively part of the country."

"Children are always good companions," she answered. "Nevertheless I shall miss both Mr. Thornton and yourself very much when you go."

"I shall be sorry when the time comes," I said. "I never expected to enjoy this visit as I have done; still you won't be quite companionless when we are gone, you'll always have Mr. Copperthorne."

"Yes; we shall always have Mr. Copperthorne." She spoke with a weary intonation.

"He's a pleasant companion," I remarked; "quiet, well informed, and amiable. I don't wonder that old Mr. Thurston is so fond of him."

As I spoke in this way I watched my companion intently. There was a slight flush on her dark cheeks, and she drummed her fingers impatiently against the arms of the chair.

"His manner may be a little cold sometimes—" I was continuing, but she interrupted me, turning on me furiously, with an angry glare in her black eyes.

"What do you want to talk to me about him for?" she asked.

"I beg pardon," I answered, submissively, "I did not know it was a forbidden subject."

"I don't wish ever to hear his name," she cried, passionately. "I hate it and I hate him. Oh, if I had only some one who loved me — that is, as men love away over the seas in my own land, I know what I should say to him."

"What would you say?" I asked, astonished at this extraordinary outburst.

She leaned forward until I seemed to feel the quick pants of her warm breath upon my face.

"Kill Copperthorne," she said. "That is what I should say to him. Kill Copperthorne. Then you can come and talk of love to me."

Nothing can describe the intensity of fierceness with which she hissed these words out from between her white teeth.

She looked so venomous as she spoke that I involuntarily shrank away from her. Could this pythoness be the demure young lady who sat every day so primly and quietly at the table of Uncle Jeremy? I had hoped to gain some insight into her character by my leading question, but I had never expected to conjure up such a spirit as this. She must have seen the horror and surprise which was depicted on my face, for her manner changed and she laughed nervously.

"You must really think me mad," she said. "You see it is the Indian training breaking out again. We do nothing by halves over there — either loving or hating."

"And why is it that you hate Mr. Copperthorne?" I asked.

"Ah, well," she answered, in a subdued voice, "perhaps hate is rather too strong a term after all. Dislike would be better. There are some people you cannot help having an antipathy to, even though you are unable to give any exact reason."

It was evident that she regretted her recent outburst and was endeavouring to explain it away.

As I saw that she wished to change the conversation, I aided her to do so, and made some remark about a book of Indian prints which she had taken down before I came in, and which still lay upon her lap. Uncle Jeremy's collection was an extensive one, and was particularly rich in works of this class.

"They are not very accurate," she said, turning over the many-coloured leaves. "This is good, though," she continued, picking out a picture of a chieftain clad in chain mail with a picturesque turban upon his head. "This is very good indeed. My father was dressed like that when he rode down on his white charger and led all the warriors of the Dooab to do battle with the Feringhees. My father was chosen out from amongst them all, for they knew that Achmet Genghis Khan was a great priest as well as a great soldier. The people would be led by none but a tried Borka. He is dead now, and of all those who followed his banner there are none who are not scattered or slain, whilst I, his daughter, am a servant in a far land."

"No doubt you will go back to India some day," I said, in a somewhat feeble attempt at consolation.

She turned the pages over listlessly for a few moments without answering. Then she gave a sudden little cry of pleasure as she paused at one of the prints.

"Look at this," she cried, eagerly. "It is one of our wanderers. He is a Bhuttotee. It is very like."

The picture which excited her so was one which represented a particularly uninviting-looking native with a small instrument which looked like a miniature pickaxe in one hand, and a striped handkerchief or roll of linen in the other.

"That handkerchief is his roomal," she said. "Of course he wouldn't go about with it openly like that, nor would he bear the sacred axe, but in every other respect he is as he should be. Many a time have I been with such upon the moonless nights when the Lughaees were on ahead and the heedless stranger heard the Pilhaoo away to the left and knew not what it might mean. Ah! that was a life that was worth the living!"

"And what may a roomal be — and the Lughaee and all the rest of it?" I asked.

"Oh, they are Indian terms," she answered, with a laugh. "You would not understand them."

"But," I said, "this picture is marked as Dacoit, and I always thought that a Dacoit was a robber."

"That is because the English know no better," she observed. "Of course, Dacoits are robbers, but they call many people robbers who are not really so Now this man is a holy man and in all probability a Gooroo."

She might have given me more information upon Indian manners and customs, for it was a subject upon which she loved to talk; but suddenly as I watched her I saw a change come over her face, and she gazed with a rigid stare at the window behind me. I looked round, and there peering stealthily round the corner at us was the face of the amanuensis. I confess that I was startled myself at the sight, for, with its corpse-like pallor, the head might have been one which had been severed from his shoulders. He threw open the sash when he saw that he was observed.

"I'm sorry to interrupt you," he said, looking in, "but don't you think, Miss Warrender, that it is a pity to be boxed up on such a fine day in a close room? Won't you come out and take a stroll?"

Though his words were courteous they were uttered in a harsh and almost menacing voice, so as to sound more like a command than a request. The governess rose, and without protest or remark glided away to put on her bonnet. It was another example of Copperthorne's authority over her. As he looked in at me through the open window a mocking smile played about his thin lips, as though he would have liked to have taunted me with this display of his power. With the sun shining in behind him he might have been a demon in a halo. He stood in this manner for a few moments gazing in at me with concentrated malice upon his face. Then I heard his heavy footfall scrunching along the gravel path as he walked round in the direction of the door.

V

For some days after the interview in which Miss Warrender confessed her hatred of the secretary, things ran smoothly at Dunkelthwaite. I had several long conversations with her as we rambled about the woods and fields with the two little children, but I was never able to bring her round to the subject of her outburst in the library, nor did she tell me anything which threw any light at all upon the problem which interested me so deeply. Whenever I made any remark which might lead in that direction she either answered me in a guarded manner or else discovered suddenly that it was high time that the children were back in their nursery, so that I came to despair of ever learning anything from her lips.

During this time I studied spasmodically and irregularly. Occasionally old Uncle Jeremy would shuffle into my room with a roll of manuscript in his hand, and would read me extracts from his great epic poem. Whenever I felt in need of company I used to go a-visiting to John's laboratory, and he in his turn would come to my chamber if he were lonely. Sometimes I used to vary the monotony of my studies by taking my books out into an arbour in the shrubbery and working there during the day. As to Copperthorne, I avoided him as much as possible, and he, for his part, appeared to be by no means anxious to cultivate my acquaintance.

One day about the second week in June, John came to me with a telegram in his hand and look of considerable disgust upon his face. "Here's a pretty go!" he cried. "The governor wants me to go up at once and meet him in London. It's some legal business, I suppose. He was always threatening to set his affairs in order, and now he has got an energetic fit and intends to do it."

"I suppose you won't be gone long?" I said.

"A week or two perhaps. It's rather a nuisance, just when I was in a fair way towards separating that alkaloid."

"You'll find it there when you come back," I said laughing. "There's no one here who is likely to separate it in your absence."

"What bothers me most is leaving you here," he continued. "It seems such an inhospitable thing to ask a fellow down to a lonely place like this and then to run away and leave him."

"Don't you mind about me," I answered, "I have too much to do to be lonely. Besides, I have found attractions in this place which I never expected. I don't think any six weeks of my life have ever passed more quickly than the last."

"Oh, they passed quickly, did they?" said John, and sniggered to himself. I am convinced that he was still under the delusion that I was hopelessly in love with the governess.

He went off that day by the early train, promising to write and tell us his address in town, for he did not know yet at which hotel his father would put up. I little knew what a difference this trifle would make, nor what was to occur before I set eyes upon my friend once more. At the time I was by no means grieved at his departure. It brought the four of us who were left into closer apposition, and seemed to favour the solving of that problem in which I found myself from day to day becoming more interested.

About a quarter of a mile from the house of Dunkelthwaite there is a straggling little village of the same name, consisting of some twenty or thirty slate-roofed cottages, with an ivy-clad church hard by and the inevitable beerhouse. On the afternoon of the very day on which John left us, Miss Warrender and the two children walked down to the post-office there, and I volunteered to accompany them.

Copperthorne would have liked well to have either prevented the excursion or to have gone with us, but fortunately Uncle Jeremy was in the throes of composition, and the services of his secretary were indispensable to him. It was a pleasant walk, I remember, for the road was well shaded by trees, and the birds were singing merrily overhead. We strolled along together, talking of many things, while the little boy and girl ran on, laughing and romping.

Before you get to the post-office you have to pass the beerhouse already mentioned. As we walked down the village street we became conscious that a small knot of people had assembled in front of this building. There were a dozen or so ragged boys and draggle-tailed girls, with a few bonnetless women, and a couple of loungers from the bar – probably as large an assemblage as ever met together in the annals of that quiet neighbourhood. We could not see what it was that was exciting their curiosity, but the children scampered on and quickly returned brimful of information.

"Oh, Miss Warrender," Johnnie cried, as he dashed up, panting and eager, "there's a black man there like the ones you tell us stories about!"

"A gipsy, I suppose," I said.

"No, no," said Johnnie, with decision; "he is blacker than that, isn't he, May?"

"Blacker than that," the little girl echoed.

"I suppose we had better go and see what this wonderful apparition is," I said.

As I spoke I glanced at my companion. To my surprise, she was very pale, and her great black eyes appeared to be luminous with suppressed excitement.

"Aren't you well?" I asked.

"Oh, yes. Come on!" she cried, eagerly, quickening her step; "come on!"

It was certainly a curious sight which met our eyes when we joined the little circle of rustics. It reminded me of the description of the opium-eating Malay whom De Quincey saw in the farm-house in Scotland. In the centre of the circle of homely Yorkshire folk there stood an Oriental wanderer, tall, lithe, and graceful, his linen clothes stained with dust and his brown feet projecting through his rude shoes. It was evident that he had travelled far and long. He had a heavy stick in his hand, on which he leaned, while his dark eyes looked thoughtfully away into space, careless apparently of the throng around him. His picturesque attire, with his coloured turban and swarthy face, had a strange and incongruous effect amongst all the prosaic surroundings.

"Poor fellow!" Miss Warrender said to me, speaking in an excited, gasping voice. "He is tired and hungry, no doubt, and cannot explain his wants. I will speak to him;" and, going up to the Indian, she said a few words in his native dialect.

Never shall I forget the effect which those few syllables produced. Without a word the wanderer fell straight down upon his face on the dusty road and absolutely grovelled at the feet of my companion. I had read of Eastern forms of abasement when in the presence of a superior, but I could not have imagined that any human could have expressed such abject humility as was indicated in this man's attitude.

Miss Warrender spoke again in a sharp and commanding voice, on which he sprang to his feet and stood with his hands clasped and his eyes cast down, like a slave in the presence of his mistress. The little crowd, who seemed to think that the sudden prostration had been the prelude to some conjuring feat or acrobatic entertainment, looked on amused and interested.

"Should you mind walking on with the children and posting the letters?" the governess said. "I should like to have a word with this man."

I complied with her request, and when I returned in a few minutes the two were still conversing. The Indian appeared to be giving a narrative of his adventures or detailing the causes of his journey, for he spoke rapidly and excitedly, with quivering fingers and gleaming eyes. Miss Warrender listened intently, giving an occasional start or exclamation, which showed how deeply the man's statement interested her.

"I must apologise for detaining you so long in the sun," she said, turning to me at last. "We must go home, or we shall be late for dinner."

With a few parting sentences, which sounded like commands, she left her dusky acquaintance still standing in the village street, and we strolled homewards with the children.

"Well?" I asked, with natural curiosity, when we were out of earshot of the visitors. "Who is he, and what is he?"

"He comes from the Central Provinces, near the land of the Mahrattas. He is one of us. It has been quite a shock to me to meet a fellow-countryman so unexpectedly; I feel quite upset."

"It must have been pleasant for you," I remarked.

"Yes, very pleasant," she said, heartily.

"And why did he fall down like that?"

"Because he knew me to be the daughter of Achmet Genghis Khan," she said, proudly.

"And what chance has brought him here?"

"Oh, it's a long story," she said, carelessly. "He has led a wandering life. How dark it is in this avenue, and how the great branches shoot across! If you were to crouch on one of those you could drop down on the back of any one who passed, and they would never know that you were there until they felt your fingers on their throat."

"What a horrible idea!" I exclaimed.

"Gloomy places always give me gloomy thoughts," she said, lightly. "By the way, I want you to do me a favour, Mr. Lawrence."

"What is that?" I asked.

"Don't say anything at the house about this poor compatriot of mine. They might think him a rogue and a vagabond, you know, and order him to be driven from the village."

"I'm sure Mr. Thurston would do nothing so unkind."

"No; but Mr. Copperthorne might."

"Just as you like," I said; "but the children are sure to tell."

"No, I think not," she answered.

I don't know how she managed to curb their little prattling tongues, but they certainly preserved silence upon the point, and there was no talk that evening of the strange visitor who had wandered into our little hamlet.

I had a shrewd suspicion that this stranger from the tropics was no chance wanderer, but had come to Dunkelthwaite upon some set errand. Next day I had the best possible evidence that he was still in the vicinity, for I met Miss Warrender coming down the garden walk with a basketful of scraps of bread and of meat in her hand. She was in the habit of taking these leavings to sundry old women in the neighbourhood, so I offered to accompany her.

"Is it old Dame Venables or old Dame Taylforth to-day?" I asked.

"Neither one nor the other," she said, with a smile. "I'll tell you the truth, Mr. Lawrence, because you have always been a good friend to me, and I feel I can trust you. These scraps are for my poor countryman. I'll hang the basket here on this branch, and he will get it."

"Oh, he's still about, then," I observed.

"Yes, he's still in the neighbourhood."

"You think he will find it?"

"Oh, trust him for that," she said. "You don't blame me for helping him, do you? You would do the same if you lived among Indians and suddenly came upon an Englishman. Come to the hothouse and look at the flowers."

We walked round to the conservatory together. When we came back the basket was still hanging to the branch, but the contents were gone. She took it down with a laugh and carried it in with her.

It seemed to me that since this interview with her countryman the day before her spirits had become higher and her step freer and more elastic. It may have been imagination, but it appeared to me also that she was not as constrained as usual in the presence of Copperthorne, and that she met his glances more fearlessly, and was less under the influence of his will.

And now I am coming to that part of this statement of mine which describes how I first gained an insight into the relation which existed between those two strange mortals, and learned the terrible truth about Miss Warrender, or of the Princess Achmet Genghis, as I should prefer to call her, for assuredly she was the descendant of the fierce fanatical warrior rather than of her gentle mother.

To me the revelation came as a shock, the effect of which I can never forget. It is possible that in the way in which I have told the story, emphasising those facts which had a bearing upon her, and omitting those which had not, my readers have already detected the strain which ran in her blood. As for myself, I solemnly aver that up to the last moment I had not the smallest suspicion of the truth. Little did I know what manner of woman this was, whose hand I pressed in friendship, and whose voice was music to my ears. Yet it is my belief, looking back, that she was really well disposed to me, and would not willingly have harmed me.

It was in this manner that the revelation came about. I think I have mentioned that there was a certain arbour in the shrubbery in which I was accustomed to study during the daytime. One night, about ten o'clock, I found on going to my room that I had left a book on gynæcology in this summer-house, and as I intended to do a couple of hours' work before turning in, I started off with the intention of getting it. Uncle Jeremy and the servants had already gone to bed, so I slipped downstairs very quietly and turned the key gently in the front door. Once in the open air, I hurried rapidly across the lawn, and so into the shrubbery, with the intention of regaining my property and returning as rapidly as possible.

I had hardly passed the little wooden gate and entered the plantation before I heard the sound of talking, and knew that I had chanced to stumble upon one of those nocturnal conclaves which I had observed from my window. The voices were those of the secretary and of the governess, and it was clear to me, from the direction in which they sounded, that they were sitting in the arbour and conversing together without any suspicion of the presence of a third person. I have ever held that eavesdropping, under any circumstances, is a dishonourable practice, and curious as I was to know what passed between these two, I was about to cough or give some other signal of my presence, when suddenly I heard some words of Copperthorne's which brought me to a halt with every faculty overwhelmed with horrified amazement.

"They'll think he died of apoplexy," were the words which sounded clearly and distinctly through the peaceful air in the incisive tones of the amanuensis.

I stood breathless, listening with all my ears. Every thought of announcing my presence had left me. What was the crime which these ill-assorted conspirators were hatching upon this lovely summer's night.

I heard the deep sweet tones of her voice, but she spoke so rapidly, and in such a subdued manner, that I could not catch the words. I could tell by the intonation that she was under the influence of deep emotion. I drew nearer on tip-toe, with my ears straining to catch every sound. The moon was not up yet, and under the shadows of the trees it was very dark. There was little chance of my being observed.

"Eaten his bread, indeed!" the secretary said, derisively. "You are not usually so squeamish. You did not think of that in the case of little Ethel."

"I was mad! I was mad!" she ejaculated in a broken voice. "I had prayed much to Buddha and to the great Bhowanee, and it seemed to me that in this land of unbelievers it would be a great and glorious thing for me, a lonely woman, to act up to the teachings of my great father. There are few women who are admitted into the secrets of our faith, and it was but by an accident that the honour came upon me. Yet, having once had the path pointed out to me, I have walked straight and fearlessly, and the great Gooroo Ramdeen Singh has said that even in my fourteenth year I was worthy to sit upon the cloth of the Tupounee with the other Bhuttotees. Yet I swear by the sacred pickaxe that I have grieved much over this, for what had the poor child done that she should be sacrificed!"

"I fancy that my having caught you has had more to do with your repentance than the moral aspect of the case," Copperthorne said, with a sneer. "I may have had my misgivings before, but it was only when I saw you rising up with the handkerchief in your hand that I knew for certain that we were honoured by the presence of a Princess of the Thugs. An English scaffold would be rather a prosaic end for such a romantic being."

"And you have used your knowledge ever since to crush all the life out of me," she said, bitterly. "You have made my existence a burden to me."

"A burden to you!" he said, in an altered voice. "You know what my feelings are towards you. If I have occasionally governed you by the fear of exposure it was only because I found you were insensible to the milder influence of love."

"Love!" she cried, bitterly. "How could I love a man who held a shameful death for ever before my eyes. But let us come to the point. You promise me my unconditional liberty if I do this one thing for you?"

"Yes," Copperthorne answered; "you may go where you will when this is done. I shall forget what I saw here in the shrubbery."

"You swear it?"

"Yes, I swear it."

"I would do anything for my freedom," she said.

"We can never have such a chance again," Copperthorne cried. "Young Thurston is gone, and this friend of his sleeps heavily, and is too stupid to suspect. The will is made out in my favour, and if the old man dies every stock and stone of the great estate will be mine."

"Why don't you do it yourself, then?" she asked.

"It's not in my line," he said. "Besides, I have not got the knack. That roomal, or whatever you call it, leaves no mark. That's the advantage of it."

"It is an accursed thing to slay one's benefactor."

"But it is a great thing to serve Bhowanee, the goddess of murder. I know enough of your religion to know that. Would not your father do it if he were here?"

"My father was the greatest of all the Borkas of Jublepore," she said, proudly. "He has slain more than there are days in the year."

"I wouldn't have met him for a thousand pounds," Copperthorne remarked, with a laugh. "But what would Achmet Genghis Khan say now if he saw his daughter hesitate with such a chance before her of serving the gods? You have done excellently so far. He may well have smiled when the infant soul of young Ethel was wafted up to this god or ghoul of yours. Perhaps this is not the first sacrifice you have made. How about the daughter of this charitable German merchant? Ah, I see in your face that I am right again! After such deeds you do wrong to hesitate now when there is no danger and all shall be made easy to you. Besides that, the deed will free you from your existence here, which cannot be particularly pleasant with a rope, so to speak, round your neck the whole time. If it is to be done it must be done at once. He might rewrite his will at any moment, for he is fond of the lad, and is as changeable as a weather-cock."

There was a long pause, and a silence so profound that I seemed to hear my own heart throbbing in the darkness.

"When shall it be done?" she asked at last.

"Why not to-morrow night?"

"How am I to get to him?"

"I shall leave his door open," Copperthorne said. "He sleeps heavily, and I shall leave a night-light burning, so that you may see your way."

"And afterwards?"

"Afterwards you will return to your room. In the morning it will be discovered that our poor employer has passed away in his sleep. It will also be found that he has left all his worldly goods as a slight return for the devoted labours of his faithful secretary. Then the services of Miss Warrender the governess being no longer required, she may go back to her beloved country or to anywhere else that she fancies. She can run away with Mr. John Lawrence, student of medicine, if she pleases."

"You insult me," she said, angrily; and then, after a pause. "You must meet me to-morrow night before I do this."

"Why so?" he asked.

"Because there may be some last instructions which I may require."

"Let it be here, then, at twelve," he said.

"No, not here. It is too near the house. Let us meet under the great oak at the head of the avenue."

"Where you will," he answered, sulkily; "but mind, I'm not going to be with you when you do it."

"I shall not ask you," she said, scornfully. "I think we have said all that need be said to-night."

I heard the sound of one or other of them rising to their feet, and though they continued to talk I did not stop to hear more, but crept quietly out from my place of concealment and scudded across the dark lawn and in through the door, which I closed behind me. It was only when I had regained my room and had sunk back into my armchair that I was able to collect my scattered senses and to think over the terrible conversation to which I had listened. Long into the hours of the night I sat motionless, meditating over every word that I had heard and endeavouring to form in my mind some plan of action for the future.

VI

The Thugs! I had heard of the wild fanatics of that name who are found in the central part of India, and whose distorted religion represents murder as being the highest and purest of all the gifts which a mortal can offer to the Creator. I remember an account of them which I had read in the works of Colonel Meadows Taylor, of their secrecy, their organisation, their relentlessness, and the terrible power which their homicidal craze has over every other mental or moral faculty. I even recalled now that the roomal – a word which I had heard her mention more than once – was the sacred handkerchief with which they were wont to work their diabolical purpose. She was already a woman when she had left them, and being, according to her own account, the daughter of their principal leader, it was no wonder that the varnish of civilisation had not eradicated all her early impressions or prevented the breaking out of occasional fits of fanaticism. In one of these apparently she had put an end to poor Ethel, having carefully prepared an alibi to conceal her crime, and it was Copperthorne's accidental discovery of this murder which gave him his power over his strange associate. Of all deaths that by hanging is considered among these tribes to be the most impious and degrading, and her knowledge that she had subjected herself to this death by the law of the land was evidently the reason why she had found herself compelled to subject her will and tame her imperious nature when in the presence of the amanuensis.

As to Copperthorne himself, as I thought over what he had done, and what he proposed to do, a great horror and loathing filled my whole soul. Was this his return for the kindness lavished upon him by the poor old man? He had already cozened him into signing away his estates, and now, for fear some prickings of conscience should cause him to change his mind, he had determined to put it out of his power ever to write a codicil. All this was bad enough, but the acme of all seemed to be that, too cowardly to effect his purpose with his own hand, he had made use of this unfortunate woman's horrible conceptions of religion in order to remove Uncle Jeremy in such a way that no suspicion could possibly fall upon the real culprit. I determined in my mind that, come what might, the amanuensis should not escape from the punishment due to his crimes.

But what was I to do? Had I known my friend's address I should have telegraphed for him in the morning, and he could have been back in Dunkelthwaite before nightfall. Unfortunately John was the worst of correspondents, and though he had been gone for some days we had had no word yet of his whereabouts. There were three maid-servants in the house, but no man, with the exception of old Elijah; nor did I know of any upon whom I could rely in the neighbourhood. This, however, was a small matter, for I knew that in personal strength I was more than a match for the secretary, and I had confidence enough in myself to feel that my resistance alone would prevent any possibility of the plot being carried out.

The question was, what were the best steps for me to take under the circumstances? My first impulse was to wait until morning, and then to quietly go or send to the nearest police-station and summon a couple of constables. I could then hand Copperthorne and his female accomplice over to justice and narrate the conversation which I had overheard. On second thoughts this plan struck me as being a very impracticable one. What grain of evidence had I against them except my story? which, to people who did not know me, would certainly appear a very wild and improbable one. I could well imagine too the plausible voice and imperturbable manner with which Copperthorne would oppose the accusation, and how he would dilate upon the ill-will which I bore both him and his companion on account of their mutual affection. How easy it would be for him to make a third person believe that I was trumping up a story in the hope of injuring a rival, and how difficult for me to make any one credit that this clerical-looking gentleman and this stylishly-dressed young lady were two beasts of prey who were hunting in couples! I felt that it would be a great mistake for me to show my hand before I was sure of the game.

The alternative was to say nothing and to let things take their course, being always ready to step in when the evidence against the conspirators appeared to be conclusive. This was the course which recommended itself to my young adventurous disposition, and it also appeared to be the one most likely to lead to conclusive results. When at last at early dawn I stretched myself upon my bed and I had fully made up my mind to retain my knowledge in my own breast, and to trust to myself entirely for the defeat of the murderous plot which I had overheard.

Old Uncle Jeremy was in high spirits next morning after breakfast, and insisted upon reading aloud a scene from Shelley's "Cenci," a work for which he had a profound admiration. Copperthorne sat silent and inscrutable by his side, save when he threw in a suggestion or uttered an exclamation of admiration. Miss Warrender appeared to be lost in thought, and it seemed to me more than once that I saw tears in her dark eyes. It was strange for me to watch the three of them and to think of the real relation in which they stood to each other. My heart warmed towards my little red-faced host with the quaint head-gear and the old-fashioned ways. I vowed to myself that no harm should befall him while I had power to prevent it.

The day wore along slowly and drearily. It was impossible for me to settle down to work, so I wandered restlessly about the corridors of the old-fashioned house and over the garden. Copperthorne was with Uncle Jeremy upstairs, and I saw little of him. Twice when I was striding up and down outside I perceived the governess coming with the children in my direction, but on each occasion I avoided her by hurrying away. I felt that I could not speak to her without showing the intense horror with which she inspired me, and so betraying my knowledge of what had transpired the night before. She noticed that I shunned her, for at luncheon, when my eyes caught hers for a moment, she flashed across a surprised and injured glance, to which, however, I made no response.

The afternoon post brought a letter from John telling us that he was stopping at the Langham. I knew that it was now impossible for him to be of any use to me in the way of sharing the responsibility of whatever might occur, but I nevertheless thought it my duty to telegraph to him and let him know that his presence was desirable. This involved a long walk to the station, but that was useful as helping me to while away the time, and I felt a weight off my mind when I heard the clicking of the needles which told me that my message was flying upon its way.

When I reached the avenue gate on my return from Ingleton I found our old serving-man Elijah standing there, apparently in a violent passion.

"They says as one rat brings others," he said to me, touching his hat, "and it seems as it be the same with they darkies."

He had always disliked the governess on account of what he called her "uppish ways."

"What's the matter, then?" I asked.

"It's one o' they furriners a-hidin' and a-prowlin'," said the old man. "I seed him here among the bushes, and I sent him off wi' a bit o' my mind. Lookin' after the hens as like as not, or maybe wantin' to burn the house and murder us all in our beds. I'll go down to the village, Muster Lawrence, and see what he's after," and he hurried away in a paroxysm of senile anger.

This little incident made a considerable impression on me, and I thought seriously over it as I walked up the long avenue. It was clear that the wandering Hindoo was still hanging about the premises. He was a factor whom I had forgotten to take into account. If his compatriot enlisted him as an accomplice in her dark plans, it was possible that the three of them might be too many for me. Still it appeared to me to be improbable that she should do so, since she had taken such pains to conceal his presence from Copperthorne.

I was half tempted to take Elijah into my confidence, but on second thoughts I came to the conclusion that a man of his age would be worse than useless as an ally.

About seven o'clock I was going up to my room when I met the secretary, who asked me whether I could tell him where Miss Warrender was. I answered that I had not seen her.

"It's a singular thing," he said, "that no one has seen her since dinner-time. The children don't know where she is. I particularly want to speak to her."

He hurried on with an agitated and disturbed expression upon his features.

As to me, Miss Warrender's absence did not seem a matter of surprise. No doubt she was out in the shrubbery somewhere, nerving herself for the terrible piece of work which she had undertaken to do. I closed my door behind me and sat down, with a book in my hand, but with my mind too much excited to comprehend the contents. My plan of campaign had been already formed. I determined to be within sight of their trysting-place, to follow them, and to interfere at the moment when my interference would have most effect. I had chosen a thick, knobby stick, dear to my student heart, and with this I knew that I was master of the situation, for I had ascertained that Copperthorne had no firearms.

I do not remember any period of my life when the hours passed so slowly as did those which I spent in my room that night. Far away I heard the mellow tones of the Dunklethwaite clock as it struck the hours of eight and then of nine, and then, after an interminable pause, of ten. After that it seemed as though time had stopped altogether as I paced my little room, fearing and yet longing for the hour as men will when some great ordeal has to be faced. All things have an end, however, and at last there came pealing through the still night air the first clear stroke which announced the eleventh hour. Then I rose, and, putting on my soft slippers, I seized my stick and slipped quietly out of my room and down the creaking old-fashioned staircase. I could hear the stertorous snoring of Uncle Jeremy upon the floor above. I managed to feel my way to the door through the darkness, and having opened it passed out into the beautiful starlit night.

I had to be very careful of my movements, because the moon shone so brightly that it was almost as light as day. I hugged the shadow of the house until I reached the garden hedge, and then, crawling down in its shelter, I found myself safe in the shrubbery in which I had been the night before. Through this I made my way, treading very cautiously and gingerly, so that not a stick snapped beneath my feet. In this way I advanced until I found myself among the brushwood at the edge of the plantation and within full view of the great oak-tree which stood at the upper end of the avenue.

There was someone standing under the shadow of the oak. At first I could hardly make out who it was, but presently the figure began to move, and, coming out into a silvery patch where the moon shone down between two branches, looked impatiently to left and to right. Then I saw that it was Copperthorne, who was waiting alone. The governess apparently had not yet kept her appointment.

As I wished to hear as well as to see, I wormed my way along under the dark shadows of the trunks in the direction of the oak. When I stopped I was not more than fifteen paces from the spot where the tall gaunt figure of the amanuensis looked grim and ghastly in the shifting light. He paced about uneasily, now disappearing in the shadow, now reappearing in the silvery patches where the moon broke through the covering above him. It was evident from his movements that he was puzzled and disconcerted at the non-appearance of his accomplice. Finally he stationed himself under a great branch which concealed his figure, while from beneath it he commanded a view of the gravel drive which led down from the house, and along which, no doubt, he expected Miss Warrender to come.

I was still lying in my hiding-place, congratulating myself inwardly at having gained a point from which I could hear all without risk of discovery, when my eye lit suddenly upon something which made my heart rise to my mouth and almost caused me to utter an ejaculation which would have betrayed my presence.

I have said that Copperthorne was standing immediately under one of the great branches of the oak-tree. Beneath this all was plunged in the deepest shadow, but the upper part of the branch itself was silvered over by the light of the moon. As I gazed I became conscious that down this luminous branch something was crawling – a flickering, inchoate something, almost indistinguishable from the branch itself, and yet slowly and steadily writhing its way down it. My eyes, as I looked, became more accustomed to the light, and then this indefinite something took form and substance. It was a human being – a man – the Indian whom I had seen in the village. With his arms and legs twined round the great limb, he was shuffling his way down as silently and almost as rapidly as one of his native snakes.

Before I had time to conjecture the meaning of his presence he was directly over the spot where the secretary stood, his bronzed body showing out hard and clear against the disc of moon behind him. I saw him take something from round his waist, hesitate for a moment, as though judging his distance, and then spring downwards, crashing through the intervening foliage. There was a heavy thud, as of two bodies falling together, and then there rose on the night air a noise as of some one gargling his throat, followed by a succession of croaking sounds, the remembrance of which will haunt me to my dying day.

Whilst this tragedy had been enacted before my eyes its entire unexpectedness and its horror had bereft me of the power of acting in any way. Only those who have been in a similar position can imagine the utter paralysis of mind and body which comes upon a man in such straits, and prevents him from doing the thousand and one things which may be suggested afterwards as having been appropriate to the occasion. When those notes of death, however, reached my ears I shook off my lethargy and ran forward with a loud cry from my place of concealment. At the sound the young Thug sprang from his victim with a snarl like a wild beast driven from a carcase, and made off down the avenue at such a pace that I felt it to be impossible for me to overtake him. I ran to the secretary and raised his head. His face was purple and horribly distorted. I loosened his shirt-collar and did all I could to restore him, but it was useless. The roomal had done its work, and he was dead.

I have little more to add to this strange tale of mine. If I have been somewhat long-winded in the telling of it, I feel that I owe no apology for that, for I have simply set the successive events down in a plain unvarnished fashion, and the narrative would be incomplete without any one of them. It transpired afterwards that Miss Warrender had caught the 7.20 London train, and was safe in the metropolis before any search could be made for her. As to the messenger of death whom she had left behind to keep her appointment with Copperthorne under the old oak-tree, he was never either heard of or seen again. There was a hue and cry over the whole countryside, but nothing came of it. No doubt the fugitive passed the days in sheltered places, and travelled rapidly at night, living on such scraps as can sustain an Oriental, until he was out of danger.

John Thornton returned next day, and I poured all the facts into his astonished ears. He agreed with me that it was best perhaps not to speak of what I knew concerning Copperthorne's plans and the reasons which kept him out so late upon that summer's night. Thus even the county police have never known the full story of that strange tragedy, and they certainly never shall, unless, indeed, the eyes of some of them should chance to fall upon this narrative. Poor Uncle Jeremy mourned the loss of his secretary for months, and many were the verses which he poured forth in the form of epitaphs and of "In Memoriam" poems. He has been gathered to his fathers himself since then, and the greater part of his estate has, I am glad to say, descended to the rightful heir, his nephew.

There is only one point on which I should like to make a remark. How was it that the wandering Thug came to Dunkelthwaite? This question has never been cleared up; but I have not the slightest doubt in my own mind, nor I think can anyone have who considers the facts of the case, that there was no chance about his appearance. The sect in India were a large and powerful body, and when they came to look around for a fresh leader, they naturally bethought them of the beautiful daughter of their late chief. It would be no difficult matter to trace her to Calcutta, to Germany, and finally to Dunkelthwaite. He had come, no doubt, with the message that she was not forgotten in India, and that a warm welcome awaited her if she chose to join her scattered tribesmen. This may seem far-fetched, but it is the opinion which I have always entertained upon the matter.

I began this statement by a quotation from a letter, and I shall end it by one. This was from an old friend, Dr. B.C. Haller, a man of encyclopædic knowledge, and particularly well versed in Indian manners and customs. It is through his kindness that I am able to reproduce the various native words which I heard from time to time from the lips of Miss Warrender, but which I should not have been able to recall to my memory had he not suggested them to me. This is a letter in which he comments upon the matter, which I had mentioned to him in conversation some time previously:

"My dear Lawrence, – I promised to write to you re Thuggee, but my time has been so occupied that it is only now that I can redeem my pledge. I was much interested in your unique experience, and should much like to have further talk with you upon the subject. I may inform you that it is most unusual for a woman to be initiated into the mysteries of Thuggee, and it arose in this case probably from her having accidently or by design tasted the sacred goor, which was the sacrifice offered by the gang after each murder. Any one doing this must become an acting Thug, whatever the rank, sex, or condition. Being of noble blood she would then rapidly pass through the different grades of

Tilhaee, or scout, Lughaee, or grave-digger, Shumsheea, or holder of the victim's hands, and finally of Bhuttotee, or strangler. In all this she would be instructed by her Gooroo, or spiritual adviser, whom she mentions in your account as having been her own father, who was a Borka, or an expert Thug. Having once attained this position, I do not wonder that her fanatical instincts broke out at times. The Pilhaoo which she mentions in one place was the omen on the left hand, which, if it is followed by the Thibaoo, or omen on the right, was considered to be an indication that all would go well. By the way, you mention that the old coachman saw the Hindoo lurking about among the bushes in the morning. Do you know what he was doing? I am very much mistaken if he was not digging Copperthorne's grave, for it is quite opposed to Thug customs to kill a man without having some receptacle prepared for his body. As far as I know only one English officer in India has ever fallen a victim to the fraternity, and that was Lieutenant Monsell, in 1812. Since then Colonel Sleeman has stamped it out to a great extent, though it is unquestionable that it flourishes far more than the authorities suppose. Truly 'the dark places of the earth are full of cruelty,' and nothing but the Gospel will ever effectually dispel that darkness. You are very welcome to publish these few remarks if they seem to you to throw any light upon your narrative.

"Yours very sincerely,
"B.C. HALLER."

THE STONE OF BOXMAN'S DRIFT

———————◆———————

The sun had sunk down behind the distant Griqualand mountains and had left a few bright slashes upon the western sky, which faded slowly from scarlet into pink and from that into the prevailing grey. A deep purplish haze lay over veldt, and kopje, and kloof. Through the gathering twilight the Vaal river lay like a silver serpent, winding its way through valley and gorge, until it lost itself amid the mists of the horizon. Here and there along its course a group of glittering twinkling yellow lights, like golden pendants on a silver string, marked the position of the score of hamlets and townships which are studded along its banks.

But how come towns and hamlets to be there? To the north stretch the wilds of Bechuanaland, where the savage and the wild beast are still contending their world-old quarrel. It is the desolate kingdom of the two-footed man-slayer and of the four-footed man-eater. To the south lies a barren and unprofitable region, where water is scarce, and the dry withered veldt grass can hardly support the flocks of gaunt ill-fed sheep which roam over it. The east and west are still the homes of three Kaffir tribes, who have slowly and sullenly retreated before the advancing tide of civilisation. How comes it, then, that men are so ready to risk their lives and their property in the valley of the Vaal? The answer is the old, old one. It is the search for riches that brings them there. Of all the thousands who live down there, there is not one who does not hope that a single stroke of a pick may send him home some day a wealthy man, to take his place among the magnates of his native shire. To the eyes of hope these scattered shanties and dilapidated huts are the porticos which lead up to honour, position, wealth, all that can place a man above his fellows. For in this desolate valley, amid the sordid clay and gravel, lies buried that which can lend state to the stately monarch, and beauty to the beautiful woman; that which rejoices the soul of the covetous and pleases the eyes of the fastidious. As surely as California is the home of gold, and Nevada of silver, so is this wild and desolate African valley the chosen seat and throne of the most precious of the products of nature, the regal diamond.

Who can say by what convulsion and cataclysm of nature they come to be there? those sparkling fragments of carbon, lying scattered broadcast among the gneiss and the felspar, and other humbler crystalline brethren. A poor Boer, trekking through in his waggon, observes his children playing with a glittering stone. Struck by its appearance, he takes it with him to Natal, where it is pronounced to be a diamond of the purest water. The news spreads fast over the whole habitable globe. There is in very truth a valley as marvellous as that of Sindbad, where a king's ransom may be picked up for the stooping. From every country, by land and by water, on foot, on horseback, in buggy or in waggon, the searchers after wealth converge upon it. Neither savage man nor savage beast can deter them from their purpose. And so the mining camps spring up and the pits are dug, and nature's hidden wealth is torn from her, and pressed into the service of restless avaricious man.

But where money is all other things must come even in the heart of savage Africa. The store enlarges and becomes an emporium, while the liquor saloon expands into the hotel. The bank, the police-station, and the church are all found to be necessary adjuncts of civilisation. Thus, at the time of which I write, the hamlet of Dutoitspan had grown into the flourishing city of Kimberley, while all the other camps, which extended for sixty miles or more along the Vaal river, bore evident signs of prosperity, as befitted a settlement which was turning out a million or more of money every year. Luxuries were very dear, but they were attainable. Frock coats and felt hats were occasionally to be seen in the streets. Now and again the rough inhabitants rose superior to the law, and argued with six-shooters, or emphasised their remarks with knives, but in spite of these occasional outbreaks, Peniel, Winter Rush, Blue Jacket, or Hebron were by no means rowdy localities. The work was too hard and constant to allow of dissipation. A successful digger might at long intervals indulge in a night's orgy, and be found lying heavy with whisky on the roadway in the morning, but the necessity of working his claim was too urgent to allow him to devote much of his time to the consumption of alcohol. Vice is not seldom the offspring of idleness, and here all were busy.

A mile or so from the camp at Winter Rush there is a small gulch, or ravine, named Boxman's Drift, which is a mere rocky cleft in the hill, with a small stream running down the centre. This locality had been frequently prospected, and several experimental pits sunk in it, but with so little success that it had long been abandoned as useless. It chanced, however, in 1872, that two Englishmen, finding every other claim occupied, erected a hut in this lonely gulch, and succeeded, either through hard work or good luck, in making their workings pay their way. Indeed, after a year or two they struck pay gravel, and were able to enlarge their claim and to hire a couple of Kaffirs to assist them in the work. They were steady, industrious men, quiet in their habits, loyal to each other, and accustomed to work from daybreak to sunset during six days out of the seven. On the evening in question they had remained in their pit digging and washing, until light failed them, when the elder, Bill Stewart, clambered reluctantly out, and reaching down a powerful hand, pulled his partner up after him.

"I'll tell you what it is, Bill," said the latter, a slim, flaxen-haired man in the prime of life, "if we are going to make this pit much deeper we shall need a cord and a windlass. It's all very well for giants like you, but it would take me all my time to get out if I were alone."

"We'll set Pompey to cut steps," the other answered. "Talking about deep places, d'ye see that flaw in the rock?" pointing with his shovel to a dark crack which zigzagged along one side of the valley. "That's deep enough. It's my belief that it extends to somewhere near the centre of the earth – or maybe right through to old England. 'Twould save postage if we could drop our letters through."

"Aye, it's very deep," said his companion. "The day you went to Kimberley I tried it with a beer-bottle bent on to a hundred fathoms of string, but I never touched bottom."

"I'll try the beer-bottle without the string, for I am as dry as a chip," said Bill Stewart, slinging his tools over his shoulder. "Have you the take, Headley?"

"All safe."

"Then come along, and we'll reckon it up at the hut."

The hut in question was a square wooden shanty which had been erected on entirely novel architectural principles by Stewart, or Big Bill, as he was usually called in the camps. He was a stolid, slow-tempered man; but if there was a subject upon which he was thin-skinned it was when any one ventured to hint that there was any room for improvement in Azalea Cottage, as he grandiloquently termed it. It was in vain to quote against it any obvious defect, for Bill would at once proceed to prove that that had been specially introduced, and was the result of his own care and forethought.

"Crooked," he would say; "yes, it's not one of your twopenny-halfpenny square-faced blocks that look as if they were turned out by a machine at so much a dozen. It's a select house, sir. There is style about it. Chinks! Why, yes, sir, I like chinks. They promote ventilation, and all good architects aim at that. I took some trouble to work all those chinks in. Holes in the roof? Well, it's an advantage to know when it's raining without going outside to look. Besides, it's handy when the fire smokes. We'd all have been smothered if I hadn't thought to leave those holes there." These were Bill Stewart's usual answers to the casual and inquisitive stranger; but should the banter proceed too far, an angry light would appear in his big blue eyes. "That house, sir," he would remark, "is good enough for my pard, Headley Dean, who is a gentleman born, and so I guess it's good enough for you!" At which descent to personalities the stranger, if he were a wise man, would shift the conversation to the price of stones, or the latest blunder of the Cape Town Government.

The two partners, as they sat opposite to one another on either side of the blazing fire, were a remarkable contrast to each other. Headley Dean, with his crisp, neatly-trimmed hair and beard, his quick, glancing eyes, and his nervous, impulsive ways, had something of the Celt, both in his appearance and in his manner. Eager, active, energetic, he gave the impression of a man who must succeed in the world, but who might be a little unscrupulous in his methods of doing so. Big Bill, on the other hand, quiet, unimpressionable, and easy-going, with a sweeping yellow beard and open Saxon countenance, may have had a stronger and deeper nature than his partner, but was inferior to him in fertility of resource, and in decision of character in all the minor matters of life. This superior readiness made the big man look up to the other and bow to his opinions in a manner that was almost ludicrous considering the relative size and physical strength of the pair.

"Well, and how much have we taken?" asked Stewart, stretching his mud-bespattered boots up to the blaze.

"Not very much," said the other, stirring his pannikin of tea and looking down at the small, flat box in which the day's takings had been placed. "There are fourteen stones of a sort, but there's not one worth more than a few shillings. If we get three pound for the lot it's as much as they are worth."

Bill Stewart whistled. "Our working expenses are close on two pound a day," he remarked. "We won't make a fortune at this rate!"

Headley Dean took a flat tin case from a shelf, and having unlocked it, laid it upon the table. It was divided into compartments, and was half-full of diamonds, arranged in their different classes. He proceeded to examine each of the stones taken that day, and to assign them to their various categories.

"These three are off-coloured," said he. "That makes a hundred and eighteen off-coloured stones which we hold."

"Better sell," suggested Bill Stewart, lighting his pipe with an ember.

"Better do nothing of the sort!" replied his partner, curtly. "You might as well give them away. Why, the market is at its very lowest!"

"Hold on to them then," said the other, puffing philosophically.

"I intend to. Here are twin stones. They are no great shakes. And here are four flawed ones, and two smoky. Only one pure coloured stone among the lot, and it so small as to be almost worthless. Yet we hear of other fellows getting unexpected pieces of luck. Look at that fellow over at Murphy turning up a twenty thousand pounder out of a claim that had ruined four men before him! Why are we never to have a show? Why are we to be always at this drudgery while the best years of our life are passing over our heads? And you can sit there and smoke, and look as contented as though we hadn't a wish unsatisfied." He locked up the box with a vicious snap, and replaced it with a bang upon the shelf.

"Well, pard," said the big miner, "to tell the truth, I think we have a deal to be thankful for. If we don't win we don't lose. We pay the boys and the licences, and we bank a few hundreds. There's many a dead-broke down there in the valley would be glad to swap with us. If we hang on long enough we must come on a streak of luck. You keep your beak in the air and wait for it."

"It's a precious long time coming," the other remarked, peevishly.

"All the more welcome when it does come. Now, suppose – just suppose we was to hit on a real hundred carat pure-water stone, and your share was to be ten thousand, and my share was to be ten thousand, what would you do with your share, eh?"

"What would I do?" said Dean, nursing his knee, and staring into the fire with glistening eyes. "What would I not do? I would take my natural position in the world once more as a gentleman. I would wash the dirt of labour from my hands for ever. Is it not the hope of some such chance that spurs me on to dig like a mole in this filthy gravel, or to stay day after day knee-deep in the mud of the gulches? I should return to society and to the world."

"Hum! That's just it," Big Bill remarked, ruefully. "You and me's been thick enough in these days, but if our luck were to come you'd mount a play hat and a boiled shirt and sail right away into society, which might be glad enough to see you, but would look twice at your pardner. It would be Sir Edward this, or My Lord that, and goodbye to old Bill Stewart."

"Nonsense, man," said Headley Dean, "success would never alter me. We have worked together and we shall rise together. Here's my hand on it. But you — what would you do with your money in case we had any such piece of luck?"

"Build a house," his companion answered, with decision. "Build a house, and boss the job myself. It should be in the country just in the very snuggiest and blue-bloodiest bit of England. It should be like the houses of the nobles and gentry, big and square, with about half a hundred flagstaffs stuck on the roof, and a Union Jack flying from each. None of your grey stone, you understand, but the blazing bricks, with ivy and ancestral oaks and balconies, and the family tree stuck up above the hall door, all in the best o' taste."

Headley Dean laughed languidly at his comrade's ideal country house.

"It would be something between a grand-stand and a private lunatic asylum," he remarked. "But I fear you won't have the chance of building it just yet awhile. Have you seen my pipe?"

"Yes; I seed it lying in the claim just as we struck work."

"Strange, I have no remembrance of using it to-day. Well, I suppose I must clamber down and fetch it, unless you happen to be going that way."

"I don't leave Azalea Cottage to-night," said Bill Stewart, with decision.

His partner glanced at him with surprise, for it was seldom that his good-natured companion refused to execute his small errands.

"Then I suppose I must go myself," he remarked, somewhat sulkily, and strode off into the darkness.

The big miner, left to himself, rose and began pacing up and down the room, chuckling softly and rubbing his broad palms together with delight. So amused was he that he was compelled at last to lean up against the doorpost shaking with suppressed merriment. When, however, the sound of hurrying feet announced his companion's return he managed to resume his gravity, and reseated himself on the chair by the fire.

"Bill!" cried Headley Dean, bursting into the room with a face white with emotion. "Bill!"

"What now, pard?"

"Come down to the pit with me Bill! Never mind your hat, but come at once. Come, come!" He tugged at his companion's coat with nervous trembling fingers.

"What's up now?"

"Don't ask questions, but come." With feverish energy he rushed out of the hut, half leading, half dragging his friend, and retraced his steps to the diamond pit. The night was dark and the path was steep, but the two never slackened their pace until they were at the brink of the claim. "Look there!" said Headley Dean, pointing downwards with a quivering finger.

It was indeed a strange and impressive sight. The pit was full of light – a vague, greenish, glimmering light, which pervaded its whole extent without appearing to radiate from any central point. Every stick and stone, and even the missing pipe, were visible in the dim ghostly illumination. Had the floor and walls been strewn with phosphorus they could not have been brighter.

Bill Stewart gave a long whistle as he gazed down at this extraordinary phenomenon. "Why, pard," said he at last, though in no very excited tones, "it must be a carbuncle."

"An enormous one! A gigantic one!" said the other in a subdued whisper. "In letting myself down into the pit I took a grip of the small bush which used to grow on the side of the ridge. It came away in my hand, and at once the pit was filled with that wondrous light."

"Think of that now! The stone must have been under the roots of the bush. Suppose I go down and hoist you up on my back, so that you may examine the place."

"I am almost afraid to," cried Dean; "what a blow if it should prove to be anything else!"

"Nonsense, man, what else could it be? There's nothing else in all nature that gives a light like that except a carbuncle. Come along down, and we'll soon pick out our little twinkler."

The two scrambled down into the pit, and Stewart, picking up his partner in his herculean grip, held him up against the side of the wall. With eager nervous fingers Dean felt all over the place where the bush had been, thrusting his hand into every cleft and cranny. "There's no stone here," he said at last, in a disconsolate voice.

"Oh, but there is, though," cried the other from below. "There must be."

"I have searched every square inch of it," Dean answered moodily.

"Well, if this doesn't lick cock-fighting! I tell you there is a stone there. Look again."

"Let me down!" cried Dean, excitedly. "Don't you see what's over my head! Let me down!"

"What is it now? What's over your head?"

"Why, my shadow! Don't you see it against the wall?"

"What then?" asked his slow-witted comrade.

"If the shadow is above, the light must be below. Why, of course it must come from the roots of the fallen bush. What a fool I was not to think of it! Here's the bush – yes, and here's the stone! Hurrah! hurrah!" He capered about the bottom of the pit, holding up above his head a great blazing scintillating crystal.

"It is a beauty, ain't it?" said Stewart, with his hands in his pockets. "I never seed a finer. But there's one thing it can't do. It can't stop us from getting cold if we stand all night in this damp hole. We can admire it a great deal more at our ease if we march it up to the cottage."

This matter-of-fact advice had the effect of steadying his partner's excited nerves. "You are right, Bill," he said. "We must get it to a place of safety." Clambering to the surface, they made their way back to the hut, where they proceeded to make a more minute examination of their prize.

It was rather larger than a pigeon's egg in size, and of a lustrous ruby tint, save on one side where there was an opaque discolouration. Held up to the light it proved to be beautifully transparent, save at that one point. Headley Dean produced a delicate pair of scales from a drawer, and weighed it with the utmost care and nicety.

"A hundred and fourteen carats," he said. "The largest stone that has been found during my time. One small flaw at the side, but that can be got over in the cutting. It is worth a small fortune in itself."

"Of course it is," said Big Bill gleefully. "There won't be no more tin pannikins for us, pard."

Headley Dean had stowed the stone away in his innermost pocket, and was sitting lost in thought, his heavy brows drawn down over his keen, shifting eyes, and his clenched hand drumming against the table. His partner's chatter fell meaningless upon his heedless ear. A dark thought had come into his mind, and he had not cast it out. It had fastened there, and was rapidly sprouting and growing until his whole better nature was clouded and obscured.

"It's too big a stone to sell in these parts," remarked Stewart. "We must realise all we have here, and make tracks for London. That's the place for dealers and big prices! Then you can go straight into your natural *spear*, as I think I've heard you call it, and I'll get started on the house. But, bless you! we won't lose sight of each other on that account. For half the time I'll be in London a-visiting you in your natural spear, and the other half you'll spend with me, a-walking under the oaks."

Still the gloom grew deeper upon his partner's face as the devil of avarice whispered in his ear. He put his hand upon the little hard lump where the carbuncle lay hid, and his brows grew darker and his eyes more keen.

"Twenty thousand," said Big Bill, "or maybe thirty thousand. What's half that? Two's into thirty – fifteen! Yes, fifteen thousand pounds apiece. How much is that at five per cent? Five tens's fifty, and fifteen fifties" – he counted on his great red fingers, like an overgrown schoolboy – "seven hundred and fifty pounds a year! How's that for a fortune? But what on earth's the matter with you, pard? Have a drop. This bit o' excitement has been too much for you."

"No, no," said Headley Dean, pushing back the bottle which his partner held towards him. "I don't want any brandy; I want to put this matter in its right light, though, so that we may know exactly how we stand, that there may be no misunderstanding. I think you rather mistake our relations to one another in the matter. Of course, you know very well that I want everything to be honourable between us, and that I would not willingly take advantage of you in any way."

"In course you wouldn't!" cried the big miner, heartily.

"Still, on the other hand, business is business, even between the best of friends. If we had been at work together during working hours, and had come on this stone, why of course it would have belonged to us both in equal shares. But this, you see, is quite a different matter."

"Eh?" cried Stewart.

"Quite a different matter. It was an accident at a time when I was not looking for a stone, and when you were not present. You see that, don't you? I'm sure I only want to do what is fair. Suppose you were to pick up a purse of gold in the drift, I could not claim half because I was your partner. It would be a thing outside our agreement. And so is this a thing outside our agreement. Still, of course I would not be mean about it. If I get a fair price for the stone you shall certainly have a share. I only wish you to understand that you have no right to claim a full half." He spoke with his face averted and his eyes still fixed on the fire, for, clothe it as he would with sophistry, he was too sensitive not to feel deeply the ignomiry of his position.

His partner sat for some minutes in a silence which was far

more suggestive then any words. The ticking of the Kimberley-made clock and the crackling of the fire appeared to be almost oppressively loud in the complete stillness. At last Stewart spoke in a slow, measured voice, very unlike his usual cheery tones.

"You don't intend that I should have half the price of the stone?" he said.

"You have no right to it."

"Oh!" No physical pain could have wrung from the stalwart miner the groan which was elicited by this unlooked-for treachery. Not another word passed his lips, but, putting on his broad hat and drawing it down over his brows, he passed away out of the hut and into the night. His heavy footsteps might be heard scrunching their way among the shingle which lined Boxman's Drift, until they slowly died away in the distance.

Headley Dean continued to sit by the fire and to brood over the incident of the evening. What though his innermost conscience told him that he had acted shamefully, he was still ready with some sophism, some subtle distinction between what should and what should not be divisible between partners, to bolster up his misdeed. If his heart failed him for a moment he had but to draw the beautiful glowing carbuncle from his pocket to find an argument which would silence every doubt. How could he bear to part with half of it, he who had discovered it all! What use was a paltry income of seven hundred pounds? With fifteen hundred some little show might be kept up. If Bill had a share of the money he would only waste it on some tomfoolery. Still, he should of course give him something, five hundred down, or even a thousand. No one could say that that was not generous.

This was the train of thought which passed through Dean's head as he sat waiting for his companion's return. An hour passed, and then another, but there were no signs of the absentee. The young miner went to the door and peered out into the darkness. All was very still save the melancholy whooping of a veldt-owl somewhere down the kloof.

"What can have become of the fellow?" he muttered to himself. "He must have turned sulky, and gone off to Winter Rush or to Peniel for the night. Well, anyhow, I can't sit up all night, for I must be off to Kimberley by the early coach in the morning."

With this reflection he threw himself down on his bunk without undressing, with the precious carbuncle still pressed close to his heart. For an hour or more he lay awake, listening for a footstep which never came, but at last he sank into a troubled and uneasy sleep.

He woke in the morning with a strange sense of sadness and

depression. The door of the hut was half-open, and the keen fresh air of the drift was blowing in through it, yet he felt heavy and weary. He sat up for a moment with his hand on his forehead, endeavouring to collect his thoughts. What misfortune had occurred to him that he should feel like this? His eye fell upon the empty bunk opposite, where the burly form of his partner was wont to lie. Ah, of course, he remembered it all now. It was no misfortune, but a crowning piece of good luck. Why, then, should he feel so sad at heart? He had never felt like that when he was a poor adventurer. He drew the stone again from its place of concealment; and again its lurid brilliance, which caught and reflected the clear morning light, reconciled him to the dull prickings of his conscience.

He had determined to set off for Kimberley by the early coach, in order that he might submit his stone to an expert, and have a definite opinion as to its value. Having ascertained that, his next step would be to convey it to London, and there dispose of it. Full of his purpose, he snatched a hurried breakfast, and started off down the drift with the precious jewel in his hand. As he walked he held it up against the rising sun, and marvelled to see how it shimmered and glittered and gleamed. So intent was he upon it that he did not observe until he was close upon him that his injured partner was standing silent and thoughtful with his arms folded across his broad chest, beside the diamond pit.

"Ah, good morning, Bill," said Headley Dean, with out-stretched hand; "I sat up late waiting for you."

But Stewart took no notice of the proffered hand. "If any man had told me —" he began; "but there! there's no use talking about it. Are you still of the same mind you were in last night?"

"What, about the stone? Why, Bill, you know miner's law, and you know you have no claim on the stone. Any one would tell you that. Why should you turn rusty about it? It's a mere matter of business. Besides, you shall have a thousand — I promise you that. I am going down to Kimberley to have it valued."

"Look here, Headley Dean," said Bill Stewart, talking very slowly and deliberately. "I've known you as an honest man for six years, and if anyone had come to me and told me that you were no better than a thief I'd have knocked him flat. Yes, thief is the word, though you may colour up at it. I won't believe now that it's *you* that's dishonest. It isn't the old Headley Dean that I knew. It's some evil spirit that has taken possession of him. I shall protect you against it in spite of yourself, pard. You shall not do a thing that will be a shame to you for ever. Give me the stone!"

"What, would you rob me by violence?" cried Dean, for

his partner was advancing upon him with a very determined expression upon his stolid face. "I won't stand it, Stewart. Keep your hands off me!"

"Give me the stone!"

"Never."

"Then I shall take it;" and in a moment the big miner had seized his companion by the hand which held the diamond. Headley Dean was a far less muscular man, but his nervous energy and his strength of purpose enabled him to struggle for a few moments with the giant. Then his fingers opened, the carbuncle flew out of them, and, bounding down the slope of the valley, vanished over the side of the unfathomable volcanic crack.

For an instant the two stood silent and spellbound, staring at the spot where the stone had disappeared. Then, with a cry of rage and disappointment, Headley Dean rushed to the head of the fissure and gazed down into the narrow cleft. All was black and silent beneath him. Far down in those dark inaccessible depths the great Boxman's Drift carbuncle would flicker and gleam at the bottom of the terrible chasm until some fresh convulsion of nature would in the course of ages bring it again within the reach of man. And he – he had lost his stone, he had lost his honour, he had lost his friend, he had lost his self-respect. What was there left to him? He turned sharply upon his heel, and with his head sunk upon his breast he went back without a word to the cottage.

Now that the demoralising presence of the stone had been removed he saw clearly enough the meanness and unutterable vileness of his own conduct. He was not by nature a dishonest man, nor was he devoid of a code of honour from which he had never before deviated. But his principles were not very firm, and the sudden temptation had been too strong for him. To do him justice, his remorse and grief at his own conduct were now so strong that they entirely overcame his sorrow at the loss he had sustained. It was for himself he mourned and not for the stone. There was no reparation which he would not willingly offer to undo the past and make up for the shameful injustice which he had done his partner. Anything to feel the grip of his hard hand once more, and to know that he was forgiven. What were all the diamonds in Africa compared to one's own self-respect and the friendship of such a man? He could see it clearly enough now that it was too late. With his elbows upon his knees, and his face buried in his hands, he racked his brain to find some method of showing his sincere repentance and of repairing the evil that he had done.

A heavy footfall was heard outside the cottage, and the big miner came lounging in.

Headley Dean rose and faced him with downcast eyes and trembling lip. "I hardly know what to say to you, Bill," he said, in a low, broken voice. "I have behaved abominably—shamefully. The stone was, as you said, like an evil spirit, which brought all the bad that is in me to the surface. If I could repair the past by cutting my right hand off I would do it without hesitatiion. No doubt you think I am saying this just because I have lost the stone. It is only natural you should think so. There's one thing I'll do, though, to show that I am in earnest. We have in that tin box a thousand pounds' worth of diamonds, which belong to us jointly. You may do what you will with my share. You would scorn to take it yourself, no doubt, but you may give it to the hospital at Kimberley. I at least shall never touch them."

Bill walked over to the fire and lit his pipe. "You say if you had the stone you would go fair halves?" said he.

"If I had it you should have the disposing of it," Dean answered.

"I bear no malice," said Stewart. "Shake hands on it."

The great red hand of the big miner enclosed the nervous white one of his partner. When they separated Headley Dean stood staring and rigid and pale to the very lips, for there, in the centre of the palm of his outstretched hand, lay the very stone which he had just seen disappear into the bowels of the earth.

"Whoa!" cried Big Bill, supporting him into a chair. "You ain't strong enough to bear up against this sort o' surprise. There, the colour's coming back to your cheeks. Why, bless you! there's nothing very wonderful about it. That chasm ain't the same depth all along. Where you measured there's no bottom to it, but where the stone fell in it ain't more 'n forty feet deep. It was too narrow for me or you to go down, but I got little Kaffir Jim and lowered him down with a rope. He got it in no time. He tells me it was a-shinin' as bright as ever, but the curve of the rock hid it from the top. So, you see, it ain't lost yet!"

Headley Dean could but sit and listen and gaze at the wondrous gem. The sudden revulsion of feeling had stupefied him.

"The fun of the thing," said Bill Stewart, chuckling heartily to himself, "is that this is the third time as that 'ere stone has been discovered. I found it three nights back, but I had often noticed, pard, what a relish and a pleasure it was to you to find a stone, and, being myself of a kind o' coarse and common nature, that don't feel these things so much, I made up my mind that you should find it for yourself. I therefore put your pipe in the pit —

like you put the cheese in a mouse-trap – and I pulled the bush out, knowing you always use it for getting up and down, and I hid the stone amongst the roots. Thinks I, 'When pard goes down out will come the bush, and he'll be fairly dazzled,' for I knew the thing would shine in the dark. Well, you goes, and you finds it, and then you begins playing a game on your pard, and we gets skylarking and the stone gets down the crevice, and Kaffir Jim fetches it up, and here we are, all snug and comfortable. Who's game to come to Kimberley and have it valued?"

"You shall do what you will with the gem," said Headley Dean, laying it upon the table; "I have forfeited all part and share in it."

"All right, Boss," Stewart answered, shoving it away into his trousers pocket, "we'll talk about that during our voyage to London. If this here stone is not going to put you into your natural spear, why, souse it goes into the Atlantic Ocean, and then what becomes of my house and flagstaff, etc. They all depend on the stone of Boxman's Drift."

*   *   *   *

There is no need to say more. The gem realised even more than had been anticipated, and the two partners are now well-to-do country gentlemen in one of the inland shires. Big Bill has built a house which is a source of never-failing delight to himself, and of wonder to the whole countryside. Headley Dean lives hard by, a quiet and contented man. The two old friends are much together, and have many a chat about their old African experiences, but it may safely be said that they never did, and never will, allude to the one eventful estrangement which had occurred between them.

A PASTORAL HORROR

———◆———

Far above the level of the Lake of Constance, nestling in a little corner of the Tyrolese Alps, lies the quiet town of Feldkirch. It is remarkable for nothing save for the presence of a large and well-conducted Jesuit school and for the extreme beauty of its situation. There is no more lovely spot in the whole of the Vorarlberg. From the hills which rise behind the town, the great lake glimmers some fifteen miles off, like a broad sea of quicksilver. Down below in the plains the Rhine and the Danube prattle along, flowing swiftly and merrily, with none of the dignity which they assume as they grow from brooks into rivers. Five great countries or principalities, – Switzerland, Austria, Baden, Wurtemburg, and Bavaria – are visible from the plateau of Feldkirch.

Feldkirch is the centre of a large tract of hilly and pastoral country. The main road runs through the centre of the town, and then on as far as Anspach, where it divides into two branches, one of which is larger than the other. This more important one runs through the valleys across Austrian Tyrol into Tyrol proper, going as far, I believe, as the capital of Innsbruck. The lesser road runs for eight or ten miles amid wild and rugged glens to the village of Laden, where it breaks up into a network of sheep-tracks. In this quiet spot, I, John Hudson, spent nearly two years of my life, from the June of '65 to the March of '67, and it was during that time that those events occurred which for some weeks brought the retired hamlet into an unholy prominence, and caused its name for the first, and probably for the last time, to be a familiar word to the European press. The short account of these incidents which appeared in the English papers was, however, inaccurate and misleading, besides which, the rapid advance of the Prussians, culminating in the battle of Sadowa, attracted public attention away from what might have moved it deeply in less troublous times. It seems to me that the facts may be detailed now, and be new to the great majority of readers, especially as I was myself intimately connected with the drama, and am in a position to give many particulars which have never before been made public.

And first a few words as to my own presence in this out of the way spot. When the great city firm of Sprynge, Wilkinson, and Spragge failed, and paid their creditors rather less than eighteen-pence in the pound, a number of humble individuals were ruined, including myself. There was, however, some legal objection which held out a chance of my being made an exception to the other creditors, and being paid in full. While the case was being brought out I was left with a very small sum for my subsistence.

I determined, therefore, to take up my residence abroad in the interim, since I could live more economically there, and be spared the mortification of meeting those who had known me in my more prosperous days. A friend of mine had described Laden to me some years before as being the most isolated place which he had ever come across in all his experience, and as isolation and cheap living are usually synonymous, I bethought use of his words. Besides, I was in a cynical humour with my fellow-man, and desired to see as little of him as possible for some time to come. Obeying, then, the guidances of poverty and of misanthropy, I made my way to Laden, where my arrival created the utmost excitement among the simple inhabitants. The manners and customs of the red-bearded Englander, his long walks, his check suit, and the reasons which had led him to abandon his fatherland, were all fruitful sources of gossip to the topers who frequented the Gruner Mann and the Schwartzer Bar – the two alehouses of the village.

I found myself very happy at Laden. The surroundings were magnificent, and twenty years of Brixton had sharpened my admiration for nature as an olive improves the flavour of wine. In my youth I had been a fair German scholar, and I found myself able, before I had been many months abroad, to converse even on scientific and abstruse subjects with the new curé of the parish.

This priest was a great godsend to me, for he was a most learned man and a brilliant conversationalist. Father Verhagen – for that was his name – though little more than forty years of age, had made his reputation as an author by a brilliant monograph upon the early Popes – a work which eminent critics have compared favourably with Von Ranke's. I shrewdly suspect that it was owing to some rather unorthodox views advanced in this book that Verhagen was relegated to the obscurity of Laden. His opinions upon every subject were ultra-Liberal, and in his fiery youth he had been ready to vindicate them, as was proved by a deep scar across his chin, received from a dragoon's sabre in the abortive insurrection at Berlin. Altogether the man was an interesting one, and though he was by nature somewhat cold and reserved, we soon established an acquaintanceship.

The atmosphere of morality in Laden was a very rarefied one. The position of Intendant Wurms and his satellites had for many years been a sinecure. Non-attendance at church upon a Sunday or feast-day was about the deepest and darkest crime which the most advanced of the villagers had attained to. Occasionally some hulking Fritz or Andreas would come. lurching home at ten o'clock at night, slightly under the influence of Bavarian beer, and might even abuse the wife of his bosom if she ventured to remonstrate, but such cases were rare, and when they occurred the Ladeners looked at the culprit for some time in a half admiring, half horrified manner, as one who had committed a gaudy sin and so asserted his individuality.

It was in this peaceful village that a series of crimes suddenly broke out which astonished all Europe, and for atrocity and for the mystery which surrounded them surpassed anything of which I have ever heard or read. I shall endeavour to give a succinct account of these events in the order of their sequence, in which I am much helped by the fact that it has been my custom all my life to keep a journal – to the pages of which I now refer.

It was, then, I find upon the 19th of May in the spring of 1866, that my old landlady, Frau Zimmer, rushed wildly into the room as I was sipping my morning cup of chocolate and informed me that a murder had been committed in the village. At first I could hardly believe the news, but as she persisted in her statement, and was evidently terribly frightened, I put on my hat and went out to find the truth. When I came into the main street of the village I saw several men hurrying along in front of me, and following them I came upon an excited group in front of the little stadthaus or town hall – a barn-like edifice which was used for all manner of public gatherings. They were collected round the body of one Maul, who had formerly been a steward upon one of the steamers running between Lindau and Fredericshaven, on the Lake of Constance. He was a harmless, inoffensive little man, generally popular in the village, and, as far as was known, without an enemy in the world. Maul lay upon his face, with his fingers dug into the earth, no doubt in his last convulsive struggles, and his hair all matted together with blood, which had streamed down over the collar of his coat. The body had been discovered nearly two hours, but no one appeared to know what to do or whither to convey it. My arrival, however, together with that of the curé, who came almost simultaneously, infused some vigour into the crowd. Under our direction the corpse was carried up the steps, and laid on the floor of the town hall, where, having made sure that life was extinct, we proceeded to examine the injuries, in conjunction with Lieutenant Wurms, of the police. Maul's face was perfectly placid, showing that he had had no thought of danger until the fatal blow was struck. His watch and purse had not been taken. Upon washing the clotted blood from the back of his head a singular triangular wound was found, which had smashed the bone and penetrated deeply into the brain. It had evidently been inflicted by a heavy blow from a sharp-pointed pyramidal instrument. I believe that it was Father Verhagen, the curé, who suggested the probability of the weapon in question having been a short mattock or small pickaxe, such as are to be found in every Alpine cottage. The Intendant, with praiseworthy promptness, at once obtained one and striking a turnip, produced just such a curious gap as was to be seen in poor Maul's head. We felt that we had come upon the first link of a chain which might guide us to the assassin. It was not long before we seemed to grasp the whole clue.

A sort of inquest was held upon the body that same afternoon, at which Pfiffor, the maire, presided, the curé, the Intendant, Freckler, of the post office, and myself forming ourselves into a sort of committee of investigation. Any villager who could throw a light upon the case or give an account of the movements of the murdered man upon the previous evening was invited to attend. There was a fair muster of witnesses, and we soon gathered a connected series of facts. At half-past eight o'clock Maul had entered the Gruner Mann public-house, and had called for a flagon of beer. At that time there were sitting in the tap-room Waghorn, the butcher of the village, and an Italian pedlar named Cellini, who used to come three times a year to Laden with cheap jewellery and other wares. Immediately after his entrance the landlord had seated himself with his customers, and the four had spent the evening together, the common villagers not being admitted beyond the bar. It seemed from the evidence of the landlord and of Waghorn, both of whom were most respectable and trustworthy men, that shortly after nine o'clock a dispute arose between the deceased and the pedlar. Hot words had been exchanged, and the Italian had eventually left the room, saying that he would not stay any longer to hear his country decried. Maul remained for nearly an hour, and being somewhat elated at having caused his adversary's retreat, he drank rather more than was usual with him. One witness had met him walking towards his home, about ten o'clock, and deposed to his having been slightly the worse for drink. Another had met him just a minute or so before he reached the spot in front of the stadthaus where the deed was done. This man's evidence was most important. He swore confidently that while passing the town hall, and before meeting Maul, he had seen a figure standing in the shadow of the building, adding that the person appeared to him, as far as he could make him out, to be not unlike the Italian.

Up to this point we had then established two facts – that the Italian had left the Gruner Mann before Maul, with words of anger on his lips; the second, that some unknown individual had been seen lying in wait on the road which the ex-steward would have to traverse. A third, and most important, was reached when the woman with whom the Italian lodged deposed that he had not returned the night before until half-past ten, an unusually late hour for Laden. How had he employed the time, then, from shortly after nine, when he left the public-house, until half-past ten, when he returned to his rooms? Things were beginning to look very black, indeed, against the pedlar.

It could not be denied, however, that there were points in the man's favour, and that the case against him consisted entirely of circumstantial evidence. In the first place, there was no sign of a mattock or any other instrument which could have been used for such a purpose among the Italian's goods; nor was it easy to understand how he could come by any such a weapon, since he did not go home between the time of the quarrel and his final return. Again, as the curé pointed out, since Cellini was a comparative stranger in the village, it was very unlikely that he would know which road Maul would take in order to reach his home. This objection was weakened, however, by the evidence of the dead man's servant, who deposed that the pedlar had been hawking his wares in front of their house the day before, and might very possibly have seen the owner at one of the windows. As to the prisoner himself, his attitude at first had been one of defiance, and even of amusement; but when he began to realise the weight of evidence against him, his manner became cringing, and he wrung his hands hideously, loudly proclaiming his innocence. His defence was that after leaving the inn, he had taken a long walk down the Anspach-road in order to cool down his excitement, and that this was the cause of his late return. As to the murder of Maul, he knew no more about it than the babe unborn.

I have dwelt at some length upon the circumstances of this case, because there are events in connection with it which makes it peculiarly interesting. I intend now to fall back upon my diary, which was very fully kept during this period, and indeed during my whole residence abroad. It will save me trouble to quote from it, and it will be a teacher for the accuracy of facts.

May 20th. – Nothing thought of and nothing talked of but the recent tragedy. A hunt has been made among the woods and along the brook in the hope of finding the weapon of the assassin. The more I think of it, the more convinced I am that Cellini is the man. The fact of the money being untouched proves that the crime was committed from motives of revenge, and who would bear more spite towards poor innocent Maul except the vindictive hot-blooded Italian whom he had just offended. I dined with Pfiffor in the evening, and he entirely agreed with me in my view of the case.

May 21st. – Still no word as far as I can hear which throws any light upon the murder. Poor Maul was buried at twelve o'clock in the neat little village churchyard. The curé led the service with great feeling, and his audience, consisting of the whole population of the village, were much moved, interrupting him frequently by sobs and ejaculations of grief. After the painful ceremony was over I had a short walk with our good priest. His naturally excitable nature has been considerably stirred by recent events. His hand trembles and his face is pale.

"My friend," said he, taking me by the hand as we walked together, "you know something of medicine." (I had been two years at Guy's). "I have been far from well of late."

"It is this sad affair which has upset you," I said.

"No," he answered, "I have felt it coming on for some time, but it has been worse of late. I have a pain which shoots from here to there," he put his hand to his temples. "If I were struck by lightning, the sudden shock it causes me could not be more great. At times when I close my eyes flashes of light dart before them, and my ears are for ever ringing. Often I know not what I do. My fear is lest I faint some time when performing the holy offices."

"You are overworking yourself," I said, "you must have rest and strengthening tonics. Are you writing just now? And how much do you do each day?"

"Eight hours," he answered. "Sometimes ten, sometimes even twelve, when the pains in my head do not interrupt me."

"You must reduce it to four," I said authoritatively. "You must also take regular exercise. I shall send you some quinine which I have in my trunk, and you can take as much as would cover a gulden in a glass of milk every morning and night."

He departed, vowing that he would follow my directions.

I hear from the maire that four policemen are to be sent from Anspach to remove Cellini to a safer gaol.

May 22nd. – To say that I was startled would give but a faint idea of my mental state. I am confounded, amazed, horrified beyond all expression. Another and a more dreadful crime has been committed during the night. Freckler has been found dead in his house – the very Freckler who had sat with me on the committee of investigation the day before. I write these notes after a long and anxious day's work, during which I have been endeavouring to assist the officers of the law. The villagers are so paralysed with fear at this fresh evidence of an assassin in their midst that there would be a general panic but for our exertions. It appears that Freckler, who was a man of peculiar habits, lived alone in an isolated dwelling. Some curiosity was aroused this morning by the fact that he had not gone to his work, and that there was no sign of movement about the house. A crowd assembled, and the doors were eventually forced open. The unfortunate Freckler was found in the bed-room upstairs, lying with his head in the fireplace. He had met his death by an exactly similar wound to that which had proved fatal to Maul, save that in this instance the injury was in front. His hands were clenched, and there was an indescribable look of horror, and, as it seemed to me, of surprise upon his features. There were marks of muddy footsteps upon the stairs, which must have been caused by the murderer in his ascent, as his victim had put on his slippers before retiring to his bed-room. These prints, however, were too much blurred to enable us to get a trustworthy outline of the foot. They were only to be found upon every third step, showing with what fiendish swiftness this human tiger had rushed upstairs in search of his victim. There was a considerable sum of money in the house, but not one farthing had been touched, nor had any of the drawers in the bed-room been opened.

As the dismal news became known the whole population of the village assembled in a great crowd in front of the house – rather, I think, from the gregariousness of terror than from mere curiosity. Every man looked with suspicion upon his neighbour. Most were silent, and when they spoke it was in whispers, as if they feared to raise their voices. None of these people were allowed to enter the house, and we, the more enlightened members of the community, made a strict examination of the premises. There was absolutely nothing, however, to give the slightest clue as to the assassin. Beyond the fact that he must be an active man, judging from the manner in which he ascended the stairs, we have gained nothing from this second tragedy. Intendant Wurms pointed out, indeed, that the dead man's rigid right arm was stretched out as if in greeting, and that, therefore, it was probable that this late visitor was someone with whom Freckler was well acquainted. This, however, was, to a large extent, conjecture. If anything could have added to the horror created by the dreadful occurrence, it was the fact that the crime must have been committed at the early hour of half-past eight in the evening – that being the time registered by a small cuckoo clock, which had been carried away by Freckler in his fall.

No one, apparently, heard any suspicious sounds or saw any one enter or leave the house. It was done rapidly, quietly, and completely, though many people must have been about at the time. Poor Pfiffor and our good curé are terribly cut up by the awful occurrence, and, indeed, I feel very much depressed myself now that all the excitement is over and the reaction set in. There are very few of the villagers about this evening, but from every side is heard the sound of hammering – the peasants fitting bolts and bars upon the doors and windows of their houses. Very many of them have been entirely unprovided with anything of the sort, nor were they ever required until now. Frau Zimmer has manufactured a huge fastening which would be ludicrous if we were in a humour for laughter.

I hear to-night that Cellini has been released, as, of course, there is no possible pretext for detaining him now; also that word has been sent to all the villages near for any police that can be spared.

My nerves have been so shaken that I remained awake the greater part of the night, reading Gordon's translation of Tacitus by candlelight. I have got out my navy revolver and cleaned it, so as to be ready for all eventualities.

Mary 23rd. – The police force has been recruited by three more men from Anspach and two from Thalstadt at the other side of the hills. Intendant Wurms has established an efficient system of patrols, so that we may consider ourselves reasonably safe. To-day has cast no light upon the murders. The general opinion in the village seems to be that they have been done by some stranger who lies concealed among the woods. They argue that they have all known each other since childhood, and that there is no one of their number who would be capable of such actions. Some of the more daring of them have made a hunt among the pine forests to-day, but without success.

May 24th. – Events crowd on apace. We seem hardly to have recovered from one horror when something else occurs to excite the popular imagination. Fortunately, this time it is not a fresh tragedy, although the news is serious enough.

The murderer has been seen, and that upon the public road, which proves that his thirst for blood has not been quenched yet, and also that our reinforcements of police are not enough to guarantee security. I have just come back from hearing Andreas Murch narrate his experience, though he is still in such a state of trepidation that his story is somewhat incoherent. He was belated among the hills, it seems, owing to mist. It was nearly eleven o'clock before he struck the main road about a couple of miles from the village. He confesses that he felt by no means comfortable at finding himself out so late after the recent occurrences. However, as the fog had cleared away and the moon was shining brightly, he trudged sturdily along. Just about a quarter of a mile from the village the road takes a very sharp bend. Andreas had got as far as this when he suddenly heard in the still night the sound of footsteps approaching rapidly round this curve. Overcome with fear, he threw himself into the ditch which skirts the road, and lay there motionless in the shadow, peering over the side. The steps came nearer and nearer, and than a tall dark figure came round the corner at a swinging pace, and passing the spot where the moon glimmered upon the white face of the frightened peasant, halted in the road about twenty yards further on, and began probing about among the reeds on the roadside with an instrument which Andreas Murch recognised with horror as being a long mattock. After searching about in this way for a minute or so, as if he suspected that someone was concealed there, for he must have heard the sound of the footsteps, he stood still leaning upon his weapon. Murch describes him as a tall, thin man, dressed in clothes of a darkish colour. The lower part of his face was swathed in a wrapper of some sort, and the little which was visible appeared to be of a ghastly pallor. Murch could not see enough of his features to identify him, but thinks that it was no one whom he had ever seen in his life before. After standing for some little time, the man with the mattock had walked swiftly away into the darkness, in the direction in which he imagined the fugitive had gone. Andreas, as may be supposed, lost little time in getting safely into the village, where he alarmed the police. Three of them, armed with carbines, started down the road, but saw no signs of the miscreant. There is, of course, a possibility that Murch's story is exaggerated and that his imagination has been sharpened by fear. Still, the whole incident cannot be trumped up, and this awful demon who haunts us is evidently still active.

There is an ill-conditioned fellow named Hiedler, who lives in a hut on the side of the Spiegelberg, and supports himself by chamois hunting and by acting as guide to the few tourists who find their way here. Popular suspicion has fastened on this man, for no better reason than that he is tall, thin, and known to be rough and brutal. His chalet has been searched to-day, but nothing of importance found. He has, however, been arrested and confined in the same room which Cellini used to occupy.

At this point there is a gap of a week in my diary, during which time there was an entire cessation of the constant alarms which have harassed us lately. Some explained it by supposing that the terrible unknown had moved on to some fresh and less guarded scene of operations. Others imagine that we have secured the right man in the shape of the vagabond Hiedler. Be the cause what it may, peace and contentment reign once more in the village, and a short seven days have sufficed to clear away the cloud of care from men's brows, though the police are still on the alert. The season for rifle shooting is beginning, and as Laden has, like every other Tyrolese village, butts of its own, there is a continual pop, pop, all day. These peasants are dead shots up to about four hundred yards. No troops in the world could subdue them among their native mountains.

My friend Verhagen, the curé, and Pfiffor, the maire, used to go down in the afternoon to see the shooting with me. The former says that the quinine has done him much good and that his appetite is improved. We all agree that it is good policy to encourage the amusements of the people so that they may forget all about this wretched business. Vaghorn, the butcher, won the prize offered by the maire. He made five bulls, and what we should call a magpie out of six shots at 100 yards. This is English prize-medal form.

June 2nd. – Who could have imagined that a day which opened so fairly could have so dark an ending? The early carrier brought me a letter by which I learned that Spragge and Co. have agreed to pay my claim in full, although it may be some months before the money is forthcoming. This will make a difference of nearly £400 a year to me – a matter of moment when a man is in his seven-and-fortieth year.

And now for the grand events of the hour. My interview with the vampire who haunts us, and his attempt upon Frau Bischoff, the landlady of the Gruner Mann – to say nothing of the narrow escape of our good curé. There seems to be something almost supernatural in the malignity of this unknown fiend, and the impunity with which he continues his murderous course. The real reason of it lies in the badly lit state of the place – or rather the entire absence of light – and also in the fact that thick woods stretch right down to the houses on every side, so that escape is made easy. In spite of this, however, he had two very narrow escapes to-night – one from my pistol, and one from the officers of the law. I shall not sleep much, so I may spend half an hour in jotting down these strange doings in my dairy. I am no coward, but life in Laden is becoming too much for my nerves. I believe the matter will end in the emigration of the whole population.

To come to my story, then. I felt lonely and depressed this evening, in spite of the good news of the morning. About nine o'clock, just as night began to fall, I determined to stroll over and call upon the curé, thinking that a little intellectual chat might cheer me up. I slipped my revolver into my pocket, therefore – a precaution which I never neglected – and went out, very much against the advice of good Frau Zimmer. I think I mentioned some months ago in my diary that the curé's house is some little way out of the village upon the brow of a small hill. When I arrived there I found that he had gone out – which, indeed, I might have anticipated, for he had complained lately of restlessness at night, and I had recommended him to take a little exercise in the evening. His housekeeper made me very welcome, however, and having lit the lamp, left me in the study with some books to amuse me until her master's return.

I suppose I must have sat for nearly half an hour glancing over an odd volume of Klopstock's poems, when some sudden instinct caused me to raise my head and look up. I have been in some strange situations in my life, but never have I felt anything to be compared to the thrill which shot through me at that moment. The recollection of it now, hours after the event, makes me shudder. There, framed in one of the panes of the window, was a human face glaring in, from the darkness, into the lighted room – the face of a man so concealed by a cravat and slouch hat that the only impression I retain of it was a pair of wild-beast eyes and a nose which was whitened by being pressed against the glass. It did not need Andreas Murch's description to tell me that at last I was face to face with the man with the mattock. There was murder in those wild eyes. For a second I was so unstrung as to be powerless; the next I cocked my revolver and fired straight at the sinister face. I was a moment too late. As I pressed the trigger I saw it vanish, but the pane through which it had looked was shattered to pieces. I rushed to the window, and then out through the front door, but everything was silent. There was no trace of my visitor. His intention, no doubt, was to attack the curé, for there was nothing to prevent his coming through the folding window had he not found an armed man inside.

As I stood in the cool night air with the curé's frightened housekeeper beside me, I suddenly heard a great hubbub down in the village. By this time, alas! such sounds were so common in Laden that there was no doubting what it forboded. Some fresh misfortune had occurred there. To-night seemed destined to be a night of horror. My presence might be of use in the village, so I set off there, taking with me the trembling woman, who positively refused to remain behind. There was a crowd round the Gruner Mann public-house, and a dozen excited voices were explaining the circumstances to the curé, who had arrived just before us. It was as I had thought, though happily without the result which I had feared. Frau Bischoff, the wife of the proprietor of the inn, had, it seems, gone some twenty minutes before a few yards from her door to draw some water, and had been at once attacked by a tall disguised man, who had cut at her with some weapon. Fortunately he had slipped, so that she was able to seize him by the wrist and prevent his repeating his attempt, while she screamed for help. There were several people about at the time, who came running towards them, on which the stranger wrested himself free, and dashed off into the woods, with two of our police after him. There is little hope of their overtaking or tracing him, however, in such a dark labyrinth. Frau Bischoff had made a bold attempt to hold the assassin, and declares that her nails made deep furrows in his right wrist. This, however, must be mere conjecture, as there was very little light at the time. She knows no more of the man's features than I do. Fortunately she is entirely unhurt. The curé was horrified when I informed him of the incident at his own house. He was returning from his walk, it appears, when hearing cries in the village, he had hurried down to it. I have not told anyone else of my own adventure, for the people are quite excited enough already.

As I said before, unless this mysterious and bloodthirsty villain is captured, the place will become deserted. Flesh and blood cannot stand such a strain. He is either some murderous misanthrope who has declared a vendetta against the whole human race, or else he is an escaped maniac. Clearly after the unsuccessful attempt upon Frau Bischoff he had made at once for the curé's house, bent upon slaking his thirst for blood, and thinking that its lonely situation gave hope of success. I wish I had fired at him through the pocket of my coat. The moment he saw the glitter of the weapon he was off.

June 3rd. – Everybody in the village this morning has learned about the attempt upon the curé last night. There was quite a crowd at his house to congratulate him on his escape, and when I appeared they raised a cheer and hailed me as the "tapferer Englander." It seems that his narrow shave must have given the ruffian a great start, for a thick woollen muffler was found lying on the pathway leading down to the village, and later in the day the fatal mattock was discovered close to the same place. The scoundrel evidently threw those things down and then took to his heels. It is possible that he may prove to have been frightened away from the neighbourhood altogether. Let us trust so!

June 4th. – A quiet day, which is as remarkable a thing in our annals as an exciting one elsewhere. Wurms has made strict inquiry, but cannot trace the muffler and mattock to any inhabitant. A description of them has been printed, and copies sent to Anspach and neighbouring villages for circulation among the peasants, who may be able to throw some light upon the matter. A thanksgiving service is to be held in the church on Sunday for the double escape of the pastor and of Martha Bischoff. Pfiffer tells me that Herr von Weissendorff, one of the most energetic detectives in Vienna, is on his way to Laden. I see, too, by the English papers sent me, that people at home are interested in the tragedies here, although the accounts which have reached them are garbled and untrustworthy.

How well I can recall the Sunday morning following upon the events which I have described, such a morning as it is hard to find outside the Tyrol! The sky was blue and cloudless, the gentle breeze wafted the balsamic odour of the pine woods through the open windows, and away up on the hills the distant tinkling of the cow bells fell pleasantly upon the ear, until the musical rise and fall which summoned the villagers to prayer drowned their feebler melody. It was hard to believe, looking down that peaceful little street with its quaint topheavy wooden houses and old-fashioned church, that a cloud of crime hung over it which had horrified Europe. I sat at my window watching the peasants passing with their picturesquely dressed wives and daughters on their way to church. With the kindly reverence of Catholic countries, I saw them cross themselves as they went by the house of Freckler and the spot where Maul had met his fate. When the bell had ceased to toll and the whole population had assembled in the church, I walked up there also, for it has always been my custom to join in the religious exercises of any people among whom I may find myself.

When I arrived at the church I found that the service had already begun. I took my place in the gallery which contained the village organ, from which I had a good view of the congregation. In the front seat of all was stationed Frau Bischoff, whose miraculous escape the service was intended to celebrate, and beside her on one side was her worthy spouse, while the maire occupied the other. There was a hush through the church as the curé turned from the altar and ascended the pulpit. I have seldom heard a more magnificent sermon. Father Verhagen was always an eloquent preacher, but on that occasion he surpassed himself. He chose for his text:— "In the midst of life we are in death," and impressed so vividly upon our minds the thin veil which divides us from eternity, and how unexpectedly it may be rent, that he held his audience spell-bound and horrified. He spoke next with tender pathos of the friends who had been snatched so suddenly and so dreadfully from among us, until his words were almost drowned by the sobs of the women, and, suddenly turning he compared their peaceful existence in a happier land to the dark fate of the gloomy-minded criminal, steeped in blood and with nothing to hope for either in this world or the next — a man solitary among his fellows, with no woman to love him, no child to prattle at his knee, and an endless torture in his own thoughts. So skilfully and so powerfully did he speak that as he finished I am sure that pity for this merciless demon was the prevailing emotion in every heart.

The service was over, and the priest, with his two acolytes before him, was leaving the altar, when he turned, as was his custom, to give his blessing to the congregation. I shall never forget his appearance. The summer sunshine shining slantwise through the single small stained glass window which adorned the little church threw a yellow lustre upon his sharp intellectual features with their dark haggard lines, while a vivid crimson spot reflected from a ruby-coloured mantle in the window quivered over his uplifted right hand. There was a hush as the villagers bent their heads to receive their pastor's blessing — a hush broken by a wild exclamation of surprise from a woman who staggered to her feet in the front pew and gesticulated frantically as she pointed at Father Verhagen's uplifted arm. No need for Frau Bischoff to explain the cause of that sudden cry, for there — there in full sight of his parishioners, were lines of livid scars upon the cure's white wrist — scars which could be left by nothing on earth but a desperate woman's nails. And what woman save her who had clung so fiercely to the murderer two days before!

That in all this terrible business poor Verhagen was the man most to be pitied I have no manner of doubt. In a town in which there was good medical advice to be had, the approach of the homicidal mania, which had undoubtedly proceeded from over-work and brain worry, and which assumed such a terrible form, would have been detected in time and he would have been spared the awful compunction with which he must have been seized in the lucid intervals between his fits – if, indeed, he had any lucid intervals. How could I diagnose with my smattering of science the existence of such a terrible and insidious form of insanity, especially from the vague symptoms of which he informed me. It is easy now, looking back, to think of many little circumstances which might have put us on the right scent; but what a simple thing is retrospective wisdom! I should be sad indeed if I thought that I had anything with which to reproach myself.

We were never able to discover where he had obtained the weapon with which he had committed his crimes, nor how he managed to secrete it in the interval. My experience proved that it had been his custom to go and come through his study window without disturbing his housekeeper. On the occasion of the attempt on Frau Bischoff he had made a dash for home, and then, finding to his astonishment that his room was occupied, his only resource was to fling away his weapon and muffler, and to mix with the crowd in the village. Being both a strong and an active man, with a good knowledge of the footpaths through the woods, he had never found any difficulty in escaping all obser-vation.

Immediately after his apprehension, Verhagen's disease took an acute form, and he was carried off to the lunatic asylum at Feldkirch. I have heard that some months afterwards he made a determined attempt upon the life of one of his keepers, and afterwards committed suicide. I cannot be positive of this, how-ever, for I heard it quite accidentally during a conversation in a railway carriage.

As for myself, I left Laden within a few months, having re-ceived a pleasing intimation from my solicitors that my claim had been paid in full. In spite of my tragic experience there, I had many a pleasing recollection of the little Tyrolese village, and in two subsequent visits I renewed my acquaintance with the maire, the Intendant, and all my old friends, on which occasion, over long pipes and flagons of beer, we have taken a grim pleasure in talking with bated breath of that terrible month in the quiet Vorarlberg hamlet.

OUR MIDNIGHT VISITOR

I

On the western side of the island of Arran, seldom visited, and almost unknown to tourists, is the little island named Uffa. Between the two lies a strait or roost, two miles and a half broad, with a dangerous current which sets in from the north. Even on the calmest day there are ripples, and swirls, and dimples on the surface of the roost, which suggest hidden influences, but when the wind blows from the west, and the great Atlantic waves choke up the inlet and meet their brethren which have raced round the other side of the island, there is such seething and turmoil that old sailors say they have never seen the like. God help the boat that is caught there on such a day!

My father owned one-third part of the island of Uffa, and I was born and bred there. Our farm or croft was a small one enough, for if a good thrower were to pick up a stone on the shore at Carracuil (which was our place) he could manage, in three shies, to clear all our arable land, and it was hardly longer than it was broad. Behind this narrow track, on which we grew corn and potatoes, was the homesteading of Carracuil – a rather bleak-looking grey stone house with a red-tiled byre buttressed against one side of it, and behind this again the barren undulating moorland stretched away up to Beg-na-sacher and Beg-na-phail, two rugged knolls which marked the centre of the island. We had grazing ground for a couple of cows, and eight or ten sheep, and we had our boat anchored down in Carravoe. When the fishing failed, there was more time to devote to the crops, and if the season was bad, as likely as not the herring would be thick on the coast. Taking one thing with another a crofter in Uffa had as much chance of laying by a penny or two as most men on the mainland.

Besides our own family, the MacDonalds of Carracuil, there were two others on the island. These were the Gibbs of Arden and the Fullartons of Corriemains. There was no priority claimed among us, for none had any legend of the coming of the others. We had all three held our farms by direct descent for many generations, paying rent to the Duke of Hamilton and all prospering in a moderate way. My father had been enabled to send me to begin the study of medicine at the University of Glasgow, and I had attended lectures there for two winter sessions, but whether from caprice or from some lessening in his funds, he had recalled me, and in the year 1865 I found myself cribbed up in this little island with just education enough to wish for more, and with no associate at home but the grim, stern old man, for my mother had been dead some years, and I had neither brother nor sister.

There were two youths about my own age in the island, Geordie and Jock Gibbs, but they were rough, loutish fellows, good-hearted enough, but with no ideas above fishing and farming. More to my taste was the society of Minnie Fullarton, the pretty daughter of old Fullarton of Corriemains. We had been children together, and it was natural that when she blossomed into a buxom, fresh-faced girl, and I into a square-shouldered, long-legged youth, there should be something warmer than friendship between us. Her elder brother was a corn chandler in Ardrossan, and was said to be doing well, so that the match was an eligible one, but for some reason my father objected very strongly to our intimacy and even forbade me entirely to meet her. I laughed at his commands, for I was a hot-headed, irreverent youngster, and continued to see Minnie, but when it came to his ears, it caused many violent scenes between us, which nearly went the length of blows. We had a quarrel of this sort just before the equinoctial gales in the spring of the year in which my story begins, and I left the old man with his face flushed, and his great bony hands shaking with passion, while I went jauntily off to our usual trysting-place. I have often regretted since that I was not more submissive, but how was I to guess the dark things which were to come upon us?

I can remember that day well. Many bitter thoughts rose in my heart as I strode along the narrow pathway, cutting savagely at the thistles on either side with my stick. One side of our little estate was bordered by the Combera cliffs, which rose straight out of the water to the height of a couple of hundred feet. The top of these cliffs was covered with green sward and commanded a noble view on every side. I stretched myself on the turf there and watched the breakers dancing over the Winner sands and listened to the gurgling of the water down beneath me in the caves of the Combera. We faced the western side of the island, and from where I lay I could see the whole stretch of the Irish Sea, right across to where a long hazy line upon the horizon marked the northern coast of the sister isle. The wind was blowing freshly from the north-west and the great Atlantic rollers were racing merrily in, one behind the other, dark brown below, light green above, and breaking with a sullen roar at the base of the cliffs. Now and again a sluggish one would be overtaken by its successor, and the two would come crashing in together and send the spray right over me as I lay. The whole air was prickly with the smack of the sea. Away to the north there was a piling up of clouds, and the peak of Goatfell in Arran looked lurid and distinct. There were no craft in the offing except one little eager, panting steamer making for the shelter of the Clyde, and a trim brigantine tacking along the coast. I was speculating as to her destination when I heard a light springy footstep, and Minnie Fullarton was standing beside me, her face rosy with exercise and her brown hair floating behind her.

"Wha's been vexing you, Archie?" she asked with the quick intuition of womanhood. "The auld man has been speaking aboot me again; has he no'?"

It was strange how pretty and mellow the accents were in her mouth which came so raspingly from my father. We sat down on a little green hillock together, her hand in mine, while I told her of our quarrel in the morning.

"You see they're bent on parting us," I said; "but indeed they'll find they have the wrong man to deal with if they try to frighten me away from you."

"I'm no' worth it, Archie," she answered, sighing. "I'm ower hamely and simple for one like you that speaks well and is a scholar forbye."

"You're too good and true for any one, Minnie," I answered, though in my heart I thought there was some truth in what she said.

"I'll no' trouble anyone lang," she continued, looking earnestly into my face. "I got my call last nicht; I saw a ghaist, Archie."

"Saw a ghost!" I ejaculated.

"Yes, and I doubt it was a call for me. When my cousin Steevie deed he saw one the same way."

"Tell me about it, dear," I said, impressed by her solemnity.

"There's no' much to tell: it was last nicht aboot twelve, or maybe one o'clock. I was lying awake thinking o' this and that wi' my een fixed on the window. Suddenly I saw a face looking in at me through the glass – an awfu'-like face, Archie. It was na the face of any one on the island. I canna tell what it was like – it was just awfu'. It was there maybe a minute looking tae way and tither into the room. I could see the glint o' his very een – for it was a man's face – and his nose was white where it was pressed against the glass. My very blood ran cauld and I couldna scream for fright. Then it went awa' as quickly and as sudden as it came."

"Who could it have been?" I exclaimed.

"A wraith or a bogle," said Minnie positively.

"Are you sure it wasn't Tommy Gibbs?" I suggested.

"Na, na, it wasna Tammy. It was a dark, hard, dour sort of face."

"Well," I said, laughing, "I hope the fellow will give me a look up, whoever he is. I'll soon learn who he is and where he comes from. But we won't talk of it, or you'll be frightening yourself tonight again. It'll be a dreary night as it is."

"A bad nicht for the puir sailors," she answered sadly, glancing at the dark wrack hurrying up from the northward, and at the white line of breakers on the Winner sands. "I wonder what yon brig is after! Unless it gets roond to Lamlash or Brodick Bay, it'll find itself on a nasty coast."

She was watching the trim brigantine which had already attracted my attention. She was still standing off the coast, and evidently expected rough weather, for her foresail had been taken in and her topsail reefed down.

"It's too cold for you up here!" I exclaimed at last, as the clouds covered the sun, and the keen north wind came in more frequent gusts. We walked back together, until we were close to Carracuil, when she left me, taking the footpath to Corriemains, which was about a mile from our bothy. I hoped that my father had not observed us together, but he met me at the door, fuming with passion. His face was quite livid with rage, and he held his shot-gun in his hands. I forget if I mentioned that in spite of his age he was one of the most powerful men I ever met in my life.

"So you've come!" he roared, shaking the gun at me. "You great gowk – " I did not wait for the string of adjectives which I knew was coming.

"You keep a civil tongue in your head," I said.

"You dare!" he shouted, raising his arm as if to strike me. "You wunna come in here. You can gang back where you come frae!"

"You can go to the devil!" I answered, losing my temper completely, on which he jabbed at me with the butt-end of the gun, but I warded it off with my stick. For a moment the devil was busy in me, and my throat was full of oaths, but I choked them down, and, turning on my heel, walked back to Corriemains, where I spent the day with the Fullartons. It seemed to me that my father, who had long been a miser, was rapidly becoming a madman – and a dangerous one to boot.

II

My mind was so busy with my grievance that I was poor company, I fear, and drank perhaps more whisky than was good for me. I remember that I stumbled over a stool once and that Minnie looked surprised and tearful, while old Fullarton sniggered to himself and coughed to hide it. I did not set out for home till half-past nine, which was a very late hour for the island. I knew my father would be asleep, and that if I climbed through my bedroom window I should have one night in peace.

It was blowing great guns by this time, and I had to put my shoulder against the gale as I came along the winding path which led down to Carracuil. I must still have been under the influence of liquor, for I remember that I sang uproariously and joined my feeble pipe to the howling of the wind. I had just got to the enclosure of our croft when a little incident occurred which helped to sober me.

White is a colour so rare in nature that in an island like ours, where even paper was a precious commodity, it would arrest the attention at once. Something white fluttered across my path and stuck flapping upon a furze bush. I lifted it up and discovered, to my very great surprise, that it was a linen pocket-handkerchief – and scented. Now I was very sure that beyond my own there was no such thing as a white pocket-handkerchief in the island. A small community like ours knew each other's wardrobes to a nicety. But as to scent in Uffa – it was preposterous! Who did the handkerchief belong to then? Was Minnie right, and was there really a stranger in the island? I walked on very thoughtfully, holding my discovery in my hand and thinking of what Minnie had seen the night before.

When I got into my bedroom and lit my rushlight I examined it again. It was clean and new, with the initials A.W. worked in red silk in the corner. There was no other indication as to who it might belong to, though from its size it was evidently a man's. The incident struck me as so extraordinary that I sat for some time on the side of my bed turning it over in my befuddled mind, but without getting any nearer a conclusion. I might even have taken my father into confidence, but his hoarse snoring in the adjoining room showed that he was fast asleep. It is as well that it was so, for

I was in no humour to be bullied, and we might have had words. The old man had little longer to live, and it is some solace to me now that that little was unmarred by any further strife between us.

I did not take my clothes off, for my brain was getting swimmy after its temporary clearness, so I dropped my head upon the pillow and sank into profound slumber. I must have slept about four hours when I woke with a violent start. To this day I have never known what it was that roused me. Everything was perfectly still, and yet I found all my faculties in a state of extreme tension. Was there someone in the room? It was very dark, but I peered about, leaning on my elbow. There was nothing to be seen, but still that eerie feeling haunted me. At that moment the flying scud passed away from the face of the moon and a flood of cold light was poured into my chamber. I turned my eyes up instinctively, and – good God! – there at the window was the face, an evil, malicious face, hard-cut, and distinct against the silvery radiance, glaring in at me as Minnie had seen it the night before. For one moment I tingled and palpitated like a frightened child, the next both glass and sash were gone and I was rolling over and over on the gravel path with my arms round a tall strong man – the two of us worrying each other like a pair of dogs. Almost by intuition I knew as we went down together that he had slipped his hand into his side pocket, and I clung to that wrist like grim death. He tried hard to free it but I was too strong for him, and we staggered on to our feet again in the same position, panting and snarling.

"Let go my hand, damn you!" he said.

"Let go that pistol then," I gasped.

We looked hard at each other in the moonlight, and then he laughed and opened his fingers. A heavy glittering object, which I could see was a revolver, dropped with a clink on to the gravel. I put my foot on it and let go my grip of him.

"Well, matey, how now?" he said with another laugh. "Is that an end of a round, or the end of the battle. You islanders seem a hospitable lot. You're so ready to welcome a stranger, that you can't wait to find the door, but must come flying through the window like infernal fireworks."

"What do you want to come prowling round people's houses at night for, with weapons in your pocket?" I asked sternly.

"I should think I needed a weapon," he answered, "when there are young devils like you knocking around. Hullo! here's another of the family."

I turned my head, and there was my father, almost at my elbow.

He had come round from the front door. His grey woollen nightdress and grizzled hair were streaming in the wind, and he was evidently much excited. He had in his hand the double-barrelled gun with which he had threatened me in the morning. He put this up to his shoulder, and would most certainly have blown out either my brains or those of the stranger, had I not turned away the barrel with my hand.

"Wait a bit, father," I said, "let us hear what he has to say for himself. And you," I continued, turning to the stranger, "can come inside with us and justify yourself if you can. But remember we are in a majority, so keep your tongue between your teeth."

"Not so fast, my young bantam," he grumbled; "you've got my six-shooter, but I have a Derringer in my pocket. I learned in Colorado to carry them both. However, come along into this shanty of yours, and let us get the damned palaver over. I'm wet through, and most infernally hungry."

My father was still mumbling to himself, and fidgeting with his gun, but he did not oppose my taking the stranger into the house. I struck a match, and lit the oil lamp in the kitchen, on which our prisoner stooped down to it and began smoking a cigarette. As the light fell full on his face, both my father and I took a good look at him. He was a man of about forty, remarkably handsome, of rather a Spanish type, with blue-black hair and beard, and sun-burned features. His eyes were very bright, and their gaze so intense that you would think they projected somewhat, unless you saw him in profile. There was a dash of recklessness and devilry about them, which, with his wiry, powerful frame and jaunty manner, gave the impression of a man whose past had been an adventurous one. He was elegantly dressed in a velveteen jacket, and greyish trousers of a foreign cut. Without in the least resenting our prolonged scrutiny, he seated himself upon the dresser, swinging his legs, and blowing little blue wreaths from his cigarette. His appearance seemed to reassure my father, or perhaps it was the sight of the rings which flashed on the stranger's left hand every time he raised it to his lips.

"Ye munna mind Archie, sir," he said in a cringing voice. "He was aye a fashious bairn, ower quick wi' his hands, and wi' mair muscle than brains. I was fashed mysel' wi' the sudden stour, but as tae shootin' at ye, sir, that was a' an auld man's havers. Nae doobt ye're a veesitor, or maybe it's a shipwreck — it's no a ship-wreck, is't?" The idea awoke the covetous devil in my father's soul, and it looked out through his glistening eyes, and set his long stringy hands a-shaking.

"I came here in a boat," said the stranger shortly. "This was the first house I came to after I left the shore, and I'm not likely to forget the reception you have given me. That young hopeful of yours has nearly broken my back."

"A good job too!" I interrupted hotly, "why couldn't you come up to the door like a man, instead of skulking at the window?"

"Hush, Archie, hush!" said my father imploringly; while our visitor grinned across at me as amicably as if my speech had been most conciliatory.

"I don't blame you," he said – he spoke with a strange mixture of accents, sometimes with a foreign lisp, sometimes with a slight Yankee intonation, and at other times very purely indeed. "I have done the same, mate. Maybe you noticed a brigantine standing on and off the shore yesterday?"

I nodded my head.

"That was mine," he said. "I'm owner, skipper, and everything else. Why shouldn't a man spend his money in his own way. I like cruising about, and I like new experiences. I suppose there's no harm in that. I was in the Mediterranean last month, but I'm sick of blue skies and fine weather. Chios is a damnable paradise of a place. I've come up here for a little fresh air and freedom. I cruised all down the western isles, and when we came abreast of this place of yours it rather took my fancy, so I hauled the foreyard aback and came ashore last night to prospect. It wasn't this house I struck, but another farther to the west'ard; however, I saw enough to be sure it was a place after my own heart – a real quiet corner. So I went back and set everything straight aboard yesterday, and now here I am. You can put me up for a few weeks, I suppose. I'm not hard to please, and I can pay my way; suppose we say ten dollars a week for board and lodging, and a fortnight to be paid in advance."

He put his hand in his pocket and produced four shining napoleons, which he pushed along the dresser to my father, who grabbed them up eagerly.

"I'm sorry I gave you such a rough reception," I said, rather awkwardly. "I was hardly awake at the time."

"Say no more, mate, say no more!" he shouted heartily, holding out his hand and clasping mine. "Hard knocks are nothing new to me. I suppose we may consider the bargain settled then?"

"Ye can bide as lang as ye wull, sir," answered my father, still fingering the four coins. "Archie and me'll do a' we can to mak' your veesit a pleasant ane. It's no' such a dreary place as ye might think. When the Lamlash boats come in we get the papers and a' the news."

It struck me that the stranger looked anything but overjoyed by this piece of information. "You don't mean to say that you get the papers here," he said.

" 'Oo aye, the *Scotsman* an' the *Glasgey Herald*. But maybe you would like Archie and me to row ower to your ship in the morn, an' fetch your luggage."

"The brig is fifty miles away by this time," said our visitor. "She is running before the wind for Marseilles. I told the mate to bring her round again in a month or so. As to luggage, I always travel light in that matter. If a man's purse is only full he can do with very little else. All I have is in a bundle under your window. By the way, my name is Digby – Charles Digby."

"I thought your initials were A.W.," I remarked.

He sprang off the dresser as if he had been stung, and his face turned quite grey for a moment. "What the devil do you mean by that?" he said.

"I thought this might be yours," I answered, handing him the handkerchief I had found.

"Oh, is that all!" he said with rather a forced laugh. "I didn't quite see what you were driving at. That's all right. It belongs to Whittingdale, my second officer. I'll keep it until I see him again. And now suppose you give me something to eat, for I'm about famished."

We brought him out such rough fare as was to be found in our larder, and he ate ravenously, and tossed off a stiff glass of whisky and water. Afterwards my father showed him into the solitary spare bedroom, with which he professed himself well pleased, and we all settled down for the night. As I went back to my couch I noticed that the gale had freshened up, and I saw long streamers of seaweed flying past my broken window in the moonlight. A great bat fluttered into the room, which is reckoned a sure sign of misfortune in the islands – but I was never superstitious, and let the poor thing find its way out again unmolested.

III

In the morning it was still blowing a whole gale, though the sky was blue for the most part. Our guest was up betimes and we walked down to the beach together. It was a sight to see the great rollers sweeping in, overtopping one another like a herd of oxen, and then bursting with a roar, sending the Carracuil pebbles flying before them like grapeshot, and filling the whole air with drifting spume.

We were standing together watching the scene, when looking

round I saw my father hurrying towards us. He had been up and out since early dawn. When he saw us looking, he began waving his hands and shouting, but the wind carried his voice away. We ran towards him however, seeing that he was heavy with news.

"The brig's wrecked, and they're a' drowned!" he cried as we met him.

"What!" roared our visitor.

If ever I heard exceeding great joy compressed into a monosyllable it vibrated in that one.

"They're a' drowned and naething saved!" repeated my father. "Come yoursel' and see."

We followed him across the Combera to the level sands on the other side. They were strewn with wreckage, broken pieces of bulwark and handrail, panelling of a cabin, and an occasional cask. A single large spar was tossing in the waves close to the shore, occasionally shooting up towards the sky like some giant's javelin, then sinking and disappearing in the trough of the great scooping seas. Digby hurried up to the nearest piece of timber, and stooping over it examined it intently.

"By God!" he said at last, taking in a long breath between his teeth, "you are right. It's the *Proserpine*, and all hands are lost. What a terrible thing!"

His face was very solemn as he spoke, but his eyes danced and glittered. I was beginning to conceive a great repugnance and distrust towards this man.

"Is there no chance of anyone having got ashore?" he said.

"Na, na, nor cargo neither," my father answered with real grief in his voice. "Ye dinna ken this coast. There's an awful undertow outside the Winners, and it's a' swept round to Holy Isle. De'il take it, if there was to be a shipwreck what for should they no' run their ship agroond to the east'ard o' the point and let an honest mun have the pickings instead o' they rascally loons in Arran? An empty barrel might float in here, but there's no chance o' a sea-chest, let alane a body."

"Poor fellows!" said Digby. "But there – we must meet it some day, and why not here and now? I've lost my ship, but thank Heaven I can buy another. It is sad about them, though – very sad. I warned Lamarck that he was waiting too long with a low barometer and an ugly shore under his lee. He has himself to thank. He was my first officer, a prying, covetous, meddlesome hound."

"Don't call him names," I said. "He's dead."

"Well said, my young prig!" he answered. "perhaps you wouldn't be so mealy-mouthed yourself if you lost five thousand pounds before breakfast. But there – there's no use crying over spilt milk. *Vogue la galère!* as the French say. Things are never so bad but that they might be worse."

My father and Digby stayed at the scene of the wreck, but I walked over to Corriemains to reassure Minnie's mind as to the apparition at the window. Her opinion, when I had told her all, coincided with mine, that perhaps the crew of the brig knew more about the stranger than he cared for. We agreed that I should keep a close eye upon him without letting him know that he was watched.

"But oh, Archie," she said, "ye munna cross him or anger him while he carries them awfu' weapons. Ye maun be douce and saft, and no' gainsay him."

I laughed, and promised her to be very prudent, which re-assured her a little. Old Fullarton walked back with me in the hope of picking up a piece of timber, and both he and my father patrolled the shore for many days, without, however, finding any prize of importance, for the under current off the Winners was very strong, and everything had probably drifted right round to Lamlash Bay in Arran.

It was wonderful how quickly the stranger accommodated himself to our insular ways, and how useful he made himself about the homesteading. Within a fortnight he knew the island almost as well as I did myself. Had it not been for that one unpleasant recollection of the shipwreck which rankled in my remembrance, I could have found it in my heart to become fond of him. His nature was a tropical one – fiercely depressed at times, but sunny as a rule, bursting continually into jest and song from pure instinct, in a manner which is unknown among us North-erners. In his graver moments he was a most interesting com-panion, talking shrewdly and eloquently of men and manners, and his own innumerable and strange adventures. I have seldom heard a more brilliant conversationalist. Of an evening he would keep my father and myself spell-bound by the kitchen fire for hours and hours, while he chatted away in a desultory fashion and smoked his cigarettes. It seemed to me that the packet he had brought with him on the first night must have consisted entirely of tobacco. I noticed that in these conversations, which were mostly addressed to my father, he used, unconsciously perhaps, to play upon the weak side of the old man's nature. Tales of cunning, of smartness, of various ways in which mankind had been cheated and money gained, came most readily to his lips, and were relished by an eager listener. I could not help one night remarking upon it, when my father had gone out of the room, laughing hoarsely, and vibrating with amusement over some story of how the Biscayan peasants will strap lanterns to a bullock's horns, and taking the beast some distance inland on a stormy night, will make it prance and rear so that the ships at sea may imagine it to be the lights of a vessel, and steer fearlessly in that direction, only to find themselves on a rockbound coast.

"You shouldn't tell such tales to an old man," I said.

"My dear fellow," he answered very kindly, "you have seen nothing of the world yet. You have formed fine ideas no doubt, and notions of delicacy and such things, and you are very dogmatic about them, as clever men of your age always are. I had notions of right and wrong once, but it has been all knocked out of me. It's just a sort of varnish which the rough friction of the world soon rubs off. I started with a whole soul, but there are more gashes and seams and scars in it now than there are in my body, and that's pretty fair as you'll allow" – with which he pulled upon his tunic and showed me his chest.

"Good heavens!" I said, "How on earth did you get those?"

"This was a bullet," he said, pointing to a deep bluish pucker underneath his collar bone. "I got it behind the barricades in Berlin in '48. Langenback said it just missed the subclavian artery. And this," he went on, indicating a pair of curious elliptical scars upon his throat, "was the bite from a Sioux chief, when I was under Custer on the plains – I've got an arrow wound on my leg from the same party. This is from a mutinous Lascar aboard ship, and the others are mere scratches – Californian vaccination marks. You can excuse my being a little ready with my own irons, though, when I've been dropped so often."

"What's this?" I asked, pointing to a little chamois-leather bag which was hung by a strong cord round his neck. "It looks like a charm."

He buttoned up his tunic again hastily, looking extremely disconcerted. "It is nothing," he said brusquely. "I am a Roman Catholic, and it is what we call a scapular." I could hardly get another word out of him that night, and even next day he was reserved and appeared to avoid me. This little incident made me very thoughtful, the more so as I noticed shortly afterwards when standing over him, that the string was no longer round his neck. Apparently he had taken it off after my remark about it. What could there be in that leather bag which needed such secrecy and precaution! Had I but known it, I would sooner have put my left hand in the fire than have pursued that inquiry.

One of the peculiarities of our visitor was that in all his plans for the future, with which he often regaled us, he seemed entirely untrammelled by any monetary considerations. He would talk in the lightest and most off-hand way of schemes which would involve the outlay of much wealth. My father's eyes would glisten as he heard him talk carelessly of sums which to our frugal minds appeared enormous. It seemed strange to both of us that a man who by his own confession had been a vagabond and adventurer all his life, should be in possession of such a fortune. My father was inclined to put it down to some stroke of luck on the American goldfields. I had my own ideas even then — chaotic and half-formed as yet, but tending in the right direction.

It was not long before these suspicions began to assume a more definite shape, which came about in this way. Minnie and I made the summit of the Combera cliff a favourite trysting-place, as I think I mentioned before, and it was rare for a day to pass without our spending two or three hours there. One morning, not long after my chat with our guest, we were seated together in a little nook there, which we had chosen as sheltering us from the wind as well as from my father's observation, when Minnie caught sight of Digby walking along the Carracuil beach. He sauntered up to the base of the cliff, which was boulder-studded and slimy from the receding tide, but instead of turning back he kept on climbing over the great green slippery stones, and threading his way among the pools until he was standing immediately beneath us so that we looked straight down at him. To him the spot must have seemed the very acme of seclusion, with the great sea in front, the rocks on each side, and the precipice behind. Even had he looked up, he could hardly have made out the two human faces, which peered down at him from the distant ledge. He gave a hurried glance round, and then slipping his hand into his pocket, he pulled out the leather bag which I had noticed, and took out of it a small object which he held in the palm of his hand and looked at long, and, as it were, lovingly. We both had an excellent view of it from where we lay. He then replaced it in the bag, and shoving it down to the very bottom of his pocket picked his way back more cheerily than he had come.

Minnie and I looked at each other. She was smiling; I was serious.

"Did you see it?" I asked.

"Yon? Aye, I saw it."

"What did you think it was then?"

"A wee bit of glass," she answered, looking at me with wondering eyes.

"No," I cried excitedly, "glass could never catch the sun's rays so. It was a diamond, and if I mistake not, one of extraordinary value. It was as large as all I have seen put together, and must be worth a fortune."

A diamond was a mere name to poor, simple Minnie, who had never seen one before, nor had any conception of their value, and she prattled away to me about this and that, but I hardly heard her. In vain she exhausted all her little wiles in attempting to recall my attention. My mind was full of what I had seen. Look where I would, the glistening of the breakers, or the sparkling of the mica-laden rocks, recalled the brilliant facets of the gem which I had seen. I was moody and distraught, and eventually let Minnie walk back to Corriemains by herself while I made my way to the home-steading. My father and Digby were just sitting down to the mid-day meal, and the latter hailed me cheerily.

"Come along, mate," he cried, pushing over a stool, "we were just wondering what had become of you. Ah! you rogue, I'll bet my bottom dollar it was that pretty wench I saw the other day who kept you."

"Mind your own affairs," I answered angrily.

"Don't be thin-skinned," he said; "young people should control their tempers, and you've got a mighty bad one, my lad. Have you heard that I am going to leave you."

"I'm sorry to hear it," I said frankly; "when do you intend to go?"

"Next week," he answered, "but don't be afraid; you'll see me again. I've had too good a time here to forget you easily. I'm going to buy a good steam yacht – 250 tons or thereabouts – and I'll bring her round in a few months and give you a cruise."

"What would be a fair price for a craft of that sort?" I asked.

"Forty thousand dollars," said our visitor, carelessly.

"You must be very rich," I remarked, "to throw away so much money on pleasure."

"Rich!" echoed my companion, his Southern blood mantling up for a moment. "Rich, why man, there is hardly a limit – but there, I was romancing a bit. I'm fairly well off, or shall be very shortly."

"How did you make your money?" I asked. The question came so glibly to my lips that I had no time to check it, though I felt the moment afterwards that I had made a mistake. Our guest drew himself into himself at once, and took no notice of my query, while my father said:

"Hush, Archie laddie, ye munna speer they questions o' the gentleman!" I could see, however, from the old man's eager grey eyes, looking out from under the great thatch of his brows, that he was meditating over the same problem himself.

During the next couple of days I hesitated very often as to whether I should tell my father of what I had seen and the opinions I had formed about our visitor; but he forestalled me by making a discovery himself which supplemented mine and explained all that had been dark. It was one day when the stranger was out for a ramble, that, entering the kitchen, I found my father sitting by the fire deeply engaged in perusing a newspaper, spelling out the words laboriously, and following the lines with his great forefinger. As I came in he crumpled up the paper as if his instinct were to conceal it, but then spreading it out again on his knee he beckoned me over to him.

"Wha d'ye think this chiel Digby is?" he asked. I could see by his manner that he was much excited.

"No good," I answered.

"Come here, laddie, come here!" he croaked. "You're a braw scholar. Read this tae me alood – read it and tell me if you dinna think I've fitted the cap on the right heid. It's a *Glasgey Herald* only four days auld – a Loch Ranza feeshin' boat brought it in the morn. Begin frae here – 'Oor Paris Letter.' Here it is, 'Fuller details;' read it a' to me."

I began at the spot indicated, which was a paragraph of the ordinary French correspondence of the Glasgow paper. It ran in this way. "Fuller details have now come before the public of the diamond robbery by which the Duchesse de Rochevieille lost her celebrated gem. The diamond is a pure brilliant weighing eighty three and a half carats, and is supposed to be the third largest in France, and the seventeenth in Europe. It came into the possession of the family through the great grand-uncle of the Duchess, who fought under Bussy in India, and brought it back to Europe with him. It represented a fortune then, but its value now is simply enormous. It was taken, as will be remembered, from the jewel case of the Duchess two months ago during the night, and though the police have made every effort, no real clue has been obtained as to the thief. They are very reticent upon the subject, but it seems that they have reason to suspect one Achille Wolff, an Americanised native of Lorraine, who had called at the Château a short time before. He is an eccentric man, of Bohemian habits, and it is just possible that his sudden disappearance at the time of the robbery may have been a coincidence. In appearance he is described as romantic-looking, with an artistic face, dark eyes and hair, and a brusque manner. A large reward is offered for his capture."

When I finished reading this, my father and I sat looking at each other in silence for a minute or so. Then my father jerked his finger over his shoulder. "Yon's him," he said.

"Yes, it must be he," I answered, thinking of the initials on the handkerchief.

Again we were silent for a time. My father took one of the faggots out of the grate and twisted it about in his hands. "It maun be a muckle stane" he said. "He canna hae it aboot him. Likely he's left it in France."

"No, he has it with him," I said, like a cursed fool as I was.

"Hoo d'ye ken that?" asked the old man, looking up quickly with eager eyes.

"Because I have seen it."

The faggot which he held broke in two in his grip, but he said nothing more. Shortly afterwards our guest came in, and we had dinner, but neither of us alluded to the arrival of the paper.

IV

I have often been amused, when reading stories told in the first person, to see how the narrator makes himself out as a matter of course to be a perfect and spotless man. All around may have their passions, and weaknesses, and vices, but he remains a cold and blameless nonentity, running like a colourless thread through the tangled skein of the story. I shall not fall into this error. I see myself as I was in those days, shallow-hearted, hot-headed, and with little principle of any kind. Such I was, and such I depict myself.

From the time that I finally identified our visitor Digby with Achille Wolff the diamond robber, my resolution was taken. Some might have been squeamish in the matter, and thought that because he had shaken their hand and broken their bread he had earned some sort of grace from them. I was not troubled with sentimentality of this sort. He was a criminal escaping from justice. Some providence had thrown him into our hands, and an enormous reward awaited his betrayers. I never hesitated for a moment as to what was to be done.

The more I thought of it the more I admired the cleverness with which he had managed the whole business. It was clear that he had had a vessel ready, manned either by confederates or by unsuspecting fishermen. Hence he would be independent of all those parts where the police would be on the look-out for him. Again, if he had made for England or for America, he could hardly have escaped ultimate capture, but by choosing one of the most desolate and lonely spots in Europe he had thrown them off his track for a time, while the destruction of the brig seemed to destroy the last clue as to his whereabouts. At present he was entirely at our mercy, since he could not move from the island without our help. There was no necessity for us to hurry therefore, and we could mature our plans at our leisure.

Both my father and I showed no change in our manner towards our guest, and he himself was as cheery and light-hearted as ever. It was pleasant to hear him singing as we mended the nets or caulked the boat. His voice was a very high tenor and one of the most melodious I ever listened to. I am convinced that he could have made a name upon the operatic stage, but like most versatile scoundrels, he placed small account upon the genuine talents which he possessed, and cultivated the worse portion of his nature. My father used sometimes to eye him sideways in a strange manner, and I thought I knew what he was thinking about – but there I made a mistake.

One day, about a week after our conversation, I was fixing up one of the rails of our fence which had been snapped in the gale, when my father came along the seashore, plodding heavily among the pebbles, and sat down on a stone at my elbow. I went on knocking in the nails, but looked at him from the corner of my eye, as he pulled away at his short black pipe. I could see that he had something weighty on his mind, for he knitted his brows, and his lips projected.

"D'ye mind what was in yon paper?" he said at last, knocking his ashes out against the stone.

"Yes," I answered shortly.

"Well, what's your opeenion?" he asked.

"Why, that we should have the reward, of course!" I replied.

"The reward!" he said, with a fierce snarl. "You would tak' the reward. You'd let the stane that's worth thoosands an' thoosands gang awa' back tae some furrin Papist, an' a' for the sake o' a few pund that they'd fling till ye, as they fling a bane to a dog when the meat's a' gone. It's a clean flingin' awa' o' the gifts o' Providence."

"Well, father," I said, laying down the hammer, "you must be satisfied with what you can get. You can only have what is offered."

"But if we got the stane itsel'," whispered my father, with a leer on his face.

"He'd never give it up," I said.

"But if he deed while he's here – if he was suddenly –"

"Drop it, father, drop it!" I cried, for the old man looked like a fiend out of the pit. I saw now what he was aiming at.

"If he deed," he shouted, "wha saw him come, and wha wad speer where he'd ganged till? If an accident happened, if he came by a dud on the heid, or woke some nicht to find a knife at his thrapple, wha wad be the wiser?"

"You mustn't speak so, father," I said, though I was thinking many things at the same time.

"It may as well be oot as in," he answered, and went away rather sulkily, turning round after a few yards and holding up his finger towards me to impress the necessity of caution.

My father did not speak of this matter to me again, but what he said rankled in my mind. I could hardly realise that he meant his words, for he had always, as far as I knew, been an upright, righteous man, hard in his ways, and grasping in his nature, but guiltless of any great sin. Perhaps it was that he was removed from temptation, for isothermal lines of crime might be drawn on the map through places where it is hard to walk straight, and there are others where it is as hard to fall. It was easy to be a saint in the island of Uffa.

One day we were finishing breakfast when our guest asked if the boat was mended (one of the thole-pins had been broken). I answered that it was.

"I want you two," he said, "to take me round to Lamlash to-day. You shall have a couple of sovereigns for the job. I don't know that I may not come back with you – but I may stay."

My eyes met those of my father for a flash. "There's no' vera much wind," he said.

"What there is, is in the right direction," returned Digby, as I must call him.

"The new foresail has no' been bent," persisted my father.

"There's no use throwing difficulties in the way," said our visitor angrily. "If you won't come, I'll get Tommy Gibbs and his father, but go I shall. Is it a bargain or not?"

"I'll gang," my father replied sullenly, and went down to get the boat ready. I followed, and helped him to bend on the new foresail. I felt nervous and excited.

"What do you intend to do?" I asked.

"I dinna ken," he said irritably. "Gin the worst come to the worst we can gie him up at Lamlash – but oh, it wad be a peety, an awfu' peety. You're young an' strong, laddie; can we no' master him between us?"

"No," I said, "I'm ready to give him up, but I'm damned if I lay a hand on him."

"You're a cooardly, white-livered loon!" he cried, but I was not to be moved by taunts, and left him mumbling to himself and picking at the sail with nervous fingers.

It was about two o'clock before the boat was ready, but as there

was a slight breeze from the north we reckoned on reaching
Lamlash before nightfall. There was just a pleasant ripple upon
the dark blue water, and as we stood on the beach before shoving
off, we could see the Carlin's leap and Goatfell bathed in a purple
mist, while beyond them along the horizon loomed the long line
of the Argyleshire hills. Away to the south the great bald summit
of Ailsa crag glittered in the sun, and a single white fleck showed
where a fishing-boat was beating up from the Scotch coast. Digby
and I stepped into the boat, but my father ran back to where I had
been mending the rails, and came back with the hatchet in his
hand, which he stowed away under the thwarts.

"What d'ye want with the axe?" our visitor asked.

"It's a handy thing to hae aboot a boat," my father answered
with averted eyes, and shoved us off. We set the foresail, jib, and
mainsail, and shot away across the Roost, with the blue water
splashing merrily under our bows. Looking back, I saw the coast-
line of our little island extend rapidly on either side. There was
Carravoe which we had left, and our own beach of Carracuil and
the steep brown face of the Combera, and away behind the
rugged crests of Beg-na-phail and Beg-na-sacher. I could see the
red tiles of the byre of our homesteading, and across the moor a
thin blue reek in the air which marked the position of Corriemains. My heart warmed towards the place which had been my
home since childhood.

We were about half-way across the Roost when it fell a dead
calm, and the sails flapped against the mast. We were perfectly
motionless except for the drift of the current, which runs from
north to south. I had been steering and my father managing the
sails, while the stranger smoked his eternal cigarettes and admired the scenery; but at his suggestion we now got the sculls out
to row. I shall never know how it began, but as I was stooping
down to pick up an oar I heard our visitor give a great scream that
he was murdered, and looking up I saw him with his face all in a
sputter of blood leaning against the mast, while my father made at
him with the hatchet. Before I could move hand or foot Digby
rushed at the old man and caught him round the waist. "You
grey-headed devil," he cried in a husky voice. "I feel that you have
done for me. But you'll never get what you want. No — never!
never! never!" Nothing can ever erase from my memory the
intense and concentrated malice of those words. My father gave a
raucous cry, they swayed and balanced for a moment and then
over they went into the sea. I rushed to the side, boat-hook in
hand, but they never came up. As the long rings caused by the
splash widened out however and left an unruffled space in the

centre, I saw them once again. The water was very clear, and far far down I could see the shimmer of two white faces coming and going, faces which seemed to look up at me with an expression of unutterable horror. Slowly they went down, revolving in each other's embrace until they were nothing but a dark loom, and then faded from my view for ever. There they shall lie, the Frenchman and the Scot, till the great trumpet shall sound and the sea give up its dead. Storms may rage above them and great ships labour and creak, but their slumber shall be dreamless and unruffled in the silent green depths of the Roost of Uffa. I trust when the great day shall come that they will bring up the cursed stone with them, that they may show the sore temptation which the devil had placed in their way, as some slight extenuation of their errors while in this mortal flesh.

It was a weary and awesome journey back to Carravoe. I remember tug-tugging at the oars as though to snap them in trying to relieve the tension in my mind. Towards evening a breeze sprang up and helped me on my way, and before nightfall I was back in the lonely homesteading once more, and all that had passed that spring afternoon lay behind me like some horrible nightmare.

I did not remain in Uffa. The croft and the boat were sold by public roup in the market-place of Ardrossan, and the sum realised was sufficient to enable me to continue my medical studies at the University. I fled from the island as from a cursed place, nor did I ever set foot on it again. Gibbs and his son, and even Minnie Fullarton too, passed out of my life completely and for ever. She missed me for a time, no doubt, but I have heard that young McBane, who took the farm, went a-wooing to Corriemains after the white fishing, and as he was a comely fellow enough he may have consoled her for my loss. As for myself, I have settled quietly down into a large middle-class practice in Paisley. It has been in the brief intervals of professional work that I have jotted down these reminiscences of the events which led up to my father's death. Achille Wolff and the Rochevieille diamond are things of the past now, but there may be some who will care to hear of how they visited the island of Uffa.

THE VOICE OF SCIENCE

Mrs. Esdaile, of the Lindens, Birchespool, was a lady of quite remarkable scientific attainments. As honorary secretary of the ladies' branch of the local Eclectic Society, she shone with a never-failing brilliance. It was even whispered that on the occasion of the delivery of Professor Tomlinson's suggestive lecture "On the Perigenesis of the Plastidule" she was the only woman in the room who could follow the lecturer even as far as the end of his title. In the seclusion of the Lindens she supported Darwin, laughed at Mivart, doubted Haeckel, and shook her head at Weissman, with a familiarity which made her the admiration of the University professors and the terror of the few students who ventured to cross her learned but hospitable threshold. Mrs. Esdaile had, of course, detractors. It is the privilege of exceptional merit. There were bitter feminine whispers as to the cramming from encyclopædias and text-books which preceded each learned meeting, and as to the care with which in her own house the conversation was artfully confined to those particular channels with which the hostess was familiar. Tales there were, too, of brilliant speeches written out in some masculine hand, which had been committed to memory by the ambitious lady, and had afterwards flashed out as extempore elucidations of some dark, half-explored corner of modern science. It was even said that these little blocks of information got jumbled up occasionally in their bearer's mind, so that after an entomological lecture she would burst into a geological harangue, or *vice versa*, to the great confusion of her audience. So ran the gossip of the malicious, but those who knew her best were agreed that she was a very charming and clever little person.

It would have been a strange thing had Mrs. Esdaile not been popular among local scientists, for her pretty house, her charming grounds, and all the hospitality which an income of two thousand a year will admit of, were always at their command. On her pleasant lawns in the summer, and round her drawing-room fire in the winter, there was much high talk of microbes, and leucocytes, and sterilised bacteria, where thin, ascetic materialists from the University upheld the importance of this life against round, comfortable champions of orthodoxy from the Cathedral Close. And in the heat of thrust and parry, when scientific proof ran full tilt against inflexible faith, a word from the clever widow, or an opportune rattle over the keys by her pretty daughter Rose, would bring all back to harmony once more.

Rose Esdaile had just passed her twentieth year, and was looked upon as one of the beauties of Birchespool. Her face was, perhaps, a trifle long for perfect symmetry, but her eyes were fine, her expression kindly, and her complexion beautiful. It was an open secret, too, that she had under her father's will five hundred a year in her own right. With such advantages a far plainer girl than Rose Esdaile might create a stir in the society of a provincial town.

A scientific conversazione in a private house is an onerous thing to organise, yet mother and daughter had not shrunk from the task. On the morning of which I write, they sat together surveying their accomplished labours, with the pleasant feeling that nothing remained to be done save to receive the congratulations of their friends. With the assistance of Rupert, the son of the house, they had assembled from all parts of Birchespool objects of scientific interest, which now adorned the long tables in the drawing-room. Indeed, the full tide of curiosities of every sort which had swelled into the house had overflowed the rooms devoted to the meeting, and had surged down the broad stairs to invade the dining-room and the passage. The whole villa had become a museum. Specimens of the flora and fauna of the Philippine Islands, a ten-foot turtle carapace from the Gallapagos, the os frontis of the Bos montis as shot by Captain Charles Beesly in the Thibetan Himalayas, the bacillus of Koch cultivated on gelatine – these and a thousand other such trophies adorned the tables upon which the two ladies gazed that morning.

"You've really managed it splendidly, ma," said the young lady, craning her neck up to give her mother a congratulatory kiss. "It was so brave of you to undertake it."

"I think that it will do," purred Mrs. Esdaile complacently. "But I do hope that the phonograph will work without a hitch. You know at the last meeting of the British Association I got Professor Standerton to repeat into it his remarks on the life history of the Medusiform Gonophore."

"How funny it seems," exclaimed Rose, glancing at the square box-like apparatus, which stood in the post of honour on the central table, "to think that this wood and metal will begin to speak just like a human being."

"Hardly that, dear. Of course the poor thing can say nothing except what is said to it. You always know exactly what is coming. But I do hope that it will work all right."

"Rupert will see to it when he comes up from the garden. He understands all about them. Oh, ma, I feel so nervous."

Mrs. Esdaile looked anxiously down at her daughter, and passed her hand caressingly over her rich brown hair. "I understand," she said, in her soothing, cooing voice, "I understand."

"He will expect an answer to-night, ma."

"Follow your heart, child. I am sure that I have every confidence in your good sense and discretion. I would not dictate to you upon such a matter."

"You are so good, ma. Of course, as Rupert says, we really know very little of Charles – of Captain Beesly. But then, ma, all that we do know is in his favour."

"Quite so, dear. He is musical, and well-informed, and good-humoured, and certainly extremely handsome. It is clear, too, from what he says, that he has moved in the very highest circles."

"The best in India, ma. He was an intimate friend of the Governor-General's. You heard yourself what he said yesterday about the D'Arcies, and Lady Gwendoline Fairfax, and Lord Montague Grosvenor."

"Well, dear," said Mrs. Esdaile resignedly, "you are old enough to know your own mind. I shall not attempt to dictate to you. I own that my own hopes were set upon Professor Stares."

"Oh, ma, think how dreadfully ugly he is."

"But think of his reputation, dear. Little more than thirty, and a member of the Royal Society."

"I couldn't ma. I don't think I could, if there was not another man in the world. But, oh, I do feel so nervous; for you can't think how earnest he is. I must give him an answer to-night. But they will be here in an hour. Don't you think that we had better go to our rooms?"

The two ladies had risen, when there came a quick masculine step upon the stairs, and a brisk young fellow, with curly black hair, dashed into the room.

"All ready?" he asked, running his eyes over the lines of relic-strewn tables.

"All ready, dear," answered his mother.

"Oh, I am glad to catch you together," said he, with his hands buried deeply in his trouser pockets, and an uneasy expression on his face. "There's one thing that I wanted to speak to you about. Look here, Rosie; a bit of fun is all very well; but you wouldn't be such a little donkey as to think seriously of this fellow Beesly?"

"My dear Rupert, do try to be a little less abrupt," said Mrs. Esdaile, with a deprecating hand outstretched.

"I can't help seeing how they have been thrown together. I don't want to be unkind, Rosie; but I can't stand by and see you wreck your life for a man who has nothing to recommend him but his eyes and his moustache. Do be a sensible girl, Rosie, and have nothing to say to him."

"It is surely a point, Rupert, upon which I am more fitted to decide than you can be," remarked Mrs. Esdaile, with dignity.

"No, mater, for I have been able to make some inquiries. Young Cheffington, of the Gunners, knew him in India. He says—"

But his sister broke in upon his revelations. "I won't stay here, ma, to hear him slandered behind his back," she cried, with spirit. "He has never said anything that was not kind of you, Rupert, and I don't know why you should attack him so. It is cruel, unbrotherly." With a sweep and a whisk she was at the door, her cheek flushed, her eyes sparkling, her bosom heaving with this little spurt of indignation, while close at her heels walked her mother with soothing words, and an angry glance thrown back over her shoulder. Rupert Esdaile stood with his hands burrowing deeper and deeper into his pockets, and his shoulders rising higher and higher to his ears, feeling intensely guilty, and yet not certain whether he should blame himself for having said too much or for not having said enough.

Just in front of him stood the table on which the phonograph, with wires, batteries, and all complete, stood ready for the guests whom it was to amuse. Slowly his hands emerged from his pockets as his eye fell upon the apparatus, and with languid curiosity he completed the connection, and started the machine. A pompous, husky sound, as of a man clearing his throat proceeded from the instrument, and then in high, piping tones, thin but distinct, the commencement of the celebrated scientist's lecture. "Of all the interesting problems," remarked the box, "which are offered to us by recent researches into the lower orders of marine life, there is none to exceed the retrograde metamorphosis which characterises the common barnacle. The differentiation of an amorphous protoplasmic mass —" Here Rupert Esdaile broke the connection again, and the funny little tinkling voice ceased as suddenly as it began.

The young man stood smiling, looking down at this garrulous piece of wood and metal, when suddenly the smile broadened, and a light of mischief danced up into his eyes. He slapped his thigh, and danced round in the ecstasy of one who has stumbled on a brand-new brilliant idea. Very carefully he drew forth the slips of metal which recorded the learned Professor's remarks, and laid them aside for future use. Into the slots he thrust virgin plates, all ready to receive an impression, and then, bearing the phonograph under his arm, he vanished into his own sanctum. Five minutes before the first guests had arrived the machine was back upon the table, and all ready for use.

There could be no question of the success of Mrs. Esdaile's conversazione. From first to last everything went admirably. People stared through microscopes, and linked hands for electric shocks, and marvelled at the Gallapagos turtle, the os frontis of the Bos montis, and all the other curiosities which Mrs. Esdaile had taken such pains to collect. Groups formed and chatted round the various cases. The Dean of Birchespool listened with a protesting lip, while Professor Maunders held forth upon a square of triassic rock, with side-thrusts occasionally at the six days of orthodox creation; a knot of specialists disputed over a stuffed ornithorhynchus in the corner; while Mrs. Esdaile swept from group to group, introducing, congratulating, laughing, with the ready, graceful tact of a clever woman of the world. By the window sat the heavily-moustached Captain Beesly, with the daughter of the house, and they discussed a problem of their own, as old as the triassic rock, and perhaps as little understood.

"But I must really go and help my mother to entertain, Captain Beesly," said Rose at last, with a little movement as if to rise.

"Don't go, Rose. And don't call me Captain Beesly; call me Charles. Do, now!"

"Well, then, Charles."

"How prettily it sounds from your lips! No, now, don't go. I can't bear to be away from you. I had heard of love, Rose; but how strange it seems that I, after spending my life amid all that is sparkling and gay, should only find out now, in this little provincial town, what love really is!"

"You say so; but it is only a passing fancy."

"No, indeed. I shall never leave you, Rose – never, unless you drive me away from your side. And you would not be so cruel – you would not break my heart?"

He had very plaintive, blue eyes, and there was such a depth of sorrow in them as he spoke that Rose could have wept for sympathy.

"I should be very sorry to cause you grief in any way," she said, in a faltering tone.

"Then promise –"

"No, no; we cannot speak of it just now, and they are collecting round the phonograph. Do come and listen to it. It is so funny. Have you ever heard one?"

"Never."

"It will amuse you immensely. And I am sure that you would never guess what it is going to talk about."

"What then?"

"Oh, I won't tell you. You shall hear. Let us have these chairs by the open door; it is so nice and cool."

The company had formed an expectant circle round the instrument. There was a subdued hush as Rupert Esdaile made the connection, while his mother waved her white hand slowly from left to right to mark the cadence of the sonorous address which was to break upon their ears.

"How about Lucy Araminta Pennyfeather?" cried a squeaky little voice. There was a rustle and a titter among the audience. Rupert glanced across at Captain Beesly. He saw a drooping jaw, two protruding eyes, and a face the colour of cheese.

"How about little Martha Hovedean of the Kensal Choir Union?" cried the piping voice.

Louder still rose the titters. Mrs. Esdaile stared about her in bewilderment. Rose burst out laughing, and the Captain's jaw drooped lower still, with a tinge of green upon the cheese-like face.

"Who was it who hid the ace in the artillery card-room at Peshawur? Who was it who was broke in consequence? Who was it –"

"Good gracious!" cried Mrs. Esdaile, "what nonsense is this? The machine is out of order. Stop it, Rupert. These are not the Professor's remarks. But, dear me, where is our friend Captain Beesly gone?"

"I am afraid that he is not very well, ma," said Rose. "He rushed out of the room."

"There can't be much the matter," quoth Rupert. "There he goes, cutting down the avenue as fast as his legs will carry him. I do not think, somehow, that we shall see the Captain again. But I must really apologise. I have put in the wrong slips. These, I fancy are those which belong to Professor Standerton's lecture."

Rose Esdaile has become Rose Stares now, and her husband is one of the most rising scientists in the provinces. No doubt she is proud of his intellect and of his growing fame, but there are times when she still gives a thought to the blue-eyed Captain, and marvels at the strange and sudden manner in which he deserted her.

———————❖———————

THE COLONEL'S CHOICE

There was some surprise in Birchespool when so quiet and studious a man as Colonel Bolsover became engaged to the very dashing and captivating Miss Hilda Thornton. And in truth this surprise was mingled with some feeling of pity for the gallant officer. It was not that anything really damaging could be alleged against the young lady. Her birth at least was excellent, and her accomplishments undeniable. But for some years she had been mixed up with a circle of people whose best friends could not deny that they were fast. "Smart" they preferred to call themselves, but the result was much the same.

Hilda Thornton was a very lovely woman of the blonde, queenly, golden-haired type. She was the belle of the garrison, and each fresh subaltern who came up from Woolwich or from Sandhurst bowed down and adored her. Yet subalterns grew into captains and captains into majors without a change in her condition. An interminable succession of sappers, gunners, cavalrymen and linesmen filed past through the social life of Birchespool, but Miss Hilda Thornton remained Miss Hilda still. Already she had begun to show a preference for subdued lights, and to appear some years younger in the evening than in the morning, when good, simple-hearted Colonel Bolsover, in one of his brief sallies into the social world, recognising in her all that was pure and fresh, with much diffidence made her the offer of an honoured name, a good position, and some two thousand a year. It is true that there were a grizzled head and an Indian constitution to set off against these advantages, but the young lady showed no hesitation, and the engagement was the talk next day of all the mess-rooms and drawing-rooms of the little town.

But even now it was felt that there was a doubt as to her ultimate marriage. Spinsters whispered dark prophecies upon the subject, and sporting ensigns had money on the event. Twice already had

Hilda approached the happy state, and twice there had been a ring returned, and a pledge unfulfilled. The reason of these fiascos had never been made plain. There were some who talked of the fickleness and innate evil of mankind. Others spoke of escapes, and hinted at sinister things which had come to the horrified ears of her admirers, and had driven them from her side. Those who knew most said least, but they shook their heads sadly when the colonel's name was mentioned.

Just six days before the time fixed for the marriage Colonel Bolsover was seated in his study with his cheque-book upon the desk in front of him, glancing over the heavy upholsterer's bills, which had already commenced to arrive, when he received a visit from his very old friend, Major Barnes, of the Indian horse. They had done two campaigns together on the frontier, and it was a joy to Bolsover to see the dark, lean face and the spare, wiry figure of the Bengal Lancer.

"My dear boy," he cried, with outstretched hands. "I did not even know that you were in England."

"Six months' furlough," answered his old comrade, returning his greeting warmly. "Had a touch of liver in Peshawar, and a board thought that a whiff of the old air might stiffen me up. But you are looking well, Bolsover."

"So I should Barnes. I have had some good fortune lately, better fortune than I deserve. Have you heard it? You may congratulate me, my boy. I am a Benedict from next Wednesday."

The Indian soldier grasped the hand which was held out to him, but his grip was slack and his eyes averted.

"I'm sure I hope it is all for the best, Bolsover."

"For the best? Why, man, she is the most charming girl in England. Come in this evening and be introduced."

"Thank you, Bolsover, I think that I have already met the young lady. Miss Hilda Thornton, I believe? I dined with the Sappers last night and heard the matter mentioned."

Barnes was talking in a jerky, embarrassed style, which was very different to his usual free and frank manner. He paused to pick his words, and scraped his chin with his finger and thumb. The colonel glanced at him with a questioning eye.

"There's something wrong, Jock," said he.

"Well, old chap, I have been thinking – we have been thinking – several of your old chums, that is to say – I wish to the Lord they would come and do their own talking –"

"Oh, you're a deputy?" Bolsover's mouth set, and his brows gathered.

"Well, you see, we were talking it over, you know, Bolsover, and it seemed to us that marriage is a very responsible kind of thing, you know."

"Well, you ought to know," said the colonel, with a half smile. "You have been married twice."

"Ah, yes, but in each case I give you my word, Bolsover, that I acted with prudence. I knew all about my wife and her people: upon my honour I did!"

"I don't quite see what you are driving at, Barnes."

"Well, old chap, I am rather clumsy at anything of this sort. It's out of my line, but you will forgive me, I am sure. But we can't see a chum in danger without a word to warn him. I knew Tresillian in India. We shared one tent in the Afghan business. Tresillian knew Miss Thornton, no one better. I have reason to believe that when he was quartered here five years ago—"

Colonel Bolsover sprang from his chair, and threw up a protesting hand.

"Not another word, Barnes," said he. "I have already heard too much. I believe that you mean well to me, but I cannot listen to you upon this subject. My honour will not permit it."

Barnes had risen from his chair, and the two old soldiers looked into each other's eyes.

"You are quite resolved upon this, Bolsover?"

"Absolutely."

"Nothing would shake you?"

"Nothing on earth."

"Then that's an end of it. I won't say another word. I may be wrong and you may be right. I am sure that I wish you every happiness from the bottom of my heart."

"Thank you, Jock. But you'll stay tiffin. It's almost ready."

"No, thank you, my boy. I have a cab at the door, and I am off to town. I ought to have started by the early train, but I felt that I could not leave Birchespool without having warned—that is to say congratulated you upon the event. I must run now, but you'll hear from me by Friday."

Such was the embassy of Major Jack Barnes, the one and only attempt which was made to shake the constancy of Percy Bolsover. Within a week Hilda Thornton was Hilda Thornton no longer; and amid a pelting storm of rice the happy couple made their way to the Birchespool railway station, *en route* for the Riviera.

For fifteen months all went well with the Bolsovers. They had taken a large detached villa which stood in its own grounds on the outskirts of Birchespool, and there they entertained, with a

frequency and a lavishness which astonished those who had
known the soldierly simplicity of the colonel's bachelor days.
Indeed he had not altered in his tastes. A life of frivolity was
thoroughly repellent to him. But he was afraid of transplanting
his wife too suddenly into an existence which might seem to her to
be austere. After all he was nearly twenty years her senior, and
was it reasonable to suppose that she could conform her tastes to
his? He must sacrifice his own tastes. It was a duty. He must shake
off his old ways and his old comforts. He set himself to the task
with all the energy and thoroughness of an old soldier, until
Bolsover's dances and Bolsover's dinners were one of the features
of social life in Birchespool.

It was in the second winter after their marriage that the great
ball was given in the little town on account of a very august and
Royal visitor. The cream of the county had joined with the
garrison to make it a brilliant success. Beautiful women were
there in plenty. But Bolsover thought as he gazed upon the
dancers that there was none who could compare with his own
wife. In a grey tulle toilette, trimmed with apple-blossom, with a
diamond aigrette twinkling from amid her golden hair, she might
have stood as the very type and model of the blonde regal Anglo-
Saxon beauty. In this light the first faint traces of time were
smoothed away, and, with a gleam of pleasure in her eyes, and a
dash of colour in her cheeks, she was so lovely that even the Royal
and august, though reported to be very blasé in the matter of
beauty, was roused to interest. The colonel stood among the
palms and the rhododendrons, following her with his eyes, and
thrilling with pride as he noticed how heads turned and quick
whispers were exchanged as she passed through the crowd.

"You are to be congratulated, colonel," said Lady Shipton, the
wife of the general of the brigade. "Madame is quite our belle
to-night."

"I am very flattered to hear you say so," said the colonel,
rubbing his hands in his honest delight.

"Ah, you know that you think so yourself," said the lady, archly,
tapping his arm with her fan. "I have been watching your eyes."

The colonel coloured slightly and laughed. "She certainly
seems to be enjoying herself," he remarked. "She is a little hard to
please in the matter of partners, and when I see her dance twice
with the same I know that she is satisfied."

The lady looked, and a slight shadow crossed her face.

"Oh, her partner!" she exclaimed. "I did not notice him."

"He looks like a man who has been hard hit at some time,"
observed the colonel. "Do you know him?"

"Yes. He used to be stationed here before you came. Then he got an appointment and went to India. Captain Tresillian is his name, of the Madras Staff corps."

"Home on leave, I suppose!"

"Yes. He only arrived last week."

"He needed a change," observed the colonel. "But the band is rather overpowering here. This next is the 'Lancers.' May I have the pleasure?"

The face which had attracted the colonel's attention was indeed a remarkable one — swarthy, keen, and hawklike, with sunken cheeks and deep set eyes, which were Italian rather than English in their blackness and brightness. The Celtic origin of his old Cornish blood showed itself in his thin, wiry figure, his nervous, mobile features, and the little petulant gestures with which he lent emphasis to his remarks. Hilda Bolsover had turned pale to the lips at the sight of him as she entered the ballroom, but now they had danced two consecutive dances, and the third they had sat out under the shadow of the palms. There the colonel found them as he strolled round the room while the dancers were forming up for the cotillon.

"Why, Hilda, this is one of your favourites," said he. "You are surely not going to miss it?"

"Thank you, Percy; but I am a little tired. May I introduce you to my old friend, Captain Tresillian, of the Indian army! You may have heard me speak of him. I have known him for ever so many years."

Colonel Bolsover held out his hand cordially, but the other swung round his shoulder, and gazed vacantly across the ballroom as though he had heard nothing. Then suddenly, with a half shrug, like a man who yields to his fate, he turned and took the hand which was offered to him. The colonel glanced at him in some surprise, for his manner was strange, his eyes wild, and his grasp burned like that of a man in a fever.

"You have not been home long, I believe?"

"Got back last week in the Jumna."

"Had you been away long?"

"Only three years."

"Oh! Then you found little changed at home?"

Captain Tresillian burst into a harsh laugh.

"Oh, yes; I find plenty of change at home. Plenty of change. Things are very much altered."

His swarthy face had darkened, and his thin, dark hands were nervously opening and shutting.

"I think, Percy," said Hilda Bolsover, "that the carriage will be waiting now. Good night, Captain Tresillian. I am sure that we shall be happy to see you at Melrose Lodge."

"Most certainly," cried the colonel. "Any friend of my wife's is a welcome guest. When may we hope to see you?"

"Yes, yes; I shall certainly call," the other answered, "I am very much obliged to you. Good night."

"Do you know, Hilda," remarked the colonel, as they rattled homewards that night in their brougham, "I notice something very strange in the manner of your friend, Captain Tresillian. He struck me as a very nice fellow, you know, but his talk and his look were just a little wild at times. I should think he has had a touch of the sun in India."

"Very possibly. He has had some trouble, too, I believe."

"Ah, that might account for it. Well, we must try and make the place as pleasant to him as we can."

Hilda said nothing, but she put her arms round her husband's neck and kissed him.

The very next day and for many days after Captain Tresillian called at Melrose Lodge. He walked with Hilda, he rode with her, he chatted with her in the garden, and he escorted her out when the colonel was away at his duties. In a week there was gossip about it in Birchespool: in a month it was the notorious patent scandal of the town. Brother veterans sniggered about it, women whispered, some pitied, some derided; but amid all the conflict of opinions Bolsover alone seemed to be absolutely unconcerned. Once only Lady Shipton ventured to approach the subject with him, but he checked her as firmly as, if more gently than, he had his old friend in the days of his engagement. "I have implicit faith in her," he said. "I know her better than anyone else can do."

But there came a day when the colonel, too, found that he could no longer disregard what was going on beneath his roof. He had come back late one afternoon, and had found Captain Tresillian installed as usual in the drawing-room, while his wife sat pouring out tea at the small table by the fire. Their voices had sounded in brisk talk as he had entered, but this had tailed off to mere constraint and formalities. Bolsover took his seat by the window, thoughtfully stirring the cup of tea which his wife had handed to him, and glancing from time to time at Tresillian. He noticed him draw his note-book from his pocket, and scribble a few words upon a loose page. Then he saw him rise with his empty cup, step over to the table with it, and hand both it and the note to her. It was neatly done, but her fingers did not close upon it quickly enough, and the little slip of white paper fluttered down to the ground. Tresillian stooped for it, but Bolsover had taken a step forward, and had snatched it from the carpet.

"A note for you, Hilda," said he quietly, handing it to her. His words were gentle, but his mouth had set very grimly, and there was a dangerous glitter in his eyes.

She took it in her hand and then held it out to him again.

"Won't you read it out to me?" said she.

He took it and hesitated for an instant. Then he threw it into the fire. "Perhaps it is better unread," said he. "I think, Hilda, you had best step up to your room."

There was something in his quiet, self-contained voice which dominated and subdued her. He had an air and a manner which was new to her. She had never seen the sterner side of his character. So he had looked and spoken on the fierce day before the Delhi Gates, when the Sepoy bullets were hopping like peas from the tires of his gun, and Nicholson's stormers were massing in the trenches beneath him. She rose, shot a scared, half-reproachful glance at Tresillian, and left the two men to themselves.

The colonel closed the door quickly behind her, and then turned to his visitor.

"What have you to say?" he asked, sternly and abruptly.

"There was no harm in the note." Tresillian was leaning with his shoulder against the mantelpiece, a sneering, defiant expression upon his dark, haggard face.

"How dare you write a note surreptitiously to my wife? What had you to say which might not be spoken out?"

"Well, really, you had the opportunity of reading it. You would have found it perfectly innocent. Mrs. Bolsover, at any rate, was not in the least to blame."

"I do not need your assurance on that point. It is in her name as much as in my own that I ask you what you have to say."

"I have nothing to say, except that you should have read the note when you had the chance."

"I am not in the habit of reading my wife's correspondence. I have implicit confidence in her, but it is one of my duties to protect her from impertinence. When I first joined the service there was a way by which I could have done so. Now I can only say that I think you are a blackguard, and that I shall see that you never again cross my threshold, or that of any other honest man in this town, if I can help it."

"You show your good taste in insulting me when I am under your roof," sneered the other. "I have no wish to enter your house, and as to the other thing you will find me very old-fashioned in my ideas if you should care to propose anything of the kind. I wish you good-day."

He took up his hat and gloves from the piano, and walked to the door. There he turned round with his hand upon the handle and faced Bolsover with a face which was deeply lined with passion and with misery.

"You asked me once whether I found things different in England. I told you that I did. Now I will tell you why. When I was in England last I loved a girl and she loved me – she loved me, you understand. There was a secret engagement between us. I was poor, with nothing but my pay, and she had been accustomed to every luxury. It was to earn enough to be able to keep her that I volunteered in India, that I worked for the Staff, that I saved and saved, and lived as I believe no British officer ever lived in India yet. I had what I thought was enough at last, and I came back with it. I was anxious, for I had had no word from my girl. What did I find? That she had been bought by a man twice my age – bought as you would buy –." He choked and put out a hand to his throat before he could find his voice. "You complain – you pose as being injured," he cried. "I call God to witness which has most reason to cry out, you or I."

Colonel Bolsover turned and rang the bell. Before the servant could come, however, his visitor was gone, and he heard the quick scrunch of his feet on the gravel without. For a time he sat with his chin on his hands, lost in thought. Then he rose and ascended to his wife's boudoir.

"I want to have a word with you, Hilda," said he, taking her hand, and sitting down beside her on the settee. "Tell me truly now, are you happy with me?"

"Why, Percy, what makes you ask?"

"Are you sorry that you married me? Do you regret it? Would you wish to be free?"

"Oh! Percy, don't ask such questions."

"You never told me that there was anything between you and that man before he went to India."

"It was quite informal. It was nothing – a mere friendship."

"He says an engagement."

"No, no; it was not quite that."

"You were fond of him?"

"Yes; I was fond of him."

"Perhaps you are so still?"

She turned away her face, and played with the jingling ornaments of her chatelaine. Her husband waited for an answer, and a spasm of pain crossed his face as no answer came.

"That will do," said he, gently disengaging his hand from hers. "At least you are frank. I had hoped for too much. I was a fool.

But all may yet be set right. I shall not mar your life, Hilda, if I can help it."

The next day the authorities at the War office were surprised to receive a strongly-worded letter from so distinguished an artillery officer as Percy Bolsover, asking to be included in an expedition which was being fitted out in the North-west of India, and which notoriously promised a great deal of danger and very little credit. There was some delay in the answer, and before it arrived the colonel had reached his end in another and a more direct fashion.

No one will ever know how the fire broke out at Melrose Lodge. It may have been the paraffin in the cellars, or it may have been the beams behind the grate. Whatever the cause the colonel was wakened at two on a winter morning by the choking, suffocating smell of burning wood, and rushing out of his bedroom found that the stairs and all beneath him was already a sea of fire. Shouting to his wife he dashed upstairs, and roused the frightened maids, who came screaming, half-dressed, down into his bedroom.

"Come, Hilda," he cried, "we may manage the stairs."

They rushed down together as far as the first landing, but the fire spread with terrible rapidity; the dry woodwork was blazing like tinder, and the swirl of mingled smoke and flame drove them back into the bedroom. The colonel shut the door, and rushed to the window. A crowd had already assembled in the road and the garden, but there were no signs of the engines. A cry of horror and of sympathy went up from the people as they saw the figures at the window, and understood from the flames which were already bursting out from the lower floor that their retreat was already cut off.

But the colonel was too old a soldier to be flurried by danger, or at a loss for a plan. He opened the folding windows and dragging the feather-bed across the floor he hurled it out.

"Hold it under the window," he cried. And a cheer from below showed that they understood his meaning.

"It is not more than forty feet," said he, coolly. "You are not afraid, Hilda?"

She was as calm as he was. "No, I am not afraid," she answered.

"I have a piece of rope here. It is not more than twenty feet, but the feather bed will break the fall. We will pass the maids down first, Hilda. Noblesse oblige!"

There was little time to spare, for the flames were crackling like pistol shots at the further side of the door and shooting little red tongues through the slits. The rope was slung round one maid, under her arms, and she was instructed to slip out from it, and to fall when she had been lowered as far as it would go. The first was unfortunate, for she fell obliquely, bounded from the edge of the bed, and her screams told those above her of her mishap. The second fell straight, and escaped with a shaking. There were only the husband and wife now.

"Step back from the window, Hilda," said he. He kissed her on the forehead, as a father might a child. "Good-bye, dear," he said. "Be happy."

"But you will come after me, Percy?"

"Or go before you," said he, with a quiet smile. "Now, dear, slip the rope round you. May God watch over you and guard you!"

Very gently he lowered her down, leaning far over the window, that another three feet might be taken from her fall. Bravely and coolly she eyed the bed beneath her, put her feet together, and came down like an arrow into the centre of it. A cheer from beneath told him that she was unhurt. At the same instant there was a crash and a roar behind him, and a great yellow blast of flame burst roaring into the room. The colonel stood framed in the open window, looking down upon the crowd. He leaned with one shoulder against the stonework, with the droop of the head of a man who is lost in thought. Behind him was a lurid background of red flame, and a long venomous tongue came flickering out over his head. A hundred voices screamed to him to jump. He straightened himself up like a man who has taken his final resolution, glanced down at the crowd, and then, turning, sprang back into the flames.

And that was the colonel's choice. It was "Accidental death" at the inquest, and there was talk of the giddiness of suffocation and the slipping of feet; but there was one woman at least who could tell how far a man who truly loves will carry his self sacrifice.

A SORDID AFFAIR

"My dear, what a perfectly charming bodice! I mean the Louis Quinze with the vest of white chiffon de soie."

"Ah, but do look at that skirt of old rose silk, brocaded à la Pompadour, and trimmed with duchesse lace!"

"But you know, Alice, my favourite of them all is that satin foulard, the grey one, gouffred at the neck. It is so lovely, I think, and exactly my measurements, for I went in and inquired."

"Then why not have it?"

"My dear! Fifteen guineas! It was dreadful. Now, if it had been ten I might have managed it."

The speakers were two well-dressed ladies, standing in front of one of the largest plate-glass windows in Bond Street, and gazing up at the dense group of slim, headless figures in prim, straight-cut, tailor-made costumes, or in evening dresses of the many strange neutral tints which were the rage of the moment. They had raised their voices in their excitement, and gave little clutches at each other's wrists as they compared notes about the treasures in front of them. Close behind them stood a plainly-clad middle-aged woman with a sad wrinkled face, and the air of one who has found the world anything but a playground. She had stood gazing with a very critical eye at the various costumes, and listening with a half smile to the comments of the ladies beside her, but at their last remark she looked earnestly at the speaker, and put her hand out timidly towards her to attract her attention.

"If you please, ma'am," she said, "I could do that for you."

The lady looked round in surprise. "What could you do, my good woman?"

"A dress the exact same as that one at every point for ten pounds."

"You could do it?"

"Yes, ma'am. You'll excuse my speaking to you, but I could not help hearing what you said, and I know that I could give you satisfaction. I did all Madame Davoust's work when she was court dressmaker."

The lady looked inquiringly at her companion. "What do you say, Louise?"

"Well, my dear, if you wish such a dress. You need not pay unless you are satisfied with it."

"No, of course not. What is your name, please?"

"Mrs. Raby."

"Well then, Mrs. Raby, you quite understand that I shall require the dress to be absolutely as well finished as the one in the window, material and cut identical."

"Yes, madam."

"And it must be ready by next Monday before ten o'clock."

"Very well, madam."

"And your price is ten pounds, inclusive."

"Ten pounds, madam."

"I have your solemn promise that the dress shall be the same, and that I shall have it on Monday by ten?"

"I promise you, madam."

"Well, then, you may call this afternoon, and take your measurements. Mrs. Clive is the name, 73, Palace Gardens." She gave a nod, and turned again to her companion, while the dressmaker, with another very critical glance at the dress in the window, hurried off upon her way.

A busy morning lay before her, for her foulard was to be purchased at one shop, her linings at another, her braid and her buttons at yet another, all down in the depths of the City, far away from West-end prices. At last, with her arms full of brown paper parcels, she gained her 'bus, and drove out to Brompton, where in a quiet side street of two-storeyed houses, a small brass plate, "Mrs. Raby, costumier and dressmaker," showed where she carried on her modest business.

In the front room an assistant was whirring away upon a hand sewing machine, running a seam down the edge of a dress, while all round her lay heaped masses of cloth, grey strips of lining, and rolls of braid.

"Whose is that, Anna?" asked Mrs. Raby.

"It is Mrs. Summerton's." The assistant was a broad-faced, good-humoured girl, with red hair and freckles.

"Ah, you must be very careful with it. She is most particular. The front cut straight, and the back gored and cut on the cross."

"Yes, Mrs. Raby. It's coming out fine."

"I have a new order, a foulard dress, which must be ready by

Monday. This is the stuff, and I shall have the measurements this evening. It will take us all our time. Is Mr. Raby in?"

"Yes, he came in half an hour ago."

"Where is he?"

"In the back room."

Mrs. Raby closed the door, and went into the next apartment. A small man, black bearded and swarthy, was seated at a side table, stooping over a box of colours and a small oval piece of ivory, upon which he was beginning to paint a background. He was a peaky, irritable-looking person, with sunken cheeks, a nervous manner, and a very large piece of blue-ribbon in his button-hole.

"It is no use, Helen," he said. "I can't paint until I have an order."

"But however are you to get an order if you don't show folk what you can do. Why don't you paint me, John, and hang me up in a case outside the door."

"I want something that will look nice and attractive," said he, petulantly.

She laughed good-humouredly. "Paint me as you remember me when you first met me, then," said she.

"Ah, you were different then."

"Well, if I am, you ought to know, John, what it is that has changed me. It has not been an easy life for me these twenty years."

"Well, I'm sure I don't know what more I can do. I've taken the ribbon to please you."

"Yes, John, dear, you've dropped the drink, and God bless you for it."

"Six months since I had a taste."

"And aren't you the better for it, in health and happiness and everything? I always knew that if you were to get away from those other clerks you would be all right. Now you are a clerk no longer. You're an artist."

"Yes, but I earned my money as a clerk, and I have made none as an artist. I don't see that I am the gainer by the change."

"Ah, I'd rather starve, dear, and have you a sober man. Besides, I can earn enough for both while you are gradually getting a few customers."

"Sitters!"

"Oh, yes, sitters. But you must go to them or they will never come to you. Why, look at me! I heard two ladies talking in the street, and by pushing myself in I got a ten-pound job."

"Did you, though."

"Yes, this very morning. My stuff will cost from five to six, but there should be four pound profit." She took a key from her pocket, unlocked a drawer in a side table, and taking a tin box out unlocked that also.

"We have fifteen pounds here," said she, turning out a small heap of gold. "We'll make it twenty soon, and then I think I may afford to take on another assistant."

Her husband looked wistfully at the gold. "It seems hard that you should put away all that money, and I should go about without a half-crown in my pocket," said he.

"I don't want your pocket to be empty, John, but you don't need more than sixpence. It is only putting yourself in the way of temptation."

"Well, anyway, I ought to be head in my own family. Why don't you give me the key, and let me have the keeping of the money."

"No, no, John; it is my earning and I'll have the keeping. What you want I'll buy for you, but what I save I must have in my own hands."

"A pretty thing, too!" He went back to his painting with a snarl, while she very carefully locked up her small treasure again, and then returned to the work-room. She had hardly turned her back when he sprang from his seat, rushed to the table and took two wicked little tugs at the drawer, but all was fast, so he slunk back, cursing under his breath, to his paints and his ivory.

That afternoon Mrs. Raby called at Palace Gardens, obtained her measurements, and forthwith got to work with might and main upon the dress. It was a Thursday, and she had only two and a half working days before her, but she had given her promise, and she was a woman who would keep her word, if flesh and blood could do it. On Saturday morning it must be ready for the trying on, and on the Monday by ten o'clock it must be actually delivered. So away she went cutting, and stitching, gouffring, and tabbing, and looping, and hemming, working late, and working early, until on the second day a dozen separate pieces were all brought together like a child's puzzle, a square there, a triangle here, a long narrow slip down the front, and there, out of what to a masculine eye would have seemed the merest scraps, there rose the daintiest, neatest little dress that heart could wish, still loosely pinned together, but taking already its ultimate outlines. In this state it was carried to Palace Gardens, tried on, and then brought back to be finally completed. By twelve o'clock at night it was finished, and all Sunday it stood upon the frame in the work-room looking so fresh and neat and perfect, that the wife, in the pride of her heart, could not forbear from running in every hour or so, and coaxing her husband in with her, to look and to admire.

He had been a sorry helpmate to her. It was not work which had placed those marks of care upon his face. As a clerk in the wholesale cocoa firm, he had for years been having some three pounds a week, but of the three it was seldom that one found its way to his wife, who planned, and worked, and managed as only a devoted woman can. At last she had herself turned to business, and had made herself independent of him, or, rather, had made him dependent upon her. A long course of secret drunkenness had ended in a raging attack of delirium tremens, which could not be concealed from his employers, and which brought about his instant dismissal from his situation. But it was no misfortune in the eyes of his wife. She had long made up her mind that his weak nature was not to be reformed while he was surrounded by temptation. Now, at last, she had him to herself. Some occupation must be found for him which would hold him within her influence. It was always with others that she laid the blame, never with him, for her eyes were blind to the shattered irritable wreck, and could only see the dark-haired bashful lad who had told her twenty years ago how he loved her. Could she keep out those evil influences, all would yet be well. Her woman's wit was set to do it. He had long had some leanings towards art, so now she bought him paints and paper and all that an artist could require. She had prayed and argued until he had taken the blue ribbon, and for six whole months she had stood between him and danger, shutting off what was evil, encouraging the little that was good, like some tender gardener watching over a sickly plant. And now at last all seemed bright before her. Her husband had forsworn his fatal habits. She had saved a little money, and there was a prospect of saving more. Soon she might hope for a second assistant, and even spend a few pounds in advertisements. As she went into her work-room for the last time that Sunday night, holding out the lamp in her work-worn hand, and looked at the delicate tint and dainty curves, it seemed to her that the long struggle was at last drawing to an end, and that the evening would be mellow if the day had been stormy.

She slept heavily that night, for she had worked almost continuously until the dress was finished. It was nearly eight o'clock when she woke. Her husband was not lying by her side. His clothes and boots were gone. She smiled to think how completely she had overslept herself, and, rising, she dressed, hurriedly putting on her outdoor things so that she might be ready to start immediately after breakfast to keep her appointment. As she descended the stair she noticed that the work-room door was open. She entered with a sudden strange sinking at the heart. The new dress had disappeared.

Mrs. Raby sat down on a packing case, and sank her face in her hands. The blow was so sudden, so unexpected! But she was a practical woman, and there was no use in sitting groaning. She walked through the house. Her husband, as she expected, was nowhere to be seen. Then she wrote a short note to the assistant, left it on the workroom table, and leaving the door upon the latch, set out upon her hopeless and piteous chase.

Just round the corner, in the Brompton Road, was a pawnbroker's shop, and into it she hastened. A heavy, red-bearded man, who was reading the morning paper in the corner, cocked his eye at her as she entered.

"What can I do for you, ma'am?"

"Would you kindly tell me, sir, if any one has been here this morning to pledge a grey dress?"

The pawnbroker called to his assistant, a young, pasty-faced man, who emerged from among the countless suits of clothes and piles of miscellaneous things which blocked the shop.

"There was some one here with a grey dress, Alec, was there not?" he asked.

"Yes, sir! that was the one that you thought might be a police matter."

"Ah, yes, of course. A small, dark man, with black hair?"

"That's it, sir."

"He was here at quarter-past seven, just after opening time. I wasn't down yet, but my assistant told me that the dress was a very good and new one, and that the man's manner was just a bit suspicious."

"You didn't take it, then?"

"No."

"You don't know where he went?"

"No idea."

The red-bearded man plunged back into his morning paper, and the woman hurried on upon her quest. Should she turn up the street or down. The sight of a distant glimmer of gilt balls decided her, and she found herself in another office. They had seen nothing there either of her husband or of the dress.

She paused irresolute outside the door. Then she reflected that if her husband had come up the road he would certainly have come there. He must have turned down then. She entered the first pawnbroker's in that direction, and there was the grey foulard dress hanging up upon a hook right in front of her. She gave a cry of joy at the sight of it. It was not yet nine, and there was time to keep her appointment.

"That's my dress," she gasped.

The pawnbroker gazed at her curiously. "It was pawned this morning, ma'am, by a small, dark man."

"Yes, sir, that was my husband. How much did he get on it?"

"Three pound, five."

She had put some money into her pocket when she left home. Now she laid four sovereigns upon the counter.

"Please let me have it at once."

"Where's the ticket?"

"The ticket? I have none."

"Then you can't have the dress."

"But it is my dress, and here is the money. Why can I not have it?"

"I am very sorry for you, marm. But we must stick to the law. Suppose I take your money and give you your dress, and suppose then your husband comes here with the ticket and demands his pledge, what could I say to him? He could put his own price on it, and I should have to pay him."

"But I promise you he won't come. Do, do, let me have the dress. I've promised it to a customer at ten."

"I tell you that I can't, and there's an end of it," said the pawnbroker, turning upon his heel.

It was heartbreaking to be within touch of it, and not to be allowed to take it. And yet she could not blame the pawnbroker. She could see that he could not act otherwise. What remained then? To find her husband. But how could she tell in which of a hundred public-houses he was making amends for his long abstention. She paced wildly up and down the pavement. What would this lady think of her? She had given a promise, and a promise had always been a sacred thing with her. Was there no way in which she could manage? And then suddenly an idea came to her, and she ran as hard as she could back to her own house, rushed into the back room, opened her drawer, poured her little heap of savings into her purse, and hastened out to catch an eastward bound 'bus.

At Bond Street she got out and sped on to the window where she had first undertaken this unhappy contract. Thank God, the dress was still unsold in the window. She remembered that the lady had said that the measurements were correct. In five minutes more her whole savings had gone into the till of the wealthy retail firm, and she, with her great cardboard-box was driving at the top of her speed to Palace Gardens.

"My dear Alice," remarked her friend, who had dropped in early that morning, in order to criticise the costume, "you see it never does to trust people in that class of life. She said ten o'clock, and now it is five minutes past. They have no idea of the nature of a promise."

"No, I suppose not. Still, she is sure to come, for I have not paid her anything yet. Ah, here she is coming up the stair, so she is not so very late after all."

The dress was duly unpacked, and Mrs. Alice Clive put it on at once, while her friend and the dressmaker walked slowly round her with sidelong heads, eyeing it up and down.

"Well, dear, how do you like it. It feels very comfortable and seems to sit well about the shoulders."

"Oh yes, I think it will do. I don't think, however, that the foulard is quite of the same quality as that which we saw in the shop."

"I assure you, madam, that it is."

"Well, Mrs. Raby, I am sure you will acknowledge that the lace is inferior."

"No, it is precisely the same."

The lady critic shrugged her shoulders. "At least, there is no question as to the inferiority of the cut," said she, "I cannot refuse to believe my own eyes."

"Well, at least, it is not dear at that price," said her friend.

"It is entirely a matter of taste," the other rejoined, "but I confess that I would rather pay fifteen guineas for the other than ten for this."

"Well, well, on the whole I am pretty well satisfied," said she, Mrs. Clive, and paid over the ten pounds to the silent weary woman who stood before her.

But strange and wondrous are the ways of women, and where is the man who shall grasp them. As she walked home, tired, foot-sore, the loser in time and in money, with all her little hopes shattered to ruins, and all to be built up once more, she saw a crowd of jeering boys at the corner of the Brompton Road, and peeping over their shoulders, she caught a glimpse of a horrid crawling figure, a hatless head, and a dull, vacant, leering face. In an instant she had called a cab.

"It is my husband," said she, "he is ill. Help me to get him into the cab, policeman. We live quite close to here."

They thrust him into a four-wheeler, and she got in beside him, holding him up with her arms. His coat was covered with dust, and he mumbled and chuckled like an ape. As the cab drove on, she drew his head down upon her bosom, pushing back his straggling hair, and crooned over him like a mother over a baby.

"Did they make fun of him, then?" she cried. "Did they call him names? He'll come home with his little wifey, and he'll never be a naughty boy again."

Oh, blind, angelic, foolish love of woman! Why should men demand a miracle while you remain upon earth?

A REGIMENTAL SCANDAL

It was a very painful business. I don't think any of us have forgotten it or are at all likely to. The morality of the third Carabiniers was as loose as their discipline was tight, and if a man rode straight and was keen on soldiering he might work out his private record to his own mind. But still there is a limit to what even such a thoroughgoing old sportsman as the Colonel could stand, and that limit was passed on the instant that there was a breath of suspicion about fair play at the card table.

Take the mess. They had ridden through the Decalogue as gaily as through Arabi's guns at Kassassin. Professionally they had made free with other men's lives. But the unwritten laws of honour lay unbroken amid the shattered commandments. They were short and sharp, and woe to the man who transgressed them. Sporting debts must be paid. There was no such thing as a white feather. Above all, a man must play fair. It was a simple code of ethics, but it commanded an absolute obedience which might have been refused to a more elaborate system.

If there was one man in the mess who could be held up by the youngsters as the embodiment of honour it was Major Errington. He was older than the chief, and having served twice as a volunteer war correspondent and once as a military attaché, he had been shot over by Berdan's and Manuffcher repeaters, which seemed to us a much more gaudy thing than Jezails or even Egyptian Remingtons. We had all done Egypt and we had all done the Soudan, but when he would begin his modest after-mess anecdote with: "I remember when Gourko crossed the Balkans," or "I was riding beside the Red Prince's staff just two days before Gravelotte," we would feel quite ashamed of our poor "Fuzzies" and "Pathans," and yearn to replace the foreign office by a committee of subalterns of the Carabiniers, all pledged to a spirited policy.

Then our Major was so humble and gentle with it all. That was his only fault as a soldier. He could fight – none better – but he could not be stern. No matter how heinous the crime of the defaulter who was brought before him, and no matter how resolutely he might purse up his features into a frown, there was still something so very human always gleaming from his eyes that the most drunken deserter could not but feel that this, instead of being a commanding officer, was merely a man and a brother. Though far the richest man in the regiment, for he had ample private means, he lived always in the simplest fashion. Some even set him down as parsimonious, and blamed him for it. But most of us saw in it only another example of the Major's delicacy which made him fear to make others feel poor by showing himself rich. It was no wonder that he was popular. We subalterns worshipped him, and it was to him that we brought all those tiffs and bickerings and misunderstandings which need a little gentle wisdom to set them right. He would sit patiently, with his cheroot reeking from the corner of his mouth and his eyes fixed upon the ceiling, listening to our details, and then would come the quick, "I think that you ought to withdraw the expression, Jones," or "Under the circumstances, you were quite justified, Hall," which settled the matter forever. If we had been told that the chief had burgled the regimental plate or that the chaplain had invited the secularist Sergeant Major to tea, we should have been less astonished than at the rumour that Major Errington had been guilty of anything which was dishonourable.

It came about in this way. The chief was a born plunger. Horses, cards, dice – they were all the same to him. He would bet on, or he would bet against, give the odds or take them, but bet he would. It was all very well as long as he stuck to shilling points and half-crown rubs at whist, or made his little book upon the regimental cup; but when he took to American railway scrip, and laid out all his savings on seven per cent bonds which were selling at sixty-two, he started a game where the odds are all on the bank and the dealer sits somewhere near Wall Street. It was no use telling the old man that Monte Carlo was a sound family investment in comparison. He held on grimly until the inevitable came round. The line was squelched by a big capitalist, who wished to buy it, and our chief was left on the very edge of the bankruptcy court, uncertain from week to week how long it might be before he would need to send in his papers. He said nothing, for he was as proud as Lucifer, but he looked bleary about the eyes in the morning, and his tunic did not fit him quite as tight as it used to. Of course, we were very sorry for the poor old chief, but we were sorrier still for his daughter Violet. We were all in love with Violet Lovell, and her grief was a blight to the regiment. She wasn't such a very pretty girl, either, but she was fresh and bright and sprightly as an English spring, and so sweet, and good, and sympathetic, that she was just the type of womanhood for all of us. She was one of those girls about whom when once you come to know them, you never think whether they are pretty or not. You only know that it is pleasant to be near them, to see their happy faces, to hear their voices, and to have life made sweeter and more beautiful by their presence. That was how we all felt toward Violet – from the old Major to the newly-joined subaltern, with a brand new razor case upon his dressing table. So when that bright face clouded over as the shadow of her father's troubles fell upon it, we clouded over also, and the mess of the Carabiniers sank into a state from which even the caterer's Deutz and Guelderman of '81 was unable to redeem it.

The Major was the most stricken of all. I think that he took the whole matter to heart even more than the Colonel did, although it had been against his strenuous advice that those cursed bonds had been bought. He was an old friend of the chief and he knew that the disgrace of bankruptcy would be the old man's death blow; but he was fonder still of the chief's daughter – none of us ever knew how much so, for he was a shy, silent man, and, in his English fashion, he hid away his emotions as though they were shameful vices. Yet, with all his care, we got a little peep into his heart, if only through his grey eyes when he looked at her, and we knew that he was very fond of our Violet.

The chief used to go to his own room after mess, and whoever wished was welcome to follow him there. Major Errington always went, and the two would play écarte by the hour, while we others either made a four at whist, or smoked and looked on. It was worth looking at too. The chief was a fine écarte player, and they were doing all they knew, for they had taken to playing high points. Of course, the chief, bankruptcy or no, was always ready to plank down whatever he had in his pocket upon the turn of a card. But it was something new in Errington. There had been a time when he had refused to play for money at all. Now he closed at once with every challenge, and even seemed to goad his opponent on to higher stakes still. And he played with the air of a man who was anxious about the game – too anxious to be quite good form, considering that there was money upon the table. He was flustered and unlike himself, and more than once he misplayed the cards completely; but still luck was absolutely in his favour and he won. It went against us to see the old man, who had been so hard hit, losing the money which he needed badly to the richest man in the regiment; but still the Major was the soul of honour, and if he did it there must be some very good reason behind it all.

But there was one of our subalterns who was not so sure about that. Second Lieutenant Peterkin was young and small and newly joined, but he was as keen as a razor edge, with the wits of a racing tout of 50 crammed into a boy's body. He had made a book himself at 9, ridden a winner at 10 and owned one at 13, so that by the time he came our way he was as blasé and shrewd and knowing as any man in the corps. But he had pluck and he was good humoured, so we all got along with him pretty well until he breathed that first word of suspicion against the Major.

It was in the billiard-room one morning and there were six of us there, all subalterns except Austen, who was the junior captain. Austen and Peterkin were knocking the balls about and we others were helping them by sitting on the corner pockets. Suddenly Austen chucked down his cue with a clatter into the corner.

"You're a damned little liar, Peterkin," he remarked.

This was interesting, as we had not listened to the context. We came off our perches and stared. Peterkin took up the chalk and gently rubbed the tip of his cue.

"You'll be sorry for having said that, Captain Austen," said he.

"Shall I?"

"Yes, and you'll apologise to me for it."

"Oh indeed!"

"All I ask is that you test the matter for yourself tonight, and that tomorrow we all meet here again at this hour, and that you let these gentlemen know what you think then."

"They have nothing to do with it."

"Excuse me, Captain Austen, they have everything to do with it. You used an expression to me a few moments ago in their presence, and you must withdraw it in their presence also. I shall tell them what the matter was about, and then —"

"Not a word!" cried Austen, angrily. "Don't dare to repeat such a libel!"

"Just as you like, but in that case you must agree to my conditions."

"Well, I'll do it. I'll watch tonight, and I'll meet you here tomorrow; but I warn you, young Peterkin, that when I have shown up this mare's nest of yours the regiment will be too hot to hold you!" He stalked out of the room in a passion, while Peterkin chuckled to himself and began to practise the spot stroke, deaf to our questions as to what was the matter.

We were all there to keep our appointment next day. Peterkin had nothing to say, but there was a twinkle in his little, sharp eyes, especially when Austen came in with a very crestfallen expression upon his face.

"Well," said he, "If I hadn't seen with my own eyes I should never have believed it, never! Peterkin, I withdraw what I said yesterday. You were right. By God, to think that an officer of this regiment should stoop so low!"

"It's a bad business," said Peterkin. "It was only by chance I noticed it."

"It's a good thing you did. We must have a public exposure."

"If it's a matter affecting the honour of any fellow of the mess it would surely be best to have Major Errington's opinion," said Hartridge.

Austen laughed bitterly. "You fellows may as well be told," said he. "There's no use in any mystification. Major Errington has, as you may know, been playing high stakes at écarte with the chief. He has been seen, on two evenings in succession, first by Peterkin and then by me, to hide cards and so strengthen his hand after dealing. Yes, yes, you may say what you like, but I tell you that I saw it with my own eyes. You know how short-sighted the chief is. Errington did it in the most barefaced way, when he thought no one was looking. I shall speak to the chief about it. I consider it to be my duty."

"You had better all come to-night," said Peterkin, "but don't sit near the table, or pretend to be watching. Six witnesses will surely be enough to settle it."

"Sixty wouldn't make me believe it," said Hartridge.

Austen shrugged his shoulders. "Well, you must believe your own eyes, I suppose. It's an awkward thing for a few subalterns to bring such a serious charge against a senior major of twenty years' service. But the chief shall be warned, and he may take such steps as he thinks best. It's been going on too long, and to-night should finish it for good and all."

So that night we were all in the Colonel's room, when the card table was pushed forward and the two seniors sat down to their écarte as usual. We others sat round the fire with a keen eye on the players. The Colonel's face was about two shades redder than usual, and his stiff hair bristled up, as it would when he was angry. Austen, too, looked ruffled. It was clear that he had told the chief, and that the chief had not taken it very sweetly.

"What points?" asked the Major.

"Pound a game, as before."

"Pound a trick, if you like," suggested the Major.

"Very good. A pound a trick." The chief put on his pince-nez and shot a keen questioning glance at his antagonist. The Major shuffled and pushed the cards over to be cut.

The first three games were fairly even. The Major held the better cards, but the chief played far the finer game. The fourth game and deal had come round to the Major again, and as he laid the pack down he spread his elbows out so as to screen his hands from me. Austen gave his neighbour a nudge and we all craned our necks. A hand whisked over the pack and Peterkin smiled.

The chief played a knave and the Major took it with a queen. As he put forward his hand to pick up the trick the Colonel sprang suddenly out of his chair with an oath.

"Lift up your sleeve, sir," he cried. "By –, you have a card under it!"

The Major had sprung up also, and his chair toppled backward onto the floor. We were all on our feet, but neither of the men had a thought for us. The Colonel leaned forward with his thick red finger upon a card which lay face downward upon the table. The Major stood perfectly composed, but a trifle paler than usual.

"I observe that there was a card there, sir," said he, "but surely you do not mean to insinuate that –"

The Colonel threw his hand down upon the table.

"It's not the first time," said he.

"Do you imagine that I would take an unfair advantage of you?"

"Why, I saw you slip the card from the pack – saw it with my own eyes."

"You should have known me better after twenty years," said Major Errington, gently. "I say sir, that you should have known me better, and that you should have been less ready to come to such a conclusion. I have the honour to wish you good evening, sir." He bowed very gravely and coldly and walked from the room.

But he had hardly closed the door when the curtains at the other end, which separated the card room from the little recess where Miss Lovell was pouring out our coffee, were opened, and she stepped through. She had not a thought for any of us, but walked straight up to her father.

"I couldn't help hearing you, Dad," said she. "I am sure that you have done him a cruel injustice."

"I have done him no injustice. Captain Austen, you were watching. You will bear me out."

"Yes, sir, I saw the whole affair. I not only saw the card taken, but I saw which it was that he discarded from his hand. It was this one." He leaned forward and turned up the top card.

"That one!" shouted the chief; "why that is the king of trumps."

"So it is."

"But who in his senses would discard the king of trumps; what did he exchange?" He turned up the card on the table. It was an eight. He whistled and passed his fingers through his hair.

"He weakened his hand," said he. "What was the meaning of that?"

"The meaning is that he was trying to lose, Dad."

"Upon my word, sir, now that I come to think of it, I am convinced that Miss Lovell is perfectly correct," said Captain Austen. "That would explain why he suggested high points, why he played such a vile game, and why, when he found that he had such good cards in his hand that he could not help winning, he thought himself justified in getting rid of some of them. For some reason or other he was trying to lose."

"Good Lord!" groaned the Colonel, "what can I say to put matters straight?" and he made for the door.

And so our little card scandal in the Carabiniers was brought to an honourable ending, for all came out as it had been surmised. Ever since the Colonel's financial misfortunes his comrade's one thought had been to convey help to him, but finding it absolutely impossible to do it directly he had tried it by means of the card table. Finding his efforts continually foiled by the run of good cards in his hands he had broken our usual calm by his clumsy attempts to weaken himself. However, American railway bonds are up to 87 now, owing to the providential death of the American millionaire, and the Colonel is no longer in need of any man's help. The Major soon forgave him for his mistake, and for a time hoped that Violet would have been the pledge of reconciliation – and no match would have been more popular in the regiment – but she destroyed the symmetry of things by marrying a young Madras Staff Corps man, home on leave, so our senior major is still a bachelor, and likely to remain so.

THE RECOLLECTIONS OF CAPTAIN WILKIE

I

"Who can he be?" thought I, as I watched my companion in the second-class carriage of the London and Dover Railway.

I had been so full of the fact that my long-expected holiday had come at last, and that for a few days at least the gaieties of Paris were about to supersede the dull routine of the hospital wards, that we were well out of London before I observed that I was not alone in the compartment. In these days we have all pretty well agreed that "Three is company and two is none" upon the railway. At the time I write of, however, people were not so morbidly sensitive about their travelling companions. It was rather an agreeable surprise to me to find that there was some chance of whiling away the hours of a tedious journey. I therefore pulled my cap down over my eyes, took a good look from beneath it at my vis-à-vis, and repeated to myself, "Who can he be?"

I used rather to pride myself on being able to spot a man's trade or profession by a good look at his exterior. I had the advantage of studying under a Professor at Edinburgh who was a master of the art, and used to electrify both his patients and his clinical classes by long shots, sometimes at the most unlikely of pursuits, and never very far from the mark. "Well, my man," I have heard him say, "I can see by your fingers that you play some musical instrument for your livelihood, but it is a rather curious one — something quite out of my line." The man afterwards informed us that he earned a few coppers by blowing *Rule Britannia* on a coffee-pot, the spout of which was pierced to form a rough flute. Though a novice in the art compared to the shrewd Professor, I was still able to astonish my ward companions on occasion, and I never lost an opportunity of practising myself. It was not mere curiosity, then, which led me to lean back on the cushions and analyse the quiet middle-aged man in front of me.

I used to do the thing systematically, and my train of reflections ran somewhat in this wise: "General appearance vulgar, fairly opulent, and extremely self-possessed — looks like a man who could outchaff a bargee, and yet be at his ease in the best middle-class society. Eyes well set together, and nose rather prominent — would be a good long-range marksman. Cheeks flabby, but the softness of expression redeemed by a square-cut jaw and a well-set lower lip. On the whole, a powerful type. Now for the hands — rather disappointed there. Thought he was a self-made man by the look of him, but there is no callus in the palm, and no thickening at the joints. Has never been engaged in any real physical work, I should think. No tanning on the backs of the hands; on the contrary, they are very white, with blue projecting veins and long delicate fingers. Couldn't be an artist with that face, and yet he has the hands of a man engaged in delicate manipulations. No red acid spots upon his clothes, no ink-stains, no nitrate-of-silver marks upon the hands (this helps to negative my half-formed opinion that he was a photographer). Clothes not worn in any particular part. Coat made of tweed, and fairly old; but the left elbow, as far as I can see it, has as much of the fluff left on as the right, which is seldom the case with men who do much writing. Might be a commercial traveller, but the little pocket-book in the waistcoat is wanting, nor has he any of those handy valises suggestive of samples."

I give these brief headings of my ideas merely to demonstrate my method of arriving at a conclusion. As yet I had obtained nothing but negative results; but now, to use a chemical metaphor, I was in a position to pour off this solution of dissolved possibilities and examine the residue. I found myself reduced to a very limited number of occupations. He was neither a lawyer nor a clergyman, in spite of a soft felt hat, and a somewhat clerical cut about the necktie. I was wavering now between pawnbroker and horse-dealer; but there was too much character about his face for the former; and he lacked that extraordinary equine atmosphere which hangs over the latter even in his hours of relaxation; so I formed a provisional diagnosis of betting man of methodistical proclivities, the latter clause being inserted in deference to his hat and necktie.

Pray, do not think that I reasoned it out like this in my own mind. It is only now, sitting down with pen and paper, that I can see the successive steps. As it was, I had formed my conclusion within sixty seconds of the time when I drew my hat down over my eyes and uttered the mental ejaculation with which my narrative begins.

I did not feel quite satisfied even then with my deductions. However, as a leading question would – to pursue my chemical analogy – act as my litmus paper, I determined to try one. There was a *Times* lying by my companion, and I thought the opportunity too good to be neglected.

"Do you mind my looking at your paper?" I asked.

"Certainly, sir, certainly," said he most urbanely, handing it across.

I glanced down its columns until my eye rested upon the list of the latest betting.

"Hullo!" I said, "they are laying odds upon the favourite for the Cambridgeshire. – But perhaps," I added, looking up, "you are not interested in these matters?"

"Snares, sir!" said he violently, "wiles of the enemy! Mortals are but given a few years to live; how can they squander them so! – They have not even an eye to their poor worldly interests," he added in a quieter tone, "or they would never back a single horse at such short odds with a field of thirty."

There was something in this speech of his which tickled me immensely. I suppose it was the odd way in which he blended religious intolerance with worldly wisdom. I laid the *Times* aside with the conviction that I should be able to spend the next two hours to better purpose than in its perusal.

"You speak as if you understood the matter, at any rate," I remarked.

"Yes, sir," he answered; "few men in England understood these things better in the old days before I changed my profession. But that is all over now."

"Changed your profession?" said I interrogatively.

"Yes; I changed my name too."

"Indeed?" said I.

"Yes; you see, a man wants a real fresh start when his eyes become opened, so he has a new deal all round, so to speak. Then he gets a fair chance."

There was a short pause here, as I seemed to be on delicate ground in touching on my companion's antecedents, and he did not volunteer any information. I broke the silence by offering him a cheroot.

"No; thanks," said he; "I have given up tobacco. It was the hardest wrench of all, was that. It does me good to smell the whiff of your weed. – Tell me," he added suddenly, looking hard at me with his shrewd grey eyes, "why did you take stock of me so carefully before you spoke?"

"It is a habit of mine," said I. "I am a medical man, and

observation is everything in my profession. I had no idea you were looking."

"I can see without looking," he answered. "I thought you were a detective, at first; but I couldn't recall your face at the time I knew the force."

"Were you a detective, then?" said I.

"No," he answered with a laugh; "I was the other thing – the detected, you know. Old scores are wiped out now, and the law cannot touch me, so I don't mind confessing to a gentleman like yourself what a scoundrel I have been in my time."

"We are none of us perfect," said I.

"No; but I was a real out-and-outer. A 'fake,' you know, to start with, and afterwards a 'cracksman.' It is easy to talk of these things now, for I've changed my spirit. It's as if I was talking of some other man, you see."

"Exactly so," said I. Being a medical man I had none of that shrinking from crime and criminals which many men possess. I could make all allowances for congenital influence and the force of circumstances. No company, therefore, could have been more acceptable to me than that of the old malefactor; and as I sat puffing at my cigar, I was delighted to observe that my air of interest was gradually loosening his tongue.

"Yes; I'm a changed man now," he continued, "and of course I am a happier man for that. And yet," he added wistfully, "there are times when I long for the old trade again, and fancy myself strolling out on a cloudy night with my jemmy in my pocket. I left a name behind me in my profession, sir. I was one of the old school, you know. It was very seldom that we bungled a job. We used to begin at the foot of the ladder, in my younger days, and then work our way up through the successive grades, so that we were what you might call good men all round."

"I see," said I.

"I was always reckoned a hard-working, conscientious man, and had talent too – the very cleverest of them allowed that. I began as a blacksmith, and then did a little engineering and carpentering, and then I took to sleight-of-hand tricks, and then to picking pockets. I remember, when I was home on a visit, how my poor old father used to wonder why I was always hovering around him. He little knew that I used to clear everything out of his pockets a dozen times a day, and then replace them, just to keep my hand in. He believes to this day that I am in an office in the City. There are few of them could touch me in that particular line of business, though."

"I suppose it is a matter of practice?" I remarked.

"To a great extent. Still, a man never quite loses it, if he has once been an adept. – Excuse me; you have dropped some cigar ash on your coat," and he waved his hand politely in front of my breast, as if to brush it off. – "There," he said, handing me my gold scarf pin, "You see I have not forgot my old cunning yet."

He had done it so quickly that I hardly saw the hand whisk over my bosom, nor did I feel his fingers touch me, and yet there was the pin glittering in his hand. "It is wonderful!" I said as I fixed it again in its place.

"Oh, that's nothing! But I have been in some really smart jobs. I was in the gang that picked the new patent safe. You remember the case. It was guaranteed to resist anything; and we managed to open the first that was ever issued, within a week of its appearance. It was done with graduated wedges, sir, the first so small that you could hardly see it against the light, and the last strong enough to prise it open. It was a cleverly managed affair."

"I remember it," said I. "But surely someone was convicted for that?"

"Yes, one was nabbed. But he didn't split, nor even let on how it was done. It would have been as much as his life was worth. – Perhaps I am boring you, talking about these old wicked days of mine?"

"On the contrary," I said, "you interest me extremely."

"I like to get a listener I can trust. It's a sort of blow-off, you know, and I feel lighter after it. When I am among my new and highly respectable acquaintances, I dare hardly think of what has gone before. – Now, I'll tell you about another job I was in. To this day, I cannot think about it without laughing."

I lit another cigar, and composed myself to listen.

"It was when I was a youngster," said he. "There was a big City man in those days who was known to have a very valuable gold watch. I followed him about for several days before I could get a chance; but when I did get one, you may be sure I did not throw it away. He found, to his disgust, when he got home that day, that there was nothing in his fob. I hurried off with my prize, and got it stowed away in safety, intending to have it melted down next day. Now, it happened that this watch possessed a special value in the owner's eyes because it was a sort of ancestral possession – presented to his father on coming of age, or something of that sort. I remember there was a long inscription on the back. He was determined not to lose it if he could help it, and accordingly he put an advertisement in an evening paper offering thirty pounds reward for its return, and promising that no questions should be asked. He gave the address of his house, 31 Caroline Square, at the end of the advertisement. The thing sounded good enough, so I set off for Caroline Square, leaving the watch in a parcel at a public-house which I passed on the way. When I got there, the gentleman was at dinner; but he came out quick enough when he heard that a young man wanted to see him. I suppose he guessed who the young man would prove to be. He was a genial-looking old fellow, and he led me away with him into his study.

"Well, my lad," said he, "what is it?"

"I've come about that watch of yours," said I. "I think I can lay my hands on it."

"Oh, it was you that took it!" said he.

"No," I answered; "I know nothing whatever about how you lost it. I have been sent by another party to see you about it. Even if you have me arrested, you will not find out anything."

"Well," he said, "I don't want to be hard on you. Hand it over, and here is my cheque for the amount."

"Cheques won't do," said I; "I must have it in gold."

"It will take me an hour or so to collect it in gold," said he.

"That will just suit," I answered, "for I have not got the watch with me. I'll go back and fetch it, while you raise the money."

"I started off, and got the watch where I had left it. When I came back, the old gentleman was sitting behind his study table, with the little heap of gold in front of him.

"Here is your money," he said, and pushed it over.

"Here is your watch," said I.

"He was evidently delighted to get it back; and after examining it carefully, and assuring himself that it was none the worse, he put it into the watch-pocket of his coat with a grunt of satisfaction.

" 'Now, my lad,' he said, 'I know it was you that took the watch. Tell me how you did it, and I don't mind giving you an extra five-pound note.'

" 'I wouldn't tell you in any case,' said I; 'but especially I wouldn't tell you when you have a witness hid behind that curtain.' You see, I had all my wits about me, and it didn't escape me that the curtain was drawn tighter than it had been before.

" 'You are too sharp for us,' said he good-humouredly. 'Well, you have got your money, and that's an end of it. I'll take precious good care you don't get hold of my watch again in a hurry. – Good-night. – No; not that door,' he added as I marched towards a cupboard. 'This is the door,' and he stood up and opened it. I brushed past him, opened the hall door, and was round the corner of the square in no time. I don't know how long the old gentleman took to find it out, but in passing him at the door, I managed to pick his pocket for the second time, and next morning the family heirloom was in the melting-pot after all. – That wasn't bad, was it?"

The old war-horse was evidently getting his blood up now. There was a tone of triumph in the conclusion of his anecdote which showed that, sometimes at least, his pride in his smartness surpassed his repentance of his misdeeds. He seemed pleased at the astonishment and amusement I expressed at his adroitness.

"Yes," he continued with a laugh, "it was a capital joke. But sometimes the fun lies all the other way. Even the sharpest of us comes to grief at times. There was one rather curious incident which occurred in my career. You may possibly have seen the anecdote, for it got into print at the time."

"Pray, let me hear it," said I.

II

"Well, it is hard lines telling stories against one's self, but this was how it happened. I had made a rather good haul, and invested some of the swag in buying a very fine diamond ring. I thought it would be something to fall back upon when all the ready was gone and times were hard. I had just purchased it, and was going back to my lodgings in the omnibus, when, as luck would have it, a very stylishly dressed young lady came in and took her seat beside me. I didn't pay much attention to her at first; but after a time something hard in her dress knocked up against my hand, which my experienced touch soon made out to be a purse. It struck me that I could not pass the time more profitably or agreeably than by making this purse my own. I had to do it very carefully; but I managed at last to wriggle my hand into her rather tight pocket, and I thought the job was over. Just at this moment she rose abruptly to leave the 'bus, and I had hardly time to get my hand with the purse in it out of her pocket without detection. It was not until she had been gone some time that I found out that, in drawing out my hand in that hurried manner, the new and ill-fitting ring I wore had slipped over my finger and remained in the young lady's pocket. I sprang out, and ran in the direction in which she had gone, with the intention of picking her pocket once again. She had disappeared, however; and from that day till this I have never set eyes on her. To make the matter worse, there was only four-pence-halfpenny in coppers inside the purse. Serve me right for trying to rob such a pretty girl; still, if I had that two hundred quid now, I should not be reduced to – Good heavens, forgive me! What am I saying?"

He seemed inclined to relapse into silence after this; but I was determined to draw him out a little more, if I could possibly manage it. "There is less personal risk in the branch you have been talking of," I remarked, "than there is in burglary."

"Ah!" he said, warming to his subject once again, "it is the higher game which is best worth aiming at. – Talk about sport, sir, talk about fishing or hunting! why, it is tame in comparison! Think of the great country-house with its men-servants and its dogs and its fire-arms, and you with only your jemmy and your centre-bit, and your mother-wit, which is best of all. It is the triumph of intellect over brute-force, sir, as represented by bolts and bars."

"People generally look upon it as quite the reverse," I remarked.

"I was never one of those blundering life-preserver fellows," said my companion. "I did try my hand at garrotting once; but it was against my principles, and I gave it up. I have tried everything. I have been a bedridden widow with three young children; but I do object to physical force."

"You have been what?" said I.

"A bedridden widow. Advertising, you know, and getting subscriptions. I have tried them all. – You seem interested in these experiences," he continued; "so I will tell you another anecdote. It was the narrowest escape for penal servitude that ever I had in my life. A pal and I had gone down on a country beat – it doesn't signify where it was – and taken up our headquarters in a little provincial town. Somehow it got noised abroad that we were there, and householders were warned to be careful, as suspicious characters had been seen in the neighbourbood. We should have changed our plans when we saw the game was up; but my chum was a plucky fellow, and wouldn't consent to back down. Poor little Jim! He was only thirty-four round the chest, and about twelve at the biceps; but there is not a measuring tape in England could have given the size of his heart. He said we were in for it, and we must stick to it; so I agreed to stay, and we chose Morley Hall, the country-house of a certain Colonel Morley, to begin with.

"Now, this Colonel Morley was about the last man in the world that we should have meddled with. He was a shrewd, cool-headed fellow, who had knocked about and seen the world, and it seems that he took a special pride in the detection of criminals. However, we knew nothing of all this at that time; so we set forth hopefully to have a try at the house.

"The reason that made us pick him out among the rest was that he had a good-for-nothing groom, who was a tool in our hands.

This fellow had drawn up a rough plan of the premises for us. The place was pretty well locked up and guarded, and the only weak point we could see was a certain trap-door, the padlock of which was broken, and which opened from the roof into one of the lumber-rooms. If we could only find any method of reaching the roof, we might force a way securely from above. We both thought the plan rather a good one, and it had a spice of originality about it which pleased us. It is not the mere jewels or plate, you know, that a good cracksman thinks about. The neatness of the job, and his reputation for smartness, are almost as important in his eyes.

"We had been very quiet for a day or two, just to let suspicion die away. Then we set out one dark night, Jim and I, and got over the avenue railings and up to the house without meeting a soul. It was blowing hard, I remember, and the clouds hurrying across the sky. We had a good look at the front of the house, and then Jim went round to the garden side. He came running back in a minute or two in a great state of delight. 'Why, Bill,' he said, gripping me by the arm, 'there never was such a bit of luck! They've been repairing the roof or something, and they've left the ladder standing.' We went round together, and there, sure enough, was the ladder towering above our heads, and one or two labourers' hods lying about, which showed that some work had been going on during the day. We had a good look round, to see that everything was quiet, and then we climbed up, Jim first, and I after him. We got to the top, and were sitting on the slates, having a bit of a breather, before beginning business, when you can fancy our feelings to see the ladder that we came up by suddenly stand straight up in the air, and then slowly descend until it rested in the garden below! At first, we hoped it might have slipped, though that was bad enough; but we soon had that idea put out of our head.

" 'Hullo, up there!' cried a voice from below.

"We craned our heads over the edge, and there was a man, dressed, as far as we could make out, in evening dress, and standing in the middle of the grass plot. We kept quiet.

" 'Hullo!' he shouted again. 'How do you feel yoursleves? Pretty comfortable, eh? Ha! ha! You London rogues thought we were green in the country. What's your opinion now?'

"We both lay still, though feeling pretty considerably small, as you may imagine.

" 'It's all right; I see you,' he continued. 'Why, I have been waiting behind that lilac bush every night for the last week, expecting to see you. I knew you couldn't resist going up that ladder, when you found the windows were too much for you. – Joe! Joe!'

" 'Yes, sir,' said a voice, and another man came from among the bushes.

" 'Just you keep your eye on the roof, will you, while I ride down to the station and fetch up a couple of constables? – *Au revoir*, gentlemen! You don't mind waiting, I suppose?' And Colonel Morley – for it was the owner of the house himself – strode off; and in a few minutes we heard the rattle of his horse's hoofs going down the avenue.

"Well, sir, we felt precious silly, as you may imagine. It wasn't so much having been nabbed that bothered us, as the feeling of being caught in such a simple trap. We looked at each other in blank disgust, and then, to save our lives, we couldn't help bursting into laughter at our own fix. However, it was no laughing matter; so we set to work going round the roof, and seeing if there was a likely waterpipe or anything that might give us a chance of escape. We had to give it up as a bad job; so we sat down again, and made up our minds to the worst. Suddenly an idea flashed into my head, and I groped my way over the roof until I felt wood under my feet. I bent down, and found that the Colonel had actually forgotten to secure the padlock! You will often notice, as you go through life, that it is the shrewdest and most cunning man who falls into the most absurd mistakes; and this was an example of it. You may guess that we did not lose much time, for we expected to hear the constables every moment. We dropped through into the lumber-room, slipped down-stairs, tore open the library shutters, and were out and away before the astonished groom could make out what had happened. There wasn't time enough to take any little souvenir with us, worse luck. I should have liked to have seen the Colonel's face when he came back with the constables and found that the birds were flown."

"Did you ever come across the Colonel again?" I asked.

"Yes; we skinned him of every bit of plate he had, down to the salt-spoons, a few years later. It was partly out of revenge, you see, that we did it. It was a very well-managed and daring thing, one of the best I ever saw, and all done in open daylight too."

"How in the world did you do it?" I asked.

"Well, there were three of us in it – Jim was one; and we set about it in this way. We wanted to begin by getting the Colonel out of the way, so I wrote him a note purporting to come from Squire Brotherwick, who lived about ten miles away, and was not always on the best of terms with the master of Morley Hall. I dressed myself up as a groom and delivered the note myself. It was to the effect that the Squire thought he was able to lay his hands on the scoundrels who had escaped from the Colonel a couple of years before, and that if the Colonel would ride over, they would have little difficulty in securing them. I was sure that this would have the desired effect; so, after handing it in, and remarking that I was the Squire's groom, I walked off again, as if on the way back to my master's.

"After getting out of sight of the house, I crouched down behind a hedge; and, as I expected, in less than a quarter of an hour the Colonel came swinging past me on his chestnut mare. Now, there is another accomplishment I possess which I have not mentioned to you yet, and that is, that I can copy any hand-writing that I see. It is a very easy trick to pick up, if you only give your mind to it. I happened to have come across one of Colonel Morley's letters some days before, and I can write so that even now I defy an expert to detect a difference between the hands. This was a great assistance to me now, for I tore a leaf out of my pocket-book and wrote something to this effect:

" 'As Squire Brotherwick has seen some suspicious characters about, and the house may be attempted again, I have sent down to the bank, and ordered them to send up their bank-cart to convey the whole of the plate to a place of safety. It will save us a good deal of anxiety to know that it is in absolute security. Have it packed up and ready, and give the bearer a glass of beer.'

"Having composed this precious epistle, I addressed it to the butler, and carried it back to the Hall, saying that their master had overtaken me on the way and asked me to deliver it. I was taken in and made much of downstairs; while a great packing-case was dragged into the hall, and the plate stowed away among cotton-wool and stuffing. It was nearly ready, when I heard the sound of wheels upon the gravel, and sauntered round just in time to see a business-like closed car drive up to the door. One of my pals was sitting very demurely on the box; while Jim, with an official-looking hat, sprang out and bustled into the hall.

" 'Now, then,' I heard him say, 'look sharp! What's for the bank? Come on!'

" 'Wait a minute, sir,' said the butler.

" 'Can't wait. There's a panic all over the country, and they are clamouring for us everywhere. Must drive on to Lord Blackbury's place, unless you are ready.'

" 'Don't go, sir!' pleaded the butler. 'There's only this one rope to tie. — There; it is ready now. You'll look after it, won't you?'

" 'That we will. You'll never have any more trouble with it now,' said Jim, helping to push the great case into the car.

" 'I think I had better go with you and see it stowed away in the bank,' said the butler.

" 'All right!' said Jim, nothing abashed. 'You can't come in the car, though, for Lord Blackbury's box will take up all the spare room – Let's see – it's twelve o'clock now. Well, you be waiting at the bank door at half-past one, and you will just catch us.'

" 'All right – half-past one,' said the butler.

" 'Good-day!' cried my chum; and away went the car, while I made a bit of a short cut and caught it round a turn of the road. We drove right off into the next county, got a down-train to London; and before midnight, the Colonel's silver was fused into a solid lump."

I could not help laughing at the versatility of the old scoundrel. "It was a daring game to play," I said.

"It is always the daring game which succeeds best," he answered.

At this point the train began to show symptoms of slowing down, and my companion put on his overcoat and gave other signs of being near the end of his journey. "You are going on to Dover?" he said.

"Yes,"

"For the Continent?"

"Yes."

"How long do you intend to travel?"

"Only for a week or so."

"Well, I must leave you here. You will remember my name, won't you? John Wilkie, I am pleased to have met you. – Is my umbrella behind you?" he added, stretching across. – "No; I beg your pardon. Here it is in the corner;" and with an affable smile, the ex-cracksman stepped out, bowed, and disappeared among the crowd upon the platform.

I lit another cigar, laughed as I thought of my late companion, and lifted up the *Times* which he had left behind him. The bell had rung, the wheels were already revolving, when, to my astonishment, a pallid face looked in at me through the window. It was so contorted and agitated, that I hardly recognised the features which I had been gazing upon during the last couple of hours. "Here, take it," he said – "take it. It's hardly worth my while to rob you of seven pounds four shillings; but I couldn't resist once more trying my hand;" and he flung something into the carriage and disappeared.

It was my old leather purse, with my return ticket, and the whole of my travelling expenses. How he had taken it he knows best himself; I suppose it was while he was bending over in search of an imaginary umbrella. His newly re-awakened conscience had then pricked him, so that he had been driven to instant restitution.

THE CONFESSION

The Convent of the Third Order of Dominican Nuns — a large whitewashed building with little deep-set windows — stands at the corner of the Rua de St. Pedro in Lisbon. Inside the high wooden porch there is a life-size wooden statue of Saint Dominic, founder of the order, and the stranger is surprised to observe the curious scraps which are scattered over the pedestal. These singular votive offerings vary from week to week. For the most part they consist of cups of wine, splinters of firewood, crumbs of cheese, and berries of coffee, but occasionally a broken tin saucepan or a cracked plate is to be found among them. With simple faith the sisters, when their household stores run low, lay a piece of whatever it is they lack in front of their saint, as a reminder to him that they look to him for help; and sure enough upon the next day there arrives the wood, the wine, the new saucepan, or whatever else it is that they need. Whether this is due to a miracle, or to the help of the pious laity outside, may be a question to others, but it is none to the simple-minded Sisters of Saint Dominic. To them their whole existence is one continued miracle, and they point to the shelves of their own larder as a final refutation of every heretical doubt.

And had they been asked, these gentle fanatics, why their order above all others should be chosen for this constant supernatural care, they would have answered that it was a heavenly recognition of the sanctity of their Mother Superior. For twenty years Sister Monica had worked among those fallen classes which it is the special mission of the Dominican nuns to rescue. There was not an alley in Lisbon which had not been brightened by the flutter of her long white gown. And still as lady abbess she went on working and praying, with a tireless energy which put the young novices to shame. No one could compute how many there were who had been drawn from a life of sin through her exertions. For she had, above all things, the power of showing sympathy and of drawing the confidence of those who had suffered. They said that it was a sign that she had suffered herself; but none knew her early history, for she had come from the mountains of the north, and she spoke seldom and briefly of her own life. Her wax-like face was cold and serene, but there came a look sometimes into her large dark eyes which made the wretched and the poor feel that there was no depth of sorrow where the Abbess Monica had not been before them.

In the placid life of the convent, there is one annual event which is preceded by six months of expectation and followed by six of reminiscence. It is the yearly mission or "retreat," when some reverend preacher comes among them, and, through a week of prayer and exhortation, stimulates these pious souls to a finer shade of spirituality. Only a saint could hope to influence so saint-like a congregation, and it is the last crown to the holy and earnest priest that he should have given a retreat to the Sisters of Saint Dominic. On one year it had been Espinas, the Franciscan; on another Father Menas, the famous Abbot of Alcantara. But neither of these had caused the suppressed excitement which filled the convent when it passed from cell to cell that the retreat this year was to be given by no less a man than Father Garcia, the Jesuit.

For Father Garcia was a priest whose name was famous through all Catholic Europe as being a worthy successor to those great men, the Xaviers and Loyolas, who founded the first company of Jesus. He was a preacher; he was a writer; above all he was a martyr, for he had carried the gospel into Thibet and had come back with splintered fingers and twisted wrists as a sign of his devotion. Those mutilated hands raised in exhortation had moved his hearers more than the exhortation itself. In person he was tall, dark, and bent, worn to the bone with self-discipline, with a keen, eager face, and the curved predatory nose of the aggressive Churchman. Once that dark, deep-lined face had grace and beauty; now it had character and power; but in youth or age it was a face which neither man nor woman could look upon with indifference. A pagan sword-cut, which had disfigured the cheek, gave it an additional grace in the eyes of the faithful. So warped, and worn, and haggard was the man's whole appearance, that one might have doubted whether such a frame could contain so keen and earnest a spirit, had it not been for those flashing dark eyes which burned in the heavy shadows of the tufted brows.

It was those eyes which dominated his hearers, whether they

consisted of the profligate society of Lisbon or of the gentle nuns of St. Dominic. When they gleamed fiercely as he denounced sin and threatened the sinner, or when, more seldom, they softened into a serene light as he preached the gospel of love, they forced those who saw them into the emotion which they expressed. Standing at the foot of the altar, with his long black figure and his eager face, he swayed the dense crowd of white-cowled women with every flash of those terrible eyes and with every sweep of that mutilated hand. But most of all he moved the Abbess. Her eyes were never taken from his face, and it was noticed that she, who had seemed for so long to have left all the emotions of this world beneath her, sat now with her wax-like face as white as the cowl which framed it, and that after every sermon she would tremble and shake until her rosary rattled against the wooden front of her prie-dieu. The lay-sister of the refectory, who had occasion to consult the Lady Abbess upon one of those nights, could scarcely believe her eyes when she saw her self-contained Superior sobbing her heart out, with her face buried in her little hard pillow.

At last the week of the retreat was over, and upon the Saturday night each nun was to make her general confession as a preparation for the Communion upon the Sunday morning. One after another these white-gowned figures, whose dress was emblematic of their souls, passed into the confessional, whispered through the narrow grating the story of their simple lives, and listened in deep humility and penitence to the wise advice and gentle admonitions which the old priest, with eyes averted, whispered back to them. So in their due order, lay-sisters, novices, sisters, they came back into the chapel, and waited only for the return of their Abbess to finish the day with the usual vespers.

The Abbess Monica had entered the little dark confessional, and saw through the foot-square wire-latticed opening the side of a grey head, one listening ear, and a claw-like hand which covered the rest of the face. A single candle was burning dimly by the Jesuit's side, and she heard the faint rustle as he turned over the leaves of his breviary. With the air of one who discloses the most terrible crimes, she knelt, with her head abased in sweet humility, and murmured the few trivial faults which still united her to humanity. So slight they were, and so few, that the priest was wondering in his mind what penance there was which would not be out of all proportion to her innocence, when the penitent hesitated, as if she still had something to say but found it difficult to say it.

"Courage, my sister," said Father Garcia: "what is there which still remains?"

"What remains," said she, "is the worst of all."

"And yet it may not be very serious," said the confessor reassuringly: "have no fear, my sister, in confiding it to me."

But still the Abbess hesitated, and when at last she spoke it was in a whisper so low that the hand beyond the grating gathered itself round the ear.

"Reverend father," she said, "we who wear the garb of the holy Dominic have vowed to leave behind us all thoughts of that which is worldly. And yet I, who am the unworthy Abbess, to whom all others have a right to look for an example, have during all this week been haunted by the memory of one whom I loved – of a man whom I loved, father – in the days so many years ago before I took the veil."

"My sister," said the Jesuit, "our thoughts are not always ours to command. When they are such as our conscience disapproves we can but regret them and endeavour to put them away."

"There lies the blackness of my sin, father. The thoughts were sweet to me, and I could not in my heart wish to put them away. When I was in my cell I did indeed struggle with my own weakness, but at the first words which fell from your lips—"

"From my lips!"

"It was your voice, father, which made me think of what I had believed that I had at last forgotten. Every tone of your voice brought back the memory of Pedro."

The confessor started at this indiscretion by which the penitent had voluntarily uttered the name of her lover. She heard his breviary flutter down upon the ground, but he did not stoop to pick it up. For some little time there was a silence, and then with head averted he pronounced the penance and the absolution.

She had risen from the cushion, and was turning to go, when a little gasping cry came from beside her. She looked down at the grating, and shrank in terror from the sight. A convulsed face was looking out at her, framed in that little square of oak. Two terrible eyes looked out of it – two eyes so full of hungry longing and hopeless despair that all the secret miseries of thirty years flashed into that one glance.

"Julia!" he cried.

And she leaned against the wooden partition of the confessional, her hand upon her heart, her face sunk. Pale and white-clad, she looked a drooping lily.

"It *is* you, Pedro," said she at last. "We must not speak. It is wrong."

"My duty as a priest is done," said he. "For God's sake give me a few words. Never in this world shall we two meet again."

She knelt down upon the cushion, so that her pale pure face was near to those terrible eyes which still burned beyond the grating.

"I did not know you, Pedro. You are very changed. Only your voice is the same."

"I did not know you either — not until you mentioned my old name. I did not know that you had taken the veil."

She heaved a gentle sigh.

"What was there left for me to do?" she said. "I had nothing to live for when you had left me."

His breath came quick, and harsh through the grating. "When I left you? When you ordered me away," said he.

"Pedro, you know that you left me."

The eager, dark face composed itself suddenly, with the effort of a strong man who steadies himself down to meet his fate.

"Listen, Julia," said he. "I saw you last upon the Plaza. We had but an instant, because your family and mine were enemies. I said that if you put your lamp in your window I would take it as a sign that you wished me to remain true to you, but that if you did not I should vanish from your life. You did not put it."

"I did put it, Pedro."

"Your window was the third from the top?"

"It was the first. Who told you that it was the third?"

"Your cousin Alphonso — my only friend in the family."

"My cousin Alphonso was my rejected suitor."

The two claw-like hands flew up into the air with a horrible spasm of hatred.

"Hush, Pedro, hush!" she whispered.

"I have said nothing."

"Forgive him!"

"No, I shall never forgive him. Never! never!"

"You did not wish to leave me, then?"

"I joined the order in the hope of death."

"And you never forgot me?"

"God help me, I never could."

"I am so glad that you could not forget me. Oh, Pedro, your poor, poor hands! My loss has been the gain of others. I have lost my love, and I have made a saint and a martyr."

But he had sunk his face, and his gaunt shoulders shook with his agony.

"What about our lives!" he murmured. "What about our wasted lives!"

The Sisters of St. Dominic still talk of the last sermon which

Father Garcia delivered to them – a sermon upon the terrible mischances of life, and upon the hidden sweetness which may come from them, until the finest flower of good may bloom upon the foulest stem of evil. He spoke of the soul-killing sorrow which may fall upon us, and how we may be chastened by it, if it be only that we learn a deeper and truer sympathy for the sorrow of our neighbour. And then he prayed himself, and implored his hearers to pray, that an unhappy man and a gentle woman might learn to take sorrow in such a spirit, and that the rebellious spirit of the one might be softened and the tender soul of the other made strong. Such was the prayer which a hundred of the sisters sent up; and if sweetness and purity can aid it, their prayer may have brought peace once more to the Abbess Monica and to Father Garcia of the Order of Jesus.

THE RETIREMENT OF
SIGNOR LAMBERT

———◆———

Sir William Sparter was a man who had raised himself in the course of a quarter of a century from earning four-and-twenty shillings a week as a fitter in Portsmouth Dockyard to being the owner of a yard and a fleet of his own. The little house in Lake Road, Landport, where he, an obscure mechanic, had first conceived the idea of the boilers which are associated with his name, is still pointed out to the curious. But now, at the age of fifty, he owned a mansion in Leinster Gardens, a country house at Taplow, and a shooting in Argyleshire, with the best stable, the choicest cellars, and the prettiest wife in town.

As untiring and inflexible as one of his own engines, his life had been directed to the one purpose of attaining the very best which the world had to give. Square-headed and round-shouldered, with massive, clean-shaven face and slow deep-set eyes, he was the very embodiment of persistency and strength. Never once from the beginning of his career had public failure of any sort tarnished its brilliancy.

And yet he had failed in one thing, and that the most important of all. He had never succeeded in gaining the affection of his wife. She was the daughter of a surgeon and the belle of a northern town when he married her. Even then he was rich and powerful, which made her overlook the twenty years which divided them. But he had come on a long way since then. His great Brazilian contract, his conversion into a company, his baronetcy – all these had been since his marriage. Only in the one thing he had never progressed. He could frighten his wife, he could dominate her, he could make her admire his strength and respect his consistency, he could mould her to his will in every other direction, but, do what he would he could not make her love him.

But it was not for want of trying. With the unrelaxing patience which made him great in business, he had striven, year in and year out, to win her affection. But the very qualities which had helped him in his public life made him unendurable in private. He was tactless, unsympathetic, overbearing, almost brutal sometimes, and utterly unable to think out those small attentions in word and deed which women value far more than the larger material benefits. The hundred pound cheque tossed across a breakfast table is a much smaller thing to a woman than the five-shilling charm which represents some thought and some trouble upon the part of the giver.

Sparter failed to understand this. With his mind full of the affairs of his firm, he had little time for the delicacies of life, and he endeavoured to atone by periodical munificence. At the end of five years he found that he had lost rather than gained in the lady's affections. Then at this unwonted sense of failure the evil side of the man's nature began to stir, and he became dangerous. But he was more dangerous still when a letter of his wife came, through the treachery of a servant, into his hands, and he realised that if she was cold to him she had passion enough for another. His firm, his ironclads, his patents, everything was dropped, and he turned his huge energies to the undoing of the man who had wronged him.

He had been cold and silent during dinner that evening, and she had wondered vaguely what had occurred to change him. He had said nothing while they sat together over their coffee in the drawing-room. Once or twice she had glanced at him in surprise, and had found those deep-set grey eyes fixed upon her with an expression which was new to her. Her mind had been full of someone else, but gradually her husband's silence and the inscrutable expression of his face forced themselves upon her attention.

"You don't seem yourself, to-night, William. What is the matter?" she asked. "I hope there has been nothing to trouble you."

He was still silent, and leant back in his armchair watching her beautiful face, which had turned pale with the sense of some impending catastrophe.

"Can I do anything for you, William?"

"Yes, you can write a letter."

"What is the letter?"

"I will tell you presently."

The last murmur died away in the house, and they heard the discreet step of Peterson, the butler, and the snick of the lock as he made all secure for the night. Sir William Sparter sat listening for a little. Then he rose.

"Come into my study," said he.

The room was dark, but he switched on the green-shaded electric lamp which stood upon the writing-table.

"Sit here at the table," said he. He closed the door and seated himself beside her. "I only wanted to tell you, Jacky, that I know all about Lambert and the Warburton Street studio."

She gasped and shivered, flinching away from him with her hands out as if she feared a blow.

"Yes, I know everything," said he, and his quiet tone carried such conviction with it that she could not question what he said. She made no reply, but sat with her eyes fixed upon his grave, impassive face. A clock ticked loudly upon the mantelpiece, but everything else was silent in the house. She had never noticed that ticking before, but now it was like the hammering of a nail into her head. He rose and put a sheet of paper before her. Then he drew one from his own pocket and flattened it out upon the corner of the table.

"I have a rough draft here of the letter which I wish you to copy," said he. "I will read it to you if you like. 'My own dearest Cecil, — I will be at No. 29 at half-past six, and I particularly wish you to come before you go down to the Opera. Don't fail me, for I have the very strongest reasons for wishing to see you. Ever yours, Jacqueline.' Take up a pen, and copy that letter."

"William, you are plotting some revenge. Oh, Willie, if I have wronged you, I am so sorry —"

"Copy that letter!"

"How can you be so harsh to me, William. You know very well —"

"Copy that letter!"

"I begin to hate you, William. I believe that it is a fiend, not a man, that I have married."

"Copy that letter!"

Gradually the inflexible will and the unfaltering purpose began to prevail over the creature of nerves and moods. Reluctantly, mutinously, she took the pen in her hand.

"You wouldn't harm him, William!"

"Copy the letter!"

"Will you promise to forgive me, if I do?"

"Copy it!"

She looked at him with the intention of defying him, but those masterful, grey eyes dominated her. She was like a half-hypnotised creature, resentful, and yet obedient.

"There, will that satisfy you?"

He took the note from her and placed it in an envelope.

"Now address it to him!"

She wrote "Cecil Lambert, Esq., 133B, Half Moon Street, W.," in a straggling agitated hand. Her husband very deliberately blotted it and placed it carefully in his pocket-book.

"I hope that you are satisfied now," said she with weak petulance.

"Quite," said he gravely. "You can go to your room. Mrs. McKay has my orders to sleep with you, and to see that you write no letters."

"Mrs. McKay! Do you expose me to the humiliation of being watched by my own servants!"

"Go to your room."

"If you imagine that I am going to be under the orders of the house-keeper—"

"Go to your room."

"Oh, William, who would have thought in the old days that you could ever have treated me like this. If my mother had ever dreamed —"

He took her by the arm, and led her to the door.

"Go to your room!" said he, and she passed out into the darkened hall. He closed the door and returned to the writing-table. Out of a drawer he took two things which he had purchased that day, the one a paper and the other a book. The former was a recent number of the "Musical Record," and it contained a biography and picture of the famous Signor Lambert, whose wonderful tenor voice had been the delight of the public and the despair of his rivals. The picture was that of a good-natured, self-satisfied creature, young and handsome, with a full eye, a curling moustache, and a bull neck. The biography explained that he was only in his twenty-seventh year, that his career had been one continued triumph, that he was devoted to his art, and that his voice was worth to him, at a very moderate computation, some twenty thousand pounds a year. All this Sir William Sparter read very carefully, with his great brows drawn down, and a furrow like a gash between them, as his way was when his attention was concentrated. Then he folded the paper up again, and he opened the book.

It was a curious work for such a man to select for his reading—a technical treatise upon the organs of speech and voice-production. There were numerous coloured illustrations, to which he paid particular attention. Most of them were of the internal anatomy of the larynx, with the silvery vocal chords shining from under the pink aretenoid cartilages. Far into the night Sir William Sparter, with those great virile eyebrows still bunched together,

pored over these irrelevant pictures, and read and re-read the
text in which they were explained.

Dr. Manifold Ormonde, the famous throat specialist, of
Cavendish Square, was surprised next morning when his butler
brought the card of Sir William Sparter into his consulting room.
He had met him at dinner at the table of Lord Marvin a few nights
before, and it had struck him at the time that he had seldom seen a
man who looked such a type of rude, physical health. So he
thought again, as the square, thick-set figure of the shipbuilder
was ushered in to him.

"Glad to meet you again, Sir William," said the specialist. "I
hope there is nothing wrong with your health."

"Nothing, thank you."

"Or with Lady Sparter's?"

"She is quite well."

He sat down in the chair which the Doctor had indicated, and
he ran his eyes slowly and deliberately round the room. Dr.
Ormonde watched him with some curiosity, for he had the air of a
man who looks for something which he had expected to see.

"No, I didn't come about my health," said he at last. "I came for
information."

"Whatever I can give you is entirely at your disposal."

"I have been studying the throat a little of late. I read
McIntyre's book about it. I suppose that is all right."

"An elementary treatise, but accurate as far as it goes."

"I had an idea that you would be likely to have a model or
something of the kind."

For answer the Doctor unclasped the lid of a yellow, shining
box upon his consulting-room table, and turned it back upon the
hinge. Within was a very complete model of the human vocal
organs.

"You are right, you see," said he.

Sir William Sparter stood up, and bent over the model.

"It's a neat little bit of work," said he, looking at it with the
critical eyes of an engineer. "This is the glottis, is it not? And here
is the epiglottis."

"Precisely. And here are the cords."

"What would happen if you cut them?"

"Cut what?"

"These things – the vocal cords."

"But you could not cut them. They are out of the reach of all
accident."

"But if such a thing did happen?"

"There is no such case upon record, but of course, the person would become dumb – for the time, at any rate."

"You have a large practice among singers, have you not?"

"The largest in London."

"I suppose you agree with what this man McIntyre says, that a fine voice depends partly upon the cords."

"The volume of sound would depend upon the lung capacity, but the clearness of the note would correspond with the complete control which the singer exercised over the cords."

"Any roughness or notching of the cords would ruin the voice?"

"For singing purposes, undoubtedly – but your researches seem to be taking a very curious direction."

"Yes," said Sir William, as he picked up his hat, and laid a fee upon the corner of the table. "They *are* a little out of the common, are they not?"

Warburton Street is one of the network of thoroughfares which connect Chelsea with Kensington, and it is chiefly remarkable for a number of studios, in which it is rumoured that other arts besides that of painting are occasionally cultivated. The possession of a comfortable room, easily accessible and at a moderate rent, may be useful to other people besides artists amid the publicity of London. At any rate, Signor Cecil Lambert, the famous tenor, owned such an apartment, and his neat little dark green brougham might have been seen several times a week waiting at the head of the long passage which led down to the chambers in question.

When Sir William Sparter, muffled in his overcoat, and carrying a small black leather bag in his hand, turned the corner he saw the lamps of the carriage against the kerb, and knew that the man whom he had come to see was already at the place of assignation. He passed the empty brougham, and walked up the tile-paved passage with the yellow gas lamp shining at the far end of it.

The door was open, and led into a large empty hall, laid down with cocoa-nut matting and stained with many footmarks. The place was a rabbit warren by daylight, but now, when the working hours were over, it was deserted. A house-keeper in the basement was the only permanent resident. Sir William paused, but everything was silent and everything was dark, save for one door which was outlined in thin yellow slashes. He pushed it open and entered. Then he locked it upon the inside and put the key in his pocket.

It was a large room, scantily furnished, and lit by a single oil lamp upon a centre table. A gaunt easel kept up appearances in the corner, and three studies of antique figures hung upon unpapered walls. For the rest a couple of comfortable chairs, a cupboard, and a settee made up the whole of the furniture. There was no carpet, but the windows were discreetly draped. On one of the chairs at the further side of a table a man had been sitting, who had sprung to his feet with an exclamation of joy, which had changed into one of surprise, and culminated in an oath.

"What the devil do you mean by locking that door? Unlock it again, sir, this instant!"

Sir William did not even answer him. He took off his overcoat and laid it over the back of a chair. Then he advanced to the table, opened his bag, and began to take out all sorts of things – a green bottle, a dentist's gag, an inhaler, a pair of forceps, a curved bistoury, and a curious pair of scissors. Signor Lambert stood staring at him in a paralysis of rage and astonishment.

"You infernal scoundrel; who are you, and what do you want?"

Sir William had emptied his bag, and now for the first time he turned his eyes upon the singer. He was a taller man than himself, but far slighter and weaker. The engineer, though short, was exceedingly powerful, with muscles which had been toughened by hard, physical work. His broad shoulders, arching chest, and great gnarled hands gave him the outline of a gorilla. Lambert shrunk away from him, frightened by his sinister figure and by his cold, inexorable eyes.

"Have you come to rob me?" he gasped.

"I have come to speak to you. My name is Sparter."

Lambert tried to retain his grasp upon the self-possession which was rapidly slipping away from him.

"Sparter!" said he, with an attempt at jauntiness. "Sir William Sparter, I presume? I have had the pleasure of meeting Lady Sparter, and I have heard her mention you. May I ask the object of this visit?" He buttoned up his coat with twitching fingers, and tried to look fierce over his high collar.

"I've come," said Sparter, jerking some fluid from the green bottle into the inhaler, "to treat your voice."

"To treat my voice?"

"Precisely."

"You are a madman! What do you mean?"

"Kindly lie back upon the settee."

"You are raving! I see it all. You wish to bully me. You have some motive in this. You imagine that there are relations between Lady Sparter and me. I do assure you that your wife –"

"My wife has nothing to do with the matter either now or

hereafter. Her name does not appear at all. My motives are musical – purely musical, you understand. I don't like your voice. It wants treatment. Lie back upon the settee!"

"Sir William, I give you my word of honour –"

"Lie back!"

"You're choking me! It's chloroform! Help, help, help! You brute! Let me go! Let me go, I say! Oh please! Lemme – Lemme – Lem –!" His head had fallen back, and he muttered into the inhaler. Sir William pulled up the table which held the lamp and the instruments.

It was some minutes after the gentleman with the overcoat and the bag had emerged that the coachman outside heard a voice shouting, and shouting very hoarsely and angrily, within the building. Presently came the sounds of unsteady steps, and his master, crimson with rage, stumbled out into the yellow circle thrown by the carriage lamps.

"You, Holden!" he cried, "you leave my service to-night. Did you not hear me calling? Why did you not come?"

The man looked at him in bewilderment, and shuddered at the colour of his shirt-front.

"Yes, sir, I heard someone calling," he answered, "but it wasn't you sir. *It was a voice that I had never heard before.*"

"Considerable disappointment was caused at the Opera last week," said one of the best informed of our musical critics, "by the fact that Signor Cecil Lambert was unable to appear in the various rôles which had been announced. On Tuesday night it was only at the very last instant that the management learned of the grave indisposition which had overtaken him, and had it not been for the presence of Jean Caravatti, who had understudied the part, the piece must have been abandoned. Since then we regret to hear that Signor Lambert's seizure was even more severe than was originally thought, and that it consists of an acute form of laryngitis, spreading to the vocal cords, and involving changes which may permanently affect the quality of his voice. All lovers of music will hope that these reports may prove to be pessimistic, and that we may soon be charmed once more by the finest tenor which we have heard for many a year upon the London operatic stage."

A TRUE STORY OF THE
TRAGEDY OF *FLOWERY LAND*

A steam tug was puffing wheezily in front of the high-masted barque-rigged clipper. With her fresh painted glistening black sides, her sharp sloping bows and her cut-away counter she was the very picture of a fast, well-found ocean-going sailing ship, but those who knew anything about her may have made her the text of a sermon as to how the British seaman was being elbowed out of existence. In this respect she was the scandal of the river. Chinamen, French, Norwegian, Spaniards, Turks – she carried an epitome of the human race. They were working hard cleaning up the decks and fastening down the hatches, but the big burly mate tore his hair when he found that hardly a man on board could understand an order in English.

Capt. John Smith had taken his younger brother, George Smith, as a passenger and companion for the voyage, in the hope that it might be beneficial to his health. They were seated now at each side of the round table, an open bottle of champagne between them, when the mate came in answer to a summons, his eyes still smouldering after his recent outburst.

"Well, Mr. Karswell," said the captain, "we have a long six months before us, I dare say, before we raise the light of Singapore. I thought you might like to join us in a glass to our better acquaintance and to a lucky voyage.

He was a jovial, genial soul, this captain, with good humour shining from his red weather-stained face. The mate's gruffness relaxed before his kindly words and he tossed off the glass of champagne which the other had filled for him.

"How does the ship strike you, Mr. Karswell?" asked the captain.

"There's nothing the matter with the ship, sir."

"Nor with the cargo, either," said the captain. "Champagne we are carrying – a hundred dozen cases. Those and bales of cloth are our main lading. How about the crew, Mr. Karswell?"

The mate shook his head.

"They'll need thrashing into shape, and that's a fact, sir. I've been hustling and driving ever since we left the pool. Why, except oursleves here and Taffir, the second mate, there's hardly an Englishman aboard. The steward, the cook and the boy are Chinese, as I understand. Anderson, the carpenter, is a Norwegian. There's Early, the lad, he's English. Then there's one Frenchman, one Finn, one Turk, one Spaniard, one Greek and one negro, and as to the rest I don't know what they are, for I never saw the match of them before."

"They are from the Philippine Islands, half Spanish, half Malay," the captain answered. "We call them Manila men, for that's the port they all hail from. You'll find them good enough seamen, Mr. Karswell. I'll answer for it that they work well."

"I'll answer for it, too," said the big mate, with an ominous clenching of his great red fist.

Karswell was hard put to it to establish any order amongst the strange material with which he had to work. Taffir, the second mate, was a mild young man, a good seaman and a pleasant companion, but hardly rough enough to bring this unruly crew to heel. Karswell must do it or it would never be done. The others he could manage, but the Manila men were dangerous. It was a strange type, with flat Tartar noses, small eyes, low brutish foreheads and lank, black hair like the American Indians. Their faces were of a dark coffee tint, and they were all men of powerful physique. Six of these fellows were on board, Leon, Blanco, Duranno, Santos, Lopez and Marsolino, of whom Leon spoke English well and acted as interpreter for the rest. These were all placed in the mate's watch together with Watto, a handsome young Levantine, and Carlos, a Greek. The more tractable seamen were allotted to Taffir for the other watch. And so, on a beautiful July day, holiday makers upon the Kentish downs saw the beautiful craft as she swept past the Goodwins – never to be seen again, save once, by human eyes.

The Manila men appeared to submit to discipline, but there were lowering brows and sidelong glances which warned their officers not to trust them too far. Grumbles came from the forecastle as to the food and water – and the grumbling was perhaps not altogether unreasonable. But the mate was a man of hard nature and prompt resolution, and the malcontents got little satisfaction or sympathy from him. One of them, Carlos, the Spaniard, endeavoured to keep his bunk upon a plea of illness, but was dragged on deck by the mate and triced up by the arms to the bulwarks. A few minutes afterward Capt. Smith's brother came on deck and informed the captain what was going on forward. He came bustling up, and having examined the man he pronounced him to be really unwell and ordered him back to his bunk, prescribing some medicine for him. Such an incident would not tend to preserve discipline, or to uphold the mate's authority with the crew. On a later occasion this same Spaniard began fighting with Blanco, the biggest and most brutal of the Manila men, one using a knife and the other a handspike. The two mates threw themselves between them, and in the scuffle the first mate felled the Spaniard with his fist. In the meantime the barque passed safely through the bay and ran south as far as the latitude of Cape Blanco upon the African coast. The winds were light, and upon the 10th of September, when they had been six weeks out, they had only attained latitude 19 degrees south and longitude 36 degrees west. On that morning it was that the smouldering discontent burst into a most terrible flame.

The mate's watch was from one to four, during which dark hours he was left alone with the savage seamen whom he had controlled. No lion-tamer in a cage could be in more imminent peril, for death might be crouching in wait for him in any of those black shadows which mottled the moonlit deck. Night after night he had risked it until immunity had perhaps made him careless, but now at last it came. At six bells or three in the morning – about the time when the first grey tinge of dawn was appearing in the Eastern sky, two of the mulattos, Blanco and Duranno, crept silently up behind the seaman, and struck him down with handspikes. Early, the English lad, who knew nothing of the plot was looking out on the forecastle head at the time. Above the humming of the foresail above him and the lapping of the water, he heard a sudden crash, and the voice of the mate calling murder. He ran aft, and found Duranno, with horrible persistence, still beating the mate about the head. When he attempted to interfere, the fellow ordered him sternly into the deckhouse, and he obeyed. In the deckhouse the Norwegian carpenter and Candereau, the French seaman, were sleeping, both of whom were among the honest men. The boy Early told them what had occurred, his story being corroborated by the screeches of the mate from the outside. The carpenter ran out and found the unfortunate fellow with his arm broken and his face horribly mutilated.

"Who's that?" he cried, as he heard steps approaching.

"It's me – the carpenter."

"For God's sake get me into the cabin!"

The carpenter had stooped, with the intention of doing so, but Marsolino, one of the conspirators, hit him on the back of the neck and knocked him down. The blow was not a dangerous one, but the carpenter took it as a sign that he should mind his own business, for he went back with impotent tears to his deckhouse. In the meanwhile Blanco, who was the giant of the party, with the help of another mutineer, had raised Karswell, and hurled him, still yelling for help, over the bulwarks into the sea. He had been the first attacked but he was not the first to die.

The first of those below to hear the dreadful summons from the deck was the Captain's brother, George Smith — the one who had come for a pleasure trip. He ran up the companion and had his head beaten to pieces with handspikes as he emerged. Of the personal characteristics of this pleasure tripper the only item which has been handed down is the grim fact that he was so light that one man was able to throw his dead body overboard. The Captain had been aroused at the same time and had rushed from his rooms into the cabin. Thither he was followed by Leon, Watto and Lopez, who stabbed him to death with their knives. There remained only Taffir, the second mate, and his adventures may be treated with less reticence since they were happier in their outcome.

He was awakened in the first grey of dawn by the sounds of smashing and hammering upon the companion. To so experienced a seaman those sounds at such an hour could have carried but one meaning, and that the most terrible which an officer at sea can ever learn. With a sinking heart, he sprang from his bunk and rushed to the companion. It was choked by the sprawling figure of the captain's brother, upon whose head a rain of blows was still descending. In trying to push his way up, Taffir received a crack which knocked him backwards. Half distracted he rushed back into the cabin and turned down the lamp, which was smoking badly — a graphic little touch which helps us to realise the agitation of the last hand which lit it. He then caught sight of the body of the captain pierced with many stabs and lying in his blood-mottled nightgown upon the carpet. Horrified at the sight he ran back into his berth and locked the door, waiting in a helpless quiver of apprehension for the next move of the mutineers. He may not have been of a very virile character, but the circumstances were enough to shake the most stout-hearted. It is not an hour at which a man is at his best, that chill hour of the opening dawn, and to have seen the two men, with whom he had supped the night before, lying in their blood, seems to have completely unnerved him. Shivering and weeping he listened with straining ears for the footsteps which would be the fore-runners of death.

At last they came, and of half a dozen men at least, clumping heavily down the brass-clamped steps of the companion. A hand beat roughly upon his door and ordered him out. He knew that his frail lock was no protection, so he turned the key and stepped forth. It might well have frightened a stouter man, for the murderers were all there. Leon, Carlos, Santos, Blanco, Dur-anno, Watto, dreadful looking folk most of them at the best of times, but now, armed with their dripping knives and crimson cudgels, and seen in that dim morning light, as terrible a group as ever a writer of romance conjured up in his imagination. The Manila men stood in a silent semi-circle round the door, with their savage Mongolian faces turned upon him.

"What are you going to do with me?" he cried. "Are you going to kill me?" He tried to cling to Leon as he spoke, for as the only one who could speak English he had become the leader.

"No," said Leon. "We are not going to kill you. But we have killed the captain and the mate. Nobody on board knows any-thing of navigation. You must navigate us to where we can land."

The trembling mate, hardly believing the comforting assur-ance of safety, eagerly accepted the commission.

"Where shall I navigate you to?" he asked.

There was a whispering in Spanish among the dark-faced men, and it was Carlos who answered in broken English.

"Take up River Platte," said he. "Good country! Plenty Spanish!" And so it was agreed.

And now a cold fit of disgust seemed to have passed through those callous ruffians for they brought down mops and cleaned out the cabin. A rope was slung round the captain and he was hauled on deck. Taffir, to his credit be it told, interfering to impart some decency to the ceremony of his burial. "There goes the captain!" cried Watto, the handsome Levantine lad, as he heard the splash of the body. "He'll never call us names any more!" Then all hands were called into the saloon with the exception of Candereau, the Frenchman, who remained at the wheel. Those who were innocent had to pretend approval of the crime to save their own lives. The captain's effects were laid out upon the table and divided into seventeen shares. Watto insisted that it should only be eight shares, as only eight were concerned in the mutiny, but Leon with greater sagacity argued that everyone should be equally involved in the crime by taking their share of the booty. There were money and clothes to divide, and a big box of boots which represented some little commercial venture of the captain's. Everyone was stamping about in a new pair. The actual money came to about ten pounds each and the watch was set aside to be sold and divided later. Then the mutineers took permanent possession of the cabin, the course of the ship was altered for South America, and the ill-fated barque began the second chapter of her infamous voyage.

The cargo had been breached and the decks were littered with open cases of champagne, from which everyone helped himself as he pleased. There was a fusillade of popping corks all day, and the air was full of the faint, sweet, sickly smell of the wine. The second mate was nominally commander, but he was commander without the power to command. From morning to night he was threatened and insulted, and it was only Leon's interference and the well-grounded conviction that they could never make the land without him, which saved him from their daily menaces. They gave a zest to their champagne carousals by brandishing their knives in his face. All the honest men were subjected to the same treatment. Santos and Watto came to the Norwegian carpenter's whetstone to sharpen their knives, explaining to him as they did so that they would soon use them on his throat. Watto, the handsome lad, declared that he had already killed sixteen men. He wantonly stabbed the inoffensive Chinese steward through the fleshy part of the arm. Santos said to Candereau, the Frenchman, "In two or three days I shall kill you."

"Kill me then!" cried Candereau with spirit.

"This knife," said the bully, "will serve you the same that it has the captain."

There seems to have been no attempt upon the part of the nine honest men to combine against the eight rogues. As they were all of different races and spoke different languages it is not surprising that they were unable to make head against the armed and unanimous mutineers.

And then there befell one of those incidents which break the monotony of long sea voyages. The topsails of a ship showed above the horizon and soon there rose her hull. Her course would take her across her bows, and the mate asked leave to hail her, as he was doubtful as to his latitude.

"You may do so," said Leon. "But if you say a word about us you are a dead man."

The strange ship hauled her yard aback when she saw that the other wished to speak to her, and the two lay rolling in the Atlantic swell within a hundred yards of each other.

"We are the *Friend*, of Liverpool," cried an officer. "Who are you?"

"We are the *Louisa*, seven days out from Dieppe for Valparaiso," answered the unhappy mate, repeating what the mutineers whispered to him. The longitude was asked and given, and the two vessels parted company. With yearning eyes the harassed man looked at the orderly decks and the well served officer of the Liverpool ship, while he in turn noticed with surprise those signs of careless handling which would strike the eye of a sailor in the rig and management of the *Flowery Land*. Soon the vessel was hull down upon the horizon, and in an hour the guilty ship was again alone in the vast ring of the ocean.

This meeting was very nearly being a fatal one to the mate, for it took all Leon's influence to convince the other ignorant and suspicious seamen that they had not been betrayed. But a more dangerous time still was before him. It must have been evident to him that when they had made their landfall then was the time when he was no longer necessary to the crew and when they were likely to silence him forever. That which was their goal was likely to prove his death warrant. Every day brought him nearer to this inevitable crisis, and then at last on the night of the 2nd of October the look-out man reported land ahead. The ship was at once put about, and in the morning the South American coast was a dim haze upon the western horizon. When the mate came upon deck he found the mutineers in earnest conclave about the fore-hatch, and their looks and gestures told him that it was his fate which was being debated. Leon was again on the side of mercy. "If you like to kill the carpenter and the mate, you can: I shall not do it," said he. There was a sharp difference of opinion upon the matter, and the poor, helpless mate waited, like a sheep near a knot of butchers.

"What are they going to do with me?" he cried to Leon, but received no reply. "Are they going to kill me?" he asked Marsolino.

"I am not, but Blanco is," was the discouraging reply.

However, the thoughts of the mutineers were happily diverted by other things. First they clewed up the sails and dropped the boats alongside. The mate having been deposed from his command there was no commander at all, so that everything was chaos. Some got into the boats and some remained upon the decks of the vessel. The mate found himself in one boat which contained Watto, Paul the Sclavonian, Early the ship's boy and the Chinese cook. They rowed a hundred yards away from the ship, but were recalled by Blanco and Leon. It shows how absolutely the honest men had lost their spirit, that though they were four to one in this particular boat they meekly returned when they were recalled. The Chinese cook was ordered on deck, and the others were allowed to float astern. The unfortunate steward had descended into another boat, but Duranno pushed him overboard. He swam for a long time begging hard for his life, but Leon and Duranno pelted him with empty champagne bottles from the deck until one of them struck him on the head and sent him to the bottom. The same men took Cassap, the little Chinese boy, into the cabin. Candereau, the French sailor heard him cry out: "Finish me quickly then!" and they were the last words that he ever spoke.

In the meantime the carpenter had been led into the hold by the other mutineers and ordered to scuttle the ship. He bored four holes forward and four aft, and the water began to pour in. The crew sprang into the boats, one small one, and one large one, the former in tow of the latter. So ignorant, and thoughtless were they that they were lying alongside as the ship settled down in the water, and would infallibly have been swamped if the mate had not implored them to push off. The Chinese cook had been left on board, and had clambered into the tops so that his gesticulating figure was almost the last that was seen of the ill-omened *Flowery Land* as she settled down under the leaping waves. Then the boats, well laden with plunder, made slowly for the shore.

It was 4 in the afternoon upon the 4th of October that they ran their boats upon the South American beach. It was a desolate spot, so they tramped inland, rolling along with the gait of seamen ashore, their bundles upon their shoulders. Their story was that they were the shipwrecked crew of an American ship from Peru to Bordeaux. She had foundered a hundred miles out, and the captain and officers were in another boat which had parted company. They had been five days and nights upon the sea. Toward evening they came upon the estancia of a lonely farmer to whom they told their tale, and from whom they received every hospitality. Next day they were all driven over to the nearest town of Rocha. Candereau and the mate got an opportunity of escaping that night, and within twenty-four hours their story had been told to the authorities and the mutineers were all in the hands of the police.

Of the twenty men who had started from London in the *Flowery Land* six had met their deaths from violence. There remained fourteen, of whom eight were mutineers, and six were destined to be the witnesses against them. No more striking example could be given of the long arm and steel hand of the British law than that within a few months this mixed crew, Sclavonian, negro, Manila men, Norwegian, Turk and Frenchman, gathered on the shore of the distant Argentine, were all brought face to face at the Central Criminal Court in the heart of London town.

The trial excited great attention on account of the singular crew and the monstrous nature of their crimes. The death of the officers did less to rouse the prejudice of the public and to influence the jury than the callous murder of the unoffending Chinaman. The great difficulty was that of apportioning the blame amongst so many men and of determining which had really been active in the shedding of blood. Taffir, the mate: Early, the ship's boy: Candereau, the Frenchman, and Anderson, the carpenter, all gave their evidence, some incriminating one and some another. After a very careful trial five of them, Leon, Blanco, Watto, Duranno and Lopez, were condemned to death. They were all Manila men, with the exception of Watto, who came from the Levant. The oldest of the prisoners was only five and twenty years of age. They took their sentence in a perfectly callous fashion, and immediately before it was pronounced Leon and Watto laughed heartily because Duranno had forgotten the statement which he had intended to make. One of the prisoners who had been condemned to imprisonment was at once heard to express a hope that he might be allowed to have Blanco's boots.

The sentence of the law was carried out in front of Newgate upon the 22nd of February. Five ropes jerked convulsively for an instant, and the tragedy of the *Flowery Land* had reached its fitting consummation.

AN IMPRESSION OF THE REGENCY

—◆—

It was in those stormy days of the early century when England, in an age of heroes and buffoons, had turned, in her intervals of prize-fighting and horse-racing, Almack balls and Carlton House scandals, to grasp the sceptre of the seas, and to push Napoleon's veterans out of the Peninsula. The practical jokers of St. James's Street and the gamblers of Watier's were of the same blood and class as the exquisites of Wellington, or the Foleys and Balls whose foppishness aroused the anger of Nelson until their gallantry extorted his admiration. A singular effeminacy and a desperate recklessness alternated in the same individual, and the languid lounger of the evening was easily stirred into the fierce duellist of the morning. Amid this strange society of brutality and sentiment there moved the portly figure of George, the Prince and Regent, monstrous on account of his insignificance and interesting for the inhuman absence of any points of interest. Weak and despicable, a liar and a coward, he still in some inexplicable way catches the attention of posterity as he did of his own contemporaries, and draws the eye away from better men.

George the King was in his second and more fatal period of madness, while George the Prince waited for his heritage and filled his father's place. Twice a year the Regent should go to Windsor where the lunatic was kept, and satisfy himself as to his condition. It was a formality, but in the strange lumbering British Constitution formalities were the ultimate rulers of all things, with Kings, Lords and Commons groaning under their tyranny. And so, sorely against his will, the weak, foolish man abandoned his Brighton palace and drove northwards to fulfil his odious duty at the Castle.

But he did not go alone. He was no lover of solitude at any time, and least of all when his work might be done or lightened by others. Sir Charles Tregellis shared his coach — Tregellis, the arbiter of fashions, the gentle duellist, the languid rake, the wary gambler, the masterful lounger whose drooping eyelids and supercilious eyes could dominate the most high-blooded buck in Watier's or in Brooks's. Lord Yarmouth was with them, the foxy-haired, red-whiskered sportsman, and all day they drove through the weald of Sussex and over the uplands of Surrey until in the evening, ankle deep in playing cards, they saw the Thames wind through green meadows, and the huge dark bulk of the Windsor towers loom black against the gold and carmine of a September sunset. Another coach and yet another were on the London road, for it had been given out that the Regent had need of company, and his friends were rallying to his call.

Why should the Prince see his father? It was enough to have paid his formal visit and to have received the reports of Doctor John Willis and his son. To the Regent an unpleasant duty meant a duty to be evaded. He had seen his father once, and he had never forgotten it. It came to him still, that memory, when he lay restless at night, and not all his little glasses of maraschino could banish it from his mind. The royal state had always seemed so fenced in from unpleasantness of every kind! The whole world conspired to keep trouble away. But nature would not join in the conspiracy. Nature was rough, brutal, unreasonable. This Prince had never heard one harsh or reproving word in all his life, save only from this stern old man, his father, and from the dreadful, unutterable German woman whom he had married. Once or twice, when the Commons had been asked to pay his debts, there had been unpleasant speeches, but then he did not hear them, and they only reached his ears in the mildest and least irritating form. Sycophants and courtiers filtered everything from the outer world. And now into this sheltered life, weakened and softened by indulgence, there came the brutal realities of disease. The King himself, the one man whose position was more august then his own, was struck into puling childish imbecility. George's craven heart quailed at the sight of the foolish, garrulous old man for ever pouring forth a ceaseless gabble of meaningless words. It brought home to him that there was a higher law against which all his prerogatives were vain. He shrank now from such an experience, and his quarters, with those of his friends, were placed at that wing of the castle which was farthest from the chambers of the King.

There were twelve of them at supper that night, and they sat late over the wine. The Prince drank deeply to clear away the weight which lay upon his spirits. This house of royal suffering cast its gloom upon him. And the others drank as much, or more than he, out of sympathy with their royal comrade, and because it was their good pleasure and the custom of the time. Sheridan, of the inflamed face and the ready tongue; Hertford, the husband of the reigning favourite; Yarmouth, his son; Theodore Hook, the jester; Tregellis, whose pale cheek flushed into comeliness upon the fourth bottle; Mountford, with the lewd eyes and the perfect cravat; Mackinnon, of the Guards; Banbury, who shot Sir Charles Williams behind Chalk Farm – these were the men who, out of all the virtue and wisdom of England, had in his fiftieth year gathered as intimates round the English Prince.

He lay back in his chair, as the decanters circulated, his eyes glazed and his face flushed. His waistcoat was partly undone, and his ruffled shirt came bursting through the gaps. Laziness and liquors had made him very fat, but he carried himself in his official duties with a dignified solemnity. Now in his hour of relaxation the dignity was gone, and he lolled, a coarse, swollen man, at the head of his table. At supper he had been amusing. He had two genuine gifts, the one for telling a story, and the other for singing a song, and, had he been a commoner, he had still been a good companion. But his brain had softened, and he was at a disadvantage with the seasoned men around him. A little wine would make him excited, a little more, maudlin, and then it was but a short step to irresponsibility. Already he had lost all sense of decency and restraint. He raged between his glasses at his brothers, at his wife, at the Princess Charlotte, his daughter, at the Whigs, the cursed Whigs, who would not come to heel, at the Commons, who would not vote him the money for which his duns were clamouring – at everything and everybody as far as they had ever stood in the way of his ever-varying whims. The baser of the company urged him onwards by their ready sympathy, the others looked downwards at their glasses, or raised their critical eyebrows as they glanced at each other. And then, in yet another stage of his exaltation, he lied, with palpably absurd, vainglorious lies which sprang from that same family taint which had laid his father low. Always behind the pampered, foolish Sybarite there loomed the shadow of madness.

"Yes, yes, he has done well enough," said he, for the talk had turned upon the recent victories of Wellington in the Peninsula. "He has done well enough, but he is lucky in those who serve him. Now, at Salamanca–"

They all glanced furtively at each other, for the delusion was well known to them.

"At Salamanca," he continued pompously, "where would he

have been if the heavies had not charged? And why did the heavies charge?"

"Because your Highness gave the order," said some sycophant.

"Ah ha, the thing has become public then?" said he exultantly. "York tried to hush it up, and so did Wellington, d—d jealous of me, both of them — but truth will come out.

" 'Le Marchant,' said I, 'if the heavies don't charge, the game is up.'

" 'We cannot charge unshaken infantry,' said he.

" 'Then, by God, sir, I can and I will,' said I. I rammed my spurs into my charger — a big black he was, with white stockings — and we went right into them. You can vouch for the story, Tregellis."

"I can vouch for the story," said Sir Charles, with an emphasis upon the last word, which caused a titter.

"Sir Charles expresses himself cautiously," said Mountford, eager to pose as champion of the Prince. "He will, no doubt, vouch for the fact as well."

"I had not the honour to be there," said Sir Charles wearily. "It is strange, Lord Mountford, that you should ask for a voucher for anything which the Prince has cited as a fact."

Mountford's point had been turned against his own breast so adroitly, that the befuddled Prince had not perceived it. He frowned darkly at his champion, and shook his head.

"Have you any doubt of the truth of what I have said, Lord Mountford? Eh, sir? What?"

"Not in the least, sir."

"Then I must ask you, sir, to be more guarded in your language." He pouted like an angry child, and Mountford flushed from his curling hair to his speckless, many-wreathed cravat.

"Do you return early to town, Sir Charles?" he asked quickly when the hum of conversation had been resumed.

"I shall still be here at seven," said Sir Charles, smiling gently.

"I shall walk in the Eton meadows," said Mountford, bowing.

It was the last walk he ever made without a stick. But the company cared nothing for a quarrel so discreetly conducted. The Prince was telling a story. He missed the point, but they guffawed with outrageous merriment. Hook capped it with another which was all point but met with a languid murmur of approval. The talk turned upon racing, why Sam Chifney had been warned off the turf, and why the Regent had abandoned Newmarket. There were drunken tears in his dull eyes as he told how scandalously he had been treated. And then it passed on to prize fighting. Yarmouth was a patron of the ring, and told of

Gregson, the North-Country giant, whom he had seen in Ward's ordinary in St. Martin's Lane. His father bet a hundred guineas against him in the coming fight, and the family wager was booked amidst shoutings and laughter. Then the talk came back to the never-failing topic of women, and it was seen how a coarse and material age could debase the minds of men, and soil the daintiest of subjects. A shadow of disgust passed over the pale face of Tregellis as he listened to the hiccoughed reminiscences of the maudlin Regent.

"By-the-way, sir," said he, adroitly changing the subject, "has your Highness heard of the vogue which Captain Mackinnon has obtained? No function is à la mode without his exploit. Even Lady Lieven swears that the next ball at Almack's will not be complete unless he goes round the room upon the route chairs and the instruments of the musicians."

The jaded appetite of the Regent needed eternal novelties to stimulate it. Hook had risen from the depths to the surface on account of his originality – an originality which was already losing its freshness. Every one who had any talent or peculiarity, however grotesque, was brought to Brighton. Mackinnon had never before been in the presence, and his fresh young soldier face was suffused with blushes at the words of Tregellis. The Regent looked at him with his glazed eyes.

"Let me see, I heard of you, sir, but I am d—d if I can call to mind what you can do. Didn't you kill a cat with your teeth at the Cockpit? No, that was Ingleston. Or are you the man who imitates a coach horn? No, by George, I've got it! you're the furniture man."

"Yes, sir."

"Go round any room in London on the furniture – never been beaten – haw! haw! Well, it's close enough here, and any child could do it."

"Yes, sir," said Mackinnon. "It would be easy here."

"They tried to beat him at Lady Cunningham's," cried Banbury. "They had but four chairs and a settee, but he climbed up the window and scrambled round the picture rod. He takes some pounding, I tell you."

The Regent glanced round at the furniture and staggering to his feet, he pulled of his plum-coloured silken coat.

"Coats off, gentlemen!" said he, and in an instant, young and old, they were all in their white cambric shirt-sleeves.

"We'll all do it," said he. "Every man Jack of us. By Gad, Captain Mackinnon, we'll play you at your own game. 'Pon my life a little exercise will harm none of us. Now, sir, give us a lead! You next,

Banbury! You, Yarmouth! You, Hertford! Then myself! And so, as we sit! And the man who is pounded shall drink a claret glass of maraschino for a punishment."

It was an idiotic spectacle, and yet one which was characteristic of an age when, in the highest circles, any form of ludicrous eccentricity was a more sure pass to popularity and success than wisdom or brilliancy. If wise and brilliant men – a Fox, or a Sheridan – *did* succeed in such circles, it was by reason of their vices rather than of their virtues. A Wordsworth or a Coleridge would have been powerless before a rival who crowed like a cock or had a boundless invention for practical jokes. So it was that Mackinnon, with his absurd accomplishment, had taken London society by storm, and shot over the heads of his superior officers into the select circle which shared the amusements and the vices of the repulsive George.

Mackinnon, a little flurried at this strange game of follow-my-leader for which he was to be responsible, had risen from his chair. He was a tall, thin, supple lad, with a wiry, active figure, which bore out his reputation for gymnastic skill. But there was nothing here to test his powers. As the Prince had remarked, any one could, with a little address, have made the circuit of the room without touching the floor, for the furniture was massive and abundant. From a chair he stepped on to the long brown oaken sideboard, strewn with fruit and plate. Walking along it, he found himself some few feet from an armchair, on to which he sprang. The others followed with shouts and cheers – some as active and light as himself, some stout from good living and unsteady from wine, but all entering eagerly into the royal joke. The courtly Banbury sprang with languid grace from the sideboard to the armchair, and, landing on the arm, rolled with it upon the ground. George, balanced among the dishes and wine-coolers upon the sideboard, laughed until he had to hold on to a picture to keep from falling. When he, in his turn, sprang on to the chair his two feet went through the bottom, amid shrieks of delight from his companions. "Hard forrard! Hard forrard!" cried Hook; and Mountford "yoicked" like a huntsman. On to the broken chair they bounded, one after another, until it was a bundle of splinters and upholstery. From there, with all the yapping and clamour of a hunt, they scrambled over a cabinet, and so along a chain of chairs that ended at the broad marble mantelpiece. Here was indeed a perilous passage; nothing but a high pier glass upon one side, and a five-foot drop into an ornamental fender upon the other. Mackinnon tripped over, and then Banbury, Yarmouth, Hertford, and the Prince, the last pawing nervously at the glass with fat, moist hands, which left their blurred marks across it. He had shuffled his unwieldy bulk almost into safety, when suddenly the shoutings and the cheering died away, and a strange silence fell upon the rioters. Another sound, which had grown louder upon their ears, hushed their foolish outcry.

It was a long, monotonous, bellowing call; a strangely animal uproar; one deep note repeated again and again, but rising in volume to a retching whoop. For some minutes Tregellis and others had been conscious of the sinister clamour; but now it grew louder with every instant, as if some wandering heifer were lowing down the corridor and rapidly approaching the door of their dining-room. It was so overpoweringly loud that it boomed through all their riot and reduced them to a startled silence. For it was an extraordinary noise, animal in sound, but human in origin – a grim, mindless hooting which struck cold into their hearts. They looked from one to the other, the grotesque line of coatless men, balanced upon the tables and the chairs. Who could it be who howled thus down the royal corridor? The question flashed from eye to eye, and it was the bloodless lips of George which found the answer. He had descended to a chair and stood there with frightened, staring eyes fixed upon the door. Outside there rang one last terrific whoop, as the door was flung open, and the mad King stood mowing and gabbling in the opening.

He was in a grey dressing-gown, with red slippers protruding beneath. His white hair was ruffled, a white beard fell over his chest, and his huge, protruding eyes rolled round him with the anxious eagerness of a purblind man. For a moment he stood thus, his hand upon the door, a piteous, venerable figure. Then the white beard dropped, the mouth opened wide, and again that discordant, horrible, long-drawn cry boomed through the room. At the same instant the frightened roisterers saw moving figures in the corridor over his shoulder, the startled faces of hurrying doctors, and heard the patter and rustle of their feet. Eager hands clutched at the old King, he was plucked backwards, and the door slammed behind his struggling screaming form. There was a heavy thud within the dining-room. Tregellis sprang for the brandy decanter.

"Loosen his shirt," said he; "hold up his head." And a little group of flushed, half-drunken men propped up the gross and senseless form of the Heir-apparent.

THE CENTURION

[Being the fragment of a letter from Sulpicius Balbus, Legate of the Tenth Legion, to his uncle, Lucius Piso, in his villa near Baiae, dated The Kalends of the month of Augustus in the year 824 of Rome.]

I promised you, my dear uncle, that I would tell you anything of interest concerning the siege of Jerusalem; but, indeed, these people whom we imagined to be unwarlike have kept us so busy that there has been little time for letter-writing. We came to Judæa thinking that a mere blowing of trumpets and a shot would finish the affair, and picturing a splendid triumph in the *via sacra* to follow, with all the girls in Rome throwing flowers and kisses to us. Well, we may get our triumph, and possibly the kisses also, but I can assure you that not even you who have seen such hard service on the Rhine can ever have experienced a more severe campaign than this has been. We have now won the town, and to-day their temple is burning, and the smoke sets me coughing as I sit writing in my tent. But it has been a terrible business, and I am sure none of us wish to see Judæa again.

In fighting the Gauls, or the Germans, you are against brave men, animated by the love of their country. This passion acts more, however, upon some than others, so that the whole army is not equally inflamed by it. These Jews, however, besides their love of country, which is very strong, have a desperate religious fervour, which gives them a fury in battle such as none of us have ever seen. They throw themselves with a shriek of joy upon our swords and lances, as if death were all that they desired.

If one gets past your guard may Jove protect you, for their knives are deadly, and if it comes to a hand-to-hand grapple they are as dangerous as wild beasts, who would claw out your eyes or your throat. You know that our fellows of the Tenth Legion have been, ever since Cæsar's time, as rough soldiers as any with the Eagles, but I can assure you that I have seen them positively cowed by the fury of these fanatics. As a matter of fact we have had least to bear, for it has been our task from the beginning to guard the base of the peninsula upon which this extraordinary town is built. It has steep precipices upon all the other sides, so that it is only on this one northern base that fugitives could escape or a rescue come. Meanwhile, the fifth, fifteenth, and the twelfth or Syrian legions have done the work, together with the auxiliaries. Poor devils! we have often pitied them, and there have been times when it was difficult to say whether we were attacking the town or the town was attacking us. They broke down our tortoises with their stones, burned our turrets with their fire, and dashed right through our whole camp to destroy the supplies in the rear. If any man says a Jew is not a good soldier, you may be sure that he has never been in Judæa.

However, all this has nothing to do with what I took up my stylus to tell you. No doubt it is the common gossip of the forum and of the baths how our army, excellently handled by the princely Titus, carried one line of wall after the other until we had only the temple before us. This, however, is – or was, for I see it burning even as I write – a very strong fortress. Romans have no idea of the magnificence of this place. The temple of which I speak is a far finer building than any we have in Rome, and so is the Palace, built by Herod or Agrippa, I really forget which. This temple is two hundred paces each way, with stones so fitted that the blade of a knife will not go between, and the soldiers say there is gold enough within to fill the pockets of the whole army. This idea puts some fury into the attack, as you can believe, but with these flames I fear a great deal of the plunder will be lost.

There was a great fight at the temple, and it was rumoured that it would be carried by storm to-night, so I went out on the rising ground whence one sees the city best. I wonder, uncle, if in your many campaigns you have ever smelt the smell of a large beleaguered town. The wind was south to-night, and this terrible smell of death came straight to our nostrils. There were half a million people there, and every form of disease, starvation, decomposition, filth and horror, all pent in within a narrow compass. You know how the lion sheds smell behind the Circus Maximus, acid and foul. It is like that, but there is a low, deadly, subtle odour which lies beneath it and makes your very heart sink within you. Such was the smell which came up from the city to-night.

As I stood in the darkness, wrapped in my scarlet chlamys – for the evenings here are chill – I was suddenly aware that I was not alone. A tall, silent figure was near me, looking down at the town

even as I was. I could see in the moonlight that he was clad as
an officer, and as I approached him I recognised that it was
Longinus, third tribune of my own legion, and a soldier of great
age and experience. He is a strange, silent man, who is respected
by all, but understood by none, for he keeps his own council and
thinks rather than talks. As I approached him the first flames
burst from the temple, a high column of fire, which cast a glow
upon our faces and gleamed upon our armour. In this red light I
saw that the gaunt face of my companion was set like iron.

"At last!" said he. "At last!"

He was speaking to himself rather than to me, for he started
and seemed confused when I asked him what he meant.

"I have long thought that evil would come to the place," said he.
"Now I see that it has come, and so I said 'At last!' "

"For that matter," I answered, "we have all seen that evil would
come to the place, since it has again and again defied the authority
of the Cæsars."

He looked keenly at me with a question in his eyes. Then he
said:

"I have heard, sir, that you are one who has a full sympathy in
the matter of the gods, believing that every man should worship
according to his own conscience and belief."

I answered that I was a Stoic of the school of Seneca, who held
that this world is a small matter and that we should care little for
its fortunes, but develop within ourselves a contempt for all but
the highest.

He smiled in grim fashion at this.

"I have heard," said he, "that Seneca died the richest man of all
Nero's Empire, so he made the best of this world in spite of his
philosophy."

"What are your own beliefs?" I asked. "Are you, perhaps, one
who has fathomed the mysteries of Isis, or been admitted to the
Society of Mythras?"

"Have you ever heard," he asked, "of the Christians?"

"Yes," said I. "There were some slaves and wandering men in
Rome who called themselves such. They worshipped, so far as I
could gather, some man who died over here in Judæa. He was put
to death, I believe, in the time of Tiberius."

"That is so," he answered. "It was at the time when Pilate was
procurator – Pontius Pilate, the brother of old Lucius Pilate, who
had Egypt in the time of Augustus. Pilate was of two minds in the
matter, but the mob was as wild and savage as these very men that
we have been contending with. Pilate tried to put them off with a
criminal, hoping that so long as they had blood they would be

satisfied. But they chose the other, and he was not strong enough to withstand them. Ah! it was a pity – a sad pity!"

"You seem to know a good deal about it." said I.

"I was there," said the man simply, and became silent, while we both looked down at the huge column of flame from the burning temple. As it flared up we could see the white tents of the army and all the country round. There was a low hill just outside the city, and my companion pointed to it.

"That was where it happened," said he. "I forget the name of the place, but in those days – it was more than thirty years ago – they put their criminals to death there. But He was no criminal. It is always His eyes that I think of – the look in His eyes."

"What about the eyes, then?"

"They have haunted me ever since. I see them now. All the sorrow of earth seemed mirrored in them. Sad, sad, and yet such a deep, tender pity! One would have said that it was He who needed pity had you seen His poor battered, disfigured face. But He had no thought for Himself – it was the great world pity that looked out of His gentle eyes. There was a noble maniple of the legion there, and not a man among them who did not wish to charge the howling crowd who were dragging such a man to His death."

"What were you doing there?"

"I was Junior Centurion, with the gold vinerod fresh on my shoulders. I was on duty on the hill, and never had a job that I liked less. But discipline has to be observed, and Pilate had given the order. But I thought at the time – and I was not the only one – that this man's name and work would not be forgotten, and that there would be a curse on the place that had done such a deed. There was an old woman there, His mother, with her grey hair down her back. I remember how she shrieked when one of our fellows with his lance put Him out of his pain. And a few others, women and men, poor and ragged, stood by Him. But, you see, it has turned out as I thought. Even in Rome, as you have observed, His followers have appeared."

"I rather fancy," said I, "that I am speaking to one of them."

"At least, I have not forgotten," said he. "I have been in the wars ever since with little time for study. But my pension is overdue, and when I have changed the sagum for the toga, and the tent for some little farm up Como way, then I shall look more deeply into these things, if, perchance, I can find some one to instruct me."

And so I left him. I only tell you all this because I remember that you took an interest in the man, Paulus, who was put to death for preaching this religion. You told me that it had reached

Cæsar's palace, and I can tell you now that it has reached Cæsar's soldiers as well. But apart from this matter I wish to tell you some of the adventures which we have had recently in raiding for food among the hills, which stretch as far south as the river Jordan. The other day . . .

[*Here the fragment is ended.*]

THE DEATH VOYAGE

It was a winter evening, and as I sat by a dwindling fire in the twilight my mind hit upon a strange line of thought. Musing over the great crises of history, I could see that the chief actor in each had always come to a dividing of the ways where it was within his choice to take the one path or the other. He took the one, and the annals tell us what came of it. But suppose that he had taken the other. Is it possible for the human imagination to follow up the course of events which would have resulted from that? A series of fascinating alternatives passed through my brain, each involving a problem of its own. Had Cæsar remained faithful as a General of the Republic and refused to cross the Rubicon, would not the whole story of Imperial Rome have been different? Had Washington persuaded his fellow-countrymen to wait patiently until a Liberal majority in the British Parliament righted their wrongs – would not Britain and all her Dominions now be an annexe to the great central Power of America? If Napoleon had made peace before entering upon the Russian campaign – and so on, and so on. As I brooded thus, a modern instance came into my mind, and so, half sleeping, and with my eyes fixed upon the red embers, there came a series of pictures, a vision if one may so call it, which, with realistic detail duly added, might be translated into some such narrative as this.

It was a dull November day in the little Belgian town of Spa. It was very easy to see that some great event had occurred – some event which had stirred the townspeople to their depth. Business had ceased, and they stood in excited gossiping groups along the sidewalks. Among them there wandered great numbers of German soldiers in their grey-green uniforms, some of them so worn with service that they presented every shade of colour. These men were as excited as the civilians, and choked the streets with their noisy, gesticulating assemblies. Boys carrying newspapers rushed wildly here and there. The whole place was like an ants' nest stirred up suddenly by some intrusive stick.

Suddenly the groups fell apart to give space for a huge motor-car, containing four officers and two civilians, who were clearly men of importance, to judge by the attention which they excited. The lion-like face, which looked fiercely out at the undisciplined groups of soldiers, was one which was familiar to every bystander, since Spa had been for so long the centre of German military activity. It was old Marshal von Berg himself. Beside him, lost in thought, sat a high naval officer, his clean-shaven face seamed with furrows of care. It was the famous Admiral von Speer. Two other high Generals and two statesmen fresh from Berlin completed the group. The car roared down the main street, turned hard to the right, swung round between the pillars of an ornamental gate, and halted presently before the stuccoed front of the Villa Froneuse. Sentries on either side of the door presented arms, a red-plushed butler appeared in the opening, and the illustrious deputation vanished into the house, while curious faces and staring eyes lined the railing, for it was rumoured that some eventful decision was to be reached that day, and that the moment of fate had arrived.

The deputation was ushered into the large hall, decorated in white and gold, and from the end of it they entered a spacious lounge or study, where they seated themselves round a table.

"The Emperor was expecting you," said the butler; "he will be with you presently." He walked silently as one who is at a funeral, and closed the door gently behind him.

The party was clearly ill at ease. They looked at each other in a questioning way. It was the naval officer who broke the silence.

"Perhaps it would be best, sir, if you opened the matter," said he to the great soldier. "His Majesty knows that what you advise comes from a loyal heart."

"Do you imply, Admiral, that our advice is anything but loyal?" asked one of the Berlin statesmen.

The Admiral shrugged his shoulders.

"You come from the centre of disturbance. For the moment we can learn nothing from Berlin. We only know that forces behind the line have brought our affairs to ruin."

"If you mean to say—" cried the civilian hotly, but Von Berg interrupted with a wave of his arm.

"We have had discussion enough," he growled. "But I am a soldier, not a talker. Do you speak, Von Stein, and we will check what you say."

"It is no pleasant task," answered the civilian, a large, heavy, blond man with a flowing yellow beard. "Still, if you so desire it –"

The door opened and a man entered. The six men round the table sprang to their feet, and their heels all clicked together. The Emperor bowed stiffly, and motioned that they should be seated. His keen grey eyes glanced from the face of one to the other, as if to gather what their message might be. Then with a wry smile he seated himself alone at the farther end of the table.

"Well, gentlemen," he said, "I hear that you have been determining the fate of your Emperor. May I ask the result of your deliberations?"

"Your Majesty," said Von Stein in answer, "we have carefully considered the situation, and we are all of one mind. We feel that your Majesty's safety is endangered if you remain here. We cannot answer for what may happen."

The Emperor shrugged his shoulders. "If Germany falls it can matter little what happens to individuals," said he.

"Germany may stumble, your Majesty, but she can never fall. Sixty million of people cannot be wiped from the map. There will soon come a period of reconstruction, and who can say how necessary the presence of your Majesty may be at such a time?"

"What are your views, Field-Marshal?" the Emperor asked.

Von Berg shrugged his massive shoulders and shook his head disconsolately.

"I have had reports from the seven armies to-day, your Majesty. The greater part of the soldiers are still ready to fight the enemy. They refuse, however, to fight their own comrades, and many of the battalions are out of hand."

"And the navy, Admiral?"

"It is hopeless, your Majesty. The red flag flies on every ship in Kiel and Wilhelmshaven. The officers have been set ashore. There is little violence, but the Soviets command the vessels."

"And the civilians, Herr von Stein?"

"They will support the war no longer, your Majesty. They are weary of it all, and ask only for peace."

"Do they realise the consequences if we lay down our arms?"

"Erzberger and his party are at the French headquarters making such terms as they can. Perhaps, sire, it may not be as bad as you think."

"We need not deceive ourselves. We have only to ask ourselves what our own terms would have been had we been the victors. It means the loss of our fleet, of our colonies, and of all that was built up under my care in the last twenty-five years. And why, why has this terrible thing come upon us?"

"Because the nation behind the line has failed us."

"But why has it failed us?" There was a cold gleam of anger in the Emperor's eyes, and he looked from one to the other for an answer.

"They were tried too high, your Majesty. There is a limit to human endurance. They could go no farther."

"It is false," cried the Emperor, hotly, and he struck the table with his hand. "It is because you did not trust them. It is because they were for ever misinformed, as I was misinformed, so that they lost all confidence in you and me and everyone."

"Misinformed, your Majesty?"

"Yes, misinformed at every turn. I might well use a stronger word. I am not accusing you individually, gentlemen. I speak of the various services which you represent — though indeed you are yourselves not guiltless in the matter, and you have helped, each of you, to supply me with information which was false, so that all my plans were built upon an unsound foundation. We might have had peace with honour at any time had I known all that I know now."

The members of the Council moved uneasily in their seats. It was the second civilian, a small, dark, bristle-haired man, clean-cut and alert like a well-bred terrier, who was the first to speak.

"Your Majesty may perhaps be putting blame upon us which might be justly borne by more august shoulders," said he.

"Be silent," said Von Berg roughly. "We want none of your Berlin insolence here."

"We want the truth, which the Emperor has so seldom had in the past," cried the Radical Deputy. "Has he not told us so himself? Has not everyone said what would please him rather than what is true, and has he not been too confiding and complaisant in accepting such assurances?"

"Enough, Brunner!" cried the Admiral, angrily. "We are here to hear the Emperor, not to listen to speeches from the Left bench. But, your Majesty, your accusation is a grave one. How and when have your counsellors failed you?"

"At every turn," said the Emperor, bitterly. "There is hardly one vital promise ever made to me or to the nation which has not proved to be false. Take your own service, Admiral Von Speer. Is it not a fact that your authorities assured us that if we had indiscriminate U-boat warfare from February, 1917, onwards we must starve England out and so win? Was it not said again and again? Now it is November, 1918, and where is this starvation of England?"

"Events were too strong for us, your Majesty."

"A wise counsellor foresees events. And you, Von Berg, did not you and Ludendorff assure me that when the Russians broke away, and our Eastern armies were available in the West, we would drive the French behind Paris and the British into the sea?"

"We nearly did so, your Majesty."

"There was no qualification in your assurances. You all declared that it would be so. And did not every military leader assure me in 1914 that the British might be disregarded upon the land, and yet these papers" – he beat upon a wallet which lay upon the table – "show me that in the last four months they have taken from us more prisoners and guns than all the Allies put together? Can you excuse such miscalculations as that?"

The great soldier sank his eyes.

"I have never underrated the British," he said.

"But my advisers did. And the Americans! Did not my statesmen say that they would not come into the War? Did not my sailors say that they could not bring an army to Europe? Did not my soldiers say that they had no army to bring? And now" – he caught up the wallet and shook it at the Council – "they have over a million men available, and there are American naval guns which are sweeping the roads between Montmedy and Conflans, the only line of retreat of my Eastern armies. This could not happen. That could not happen. But it has all happened. Is it a wonder that the people should lose heart when every promise is broken?"

A thin austere General in spectacles, who had not yet spoken, now joined in the debate. His voice was cold, harsh, and precise – a man of definite routine and fixed ideas.

"Your Majesty, any recriminations now are out of place. The question is immediate and pressing. There are Bolsheviks within fifteen miles of Spa, and if you should fall into their hands no one can foresee the consequences. Your life is in danger, and the responsibility for your person rests with us."

"What then do you advise, General von Groner?"

"We are unanimous, sir, that you should at once cross the Dutch border. General van Hentz suggested it. It is but a few miles, and your own special train waits in the station."

"And where should I go when I cross the border?"

"We have gone so far, your Majesty, as to telegraph to the Dutch Government. We have not yet received a reply. But we cannot wait. Your own train affords every accommodation, and carries your personal servants. All else can be settled later. Let us hear you are at Eyden, and our minds will be at ease."

The Emperor sat for some little time in silence.

"Would this not appear," said he at last, "as if I were deserting my people and my army at a moment of need? There is my personal honour to be considered."

"So long, sire, as you are acting upon the advice of your Council you can hardly be called to account," said Von Groner.

"A man's honour is his own private affair, and no one can lessen his responsibility." the Emperor answered. "I think that I may now dismiss you, gentlemen. You have advised me to the best of your ability, and the rest remains with me. If you will wait, Von Berg, and you, Admiral, I would have a last word with you."

The others bowed and filed out from the room. The Emperor advanced towards his two great servants, both of whom had risen to their feet.

"In you," he said, placing his hand upon the old Field-Marshal's sleeve – "and in you, Admiral, I recognise two men who represent the honour of my army and my navy. You of all men are judges upon such a point. Tell me now, as between man and man, since there is no longer any question of Emperor and subject, would you advise me to go to Holland?"

"We would," the two men said in a breath.

"Would you consider that in doing so my honour was quite untouched?"

"Undoubtedly, your Majesty. We have now to treat for terms. The American President has ventured to say that he will not treat with you. Everything will be at a deadlock until you go. You are best serving the country by sacrificing your own feelings and vanishing from the scene."

The Emperor pondered for a minute or more with his brows drawn down over his eyes, and a deep frown of concentrated thought upon his face. At last he broke silence.

"Let us go back a hundred years for our lesson. Suppose the Emperor Napoleon had refused to give himself up, or resign, what would have followed?"

"A hopeless war with senseless slaughter, which would have ended in his death or capture."

"You misunderstand me. Suppose that he had never left the Field of Waterloo, but had thrown himself inside a square of his old Guard, and had perished with them. What then?"

"What would have been gained, sire?"

"Nothing perhaps to France, save as an example. But would his memory not be greater? Would he not seem now like some wonderful angel of destruction who had set foot upon the earth, if we were not disabused by that anti-climax of St. Helena?"

The Field-Marshal shook his rugged head.

"Your Majesty is a better historical student than I," said he. "I fear that I have enough upon my hands now without going back a hundred years."

"And you, Von Speer? Have you nothing to say?"

"If you insist upon an answer, your Majesty, I think that Napoleon should have died at Waterloo."

The Emperor grasped him by the hand.

"You are a kindred soul. I have your assurance that my honour is safe whatever course I take. But there is something even higher than honour. There is that super-honour which we call heroism, when a man does more than is required of him. Napoleon failed to find that quality. And now I wish you farewell, gentlemen. Be assured that I will think carefully over what you have told me, and I will then announce my action."

The Emperor sat with his head resting upon his hands, listening first to the clank of spurred feet in the hall, and then to the rumble of the heavy motor. For half an hour or more he was motionless, lost in thought. Then he sprang suddenly to his feet and raised his face and hands to heaven. "God give me the strength!" he cried. He rang the electric bell and a footman appeared.

"Tell Captain von Mann that I await him."

A moment later a young, fresh-faced officer with quick, intelligent eyes had entered the room and saluted.

"Sigurd," said the Emperor, "there are likely to be very serious times before us. I hereby free you from any personal allegiance to me. From what I hear Prince Max of Baden has probably of his own initiative freed all Germany by now."

"I have no wish to be freed. You are always my master and my Emperor."

"But I would not involve you in a tragic fate."

"I wish to be involved."

"But if it means death?"

"Even so."

"What I say I mean in a literal sense. You will die if you follow me far enough."

"I ask for no better fate."

The Emperor grasped the young man's hand. "Then we are comrades in a great venture," he cried. "Now, sit beside me here at the table and let us discuss our plans. No ignoble suicide will end your Emperor's career. There are nobler ways of dying, and it is for me to find them."

*　　*　　*

There was a curious scene at the Spa station that night, though none save the three actors in it were aware of it. It was in the station-master's room, which had the door barred and the curtain drawn. Three men sat round a circular table with a strong lamp above them beating down upon their heads. Outside the trains clanked and whistled and roared, while the hubbub upon the platform showed that all was anarchy and confusion. Yet, regardless of all this, the man whose very duty it was to set the matter right sat at the table with such a look of astonishment upon his face that it was clear that he was oblivious to the turmoil outside. The station-master, Baumgarten, was a smart, alert, youngish man, such a man as one would expect to find attached to army headquarters, and he was giving his whole attention now to what the elder of his two visitors was explaining. This man, who, like his companion, was dressed in civilian dress, a loose-fitting suit of grey tweeds, was studying a railway map, while his younger companion looked over his shoulder.

"There is but one change, Your Majesty," said the station-master.

"So I see," answered the Emperor, placing his finger upon Cologne. "Once through that point we are safe. But it is all-important that we should not be recognised."

"Alas, sire, your face is so well known that it is impossible you should escape notice."

"Think, man, think!" cried the younger man impatiently; "surely you can plan it out."

Baumgarten scratched his puzzled head and paced the room in perplexity. Then suddenly there came an inspiration. He stopped and turned to the table.

"There is a refrigerator car, your Majesty. It has just come through with vegetables from Holland. We can shut off the refrigerating apparatus. It is of course closed and windowless. If your Majesty would condescend —"

"Drop titles," said the Emperor, looking round him suspiciously.

"Well, sir, if you would consent to travel in so humble a fashion we could have it marked 'Not to be opened,' and sent through to Kiel with the next train."

"Excellent. It could not be better. See that some food and water are placed in it."

"And a bed, your — a bed, sir."

"Tut, tut! Straw will serve us well. Can we get on at once?"

"Within half an hour. But how can you cross the platform here unseen?"

"I had anticipated that difficulty," said the aide-de-camp. He drew a bandage from his pocket. "If, sir, you would not mind acting the part of an officer who is wounded in the face, I could easily disguise you."

"My wound is in the heart," said the Emperor. "But how about the civil clothes?"

"People will not stop to reason in such times as these." With a few deft twists the young man passed the bandage over the Emperor's brow, and then diagonally across the tell-tale moustache. "Now, sir, I think you are safe."

"Well done, Sigurd. We will wait here, Herr Baumgarten, and when you give the word, we are ready."

And so it was that thirty-six hours later the station-master of Kiel, known to be a loyalist, opened the locked doors of a refrigerator van, from which emerged a middle-aged man, bandaged as from a severe face wound, and his young companion, who looked after him with touching care. The pair were cold and stiff, but the station-master hustled them rapidly into his own room, where hot coffee was waiting, and a warm stove. "Anything I can do, sire? You have but to command."

"Presently you shall learn," said the Emperor. "Meanwhile you will take this note, or send it by a trusty hand, to Admiral von Drotha. When he comes you will show him in to us."

An hour later a very amazed officer in the uniform of the Imperial Navy entered the humble room. He was quivering with emotion and eager zeal, with *"Zum befehl"* in every feature. He sank upon his knee before the Emperor, who raised him to his feet.

"My dear Admiral, the days of such things are past. Has not Prince Max declared that I have abdicated, though I confess that it was news to me? This is my throne now." He waved his hand towards the station chair.

"You are always our Emperor."

"Yes, here, here," and the speaker struck his breast, "I am always the Emperor. God has given me the charge and only He can relieve me from it. But in these times I ask for no response and no favour from others, save only one. But it is a supreme and onerous one. I wonder if your loyalty will rise to it?"

"It will rise to any height, sire. What is it?"

"That you should die with me."

"Sire, it is my greatest ambition." Tears of devotion ran down the face of the honest sailor. The Emperor also passed his hand across his eyes.

"I have had false friends," he said, "but there are true hearts also in the world. Now sit here, Admiral. These are rather different surroundings from the Potsdam palace, where last we met. But we have privacy, and that is essential. I have come to Kiel to lead my fleet out against the English."

The Admiral gasped.

"But, sire, the men are in mutiny. They have driven the officers ashore. How can we man our ships?"

"They will come. They will come. They are Germans, and will not let their Emperor go out to die alone – for I am going, Admiral, if it is only one torpedo boat which takes me out."

"And I am the commander of that torpedo boat," cried the Admiral.

"And I on the deck," said Sigurd von Mann.

"But what do you propose, sire? You have some definite plan in your head."

"Yes, Admiral, I have thought out every detail. In the first place, can you name any large room where some hundreds of men can be privately assembled?"

"Yes, sire. Count von Waldorf has a dancing hall attached to his villa, which would exactly meet your requirement. The Count, I need not say, is loyal to the core."

"If we could pass the word round to all the officers and assemble them there, I would appeal for their support and co-operation."

"Sire, I know the feelings of my comrades. To ask such a question is pure loss of time. There is not a man of the officers' corps of the German navy who would shrink from following you. You have only to signify your desire, and they are ready to meet it."

"Then so much time is gained, and every hour now is of importance. Everything is cracking both on the line and behind it. We must act at once or we may be stopped. What of the men?"

"I fear, sire, that they will not come. It might even be dangerous for them to know that you are in the town."

"Danger is nothing. When death is the certain end, who cares for danger upon the way? I take your word, Admiral, as to the officers. Are there any who are loyal and trustworthy among the men?"

"There are many such, sire. But they are in a minority."

"They will serve as our messengers. Collect as many as you can. Send by their hand letters to every vessel. Ask the men to send their delegates, three for a large ship, two for a light cruiser, one for a small unit, to the saloon of which you speak. Say that at three o'clock their Emperor would wish to speak with them. Call me

Wilhelm von Hohenzollern if you wish. It matters not what they call me so long as they will come."

"Sire, they will come. And a bodyguard of your faithful officers will surround you. They will only approach you over our bodies."

"Not an officer, Admiral. I must trust the men, or our cause is lost. You and Captain von Mann. None others. Send me a closed motor-car, and warn your friend Count von Waldorf that I am coming. I will see you again at three o'clock."

Long before the time mentioned all Kiel was buzzing with excitement. The news had spread like wildfire that the Emperor was in the town, and that he was in the Villa Waldorf. Great crowds assembled in the streets, and here or there a red flag fluttered over them, but there was no demonstration. Utter amazement was the prevailing sentiment. That he should come here of all places – the very centre of revolutionary disturbance. That he should put his head into the lion's mouth. Amazing! Still more wonderful was it when an open car bearing a bearded officer in an Admiral's uniform made its way slowly through the crowd, and its occupant entered the villa. That thin, eager face was well known to all – the face of Henry, younger brother of William, and head Admiral of the Fleet. What was going on? What could it mean? Were they planning a *coup d'état*? If so, they would soon find out that revolutions are not so easily set aside. So growled the crowd as it stood watching the white stuccoed face of the palatial villa.

And now the delegates began to assemble. In twos and threes they elbowed their way through the crowd, amid a good deal of rough chaff. Many had red handkerchiefs slung ostentatiously round their necks, or red ribbons in their caps. Soon the great hall, with its splendid hangings and polished oak floor, began to fill up. The red velvet seats which lined it were filled with sailors, and the body of the hall was also crammed. Everyone was smoking, and the air was a blue haze. Someone started a revolutionary song, and it rolled and echoed round the high vaulted roof. In the very midst of it the Emperor appeared.

The song was cut off in an instant, and every eye was upon that small upright figure with the dangling arm, and upon that earnest, care-worn face which looked down upon them from the band dais at the end. He was clad now in a rough blue pilot jacket, and seemed far more a man of the sea, one of their own kind, than ever he had done in his lordly trappings. A kindly wave of human sympathy went out to him. Those who were seated rose to their feet. Two men who had uttered shrill whistles of disapproval were bundled out of the hall.

The Emperor moved to the front and laid his hand upon the gilt rail. His brother Henry, Admiral von Drotha, and young Sigurd von Mann stood behind him. When he spoke it was in a firm voice, which rang through the hall.

"I speak," said he, "as a German to Germans. I thought it right to come here and see you face to face. I am not talking politics. There is no question of Empire or Republic in my mind. I have but one thought, my personal honour, the honour of my fleet, and the honour of my country."

There was no question that he had already captured his rough audience, as earnest honesty will always capture an audience. The sea of weather-beaten faces were all strained with attention. Their eyes were riveted upon the speaker.

"They are surrendering at Berlin. Is that any reason why we should surrender at Kiel? The army has fought most bravely, but it is worn out, and can fight no more. It is not I who have left the army, but the army has left me. The navy, too, has fought bravely. But it is not worn out. It has fought no general action."

"Skagerack!" cried many voices.

"Yes, you did well at Skagerack. But your battle was not with the British Fleet. It was with two or three squadrons at the most. We have still to pit our strength fairly against theirs. I am told that it is hopeless. I am told that their numbers make it impossible. There is nothing hopeless or impossible to brave men. And if it is hopeless or impossible, is it not at the worst better that we and our ships should lie at the bottom of the North Sea than that they should be surrendered without a blow? Would you stand by and let such a thing be, you men of the German Fleet? Or are you ready to die with your Emperor?"

He flung out his arm in an eloquent gesture of appeal, and then a proud, happy smile passed over his face. For he had won his cause. A forest of outstretched hands, a lake of flushed, eager faces, a roar of deep-toned voices – the navy would die with its Kaiser!

"Quick, William! Strike at once!" whispered his brother.

"You will come with me. I knew that you would. Then carry my word to your comrades. Say that no unwilling man need come. Let them stay ashore. But you and I and all true German hearts will sail together upon the death voyage of the German Fleet. Go, and do what I have told you."

There was a rush of heavy feet, and in a few minutes the hall was cleared, and every exit filled with pushing, struggling men.

In some strange way the crowd outside had in an instant learned what was afoot, and had caught the flame. The whole town was in an uproar of cheering. Flags broke out on every flagstaff, the German war flag on the same pole as the red ensign of revolution. On that the sailors were firm. The war flag might go up, but the red flag should not come down. All day and all night the Soviets held their heated meetings, where again and again dissentients were struck down by those who wished to go. News came back from Wilhelmshaven that the excitement had spread there, that all officers had been recalled to their ships, that the crews were at their quarters, and that the engineers were stoking their fires. Soon the fleet would be ready to start.

The next few days saw an uninterrupted flow of vessels through the Canal, to join the main fleet which lay in the Jade. Some delay was caused by the breakdown of a light cruiser, which blocked the passage near Neu Wittenbeck, but this was finally overcome, and by the evening of the third day the ships had collected, either in the vicinity of the Jade or in the Wilhelmshaven Roads. That night a Council was held in the wardroom of the new battleship *Bayern*, at which all the German chiefs were present, including the Emperor, who insisted upon taking a subordinate place, while von Speer, who had hastened from Spa at the first whisper of what had happened, presided over the deliberations. Vice-Admirals and Captains of capital ships – forty in all – crowded the room – gloom, and yet determination, upon every face.

"I understand, your Majesty, that your commands are that there shall be a fight to a finish?"

"That is my wish, and my order," the Emperor answered. "The fleet is to be sunk, and it is better that it take as many of the enemy as possible with it."

"We have to face the cost," said the Admiral. "It means the death of your Majesty."

"I desire no better fate."

"And of twenty-five thousand officers and men."

"Is there anyone in this Council who shrinks from it?" asked the Emperor.

There was silence. All were ready. The fleet was ready.

"But with all respect," said the young Vice-Admiral, "is it necessary that we talk as if defeat were inevitable? We held the English at Skagerack. May we not do so again?"

"Besides," said another, "our fleet is now stronger, far stronger than then. Have we not added the *Bayern* and *Baden*, great ships with fifteen-inch guns, whereas we had nothing over twelve at

Skagerack? And the *Hindenburg*, too! Is she not an addition? And the new fire control? May we not have a surprise for the English?"

"It is too late," said Von Speer. "If we won the victory, we have no fatherland to which to return." He took a telegram from his pocket and read it aloud: " 'The provisional Government severely condemns the mad project of a *sortie* upon the part of the fleet, which can lead to no result save unnecessary loss of ships and men. The report of it has seriously impeded the negotiations for an Armistice. Your allegiance to the Government demands that you instantly order the ships to return to their anchorage.' "

A growl of indignation rose from the officers, as their Admiral replaced the paper in his pocket.

"I think you will agree with me, gentlemen, that our allegiance is due to our Emperor, and to him alone."

"Have you answered it?" asked the Emperor.

"No, sire. Our deeds will answer it. But I have drawn up a message here, which, with your consent, I would wish to send to the British Commander-in-Chief. It runs thus: 'The High Seas Fleet does not consent to any Armistice. It proposes to come out at once and hopes on Monday to be seventy miles due west of Heligoland, if the mine clearing permits. Should we be delayed you will no doubt have the courtesy to wait for us.' "

"Excellent!" cried the Emperor, and all the Council clapped their hands.

"Then it shall go at once," said the Admiral.

"Might not the enemy lay their submarines at the spot?" asked one captain.

"We shall not be too exact as to the spot. Our light cruisers will guide the enemy to where we are. But as to what you say, Captain Muller, concerning the addition to our fleet, and to the Skagerack, it is well to have no illusions. The enemy has not been idle. We are in close touch with all that he has done. If we can build and improve and organise, so can they. You are aware that they lost two great ships because there was no cut-off from the turrets to the magazines. That has now been remedied. The protection of their decks and the roofs of their turrets is stronger now against plunging fire. Their shells have more explosive power. They have added many powerful ships to their squadrons. I have their names here. There are the *Ramillies*, the *Resolution*, the *Renown*, the *Repulse*, all with fifteen-inch guns. They have a squadron, too, of American battleships, and American naval history shows that they will be well handled and well fought. The odds against us are greater than ever. We can but swear to fight to the death. For myself I swear it."

He raised his hand as he spoke, and every officer in the room, including the Emperor, did the same. "We swear it," they cried. Nobly, as this record will show, did they fulfil their oath. That was the final word of the last council of war ever held in the High Seas Fleet. With set and sombre faces they bade each other farewell, the Captains returning to their vessels, while the Admirals remained to plan their future with their leader.

It was just one day later that two Admirals sat talking very earnestly together in the cabin of the Commander-in-Chief of the Grant Fleet. One was that Commander himself. The other was the American Bradman, whose fine squadron, comprising the *New York, Wyoming, Florida, Delaware, Arkansas,* and *Texas*, was the latest addition to the most formidable collection of war vessels ever assembled in the history of the world. Through the open porthole of Beaton's cabin one could see them riding at anchor with the Stars and Stripes flying over them, while beyond line after line of mighty battleships, of giant cruisers, and of smaller craft, under St. George's flag, choked the broad steam. Beyond lay the low, barren shore – as sad and bleak a prospect as any in the world.

Beaton, his handsome face wearing a puzzled frown, was reading aloud to his colleague the German wireless message.

"What do you make of that, Bradman?" he asked, looking up at his companion.

"Say, it's just fine on the face of it!" the American answered. "Too good to be true, I guess."

"I don't know. They have not much choice, have they? I think it is what we should do if things were reversed. They can scuttle their own ships in harbour – or they can come outside and have them scuttled by our guns, taking a few of our own to the bottom with them. It seems to me to be reasonable, and the first thing that brave men would think of."

"Maybe so. But it might be a trap all the same."

"Well, we won't walk into a minefield if we can help it. Our light craft will look out for that. Anyhow, I think we should let them have an answer." He took up a pencil and scribbled upon a card: "Very good. We shall be there." "How's that?"

"That's the idea."

Beaton rang the gong and handed the message to a young officer in attendance. "No need for code, Duncan. Send it as it stands." Then as the door closed he turned to the great map of the North Sea, which was now so crisscrossed with pencil marks and bearings as to be almost worn out. "That being so, Bradman, I suppose we should take it seriously and make our preparations. The poor devils would not have a chance, for we are two to one, but from what we saw of them at Jutland, I'll promise you that they will put up a very fine fight."

"Yes, they side-stepped you there," said Bradman, with a sly twinkle.

"Maybe so. But it's difficult to take chances when on our side the war is lost if our fleet is lost, while the other fellow lays no such stake upon the table. That was our trouble at Jutland. We could not risk the rough-and-tumble of a night action. We have a free hand now, and every man in the British Fleet wants a fight to a finish."

"I'll answer for my squadron, too," said Admiral Bradman, and the two sailors bent over the chart.

The day of the great adventure and of the supreme sacrifice had come. The German Fleet had assembled now in Heligoland Bay, and shortly after dawn started upon its last terrible voyage, its mine-sweepers having for two days swept a clear passage. In front of the magnificent array were two squadrons of light cruisers, forming the screen of the fleet. Then came the battle-cruisers in double line, *Derfflinger, Seydlitz, Moltke*, and *Von der Tann*, the old squadron which had already endured so much and won the respect of every British sailor. Von Lippert was in command. They were strengthened now by the mighty *Hindenburg* but her sister ship, the *Mackensen*, was not yet ready for service. Behind the cruisers came the magnificent line of the battleships, led by the strongest squadron just out of the builder's yard, the *Bayern* flying the flag of Von Speer and carrying the Emperor on board, the *Baden*, and two others. All of these great ships carried eight fifteen-inch guns and had a speed of twenty-two knots. Behind them were the four powerful ships of the *König* class, *König, Grosser Kurfurst, Kronprinz*, and *Mark Graf*. They carried ten twelve-inch guns. Then came four *Kaisers*, ships as strong as the *Königs* and rather faster. Astern of these the great line extended across the whole visible circle of ocean, giant behind giant, the *Friedrich der Grosse, Ost Friedland, Thuringen, Heligoland, Oldenburg, Posen*, and many more, while even the very old ships, such as the *Deutschland* or the *Schleswig-Holstein*, which carried four heavy guns, but were incapable of more than sixteen knots, had fallen in behind, and panted along to share the fate of their comrades. There was no need for hurry, and the whole fleet steamed at reduced speed, while on every side the destroyers kept guard against surprise. In this they were but partially successful, as the

Posen was struck by an English submarine and had to stagger back into port in a sinking condition. The submarine itself (M 16) was destroyed by the depth charges showered around it.

The Allied Fleet had to start long before dawn in order to keep its tryst. If the German array had been formidable, this could only be described as terrific. Apart from a swarm of light cruisers and destroyers, the van was led by the *Lion*, which still bore upon her plates the dints of former battles. Behind her in single line came the *Tiger*, bearing the flag of Rear-Admiral Morton, and astern were the *Australia* and *Princess Royal*. Even more formidable were two new vessels, which, on account of their peculiar qualities, operated apart. These were the *Renown* and *Repulse*, carrying fifteen-inch guns and capable of attaining the amazing speed of thirty-two knots. The light battleship squadron, under Admiral Thoms, which had shown its fine qualities at Jutland, where for a time it had been under the fire of a large part of the German Fleet, followed the cruisers. They were as before, *Malaya*, *Valiant*, *Warspite*, and *Barham*, with *Queen Elizabeth* added, all armed with fiftteen-inch guns. Behind them in double column came the new pride of the British service, *Ramillies*, *Resolution*, *Revenge*, *Royal Sovereign*, and *Royal Oak*, twenty-three-knot vessels carrying eight fifteen-inch guns each. Behind them again was the splendid American squadron of six vessels already named, with their fourteen-inch guns and twenty-one knots of speed. The thick smoke from their funnels showed that they were coal-burning ships. So, squadron after squadron, the great armada passed out to sea, with the strange, unwieldy aeroplane-carrier, *Furious*, like a huge Noah's Ark, in the rear. Far out on each flank were heavy cruisers, *Inflexible*, *New Zealand*, *Indomitable*, and others, while swarms of light cruisers and destroyers covered the ocean up to the horizon in every direction. The heavier ships formed into six columns outside the bay, and the whole majestic procession moved at eighteen knots towards the east.

It was at two-thirty in the afternoon that two British seaplanes reported a German Zeppelin in Latitude 55.46, Longitude 5.14 East, and attacked it unsuccessfully. Following it up they saw and reported the thick fringe of scouts which preceded the High Seas Fleet. The news was wirelessed to every vessel in the Allied armada and assured them for the first time that the German challenge was not empty bravado, and that the great day had really come when this long-standing quarrel should be fought to an end. Battle flags were broken out upon every ship, and Beaton increased his speed to twenty knots, even at the risk of leaving his slower craft behind. The swift battle cruisers were sent on independently at full speed to hold the enemy until the main fleet should arrive. It was a fine day, but there was a brisk breeze from the south-east, and the great cruisers, running at twenty-eight knots, had their foredecks almost under water, and the spray as high as their funnels, while they thundered through the racing waves. At two-forty came news that the light cruiser *Phaeton* had been sunk by a German submarine. A few minutes later the same fate had befallen the *Inconstant*. Then came word that a Zeppelin had been destroyed by the anti-aircraft guns of the scout *Arethusa*.

Shortly after three cocoa and light food were served out to the crews and the bugles blew for action stations. News from the scouts was now coming in thick and fast, and the sound of heavy firing could be heard from the flagship in the south-eastern direction. Seaplane No. 7042, launched from the *Furious*, had flown the whole length of the German Fleet, and though brought down with a broken wing managed to wireless her observations of their total force, which proved to be surprisingly accurate considering the difficult circumstances of the reconnaissance. For this valuable service Flight-Lieutenant Oliver was very specially mentioned in despatches.

The great fleets were now rapidly closing and the 4th British Light Cruiser Squadron was fiercely engaged with the 9th German Squadron of scouts. As the British main fleet came roaring along down upon the battle the whole horizon was dotted with these smaller vessels, many of them smothered in foam from the shells which were falling thickly around them. At four o'clock the head of the heavy cruiser squadron was engaged with the *Derfflinger*, which led the German battle cruisers. The action had fairly begun.

And here I pause. Was it to describe that great epic, that Armageddon of the sea, that my vision was intended? Was it not rather to trace the alternate fates of that desperate and unhappy man who stood at the parting of the ways, where one led to life without honour and the other to death with heroism? And yet his tragedy was so involved with this far greater one that my dream could scarce deal with one except through the other. Therefore, with no more detail than is necessary to give reality to the picture, I will write what the eye of imagination has seen.

As each side desired to fight rather than to manœuvre, the covering squadrons of light cruisers, having done their duty in reporting the enemy, fell upon each other with the utmost fury. A whole series of desperate duels were begun at a range of seven thousand, shortening to five thousand, yards. So engrossed were the little fellows in their own combats that they paid hardly any attention to the heavier ships which passed through their mêlée, and which could each have sunk any one of them with a shot. The old rule of the sea by which ships of the line did not fire upon frigates still held good, and the scouts were left to settle their quarrel among themselves. At first the Germans had the better, for their gunnery was perfect, and their destroyers pushed boldly into the fight. The *Daring*, *Dryad*, *Calliope*, *Donegal*, and *Lancaster* were all sunk by gunfire or torpedo, while the *Carnarvon* drew out of the line in a sinking condition. On the other hand, the *Stettin* and *Berlin* were both sunk early in the fight, and the *Pillau* was put out of action. As the day wore on, fresh British light craft and destroyers joined in the fray, and weight of metal and of numbers overbore the gallant Germans. *Stuttgart*, *München*, and *Frankfurt* were all sunk by gunfire, while the British lost only *Carnarvon*, which was finally torpedoed by the *Regensburg*. This fighting was desperate and bloody, but it was a mere digression from the main business of the day. As to the destroyers, the flotillas on either side charged headlong at the capital ships of the enemy, and then, meeting half way, each strove desperately to prevent the other from reaching its mark. Like fighting dogs, half smothered in foam, they tore through the seas, their sides almost touching and the flashes of their guns licking the very paint from the bulwarks of their opponents.

On every side one saw shattered and blazing wrecks, for the oil fuel turned each stricken boat into a funeral pyre to their crew – a proper burial for men who on either side came of the Viking blood. Some destroyers, German or British, fought their way through the crowd, and succeeded in driving home their attack upon the battleships, with certain death for their reward. The *Marlborough* was struck again, as she had been at Jutland, and this time sank with all hands. *Orion*, too, was badly damaged and fell out of the line with a list of twelve degrees to port. *New York* and *Renown* were both hit, but neither sustained serious damage, for their watertight bulkheads stood firm. In every case the secondary armament disposed of the brave little assailant. The German line suffered even more heavily than the British. Captain von Hase's ship, the *Derfflinger*, had a huge hole blown in her bows, and sank by the head. *Kaiserin* and *Grosser Kurfurst* were each of them sunk, and *Oldenburg* was crippled. An American squadron, under Captain Tufneh of the *Cushing*, distinguished itself in this work. On either side no notice was taken of casualties. The stricken must look after themselves. The deadly lock of battle held the rest to their work.

Beaton had deployed his main fleet to either flank in the hope of placing an Allied ship on each side of a German, but Von Speer had rapidly altered his line ahead into double column to meet the danger. Now it was a fair gun duel, opening at seventeen thousand and closing in until only twelve thousand yards separated the giants, who moved parallel to each other with no manœuvres, save that each ship would sheer in or out to baffle the enemy's aim. The German rangefinders were the better, and they were the quicker on the mark, but the British guns were heavier, and there was little to choose in the shooting. Thus it was that numbers were bound to tell. Ship after ship in the German line went up in flame and smoke. The British had learned the lesson of Jutland, and though the heavy shells of the new fifteen-inch German guns plunged repeatedly through the roofs of turrets, exterminating the crews of the guns and putting them out of action, there was no passage for that murderous back flash, which had formerly reached the magazine and destroyed the ship. The deck protection was still too weak, however, on either side, and the destruction of ships was due again and again to plunging fire which penetrated to the vitals. Thus it was with many Germans, and thus, too, with *Tiger*, *Inflexible*, *Florida*, *Repulse*, and *Collingwood*, all of which shared the fate of the *Queen Mary*.

A grey figure, grey in dress and grey in face, stood for hours at the side of the bridge of the flagship. It was the Emperor. A Zeiss periscope with magnifying power of fifteen diameters enabled him to view the terrific scene. Hour after hour he saw and realised the awful thing that had come upon the earth. Men of the same blood and culture, men sprung from the same Northern stock, were locked in this horrible wrestle, which could only end in death. Who can say what his thoughts might have been at such a time?

They flashed back to dwell upon his splendid father, the kindly, golden-bearded giant, and upon the Englishwoman his mother. Yes, half the blood in his own veins flowed from the same source as that which was in the crews of the grey ships over yonder. By what extraordinary mishandling of chances and by what evil ordering of events had it come about that he was now in such deadly conflict with them? Why was it necessary when German industry was already conquering the world by its industry and circling the globe with its Colonies? It was useless to go back upon the past. Far off, many years ago, some wrong path was taken and this was whither it had led. It was the twilight of the Gods – the most fearsome thing in all the history of the human race. They held him responsible, and yet he knew that he was but a puppet in the hands of Fate, moving forward in some pre-destined and unavoidable fashion upon a terrible course. But who was responsible – surely there must be responsibility some-where? Was it the hand which drafted that mad ultimatum to Serbia? Was it the Czar and his premature mobilisation? Was it Von Tirpitz, with his colossal sea plans now at that moment reaching their tragic result? Was it Von Schlieffen, with his scheme of marching through Belgium, which must bring Eng-land into the war? Was it his Uncle Edward, who had always been so suspicious of him? Or was it his Chancellor's act when, in 1902, he had refused with contempt an offer of an alliance from England? Each and all of these facts seemed to his tired brain to have had something to do with this awful conclusion. At his feet lay a shattered body, the blood from which had splashed his high boots and left stains upon his grey overcoat. It was his faithful aide-de-camp, Von Mann, true to death as he had promised. And that mangled corpse, that premature death when youth was at its best, was typical of ten million others for which so many held him responsible. He shuddered as terrible visions rose before him. They were interrupted by Von Speer, who approached him on the bridge. The Admiral was hit by a splinter on the shoulder, and his face was white and drawn.

"How goes it now, Admiral?" asked the Emperor.

The sailor shrugged his shoulders.

"As to the fleet, we have lost nine battleships and four great cruisers. The *Hindenburg* has just gone up. Our own two after turrets have both been shot away, the top is off one of the fore ones, and we have only two guns in action. We are, as you can see, on fire at both ends, and only a part of our funnel is standing. There is water in the engine-room and the stokers are drowning. We can do no more."

"What of the English? I have seen several of their ships go up."

"The battle now covers a line of fifteen miles. Many of the aerials have been shot away. But it is likely that they have lost ship for ship with ourselves."

"And what now?"

"There is nothing for it but to fight our ships to the water's edge."

At this moment a midshipman ran upon the bridge with a message.

"The voice tubes are cut, sir," he cried, as he saluted. "I was told to bring it by hand."

The Admiral tore open the paper.

"It is a wireless from Beaton," he said. "It runs, 'Surely honour is satisfied. No men could have done more. Why this useless slaughter? You have only five ships left in a condition to give battle. I can stand off and outrange you, so as to sink you from a distance which you cannot reach. I should hate to kill brave men in such a way. Admit your honourable and inevitable defeat, and strike your flag.' "

"Never!" said the Emperor.

"Never!" echoed the Admiral.

But at that moment there came that which settled the matter. Some say that the salvo was fired from the *Delaware*, some that it came from the *Lion*. Out of eight shells four fell direct upon the deck of the *Bayern* and plunged down into her magazines. With a roar the mighty vessel went up into the air. In the instant of impact, conscious of what the next few seconds would bring, Emperor and Admiral shook hands. Many survivors have testified to seeing that salute. It was the last gesture of the German Imperial House and of the German High Seas Fleet. At that very moment the southern horizon was broken by the smoke of many hurrying vessels. The Harwich flotilla was arriving, fresh and eager. It was the end.

Late that night, when the sun had sunk and left only a pink glow in the west, the British commander looked proudly and yet ruefully upon the scene of that terrible epic. In every direction shattered wrecks were blazing, and men floated upon scattered spars or upon Carley rafts, while swift torpedo boats flew from one to the other on their errand of saving life. Admiral Beaton stood upon his bridge, worn and weary, darkened by all the shadows of reaction.

"Might I suggest, sir, that we send a message to the fleet?" said the high officer at his elbow.

"To what is left of the fleet," said Beaton, with a wan smile. "I hear their Emperor went down with their flagship. My message, Murdoch, would be to fly our flags half-mast in memory of a brave man."

So ran my vision of an alternative. And yet it may be that Fate was wiser, and that the path upon the level was better than that upon the hilltops.

THE PARISH MAGAZINE

It was six o'clock on a winter evening. Mr. Pomeroy, the printer, was on the point of leaving his office, which was his back room, for his home, which was his front room, when young Murphy entered. Murphy was an imperturbable youth with a fat face and sleepy eyes, who had the rare quality of always doing without question what ever he was told. It is usually a great virtue – but there are exceptions.

"There are two folk to see you," said Murphy, laying two cards upon the table.

Mr. Pomeroy glanced at them.

"Mr. Robert Anderson. Miss Julia Duncan. I don't know the names. Well, show them in."

A long, sad-faced youth entered, accompanied by a mournful young lady, clad in black. Their appearance was respectable, but depressing.

"I dare say you know this," said the youth, holding up a small, grey-covered volume, the outer cover of which was ornamented with the picture of a church. "It's the *St. Olivia's Church Magazine*. What I mean, it's the Parish Magazine. This lady and I are what you might call the editors. It has been printed by –"

"Elliot and Dark, in the City," said the lady, as her companion seemed to stumble. "But they have suddenly closed down their works. We have the month's issue all ready, but we want to add to it."

"A Supplement, if you get my meaning," said the youth. "That's the word – supplement. The thing has become too dam' –"

"What he is trying to say," cried the girl, "is that the magazine wants lighting up on the social side."

"That's it," said the youth. "Just a bit of ginger, so to speak. So we arranged a Supplement. We will put it in as a loose leaf, if you follow my meaning. It's all typewritten and clear" – here he drew a folded paper from his pocket – "and it needs no reading or correcting. Just rush it through, five hundred copies, as quickly as you can do it."

"The issue is overdue," said the lady. "We must have it out by midday to-morrow. They tell me Ferguson and Co. could easily have it ready in the time, and if you won't guarantee it, we must take it to them."

"Absolutely," said the youth.

Mr. Pomeroy picked up the typed copy and glanced at it. His eyes fell upon the words, "Our beloved Vicar, Mr. Ffolliott-Sharp, B.A." There was some allusion to a bishopric. Pomeroy threw the paper across to his assistant. "Get on with it!" he said.

"We should like to pay at once," said Miss Duncan, opening her bag. "Here is a five-pound note, and you can account for it afterwards. Of course, you don't know us, and might not trust us."

"Well, if one did not trust the Parish Magazine –" said Pomeroy, smiling.

"Absolutely," cried the youth. "But what I mean is that we want to pay now. You'll send the stuff round to me at 16, Colgrove Road. Got it? Not later than twelve. Rush it through. What?"

"It shall be there," said Pomeroy.

The pair were leaving the room when the girl turned back.

"Put your name as printer at the bottom," she said. " 'Tis the law. Besides, you may get the printing of the Magazine in the future."

"Certainly. We always print our name."

The couple passed out, and hugged each other in the passage.

"I think we put it across," said he.

"Marvellous!" said she.

"That fiver was my idea."

"Incredible!" she cried. "We've got him."

"Absolutely!" said he, and they passed out into the night.

The stolid Murphy wrought long and hard, and the Pomeroy Press was working till unconscionable hours. The assistant found the matter less dull than most which he handled, and a smile spread itself occasionally over his fat face. Surely some of this was rather unusual stuff. He had never read anything quite like it. However, "his not to reason why." He had been well drilled to do exactly what he was told. The packet was ready next morning, and before twelve o'clock it had been duly dispatched to the house mentioned. Murphy carried it himself and was surprised to find their client waiting for it at the garden gate. It took some energy, apparently, to be the editor of a Parish Magazine.

It was twenty-four hours before the bomb burst, which blew Mr. Pomeroy and his household into fragments. The first intimation of trouble was the following letter:

"Sir, –

"*We can hardly imagine that you have read the contents of the so-called Supplement to the Parish Magazine which has been distributed to the members of the congregation of St. Olivia's Church. If you had you would hardly have dared to make yourself responsible by putting your name to it. I need not say that you are likely to hear a good deal more of the matter. As to my teeth, I may say that they are remarkably sound, and that I have never been to a dentist in my life.*

"JAMES WILSON

"(*Major*)."

There was a second letter upon the breakfast table. The dazed printer picked it up. It was in a feminine hand, and read thus:–

"Sir, –

"*With regard to the infamous paragraph in the new issue of the Parish Magazine, I may say that if I have bought a new car it is no business of anyone else, and the remarks about my private affairs are most unkind and uncalled for. I understand that as you are the printer you are legally responsible. You will hear in the course of a few days from my legal advisers.*

"*Yours faithfully,*

"JANE PEDDIGREW.

"14, *Elton Square*."

"What the devil does it mean?" cried Pomeroy, staring wildly at his wife and daughter. "Murphy! Murphy!"

His assistant entered from the office.

"Have you a copy of that Supplement which you printed for the Parish Magazine?"

"Yes, sir. I delivered five hundred, but there are a few in the office."

"Bring it in! Bring it in! Quick!"

Then Mr. Pomeroy began to read aloud, and apoplexy grew nearer and nearer. The document was headed Social Notes, and began with several dates and allusions to services, which might give confidence to the superficial and rapid reader. Then it opened out in this way:–

" 'Our beloved Vicar (Mr. Ffolliott-Sharp, B.A.) is still busy trying to wangle a bishopric. This time he says in his breezy way that it is 'a perfect sitter,' but we have our doubts. It is notorious that he has pulled strings in the past, and that the said strings broke. However, he has a cousin in the Lord Chancellor's office, so there is always hope.'

"Gracious!" cried Pomeroy. "In the Parish Magazine, too!

" 'In the last fortnight sixteen hymn books have disappeared from the church. There is no need for public scandal, so if Mr. James Bagshaw, Junior, of 113, Lower Cheltenham Place, will call upon the Churchwarden, all will be arranged.'

"That's the son of old Bagshaw, of the bank," cried Pomeroy. "What can they have been dreaming of?

" 'The Vicar (the Rev. Ffolliott-Sharp, B.A.) would take this opportunity to beg the younger Miss Ormerod to desist from her present tactics. Delicacy forbids the Vicar from saying what those tactics are. It is not necessary for a young lady to attend every service, and to push herself into the front pew, which is already owned (though not paid for) by the Dawson-Braggs family. The Vicar has asked us to send marked copies of this paragraph to Mrs. Delmar, Miss Featherstone, and Miss Poppy Crew.' "

Pomeroy wiped his forehead. "This is pretty awful!" said he. Then:-

" 'Some of these Sundays Major Wilson's false teeth will drop into the collecting bag. Let him either get a new set, or else take off that smile when he walks round with the bag. With lips firmly compressed there is no reason why the present set may not last for years.'

"That's where the answer comes in," said Pomeroy, glancing at the open letter upon his table. "I expect he'll be round with a stick presently. What's this?

" 'We don't know if Miss Cissy Dufour and Captain Copperley are secretly married or not. If not, they should be. He could then enter Laburnum Villa instead of wearing out the garden gate by leaning on it!'

"Good heavens, listen to this one! 'Mr. Malceby, the grocer, is back from Hythe. But why the bag of sand among his luggage? Surely sugar gives a sufficient profit at its present price. As we are on the subject, we cannot but remark upon the increased water rate paid last quarter by the Silverside Dairy Company. What do they do with all this water? The public has a right to know.'

"Good Lord, listen to this! 'It is very wrong to say that our popular member, Sir James Tonder, was drunk at the garden party of the Mayor. It is true that he tripped over his own leg when he tried to dance the tango, but that can fairly be attributed to his own obvious physical disabilities. As a matter of fact, several guests who only drank one glass of the Mayor's chamapgne (natural 1928) were very ill in consequence, so that it is most unfair to put so uncharitable an interpretation upon one member's *faux pas*.'

"That's worth a thousand pounds in any Court," groaned Pomeroy. "My dear, Rothschild couldn't stand the actions that this paper will bring on us."

The ladies of the family had shown a regrettable inclination to laugh, but his words made them properly solemn. He continued his reading.

" 'Mrs. Peddigrew has started a six-cylinder which is listed at seven hundred and fifty pounds. How she does it nobody knows. Her late husband was a little rat of a man who did off jobs down in the City. He could not have left so much. This matter wants looking into.'

"Why, he was the vice-chairman of the Baltic," said Pomeroy. "These people are stark, staring mad. Listen to this.

" 'Evensong will be at six-thirty. Yes, Mrs. Mould, at six-thirty sharp. And Mr. King will be on the left-hand seat well within view. We can count on your attendance. If you are not a pillar of the church, you are generally sneaking behind one!' Oh, Lord, here's another.

" 'If Mr. Goldbury, of 7, Cheesman Place, will call at the Vicarage he will receive back the trouser-button which he put in the bag last Sunday. It is useless to the Vicar, whereas in its right place it might be most important to Mr. Goldbury!' There's no use laughing, you two. You won't laugh when you see the lawyer's letters. Listen to this.

" ' "Prithee why so pale, fond lover? Prithee why so pale?" The question is addressed to William Briggs, our dentist friend of Hope Street. Has the lady in pink chiffon turned you down, or is it merely that you are behind with your rent, as usual? Cheer up, William. You have our best wishes.'

"Good gracious! They grow worse and worse. Just listen to this.

" 'If any motorists get into trouble, my advice to them is to see Chief Constable Walton in his private room at the Town Hall. Cheques will, of course, not be received. But surely it is far better to pay a small sum across the table in ready cash – asking for no receipt – than to have the trouble and expense of proceedings in the Court.'

"My word, we shall have some proceedings in the Court before we are through. Here is a tit-bit which will keep the lawyers busy: 'The Voyd-Merriman wedding was a most interesting affair and we wish the young couple every happiness. We say "young" out of courtesy, for it is an open secret that the bride will never see thirty-five again. The groom also is, we should say, getting rather long in the tooth. By the way, why did he start and look over his shoulder when the clergyman spoke of "any just cause or impediment"? No doubt it was perfectly harmless, but it gave rise to some ill-natured gossip. We had pleasure in attending the reception afterwards. There was a detective to guard the presents. We really think that his services could have been dispensed with, for they would never have been in danger. Major Wilson's two brass napkin rings were the pick of the bunch. There was a cheque in an envelope from the bride's father. We have heard what the exact figure was, and we quite appreciate the need for an envelope. However, it will pay for the cab to the station. It is understood that the happy couple will get as far as Margate for their honeymoon, and if the money holds out they may extend their travels to Ramsgate. Address: the Red Cow public house, near the Station.'

"Why, these are the richest people in Rotherheath," said Pomeroy, wiping his forehead.

"There is a lot more, but that is enough to settle our hash. I think we had best sell up for what we can get and clear out of the town. My gosh, those two folk must have got out of an asylum. Anyhow, my first job must be to see them. Maybe they are millionaires who can afford to pay for their little jokes."

His mission proved, however, to be fruitless. On inquiry at the address given he found that it was an empty house. The caretaker from next door knew nothing of the matter. It was clear now why the young man had waited at the gate for his parcel. What was Pomeroy to do next? Apparently he could only sit and wait for the arrival of the writs. However, it was a very different document which was handed in at his door two evenings later. It was headed "R.S.B.Y.P." and ran thus:-

"A special meeting of the R.S.B.Y.P. will be held at 16, Stanmore Terrace, in the billiard room of John Anderson, J.P., to-night at 9 p.m. The presence of Mr. James Pomeroy, printer, is urgently needed. The matter under discussion is his liability for certain scandalous statements recently printed in the Parish Magazine."

It may well be imagined that Mr. Pomeroy was punctual at the appointment.

"Mr. Anderson is not at home himself," said the footman, "but young Mr. Robert Anderson and his friends are receiving." There was a humorous twinkle in the footman's eyes.

The printer was shown into a small waiting room, where two men, one a postman and the other apparently a small tradesman, were seated. He could not help observing that they were both as harassed and miserable as he was himself. They looked at him with dull, lack-lustre eyes, but were too dispirited to talk, nor did he feel sufficient energy to break the silence. Presently one of them and then the other was called out. Finally the footman came for him, and threw wide a door.

"Mr. James Pomeroy," cried the footman.

At the end of a large music-room, which was further adorned by a billiard table, was sitting a semicircle of young people, all very serious, and all with writing materials before them. None was above twenty-one years of age, and they were about equally divided as to sex. Among them were the two customers who had lured him to his doom. They both smiled at him most affectionately, in spite of his angry stare.

"Pray sit down, Mr. Pomeroy," said a very young man in evening dress, who acted as Chairman. "There are one or two questions which, as President of the R.S.B.Y.P., it is my duty to put to you. I believe that you have been somewhat alarmed by this incident of the Parish Magazine?"

"Of course I have," said Pomeroy, in a surly voice.

"May I ask if your sleep has been affected?"

"I have not closed my eyes since it happened."

There was a subdued murmur of applause, and several members leaned across to shake hands with Mr. Robert Anderson.

"Did it affect your future plans?"

"I had thought of leaving the town."

"Excellent! I think, fellow-members, that there is no doubt that the monthly gold medal should be awarded to Mr. Anderson and Miss Duncan for their very meritorious performance, which has been well conceived and cleverly carried out. To relieve your natural anxiety we must tell you at once, Mr. Pomeroy, that you have been the victim of a joke."

"It's likely to be a pretty costly one," said the printer.

"Not at all. No harm has been done. No leaflets have been sent out. The letters which have reached you emanate from ourselves. We are, Mr. Pomeroy, the Rotherheath Society of Bright Young People, who endeavour to make the world a merrier and more lively place by the exercise of our wit. Upon this occasion a prize was offered for whichever member or members could most effectually put the wind up some resident in this suburb. There have been several candidates, but on the whole the prize must be awarded as already said."

"But — but — it's unjustifiable!" stammered Pomeroy.

"Entirely," said the Chairman, cheerfully. "I think that all our proceedings may come under that head. On the other hand, we remind our victims that they have unselfishly sacrificed themselves for the general hilarity of the community. A special silver medal, which I will now affix to your coat, will be your souvenir of the occasion."

"And I'll speak to my father when he comes back," said Anderson. "What I mean is, there is printing and what not to be done for the firm."

"And my father really edits the Parish Magazine. That's what put it into our heads," said Miss Duncan. "Maybe we can get you the printing after all."

"And there is whisky and soda on the sideboard, and a good cigar," said the President.

So Mr. Pomeroy eventually went out into the night, thinking that after all youth will be served, and it would be a dull world without it.

THE END OF DEVIL HAWKER

---◆---

I

TOM CRIBB'S PARLOUR

There is a fascinating little print shop round the corner of Drury Lane. When you pass through the old oaken doorway and into the dim, dusty interior you seem to have wandered into some corridor leading back through time, for on every side of you are the pictures of the past. But very specially I value that table on the left where lies the great pile of portrait prints heaped up in some sort of order of date. There you see the pictures of the men who stood round the throne of the young Victoria, of Melbourne, of Peel, of Wellington, and then you come on the D'Orsay and Lady Blessington period, and the long and wonderful series of H. B., the great unknown John Doyle, who in his day was a real power in the land. Further back still you come on the bucks and prize-fighters of the Regency, the pompous Jackson, the sturdy Cribb, the empty Brummell, the chubby Alvanley. And then you may chace upon a face which you cannot pass without a second and a longer look. It is a face which Mephistopheles might have owned, thin, dark, keen, with bushy brows, and fierce, alert eyes which glare out from beneath them. There is a full-length coloured print which shows him to be tall and magnificently proportioned, with broad shoulders, slim waist, clad in a tightly-buttoned green coat, buckskin breeches, and high Hessian boots. Below is the inscription, "Sir John Hawker," and that is the "Devil Hawker" of the legends.

In his short but vivid career, the end of which is here outlined, Hawker was the bully of the town. The bravest shrank away from the angry, insolent glare of those baleful eyes. He was a famous swordsman and a remarkable pistol shot, so remarkable that three times he starred the knee-cap of his man, the most painful injury which he could inflict. But above all he was the best amateur boxer of his day, and had he taken to the ring it is likely that he would have made a name. His hitting is said to have been the most ferocious ever seen, and it was his amusement to try out novices at Cribb's rooms, which were his favourite haunt, and to teach them how to stand punishment. It gratified his pride to show his skill, and his cruel nature to administer pain to others. It was in these very rooms of Cribb that this little sketch of those days opens, where, as on a marionette stage, I would try to show you what manner of place it was and what manner of people walked London in those full-blooded, brutal, and virile old days.

First as to the place. It is at the corner of Panton Street, and you see over a broad, red-curtained door the sign, "Thomas Cribb. Dealer in Liquor and Tobacco," with "The Union Arms" printed above. The door leads into a tiled passage which opens on the left into a common bar, behind which, save on special evenings, a big, bull-faced, honest John Bull of a man may be seen with two assistants, each of the sparring partner type, handing out refreshment to the public, and imbibing gratis a great deal more than was good for their athletic figures. Already Tom is getting a waist-line which will cause his trainer and himself many a weary day at his next battle – if indeed the brave old fellow has not already come to the last of his fights, when he defended the honour of England by breaking the cast-iron jaw of Molyneaux, the black.

If instead of turning into the common bar you continue down the passage, you find a green baize door with the word "Parlour" printed across one upper panel of glass. Push it open and you are in a room which is spacious and comfortable. There are sawdust on the floor, numerous wooden armchairs, round tables for the card-players, a small bar presided over by Miss Lucy Stagg, a lady who had been accused of many things, but never of shyness, in the corner, and a fine collection of sporting pictures round the walls. At the back were swing doors with the words "Boxing Saloon" printed across them, leading into a large, bare apartment with a roped ring in the centre, and many pairs of gloves hanging upon the walls, belonging for the most part to the Corinthians who came up to have lessons from the champion.

It was early in the particular evening of which I speak, and there was no one in the parlour save Cribb himself, who expected the quality that night and was cleaning up in anticipation. Lucy wiped glasses languidly in her little bar. Beside the entrance door was a small, shrivelled weasel of a man, Billy Jakes by name, who sat behind a green baize table, in receipt of custom as a book-maker, dog fancier, or cock supplier – a privilege for which he paid Tom a good round sum every year. As no customers had appeared he wandered over to the little bar.

"Well, things are quiet to-night, Lucy."

She looked up from polishing her glasses.

"I expect they will be more lively soon, Mr. Jakes. It is full early."

"Well, Lucy, you look very pretty to-night. I expect I shall have to marry you yet."

"La, Mr. Jakes, how you do carry on!"

"Tell me, Lucy, do you want to make some money?"

"Everyone wants that, Mr. Jakes."

"How much can you lay your hands on?"

"I dare say I could find fifty pounds at a pinch."

"Wouldn't you like to turn it into a hundred?"

"Why, of course I would."

"It's Saracesca for the Oaks. I'd give you two to one, which is better than I give the others. She's a cert if ever there is one."

"Well, if you say so, Mr. Jakes. The money is upstairs in my box. But if you can really turn it into –"

Fortunately honest Tom Cribb had been within earshot of this little debate, and he now caught the man roughly by the sleeve and twirled him in the direction of his table.

"You dirty dog, doing the poor girl out of her hard-earned savings."

"All right, Tom. Only a joke! Only Bill Jakes's little joke. I wouldn't have let you lose, Lucy!"

"That's enough," said Tom. "Don't you heed him, Lucy. Keep your money in your box."

The green swing door opened out and a number of bucks, in black coats, brown coats, green coats, and purple, came filing into the room. The shrill voice of Jakes was at once uplifted, and his clamour filled the air.

"Now, my noble sportsmen," he cried, "back your opinions. There is a bag of gold waiting and you have only to put your hands in. How about Woodstock for the Derby? How about Saracesca for the Oaks? Four to one! Four to one! Two to one, bar one!"

The Corinthians gathered for a moment round the bookie's table, for his patter amused them.

"Lots of time for that, Jakes," said Lord Rufton, a big, bluff county magnate.

"But the odds are shorter every day. Now's your time, my noble gamesters! Now's the time to sow the seed! Gold to be had for the asking, waitin' there for you to pick up. I like to pay it. It pleases me to see happy faces round me. I like to see them smiling. Now's your time."

"Why, half the field may scratch before the race," said Sir Charles Trevor, the smiling, imperturbable Charles, whose estate had been sucked dry by its owner's wild excesses.

"No race, no pay. The old firm gives every gamester a run for his money. The knowing ones are all on to it. Sir John Hawker has five hundred on Woodstock."

"Well, Devil Hawker knows what he is about," said Lord Annerley, a dashing young Corinthian.

"Have fifty on the filly for the Oaks, Lord Rufton, four to one?"

"Very good, Jakes," said the nobleman, handing out a note. "I suppose I shall find you after the race?"

"Sitting here at this table, my lord. Old-established place of business. You've got a certainty, my lord."

"Well," said a young Corinthian, "if it is as certain as that I'll have fifty too."

"Right you are, my noble sportsman. I book it at three to one."

"I thought it was four."

"It was four. Now it is three. You're lucky to get in before it is two. Will you take your winnings in paper or gold?"

"Well, in gold."

"Very good, sir. You'll find me waiting at this table with a bag of gold at ten by the clock on the day after the race. It will be in a green baize bag with a grip so as you can easily carry it. By the way, I've got a fighting cock that's never been beat. Would any of you gentlemen —"

But the door had swung open and Sir John Hawker's handsome figure and sinister face filled the gap. The others moved towards the small bar. Hawker paused for a moment at the bookie's table.

"Hullo, Jakes! Doing some fool out of his money as usual?"

"Tut, tut, Sir John; you should know me by now."

"Know you, you rascal! You have had a cool two thousand out of me from first to last. I know you too well."

"All you want is to persevere. You'll soon have it all back, Sir John."

"Hold your tongue, I say. I have had enough."

"No offence, my noble sportsman. But I've a brindled terrier down at the stables, that's the best at rats in London."

"I wonder he hasn't had a nip at you, then. Hullo, Tom!"

Cribb had come forward as usual to greet his Corinthian guests.

"Good evening, Sir John. Going to put them on to-night?"

"Well, I'll see. What have you got?"

"Half-a-dozen up from old Bristol. That place is as full of milling coves as a bin is of bottles."

"I may try one of them over."

"Then play light, Sir John. You cracked the ribs of that lad from Lincoln. You broke his heart for fighting."

"It may as well be broke early as late. What's the use of him if he can't take punishment?"

Several more men had come into the room – one of them exceedingly drunk, another just a little less so. They were two of the Tom and Jerry clique who wandered day and night on the old round from the Haymarket to Panton Street and St. James's, imagining that they were seeing life. The drunken one, a young hawbuck from the Shires, was noisy and combative. His friend was trying to put some term to their adventures.

"Come, George," he coaxed, "we'll just have one drink here. Then one at the Dive and one at the Cellars, and wind up with broiled bones at Mother Simpson's."

The name of the dish started ideas in the drunken man's brain. He staggered in the direction of the landlord.

"Broiled bones," he cried, "d'you hear? I want broiled bones. Fetch me dish – large dish – of broiled bones this instant – under pain – displeasure."

Cribb, who was well accustomed to such visitors, continued his conversation with Hawker without taking the slightest notice. They were discussing a possible opponent for old Tom Shelton, the navvy, when George broke in again.

"Where the devil's those broiled bones? Here, landlord, ole Tom Cribb! Tom, give me large dish broiled bones this instant or I punch your old head." As Cribb still took not the faintest heed, George became more bellicose.

"No broiled bones!" he cried. "Very good. Prepare defend yourself."

"Don't hit him, George!" cried his more sober companion in alarm. "It's the champion."

"It's a lie. I am the champion. I'll give him smack in the chops. See if I don't."

For the first time Cribb turned a slow eye in his direction.

"No dancin' allowed here, sir," he said.

"I'm not dancing. I'm sparring."

"Well, don't do it, whatever it is."

"I'm going to fight you. Going to give ole Tom a smack in the chops."

"Some other time, sir. I'm busy."

"Where's those bones? Last time of asking."

"What bones? What is he talkin' of?"

"Sorry, Tom, but have to give you dam' good thrashing. Yes, Tom, very sorry, but must have lesson."

He made several wild strokes in the air, quite out of distance, and finally fell upon his knees. His friend picked him up.

"What d'you want to be so foolish for, George?"

"I had him nearly beat."

Tom looked reproachfully at the soberer friend.

"I am surprised at you, Mr. Trelawney."

"Couldn't help it, Tom. He would mix port and brandy."

"You must take him out."

"Come on, George, you've got to go out."

"Got to go! No, sir. Round two. Come up smilin'. Time!"

Tom Cribb gave a sign and a stalwart potman threw the pugnacious George over his shoulder and carried him out of the room, kicking violently, while his friend walked behind. Cribb laughed.

"There's seldom an evening that I don't have that sort of nuisance."

"By God," said Hawker, "they would not do it twice to me. I'd send him home and his wench wouldn't know him."

"I haven't the heart to touch them. It pleases the poor things to say they have punched the champion of England."

The room had now begun to fill up. At one end a circle had formed round the bookie's table. On the other side there was a group at the small private bar, where very broad chaff was being exchanged between some of the younger bucks and Lucy, who was well able to take care of herself. Cribb had gone inside the swing doors to prepare the boxing, while Hawker wandered from group to group, leaving among these fearless men, hard-riding horsemen of the Shires and dare-devils at every sport, a vague feeling of repulsion which showed itself in a somewhat formal response to his brief greetings. He paused at one chattering group and looked sardonically at a youth who stood somewhat apart listening to, but not joining in, the gay exchange of repartees. He was a well-built young man with a singularly beautiful head crowned by a mass of auburn curls. His figure might have stood for Adonis, were it not that one foot was slightly drawn up, which caused him to wear a rather unsightly boot.

"Good evening, Hawker," said he.

"Good evening, Byron. Is this one of your hours of idleness?"

The allusion was to a book of verse which the young nobleman had just brought out, and which had been severely handled by the critics.

The poet seemed annoyed, for he was sensitive on the point.

"At least I cannot be accused of idleness to-day," said he. "I swam three miles down stream from Lambeth, and perhaps you have not done so much."

"Well done," said Hawker. "I hear of you at Angelo's and Jackson's, too. But fencing needs a quick foot. I'd stick to the water if I were you." He glanced down at the malformed limb.

Byron's blue-grey eyes blazed with indignation.

"When I wish your advice as to my personal habits, Sir John Hawker, I will ask for it."

"No harm meant," said Hawker, carelessly. "I am a blunt fellow and always say what I think."

Lord Rufton plucked at Byron's sleeve. "That's enough said," he whispered.

"Of course," added Hawker, "if anyone does not like my ways they can always find me at White's Club or my lodgings in Charles Street."

Byron, who was utterly fearless, and ready, though he was still only a Cambridge undergraduate, to face any man in the world, was about to make some angry reply, in spite of the well-meant warnings of Lord Rufton, when Tom Cribb came bustling in and interrupted the scene.

"All ready, my lords and gentlemen. The fighting men are in their places. Jack Scroggins and Ben Burn will begin."

The company began to move towards the door of the sparring saloon. As they filed in Hawker advanced quietly and touched the reckless baronet, Sir Charles Trevor, upon the shoulder.

"I must have a word with you, Charles."

"Damn it, John, I want to get a ring-side seat."

"Never mind that. I must have a word."

The others passed in. Devil Hawker and Sir Charles had the room to themselves, save for Jakes counting his money at his distant table, and the girl Lucy coming and going in her little alcove. Hawker led Sir Charles to a central seat.

"I have to speak to you, Charles, of that three thousand you owe me. It pains me vastly, but what am I to do? I have my own debts to settle, and no easy matter."

"I have the matter in hand, John."

"But it presses."

"I'll pay it all right. Give me time."

"What time?"

"We are cutting the oaks at Selincourt. They should all be down by the fall. I can get an advance then that will clear all."

"I don't want to press you, Charles. If you would like a sporting flutter to clear your debt I'm ready to give it to you at once."

"What do you mean?"

"Well, double or quits. Six thousand or nothing. If you're not afraid to take a chance I'll let you have one."

"Afraid, John. I don't like that word."

"You were always a brave gamester, Charles. Just as you like in the matter. But you might clear yourself with a turn of the card, while, on the other hand, if all the Selincourt timber is going six thousand will be no more to you than three."

"Well, it's a sporting offer, John. You say the turn of a card. Do you mean one simple draw?"

"Why not? Sudden death. Win or lose. What say you?"

"I agree."

A pack of cards was lying on a nearby table. Hawker stretched out a long arm and picked them up.

"Will these do?"

"By all means."

He spread them out with a sweep of his hand.

"Do you care to shuffle?"

"No, John. Take them as they are."

"Shall it be a single draw?"

"By all means."

"Will you lead?"

Sir Charles Trevor was a seasoned gambler, but never before had three thousand pounds hung upon the turn of a single card. But he was a reckless plunger, and roared with laughter as he turned up the queen of clubs.

"That should do you, John."

"Possibly," said Hawker, and turned the ace of spades.

"My God!" cried Trevor, and staggered as he rose from his seat. "I thought I had cleared myself, and now it is six thousand."

"To wait until the oaks are cut," said Hawker. "In September I shall present my little bill. Meanwhile, perhaps a note of hand –"

"Do you doubt my word, John?"

"No, no, Charles. But business is business. Who knows what may happen? I'll have a note of hand."

"Very good. You'll have it by the post to-morrow. Well, I bear no grudge. The luck was yours. Shall we have a glass upon it?"

"You were always a brave loser, Charles." The two men walked together to the little bar in the corner.

Had either looked back he would have seen a sight which would have surprised him. During the whole incident the little book-maker had sat absorbed over his accounts, but with a pair of piercing eyes glancing up every now and then at the two gamblers. Little of their talk had been audible from where he sat, but their actions had spoken for themselves. Now, with amazing but furtive speed, he stole across, picked up one card from the table, and hurried back to his perch, concealing it inside his coat. The two gentlemen, having taken their refreshment, turned towards the boxing saloon, Sir Charles disappearing through the swing doors, from behind which came the thud of heavy blows, the breathing of hard-spent men, and every now and then a murmur of admiration or of criticism. Hawker was about to follow his companion when a thought struck him and he returned to the card table, gathering up the scattered cards. Suddenly he was aware that Jakes was at his elbow, and that two very shrewd and malignant eyes were looking up into his own.

"Hadn't you best count them, my noble sportsman?"

"What d'you mean?" The Devil's great black brows were drawn down, and his glance was like a rapier thrust.

"If you count them you'll find one missing."

"Why are you grinning at me, you rascal?"

"One card missing, my noble sportsman. A good winning card, too – the ace of spades. A useful card, Sir John."

"Where is it, then?"

"Little Billy Jakes has it. It's here –" and he slapped his breast pocket. "A little playing card with the mark of a thumb-nail on one corner of the back."

"You infernal blackguard!"

Jakes was no coward, but he shrank away from that terrible face.

"Hands off, my noble sportsman! Hands off, for your own sake! You can knock me about. That's easily done. But it won't end there. I've got the card. I could call back Sir Charles and fill this room in a jiffy. There would be an end of you, my beauty."

"It's all a lie – a damned lie."

"Right you are. Say so, if you like. Shall I call in the others and you can prove it a lie? Shall I show the cards to Lord Rufton and the rest?"

Hawker's dark face was moving convulsively. His hands were twitching with his desire to break the back of this little weasel across his knee. With an effort he mastered himself.

"Hold on, Jakes. We have always been great friends. What do you want? Speak low or the girl will hear."

"Now that's talking. You got six thousand just now. I want half."

"You want three thousand pounds. What for?"

"You're a man of sense. You know what for. I've a tongue and I can hold it if it's worth my while."

Hawker considered for a moment.

"Well, suppose I agree?"

"Then we can fix it so."

"Say no more. We will consider it as agreed."

He turned away, his mind full of plans by which he could gain time and disavow the whole business. But Jakes was not a man so easily fooled.

"Hold on, my noble sportsman. Hold on an instant. Just a word of writing to settle it."

"You dog! Is my word not enough?"

"No, Sir John; not by a long way. No, if you hit me I'll yell. Keep your hands off. I tell you I want your signature."

"Not a word."

"Very good, then. It's finished." Jakes started for the door of the saloon.

"Hold hard! What am I to write?"

"I'll do the writing." He turned to the little alcove where Lucy, who was accustomed to every sort of wrangling and argument was sitting among her bottles.

"Here, my dear, wake up! I want pen and ink."

"Yes, sir."

"And paper."

"There is a bill-head. Will that do? Dearie me, it's marked with wine."

"Never mind, that will do."

Jakes seated himself at a table, and scribbled while Hawker watched him with eyes of death. Jakes walked over to him with the scrawl completed. Hawker read it over in a low mutter.

" 'In consideration of your silence –' " He paused and glared.

"Well, that's true, ain't it? You don't give me half for the love of William Jakes, Esquire, do you now?"

"Curse you, Jakes! Curse you to Hell!"

"Let it out, my noble sportsman. Let it out, or you'll bust. Curse me again. Then sign that paper."

" 'The sum of three thousand pounds to be paid on the date when there is a settlement between me and Sir Charles Trevor.' Well, give me the pen and have done. There! Now give me that card."

Jakes had thrust the signed paper into his inner pocket.

"Give me the card, I say!"

"When the money is paid, Sir John. That's only fair."

"You devil!"

"Can't find the right word, can you? It's not been invented yet, I expect."

Jakes may have been very near his death at that moment. The furious passions of the bully had reached a point when even his fears of exposure could hardly hold him in check. But the saloon door had swung open and Cribb entered the room. He looked with surprise at the ill-assorted couple.

"Now, Mr. Jakes, time is up, you know. You've passed your hours."

"I know, Tom, but I had an important settling up with Sir John Hawker. Had I not, Sir John?"

"You've missed the first bout, Sir John. Come and see Jack Randall take a novice."

Hawker took a last scowl at the bookmaker and followed the champion into the saloon. Jakes gathered up his papers into his professional bag and went across to the little bar.

"A double brandy, my dear," said he to Lucy. "I've had a good evening, but it's been a bit of a strain upon my nerves."

II

WATIER'S CLUB

It was late in September that the grand old ancestral oaks of Selincourt were given over to the contractor, and that their owner, having at last a large balance at his bankers, was able to redeem the more pressing of his debts. It was only a day later that Sir John Hawker, with Sir Charles's note of hand for six thousand pounds in his pocket, found himself riding down in the high road at Six Mile Bottom near Newmarket. His mount was a great black stallion, as powerful and sinister as himself. He was brooding over his own rather precarious affairs, which involved every shilling which he could raise, when there was a click of hoofs beside him, and there was Billy Jakes upon his well-known chestnut cob.

"Good evening, my noble sportsman," said he. "I was looking out for you at the stables, and when I saw you ride away I thought it was time to come after you. I want my settlement, Sir John."

"What settlement? What are you talking of?"

"Your written promise to pay three thousand. I know you have had your money."

"I don't know what you are talking about. Keep clear of me or you will get a cut or two from this hunting crop."

"Oh, that's the game, is it? We will see about that. Do you deny your signature upon this paper?"

"Have you the paper on you?"

"What's that to you?"

It was not wise, Billy Jakes, to trust yourself alone upon a country by-road with one of the most dangerous men in England. For once your cupidity has been greater than your shrewdness. A quick glance of those deadly dark eyes to right and to left, and then the heavy hunting crop came down with a crash upon the bookmaker's head. With a cry he dropped from the cob, and he had hardly reached the ground before the Devil had sprung from the saddle, and with his left arm through his bridle rein to hold down his plunging horse he was rapidly running his right hand through the pockets of the prostrate man. With a bitter curse he realised that, however imprudent Jakes had been, he had not been such a fool as to carry the paper about with him. Hawker rose, looked down at his half-conscious enemy, and then slowly drew his spur across his face. A moment later he had sprung into his saddle and was on his way Londonwards, leaving the sprawling and bleeding figure in the dust of the highway. He laughed with exultation as he rode, for vengeance was sweet to him, and he seldom missed it. What could Jakes do? If he took him into the Criminal Courts it was only such an assault as was common enough in those days of violence. If, on the other hand, he pursued the matter of the card and the agreement, it was an old story now, and who would take the word of the notorious bookmaker against that of one of the best known men in London. Of course, it was a case of forgery and blackmail. Hawker looked down at his bloody spur and felt well content with his morning's work.

Jakes was raised to his feet by some kindly traveller and he was brought back, half conscious, to Newmarket. There for three days he kept his room and nursed both his injuries and his grievance. Upon the fourth day he reached London, and that night he made his way to the Albany and knocked at a door which bore upon a shining brass plate the name of Sir Charles Trevor.

It was the first Tuesday of the month, the day on which the committee of Watier's Club was wont to assemble. Half-a-dozen of them had sauntered into the great board-room, decorated with heavy canvases on the walls, and with highly-polished dark mahogany furniture, which showed up richly against the huge expanse of red Kidderminster carpet. The Duke of Bridgewater, a splendid rubicund old gentleman, grey-haired but virile, leaning heavily upon an amber-headed cane, came hobbling in and bowed affably to the waiting committee men.

"How is the gout, your Grace?"

"A little sharp at times. But I can still get my foot into the stirrup. Well, well, I suppose we had better get to work." He took his seat in the centre of a half-moon at one end of the room. Raising his quizzing-glass he looked round him.

"Where is Lord Foley?"

"He is racing, sir. He will not be here."

"The dog! He takes his duties too lightly. I would rather be on the Heath myself."

"I expect we all would."

"Ah, is that you, Lord Rufton? How are you? Colonel D'Acre! Bunbury, Scott, Poyntz, Vandeleur, good day to you! Where is Sir Charles Trevor?"

"He is in the members' room," said Lord Rufton. "He said he would wait your Grace's pleasure. The fact is that he has a personal interest in a case which comes before us, and he thought he should not have a hand in judging it."

"Ah, very delicate! very delicate indeed!" The Duke had taken up the agenda paper and stared at it through his glass. "Dear me, dear me! A member accused of cheating at cards! And Sir John Hawker, too! One of the best known men in the club. Too bad! Too bad! Who is the accuser?"

"A bookmaker named Jakes, your Grace."

"I know him. Has a stance at Tom Cribb's. A damned rascal if ever I saw one. However, we must look into it. Who has the matter in hand?"

"I have been asked to attend to it," said Lord Rufton.

"I am not sure," said the Duke, "that we are right in taking notice of what such a person says about a member of this club. Surely the Law Courts are open."

"I entirely agree with your Grace," said a solemn man upon the Duke's left. He was General Scott, who was said to live on toast and water and win ten thousand a year from his less sober companions. "I would point out to you, sir, that the alleged cheating was at the expense of Sir Charles Trevor, a member of the club. It was not Sir Charles, however, who moved in the matter. There was a violent quarrel between the man Jakes and Sir John Hawker, and this is the result."

"Then the bookmaker has brought the case before us for revenge," said the Duke. "We must move carefully in this matter. I think we had best see Sir Charles first. Call Sir Charles."

The tall, red-plushed footman entered and disappeared. A moment later, Sir Charles, debonair and smiling, stood before the committee.

"Good day, Sir Charles," said the Duke. "This is a very painful business."

"Very, your Grace."

"I understand from what is on the agenda paper that on May 3rd of this year you met Sir John at Cribb's parlour and you cut cards with him, at three thousand pounds a cut."

"A single cut, your Grace."

"And you lost?"

"Unfortunately."

"Well, now, did you in any way suspect foul play at the time?"

"Not in the least."

"Then you have no charge against Sir John?"

"None on my own behalf. Other people have something to say."

"Well, we can listen to them in their turn. Won't you take a chair, Sir Charles? Even if you do not vote there can be no objection to your presence. Is Sir John in attendance?"

"Yes, sir."

"And the witness?"

"Yes, sir."

"Well, gentlemen, it is clearly a very serious matter, and I understand that Sir John is a difficult person to deal with. However, we can make no exceptions, and we are numerous enough, and have, I trust, sufficient social weight to carry this affair to a conclusion." He rang for the footman. "Place a chair in the centre, please! Now tell Sir John Hawker that the committee would be honoured if he would step this way."

A moment later the formidable face and figure of the Devil had appeared at the door. With a scowl at the members present he strode forward, bowed to the Duke, and seated himself opposite the semicircle formed by the committee.

"In the first place, Sir John," said the Duke, "you will allow me to express my regret and that of your fellow-members that it should be our unpleasant duty to ask you to appear before us. No doubt the matter will prove to be a mere misunderstanding, but we felt that it was due to your own reputation as well as to that of the club that no time should be lost in setting the matter right."

"Your Grace," said Hawker, leaning foward and emphasising his remarks with his clenched hand, "I protest strongly against these proceedings. I have come here because it shall never be said that I was shy of meeting any charge, however preposterous. But

I would put it to you, gentlemen, that no man's reputation is safe if the committee of his club is prepared to take up any vague slander that may circulate against him."

"Kindly read the terms of the charge, Lord Rufton."

Lord Rufton picked up the agenda paper.

"The assertion is," he read, "that at ten o'clock on the night of Thursday, May 3rd, in the parlour of Tom Cribb's house, the Union Arms, Sir John Hawker did by means of marked cards win money from Sir Charles Trevor, both being members of Watier's Club."

Hawker sprang from his chair.

"It is a lie, a damned lie!" he cried.

The Duke held up a deprecating hand.

"No doubt, no doubt. I think, however, Sir John, that you can hardly describe it as a vague slander."

"It is monstrous. What is to prevent such a charge being level-led at your Grace? How would you like, sir, to be dragged up before your fellow-members?"

"Excuse me, Sir John," said the Duke, urbanely. "The question at present is not what might be preferred against me, but what actually is preferred against you. You will, I am sure, appreciate the distinction. What do you propose, Lord Rufton?"

"It is my unpleasant duty, Sir John," said Lord Rufton, "to array the evidence before the committee. You will, I am sure, acquit me of any personal feeling in the matter."

"I look on you, sir, as a damned mischievous busybody."

The Duke put up his pudgy, many-ringed hand in protest.

"I am afraid, Sir John, that I must ask you to be more guarded in your language. To me it is immaterial, but I happen to know that General Scott has an objection to swearing. Lord Rufton is merely doing his duty in presenting the case."

Hawker shrugged his broad shoulders.

"I protest against the whole proceedings," he said.

"Your protest will be duly entered in the minutes. We have heard before you entered the evidence of Sir Charles Trevor. He has no personal complaint. So far as I can see there is no case."

"Ha! Your Grace is a man of sense. Was ever an indignity put upon a man of honour on so small a pretext?"

"There is further evidence, your Grace," said Lord Rufton. "I will call Mr. William Jakes."

Word was passed to the gorgeous footman, who swung open the massive door, and Jakes was ushered in. It was a month or more since the assault, but the spur mark still shone red across his sallow cheek. He held his cloth cap in his hand, and rounded his back as a tribute to the company, but his little cunning eyes from under their ginger lashes twinkled as knowingly, not to say impudently, as ever.

"You are William Jakes, the bookmaker?" said the Duke.

"The greatest rascal in London," interpolated Hawker.

"There is one greater within three yards of me," the little man snarled. Then, turning to the Duke: "I'm William Jakes, your worship, known as Billy Jakes at Tattersall's. If you want to back a horse, your worship, or care to buy a gamecock or a ratter, you'll get the best price—"

"Silence, sir," said Lord Rufton. "Advance to this chair."

"Certainly, my noble sportsman."

"Don't sit. Stand beside it."

"At your service, gentlemen."

"Shall I cross-examine, your Grace? I understand, Jakes, that you were in Cribb's back parlour on the night of May 3rd of this year?"

"Lord bless you, sir, I'm there every night. It's where I meet my noble Corinthians."

"It is a sporting house, I understand."

"Well, my lord, I can't teach you much about it." There was a titter from the committee, and the Duke broke in:—

"I dare say we have all enjoyed Tom's hospitality at one time or another," he said.

"Yes, indeed, your Grace. Well I remember the night when you danced on the crossed baccy pipes."

"Keep your witness to the point," said the smiling Duke.

"Tell us now what you saw pass between Sir John Hawker and Sir Charles Trevor."

"I saw all there was to see. You can trust little Billy Jakes for that. There was to be a cutting game. Sir John reached out for the cards which lay on another table. I had seen him look over those cards in advance and turn the end of one or two with his thumbnail."

"You liar!" cried Sir John.

"It's an easy trick to mark them so that none can see. I've done — I know another man that can do it. You must keep your right thumbnail long and sharp. Well, look at Sir John's now."

Hawker sprang from his chair.

"Your Grace, am I to be exposed to these insults?"

"Sit down, Sir John. Your indignation is most natural. I suppose it is not a fact that your right thumbnail —"

"Certainly not."

"Ask to see," cried Jakes.

"Perhaps you would not mind showing your nail?"

"I will do nothing of the kind."

"Of course you are quite within your rights in refusing – quite!" said the Duke. Whether your refusal might in any way prejudice your case is a point which you have no doubt considered. Pray continue, Jakes."

"Well, they cut and Sir John won. When he turned his back I got the winning card, and saw that it was marked. I showed it to Sir John when we were alone."

"What did he say?"

"Well, my lord, I wouldn't like to repeat before such select company as this some of the things he said. He carried on shocking. But after a bit he saw the game was up and he consented to my having half shares."

"Then," said the Duke, "you became by your own admission the compounder of a felony."

Jakes gave a comical grimace.

"No breaks here! This ain't a Court, is it? Just a private house, as one might say, with one gentleman chatting easy-like with other ones. Well, then, that's just what I did do."

The Duke shrugged his shoulders.

"Really, Lord Rufton, I do not see how we can attach any importance to the word of such a witness. On his own confession he is a perfect rascal."

"Your Grace, I'm surprised at you!"

"I would not condemn any man – far less the member of an honourable club – on this man's word."

"I quite agree, your Grace," said Rufton. "There are, however, some corroborative documents."

"Yes, my noble sportsmen," cried Jakes, in a sort of ecstasy, "there's lots more to come. Billy's got a bit up his sleeve for a finish. How's that?" He pulled a pack of cards from his pocket and singled one out. "That's the pack. Look at the ace. You can see the mark yet."

The Duke examined the card.

"There is certainly a mark," he said, "which might well be made by a sharpened nail."

Sir John was up once more, his face dark with wrath.

"Really, gentlemen, there should be some limit to this foolery. Of course these are the cards. Is it not obvious that after Sir Charles and I had left, this fellow gathered them up and marked them so as to put forward a blackmailing demand? I only – I only wonder that he has not forged some document to prove that I admitted this monstrous charge."

Jakes threw up his hands in admiration. "By George, you have a nerve! I always said it. Give me Devil Hawker for nerve. Grasp the nettle, eh? Here's the document he talks about." He handed a paper to Lord Rufton.

"Would you be pleased to read it?" said the Duke.

" 'In consideration of services rendered, I promise William Jakes three thousand pounds when I settle with Sir Charles Trevor. Signed, John Hawker.' "

"A palpable forgery! I guessed as much," cried Sir John.

"Who knows Sir John's signature?"

"I do," said Sir Charles Bunbury.

"Is that it?"

"Well, I should say so."

"Tut, the fellow is a born forger," cried Hawker.

The Duke looked at the back of the paper: " 'To Thomas Cribb, Licensed Dealer in Beer, Wine, Spirits, and Tobacco.' It is certainly paper from the room alluded to."

"He could help himself to that."

"Exactly. The evidence is by no means convincing. At the same time, Sir John, I am compelled to tell you that the way in which you anticipated this evidence has produced a very unpleasant impression in my mind."

"I knew what the fellow was capable of."

"Do you admit being intimate with him?"

"Certainly not."

"You had nothing to do with him?"

"I had occasion recently to horsewhip him for insolence. Hence this charge against me."

"You knew him very slightly?"

"Hardly at all."

"You did not correspond?"

"Certainly not."

"Strange, then, that he should have been able to copy your signature if he had no letter of yours."

"I know nothing of that."

"You quarrelled with him recently?"

"Yes, sir. He was impertinent and I beat him."

"Had you any reason to think you would quarrel?"

"No, sir."

"Does it not seem strange to you, then, that he should have been keeping these cards all these weeks to buttress up a false charge against you if he had no idea that an occasion for such a charge would ever arise?"

"I cannot answer for his actions," said Hawker, in a sullen voice.

"Of course not. At the same time I am forced to repeat, Sir John, that your anticipation of this document has seemed to me exactly what might be expected from a man of strong character who knew that such a document existed."

"I am not responsible for this man's assertions, nor can I control your Grace's speculations, save to say that so far as they threaten my honour they are contemptible and absurd. I place my case in the hands of the committee. You know, or can easily learn, the character of this man Jakes. Is it possible that you can hesitate between the words of such a man and the character of one who has for years been a fellow-member of this club?"

"I am bound to say, your Grace," said Sir Charles Bunbury, "that while I associate myself with every remark which has fallen from you, I am still of opinion that the evidence is of so corrupt a character that it would be impossible for us to take action upon it."

"That is also my opinion," came from several of the committee, and there was a general murmur of acquiescence.

"I thank you, gentlemen," said Hawker, rising. "With your permission I shall bring this sitting to an end."

"Excuse me, sir: there are two more witnesses," said Lord Rufton.

"Jakes, you can withdraw. Leave the documents with me."

"Thank you, my lord. Good day, my noble sportsmen. Should any of you want a cock or a terrier—"

"That will do. Leave the room." With many bows and backward glances, William Jakes vanished from the scene.

"I should like to ask Tom Cribb one or two questions," said Lord Rufton. "Call Tom Cribb."

A moment later the burly figure of the champion came heavily into the room. He was dressed exactly like the pictures of John Bull, with blue coat with shining brass buttons, drab trousers and top boots, while his face in its broad bovine serenity was also the very image of the national prototype. On his head he wore a low-crowned curly-brimmed hat, which he now whipped off and stuffed under his arm. The worthy Tom was much more alarmed than ever he had been in the ring, and looked helplessly about him like a bull who finds himself in a strange enclosure.

"My respects, gentlemen all!" he repeated several times, touching his forelock.

"Good day, Tom," said the Duke, affably. "Take that chair. How are you?"

"Damned hot, your Grace. That is to say, very warm —"

"I want to ask you, Tom," said Lord Rufton, "do you remember the evening of May 3rd last in your parlour?"

"I heard there was some barney about it, and I've been lookin' it up," said Tom. "Yes, I remember it well, for it was the night when a novice had the better of old Ben Burn. Lor', I couldn't but laugh. Old Ben got one on the mark in the first round, and before he could get his wind —"

"Never mind, Tom. We'll have that later. Do you recognise these cards?"

"Why, those cards are out of my parlour. I get them a dozen dozen at a time, a shilling each, from Ned Summers of Oxford Street, the same what —"

"Well, that's settled, then. Now do you remember seeing Sir John here and Sir Charles Trevor that evening?"

"Yes, I do. I remember saying to Sir John that he must play light with my novices, for there was one cove, Bill Summers by name, out of Norwich, and when Sir John —"

"Never mind that, Tom. Tell us now, did you see Sir John and the bookmaker, Jakes, together that night?"

"Jakes was there for he says to the girl in the bar: 'How much money have you, my lass?' And I said, 'You dirty dog,' says I —"

"Enough, Tom. Did you see the man Jakes and Sir John together?"

"Yes, sir, when I came into the parlour after the bout between Ben Burn and Scroggins. I saw the two of them alone, and Jakes he said that they had done business together."

"Did they seem friendly?"

"Well, now you ask it, Sir John didn't seem too pleased. But, Lord love you, I'm that busy those evenings that if you dropped a shot on my head I'd hardly notice it."

"Nothing more to tell us?"

"I don't know as I have. I'd be glad to get back to my bar."

"Very good, Tom; you can go."

"I'd just remind you gentlemen that it's my benefit at the Fives Court, St. Martin's Lane, come Tuesday week." Tom bobbed his bullet head many times and departed.

"Not much in all that," remarked the Duke. "Does that finish the case?"

"There is one more, your Grace. Call the girl Lucy. She is the girl of the private bar."

"Yes, yes, I remember," cried the Duke, "that is to say, by all means. What does this young person know about it?"

"I believe that she was present." As Lord Rufton spoke, Lucy, very nervous, but cheered by the knowledge that she was in her best Sunday clothes, appeared at the door.

"Don't be nervous, my girl. Take this chair," said Lord Rufton, kindly. "Don't keep on curtseying. Sit down."

The girl sat timidly on the edge of the chair. Suddenly her eyes caught those of the august chairman.

"Why, Lord bless me!" she cried. "It's the little Duke!"

"Hush, my girl, hush!" His Grace held up a warning hand.

"Well, I never!" cried Lucy, and began to giggle and hide her blushing face in her handkerchief.

"Now, now!" said the Duke, "this is a grave business. What are you laughing at?"

"I couldn't help it, sir. I was thinking of that evening down in the private bar when you bet you could walk a chalk line with a bottle of champagne on your head."

There was a general laugh in which the Duke joined.

"I fear, gentlemen, I must have had a couple *in* my head before I ventured such a feat. Now, my good girl, we did not ask you here for the sake of your reminiscences. You may have seen some of us unbending, but we will let that pass. You were in the bar on May 3rd?"

"I'm always there."

"Cast your mind back and recall the evening when Sir Charles Trevor and Sir John Hawker proposed to cut cards for money.

"I remember it well, sir."

"After the others had left the bar, Sir John and a man named Jakes are said to have remained behind."

"I saw them."

"It's a lie! It's a plot!" cried Hawker.

"Now, Sir John, I must really beg you!" It was the Duke who was cross-questioning now. "Describe to us what you saw."

"Well, sir, they began talking over a pack of cards. Sir John up with his hand, and I was about to call for West Country Dick — he's the chucker-out, you know, sir, at the Union Arms — but no blow passed, and they talked very earnest like for a time. Then Mr. Jakes called for paper and wrote something, and that's all I know, except that Sir John seemed very upset."

"Did you ever see that piece of paper before?" The Duke held it up.

"Why, sir, it looks like Mr. Cribb's billhead."

"Exactly. Was it a piece like that which you gave to these gentlemen that night?"

"Yes, sir."

"Could you distinguish it?"

"Why, sir, now that I come to think of it, I could." Hawker

sprang up with a convulsed face. "I've had enough of this non-sense. I'm going."

"No, no, Sir John. Sit down again. Your honour demands your presence. Well, my good girl, you say you could recognise it?"

"Yes, sir, I could. There was a mark, sir. I drew some burgundy for Sir Charles, sir, and some slopped on the counter. The paper was marked with it on the side. I was in doubt if I should give them so soiled a piece."

The Duke looked very grave. "Gentlemen, this is a serious matter. There is, as you see, a red stain upon the side of the paper. Have you any remark to make, Sir John?"

"A conspiracy, your Grace! An infernal devilish plot against a gentleman's honour."

"You may go, Lucy," said Lord Rufton, and with curtsies and giggles the barmaid disappeared.

"You have heard the evidence, gentlemen," said the Duke. "Some of you may know the character of this girl, which is by all accounts excellent."

"A drab out of the gutter."

"I think not, Sir John, nor do you improve your position by such assertions. You will each have your own impression as to how far the girl's account seemed honest and carried conviction with it. You will observe that had she merely intended to injure Sir John her obvious method would have been to have said she overheard the conversation detailed by the witness Jakes. This she has not done. Her account, however, tends to corroborate –"

"Your Grace," cried Hawker. "I have had enough of this!"

"We shall not detain you much longer, Sir John Hawker," said the chairman, "but for that limited time we must insist upon your presence."

"Insist, sir?"

"Yes, sir, insist."

"This is strange talk."

"Be seated, sir. This matter must go to a finish."

"Well!" Hawker fell back into his chair.

"Gentlemen," said the Duke, "slips of paper are before you. After the custom of the club, you will kindly record your opinion and hand to me. Mr. Poyntz? I thank you. Vandeleur! Bunbury! Rufton! General Scott! Colonel Tufton! I thank you." He examined the papers. "Exactly. You are unanimous! I may say that I entirely agree with your opinion." The Duke's rosy, kindly face had set as hard as flint.

"What am I to understand by this, sir?" cried Hawker.

"Bring the club book," said the Duke.

Lord Rufton carried across a large brown volume from the side table and opened it before the chairman.

"C, D, E, F, G. Ah! here we are – H. Let us see! Houston, Harcourt, Hume, Duke of Hamilton – I have it – Hawker. Sir John Hawker, your name is for ever erased from the book of Watier's Club." He drew the pen across the page as he spoke. Hawker sprang frantically to his feet.

"Good God, sir, you cannot mean it! Consider, sir, this is social ruin! Where shall I show my face if I am cast from my club? I could not walk the streets of London. Take it back, sir! Reconsider it!"

"Sir John Hawker, we can only refer you to rule nineteen. It says, 'If any member shall be guilty of conduct unworthy of an honourable man, and the said offence be established to the unanimous satisfaction of the committee, then the aforesaid member shall be expelled the club without appeal.' "

"Gentlemen," cried Hawker, "I beg you not to be precipitate. You have had the evidence of a rascal bookmaker, and of a serving wench. Is that enough to ruin a gentleman's life? By God, sir, I am undone if this goes through."

"The matter has been considered, and is now in order. We can only refer you to rule nineteen."

"Your Grace, you cannot know what this will mean. How can I live? Where can I go? I never asked mercy of man before. But I ask it now. I implore it, gentlemen. Reconsider your decision!"

"Rule nineteen."

"It is ruin, I tell you, disgrace and ruin."

"Rule nineteen."

"Let me resign. Do not expel me."

"Rule nineteen."

It was hopeless, and Hawker knew it. He strode in front of the table.

"Curse your rules! Curse you, too, you silly, babbling jackanapes. Curse you all – you, Vandeleur, and you, Poyntz, and you, Scott, you doddering toast-and-water gamester. By God! You will live to mourn the day you put this indignity upon me. You will answer it – every man of you! I'll set my mark on you. By the Lord I will! You first, Rufton. One by one, I'll weed you out, by God! I've a bullet for each. I'll number 'em!"

"Sir John Hawker," said the Duke, "this club is for the use of members only. May I ask you to take yourself out of it?"

"And if I don't – what then?"

The Duke turned to General Scott. "Will you ask the hall-porters to step up?"

"There! I'll go," yelled Hawker. "I will not be thrown out – the laughing-stock of Jermyn Street. But you will hear more, gentlemen. You will remember me yet. Rascals! Rascals every one!"

And so it was, raving and stamping with his clenched hands waving above his head, that Devil Hawker passed out from his club and from the social life of London.

For it was his end. In vain he sent furious challenges to the members of the committee. He was outside the pale and no one would condescend to meet him. In vain he thrashed Sir Charles Bunbury in front of Limmer's Hotel. Hired ruffians were put upon his track and he was terribly thrashed in return. Even the bookmakers would have no more to do with him, and he was warned off the Turf. Down he sank, and down, drinking to uphold his spirits until he was but a bloated wreck of the man that he had been. And so at last one morning in his rooms in Charles Street that duelling pistol which had so often been the instrument of his vengeance was turned upon himself, and that dark face, terrible even in death, was found outlined against a blood-sodden pillow in the morning.

So put the print back among the pile. You may be the better for having honest Tom Cribb upon your wall, or even the effeminate Brummell. But Devil Hawker never in life or death brought luck to anyone. Leave him there where you found him, in the dusty old shop of Drury Lane.

THE LAST RESOURCE

---❖---

Kid Wilson's natural home would seem to be the Atlantic, since neither England nor America showed the least desire for his presence. However, in some way he got himself smuggled to London, and there found his level instantly on the edge of the criminal classes. Waldren and I used to meet him occasionally at a small and very disreputable joint at the back of Soho – a place which opened with the last postman and closed with the first milkman. One certainly heard conversation there which was worth while. You can never, unfortunately, make virtue as interesting as vice, for virtue is negative and vice is positive. The man who does not do certain things is the better citizen, but he has not the glamour of the man who does do them. It is sad but true.

When Kid Wilson got talking we were content to listen, for the world of which he spoke was one which was unknown to us, and yet he had, in his own rough way, the art of bringing it home to us. Sitting with his chair at a perilous angle and a black cigar thrusting out from the corner of his mouth, he would lead us into that strange underworld of the great American cities, where he was clearly a very competent guide. Looking across the water, it was not, so far as we could gather, the sheriffs or chiefs of police of whom he was afraid, but it was his own confederates and fellow-criminals who had it in for him. It was a silent lesson to us to watch him as he made his way out of our dive in the early mornings. With his hand slipped beneath his coat tails, he would take the sharp, quick glances of a hunted animal round each side of the door, before ever he ventured his unsavoury person into the street.

Either his experience or his imagination was very great, and he could hold us spellbound when he wished. On this particular night he started out upon a long story. Waldren says that it is no use my repeating it, because the snap of it depends upon the great

American language. Well, perhaps I can talk a little of that, too. Anyhow, I will try to get some suggestion of Wilson even as he spoke.

"I could have done better," said he, "if it had not been for that old skirt with the slop-pail. I'll give you what I can while it is clear in my mind.

"It's all about a certain burg in Amurrca. I won't give it a name, for it might make trouble, and what I say would fit any one of a dozen. You'll just figure it for yourselves as a wide-open burg, so wide open that it didn't seem as if any power on earth would ever get it shut again. The whole city seemed to have gone rotten, from the mayor down to the bellhops. The crooks had it in their hands, the bootleggers, the hi-jackers, the thugs, the racketeers, the hold-up men and the like. You'll understand that the bootlegger and the hi-jacker are mostly the same person, bootlegging on his own, and hi-jacking the booze of the other guys. The police were got at, the judges were made safe, the district attorney was squared, the mayor was seen. An honest juryman wouldn't have a chance with an insurance office. The gangsters would take him for a ride within a day of the verdict. It's no wonder that you would call fifty venire men before you got one that would stick. There was no safety anywhere. Even the State attorney was swinging a racket in gambling machines in drug stores. Yes, sir, the lid was fairly off that old burg. I was there helping, and I know, for I was beer-hustling myself till the police bought me up.

"It came sort of gradual. It rather amused the decent citizen at first to see these wops and dagoes laying each other out with automatics and Thompsons. There were gang quarrels, where some guy with three i's in his name would claim part of the city for his work, and another guy with three o's in his name would come muscling in. Then there would be shooting, good and proper, and whoever got hit there was one crook the less. But presently the decent citizen began to understand that he was the next bird to be shot at. That woke him up some. Then came the racketeers, and every store was put under blackmail, or the gorillas would be let loose and the stuff thrown into the street with the owner on the top of it. The money, too, was all on the side of the crooks, and money counts over in God's Own Country. Oh, yes, it was fierce, and no one could see any way out of it. But there was a way, and Gideon H. Fanshawe was the guy who found it. I'll hand it to Gideon, I will.

"He was a strange man, was Gideon H. Fanshawe. Some thought he was loco and some thought he was a genius. He was rich, very rich, for he had been junior partner of Gould and

Fanshawe, the real-estate folk. He spent his life in his library among books, sort of dreaming, but every now and then he kind of woke up out of his dream and then things began to happen. He woke up once and climbed the highest peak in Alaska. Another time he woke up and killed three burglars in his house. Then he woke up at the War-time, and no one saw him for a year, when he came back with one foot missing and a French medal. Yes, he was a queer guy and not too safe to handle – with a big think-box on the top, but a mouth like a rat-trap and a man-eating jaw. He was awake now and takin' notice, and somebody was goin' to hear about it. Lookit here, you folk, you can take it from me that there are plenty of dangerous men in Amurrca, but the most danger-ous of all is just the ordinary citizen when you drive him in a corner and there ain't no escape, except what he can horn out for himself. You've heard tell of the Vigilantes of San Francisco? Well, that's what I mean.

"For a month or more Gideon was just snooping round in his machine, interviewing this man and interviewing that man, and feeling his way. Then there were all-night meetings in his library, where the records of the big shots of the law and the police were debated and addresses taken and plans formed and everyone given the layout, and charged a grand each for the expenses. At that time I was stool-pigeon for the police, and I was had up at one or two of those meetings, where maybe a couple of hundred prominent citizens were present, and where I would be asked questions about what I knew. I was well paid, but I was told to keep my mouth shut or they would shut it for me, and, by George, those boys meant what they said.

"There was one clean honest man in office, and that was old Jack Barlow, the Chief of the Police. He wasn't what you would call a strong man – they would have had him out or shot him cold if he had been – but he was white all through. One night Gideon Fanshawe went down to see John Barlow, and I'll tell you what passed between them, but I have to tell it in my own way of talking.

"After greetings Gideon looked round the room.

" 'Lookit here, John,' he asked. 'there ain't no detectiphones? No stenog. round the corner?'

" 'Not with you, Mr. Fanshawe,' said the Chief, smiling and pushing over his box of cigars, friendly like.

" 'Word of honour, John?'

" 'Yep. You may take it so.'

" 'Now, I'm talking turkey, John. Every word has its face value. First of all, did you ever hear of the G.T.S. Society?'

" 'Can't say as I have. I'm fair hazed with all these societies.'

" 'Well, I'm here to tell you about it. There are two thousand of the best citizens in this town in it, and the letters mean "Got to Stop." '

" 'Meaning the crooks and boodlers?'

" 'Just so. Now, John, you know as well as I do that something has got to be done. We all trust you. We know you are straight. But your power has gone. Your own force is rotten from end to end. Is it not so?'

" 'I'd soon set it right, Mr. Fanshawe, if I had support. But what can I do? These people have the money and they've bought up the whole crowd.'

" 'Except yourself.'

" 'No, Mr. Fanshawe, nor a few more that I could name. But what can we do? '

" 'You can do nothing, John. That is why we are coming in to do it for you. Now, first of all – excuse my plain talking – I know what your place is worth.'

" 'Well, you can read that in the city accounts. It is about the only true figure you'll find.'

" 'Well, then' – Mr. Fanshawe drew a bundle of papers from his pocket – 'these are bearer bonds in first-class securities and you keep them.'

" 'Mr. Fanshawe, you are insulting me. How can you say I am a white man and yet put such a proposition before me?'

" 'Don't lose your hair, John. You don't quite see my meaning. You will keep these bonds, John, as a guarantee that you don't suffer through anything we may do. If you don't suffer, then you hand them back. But if you were to get fired on account of what we did, then it is clear justice that we should make good what we have caused you to lose. What have you to say against that?'

" 'Well, as you put it, that sounds fair enough, Mr. Fanshawe. If I should agree to risk my place for your sake – well, I'm a married man with a family, and I've got to live. But it all depends on what you want me to do. If it's crooked cut it out. Forget it.'

" 'If it is against the crooks it can't be crooked. First of all, John, are there any men at all under your orders who are straight?'

" 'Sure. I could name two hundred that I could swear by.'

" 'Then form these into one squad and order them to do as they are told on a night I shall name. Keep all the others at head-quarters or any other place so long as they are not on the streets. We don't want to hurt any cops if we can help it, and they'll get hurt for sure if they horn in between the crooks and us. Could you manage that?'

" 'Well, it would seem good sense.'

" 'Then I want you just to go for a joy-ride that night where no telephones can reach you, with orders to your deputy to touch nothing till you return. That gives us a free hand, and that's all we ask.'

" 'But what are you going to do, Mr. Fanshawe?'

" 'Well, just leave it at that John. If you don't know then you can't be held to be a partner. Just go and leave the rest to us. If all goes smooth, then you hand back those bonds. If there is trouble and you get fired, then you're none the worse. See?'

" 'Well, it's a bit fierce, Mr. Fanshawe. But there's my hand on it, and I'll do as you say.'

"So that was that. And when May 14th came round, honest John simply did a fade-away, while two hundred good harness bulls – that means cops in uniform – reported at the Auditorium Hall, which was the head-quarters of Gideon H. Fanshawe and his G.T.S. boys on that night.

"It was twelve o'clock when the whistle blew. All the crooks had been tabbed down days before and there was no difficulty in finding them. Three hundred automobiles full of hard-boiled citizens were after them, and the greater part were rounded up. No wrens were touched. It was reckoned wiser to deal with the men only. All over the city there were struggles and shootings, but all went as planned. By one o'clock or after there was a row of machines two deep for four blocks from the Hall, with heavily armed guards to each, and the prisoners without arms inside. Then Phil Hudson, he was the man who led the raid, a little hard guy that had been a flying ace in the War, reported to Fanshawe that all was ready and in order.

"The Auditorium Hall was all lit up, and at one end Fanshawe was seated at a high table with a dozen of his crowd, his lists and papers in front of him, and every man with a gun on the table beside him. Behind him were his guard, twenty men with shot-guns, each with the G.T.S. badge on his arm. They were mostly ex-service men in the G.T.S. Society. In the Hall were two or three hundred more of them, and some of the general public such as myself. I told you I was stool-pigeon for the police at the time, and I, like others, was there just to give a nod here or there when it was a question of some guy's identity, or shake if he was talking blah.

"Phil Hudson he came to the foot of the dais and saluted.

" 'We have all we could find, Chief,' said he. 'Some were tipped off, but not too many.'

"How many have you, Phil?'

" 'A thousand or more.'

" 'Anyone hurt?'

" 'We had to shoot up ten or twelve of them. Six citizens were shot.'

" 'Too bad! Too bad! Well, we had best get to it. Send in the mayor first.'

"Fat old Tom Baxter, a very surprised man, was led up, with a guard on each side of him. He was a silly old butter-and-egg man, never done with the wrens, and he was as corrupt as a graveyard.

" 'You shall pay for this, Mr. Fanshawe. What is the meaning of this outrage?'

" 'We are here to clean up this town, Mr. Mayor, and we begin at the top. The committee of the G.T.S. have examined the evidence in your case. You have sheltered the crooks. You have taken their money. You have used your office as it should not have been used. Take him away!"

" 'Take me away! Take me where?'

" 'To the Odeum. You'll have all your friends round you there. You won't be lonely. Remove him!"

So the mayor with a gat stuck into his ribs was walked down the aisle, and then came the whole procession. First it was Burgess, the district attorney, and a fine rage he was in.

" 'I'll have the law on you for this, Mr. Fanshawe. Are you aware that I was dragged out of my bedroom by these ruffians of yours, and that I have only my pyjama suit underneath this slicker?'

" 'Too bad! Too bad!' said Fanshawe. 'But the citizens of this town are dissatisfied with your conduct of your office, Mr. Attorney. They have examined your case and it has gone against you.'

" 'What right have you?'

" 'The right of the people. All power springs from the people, Mr. Attorney, and all power must answer to the people. You have taken money to let crooks slip through the law. You have condoned murders. You have been the paid servant of the gangsters. Take him to the Odeum.'

" 'What for?' The little overfed guy was shaking like a jelly.

" 'Let us say it is to have a photograph taken,' said Fanshawe. 'Anyhow, we want you all in a bunch. Take him away.'

" 'Then came Moltak, the big black Polack, boss of the South Side beer racket who was said to have made five million bucks in two years. He was a great giant of a man, all hair and muscles, and he glared murder at the men on the dais.

" 'I get you. I get you for this,' he cried.

" 'Looks as if we had got you, Mr. Moltak,' said Fanshawe, with his quiet smile. 'We've got twenty killings against you and your outfit. How many of them have we, Hudson?'

" 'There are seventy-six outside.'

" 'Well, we can't make distinctions. They've all got to go. I'll see you again at the Odeum, Moltak. Take him away and his whole gang along with him.'

"The fellow tried to make a rough house, but they had his arms twisted and he was helpless. There were some man-handlers, I tell you, among those ex-service men. They raced him down and he made way for Genaro. Boss of the Societas Meridionale. This slick little Southerner with his evening dress and his sissy ways was up to his eyes in murder. He had been snapped up at some swell gathering and he was very sore about it.

" 'You take me from my guests, Mr. Fanshawe. What you dare do? You take me from the best society in this town. Six judges dine with me to-night, and you drag me away from them.'

" 'Got those judges, Phil?' asked Fanshawe.

" 'Yes, Chief.'

" 'Let them go in with the others. All right, Genaro, we won't talk about it. We've got you down for near fifty murders. You didn't do them with your own hands. You had your choppers and your gunmen. But they were yours all the same. Have you the gang?'

" 'Sixty of them.'

" 'That's enough to go on with. Off with them to the Odeum.'

"All night they were being led in, gangsters of every kind, thugs, gunmen, booze-hustlers, hi-jackers, racketeers, con-men, scratchers, common yeggmen, and hold-uppers – crooks of every size and shape. Fanshawe had them all tabbed, ran his finger down the list, had the man's record in a moment, and dealt with him in a word or two. Often he had a consultation with his friends, and once or twice he looked across for a nod from me or some other who was in the inside of things. Here or there a man was set free with a few stern words of warning. Far the greater part were sent on to the Odeum. At last, just as dawn was breaking, Fanshawe rose, stretched himself, threw down his half-smoked cigar – he had smoked a chain of them through the whole night – and came down from the dais. The others followed, and so did I.

"There were crowds in the street, but the cops and the G.T.S. men had made an avenue, and Fanshawe, with his committee, drove down to the Odeum, which was only three or four blocks away. For my own part, I made my way on foot through the crowd, and reached the place after they had entered. There was a guard at the door, but MacDonovan, who was a pal of mine up at police headquarters, caught me by the shoulder as I tried to squeeze in.

" 'Not on your life, kid,' said he. 'These guys know you for what you are, and if you get among them I guess there wouldn't be enough of you left to be worth a funeral.'

" 'Can't I get a look in anywhere, Mac?'

"There was a little metal-faced door just inside, and he opened it.

" 'Get up this stair,' said he. 'You're taking a chance from the President's guards, but if you get up there you will see all there is.'

"So up I went, only to find a gat flashed into my face from a sentry at the top. I got friendly, however, and he let me stop where I could get a view.

"The Odeum is a big square dancing hall with no furniture. It just has a gallery at one end where the band would play – and that is where I was. There was the one stair leading to the gallery, with the guarded and locked door at the bottom. There were two or three other guarded doors faced with metal down below, and the windows, which were high, were all boarded up. Down in the body of the hall were about twelve hundred people, some in dress, most in any sort of rough clothes, but all of them just dancing with rage. They were shaking their fists up at the gallery and yelling out every kind of abuse and threat of what they were going to do with the G.T.S. folk when they got loose.

"Dancing mad – that was how they were – and as you looked down under the bright top lights you could just see open yelling mouths, and twisted faces, and fists held up shaking at the President. I'll hand it to him for being cool. There he sat with a few of his committee looking down in silence on the mob, as quiet as a fish in ice. On each side of him was a big brass tripod, and a velvet cloth over each such as photographers use. Half-a-dozen G.T.S. were at the back, and if ever I saw hard-bitten soldiers it was there.

"Presently Fanshawe rose and held up his hand for silence. There were some yells of hatred, but as the man stood and looked down at them with a face like death and eyes like icicles, these died away, and there was such utter stillness that there might have been no one in the room. Then he began to speak with a voice that crackled like electricity.

" 'There are a few Amurrcans in this room, more shame to them,' said he. 'They have been corrupted and led away, and yet they were the very ones chosen by the people and trusted to look after their affairs. I am sorry for them, but they have only themselves to thank. As to the rest of you, you are nearly all from foreign lands, whence you were driven by want or tyranny. You came here and Amurrca welcomed you. She could not have been more generous. Within a year she put you on an equality with the oldest citizen. She gave you all her broad lands that you might find a place for yourselves and use every gift that was in you. That is what Amurrca has done for you. And what have you done for Amurrca? You have broken her laws, made the name of her cities a scandal, corrupted her citizens with your ill-got money, broken down her legal system, killed her guardians of the peace when you could not corrupt them. In a word, you have done such things that at long last we, who are the real people, have had to come forth and show you that there is a live Amurrca which has been good and liberal and generous, but which has in it also the power which can punish those who abuse what has been given. You have forced it on us. You have left us no other way but this. Enough said! Cut loose!'

"As he spoke a man on either side pulled the cloth off the machine-guns. The hard-bitten citizens behind sprang to their positions, and in an instant the massacre began.

"I only had a glance at it. I saw them rushing for the doors. I saw them climbing to the sealed windows. I saw them piling up in the corners as rats do when a terrier is loose. I saw them running and screaming, and tripping and falling, and some hiding behind the others, and the dead piling up, and the judges all going down in one heap, and the mayor running forward with his hands up. All this I seemed to see, and then – and then –

"Well, what then?"

"Well, as I said at the beginning, the rattle of that skirt's slop-pail carried on the tapping of the guns, and then she was bobbing and scarping, and saying that she thought I had been up and out."

We sat in disgruntled silence.

"Do you mean to say," I cried, at last, "that this has all been a dream?"

"Well, you can call it that if you like," he answered, taking the sodden cigar from his mouth. "A vision, maybe, is a better word. It hasn't happened just like that yet. But wait a bit, folk, wait a bit."

Poor old Kid! We felt that the end of his story had been a bit of a flop. But his own end was dramatic enough. Only a few days later we saw the curt paragraph in a morning paper:–

"An American named Wilson was found by the police early yesterday morning in the portico of a common lodging-house in

Carlisle Street, Soho, suffering from several knife wounds. His assailants had apparently waited for him in the shadow of the door, and had attacked him as he returned, according to his wont, in the early morning. He was alive when found, but refused to make any statement, and died on his way to the hospital. There is no clue at present to the assassins, but there are reasons to believe that the tragedy is part of that gangster system which has wrought such havoc in America."

SOURCES

———◆———

"The Mystery of Sasassa Valley" – *Chambers's Journal*, 6 September 1879.

"The American's Tale" – *London Society*, Christmas number, 1880.

"Bones. The April Fool of Harvey's Sluice" – *London Society*, April 1882.

"Our Derby Sweepstakes" – *London Society*, May 1882.

"That Veteran" – *All the Year Round*, 2 September 1882.

"Gentlemanly Joe" – *All the Year Round*, 31 March 1883.

"The Winning Shot" – *Bow Bells*, 11 July 1883.

"An Exciting Christmas Eve or, My Lecture on Dynamite" – *Boy's Own Paper*, Christmas number, 1883.

"Selecting a Ghost. The Ghosts of Goresthorpe Grange" – *London Society*, December 1883.

"The Heiress of Glenmahowley" – *Temple Bar*, January 1884.

"The Cabman's Story" – *Cassell's Saturday Journal*, 17 May 1884.

"The Tragedians" – *Bow Bells*, 20 August 1884.

"The Lonely Hampshire Cottage" – *Cassell's Saturday Journal*, 2 May 1885.

"The Fate of the Evangeline" – *Boy's Own Paper*, Christmas number, 1885.

"Touch and Go: A Midshipman's Story" – *Cassell's Family Magazine*, April 1886.

"Uncle Jeremy's Household" – *Boy's Own Paper*, 8 January – 19 February 1887.

"The Stone of Boxman's Drift" – *Boy's Own Paper*, Christmas number, 1887.

"A Pastoral Horror" – *People*, 21 December 1890.

"Our Midnight Visitor" – *Temple Bar*, February 1891.

"The Voice of Science" – *Strand Magazine*, March 1891.

"The Colonel's Choice" – *Lloyd's Weekly London Newspaper*, 26 July 1891.

"A Sordid Affair" – *People*, 29 November 1891.

"A Regimental Scandal" – *Indianapolis Journal*, 14 May 1892.

"The Recollections of Captain Wilkie" – *Chambers's Journal*, 19, 26 January 1895.

"The Confession" – *Star*, 17 January 1898.

"The Retirement of Signor Lambert" – *Pearson's Magazine*, December 1898.

"A True Story of the Tragedy of 'Flowery Land' " – *Louisville Courier-Journal*, 10 March 1899.

"An Impression of the Regency" – *Universal Magazine*, January 1901. First known publication in *Frank Leslie's Popular Monthly*, New York, August 1900.

"The Centurion" – *Storyteller*, December 1922. First publication in *Hearst's International*, New York, October 1922.

"The Death Voyage" – *Strand Magazine*, October 1929. First publication in the *Saturday Evening Post*, Philadelphia, 28 September 1929.

"The Parish Magazine" – *Strand Magazine*, August 1930.

"The End of Devil Hawker" – *Strand Magazine*, November 1930. First publication in the *Saturday Evening Post*, Philadelphia, 23 August 1930.

"The Last Resource" – *Strand Magazine*, December 1930. First publication in *Liberty*, New York, 16 August 1930.